BE

Also by Stephen Baxter in Gollancz

Deep Future
Reality Dust
Evolution
Coalescent
Exultant
Time's Eye (with Arthur C. Clarke)

The Web: Gulliverzone
The Web: Webcrash

STEPHEN BAXTER

BEHEMOTH

Mammoth © Stephen Baxter 1999; Longtusk © Stephen Baxter 1999;
Icebones © Stephen Baxter 2001

This collection first published in Great Britain in 2004 by

Gollancz
An imprint of the Orion Publishing Group
Orion House, 5 Upper St Martin's Lane,
London WC2H 9EA

A CIP catalogue record for this book is
available from the British Library

ISBN 0 575 07604 6

Typeset at The Spartan Press Ltd,
Lymington, Hants

Printed in Great Britain by
Clays Ltd, St Ives plc

www.orionbooks.co.uk

BOOK 1:

SILVERHAIR

PROLOGUE

It is a frozen world.

To the south there are forests. But to the north, the trees – hundred-year-old spruce barely six feet tall, stunted by cold and wind – grow ever more thinly scattered, until they peter out altogether.

And beyond, where it is too cold for the hardiest tree, there is only the tundra: an immense, undulating plain, a white monotony broken by splinters of rock. Very little snow falls here, but unimpeded winds whip up ice crystals, giving the illusion of frequent blizzards. Even the outcropping rock has been shattered by millennia of frost to a rough, unstable scree.

Under the silent stars nothing stirs but the ruffled surface of the larger lakes, tormented by the breeze. The smaller lakes are frozen completely. From this place there is nothing but snow and ice and frozen ocean, all the way to the North Pole.

It seems impossible that anything should live here. And yet there is life.

There are birds here: snowy owls and ptarmigan, able to survive the bleakest midwinter by sheltering in holes in the snow. And later in the season many thousands more birds will migrate here from their winter homes across the planet. More life, plant and animal, lies dormant under the snow, waiting for the brief glory of summer. And to the north, on the frozen ocean itself, live polar bears and their prey: sea mammals like seals and walrus.

. . . And there is more.

The stars are scintillating now. A vicious wind is rising, and the ice fields to the north are shrouded in a grey haze.

And out of that haze something looms: a mountainous shape, seemingly too massive to move, and yet move it does. As it approaches through the obscuring mist, more of its form becomes visible: a body round as an eroded rock, head dropped down before it as it probes for saxifrage buds beneath the snow, the whole covered in a layer of thick red-brown hair.

The great head rears up. A trunk comes questing, and immense tusks sweep. An eye opens, warm, brown, intense, startlingly human.

This is not a vision from prehistory. This is real: a living thing a hundred times as massive as any human, a living thing prospering in this frozen desert.

The great trunk lifts, and the woolly mammoth trumpets her ancient songs of blood and wisdom.

Her name is Silverhair.

ONE
FAMILY

THE STORY OF THE HOTBLOODS

The first Cycle story of all (Silverhair told Icebones, her calf) – the *very* first of all – is of long, long ago, when there were no mammoths.

In fact there were no wolves or birds or seals or bears.

For the world belonged to the Reptiles.

Now, the Reptiles were the greatest beasts ever seen – so huge they made the Earth itself shake with their footfalls – and they were cunning and savage hunters.

But they didn't have things all their own way.

Our ancestors called themselves the Hotbloods.

The Hotbloods were small, timid creatures who lived underground, in burrows, the way lemmings do. The ancestors of every warm-blood creature you see today lived in those cramped dens: bear with seal, wolf with mammoth. They had huge, frightened eyes, for they would only emerge from their burrows at night, a time when the Reptiles were less active and less able to hunt them. They all looked alike, and rarely even argued, for their world was dominated by the constant threat of the Reptiles.

That was the way the world had been for ten thousand Great-Years.

It was into this world that Kilukpuk, the first of all Matriarchs, was born. If you could have seen her, small and cautious like the rest, you would never have imagined the mighty races which would one day spring from her loins. But, despite her smallness, Kilukpuk was destined to become the mother of us all.

Now Kilukpuk had a brother, called Aglu. He was hard-eyed and selfish, and was often accused of hiding when foraging parties were being readied, and of stealing others' food – even stealing from infants. But Aglu was sly, and nothing was ever proven.

Despite his faults, Kilukpuk loved her brother. She defended him from attack, and did not complain when he took the warmest place in the burrow, or stole her food, for she always dreamed he would learn the error of his ways.

Now, there came a time when a great light appeared in the night sky.

It was a ball of grey-white, and it had a huge hairy tail that streamed away from the sun. The light was beautiful, but it was deadly, for it turned night to day, and made it easy for the Reptiles to pick off the foraging Hotbloods. Great was the mourning in the burrows.

One night Kilukpuk was out alone, digging in a mound of Reptile dung for undigested nuts – when suddenly . . .

Well, Kilukpuk never knew what happened, and I don't suppose any of us will.

The Earth trembled. There was a great glow, as if dawn was approaching – but the glow was in the *west*, not the east. Clouds boiled across the sky.

Then the sky itself started to burn, and a great hail of shooting stars poured down towards the land, coming from the west.

Kilukpuk felt a new shaking of the ground. Silhouetted against the red fire glow of the west, she saw Reptiles: thousands, millions of them – and they were running.

The Reptiles had ruled the world as gods. But now they were fleeing in panic.

Kilukpuk ran back to her burrow, convinced that if even the gods were so afraid, she and her Family were sure to die.

The days that followed were filled with strangeness and terror.

A great heat swept over the land.

Then a rain began, salty and heavy, so powerful it was as if an ocean was emptying itself over their heads.

And then the clouds came, and snow fell even at the height of summer.

Kilukpuk and her Family, starved and thirsty, thought this was the end of all things. But their burrows protected the Hotbloods, while the creatures of the surface perished.

At last the cold abated, and day and night returned to the world.

No Reptiles came. There were no footfalls, no digging claws, no bellows of frustrated hunters.

At last, one night, Kilukpuk and Aglu led a party to the surface.

They found a world that was all but destroyed. The trees and bushes had been smashed down by winds and burned by fire.

There were no Reptiles, anywhere.

But the Hotbloods found food to eat in the ruined world, for they were used to living off scraps anyhow. There were roots, and bark that wasn't too badly burned, and the first green shoots of recovering plants.

Soon the Hotbloods grew fat, and, without the ground-rattling footfalls of the Reptiles to disturb them, began to sleep well during the long, hot days of that strange time.

But there came a time when some Hotbloods did not return from the nightly foraging expeditions, just as it had been before. And then, one day, Kilukpuk was wakened from a dreamless sleep by a *slam-slam-slam* that shook dirt from the roofs of the burrows.

Aglu, her brother, came running through the burrows. 'It is the Reptiles! They have returned!'

Kilukpuk gathered her calves to her. They were terrified and bewildered.

After that, things rapidly got worse. More foragers were lost on the surface. The Hotbloods became as fearful and hollow-eyed as they had ever been, and food soon began to run short in the burrows.

But Kilukpuk could not help but notice that not all the

Hotbloods were suffering so. While the others were skinny and raddled by disease, Aglu and his band of companions seemed sleek and healthy. Kilukpuk grew suspicious, though her suspicion saddened her, for she still loved her brother deeply.

At last, one night, she followed Aglu and his companions to the surface. She saw that Aglu and the others made little effort to conceal themselves – in fact they laughed and cavorted in the Moonlight.

And then they did a very strange thing.

When they had eaten their fill of the roots and green plants, Aglu and his friends climbed up low bushes and hurled themselves at the ground. They pushed pebbles off low outcrops and let them dash against the ground. They even picked up heavy branches and slammed them against the ground – all the time roaring and howling as if they were Reptiles themselves.

And, when an unwary Hotblood came poking her nose out of the ground, Aglu and his friends prepared to attack her.

Immediately Kilukpuk rose up with a roar of rage. She fell on Aglu and his followers, cuffing and kicking and biting them, scattering their pebbles and their sticks.

The Hotblood whose life had been spared ran away. Aglu's followers soon fled, leaving Kilukpuk facing her brother. She picked him up by the scruff of his neck. 'So,' she said, 'you are the mighty Reptile that has terrified my calves.'

'Let me go, Kilukpuk,' he said, wriggling. 'The Reptiles have gone. We are free—'

'Free to enslave your Cousins with fear? I should rip you to pieces myself.'

Aglu grew frightened. 'Spare me, Kilukpuk. I am your brother.'

And Kilukpuk said, 'I will spare you. For Hotblood should not kill Hotblood. But you are no brother of mine; and your mouth and fur stink of blood. Go now.'

And she threw him as hard as she could, threw him so far his body flew over the horizon, his cries diminishing.

She went back to the burrows to comfort her calves, and tell her people the danger was over: that they need not skulk in their burrows, that they could live on the land, not under it, and they could enjoy the light of day, not cower in darkness.

And Kilukpuk led her people to the sunlit land, and they began to feed on the new plants that sprouted from the richness of the burned ground.

As for Aglu, some say he was ripped apart and eaten by his own calves, and they have never forgotten the taste of that grisly repast: for they became the bear and the wolf, and the other Hotbloods which eat their own kind.

Certainly Kilukpuk never gave up her vigilance, even as she grew strong and sleek, and her fertile loins poured forth generation after generation of calves. And her calves feared nobody.

Nobody, that is, except the Lost.

CHAPTER 1
THE HEADLAND

Silverhair, standing tall on the headland, was cupped in a land of flatness: a land of far horizons, a land of blue and grey, of fog and rain, of watery light no brighter than an English winter twilight.

It was the will of Kilukpuk, of course, that Silverhair should be the first to spot the Lost. Nobody but Silverhair – Silverhair the rebel, the Cow who behaved more like a musth Bull, as Owlheart would tell her – nobody but her would even have been standing here, alone, on this headland at the south-western corner of the Island, looking out to sea with her trunk raised to test the air.

The dense Arctic silence was abruptly broken by the evocative calls of birds. Silverhair saw them on the cliff below her, prospecting for their colony: the first kittiwakes, arriving from the south. It was a sign of life, a sign of spring, and she felt her own spirits rise in response.

A few paces from Silverhair, in a hollow near the cliff edge, a solid bank of snow had gathered. Now a broad, claw-tipped paw broke its way out into the open air, and beady black eyes and nose protruded. It was a polar bear: a female. The bear climbed out, a mountain of yellow-white fur. Lean after consuming her body fat over the winter, her strong, elegant neck jutted forward; her muscles, long and flowing, worked as she glided over the crusted snow.

The bear saw Silverhair. She fixed the huge mammoth with a glare, quite fearless.

Then she stretched, circled and clambered back in

12

through the narrow hole to the cubs she had borne during the winter, leaving a hind leg waving in the air.

Amused, Silverhair looked to the south.

The black bulk of a spruce forest obscured her view of the coast itself – and of the mysterious Nest of Straight Lines which stood there, a place which could be glimpsed only when the air was clear of fog or mist or snow, a sinister place which no mammoth would willingly visit. But Silverhair could see beyond the forest, to the ocean itself.

Here and there blown snow snaked across the landfast ice that fringed the Island's coast. Two pairs of black guillemots, striking in their winter plumage, swam along the sea edge, mirrored in the calm water. Pack ice littered the Channel that lay between Island and Mainland. The ice had been smashed and broken by the wind; the glistening blue-white sheet was pocked by holes and leads exposing black, surging water.

Away from the shore the sea, of course, remained open, as it did all year round, swept clear of ice by the powerful currents that surged there. Frost-smoke rose from the open water, turned to gold by the low sun. And beyond the Channel, twilight was gathering on that mysterious Mainland itself. It was the land from which – according to mammoth legend recorded in the Cycle – the great hero Longtusk had, long ago, evacuated his Family to save them from extinction.

And as the day waned, she could see the strange gathering of lights, there on the Mainland: like stars, a crowded constellation, but these lights were orange and yellow and unwinking, and they clung to the ground like lichen. Silverhair growled and squinted, but her vision was poor. If only she could *smell* that remote place; if only it sent out deep contact rumbles rather than useless slivers of light.

And now heavy storm clouds descended on that unattainable land, obscuring the light.

In the icy breeze, the air crackled in her nostrils, and her breath froze in the fur that covered her face.

That was when she saw the Lost.

She didn't know what she was seeing then, of course.

All she saw was something adrift on the sea between the Island and Mainland. At first she thought it was just an ice floe; perhaps those unmoving shapes on the top of the floe were seals, resting as they chewed on their monotonous diet of fish and birds.

But she had never seen seals sitting up as these creatures did, never seen seals with fins as long and splayed as these – never heard voices, floating over the water and the shore of ice and rock, as petulant and peevish as these.

Even the 'ice floe' was strange, its sides and one end straight, the other end coming to a point like a tusk's, its middle hollow, cupping the seal-like creatures inside. Whatever it was, it was drifting steadily closer to the Island; it would surely come to ground somewhere south of the spruce forest, and spill those squabbling creatures on the shore there.

She knew she should return to the Family, tell them what she had seen. Perhaps Owlheart or Eggtusk, in their age and wisdom – or clever Lop-ear, she thought warmly – would know the meaning of this. But she had time to watch a little longer, to indulge the curiosity that had already caused her so much trouble during her short life.

. . . But now she heard the stomping.

It was a deep pounding, surging through the rocky ground. A human would have heard nothing, not even felt the quiver of the ground caused by those great footfalls. But Silverhair recognised it immediately, for the stomping has the longest range of all the mammoths' means of calling each other.

This was the distinctive footfall of Owlheart herself: it was the Matriarch, calling her Family together. The birth must be near.

When Silverhair had been a calf, the Island had rung to the stomping of mammoths, for there were many Families in those days, scattered across the tundra. Now there was only the remote echo of her own Matriarch's footfall. But Silverhair – nervous about the birth to come, curiosity engaged by what she had seen today – did not reflect long on this.

The new spring sun was weak, a red ball that rolled along the horizon, offering little warmth. And already, heart-breakingly soon, it was setting, having shed little heat over the snow which still covered the ground. The last light turned the mountains pink, and it caught Silverhair's loose outer fur, making it glow, so that it was as if she was surrounded by a smoky halo.

She stole one last glimpse at the strange object in the sea. It had almost passed out of sight anyway, as it drifted away from the headland.

She turned and began her journey back to her Family.

Later she would wonder if it might have been better to have ignored the Matriarch's call, descended to the shore – and, without mercy, destroyed the strange object and the creatures it contained.

CHAPTER 2
THE BIRTH

Mammoths wander. Few wander as far as Silverhair did, however.

It took her ten days to cross the Island and return to the northern tundra where her Family was gathered. She was not aware of the way the ground itself shuddered as her feet passed, and the way lemmings were rattled in their winter burrows in the snow. But the rodents were unconcerned, and went about their tiny businesses without interruption. For they knew that the mammoths, the greatest creatures in the land, would do them no harm.

Silverhair knew that the worst of the winter was over: that time of perpetual night broken only by the occasional flare of the aurora borealis, the time of the hard winds from the north that drove snow and ice crystals before them. The return of the sun had been heralded by days in which the darkness was relieved by twilight, when the black star pool above had turned to a dome of glowing purple – purple enriched by swathes of blue, pink, even some flashes of green – before sinking back to darkness again, all without a sliver of sunlight.

But every day the noon twilights had grown longer and stronger, until at last the sun itself had come peeking over the horizon. At first it was just a splinter of blinding light that quickly disappeared, as if shy. But at last it had climbed fully above the horizon, for the first time for more than a hundred days.

In the new light, to the north, she could see the sweep of the Island itself. The tundra was still largely buried in pale snow and ice, with none of the rich marsh green or splashes of flowering colour that the growth of summer would bring. And beyond, to the farthest north, she could see the bony faces of the Mountains at the End of the World, looming out of the bluish mist that lingered there, brown cones striped by the great white glaciers that spilled from rocky valleys. The Mountains were a wall of ice and rock beyond which no mammoth had ever ventured.

Along the south coast of the Island, more sheltered, the oily green-black of a spruce forest clung to the rock. The trees were intruders, encroaching on the ancient tundra which provided Silverhair's Family with the grassy food they needed.

Despite her sense of urgency, Silverhair paused frequently to feed. Her trunk was busy and active, like an independent creature, as it worked at the ground. She would wrap her trunk-fingers around the sparse tufts of grass she found under the snow, cramming the dark-green goodies into her small mouth, and grind them between her great molar teeth with a back-and-forth movement of her jaw. The grass, the last of the winter, was coarse, dry and unsatisfying, as was the rest of her diet of twigs and bark of birches, willows and larches; with a corner of her mind she looked forward to her richer summer feast to come.

And she would lift her anus flap and pass dung, briskly and efficiently, as mammoths must ten or twelve times a day. The soft brown mass settled to the ice behind her, steaming; it would enrich the soil it touched, and the seeds that had passed through Silverhair's stomach would germinate and turn the land green.

The Family had no permanent home. They would gather to migrate to new pastures, or when one of their members was in some difficulty. But they would scatter in pairs or small groups to forage for food during the day, or to sleep at night. There was never any formal arrangement about where to meet again – nor was one necessary, for the mammoths were by far the most massive beasts in the landscape, and the authoritative stomping of Owlheart, and the rumbling and calls of the Family gathered together, travelled – to a mammoth's ears – from one end of the Island to another.

On the eighth day, a line of white vapour cut across the deep blue sky, utterly straight, feathering slightly. Silverhair peered upward; the vapour trail was at the limit of her poor vision. There was a tiny, glittering form at the head of the vapour line, like a high-flying bird, but its path was un-naturally straight and unwavering, its wings stiff, as if frozen. And a sound like remote thunder came drifting down, even though there wasn't a cloud in the sky.

Silverhair had seen such things before. Nobody could tell her what it was, what it meant. After a time, the glittering mote passed out of sight, and the vapour trail slowly dispersed.

On the ninth day Silverhair was able to hear, not just the Matriarch's stomping, but also the rumbles, trumpets and growls of her people. The deep voices of mammoths – too deep for human ears – will carry far across the land, unimpeded by grassland, snow banks, even forest.

And in the evening of that day, when the wind was right, she could smell home: the rich, hot smell of fresh dung, the musk stink of wet fur.

On the tenth day she was able to see the others at last. The mammoths, gathered together, were blocky shapes looming out of the blue-tinged fog. Silverhair was something of a loner, but even so she felt her heart pump, her blood flow warm in her veins, at the thought of greeting the Family.

Warm at the thought – she admitted it – of seeing Lop-ear once more.

The mammoths were scraping away thin layers of snow with their feet and tusks to get at the saxifrage buds below. Moulting winter fur hung around them in untidy clouds, and she could see how gaunt they were, after a winter spent burning the fat of the long-gone summer. It had been a hard winter, even for this frozen desert, and standing water had been unusually difficult to find. Silverhair knew that when the weather lifted – and if the thaw did not come soon – the Matriarch would have to lead them to seek open water. It would be an arduous trek, and there was no guarantee of success, but there might be no choice.

The Family's two adult Bulls came to meet her.

Here was powerful old Eggtusk, his ears ragged from the many battles he had fought, and with the strange egg-shaped ivory growth in his tusk that had given him his name. And here, too, was Lop-ear, the younger Bull, with his dangling, parasite-damaged ear. The Bulls were launching into their greeting ceremony, and Silverhair joined in, rumbling and trumpeting, excited despite the shortness of her separation.

The three mammoths raised their trunks and tails and ran and spun around. They urinated and defecated in a tight ring, their dung merging in a circle of brown warmth on the ground. Old Eggtusk was the clumsiest of the three, of course, but what he lacked in elegance he made up for in his massive enthusiasm.

And now they touched each other. Silverhair clicked tusks with Eggtusk, and – with more enthusiasm – touched Lop-ear's face and mouth, wrapping her trunk over his head and rubbing at his scalp hair. She found the musth glands in his cheeks and slowly snaked her trunk across them, reading his subtle chemical language, while he rubbed her forehead; and then they pulled back their trunks and entangled them in a tight knot.

A human observer would have seen only three mammoths dancing in their baffling circles, trumpeting and growling and stomping, even emitting high-pitched, bird-like squeaks with their trunks. Perhaps, with patience, she might have deduced some simple patterns: the humming sound that indicated a warning, a roar that was a signal to attack, the whistling that meant that one of the Family was injured or in distress.

But mammoth speech is based not just on the sounds mammoths make – from the ground-shaking stomps, through low-pitched rumbles, bellows, trumpets and growls, to the highest chirrups of their trunks – but also on the complex dances of their bodies, and changes in how they smell or breathe or scratch, even in the deep throb of their pulses. All of this makes mammoth speech richer than any human language.

'. . . Hello!' Silverhair was calling. 'Hello! I'm so glad to see you! Hello!'

'Silverhair,' Eggtusk growled, failing to mask his pleasure at seeing her again. 'Last back as usual. By Kilukpuk's mite-ridden left ear, I swear you're more Bull than Cow.'

'Oh, Eggtusk, you can't keep that up.' And she laid her trunk over Eggtusk's head and began to tickle him behind his ear with her delicate trunk-fingers. 'Plenty of mites in this ear too.'

He growled in pleasure and shook his head; his hair, matted with mud, moved in great lanks over his eyes. 'You won't be able to run away when you have your own calf. You just bear that in mind. You should be watching and learning from your sister.'

'I know, I know,' she said. But she kept up her tickling, for she knew his scolding wasn't serious. A new birth was too rare and infrequent an event for anyone to maintain ill humour for long.

Rare and infrequent – but not so rare as what she'd seen on the sea, she thought, remembering. 'Lop-ear. You've got to come with me.' She wrapped her trunk around his and tugged.

He laughed, and flicked back his lifeless ear. 'What is it, Silverhair?'

'I saw the strangest thing in the sea. To the south, from

the headland. It was like an ice floe – but it wasn't; it was too dark for that. And there were animals on it – or rather inside it – like seals—'

Lop-ear was watching her fondly. He was a year older than Silverhair. Although he wouldn't reach his full height until he was forty years old, he was already tall, and his shoulders were broad and strong, and his brown eyes like pools of autumn sunlight.

But Eggtusk snorted. 'By Kilukpuk's snot-crusted nostril, what are you talking about, Silverhair? Why can't you wander off and find something useful – like nice warm water for us to drink?'

'The animals were cupped inside the floating thing, for it was hollow, like—' She had no language to describe what she'd seen. So she released Lop-ear's trunk and ripped a fingerful of trampled grass from the ground. Carefully, sheltering the blades from the wind, she cupped the grass. 'Like this!'

Lop-ear looked puzzled.

Eggtusk was frowning. '*Seals*, you say?'

'But they weren't seals,' she said. 'They had four flippers each – or rather, legs – that were stuck out at angles, like broken twigs. And heads, big round heads . . . You do believe me, don't you?'

Eggtusk was serious now. He said, 'I don't like the sound of that. Not one bit.'

Silverhair didn't understand. 'Why not?'

But now, from the circle of Cows, Foxeye, her sister, cried out.

Lop-ear pushed Silverhair's backside, gently, with his trunk. 'Go on, Silverhair. You can't stay with us Bulls. Your place is with your sister.'

And so Silverhair, with a mix of fascination and reluctance, walked to the centre of the Family, where the Cows were gathered around her sister.

*

At the heart of the group was massive Owlheart – Silver-hair's grandmother, the Matriarch of them all – and like a shadow behind her was Wolfnose. Wolfnose, Owlheart's mother, had once been Matriarch, but now she was so old that her name, given her for the sharpness of her sense of smell as a calf, seemed no more than a sad joke.

And before Owlheart's tree-trunk legs was a Cow, lying on her side on the ground. It was Foxeye, Silverhair's sister, who was close to birthing.

Owlheart lifted her great head and fixed Silverhair with a steady, intense glare; for a few heartbeats Silverhair saw in her the ghost of the patient predator bird after whom the Matriarch had been named. 'Silverhair! Where have you been?' She added such a deep rumble to her voice that Silverhair felt her chest quiver.

'To the headland. I was just—'

'I don't care,' said Owlheart. Given the question, it wasn't a logical answer. But then, Silverhair reflected, if you're the Matriarch, you don't have to be logical.

Now Snagtooth – Silverhair's aunt, Owlheart's daughter – was standing before her. 'About time, Silverhair,' she snapped, and she spat out a bit of enamel that had broken off the misshapen molar that was growing out of the left side of her mouth. Snagtooth was tall for a Cow: big, intimidating, unpredictably angry.

'Leave me alone, Snagtooth.'

Croptail came pushing his way between Snagtooth's legs to Silverhair. 'Silverhair! Silverhair!' Croptail was Foxeye's first calf. He was a third-molar – on his third set of teeth – born ten years earlier, a skinny, uncertain ball of orange hair with a peculiar stub of a tail. Kept away from his mother during the birth, he looked lost and frightened. 'I'm hungry, Silverhair.' He pushed his mouth into her fur, looking for her nipples.

Gently she tried to nudge him away. 'I can't feed you, child.'

The little Bull's voice was plaintive. 'But Momma is sick.'

'No she isn't. But when she has the new baby, you'll have to feed yourself. You'll have to find grass and—'

But Snagtooth was still growling at Silverhair. 'You always were unreliable. My sister would be ashamed.'

Silverhair squared up to her sour-eyed aunt. 'Don't you talk about my mother.'

'I'll say what I like.'

'It's only because you can't have calves of your own, no matter how many Bulls you take. That's why you're as bitter as last summer's bark. Everybody knows it.'

'Why, you little—'

Owlheart stepped between them, her great trunk working back and forth. 'Are you two Bulls in musth? Snagtooth, take the calf.'

'But she—'

Owlheart reared up to her full height, and towered over Snagtooth. 'Do not question me, daughter. Take him.'

Snagtooth subsided. She dug an impatient trunk into the mat of fur under Silverhair's belly, and pulled out a squealing Croptail.

At last, Silverhair was able to reach Foxeye. Her sister was lying on her side, her back legs flexing uncomfortably, the swell in her belly obvious. Her fur was muddy and matted with dew and sweat.

Silverhair entwined her trunk with her sister's. 'I'm sorry I'm so late.'

'Don't be,' said Foxeye weakly. Her small, sharp eyes were, today, brown pools of tears, and the dugs that protruded from the damp, flattened fur over her chest were swollen with milk. 'I wish Mother was here.'

Silverhair's grip tightened. 'So do I.'

The pregnancy had taken almost two full years. Foxeye's mate had been a Bull from Lop-ear's bachelor herd – and that, Silverhair thought uneasily, was the last time any of them had seen a mammoth from outside the Family. Foxeye

23

had striven to time her pregnancy so that her calf would be born in the early spring, with a full season of plant growth and feeding ahead of it before the winter closed around them once more. It had been a long, difficult gestation, with Foxeye often falling ill; but at last, it seemed, her day had come.

The great, stolid legs of Owlheart and Wolfnose stood over Foxeye, and Silverhair felt a huge reassurance that the older Cows were here to help her sister, as they had helped so many mothers before – including her own.

Foxeye's legs kicked back, and she cried out.

Silverhair stepped back, alarmed. 'Is it time?'

Owlheart laid a strong, soothing trunk on Foxeye's back. 'Don't be afraid, Silverhair. Watch now.'

The muscles of Foxeye's stomach flexed in great waves. And then, with startling suddenness, it began.

A pink-purple foetal sac thrust out of Foxeye's body. The sac was small, streamlined like a seal, and glistening with fluid. As it pushed in great surges from Foxeye's pink warmth it looked more like something from the sea, thought Silverhair, than mammoth blood and bone.

One last heave, and Foxeye expelled the sac. It dropped with a liquid noise to the ground.

Owlheart stepped forward. With clean, confident swipes of her tusks she began to cut open the foetal sac and strip it away.

Foxeye shuddered once more. The afterbirth was expelled, a steaming, bloody mass of flesh. Then Foxeye fell back against the hard, cold ground, closing her eyes, her empty belly heaving with her deep, exhausted breaths.

Silverhair watched, fascinated, as the new calf emerged from its sac. The trunk came first, a thin, dark rope. Then came the head, for a moment protruding almost comically from the sac. It was plastered with pale-orange hair, soaked with blood and amniotic fluid, and it turned this way and that. Two eyes opened, and they were bright-pink discs;

then the tiny mouth popped moistly open under the waving trunk.

'Her eyes,' Silverhair said softly.

Wolfnose, her great-grandmother, was stroking and soothing Foxeye. 'What about her eyes?'

'They're *red*.'

'So they should be. Everything is as it should be, as it has been since Kilukpuk birthed her last calves in the Swamp.'

The baby was a small bundle of bloody, matted fur, sprawled on the grass. She breathed with wet sucking noises, and her breath steamed; she let out a thin wail of protest and began to scrabble at the ground with her stumpy legs.

Owlheart's trunk tapped Silverhair's flank. 'Help her, child.'

Silverhair stepped forward nervously. She lowered her trunk and wrapped it around the calf's belly. Her skin was hot, and slick with birthing fluid that was already gathering frost. With gentle pulling, Silverhair helped the infant to stagger to her feet. The calf looked about blindly, mewling.

An infant mammoth, at birth, is already three feet tall. A human baby's body weighs less than the mammoth's brain.

'She wants her first suck,' Owlheart said softly.

With gentle tugs Silverhair guided the stumbling infant forward.

Foxeye knelt and stood, uncertainly, so that her pendulous dugs hung down before the calf. Silverhair slid her trunk under the calf's chin, and helped the calf roll her tiny trunk on to her forehead. Soon the baby's pink mouth had found her mother's nipple.

'Red eyes,' said Foxeye. 'Like the rising sun. That's her name. *Sunfire*.'

Then Silverhair, with Owlheart and Wolfnose, stood by the calf and mother. They kept the infant warm with their bodies, and used their trunks to clean the baby as she stood amid the rich hair of her mother's belly, protected by the palisade of their huge legs around her. After a time Foxeye moved away from the reaching calf, encouraging her to walk after her.

And, as she watched the infant suckle, Silverhair felt an odd pressure in her own empty dugs.

At the end of the long night, with the deep purple of dawn seeping into the eastern sky, Silverhair broke away from the Cows so she could feed and pass dung.

Wolfnose came wandering over the uneven tundra.

Silverhair, moved by an obscure concern, followed her great-grandmother.

The old Cow, her hair clumpy and matted, tugged fitfully at the trampled grass. But the co-ordination of her trunk-fingers was poor, and the wiry grass blades evaded her. Even when she managed to drag a fingerful from the hard, frozen ground and crammed it in her mouth, Silverhair could see that much of the crushed grass was spilling from her mouth, and a greenish juice trickled over her lower lip.

Silverhair, tenderly, reached forward and tucked the grass back into Wolfnose's mouth.

Wolfnose was so old now that the two great molars in her jaw – her last set – were wearing down, and soon they would no longer be able to perform the job of grinding her food. Then, no matter what the Family did for her, Wolfnose's ribs and backbone would become even more visible through her sagging flesh and clumps of hair. And, if the wolves spared her, her rheumy eyes would close for the last time.

It would be a time of sadness. But it was as it had been since the days of Kilukpuk.

Wolfnose was mumbling, even as her great jaw scraped ineffectually at the grass. 'Too long,' she said. 'Too long.'

'Too long since what?' Silverhair asked, puzzled.

'Since the last birth. That whining Bull-calf who's always under my feet—'

'Croptail.'

'Too long . . .'

Mammoths do not have clocks, or wrist-watches, or calendars; they do not count out the time in arbitrary packages of seconds and days and years, as humans do. But nevertheless the mammoths know time, on a deep level within themselves. They can measure the slow migration of shadows across the land, the turning faces of Arctic poppies, the strength of air currents. So massive are mammoths that they can *feel* the turn of the Earth on its axis, the slow pulse of the seasons as the Earth spins in its stately annual dance, making the sun arc across the sky – and, so deep and long are their memories, they are even aware of the greater cycles of the planet. There is the Great-Year, the twenty-thousand-year nod of the precessing axis of the spinning planet. And the mammoths know even the million-year cycle of the great ice sheets, which lap against the mountains like huge frozen waves.

So Silverhair knew time. She knew how she was embedded in the great hierarchy of Earth's rhythms.

And she knew that Wolfnose was right.

Wolfnose said, 'One infant, and one half-starved calf. It's not enough to keep the Family going, Grassfoot.'

Grassfoot had been the name of Silverhair's mother – Wolfnose's granddaughter – who, when Silverhair was herself still an infant younger than Croptail was now, had died. Calling Silverhair 'Grassfoot' was a mistake Wolfnose had made before.

'I know,' said Silverhair sadly. 'I know, Great-grandmother.' And, tenderly, she tucked more grass into the old Cow's trembling mouth.

After a time Owlheart came forward. Her huge head loomed over Silverhair, so close that the Matriarch's wiry hair brushed Silverhair's brow. She pulled Silverhair away from Wolfnose.

'I know you're no fool, child,' rumbled Owlheart. 'Sometimes I think you're the smartest, the best of us all.'

Silverhair was startled; she'd never been spoken to like that before.

'But,' the Matriarch went on, 'I want you to understand that there is nowhere so important for you to be, right now, as *here*, at the time of this, our first new birth for many seasons. Never mind headlands. Never mind plausible young Bulls, even. Do you know *why* you must be here?'

'To help my sister.'

The Matriarch shook her great head. 'More than that. *You must learn.* Soon you will be ready for oestrus, ready for a calf of your own. And that calf will depend on you – for its whole life, at first, and later, for the lore and wisdom you can teach it. We don't come into the world fully made, like the birds and the mice. We have to learn how to live. And it will be up to you to teach your calf. There is no greater responsibility. But you cannot teach if you do not learn yourself.' Owlheart stepped back. 'And if you do not learn, you will never become the great Matriarch I think you could be.'

At that, Silverhair's mouth dropped open, and her pink tongue rolled out with surprise. 'Me? A Matriarch?'

It was the most ridiculous thing she had ever heard.

But Owlheart held her gaze. 'It is your destiny, child,' she said sadly. 'Don't you know that yet?'

CHAPTER 3
THE WALK SOUTH

Mammoths sleep for only a few hours at a time. During the long nights of winter – and during the Arctic summer, when the sun never sets – they sleep not to a fixed pattern but whenever they feel the need.

So, when Silverhair woke, the Moon was still high in the sky, bathing the frozen land in blue light. But soon the short spring day would return. She heard a snow bunting call – a herald of spring – and a raven croaked by overhead.

Silverhair remembered the great mystery she had confronted, and – despite the new calf, despite Owlheart's rumblings – her curiosity was like a pull on her tail, dragging her south again.

Lop-ear was a little way away from the Family, digging in a patch of snow for frozen grass. Silverhair shook frost from her outer guard hair and went to him.

For fear of disturbing the others she silently wrapped her trunk around his and tugged. At first he was reluctant to move; Bull or not, he didn't have quite the powerful streak of curiosity that motivated Silverhair. But after a few heartbeats he let Silverhair lead him away.

Lop-ear spoke with high-pitched chirrups of his trunk that he knew would not carry back to the Family. 'Look at Owlheart.'

Silverhair turned to look back at the Family. She could see the massive dark forms of Owlheart and Wolfnose looming protectively over Foxeye and her new calf. And she could see Owlheart's eyes, like chips of ice in that huge brown head: an unblinking gaze, fixed on her.

'They don't call her Owlheart for nothing,' Lop-ear murmured.

Silverhair shivered. She remembered Owlheart's admonitions; she should stay and spend time with her sister and the calf. But the pull of curiosity in her was too strong. She knew she had to go and explore what she had found on that remote coast.

So she turned away, and the two of them walked on, heading south.

There was ice everywhere, beneath the starry sky. The ridged ice and snow drifts seemed to flow smoothly under their feet.

Silverhair walked steadily and evenly. Her bulk was dark and huge, herself and Lop-ear the only moving things in all this world of white and blue and black. Her walk was a sway of liquid grace, her head nodding with each step, her trunk swaying before her, its great weight obvious. And when she ran, her footsteps were firm, her powerful legs remaining stiff beneath her great weight, her feet swelling slightly as they absorbed her bulk.

They battled through a storm.

The snow and fog swirled around them, matting their hair with freezing moisture, at times making it impossible for them to see more than a few paces ahead. But Silverhair knew this was the last defiant bellow of the dying winter, and she kept her head down and used her bulk to drive herself forward across a tundra that was like a frozen ocean.

And they walked by night, when the only light came from the Moon, which cast a glittering purple glow on the fields of ice and snow. At such times the world was utterly still and silent, save for their own breathing.

To a watching human Silverhair would have looked something like an Asian elephant – but coated with the long, dark-brown hair of a musk ox – round and solid and dark and massive, looking as if she had sprouted from the unforgiving Earth itself.

From the ground under her tree-trunk legs to the top of her broad shoulders – as a human would have measured her – Silverhair was seven feet tall. She was fifteen years old. She could expect to continue growing until she was twenty-five or thirty, until she reached the height of eight or nine feet attained by Owlheart, the Matriarch of the Family. But at that she would be dwarfed by the biggest of the Bulls – like crusty old Eggtusk, who stood all of eleven feet tall at the shoulder.

Her head was large, with a high dome on her crown. Her face, with its long jaw, was surprisingly graceful. Her shoulders had a high, distinctive hump, behind which her back sloped markedly from front to rear – unlike the horizontal line of an elephant's back.

Her body was a machine designed to combat the cold.

The layer of fat under her skin – thick as a human forearm – had kept her warm through the lightless depths of the Arctic winter. Her ears and tail were small, for those thin, exposed organs would otherwise have been at risk from frostbite – but the long hairs which extended from her fleshy tail would let it serve as an effective fly-swat in the mosquito-ridden months of the short summer. There was even a small flap of skin beneath her tail, to seal her anus from the cold.

Her ears had an oddly human shape. Her eyes, too, were small like a human's, and buried deep in a nest of wrinkled skin, shielded from the worst of the weather by thick lashes.

Her tusks were six feet long. Sprouting from their deep sockets at the front of her face, they twisted before her in a loose spiral, their tips almost touching before her. The undersides of both her tusks were worn, for she used them to strip bark and dig up plants – and, in the depths of winter, they served as a snow plough to dig out vegetation for feeding, or even as an ice-breaker to expose water to drink in frozen ponds. The bluish ivory of the tusks was finely textured, with growth rings that mapped her age.

Her trunk, six feet long, served as her nose, her hand and arm, and was her main feeding apparatus. It was a tube of flesh packed with tiny muscles, capable of movement in any direction, even contraction and extension like a telescope. It had two finger-like extensions at its tip, for manipulating grass and other small objects. As it worked, the trunk's surface folded and wrinkled, betraying the complexity of its structure.

A heavy coat of fur covered her body.

Over a fine downy underwool, her guard hairs were long, coarse and thick, springy and transparent – more like lengths of fishing line than human hair. The hair on her head was just a few inches long. But it hung down in a long fringe under her chin and neck, and at the sides of her trunk. From her flanks and belly hung a skirt of guard hair almost three feet long, giving her something of the look of a Tibetan yak.

Her coat was dark orange-brown, like a musk ox's. And, in a broad cap between the eyes, there lay the patch of snow-white fur that had given Silverhair her name.

Silverhair was *mammuthus primigenius*: a woolly mammoth.

Ten thousand years before, creatures like Silverhair had populated the fringe of the retreating northern ice caps – right around the planet, through Asia from the Baltic to the Pacific, across North America from Alaska to Labrador. But those days were gone.

The isolation of this remote island, off the northern coast of Siberia, had saved Silverhair and her ancestors from the extinction which had washed over the planet, claiming her cousins and many other large animals.

But now the mammoths were trapped here, on the Island.

And Silverhair and her Family were the last of her kind, the last in all the world.

The short days and long nights wore away.

Silverhair and Lop-ear took time to care for their skin. They scratched against an outcropping of rock, luxuriantly dislodging the grasses and dirt which had become stuck in the crevices of their skin and under their hair. They used a patch of dusty, dried-out soil to powder their skin and force out parasites.

Under her thick hair, Silverhair's skin would have looked rough and callused. But it was very sensitive. Under a tough, horny outer layer there were receptors so sensitive she could pinpoint an annoying insect, and brush it off with a precise flick of her trunk or swish of her tail – or even crush it with one focused ripple of her skin.

Nevertheless Silverhair looked forward to the summer, when open puddles of water would be available, and she would be able to wallow comfortably in mud, cooling and washing out ticks and fleas and lice.

'. . . I wonder if Owlheart guessed where we were going?' Lop-ear was saying as he scratched. 'Did you see her talking to Eggtusk?'

'No. But after that lecture I'm surprised she's letting me out of the sight of the calf.'

Lop-ear raised his trunk to sniff at the frosty air. 'She was right. Raising the young is the most important thing of all. But she's obviously making an exception for you.'

'Why?'

'Perhaps because – to Owlheart – this may be more important than anything else you can do – even more important than learning about calves.' Lop-ear rested his trunk on his tusks. 'Owlheart is wise,' he said. 'She listens with more than ears. She listens with her heart and mind. That's why she's Matriarch.'

'And why,' said Silverhair miserably, 'I could never be

Matriarch, if I live until the Earth spins itself to dust.' She told Lop-ear what Owlheart had said: that it was her destiny to be Matriarch.

He said, 'She's probably right. There aren't too many candidates.'

'Foxeye—'

'Your sister is a fine mother. But she's weak, Silverhair. You know that. Other than that, there is only Snagtooth.'

Silverhair's hair bristled. 'I would leave the Family if *she* were ever Matriarch. She's mean-spirited, vindictive . . .'

'Then who else is there?'

When she thought it through like that, he was, of course, right. His logic was relentless. But it was all utterly depressing.

'I don't *want* to be a Matriarch,' she said miserably. 'I don't want all that responsibility.'

'Perhaps you really do have the spirit of Longtusk inside you.'

'That's ridiculous,' she said. But she was pleased to hear him say it.

Lop-ear lifted his trunk and rubbed her snow-white scalp with affection, a gentle touch that thrilled her. 'Like Longtusk, you're a wanderer,' said Lop-ear. 'Perhaps you too could lead us to places no one else could even dream of. And, like Longtusk, you're perverse. After all, Longtusk had to fight to win the command of his Family, didn't he? The story goes the other Bulls all but killed him, rather than accept his orders.'

'But I don't want to fight anybody.'

'Maybe not. But you fight yourself, Silverhair. How typical it is of you that you should choose to model yourself on the one Cycle hero who you could never be, Longtusk the Bull!'

He was right.

In all the great tundra of time reflected in the Cycle, there is only one Bull hero: Longtusk.

When the world warmed, and the ice fell back into the north, the Lost – the mammoths' only true enemy – had come pushing into the mammoth tundra from the south, butchering and murdering. All over the planet mammoths had died, Families and Clans falling together.

. . . All, that is, save the Family of Longtusk: for Longtusk had somehow brought his people across the cold waters here, to the Island. Nobody knew how he had done this: some said he had flown like a bird, carrying his Family on his mighty back; some said he stamped his mighty foot and caused the sea to roar from the ground. At any rate, the Lost had never followed, and the mammoths had been safe.

But Longtusk had given his life . . .

They found a deep puddle with only a thin layer of ice on top. Lop-ear broke through this easily with his tusk, and they plunged their trunks into the water. When Lop-ear had lifted a trunkful he closed his trunk by clenching its fingers, lifted the end and curled it into his mouth. Then he tilted his head back, opened his trunk and let the water gush into his mouth, a delicious and cooling stream.

They soon drained the puddle. But it was a rare treat: standing water had been scarce this winter, and the Family was counting on an early spring thaw. Mammoths need much fresh water each day. They can eat snow, but have to sacrifice precious body heat to melt it.

'Of course,' said Lop-ear, 'even if you were to become Matriarch, I'm not at all sure where you *could* lead us.'

'What do you mean?'

He led her to a patch of frost overlying harder, older ice. He picked up a twig with his trunk and began to scrape at the frost.

'Here is the Island,' he said. It was a rough oval. 'It is surrounded by sea, which we can't cross. To the north there are the Mountains at the End of the World. And to the south, here is the spruce forest.' More scratchings.

Silverhair watched him, baffled. 'What are you doing?'

He looked up. 'I'm—' There was no word for it. 'Imagine you're a bird,' he said at last. 'A guillemot, flying high over the Island.'

'But I'm not a bird.'

'In Kilukpuk's name, Silverhair, if you can imagine yourself as Longtusk you can surely stretch your mind that far!'

She stretched out her ears and spun, pretending to wheel like a bird. 'Look at me! Caw! Caw!'

'All right, Silverhair the gull. Now, you're looking down at the Island. You see it sitting in the middle of the sea, like a lump of dung in a pond. Yes?'

'Yes . . .'

'Look – now!' With his trunk, he pointed to the frost scrapings he had made.

And – looking down as if she were a mammoth-gull, concentrating hard – for a heartbeat, yes, she could see the Island, see it through his scrapings, just as if she really was a gull, balanced on the winds high above.

To Silverhair, the simple drawing was a kind of magic; she had never seen anything like it.

'Every time the Earth spins around the sun the summer is a little longer, the winter a little less harsh. And the forest encroaches a little more on the tundra.' Absently Lop-ear dug in the soil with his tusks, burrowed with his trunk and produced a scraping of grass. 'You know, Wolfnose remembers a time – when she was only a calf herself – when the spruce forest was just a few straggling saplings clinging to the coast. And *now* look how far it has spread.' With his twig, he pointed to the middle of the Island. 'You see? We are contained in this strip of the Island, between forest and mountains, like a calf that has fallen in a mud hole. And the strip is narrowing.'

'So what do we do?'

'I don't know. This Island is all we have. We have absolutely nowhere else to go.'

She admired Lop-ear's unusual mind, the clarity and

depth of thinking he was capable of. But his logic was chilling. 'It can't be true,' she said. 'What about the Sky Steppe?'

Lop-ear said, 'Do you really believe that?'

Silverhair was scandalised. 'Lop-ear, it's in the *Cycle*.'

The Cycle contains tales of a mysterious steppe which floats in the sky, where – the story goes – mammoths will one day roam free.

But Lop-ear was growling. 'Look – we can know the past because we remember it, and we can tell it to our calves, who remember it in turn . . . Through the Cycle, and the memories of our mothers, we can "remember" all the way back to Kilukpuk's Swamp. That's all sensible. But as to the future—' He tossed his twig in the air. 'We can no more know the future than we can say how that twig will fall.'

The stick rattled to the bone-hard ground, out of her sight.

'And besides,' he said, 'there might soon be nobody to go to the Sky Steppe anyhow.'

'What do you mean?'

He looked at her mournfully. 'Think about it. When was the last time you heard a contact rumble from my bachelor herd – or any other Family, come to that? How many mammoths have we seen on this trek? We haven't even found footprints or fresh dung—'

The thought was chilling; she turned away from it. 'You think too much.'

'I wish I could stop,' he said quietly.

They moved on, through cloudy day and Moonlit night.

They came to a place they knew was good for salty soil. It was frozen over, but they set to scraping at the ice with their tusks until they had exposed some of the bone-hard soil. Then they dug out a little and tucked it into their mouths; it was dry and dusty, but it contained salt and other minerals otherwise missing from the mammoths' diet.

And, nearby, under a thin layer of hoar frost, they found

a heap of mammoth dung. It was reasonably fresh, and hope briefly lifted; perhaps other Families were, after all, close.

But then Silverhair recognised the dung's sharp scent. 'Why, it's mine,' she said. 'I must have come this way before.'

Lop-ear broke open the pat of dung – it wasn't quite frozen in the centre – and began to lift chunks of it to his mouth. Mammoths will eat a little dung to sustain the colonies of bacteria that live in their guts, which help them digest grasses.

'Maybe our luck is changing, even so,' he said, around a mouthful of soil and dung.

'How?'

'Look up.'

She did so, and saw a curtain of light streaks spread across the sky – mostly yellow and crimson, fading to black, but here and there tinged with green. It extended from the horizon, all the way up the sky, almost to the zenith over their heads. The curtain rippled gently, like the guard hairs that dangle from the belly of a mammoth.

It was an aurora.

Mammoths believe the aurora is made up of the spirits of every mammoth who has ever lived, brought to life again by a wind from the sun, so joyous they dance at the very top of the air.

Lop-ear said, 'What do you think? Is Longtusk up there somewhere, looking down on us? Do you think he's come to guide our way?'

And indeed, the ghostly light of the aurora had made the Moonlit landscape glow green and blue, almost as brightly as day.

With uplifted hearts, they set off once more.

After days of walking they climbed a shallow ridge which gave them a view of the Island's south coast, and Silverhair could see the pale blue-white gleam of pack ice on the sea.

But between the two mammoths and the coast, lying over the land like a layer of guard hair, was the spruce forest. The first isolated, straggling trees were already close.

The two mammoths skirted the darker depths of the forest, staying at the northern fringe where only a few scattered, stunted trees encroached on the rocky tundra, ancient plants that grew no higher than their own bellies. It was well known that wolves inhabited the deeper forest. It was unlikely that even a pack would take on two full-grown mammoths, but inside the denser parts of the forest movement would be difficult, and it would be foolish to offer the wily predators any opportunity.

The only sound was the crunch of ice beneath their feet, the hiss of breath in their trunks, and the low moan of the wind in the trees. In the branches of a dwarf spruce a solitary capercaillie sat, unperturbed, eyeing them as they passed.

Night was falling by the time they reached the headland.

The sea opened up before them, flat and calm. A fringe of fast ice pushed out from the land, hard and glistening. Further out the sea ice was littered with trapped icebergs, sculptured mountains of ice that glowed green and blue. And Silverhair could see the rope of water that cut off the Island from the Mainland – which was, she saw, still shrouded by storm clouds, hiding the glittering and mysterious array of lights that clustered there.

As the sun waned, the colours faded to an ice-blue twilight. The air grew colder, and the sea water steamed.

It was a bleak, frozen scene. But there was life here. More seabirds were arriving from the south, fulmars and black guillemots, and they had begun their elaborate courtship in the pink, watery sunshine. Seals slid through the open water, snorting when they broke the surface.

Beneath the headland there was a valley which descended to the rocky southern coast. Silverhair and Lop-ear clambered down this valley now.

Between the walls of the valley, nothing moved save an occasional swirl of dry snow crystals lifted by the wind. The mountainside here had been blown almost clear of snow, and in the shade the rock was covered by a treacherous glaze of ice. The mammoths' broad feet gripped the ground well; the round soles were thickened into ridges for that purpose. But even so Silverhair's feet slid out from under her, and she barely managed to keep from stumbling. Once she found herself teetering on the edge of a sheet drop into a snow-filled chasm.

Surrounded by these huge walls of ice and rock, Silverhair received an unwelcome perspective on the smallness and frailty of even a mammoth's life.

At last they reached the beach. It was growing dark, and they decided to wait out the long night here.

The beach was a strange place, where neither of them felt comfortable.

For one thing it was noisy, compared to the thick stillness of the Arctic nights they were used to: there was the continual lapping of the sea at the shingle, the crunching of stones beneath their shifting feet, the snapping and groaning of the sea ice as it rose and fell in response to the oily surges of the water beneath. There was no food to be had here, for this eroded, shifting place was neither land nor sea. It was even considered a waste to pass dung here, for it would be merely washed away to sea rather than enrich the land.

They endured a long, uncomfortable night of broken sleep.

The dawn, when at last it came, was clear. The sky turned an intense blue, and the sea ice was so white that the horizon was a firm line. And as the sunrise itself approached, a shaft of deep-red light shot suddenly straight up, piercing the blue. Silverhair looked out over the sea ice, and saw that, thanks to a mirage effect, the distant pack ice seemed to be lifting into the sky, illusory towers rising and

40

falling in the heat from the sun. And when the sun rose a little higher she saw a ghostly companion rise with it, a halo scattered by ice crystals in the air.

Lop-ear, impulsively, ran to the water's edge. Breaking the thin ice there, he waded in until his legs were immersed up to his hips, and his belly hair was soaked and floating loosely on the surface.

He looked back at Silverhair. 'Come on. What are you waiting for?'

Silverhair took a hesitant step forward. She dipped one foot in the water, and steeled herself to go further.

Silverhair had an abiding dread of deep water. As a small calf, she had almost fallen into a fast-flowing glacier runoff stream. She had been washed down the stream, bobbing like a piece of rotten wood, her squeals all but drowned out by the rush of water. Only the fast brain and strong trunk of Wolfnose had saved her from being dashed against the rocks, or drowned.

Lop-ear waded clumsily back towards her; he splashed her, and the water droplets were icy. 'I'm sorry,' he said. 'I forgot. That was stupid of me.'

'It's all right. I'm just being foolish.'

Lop-ear grunted. 'There's nothing foolish about learning to avoid danger.' He quoted the Cycle. *'The wolf's first bite is its responsibility. Its second is yours.* I'm being selfish—'

'No.' And Silverhair waded forward deliberately, leading the way into the ocean.

The water immediately soaked through the hair over her legs. Close to freezing, its cold penetrated to her skin. Her hair, waving like seaweed around her belly, impeded her progress. The sheets of landfast ice crackled around her legs and chest.

Lop-ear stopped her. 'That's far enough,' he said. 'Now—'

Awkwardly he knelt down, so his chest was immersed. Then he dipped his head; soon the water was lapping over his eyes and forehead.

He lifted his head in a great spray, and she could see frost forming on his hair and eyelashes. He said, 'Did you hear me?'

With great reluctance, she dropped her head so that her trunk and right ear were immersed in the icy water. Lop-ear extended his trunk underwater and emitted a series of strange calls: deep-toned whistles and bleats, mixed with higher-pitched squeaks and squeals.

'What are you doing?'

'Calling our Cousins. The Calves of Siros. Don't you know your Cycle? The *sea cows*, Silverhair.'

She snorted. 'But the sea cows all died lifetimes ago. The Lost hunted them even harder than they hunted us. That's what the Cycle says—'

'The Cycle isn't always right.'

'Have you ever *seen* a sea cow?'

'No,' he said. 'But I've never seen the back of my own head either. Doesn't mean to say it doesn't exist.' And he thrust his trunk back into the sea and continued his plaintive call.

Reluctantly she ducked her ear back under the water.

The sea had its own huge, hollow noises, like an immense empty cavern. She heard the voices of seals: birdlike chirrups, long swooping whistles, and short popping cries that the seals bounced off the ice sheets above them, using the echoes to seek out their air holes. Then, deeper and more remote, there were the groans of whales, and still deeper calls which might come from half the world away . . .

And – briefly – there was a series of low whistles, interspersed with high-pitched squeaks and squeals.

But the sound died away.

They lifted their heads out of the water. They looked at each other.

'It was probably only an echo,' she said. 'Some undersea cliff.'

'I know. There's nothing there. But wouldn't it have been wonderful *if*—'

'Come on. Let's go and get warm.'

They turned and splashed their way out of the water. Silverhair shook her head to rid it of the frost that was forming. To get their blood flowing through their chilled skin once more, they played: they chased each other across the shingle, mock-wrestled with their trunks, and gambolled like calves.

Silverhair looked back once, at the place where they had called to the sea cows.

Far out in the Channel she thought she could see something surfacing: huge, black, sleek. But then it was gone.

It was probably just a trick of the light.

CHAPTER 4
THE MONSTER OF THE
ICE FLOE

When they were warm they continued along the beach, in search of the peculiar creatures Silverhair had spotted.

Hundreds of guillemots were arriving on the cliffs above them. This first sign of the summer's burst of fecundity seemed incongruous on such a bitterly cold morning; in fact, the nesting ledges were still covered in snow and ice. But the seabirds had to start early if they were to complete their breeding cycle before, all too soon, the snow of winter returned. And so the birds clung to the cliffs and fought over the prime nesting sites. So intense were these battles, Silverhair saw, that two birds, locked together beak to bloody beak, fell from the high cliffs and dashed themselves against the sea ice below.

Fast as a spray of blown snow an Arctic fox darted forward and grabbed both birds, killing them immediately. The fox buried his catch in the ice, and returned to the foot of the nesting cliff in search of more pickings.

From a snow bank high on the cliff a female polar bear, her fur yellow-white, pushed her way out of her den. She yawned and stretched, and Silverhair wondered if this was the bear she had seen before.

The bear clambered back up to her den, and sat by the entrance. After a time a cub appeared – small, dumpy and dazzling white – and greeted the world with terrified squeaks. A second cub emerged, then a third. The mother walked confidently down the steep cliff towards the sea, while the cubs looked on with trepidation. At last two of the cubs followed her, gingerly, sliding backwards, their claws clutching the snow. The other stayed in the den entrance and cried so loudly its mother returned with the others, and she suckled all three in the sun. Then the bear walked steadily down to the sea ice – in search of her first meal since the autumn – and her cubs clumsily followed.

The mammoths walked around a rocky spur, and came to the Nest of Straight Lines.

Lop-ear slowed, his eyes wide, his trunk held up in the air, his good ear cocked, alert for danger.

Silverhair was trembling, for this was an unnatural place. But still, she said: 'We have to go on. The strange ice floe, whatever it was, must have come to rest further on than this. Come on.'

And, without allowing herself to hesitate, she set off along the beach. After a few heartbeats she heard Lop-ear's heavy steps crackling on the shingle as he followed.

In this mysterious place, set back from the beach, a series of blocky shapes huddled against the cliff. They were dark and angular, each of them much larger even than a mammoth. The great blocks were hollowed out. Holes gaped in their sides and tops, allowing in the low sunlight; but there was no movement within.

Lop-ear said, 'Those things look like skulls to me.'

Looking again, she saw that he was right: *skulls*, but with eye sockets and gaping mouths made out of straight lines, and big enough for a mammoth to climb inside.

'They must be the skulls of giants, then,' she said.

And the most horrific aspect of the place was that the whole of it was constructed of hard, straight lines. It was the lines which had earned the place its mammoth name, for, aside from the horizon line and the trunks of trees, there are few long straight lines in nature.

In the centre of the Nest there was a great stalk: like the trunk of a tree, but not solid, made of sticks and spars through which Silverhair could see the pale dawn sky. And at the top of the stalk there was a series of big round shells, like the petals of a flower – but much bigger, so big they looked as if a mammoth could clamber inside.

The mammoths peered up at the assemblage of brooding forms, dwarfed.

'Perhaps those things up there are the ears of the giants who lived here,' said Lop-ear, awed.

'But what *happened* to the giants?'

'You know what Eggtusk says.'

'What?'

'That this place has nothing to do with giants,' he said.

'Then what?'

'*Lost*,' said Lop-ear. 'The Lost made this.'

And, as he spoke the name of the mammoths' most dread enemy of the past, it was Silverhair's turn to shiver.

By unspoken consent, they hurried on.

A flat sheet, lying on the shingle, briefly caught Silverhair's eye. It looked at first like a broken sheet of ice, but, as she came closer, she saw that it was made of wood – though she knew of no tree which produced such huge, straight-edged branches.

There were markings on the sheet.

She slowed, studying the markings. The patterns reminded her oddly of the scrapings Lop-ear had made in the frost. There was a splash of yellow, almost like a flower – or like a star, cupped in a crescent Moon. And beneath it, a collection of lines and curves that had no meaning for her:

USSR

AIR FORCE

SECURE AREA

ENTRANCE PROHIBITED

She wanted to ask Lop-ear about it; perhaps he would understand. But he had already hurried ahead, and she didn't want to linger here, alone in this unnatural place; she ran to catch him up.

With the Nest of Straight Lines behind them, they approached the half-frozen sea.

'What I saw must have been about here,' said Silverhair, trying to think.

Lop-ear looked around and raised his trunk. 'I can't smell anything.'

The two mammoths walked a little way on to the ice, which squeaked and crackled under them. The ice that clung closest to the shore, where the sea was frozen all the way to the bottom, was called landfast ice. It formed in protected bays, or else drifted in from the sea. Its width varied depending on how deep the water was. Later in the summer the landfast ice would break free and melt, or drift away with the pack ice.

The pack ice was the frozen surface of the deeper ocean. It was a blue-white sheet crumpled into pressure ridges, like lines of sand dunes sculpted in white. Further away from the land Silverhair could see black lines carved in the ice: leads, cracks exposing open water between the loose mass of floes. As the spring wore on the leads would extend in towards the coast, splitting off the ice floes. The floes would break up, or be washed out to open sea by the powerful current which ran between the Mainland and the Island.

Dark clouds hung over the open Channel, that forbidding stretch of black water; the clouds formed from the steam rising from the water.

And, on a floe far from the land, she made out a black, unmoving shape.

She trumpeted in triumph. Gulls, startled awake, cawed in response.

'There!' she cried. 'Do you see it?'

Lop-ear, patiently, stared where she did. 'I don't see a thing. Just pressure ridges, and shadows . . . *Oh*.'

'You do see it! You do! That's what I saw, floating in the sea – and now it's on the ice.'

It might have been the size of a mammoth, she supposed – but a mammoth lying inert on the floe. All Silverhair's fear had evaporated like hoar frost, so great was her gladness at rediscovering the strange object. 'Come on.' And she set out across the landfast ice.

Reluctantly, Lop-ear followed.

As they moved away from the shore, the quality of the sound changed. The soft lapping of the sea was gone, and the ice creaked and groaned as it shifted on the sea, a deep rumble like the call of a mammoth.

The pressure ridges were high here, frozen waves that came almost up to her shoulder. The ridges were topped by blue ice, scoured clean by the wind, and soft snow lay in the hollows between them. The ridges were difficult to scramble over, so Silverhair found a lead and walked along at the edge of the water, where the ice was flatter.

Frost-smoke, sparkling in the sunlight, rose from the black, oily water.

On one floe she found the grisly site of a polar bear's kill. It was a seal's breathing hole, iced over and tinged with blood. She could see a bloodstained area of ice where the bear must have dragged the seal and devoured it. And there was a hollowed-out area of snow near a pressure ridge, marked by black excrement, where the bear had probably slept after its bloody feast.

The wind picked up. Ice crystals swirled around her. When she looked up at the sun, she saw there was a halo around it. She knew she must be careful, for that was a sign the sea ice might break up.

She came to a place where the pressure ridges towered over her. Surrounded by the ridges, all she could see were the neighbouring hummocks and the sky above.

She struggled to the top of a crag of ice.

From here she could see the tops of the other ridges, and

the narrow valleys that separated them. They looked as if they had been scraped into this ice surface by some gigantic tusk.

And she realised that she had walked further out to sea than she had imagined, for she found herself staring up at an iceberg.

It was a wedge-shaped block trapped in the pack ice. She saw how its base had been sculpted into great smooth columns by the water that lapped there, and by the scouring of wind-blown particles of ice and snow. The sunlight flooded the berg with blue light, a blueness that seemed to shine from within the body of the translucent ice.

Further from the shore she saw many giant bergs, frozen in, standing stark and majestic all across the sea ice. The ice between the bergs was smooth and flat. Older bergs, silhouetted in the low light, were wind-sculpted and melted, some of them carved into spires, arches, pinnacles, caves and other fantastic shapes. Perhaps they would not survive another summer. She could see that some of the bergs had shattered into smaller pieces, and here and there she made out growlers, the hard, compact cores of melted bergs, made of compressed, greenish ice, polished smooth by the waves.

In the light of the low sun, the colours of the bergs varied from white to blue, pink and purple, even a rich muddy brown, strange-shaped scraps littering the pack ice.

And from this vantage, Silverhair saw the strange object she had come so far to find.

Dark and mysterious, the thing rested on a floe that had all but broken away from the main mass of pack ice. Only a neck of ice, ten or eleven paces wide, still connected the floe to the land.

She scrambled down the ridge to the edge of the floe. Then she hesitated, looking down with trepidation at the narrow ice bridge, and the unyielding blackness of the water below. Lop-ear came to join her.

'It's quite wide,' she said uncertainly. She took a step forward, near the centre of the bridge, and pushed at the ice with her lead foot. It creaked and bowed, meltwater pooling under her foot, but it held. 'If I keep away from the edges it should be safe.'

'Silverhair, that's terribly dangerous.'

'We've come this far—'

And without letting herself think about it any further, she stepped forward on to the bridge.

One step, then another: avoiding the rotten ice, testing every pace, she worked her way steadily across the bridge.

The water lapped only a few paces to either side of her.

At last she arrived on the floe. The ice here, though bowing a little, was relatively solid. There were even some pressure ridges, one or two of them as tall as she was.

She turned and looked back to Lop-ear. He was a compact, dark shape on a broad sheet of blue-white ice, and he seemed a long way away.

She raised her trunk and trumpeted bravely, 'Don't follow me. The bridge is fragile.'

'Come back as soon as you can, Silverhair.'

'I will.'

She turned and, with caution, made her way across the floe.

The mysterious object was, she supposed, about the size of a large adult mammoth. Overall it looked something like a huge, stretched-out eggshell. It was flat at one end, and tusk-sharp at the other, and hollow inside. But she could see that the bottom of it was smashed to pieces, perhaps by a collision with the ice.

It certainly wasn't made of ice.

She reached out a tentative trunk-finger, and stroked its surface.

She snatched back her trunk, shocked. It was *wood*: covered by some hard, shining coat – a coat that masked its smell – but wood nonetheless.

The short hairs on her scalp prickled. Something about this thing – perhaps the short, sharp lines of its construction – reminded her unpleasantly of the Nest of Straight Lines.

There was a cracking sound.

'Silverhair!' Lop-ear's voice sounded disturbingly remote.

She spun around and, in the light of the already setting sun, she saw two things simultaneously.

The narrow ice bridge back to the pack ice had collapsed, stranding her here.

And there was a monster on the ice floe.

The monster seemed to have stepped from behind a pressure ridge, where it had been hidden from her view – and she from its. She couldn't understand how it had got so close; it was as if it had no scent. It was smaller than she was – much smaller. It was, perhaps, about the size of a small seal. It had four legs. It was standing on its hind legs, like a seal balancing on its tail.

But this was no seal.

For its legs were long: longer, in proportion, even than a mammoth's. It was skinny – surely it could not withstand the cold with so little fat to insulate it – and it didn't have any fur, not even on its shiny, hairless, skull-like head. In fact it seemed to have nothing to protect it but a loose-fitting outer skin.

Its ears were small, and startlingly like a mammoth's. Its eyes were set at the front of its head, like a wolf's – a predator's eyes, the better to hunt with. And now those binocular eyes were fixed on Silverhair, in fear or calculation.

It was clutching things in its forelegs. In one paw it held something shiny, like a shard of ice. In the other, there was something soft that dripped blood. It was the liver of a walrus, she recognised. And there was blood all around the monster's small mouth.

A child of Aglu, then. And perhaps strangest of all that eerie lack of any scent.

She must show no fear. What would Longtusk have done in such a situation?

She lowered her head so her tusks would not seem a threat, and she spoke to the creature. 'I am called Silver-hair,' she said. 'And you—'

Its predator's eyes were wide, its gaze fixed on her, its small, hairless face wreathed in steam. And there was frost on its shining dome of a head. It was a male, she decided, for she could see no sign of dugs.

'I will call you Skin-of-Ice,' she said.

She took a step towards the creature, meaning to touch him with her trunk, as mammoths will when they meet; perhaps she would go through the greeting ritual with him.

But he cried out. He raised the glittering, sharp thing in his paw, and backed away.

The wind picked up, abruptly, and ice crystals whirled around her face. The floe rocked, and she stumbled.

When she looked again, the monster had gone.

She caught one last glimpse of him, hopping nimbly across the widening leads, heading for the shore far from Silverhair and Lop-ear.

The wind began to blow more strongly through the Channel. The sea became choppy, and as it drifted through the Channel the ice floe began to break up. Soon Silverhair found herself stranded in a mass of loose ice that was drifting rapidly eastwards.

Suddenly she was in peril.

But now Lop-ear was calling her, with a deep rumble that easily crossed the ice and water to her. 'This way! This way!'

She saw that a smaller floe had nudged alongside the floe she rode. It was even more fragile than the one she was on – but it was closer to the shore.

Not allowing herself to hesitate, she marched briskly across the narrow lead to the smaller floe.

Behind her the ice at the floe's edge crumbled into fragments.

This floe, much smaller than the first, was spinning slowly, and heaving from side to side in the heavy swell as the current swept it along. Then another floe came bumping alongside with a crunch of smashing ice; she hurried forward, and found herself a little closer again to land.

So she worked her way, floe by floe, across the ice, following a complex path that she hoped would lead her to the shore.

At the edge of one floe, a herd of walrus were gambolling among the loose ice. They completely ignored her. It was a mixed group, mothers with calves of various ages, and one massive male with long curved tusks protruding from his small face. Some of the walrus had their tusks hooked to the edge of the ice as they rested, to save themselves from sinking as they slept. The stink was almost overpowering, for it seemed they had been defecating on the same floe all winter. The walrus scratched hoar-frost from their bodies with surprisingly gentle flippers, and occasionally turned over in a great heap of pinkish blubbery flesh, their long ivory tusks glinting in the sun.

With their warty skin, wide moustaches and tiny heads atop their long, ponderous bodies, Silverhair found it hard to think of the walrus as anything but spectacularly ugly. She wondered sadly if one of this comfortable family had fallen victim to Skin-of-Ice. Perhaps they didn't know about it yet.

Silverhair skirted the walrus carefully.

Her progress was agonising – one step forward, another back – and she lost track of the time she had spent here, inching across the treacherous ice.

Brown mist, blown from over the open water, swirled around her, making it hard to keep to her chosen track. The loose floes spun around, crashed and tilted, and she felt as if the whole world, of ice and sea and land, was in motion.

More than once she stepped through rotten ice, and her feet took more dunkings in the water, and the fur on her legs was soon heavy and stiff with ice.

If she couldn't get back to the shore, these separating floes would, eventually, be blown out to sea. There – the Cycle taught – she would suffer death by starvation or thirst – if the floes did not crumble and drown her, and if killer whales did not ram their snouts through the thinning ice to reach her.

But gradually, she realised, she was working her way, floe by floe, step by step, back towards the shore. Lop-ear ran along faithfully, calling out the floes he spotted, evidently determined he would not abandon her.

At last, as she neared the landfast ice and got away from the fastest-flowing water, the swell subsided, and the rolling of the floes became more bearable.

And then she found herself on a hard, unyielding surface.

For a moment she stood there, unable to believe it was over, that she had reached the land. In fact, she felt giddy, so used had she become to standing on a surface that tipped and heaved beneath her. But Lop-ear's trunk was soon over her head, touching her mouth and cooing reassurance.

With relief, she trotted away from the ice's edge.

She turned and saw the floe that had so nearly carried her to her death. There was the anonymous hulk of distorted wood. And there, just visible as black dots on the ice, were the droppings she had made as she had circled the shrinking floe.

But now frost-smoke and the mist off the sea closed around the floe, and it was carried away to invisibility.

CHAPTER 5
THE TUSK

The Family was a small, bulky knot in the landscape, dark on dark. But Silverhair could hear the mammoths' rumbles and chirrups, kindly or complaining in turn; she could feel the deep sound passing through the frozen earth as those great feet lumbered back and forth; and she could smell the welcoming smell of wet mammoth fur, a rich stink that carried on the wind. She could even smell the moist, slightly stale aroma of the milk her sister was producing for her new calf.

And as they approached the Family, Silverhair saw that the Matriarch was preparing for a migration.

Owlheart was moving among her charges, gathering and encouraging them with gentle slaps of her trunk. Silverhair's sister, Foxeye, was gathering her calves around her. Foxeye herself looked unsteady on her feet, weakened by the long trial of her pregnancy and the birth. Sunfire, the new baby, stayed close to her mother, nestling in the long hairs of Foxeye's belly. The calf's milk tusks were already budding at her cheeks, white as Arctic flowers. Silverhair heard Foxeye murmuring the ancient tale of Kilukpuk's calves to her, and she remembered how her own mother – when Silverhair wasn't much older than Sunfire was now – had made her swear the ancient Oath of Kilukpuk. And there was little Croptail, scarcely more than an infant himself, his baffled resentment of his new sister visible even from afar.

Snagtooth and Wolfnose stood a little distance away, cropping the sparse, dry grass that protruded through the frost. Neither of them took much part in the proceedings: Snagtooth seemed, as usual, sullen and withdrawn, and Wolfnose, though standing straight and tall, was very still, and Silverhair knew that she was trying to spare her worn-out knees before the long trek that faced her.

And there was stolid old Eggtusk, unmistakable for that bulb of ivory on his tusk, if not for his mighty shoulders. The powerful old Bull stood shoulder to shoulder with Owlheart, supporting everything she said and did.

Silverhair's heart warmed as she looked over her Family, one by one, bedraggled as their dark winter fur blew away from their backs; suddenly the twenty days of her separation from them seemed much longer.

'We must tell them what we saw,' said Silverhair to Lop-ear. 'The strange creature on the floe—'

'No,' said Lop-ear. 'Not now.'

'Why not? Surely Owlheart and Eggtusk will be able to help us make sense of it.'

'They have other things on their minds right now. And besides . . .' He shook his great head, so that rust-brown hair fell over his eyes. 'I have a feeling it isn't something the Matriarch will be glad to hear.'

Silverhair found herself shivering at his words. She knew he had touched on the truth. When she thought back now over the incident with Skin-of-Ice, the ice floe monster, she felt little but dread. But that wasn't logical, she told herself. Everything strange seemed frightening at first; it didn't mean it was necessarily *bad* . . .

They trotted forward and joined the Family.

The greeting ceremony was affectionate but brief, for Owlheart was trying to ensure that everybody's mind was on the migration. But Silverhair, ignoring Lop-ear's advice, approached Owlheart, and told the Matriarch what she had found.

She tried to crystallise the monster for the Matriarch: walking upright on two long legs, strange objects held in the paws of the forelegs, face smeared with the blood of the walrus, helplessly thin, but coated with artificial fur – and, strangest of all, that utter lack of scent.

Owlheart listened, and caressed Silverhair's ear. 'My poor granddaughter,' she rumbled. 'If only you had a little less of Longtusk in you. But perhaps it's as well for all of us that you don't.'

'What do you mean?'

'You must tell nobody else what you saw. Do you understand?'

'But Lop-ear—'

'*Nobody.*'

And the Matriarch trotted away, trunk held high as if to detect danger, towards Eggtusk. They began to speak, a long and serious conversation punctuated by glares at Silverhair.

Silverhair sighed. She didn't know why, but it seemed she was in trouble again.

After a final bout of defecation, a final brief graze, the migration began.

The walk was not easy.

The new calf, Sunfire, was thin and sickly. At the frequent stops, Silverhair helped Foxeye with simple mammoth medicine. She would place her trunk into the calf's tiny mouth, ensuring she did not choke on her food; and, at rest times, she nudged the baby to her feet, for there was a danger that the infant's weight would press down on her lungs and prevent her breathing.

Wolfnose, too, was having a great deal of difficulty walking. All four of her legs, stiffened with arthritis, seemed as inflexible as tree-trunks as they clumped down on the frozen ground. And several bones in her back were fused into hard, painful units. She was too proud to admit to the pain, still less give in to it. But Wolfnose was clearly able to keep up only a slow pace.

The others helped by huddling her. Eggtusk and the

Matriarch herself walked along to either side, helping Wolf-nose stay upright, and Lop-ear walked behind her, gently nudging her great thighs to keep her going.

The world was silent around them, empty as a skull. The only sound was the crackle of frost under their feet, the hiss of breath through their long nostrils, and the occasional word of instruction or encouragement from the adults, or complaint from the calves. The land was mostly flat, but here and there they had to clamber over frozen hills, blocks of ice embedded in the ground.

As Silverhair walked, she could picture where she was, imagine the mammoths crawling across the great, empty belly of the Island.

The mammoths' ability to hear the deepest noises of the Earth enables them to do much more than communicate over long distances. Mammoths can *hear* the distinctive voices of the landscape: the growl of breaking waves and cracking ice at a seashore, the low humming of bare sand, the droning of the wind through mountains. All this enables them to build up a complex, three-dimensional map of the world around them, extending to regions far beyond the horizon. They are able to predict the weather – for they can hear the growl of turbulent air in the atmosphere – and even receive warnings about Earth tremors, for the booming bellow of seismic waves as they pass through the planet's rocky heart is the deepest voice of all.

So Silverhair had a kind of map in her head that encompassed the whole of the Island, and even a sense of the roundness of the Earth, spinning and nodding on its endless dance around the sun. Silverhair's mind had deep roots – deeper than any human's – roots that extended into the rocky structure of the world itself.

But her powerful ability to listen to the planet's many voices also made her uncomfortably aware that this was the *only* mammoth group she could sense, right across the Island. She could feel the sweep and extent of the rocky land, and the mammoths were stranded at the centre of this huge, echoing landscape like pebbles thrown on to an ice floe.

She felt distracted, restless, disturbed. Where *was* everybody?

They passed a family of wolves.

The wolves were lying on the ground, huddled against the cold, their white-furred backs turned to the teeth of the wind, their heads tucked into their bellies for warmth. An adult – perhaps a bitch – stood up and glared as Silverhair thudded past.

'Once,' rumbled Wolfnose, eyeing the wolf, 'I saw a mammoth brought down by a wolf pack. Long before any of you were born. He was a calf – a Bull, called Willowleg, for his legs were spindly and weak. The wolves pursued him, despite the efforts of the rest of the Family to keep them off. The wolves are smart. They took it in turns to pick up the running, so they did not tire as Willowleg did.

'At last they cornered him in a crevasse, where the rest of us could not follow. Willowleg got his back to the rock wall and fought. But there were many wolves. First they cut him down, with bites to his legs and hindquarters, and then, at last, they got in a killing bite to the throat. And then they pulled him apart.

'Wolves have Family too,' she said, her old eyes sunk in folds of skin. 'The lead male eats first, then his senior bitches, and any female which is feeding cubs.' She regarded the wide-eyed calves. 'It is the way of things. But be wary of the wolves.'

Silverhair could see the wolf's moist eyes, the gleam of her teeth in the sunlight, and imagined the calculation going on in her sharp-edged mind, the dark legacy of Aglu, brother of Kilukpuk.

Wolfnose's story was a timely warning. Of all of them, for all his greater size and strength compared with Sunfire, Croptail was probably the most vulnerable to predators like the wolves. He could no longer rely on the close protection of Foxeye – she was preoccupied with the new infant, and her instincts were in any event to push the growing Bull away – but he had not yet learned to forage effectively for himself, or to defend himself from the wolves. So Silverhair made sure she always knew where Croptail had got to, and she stopped periodically and raised her trunk, listening and sniffing for signs of danger on the wind.

The days were still cruelly short, but nevertheless lengthening, with the sun's brief arc above the horizon extending with each day that passed. The weather remained clear and bitterly cold. Wind whipped across the empty ground, blowing up particles of ice so small and hard and dry they felt like grit when they got into Silverhair's eyes.

One day, when the sun was at its height and bathing the frosty ground with a spurious gold, Owlheart called a halt. The mammoths dispersed to scrape grass from the hard ground and drop dung.

The calves found the energy to play. Sunfire pestered her older brother, placing her trunk in his mouth to test the grass he was eating, rubbing against him and even collapsing in a heap beside him. At times they chased each other, mounting mock charges and wrestling with their trunks.

Foxeye wearily admonished Croptail to be careful with his sister, but Silverhair knew such play was important in teaching the calves to develop their own abilities – and, most important, to learn about each other, for it was the bond between Family members that was the most important weapon of all in their continued survival. Anyhow, the calves' cheerful play warmed the dispirited adults.

Poor Wolfnose stood stiffly, away from the others, her great legs visibly trembling.

Owlheart called Silverhair, Lop-ear and Snagtooth to her.

Owlheart began digging at the ground. She broke the

crusted surface with her tusks and forefeet, scooping the debris out of the way with her trunk. Her left tusk was much more worn than the right: a good deal shorter, and its tip was rounded and grooved. Most mammoths favour their right tusk as their master tusk, but Owlheart, unusually, preferred the left, and that showed in the unevenness of the wear.

'The winter has been dry,' said Owlheart as she dug. 'Perhaps the thaw will come soon, but we are thirsty now. But here, in this place, there is water to be found – liquid, for most of the year. This is a place where the inner warmth of the Earth reaches to the surface, and keeps the water here beneath from freezing, even when the world is as cold as a corpse's belly . . .'

Now, looking around more carefully, Silverhair saw the ground was pitted by a series of shallow craters: pits dug in the ground by mammoths of the past.

'*Remember this place*,' Owlheart said. 'For it is a place of Earth's generous warmth, and water; and it may save your life.'

Silverhair turned, scanning the horizon. She raised her trunk and let the hairs there dangle in the prevailing wind. She studied the sky, and scraped with her tusks at the ground. She let the scents and subtle sounds of the land-scape sink into her mind.

She was *remembering*. Even as Owlheart spoke she was adding a new detail, exquisite but perhaps vitally important, to the map of scents and breezes and textures that each mammoth carried in her head.

'Now, help me dig,' said Owlheart.

Silverhair, Lop-ear and Snagtooth stepped forward, took their places around the preliminary hole dug by their Matri-arch, and began to work at the ground.

The ground was hard: even to the stone-hard tusks of mammoths, it offered stiff resistance. Save for the occasional peevish complaint by Snagtooth, there was no talking as they worked: only the scrape of tusk and stamp of foot, the hissing of breath through upraised trunks.

They worked through the night, taking breaks in turn.

As the night wore on – and as there was little sign of water, and they became steadily more exhausted – Silverhair had a growing sense of unease.

Owlheart was not a Matriarch who welcomed debate about her decisions. Nevertheless, as Owlheart took a break – standing to pass her dung a little way away from the others – Silverhair summoned up the courage to speak to her.

Owlheart was evidently weary already from her work, and her pink tongue protruded from her mouth.

'You're thirsty,' said Silverhair.

'Yes. A paradox, isn't it – that the work to find water is making me thirstier than ever.'

'Matriarch, Foxeye is still weak, Croptail is weaning and vulnerable to the wolves, Wolfnose can barely walk. The digging is exhausting all of us—'

The Matriarch's great jaw ceased its fore-and-back motion. 'You're right,' she said.

'. . . What?'

'We're in no fit state to have set off on an expedition like this. That's what you're leading up to, isn't it? But I wonder if you realise what peril we are in, little Silverhair. *Where water vanishes, sanity soon follows.* That's what the Cycle teaches. Thirst maddens us. Soon, without water, we would turn on each other . . . I have to avoid that at all costs, for we would be destroyed.

'Perhaps if we had stayed where we were, the thaw might have come to us before we all died of thirst. But that was not my judgement,' Owlheart growled. 'And that is the essence of being Matriarch, Silverhair. Sometimes there are no good choices: only a series of bad ones.'

'And so we are forced to risk all our lives on the bounty of a seep-hole,' Silverhair protested.

'*The art of travelling is to pick the least dangerous path*.' That was another line from the Cycle, a teaching of the great Matriarch, Ganesha the Wise.

Owlheart was turning away, evidently intent on resuming her interrupted feeding.

But still Silverhair wasn't done. She blurted: 'Maybe the old ways aren't the right ways any more.'

Owlheart snorted. 'Have you been talking to Lop-ear again?'

Silverhair was indignant. 'I don't need Lop-ear to tell me how to think.'

'The defiant one, aren't you? Tell me what has brought on this sudden doubt.'

And Silverhair spoke to the Matriarch again of the monster she had encountered on the ice floe. 'So you see, if there is such a strange creature in the world, who knows what else there is to find? *The world is changing*. Anyone can see that. It's why the winters are warmer, why the rich grass and shrubs are harder to find. But maybe there's some good for us in all this. If we only go searching – listen with open ears – we might discover—'

Owlheart cut her off with a slap of her trunk, hard enough to sting. 'Listen to me carefully. There is nothing for us in what you saw at the coast: nothing but misery and pain and death. Do you understand?'

'Won't you even tell me what it means?'

'We won't talk of this again, Silverhair,' said Owlheart, and she turned her massive back.

There was a commotion at Silverhair's feet. Gloomy, frustrated, she looked down. She saw a little animated bundle of orange hair, smelled the warm, cloying aroma of milk. It was Sunfire. The calf trotted over to the Matriarch's fresh dung, and began to poke into the warm, salty goodies with her trunk. Soon she was totally absorbed. Silverhair, watching fondly, wished she could be like that again, trotting after her own concerns, in a state of blissful, unmarked innocence.

Eggtusk came up. His giant, inward-curving tusks were looming over her, silhouetted against the sky. For a while he walked with her.

She saw that they had become isolated from the rest of the Family. And, with a flash of intuition, she saw why he had approached her. 'Eggtusk—'

'What?'

'The thing I saw on the ice floe, in the south. *You know what it is*, don't you?'

He regarded her. His words, coming deep from the hollow of his chest, were coupled with an unnatural stillness of his great head. It made her feel small and weak.

'Listen to me very carefully,' he said. 'Owlheart is right. You must not go there again. And pray to Kilukpuk that your monster did not recognise you, that it does not track you here.'

'Why? It looked weaker than a wolf cub.'

'Perhaps it did,' said Eggtusk sadly. 'But that little beast was stronger than you, stronger than me – than all of us put together. It was the beast which the Cycle tells us can never be fought.'

'You mean—'

'*It was a Lost*, little one. It was a Lost, on our Island. *Now* do you see?' Eggtusk seemed to be trembling, and that struck a deep dread into Silverhair's heart, for she had never seen the great Eggtusk afraid of anything before—

Snagtooth screamed.

'Circle!' snapped the Matriarch.

Almost without thinking, Silverhair found herself joining the others in a tight circle around Snagtooth, with the calves cowering inside, and the adults arrayed on the outside, their tusks and trunks pointing outward, huge and intimidating, ready to beat off any predator or threat.

But Silverhair knew that there were no predators involved here – nobody, in fact, but Snagtooth herself.

Snagtooth raised her head from the scraped-out hole. Her right tusk was snapped off, almost at the root where it was embedded in her face. Instead of the smooth spiral of ivory she had carried before, there was now only a broken stump, its edge rimmed by jagged, bone-like fragments. A dark fluid dripped from the tusk's hollow core; it was pulp, the living flesh of the tusk. And the skin around the tusk was ripped and bleeding heavily.

Each of the mammoths felt the pain of the break as if it was their own. Sunfire, the infant, squealed in horror and burrowed under her mother's skirt of hair.

Eggtusk lowered his trunk and reached into the hole in the ground. With some effort, he pulled out the rest of the broken tusk. 'She trapped it under a boulder that was frozen in the ground,' he said. 'Simple as that. By Kilukpuk's hairy anus, what a terrible thing. You always were too impatient, Snagtooth—'

Snagtooth howled. With tears coursing down the hair on her face, she made to charge him, like a Bull on musth, with her one remaining tusk.

Eggtusk, startled, held his ground and, with a twist of his own mighty tusks, deflected her easily, without harming her.

Owlheart stepped between them angrily. 'Enough. Leave her be, Eggtusk.'

Eggtusk withdrew, growling.

Owlheart laid her trunk over Snagtooth's neck, and stroked her mouth and eyes. 'He was right, you know. Your teeth are brittle – why do you think you are called Snagtooth in the first place? – and a tusk is nothing but a giant tooth . . . The best thing to do is to freeze that stump, or otherwise the pulp will grow infected, and we will cake it with clay to stop the bleeding. You two,' she said to Lop-ear and Silverhair, 'get on with your digging. It's all the more important now.'

She led Snagtooth away from the others.

With Lop-ear, Silverhair resumed her work, trying to ignore the splashes of tusk pulp and splinters of ivory which disfigured the ground.

At last – after hacking at such cost through a trunk's-length of permafrost – they broke through to seep-water. But the water was low and brackish, so thin it took long heartbeats for Silverhair to suck up as much as a trunkful.

The hole was too deep for the infants' short trunks to reach the water, so Foxeye and Silverhair let water from their own trunks trickle into the mouths of the younger ones. Sunfire was still learning to drink; she spilled more water than she swallowed.

Wolfnose could not bend so easily, and she too had difficulty reaching the water. But she refused any help, proudly; she insisted she had drunk enough by her own efforts, and walked stiffly away.

The mammoths drank as much as the seep-hole would offer them. But it wasn't enough, and there was still no sign of the spring thaw.

'We have to go on,' said Owlheart solemnly. 'Further west, to the land beneath the glaciers. There, at this time of year, meltwater will be found running over the land. That's where we must go.'

That was a land unknown to Silverhair – and a dangerous place, for sometimes the meltwater would come from the glaciers in great deluges that could carve out a new landscape, stranding or trapping unwary wanderers. That the Matriarch was prepared to take such a risk was a measure of the seriousness of the situation; but nevertheless Silverhair felt a prick of interest that she would be going somewhere new.

They slept before moving on.

The short day was soon over. A hard Moon sailed into the sky, lighting up high clouds of ice. The silence of the Arctic night settled on the Family, a huge emptiness broken only by the mewling of Sunfire at her mother's breast, and Snagtooth's growled complaints at the pain of her shattered tusk.

Silverhair could feel the cold penetrate her guard hair and underwool, through her flesh to her bones. Perhaps, she thought, this is how it will feel to grow old.

The Moon was still rising when Owlheart roused them and told them it was time to proceed.

CHAPTER 6

THE MOUNTAINS AT THE
END OF THE WORLD

Cold, dry nights, lengthening days. Sometimes a dense grey fog would descend on the mammoths, wrapping them in obscurity. Nevertheless the full summer was approaching. Each night the sun dipped to the horizon, becoming lost in the mist, but the sky grew no darker than a rich blue, speckled with stars.

There came a night when the sun did not set. By day it rolled along the horizon, distorted by refraction and mist; but even at midnight slivers of ruddy light were visible, casting shadows that crossed the land from horizon to horizon, and the sky was filled with a wan glow that lacked warmth but was sufficient to banish the stars. Silverhair knew that the axis of the planet had reached that point in its annual round where it was tipped towards the sun, and there would be no true darkness for a hundred days.

The land, here in the Island's northern plain, rolled to the horizon with a sense of immensity. There was little snow or ice; the wind blew too strongly and steadily for that. And it was a *flat* place. The sparse plants that clung to life here – tough grasses resistant to both frost and drought, small shrubs like sagebrush, wormwood, even rhododendron – all grew low, with short branches and strong root systems to resist the scouring effects of the wind. Even the dwarf willows cowered against the ground, their branches sprawled over the rock, dug in.

When the wind picked up it moaned through the sparse grass with an eerie intensity.

At last the Mountains at the End of the World hove into Silverhair's view. In the low sunlight the upper slopes of the Mountains were bathed in a vibrant pink glow, which reflected down on to the slopes beneath where blue shadows pooled, the colours mixing to indigo and mauve.

As the land rose towards the Mountains, gathering like a great rocky wave, it became steadily more stony and barren. Here nothing grew save sickly coloured lichen, useless for the mammoths to eat.

And the land showed the battle-scars left by the huge warring forces of the past: giant scratches in the rock, boulders and shattered scree thrown as if at random over the landscape, smooth-sided gouges cut into what soil remained. It was, rumbled Wolfnose, the mark of the ancient ice sheets which had once lain a mile thick over this land.

They approached a dark wall of spruce trees, unexpected so far north. Silverhair wondered if some outcropping of the Earth's inner warmth was working here to sustain these trees. The Family were forced to push further north, to skirt the trees and the barren land that surrounded them.

The light changed. It became strange: almost greenish in its unnaturally pale tinge. Looking up, Silverhair saw ice clouds scudding hard across the sky. A flock of ptarmigan in brilliant white plumage took off like a snow flurry, and flew into the Mountains. Their display calls echoed eerily from the rocky walls.

'Storm coming.'

She turned, and found the bulk of Eggtusk alongside her.

'And that's new,' he growled, indicating the neck of forest ahead of them. 'New since the last time the Family came this way.'

'When was that?'

'Before you were born. Every year the forest pushes further north, like pond scum on the great backside of Kilukpuk. Except that, unlike Kilukpuk, we can't scrape the land clean on a rock! Bah.'

Overhead, the greenish light was obscured by a layer of black, scudding clouds.

As the storm gathered they continued to skirt the forest, heading north-east, until they came to the fringe of the Mountains at the End of the World.

They walked past the eroded foothills of a mountain, which loomed above Silverhair. It was a severe black-brown cone, the glaciers were white ribbons wrapped around it. Yellow sunlight gleamed through the mountain's deep, ice-cut valleys.

High above her there was a snow avalanche: it poured down the mountain in a mighty, drawn-out whisper, and for a while she was enveloped in dancing flakes. And now the wind increased, coming through the towering rock pinnacles that rose above her, a keening lament that resonated in her skull. A whirr of ice splinters came scuttling across the rock shelf's surface; with every further step she took she crunched on crystals.

This was a noisy place. The cliff faces were alive with the crack of ice, the rustle and clatter of falling scree. Silverhair knew this was the voice of rock and ice, the frost's slow reworking of the upraised landscape.

Her spirit was lifted. The violence of the land exhilarated her.

Such was the clamour of ice and rock and wind from this huge barrier that even with their acute hearing, Silverhair's Family knew nothing of the land beyond the Mountains at the End of the World. Not even Longtusk himself had been able to glean the secrets of the lands which might lie to the north. Perhaps there was nothing beyond, nothing but mist and sky. But if this truly was the End of the World, Silverhair thought, then there could be no better marker than these Mountains.

Now they came to the snout of one of the great glaciers. The glacier was a river of ice, flowing with invisible slowness, its smooth curves tinted blue, surprisingly clean and beautiful.

The glacier had poured, creaking, down from the Mountains, carving and shattering the rock as it proceeded. But here, where it spilled on to the rocky plain, the pressure on that ice river was receding. The glacier calved into slices and towers, some of which had fallen to lie smashed in great blocks at her feet. Silverhair found herself walking amid sculptures of ice and snow, carved by the wind and rain into columns and wings and boulders, adorned with convoluted frills and laces, extraordinarily delicate and intricate.

But the land here was difficult. The mammoths were forced to thread their way between the ice blocks and the moraines: uneven mounds of sharp-edged debris, scoured by the glacier from the Mountains and deposited here. The wind was hard now, spilling off the Mountains. It plastered the mammoths' hair against their bodies, and Silverhair could feel it lashing against her eyes.

At last the glacier itself loomed above them, a wall of green ice and windswept snow.

Silverhair was stunned by the glacier's scale. The mammoths were the largest creatures in this landscape, and yet the ice wall before her was so tall its top was lost in mist that lingered above, as if reaching to the very clouds. Where the low sunlight caught the ice it shone a rich white-blue, as if stars were trapped within its structure; but loose fragments scattered over its surface sparkled like dew.

A pair of Arctic foxes sprinted past, probably a mating pair, their sleek white forms hard to see against the ice; Silverhair heard the foxes' complex calls to each other.

There was a flash, and thunder cracked; the mammoths flinched.

'Take it easy,' shouted Eggtusk, his trunk aloft, sniffing for danger. 'That was well to the south of us. Probably struck in that forest we skirted.'

Silverhair looked that way. There was another flash, and

STEPHEN BAXTER

this time she saw the lightning bolt, liquid fire that shot
down into the forest from the low clouds racing above. The
bolt struck a tree, which fell into the forest with a crash.
And a steady, reddish glow was gathering in the heart of the
forest.

Fire.

Now the rain came, a hard, driving, almost horizontal
sheet of water, laced with snow and hailstones.

The Matriarch had to shout and gesture. 'We'll climb up
towards the Mountains. Maybe we can shelter until this
passes. Silverhair, look after Foxeye and the calves. The rest
of you help Wolfnose. Hurry now.'

The Family moved to obey.

. . . Save for Lop-ear, who came up to Silverhair. 'I'm
worried about that fire,' he said. 'The grasses here are as
dry as a bone, and with that wind, it could be on us in
seconds.'

She looked towards the forest. The light of the fire did
seem to be spreading. 'But it's a long way away,' she said.
'And the rain—'

'Is hard but it's just gusting. Not enough to extinguish the
forest, or even soak the grass.'

Soft wet snow lashed around them.

Silverhair looked for the infant, Sunfire. Foxeye was
anxiously tugging at the baby's ear. But the calf was half-
lying on the frozen ground, mewling pitiably. The snow had
soaked into her sparse, spiky fur, making it lie flat against
her compact little body; Silverhair could see lumpy ribs and
backbone protruding through a too-thin layer of fat and
flesh.

She stood with Foxeye and, by pulling at Sunfire's ears
and trunk, managed to cajole the calf to her feet. Then
Silverhair and Foxeye stood one to either side of the infant,
supporting her tiny bulk against them. Silverhair could feel
the calf shiver against her own stolid legs.

They tried to move her forward, away from the spreading

flames. But the bedraggled Sunfire was too exhausted to move.

Silverhair looked back over her shoulder, anxiously. Fanned by the swirling wind, the fire had taken a firm hold in the stand of trees behind them, and an ominous red light was spreading through the gaunt black trunks. Already she could see flames licking at the dry grass of the slice of exposed tundra that lay between the mammoths and the forest.

But her awareness of the fire spread far beyond the limited sense of sight. She could smell the gathering stink of wood succumbing to the flames, the sour stench of burning sap; hear the pop and hiss of the moist wood. She understood the fire, felt it on a deep level; it was as if a flame was burning through the world map she carried in her head.

She knew they had to flee. But she and Foxeye could not handle the calf on their own. She turned, looking for help.

Poor Wolfnose was turning away from the fire, slow and stately as some giant hairy iceberg, but her stiff legs were unable to carry her as once they had. 'I'm not a calf any more, you know . . .' Owlheart, Eggtusk and Lop-ear were striving to help her. Their giant bulks were walls of soaked fur to either side of Wolfnose, and Lop-ear had settled himself behind her, and was pushing at her rear with his lowered forehead. Owlheart, helping with her mother and trumpeting instructions to the Family as a whole, was even finding time to wrap a reassuring trunk over the head of Croptail; the young Bull stuck close to the Matriarch.

But that left nobody to help Silverhair and Foxeye with the calf.

Nobody – except their aunt, Snagtooth, who stood away from the others, still mewling like a distressed calf over her shattered tusk.

Silverhair turned to Foxeye and raised her trunk. 'Wait here.'

Foxeye, exhausted herself, was close to panic. 'Silverhair – don't leave me—'

'I'll be back.' She trotted quickly over to Snagtooth.

The mud Owlheart had caked over the smashed tusk stump was beginning to streak over Snagtooth's fur and expose the mess of blood and pulp that lay beneath. Snagtooth's eyes were filled with a desolate misery, and Silverhair felt a stab of sympathy, for the wound did look agonising. But, for now, she knew she had to put that from her mind.

She grabbed her aunt's trunk and pulled. 'Come on. Foxeye needs your help.'

'I can't. You'll have to cope. I have to look after myself.' And Snagtooth snatched her trunk back.

Silverhair growled, reached up with her trunk and grabbed Snagtooth's healthy tusk. 'If there was anybody else I wouldn't care,' she rumbled. 'But there isn't anybody else.' She moved closer to Snagtooth and spoke again, loud enough to be audible over the howling of the storm, soft enough so nobody else could hear. 'Are you going to come with me, or are you going to make me drag you?'

For long heartbeats Snagtooth stared down at Silverhair. Snagtooth was older and, massive for a Cow, a good bit bigger than Silverhair. Now Silverhair wondered if Snagtooth would call her bluff and challenge her – and if she did, whether Silverhair could cope with her, despite the smashed tusk.

But Snagtooth backed down. 'Very well. But you aren't Matriarch yet, little Silverhair. I won't forget this.'

She turned away and, with evident reluctance, made her way towards Foxeye and the slumping Sunfire.

Silverhair felt chilled to the core, as if she'd taken a bellyful of snow.

It was slow going. The two groups of Family, huddled around the calf and the proud old Cow, seemed to crawl across the hard ground.

Here and there the snow was drifting into deceptively deep pockets. Mammoths always have difficulty traversing deep snow: now Silverhair felt her legs sink into the soft, slushy whiteness, and it pushed like a rising tide up around the long hair of her belly, chilling her dugs. In the deepest of the drifts she had to work hard, with Foxeye, to keep the calf's head and trunk above the level of the snow.

And all the time Silverhair could sense the fire pooling over the dry ground. The snow was having no effect now, such was the heat the fire was generating, and she knew their only chance was to outrun it. She stayed close to Sunfire, sheltering the calf from the wind and encouraging her to hurry – and she tried to contain her own rising panic.

But now they were brought to a halt.

Silverhair found herself on the bank of a stream that bubbled its way from the base of the ice and across the rocky land. She could see where the stream was already cutting into the loose soil and debris scattered over the rock, and depositing small stones from within the glacier. The mammoths' deep knowledge of their Island could not have helped them predict they would encounter this barrier, for every year the runoff streams reshaped the landscape. And the stream was wide, clearly too deep to ford or even to swim.

The mammoths stood clustered together against the wind, staring at the rushing water with dismay. Silverhair, blocked, felt baffled, frustrated, and filled with a deep dread that reached back to her near-drowning as a calf. It was a bitter irony, for a runoff stream like this was exactly what they had come looking for: and now it lay in their way.

She found Lop-ear standing with her. 'We're in trouble,' he said. 'Look around, Silverhair. The runoff here. The forest over there, where the fire is coming from. Behind us, the Mountains . . .'

Suddenly she understood.

They had got themselves trapped here, by river and Mountains and forest, as surely as if they had all plunged into a kettle hole.

Now Eggtusk came to them. 'We can't cross the stream,' he said bluntly.

'But—' said Lop-ear.

Eggtusk ignored him. 'It's not a time for debate. We have to move on. We can't go north; that way will soon take us into the Mountains. So we follow the stream south. The stream will get broad and shallow and maybe there'll be somewhere to cross. That's what Owlheart has ordered, and I agree with her.'

He turned away, preparing to go back to Wolfnose, but Lop-ear touched his trunk. 'Eggtusk, wait. Going south won't work. The fire will reach us before we—'

Eggtusk quoted the Cycle. *'The Matriarch has given her orders, and we follow.'*

Lop-ear cried, 'Not to our deaths!'

In the middle of the storm, there was a moment of shocked stillness.

Silverhair, startled, could not remember anyone continuing to argue with Eggtusk after such a warning.

Nor, evidently, could Eggtusk.

Eggtusk lifted his great head high over Lop-ear; he was an imposing mass of muscle, flesh and wiry, mud-brown hair. 'Any more talk like that and I'll silence you for good. You'll frighten the calves.'

'They should be frightened!'

Hastily Silverhair shoved her trunk into Lop-ear's pink, warm mouth to silence him. 'Come on,' she said. Pulling him with her trunk, nudging him with her flank, she led him away from a glaring Eggtusk.

But she felt a deep chill. Lop-ear, with his fast, unusual mind, could sometimes be distracted, a little strange. But she had never seen him so agitated.

. . . And what, she thought with a deep shiver, if he is

right? He's been right about so many things in the past. What if we really are just walking to our deaths?

Still Lop-ear called. But the wind snatched away his words, and nobody listened.

CHAPTER 7
THE BARRIER

With Foxeye and a reluctant Snagtooth, Silverhair shepherded a trembling, unsteady Sunfire along the bank of the runoff stream.

Although the depth and ferocity of the central channel gradually reduced, the stream spread further over the surrounding ground, and sheets of water ran over the rock. The cloudy water made the rock slick enough to cause even the tough sole of a mammoth's foot to slip, and several times poor Sunfire had to be rescued from stumbles.

Meanwhile the storm mounted in ferocity, with gigantic clatters from the sky and startling bolts of lightning and a wind that swirled unpredictably, slamming heavy wet snowflakes into Silverhair's face.

And all the time she could sense the fire as it spread through the dry old grass towards them.

Lop-ear was helping Owlheart and Eggtusk with Wolf-nose's cautious progress. But he was still calling to the sky, complaining and prophesying doom. Right now the Matriarch and the old Bull were too busy to deal with him, but Silverhair knew he would pay for his ill-discipline later.

She came to a young spruce, lying across the rocky ground near the stream. It neatly blocked the mammoths' path.

The little group broke up again. Foxeye, panting and near exhaustion, tucked her infant under her belly-hair curtain. Snagtooth, yowling complaints about her tusk, turned away from the others and scrabbled in the cold mud of the stream bank to cover her wound once more.

Silverhair stepped forward. She saw that the tree's roots

had sunk themselves into a shallow soil that was now overrun by the stream; when the soil was washed away, the tree had fallen. The tree itself would not be difficult to cross. They could all climb over, probably, or with a little effort they could even push it out of the way.

But the tree was only an outlier of the spruce forest. Other trees grew here, small and stunted and sparsely separated – and some of them, too, had been felled by the runoff – and she could see that a little further south the trees grew more densely, and she could smell the thick, damp mulch of the forest floor.

Eggtusk, with Owlheart, came up to her. Eggtusk saw the fallen tree. 'By Kilukpuk's gravel-stuffed navel. That's all we need.'

'We'll have to climb over it,' said Owlheart.

'Yes. If we get Wolfnose over first—'

But suddenly Lop-ear was here, standing head to head with Eggtusk. He was bedraggled, muttering, excited, eyes wide and full of reflected lightning. 'No. Don't you see? This is the answer. If we push this fallen tree over *there* – and then go further towards the forest to find more—'

In the flickering light of the storm, the old Bull stood as solid as if he had grown out of the rock. Owlheart and Wolfnose watched, their icy disapproval of Lop-ear's youthful antics obvious.

Eggtusk said, 'You're risking all our lives by wasting time like this.'

Silverhair hurried forward. 'What are you trying to say, Lop-ear?'

'I can't tell you!' he cried. 'I just *know*, if we push the trees together, and—'

'He's going rogue,' said Owlheart now. The Matriarch lumbered forward, and glowered down at the prancing Lop-ear. 'I always knew this calf would be trouble. All his talk of *changing* things. He's more like one of the Lost than a mammoth.'

'Listen to me!' Lop-ear was trumpeting now. He ran to Owlheart, who was turning away, and grabbed at her trunk. 'Listen to me—'

Now Eggtusk's massive bulk was between them. 'You don't touch the Matriarch like that.'

'But you must *listen*.'

'Perhaps you'll listen to this,' roared Eggtusk, and he tusked the ground.

It was a challenge.

Eggtusk and Lop-ear faced each other, trunks lowered, ears flaring, gazes locked. Lop-ear was trembling, and Eggtusk seemed to tower over him, his great incurving tusks poised over his head.

Bull mammoths have their own society, a society of bachelor herds independent of the Families of Cows and calves controlled by the Matriarchs. It is a warrior society, based on continual tests of strength and dominance. Normally, unless enraged by musth, a young Bull like Lop-ear would never challenge a giant tusker like Eggtusk – or if challenged, he would soon back down.

Now Silverhair waited for Lop-ear to stretch his trunk at Eggtusk to show his deference.

But Lop-ear made no such sign.

Silverhair rushed forward. 'Eggtusk, please. He didn't mean—'

But Owlheart was in her way, solid as a boulder. 'Stay back, child. This is a matter for the Bulls.'

Lop-ear raised his head and made the first blow, dashing his tusks against Eggtusk's. There was a knock of ivory on ivory, as if one great tree was being smashed into another.

The older Bull did not so much as flinch.

Again Lop-ear stabbed at Eggtusk's face. But this time Eggtusk dipped sideways, so that Lop-ear's thrust missed. Eggtusk brought his massive head down and slammed his forehead against Lop-ear's temple.

Lop-ear cried out, and stumbled back.

Eggtusk trumpeted and lumbered forward. Lop-ear turned to face him, both mammoths trying to stay head-on; if either was turned his opponent could easily knock him down or even stab him.

Still the rain howled around them, still the lightning split the sky, and still the gathering light and smoke-stink of the fire filled Silverhair's head. She was peripherally aware of the other mammoths: Foxeye's weary disbelief, Snagtooth's disdain, Croptail's childish excitement.

'I don't want to fight you,' said Lop-ear. He was panting hard, and blood was seeping from a wound in his temple. 'But if that's what I have to do to make you listen—'

Wordlessly Eggtusk trumpeted once more and raised his massive tusks. The sleetish rain swirled around them, and water dripped from the tusks' cruel tips.

Lop-ear lunged. But once again Eggtusk side-stepped, and he brought his own tusks crashing down on Lop-ear's domed head with a splintering crash.

Silverhair, horrified, trumpeted in alarm.

The younger Bull bellowed, and fell to his knees.

Eggtusk turned again, and his tusks slashed at Lop-ear's foreleg, cutting through fur and flesh and drawing thick blood.

For a heartbeat, two, Lop-ear did not move. His face was wreathed in steam, and his great form shuddered.

But then, once more, he clambered stiffly to his feet and turned to face Eggtusk again.

Fights between unmatched Bulls are usually resolved quickly, Silverhair knew. Usually, it would be enough for Eggtusk to raise his great tusks for a junior like Lop-ear to back away.

Usually. But this was not a normal fight.

Silverhair tugged at Owlheart's trunk. 'Matriarch, you have to stop this.'

Owlheart quoted the Cycle. '*To fight is the way of the Bull—*'

'This isn't about dominance,' Silverhair said. 'Don't you see?'

But once again Lop-ear was facing Eggtusk. The space between their staring eyes was filled with tangled hair and steaming breath.

With blood smeared over the dome of his head, Lop-ear charged again.

The Bulls met once more, in a splintering crunch of ivory. Silverhair saw that their curving tusks were locked together. This was a risky tactic for both the combatants, for the tusks could become locked inextricably, taking both mammoths to their deaths.

The Bulls wrestled. Lop-ear bellowed, resisting Eggtusk.

But the older Bull was much stronger. With a smooth, steady, irresistible effort, Eggtusk twisted his head to one side. Lop-ear pawed at the ground, but it was slick and muddy, and the pads of his feet slipped.

It was over in heartbeats.

His tusks still locked to Eggtusk's, Lop-ear crashed to the ground.

Eggtusk stood over the helpless younger Bull, his eyes hard. Silverhair saw that he might twist further, surely snapping Lop-ear's neck – or he might withdraw his tusks and stab down sharply, driving his ivory into Lop-ear's helpless carcass.

The storm cracked over their heads, and for an instant the lightning picked out the silhouette of Eggtusk's giant deformed tusk.

Eggtusk braced himself for the final thrust.

'*No.*'

The commanding rumble made Eggtusk hesitate.

The voice had been Wolfnose's. The old Cow, once the Matriarch, was coming forward. The rain dripped unheeded from her tangled hair, and only a smear of tears around her deep old eyes betrayed the pain of her legs.

Eggtusk said, 'Wolfnose . . .?'

'Let him up, Eggtusk.'

In the silence that followed, Silverhair could see that they were all waiting for the Matriarch's response. It was wrong for a Cow to interfere in the affairs of Bulls. And it was wrong for any Cow – even a former Matriarch, like Wolfnose – to usurp the authority of the Matriarch herself.

But Owlheart was keeping her counsel.

Eggtusk growled. Then he lowered his head, dropped his trunk, and allowed Lop-ear to clamber to his feet.

The younger Bull stood shakily, his hair matted with mud. He was bleeding heavily from the wounds to his leg and temple.

'This must stop,' said Wolfnose.

Eggtusk stiffened. 'But the Cycle—'

'I know the Cycle as well as any of you,' said Wolfnose. Her voice was even, yet powerful enough to be heard over the bellow of the storm. Once, Silverhair thought, this must have been a formidable Matriarch indeed. 'But,' Wolfnose went on, 'Ganesha taught us there are times when the Cycle can't help us. Look at us: lost, bedraggled, trapped . . . You will win your fight, Eggtusk. But what value is it? For we shall soon die, trapped here between forest and fire – all of us, even the infant. And then what?' She turned her great head and glared at them, one by one. 'When was the last time you saw another Family? And you? When was the last time you heard a contact rumble, at morning or evening? *What if we are alone – the last Family of all?* It's possible, isn't it? I tell you, if it's true, and if we do die here, then it all dies with us – after more generations than there are stars in the winter sky.'

And Silverhair, standing in the freezing rain, saw the truth, with sudden, devastating clarity. They had become a rabble, a few shivering, half-starved mammoths, a pathetic remnant of the great Clans which had once roamed here. A rabble so blinded by their own past and mythology they could not even act.

She stepped forward. 'Tell us what to do, Wolfnose.'

The old Cow stepped forward and laid her trunk over Lop-ear's splintered tusk. 'We must do what this bright young Bull says.'

Lop-ear – breathing hard, shivering, bloody – hesitated, as if waiting to be attacked once more. Then he turned to the runoff stream. 'The fallen tree-trunk,' he said, his voice blurred by blood and pain. 'Help me.' And he bent to the fallen tree, dug his tusks under it, and began to push it towards the stream. But it was much too heavy for him, exhausted as he was.

Wolfnose lumbered forward. With only a grimace to betray her pain, she forced her fused knees to bend, and she put her tusks alongside Lop-ear's and pushed with him.

The tree-trunk rocked, then fell back.

Silverhair ran forward. She squeezed between Wolfnose and Lop-ear, and rammed her head against the stubborn tree-trunk. With more hesitation, Eggtusk, Owlheart, and even Snagtooth joined in. Only Foxeye stayed back, shielding the calves.

Under the combined pressure of six adult mammoths, the tree-trunk soon popped out of its muddy groove in the ground, and rolled forward.

With a crunch of branches, the tree crashed over a boulder, and came to rest in the stream. It was so long it straddled almost the whole width of the stream. The water, bubbling, flowed over the tree and through its smashed branches.

The mammoths stood for a heartbeat, studying their work.

Silverhair looked back at Wolfnose. But Wolfnose was obviously drained; she stood with her trunk dangling, eyes closed, rain sleeting off her back.

Silverhair turned to Lop-ear. 'It's your idea, Lop-ear. Tell us what to do next.'

Now that he was being taken seriously, Lop-ear looked

even more nervous and agitated than before. 'More trees! That's it. Pile them on this one. Any you can find. And anything else – boulders, shrubs—'

Eggtusk growled. 'By the lemmings that burrow in the stinking armpits of Kilukpuk: what madness is this?'

Owlheart said dryly, 'We may as well see it through, Eggtusk. Come on.' And she lumbered further up the stream, to a tumbled sapling.

With the Matriarch's implicit approval, the others hurried to work.

Silverhair helped Eggtusk haul another huge tree up the stream. But most of the fallen trees were simply too massive to move.

Lop-ear led them to a small stand of saplings, most of them still upright, and began to barge the smallest of them with his head. 'These will do,' he said. 'Smash them off and take them to the stream.'

Silverhair joined in. This, at least, was familiar. Mammoths will often break and push over young trees; the apparently destructive act serves to clear the land and maintain its openness, and thus the health of the tundra.

So the barrier grew, higgledy-piggledy, with branches and stones and even whole bushes, their roots still dripping with dirt, being thrown on it. Even little Croptail helped, rolling boulders into the stream, where they clattered to rest against the growing pile of debris.

As the barrier grew, the water of the runoff was evidently having trouble penetrating the thickening mass of foliage, rocks and dirt. At last, it began to form a brimming pool behind the pile.

And, ahead of it, the stream's volume was greatly reduced, to a sluggish brook that crawled through the muddy channel. Silverhair stared in amazement, suddenly understanding what Lop-ear had intended.

Lop-ear stood on the bank of the stream. His head was smeared with blood and mud, and his belly hairs, soaked through, were beginning to stiffen with frost. But when he looked on his work he raised his trunk and trumpeted with triumph. 'That's it! *We can cross now.*'

'By Kilukpuk's fetid breath,' growled Eggtusk. 'It's muddy, and boggy – it won't be easy – but, yes, we should be able to ford there now. I never expected to say this, Lop-ear, but there may be something useful about you after all.'

'We should move fast,' said Lop-ear, apparently indifferent to Eggtusk's praise. 'The water is still rising. When it reaches the top of the barrier it will come rushing over, just as hard as before.'

'And besides,' Silverhair pointed out, 'that fire hasn't stopped burning.'

The Matriarch, who had already taken in the situation, brayed a sharp command, and the mammoths prepared for the crossing.

They got the calves across first.

Croptail had no difficulty. He slid down the muddy bank into the water, then emerged to shake himself dry and scramble up the far side to his mother's waiting trunk. Silverhair heard him squeal in delight, as if it was all a game.

Eggtusk was the key to getting Sunfire across. The great Bull plunged willingly into the river, sinking into freezing mud and water that lapped over his belly. The calf slithered down into the ditch and clambered across Eggtusk's broad, patient back.

Then, with Sunfire safely across, Lop-ear reached down and thrust forward a foot for Eggtusk to grasp with his trunk. Eggtusk pulled himself out, huffing mightily, with Lop-ear scrambling to hold his position, and Owlheart and Silverhair threw bark and twigs beneath Eggtusk's feet to help him climb.

Wolfnose was more difficult.

Owlheart tugged gently at her mother's trunk. 'Come now.'

Wolfnose opened her eyes within their nests of wrinkles, regarded her daughter, and with a sigh lifted her feet from the clinging, icy mud. The others gathered around her, Eggtusk behind her. But when she came to the slippery bank of the stream, Wolfnose stopped.

'I am weary,' said Wolfnose slowly. 'Leave me. I will sleep first.'

Owlheart stood before her, helpless; and Silverhair felt her heart sink.

But Eggtusk growled, and he began to butt Wolfnose's backside, quite disrespectfully. 'I – have – had – enough – of *this*!'

Almost against her will, Wolfnose was soon hobbling down the slippery bank. Silverhair and the others quickly gathered around her, helping her to stay on her feet. Wolfnose splashed, hard, into the cold, turbulent stream that emerged from beneath Lop-ear's impromptu dam. Once there, breathing heavily, she found it hard to scramble out. But Eggtusk plunged belly-deep into the clinging mud and shoved gamely at the old Cow's rear.

At last, with much scrambling, pushing and pulling, they had Wolfnose safely lodged on the far bank.

Not long after they had crossed, the water came brimming over the barrier, like a trunk emptying into a great mouth. The barrier fell apart, the trees scattering down the renewed stream like twigs, and it was as if the place they had forded had never been.

The storm blew itself out.

Silverhair watched as the fire came billowing across the tundra, at last reaching the bank they had left behind. But as the rain grew more liquid – and as the dry grass was consumed, with rain hissing over the scorched ground – the fire died.

Silverhair and Lop-ear emerged from the forest, and stood on the rocky ground overlooking the stream. On the far side of the stream the ground was blackened and steaming, with here and there the burned-out stump of a sapling spruce protruding from the ground.

A spectacular sheet of golden light, from broken clouds at the horizon, shimmered beneath the remaining grey clouds above.

'We'll have to move on soon,' said Lop-ear. 'There isn't anything for us to eat on this stony ground . . .'

'The fire would have killed us,' said Silverhair. She was certain she was right. Without Lop-ear's strange ingenuity, they would have perished. She looked down at the tree-trunks scattered along the length of the runoff stream. 'I don't know how you got the idea. But you saved us.'

'Yes,' Lop-ear said gloomily. 'But maybe Owlheart was right.'

'What do you mean?'

'I defied the Cycle. I defied Owlheart. I don't want that, Silverhair. I don't want to be different.'

'Lop-ear—'

'Maybe there *is* something of the Lost about me. Something dark.'

And with that, his eyes deep and troubled, he turned away.

No, thought Silverhair. No, you're wrong. Wolfnose, old and weary as she is, was able to see the value of new thinking – as was Ganesha the Wise before her.

The Cycle might not be able to guide them through the troubled times to come. It would require minds like Lop-ear's – new thinking, new solutions – if they were to survive.

She thought of the creature she had seen on the ice floe. One of the Lost, Eggtusk had said.

Her brain seethed with speculation over dangers and opportunities. Somehow, she knew, her destiny was bound up with the ugly, predatory monster she had encountered on that ice floe.

Destiny – or opportunity?

Silverhair surveyed the wreckage of the barrier a little longer. She tried to remember how it had been, what they had done to defeat the river. But already, she could not picture it.

And the runoff stream was dwindling. The glacier ice had been melted by the heat absorbed by the rock faces during the day. But as the sun sank, the rock cooled and the runoff slowed, reducing the torrents and gushes to mere trickles – which would, Silverhair realised ruefully, have been easy to cross.

She turned away and rejoined the others.

TWO
LOST

THE STORY OF THE
CALVES OF KILUKPUK

Now (Silverhair said to Icebones) every mammoth has heard of the mother of us all: Kilukpuk, the Matriarch of Matriarchs, who grew up in a burrow in the time of the Reptiles. The tale I am going to tell you is of the end of Kilukpuk's life: two thousand Great-Years ago, when the Reptiles were long gone, and the world was young and warm and empty.

Now by this time Kilukpuk had been alive for a very long time.

Though she was the mother of us all, Kilukpuk was not like us. By now she more resembled the seals of the coast, with stubby legs and a nub of trunk. She had become so huge, in fact, that her body had sunk into the ground, turning it into a Swamp within which she dwelled.

But she had a womb as fertile as the sea.

One year she bore three calves.

The first was called Probos; the second was called Siros; the third was called Hyros.

There was no eldest or youngest, for they had all been born at the same mighty instant. They all looked exactly the same. They played together happily, without envy or malice.

They were all equal.

And yet they were not.

Only one of them could be Matriarch, when Kilukpuk died.

As time wore on, the calves ceased to play with each other. They took to watching each other with suspicion and hostility, hoping to find some flaw or small crime they could report to their mother. At least, that is how Hyros and Siros behaved. For her part, Probos bore no ill-will to her sisters.

Kilukpuk floated in her Swamp, and showed no favour to any of her daughters.

Now Kilukpuk did not intend that her daughters should stay for ever in the Swamp, as she did. So, from the beginning, she had pushed her three daughters on to the land.

They had mewled and complained, wishing only to return to the comforting mud of the Swamp, and to snuggle once more against Kilukpuk's mighty dugs – which as you know were as big as the Mountains at the End of the World. But gradually the calves learned to browse at the grasses and nibble at the leaves of the trees, and ceased to miss the warm bath of the Swamp.

Now Hyros became very fond of the foliage of the lush trees of those days, and she became jealous if her sisters tried to share that particular bounty. It got to the point where Hyros started climbing trees to ensure she reached the juiciest leaves before her sisters, and she would leap from branch to branch and even between the trees to keep her sisters away, and she made a great crashing noise when she did so.

And Siros likewise became very fond of the fruits of the seas and rivers, and she became jealous if her sisters tried to share that particular bounty. It got to the point where Siros started swimming in the rivers and seas to ensure she reached the thickest reeds before her sisters, and she made a great galumphing, splashing noise while she did so.

Now, none of this troubled Probos. She knew that the grasses and sedges and herbs and bushes of the world were more than enough to feed her for the rest of her long life, and as many calves as she could imagine bearing. She tried to tell her sisters this: that they had nothing to fear from her or each other, for the world was rich enough to support all of them.

This enraged her sisters, for they thought Probos must be trying to trick them. And so, silently, separately, they hatched their plans against her.

One day, when Probos was browsing calmly on a lush patch of grass, she heard Hyros calling from a treetop: 'Oh, Probos!' She was so high up her voice sounded like a bird's cry. 'I want to show you how fond I am of you, sister. Here – I want you to have the very best and sweetest and fattest leaves I can find.' And Hyros began to hurl down great mouthfuls of bark and leaves and twigs, from the very tops of the trees.

Now Probos was a little bewildered. For the truth was, she had grown to relish the thin, aromatic flavour of the herbs and grasses. She found tree leaves thick and cloying and damp in her mouth, and the bark and twigs scratched at her lips and tongue. But she did not wish to offend her sister, and so she patiently began to eat the tree stuff.

For a day and a night Hyros fed her sister like this, unrelenting, and soon Probos's dung grew slippery with undigested masses of leaf. But still she would not offend her sister, and she patiently worked her way through the great piles on the ground.

Suddenly Hyros stopped throwing down the leaves. She thrust her small, mean face out of the foliage, and glared down at Probos, laughing. 'Look at you now! You will never be able to climb up here and steal my leaves!'

And when Probos looked down at herself, she found she had eaten so much she had grown huge – much bigger than her sisters, though not so big as Kilukpuk – so big that she could, surely, never again climb a tree. She looked up at Hyros sadly. 'Why have you tricked me, sister? I had no wish to share your leaves.'

But Hyros wasn't listening. She bounded off through her branches, laughing at what she had done.

Kilukpuk saw this, but said nothing.

A little while later, when Probos was grazing contentedly

on a patch of particularly savoury herbs, she heard Siros calling from the river. 'Oh, Probos!' Siros barely poked her nose out of the water, and her voice sounded like the bubbling of a fish. 'I want to show you how fond I am of you, sister. Here – I want you to enjoy the sweetest water of all, with me. Come. Give me your nose.'

Now Probos was a little bewildered. For the truth was, she was quite happy with the water she lapped from small streams and puddles; she found river water cold and silty and full of weeds. But she patiently kneeled down and lowered her nose to her sister in the water.

Siros immediately clamped her teeth on the end of Probos's nose and began to pull. Through a clenched jaw she said, 'Now, you stand firm, sister; this will not take long.'

For a day and a night Siros dragged at her sister's nose like this, unrelenting, and soon Probos's nose was starting to stretch, longer and longer, like growing grass. And it hurt a great deal, as you can imagine! And while this was going on, she could not eat or drink, and her dung grew thin and watery and foul-smelling. But still she would not offend her sister, and patiently she let Siros wrench at her aching nose.

Suddenly Siros stopped pulling at Probos's nose. She opened her jaws and slid back into the water, and Probos fell backwards.

Siros thrust her small, mean face out of the water, and glared up at Probos, laughing. 'Look at you now! What a ridiculous nose. With that in the way, you will never be able to slide through the water and steal my reeds!'

And when Probos looked down at herself, she found her nose had grown so long it dangled between her legs, all the way to the ground.

She looked down at Siros sadly. 'Why have you tricked me, sister? I didn't want to share your reeds or your water.'

But Siros wasn't listening. She turned and wriggled away through the water, laughing at what she had done.

Kilukpuk saw this, but said nothing.

The years passed, and at last the day came when Kilukpuk called her calves to her.

But the calves had changed.

Siros had now spent so long in the river and the sea that her skin had grown smooth, the hair flowing on it like water. And Hyros had spent so long in the trees that she had become small and agile, fast-moving and nervous.

As for Probos, she had a body like a boulder, and legs like mighty trees, and a nose she had learned to use as a trunk. And where Siros wriggled and flopped and Hyros skittered to and fro, Probos moved over the land as stately as the shadow of a cloud.

Kilukpuk hauled herself out of her Swamp. 'My teeth grow soft,' she said, 'and soon I will not be here to be your Matriarch. I know that the question of which of you shall follow me as Matriarch has much vexed you – some of you, at least. Here is what I have decided.'

And Hyros and Siros said together, 'Which of us? Oh, tell us. Which of us?'

Probos said nothing, but merely wept tears of Swamp water for her mother.

Kilukpuk said, 'You will all be Matriarch. And none of you will be Matriarch.'

Hyros and Siros fell silent, puzzled.

Kilukpuk said, 'You, Siros, are the Matriarch of the water. But the water is not yours. Even close to the land there will be many who will compete with you for fish and weeds and will hunt you down. But it is what you have stolen from your sisters, and it is what you wanted, and it is what you will have. Go now.'

And Siros squirmed around and flopped her way back to the water.

Now Kilukpuk said, 'You, Hyros, are the Matriarch of the trees. But the trees are not yours. You have made yourself small and weak and frightened, and that is how you will remain. Animals and birds will compete with you for leaves and bark and plants and will hunt you down. But it is what you have stolen from your sisters, and it is what you wanted, and it is what you will have. Go now.'

And Hyros clambered nervously to the branches of the tall trees.

That left only Probos, who waited patiently for her mother to speak. But Kilukpuk was weakening now, and her great body sank deeper into the water of the Swamp. She spat out fragments of tooth (so huge, by the way, they became glaciers where they fell). And she said to Probos, 'You stole nothing from your sisters. And yet what they stole from you has made you strong.

'Go, Probos. For the Earth is yours.

'With your great bulk you need fear no predator. With your strong and agile trunk you will become the cleverest animal in the world. Go now, Probos, Matriarch of the mammoths and all their Cousins who live on the land.'

Probos was greatly saddened; but she was a good calf who obeyed her Matriarch.

(And what Kilukpuk prophesied would come to pass, for each of Probos's calves and their calves to come. But that was for the future.)

Kilukpuk raised herself from the Swamp and called to her calves one last time. She said, 'You will rarely meet again; nor will your calves, or your calves' calves. But you will be Cousins for ever. You must not fight or kill each other. If you meet your Cousins you will assist each other, without question or hesitation or limit. You will make your calves swear this binding oath.'

Well, that was the end of the jealousy between the sisters. Hyros and Siros were remorseful, Probos was gladdened, and the three of them swore to hold true to Kilukpuk's command.

And that is why, as soon as she is old enough to speak, every calf is taught the Oath of Kilukpuk.

But as Kilukpuk sank back into her Swamp and prepared for her journey back into the Earth, she was saddened. For she knew she had not told even Probos, the best of her calves, the whole truth.

For, one day, there would be something for them *all* to fear – even mighty Probos.

CHAPTER 1
THE PLAIN OF BONES

Arctic summer: the sun arced around the sky's north pole, somehow aimlessly, and at midnight it rolled lazily along the horizon. It was a single day, long and crystalline, that would last for two months, an endless day of feeding and breeding and dying.

At midnight Silverhair, walking slowly with her Family across the thawing plain, saw that she cast a shadow, ice-sharp, that stretched to the horizon. She felt oddly weighed down by the shadow, as if it were some immense tail she must drag around with her. But the light turned everything to gold, and made the bedraggled mammoths, with their clouds of loose moulting fur, glow as if on fire.

They reached an area of tundra new to Silverhair. The mammoths, exhausted by their adventures, spread slowly over the landscape. As the thaw arrived, they found enough to drink in the meltpools that gathered over the permafrost. On days that were excessively hot – because mammoths do not sweat – they would reduce heat by panting, or they would find patches of soft snow to stand in, sometimes eating mouthfuls of it.

The changes in the land were dramatic now; for, after a month of continuous daylight, the sun was high and hot enough to melt ice. Rock began to protrude through the thawing hillsides, and blue meltwater glimmered on the frozen lakes. As snow banks melted, drips became trickles, and gullies became streams, and rivers, marshes and ponds reformed. In sheltered valleys there were already patches of sedge and grass, green and meadow-like. After months of frozen whiteness the land was becoming an intricate pattern of black and white. This emerging panorama – shimmering with moist light, draped in mist and fog – was still wreathed in silence. But already the haunting calls of Arctic loons echoed to the sky from the meltpools.

The mammoths slept and fed in comparative comfort, and time wore away, slowly and unmarked.

Croptail tried to play with his sister, Sunfire, and his antics pleased the slower-moving adults, who would reach down trunk or tusk to allow the Bull calf to wrestle. But despite her mother's attention Sunfire was feeding badly and did not seem to be putting on weight, and her coat remained shabby and tangled. She spent most of her time tucked under her mother's belly hair, with her face clamped to one dug or other, while Foxeye whispered verses from the Cycle.

Still, it was, all things considered, a happy time. But Silverhair's spirits did not rise. She took to keeping her distance from the others – even from Lop-ear. She sought out patches of higher ground, her trunk raised.

For there was something carried to her by the wind off the sea – something that troubled her to the depths of her soul.

Wolfnose joined her. The old Cow stood alongside Silverhair, feeling with her trunk for rich patches of grass, then trapping tufts between her trunk and tusks and pulling them out.

Silverhair waited patiently. Wolfnose seemed to be moving more slowly than ever, and her rheumy eyes, constantly watering, must be almost blind now. So worn were Wolfnose's teeth it took her a long time to consume her daily meals. And when she passed dung, Silverhair saw that it was thin and sour-smelling, and contained much unchewed grass and twigs, and even some indigestible soil which Wolfnose, in her gathering blindness, had scooped into her mouth.

But, even as her body failed, Wolfnose seemed to be settling into a new contentment.

'This is a good time of year,' Wolfnose rumbled at last. She quoted the Cycle, *'When the day becomes endless, we shed our cares with our winter coats.'* She ground her grass contentedly, her great jaw moving back and forth. 'But you are not happy, child. Even my old eyes can see that much. What troubles you? Is it Sunfire?'

'I know Foxeye is looking after her well.'

'Sunfire was born in a difficult spring, a little too early. Now that summer is approaching, she will flourish like the tundra flowers—'

Silverhair blurted, 'Wolfnose – what do you *smell* here?'

For answer, Wolfnose patiently finished her mouthful of grass. Then she raised her trunk and turned it this way and that.

She said at last, 'There is the salt of the sea, to the west. There is the crisp fur of wolves, the sour droppings of lemmings, the stink of the guano of the gulls at the rocky coast . . .'

'But no mammoths.' Silverhair meant the complex of smells which characterised mammoths to each other: the smells of moist hair, dung, mother's milk.

Wolfnose said, 'No. But there is—'

Silverhair trembled. *'There is the stink of death – of dead mammoths.'*

Wolfnose lowered her trunk and turned calmly to Silverhair. 'It isn't what you think.'

Silverhair snapped. 'I'll tell you what I *do* think. I think that what I can smell is the stench of some other Family's rotting corpses.' She felt an unreasonable anger at Wolfnose's calm patience.

'I'll tell you the truth,' Wolfnose said. 'I can't say what's become of the other Families. It's certainly a long time – too long – since any of us met a mammoth from another Family, and you know my fears about *that*. But the scent you detect has another meaning. Something wonderful.'

'Wonderful? Can death be wonderful?'

'Yes. Come on.'

And with that, ripping another mouthful of grass from the clumps at her feet, Wolfnose began to walk towards the west.

Silverhair, startled, came to herself and hurried to catch up with Wolfnose. It did not take long, for Wolfnose's arthritic gait was so forced and slow that Silverhair thought even a glacier could outrun her now.

She called, 'Where are we going?'

'You'll find out when we arrive.'

The thawing ground was moist and fragile under Silverhair's feet, and every footstep left a scar. In fact the plain was criss-crossed by the trails of mammoths, wolves, foxes and other animals, left from last summer and the years before. It could take ten years for the fragile tundra to grow over a single footstep.

Overhead the snow geese were winging to their breeding grounds to the north, skein after skein of them passing across the blue sky. Occasionally, over the lakes, the geese plummeted from the sky to reach water through thin ice.

The tundra was wet, almost boggy, peppered by rivers, lakes, pools and peaty hummocks. Although there was so little rain it was actually a desert, the tundra was one of the most waterlogged lands on the planet. There was little evaporation into the cold air and virtually no absorption into the soil; for, just a short trunk's reach down through the carpet of plants, the ground was always frozen. This was the permafrost: nearly a mile deep, a layer of frozen soil that had failed to melt since the Ice Age.

It was a harsh place. Few plants could survive the combination of the summer's shallow thawed-out soil and the intensely bitter winds of winter. But now, on the ground,

103

from under the melting snow, the frozen world was coming to life.

Dead-looking stems bore tiny leaves and flowers, and the land was peppered with green and white and yellow. The first insects were stirring too. There were flies in the air, and some spiders and mites toiling on the ground. Silverhair saw a caterpillar cocoon fixed to a dwarf willow. The cocoon twitched as if its occupant were impatient to begin life's brief adventure.

The edges of the receding snow patches were busy places. New arrivals – migrant birds like buntings, sanderling, turnstone and horned larks – rushed to and fro, as if in desperation, as the sun revealed fresh land with its cargo of roots and insects, ripe for the eating. The noise of the birds was startling after the long silence of the winter.

The lemmings seemed plentiful this year. Their heads popped up everywhere from their holes in the snow, and in some places their busy teeth had already denuded the land, leaving the characteristic 'lemming carpet' of shorn grass and hard black droppings.

And the lemming hunters were here too. As soon as any lemming left its ball-shaped nest, a long-tailed skua would take off after it, yelping display calls emanating from its hooked beak.

Usually the hapless rodents became nothing more than gifts in a skua's courtship display. But Silverhair saw one enterprising animal, attacked by a skua, rear up on its hind legs and flash its long teeth. The skua, alarmed, flew away, and Silverhair felt obscurely cheered. She could hear the clattering heartbeat of the little creature, as it nibbled in peace at a blade of grass.

But it was probably only a brief respite. The lemmings were hunted ruthlessly, not just by the skuas, but by snowy owls, gulls and buzzards, and even Arctic foxes and polar bears. Silverhair knew that this lemming's life, compared to her own, would be fast, vivid, but – even if by some miracle the predators spared it – tragically short.

The sun completed many rounds in the sky as the two mammoths walked on.

Wolfnose even brought Silverhair to some richer pastures, urging her to remember them for the future. 'And,' she said, 'you must understand why the grass grows so well here.'

'Why?'

'Once there were many mammoths here – many Families, many Clans. And they had favourite pastures, where their dung would be piled thick. The Clans are gone now – all save ours – but, even after so long, their dung enriches the Earth . . .'

Silverhair stared with awe at the thick-growing grass, a vibrant memorial to the great mammoth herds of long ago.

They came at last to the western coast.

The sea was still largely frozen. Sanderling and bunting searched for seeds in the snow, ducks dived through narrow leads in the thin ice, and skuas stood expectantly on prominent rocks. On the cliff below, barnacle geese were already incubating their clutches of eggs, still surrounded by the brilliant white of snow.

The smells of salt water and guano were all but overpowering. But it was here that the stink of rotten mammoth flesh was strongest of all, and Silverhair was filled with a powerful dread.

At last they came to a shallow, rounded hill. Silverhair could see that it had been badly eroded by recent rainstorms; deep gullies ran down its side, as if scored there by giant tusks.

Wolfnose edged forward, and poked at the ground with her trunk. 'This is called a *yedoma*,' she said. 'It is a hill mostly made of ice. Come now.'

She led Silverhair around the flank of the hill. The death

stink grew steadily stronger, until Silverhair could hardly bear to take another step. But Wolfnose marched stolidly on, her trunk raised, and Silverhair had no option but to follow.

And they came to a place where the *yedoma*'s collapsing flank had exposed a corpse: the corpse of a mammoth.

Wolfnose stood back, her trunk raised. 'Tell me what you see, little Silverhair,' she said gently.

Silverhair, shocked and distressed, stepped forward slowly, nosing at the ground with her trunk. 'I think it was a Bull . . .'

The dead mammoth was lying on his side. Silverhair could see that the flesh and skin on which he lay were mostly intact: she could make out his ear on that side, his flank, the skin on his legs, the long dark hair of winter tangled in frozen mud.

But the upper side of the Bull had been stripped of its flesh, by the sharp teeth of scavengers. The meat was almost completely removed from the skull, and the ribcage, and even the legs. There was no sign of the Bull's trunk. The pelvis, shoulder blade and several of the ribs were broken and scattered. Inside the ribcage nestled a dark, lumpy mass, still frozen hard; perhaps it was the heart and stomach of this dead mammoth.

The Bull, she found, still had traces of food in the ruin of his mouth: grass and sedge, just as she had eaten today. He must have died rapidly, then: too rapidly even to swallow his last meal.

The flensed skull gleamed white in the pale sunlight. Its empty eye socket seemed to stare at her accusingly.

She heard a soft growl. She turned, trumpeting.

A wolf stood there, its fur white as snow. It was a bitch; Silverhair could see swollen dugs dangling beneath her chest.

Silverhair lowered her head, trumpeted again, and lunged

at the wolf. 'Get away, cub of Aglu, or I will drive my tusks into you!'

The wolf dropped her ears and ran off.

Silverhair, breathing hard, returned to Wolfnose. 'If she returns, I will kill her.'

Wolfnose said, 'No. She has her place, as we all do. She probably has cubs to feed.'

'She has been chewing on the corpse of this Bull!'

Wolfnose trumpeted mockingly. 'And what difference does that make to him now? He has belonged to the wolves for a long time: in fact, longer than you think, little Silverhair . . .'

Silverhair returned to her inspection of the ravaged corpse. 'I don't recognise him. He must be from a Family I never met.'

'You don't understand yet,' Wolfnose said gently. 'Perhaps he was grazing at the soft edge of a gully or a river bluff. Perhaps he lost his footing, became trapped. The wolves would work at him, and in time he would die. But then, at last, he would be enveloped by the soil, saturated by water, frozen by winter's return.

'But the river mud that destroyed him also preserved him.

'For you see, if your body happens to be sealed inside ice, it can be saved. The ice, freezing, draws out the moisture that would otherwise rot your flesh . . . If you were sealed here, Silverhair, although your spirit would long have flown to the aurora, your body would live on – as long as it remained inside the ice, it would be as well preserved as this.'

'How long?'

Wolfnose said, 'I don't know. How can I know? Perhaps Great-Years. Perhaps longer . . .'

Silverhair was stunned.

She could reach down with her trunk and touch the hair of this Bull's face. The Bull might have been dead only a few days. And yet – could it be true? – he was separated from her by Great-Years.

'Now,' said Wolfnose. 'Look with new eyes; lift your trunk and *smell* . . .'

Silverhair, a little bewildered, obeyed.

And, now that her eyes and nostrils were accustomed to the stink of the ancient corpse beside her, she saw that this landscape was not as it had seemed.

It was littered with bones.

Here was a femur, a leg-bone, thrusting defiantly from the ground. Here was a set of ribs, broken and scattered, split as if some scavenger had been working to extract the marrow from their cores. And there a skull protruded from the ground, as if some great beast were burrowing upwards from within the Earth.

Wolfnose said, 'The bones and bodies are stored in the ground. But when the ice melts and they are exposed – after Great-Years of stillness and dark – there is a moment of daylight, a flash of activity. The wolves and birds soon come to take away the flesh, and the bones are scattered by the wind and the rain. And then it is done. The ancient bodies evaporate like a grain of snow on the tongue. So you see, you are fortunate to have witnessed this rare moment of surfacing, Silverhair.'

'We should Remember the one in the *yedoma*,' she said.

'Of course we should,' said Wolfnose. 'For he has no one left to do it for him.'

And so the two mammoths touched the vacant skull with their trunks, and lifted and sorted the bones. Then they gathered twigs and soil and cast it on the ancient corpse, and touched it with the sensitive pads of their back feet, and they stood over it as the sun wheeled around the sky. They were trying to Remember the spirit which had once occupied this body, this Bull with no name who might have been an ancestor of them both, just as they would have done had they come upon the body of one of their own Family.

Silverhair imagined the days of long ago – perhaps when the crushed corpse she had seen had been proud and full of life – days different from now, days when the Clan had covered the Island, days when Families had merged and mingled in the great migrations like rivers flowing together. Days when mammoths had been more numerous, on the Island and beyond, than pebbles on a beach.

She was standing on a ground filled with the bodies of mammoths, generations of them stretching back Great-Years and more, bodies that were raised to the surface, to glimmer in the sun and evaporate like dew. For the first time in her life she could *see* the great depth of mammoth history behind her: forty million years of it, stretching back to Kilukpuk herself in her Swamp, a great sweep of time and space of which she was just a part.

Like the bones of this long-dead Bull, her soul was merely the fragment of all that mystery which happened to have surfaced in the here and now. And like the Bull, her soul would be worn away and vanish in an instant.

Silverhair felt the world shift and flow around her, as if she herself were caught up by some great river of time.

And she was proud, fiercely proud, to be mammoth.

When they were done, the two mammoths turned away from the setting sun, side by side, and prepared for the long walk back to their Family.

At the last moment, Wolfnose stopped and turned back. 'Silverhair – what of the tusks?'

Somehow Silverhair had not noticed the Bull's tusks, one way or another. She trotted back to the *yedoma*.

The tusks had not been snapped away by whatever accident had befallen this Bull, for the stumps in the skull were sharply terminated, in clean, flat edges. And the tusks themselves were missing; there was no sign of them, not so much as a splinter.

She returned to Wolfnose and told her this.

For the first time, she detected fear in the voice of the old one. 'Then the Lost have been here.'

'*What?*'

'I know what you saw on the ice floe in the south, little Silverhair,' Wolfnose said gravely. 'Perhaps they came in search of flesh, like the wolf . . .'

'What do the Lost want with tusks?'

'There is no understanding the Lost,' said Wolfnose bluntly. 'There is only fleeing. Come. Let us return to Owlheart and the others.'

Their shadows stretching ahead of them, the two mammoths walked together.

CHAPTER 2

THE HOLE GOUGED OUT
OF THE SKY

Silverhair was impatient during the long journey back to the Family.

It struck her as a paradox that visiting a place of death and desolation like the Plain of Bones should leave her feeling so invigorated. But that was how she felt – as Wolfnose had surely intended.

And – besides all the philosophy – she was *young*, and the days of spring were bright and warming, and the tundra flowers were already starting to bloom, bright yellow amid the last scraps of snow and the first green shoots of new grass. Just as the Cycle promised, she felt as if she was shedding her cares with the worn-out layers of her winter coat.

Perhaps it would be this year that she would, for the first time, sing the Song of Oestrus: when her body would produce the eggs that could form a calf. She remembered the ache in her empty dugs as she had watched Foxeye suckle Sunfire for the first time. Now she could feel the blood surge in her veins, as if drawn by the sun.

She wanted to become pregnant: to bear her own calf, to shelter and feed and raise it, to teach it all she knew of the world, to add her own new thread to the Cycle's great and unending coat.

And her thoughts were full of Lop-ear. She longed to tell him what she had seen on the Plain of Bones, what it had meant to her . . .

She longed, bluntly, just to be with him once more.

She trotted across the thawing plains, her head full of warm, blood-red dreams of the young Bull.

Wolfnose had more difficulty.

Even at the best of times her pace was no match for Silverhair's. The pain in her legs and back was obvious. It took her much longer than Silverhair to feed and to pass dung, and her lengthening stops left Silverhair fretting with impatience.

Thus they proceeded, Wolfnose warring with her own failing body, Silverhair torn between eagerness for the future and responsibility for the past.

At last they came in sight of the Family.

It was a bright morning, and at the centre of a greening plain, the Family looked like a series of round, hairy boulders, dotted over the landscape. The smell of their dung and their moist coats was already strong, and Silverhair could feel the rumble of their voices as they called to each other. The mammoths were not beautiful – never had the ambiguous gift of great Matriarch Ganesha to her daughter Prima been more evident to Silverhair – but it was, in her eyes, the finest sight she could have seen.

She raised her trunk and trumpeted her joyous greeting, and – quite forgetting Wolfnose – she charged across the tundra towards the Family.

Here came Lop-ear, that damaged ear dangling unmistakably by his head, running to meet her.

Their meeting was so vigorous she was almost knocked over. They bumped their foreheads, ran in circles, defecated together and spun around. He was like a reflection in a meltpond, a reflection of her own resurgent youth and vigour. This is our time, she thought as she spun and danced; this is our summer, our day.

And it seemed perfectly natural that he should run behind her, rear up on his hind legs, place his forelegs on her back, and rest his great weight against her.

But she was not in oestrus, and he was not in musth, and – for now – the mounting was only a playful celebration.

They faced each other; Silverhair touched his scalp and tusks and mouth.

'I missed you,' he said.

'And I you. You won't believe what Wolfnose showed me—' And she began to recount all she had seen in the Plain of Bones, the ancient carcasses of mammoths just like themselves, swimming out of the ice after a Great-Year's sleep.

But, though he listened intently, and continued to stroke her trunk with his, she could see that his eyes were empty.

After a time she drew back from him. He reached for her again, but she pushed him gently away.

'Something's wrong. Is it what Owlheart said, about having something of the Lost in you?'

'No. Or at least, not just that. I'm confused, Silverhair. I'm happy to see you, glad the spring has come again. Part of me wants to jump about like a calf. But inside, I feel as if a giant black winter cloud is hanging over me.'

She scuffed at the ground, trying to retain that sense of wondrous optimism with which she had returned home. 'I don't understand—'

'Silverhair, if you were singing the Song of Oestrus now – *who would mount you*?'

And with that question she saw his concern. For there were only two Bulls here who might come into musth: Egg-tusk and Lop-ear. They'd fought once already; they might easily kill each other fighting over her.

Or over Owlheart, or Foxeye, or even Snagtooth, if their turn came.

Lop-ear said, 'And even if we resolve our dominance fights without killing each other – even if all the Cows become pregnant by one or other of us – what then?'

'What do you mean?'

113

'What of the future? When Sunfire and Croptail and any other calves grow up – and themselves come into oestrus and musth – who is to mate with *them*?' He spun, agitated, his trunk raised as if to ward off invisible enemies. 'Already his mother is pushing Croptail away. That's as it should be. Soon, in a few years, he will want to leave the Family and search for other Bulls, join a bachelor herd. Just as I did, just as Eggtusk did. But Croptail *can't* join the Bulls, for there *are* no other Bulls. He can't join a bachelor herd, for there *is* no herd – none that we have met for a long time, at any rate. And when he is in musth, there will be no Cows but his own sisters and aunts and cousins.'

She reached out to try to calm him. 'Lop-ear—'

But he spun away from her. 'Oh, Kilukpuk! I have this stuff rattling around in my skull all day and all night. I want to stop thinking!'

She was chilled by his words, even as she strove to understand. To think so clearly about the possibilities of the future, of change, is not common in mammoths; embedded in the great rhythms of time, they live in the here and now. But Lop-ear was no ordinary mammoth.

She took hold of his trunk and forced him to face her. 'Lop-ear – listen to me. Perhaps you're right, in all you say. But you are wrong to despair. When we were trapped by the fire and the runoff you found a way to save us. It wasn't a teaching from the Cycle; it wasn't something the Matriarch showed you. It was a new idea.

'Now we are facing a barrier even more formidable than that stream. There is nothing to guide us in the Cycle. There is nothing the Matriarch can advise us to do. *It's up to us*, Lop-ear. We have to seek out the new, and find a way to survive.'

'It's impossible.'

'No. As Longtusk said, *only death is the end of possibility*. What we must do is look for answers where nobody has looked before.'

'Where?'

She hesitated, and the vague determination that had long been gathering in her crystallised. 'If Eggtusk is right – that the Lost have come to this Island – then that's where we must go.'

'*The Lost?* Silverhair, are you rogue?'

'No. Just determined. Maybe the Lost aren't the monsters of the Cycle any more. Maybe there's some way they can help us.' She tightened her grasp on his trunk. 'We must go south again. Are you with me?'

For long heartbeats, he stared into her eyes. Then he said: 'Yes. Oh, Silverhair, yes. I'll follow you to the End of the World—'

There was an alarmed trumpeting.

Silverhair released Lop-ear's trunk and they both whirled, trunks held aloft.

Owlheart was running. 'Wolfnose! Wolfnose!'

Silverhair looked back to the west, the way she had come.

Wolfnose, trailing Silverhair's footsteps, had fallen to her knees.

Her heart surging, Silverhair ran after her Matriarch.

Silverhair, driven by guilt, was the first to reach Wolfnose.

The old Cow's belly and chest were resting against the ground, her legs splayed, and her trunk was pooled before her. Shanks of winter fur were scattered around her. Her eyes were closed, and it seemed to Silverhair as if she were slowly subsiding, as if the blood and life were leaking out of her into the hard ground.

She reached out and ran her trunk over the old Cow's face. The skin looked as rough as bark, but it was warm and soft to the touch, and she could hear the soft gurgle of Wolfnose's breathing.

Wolfnose opened her eyes. They were sunk in pools of black, wrinkled skin. 'Oh, little Silverhair,' she said softly.

'Are you tired?'

'Oh, yes. And hungry, so hungry. Perhaps I'll sleep now, and then feed a little more . . .'

She started to tip over.

Silverhair rushed to Wolfnose's side. Wolfnose's great weight settled against her flank, slack and lifeless, and Silverhair staggered, barely able to support her.

But now the others were here: Lop-ear, Owlheart and Eggtusk. Silverhair saw that Owlheart had, with remarkable calm and foresight, carried a trunkful of water with her. She offered dribbles of it to Wolfnose, and Silverhair saw Wolfnose's pink, cracked tongue uncurl and lap at the cool, clear liquid.

Wolfnose's eyes flickered open once more. She raised her trunk, so heavy it looked as if it were stuffed with river mud, and laid it over Owlheart's scalp. 'You're a good daughter, Grassfoot . . .'

The Matriarch said, 'I'll be a better one when you're on your feet again.'

Wolfnose shuddered, and a deep, ominous gurgling sounded from her lungs. Silverhair listened in horror; it was as if something had broken inside Wolfnose.

Wolfnose closed her eyes once more, and her trunk fell away from Owlheart's head.

Owlheart stepped back, staring at her mother in dismay.

When Eggtusk saw that Owlheart was giving up, he roared defiance. 'By Kilukpuk's piss-soaked hind leg, you're not done yet, Cow!'

He ran around Wolfnose, and pushed his head between her slack buttocks. Then he dug his heels into the ground and heaved. The massive body rocked. Eggtusk looked up and bellowed to Silverhair and Lop-ear: 'Come on, you lazy calves. Don't just stand there. Push!'

Lop-ear and Silverhair glanced at each other. Then they braced themselves and pushed at Wolfnose's sides.

Even after the trials of the winter – during which she had

116

shed more fat than was good for her – Wolfnose was a
mature Cow, and very heavy. Silverhair could feel Wolfnose's ribs grinding as they shoved the slack body upwards.

But, between them, they managed to lift her off the
ground. Wolfnose's legs straightened out, like cracking tree
branches, and her feet settled on the ground.

'That's it!' Eggtusk bellowed. 'Hold her now!'

But there was no strength in those old legs. Silverhair
staggered sideways, as Wolfnose's bulk slid against her body.

Eggtusk cried out, 'No!'

But it was too late. Wolfnose slumped to the ground, this
time falling on her side.

Eggtusk began pushing at Wolfnose's buttocks once more.
'Come on! Help me, you dung-heaps! Help me . . .' But
Wolfnose could not stand again.

Eggtusk crashed to his knees before her. Wolfnose's eyes,
flickering open and closed, swivelled towards him. Eggtusk
lifted her limp trunk on to his tusks. Draping the trunk over
his head, he put his own trunk into her mouth.

A watching human would have been startled by the
familiarity of his choking cries, and the heaving of his chest.

This was love, Silverhair thought, awed. A love of an intensity and depth and timelessness she had never imagined
possible. She knew that she would be privileged if, during
her life, she ever received or gave such devotion.

And she had never suspected it existed between Eggtusk
and Wolfnose.

But Owlheart came to him now. 'No more, Eggtusk.' And
Owlheart wrapped her trunk around his face.

Lop-ear was at Silverhair's side.

'Oh, Lop-ear,' Silverhair said, and her own vision blurred
as flat salty tears welled in her eyes. 'If she hadn't walked
with me all that way to the Plain of Bones – if I hadn't
been so careless as to rush her back, to leave her behind so
thoughtlessly . . . All I wanted was to get back, and—'

'Hush,' he said. 'She wanted to take you to the Plain.'

'I could have said no—'

'And treat her with disrespect? She wouldn't have wanted that. It's nobody's fault. It is her time.' And he twined his trunk in hers, and held her still.

Wolfnose lifted her trunk, shuddered, and slumped. Her breath sighed out of her in a long growl, like a final contact rumble.

Then she was still.

Eggtusk rocked over Wolfnose. He nudged her head with his. He placed his trunk in her mouth again, and her trunk in his, and intertwined their trunks. He even walked around behind her and placed his forelegs on her back, as if he were trying to mount her. And he raised his trunk and trumpeted his distress to the empty lands.

Before the end of the day, Owlheart led all the Family to Wolfnose's body for the Remembering. The sun was low now and it painted the Earth with gold and fire. Eggtusk, his trunk drooping as he stood over the body, was a noble shadow in Silverhair's eyes, the stiff hairs of his back catching the liquid light.

The calves were both staring at the body. Little Sunfire's trunk was raised in alarm.

Foxeye tapped at the calves with her trunk. 'Watch now,' she said, 'and learn. This is how to die.'

Silverhair found herself staring too. The loss she felt was enormous, as if a hole had been gouged out of the sky.

Owlheart stepped forward, and scraped at the bare ground with her tusks. Then she picked up a fingerful of earth and grass and dropped it on Wolfnose's unresponding flank.

Silverhair reached down, ripped up some grass, and stepped forward to do the same.

Soon all the Family were following Owlheart's lead, covering Wolfnose's body with mud, earth, grass and twigs. Eggtusk kicked and scraped at the soil, sending heaps of it over the carcass. Even the calves tried to help; little Sunfire looked comical as she tottered back and forth to the fallen body with a blade of grass or a scrap of dust.

As they worked, Silverhair felt a deeper calm settle on her soul. The Cycle said this was how the mammoths – and their Cousins, the Calves of Probos, the world over – had always honoured and remembered their dead. Now Silverhair felt the ancient truth and wisdom of the ceremonial seep into her. It was a way to show their love for the spark of Wolfnose, as it floated across the river of darkness to the aurora, leaving the daylight diminished.

When they were done, the mammoths stood a little longer over the body, and wove restlessly from side to side, the younger ones joining in without thinking.

Then Owlheart turned away, and quoted a final line from the Cycle: '*She belongs to the wolves now.*'

She led the Family away. Eggtusk walked at her side, still desolate, his trunk dangling limp between his legs.

Silverhair looked back once. The mound of Wolfnose's body looked like the *yedoma* within which she had seen the emerging, ancient corpse.

Suddenly she saw this scene as it might be Great-Years from now. She saw another mammoth, young and foolish as herself, come lumbering across the plain – to discover Wolfnose's body, stripped by time of flesh and name, emerging once more from the icy ground. It was like a vision of her own life, she thought: as intense as sunlight, as brief as the glimmer of hoar-frost.

She sought out Lop-ear. She stroked his musth gland with her trunk, but he shrank back, oddly.

She turned her face towards the south.

He hesitated. 'Now?'

'Yes. Now.'

'. . . Shouldn't we tell the others?'

'What for? They would only stop us.'

She began to walk. Resolutely, she did not look back.

After a few heartbeats she heard his heavy footfalls as he lumbered after her. She hid her grim satisfaction.

CHAPTER 3
THE TIME OF MUSTH
AND OESTRUS

Once more, their walk took them many days.

They passed through a valley flanked by eroded mountains.

It was a valley of water and light. Gently undulating meadows fell away to a central river, which was slow-moving, wide and deep, meandering through a sandy flood-plain. To the west the river's numerous tangled channels shimmered in the low sun. Above them the valley sides rose up to become dramatic peaks, the white light blazing off the ice that crowned them. The basalt walls, their sheer rock faces shattered by centuries of frost, had eroded into narrow pinnacles that stood against the sky. Every ledge was coated with orange lichen, nourished by the droppings of geese, whose cackling calls echoed down to the mammoths.

There was little snow left on the valley floor now, and trickles of water, cool and fresh, ran from the remaining snow banks. But the ground was still bare, shaded rust-red, ochre and russet; of the lush vegetation which would soon cover the valley there was still little sign.

The first bumble bees and butterflies were appearing in the air.

Silverhair suffered her first mosquito bite of the year. She snapped at the troublesome insect with her tail, but she knew that even if she reached it her effort was futile; millions of its relatives would soon be emerging from the silt at the bottom of ice-covered ponds, where they had spent the winter as larvae.

The beauty of the valley, the return of life, the calmness of their situation: all of this, as the long days wore on, was having a profound effect on Silverhair. She could feel the flesh and fat gathering comfortably on her bones, her winter coat falling away. And her body responded deeply to the season, surging with oceanic warmth.

Somewhere within her, seeds were ripening, as if in response to the death she had witnessed. It was oestrus; she was thrilled.

And she knew that Lop-ear, too, was ready. As he walked he kept his head held high, his trunk curled. He seethed with irritability and urgency. He dribbled musth from the temporal gland at the top of his head, and he left a trail of strong-smelling urine wherever he walked. He was even making a deep rumble, a sound she had only heard from much older Bulls before. But he seemed consumed by his own inner turmoil and ill-defined longing, and when he spoke to her it was only of their greater concerns: the strange encounter with the Lost that might await them in the south, the possibility of bringing the Family to these richer lands, the disturbing, nagging fact that they were finding no recent signs of other mammoth Families any-where.

He spoke of everything but *them*.

He was in musth.

And yet he couldn't see it himself.

Patiently, she kept her counsel and waited for him to understand.

After many days of walking, they came to a ridge that overlooked the southern coast of the Island.

The world to the south lay displayed before Silverhair, divided into broad stripes, dazzling in her poor vision. Below the blue-grey line of sky there was the misty bulk of the Mainland, still obscured by storm cloud. Then came the Channel, a blue-black strip of water fringed by cracked, gleaming pack ice. Below the ridge they were standing on was the shore, a shingle beach fringed by dirty landfast ice.

The all-pervasive sound rising from the coast was of broken pack ice lifting on and off the shore rocks. Further away, in the open Channel, icebergs drifted: a procession of them, mysterious and awe-inspiring, like clouds brought down to Earth. As the light shifted, their contours would suddenly glow iridescent blue. Silverhair's heart was lifted by the stately beauty and strangeness of the bergs; they were the mammoths of the sea, she thought, effortlessly dominating their surroundings, giant and dignified.

The wind here was strong, and its cold penetrated Silverhair's newly exposed underwool. She huddled close to Lop-ear, the wind whipping across her eyes. 'There are times when I wish I could keep my winter fur all year around—'

'Hush,' he said, staring. '*Look*.'

. . . And there, resting on the shore, was something she had never seen before.

At first she thought it was the splayed-open body of some giant animal. It had one end coming to a point, the other rounded. Its long, sleek flanks were encrusted with sea plants and streaks of brownish discoloration. And those flanks were torn open, she saw, perhaps ripped by the sea ice. The top of the monster was like a complex, shattered forest, with posts like tree-trunks sprouting from each other at all angles.

The thing was huge: so big she could have walked around inside its belly.

Lop-ear was silent, staring at the hulk, his trunk raised in the air.

Silverhair said, 'Do you think it's dead?'

'I don't think it was ever alive,' he said bluntly.

'What, then?'

'I think you must ask the Lost that,' he said. 'For something as ugly and unfitting as *that* could only come from their tortured souls. Perhaps it brought them here.'

123

'But it's damaged. Perhaps that's why they can't leave.'
Suddenly she raised her trunk. 'I smell something.'

'Yes.' He turned, scanning along the coast.

It was smoke.

They saw a small fire, confined to a spot on the beach
below, close to the foot of the ridge. There was, Silverhair
saw, a shape above it: like a tree, bent all the way over to
touch the ground. There were objects dangling from the
tree-thing, over the fire.

Now she could smell something else, carried on the wind.
The stink of burning flesh.

And that bent-over object wasn't a tree, she realised with
mounting horror.

It was a tusk.

'By Kilukpuk's mercy . . .'

Lop-ear was becoming agitated. 'That smell of flesh—' His
voice was tight and indistinct. 'It is all I can do to keep from
fleeing.'

'Lop-ear, listen to me.' She told him about the body in the
yedoma. The way the tusks of the ancient Bull had been
hacked away. 'Well, now I know what became of those
tusks,' she said grimly.

Now there was movement on the beach. Two creatures –
something like wolves, perhaps, but walking upright, on
their hind legs – approached the fire. One of them reached
out with its foreleg and prodded at the dangling scraps of
flesh. It was using its paw as Silverhair would her trunk, to
manipulate the burned flesh.

To rip a piece off it.

To lift it to its mouth, and bite into it. Another of the
creatures grabbed at the meat, and they fought over it,
clumsily.

She felt bile rise in her own throat.

Without speaking, the two mammoths turned and fled
from the ridge, towards the sanctity and calmness of the
north.

124

*

The sun rolled along the mist-shrouded horizon. The Moon rose, a gaunt old crescent, clearly visible in the mysterious, subdued sky of the summer midnight.

The two mammoths huddled together.

'They were Lost,' Silverhair whispered. 'Weren't they? How can I have ever imagined I could deal with them?' Every instinct, every nerve shrieked for her to fly from this place, from the Lost and their scentless, unnatural activities, their slavering like wolves over burned scraps of flesh.

But Lop-ear didn't reply.

By the wan light she could see him, apparently unconsciously, reaching into his mouth with his trunk, and tasting her musk. Tasting it for oestrus.

Suddenly it was not a time for talking. And her fear, in this strange, remote place, her residual sadness at Wolfnose's death – all of it transmuted into a powerful longing.

She rumbled, deeper and lower than ever in her life. Then her tone rose gently, becoming stronger and higher in pitch, and sinking down to silence at the end.

This was the Song of Oestrus. The call would carry many days' walk from here, and was a signal to any Bull who heard it that she was a Cow ready to mate.

But there was only one Bull she wanted to hear.

She pulled away from Lop-ear, her head held high. Then she whirled around, backing into him.

She ran across the shadow-strewn plain, the frosty grass crushing beneath her feet, her breath steaming before her face. She could feel him pursuing her, his own giant footfalls like an echo of her own – but much more than an echo, for as he neared her it was as if the other half of her own soul was joining her.

She let him catch her.

He laid his trunk over her shoulder, pulling her back. Still singing, she turned to face him. He was silhouetted in the low light, his body, newly fattened by the spring grass, broad and strong. She stepped from side to side, slowly, and every step she took was mirrored by him. She could see the musth liquid which oozed thickly from the gland on top of his head.

Then, facing her, he gently laid his trunk on her head and body. She twined her trunk around his, and their mouths met.

Thus, since the time of Probos, have mammoths and their Cousins expressed their readiness to mate.

Now, at last, she let him move behind her.

He placed his tusks and forelegs on her back, and raised himself up. She knew he was taking most of his weight on his own back legs, but even so his mass was solid, heavy, warm on her back.

And she felt him enter her.

When it was over, and his warmth was captured inside her, she entered the mating pandemonium. She rumbled, screamed, trumpeted, defecated, secreted from her musth gland, whirled in a dance that made the ground shake. If other Cows were here they would have joined in with Silver-hair's pandemonium now, celebrating the deep ancient joy of the mating. It was as if all her experiences – of death and birth and renewed life, of the immense mammoth history which lay behind her – channelled through this moment. The blood surged in her, remaking her like a larva in its cocoon, and she knew she had never been so alive, so joyous, so tied to the Earth.

This was her summer day; this was her moment. She trumpeted her defiant joy that she was *alive*.

And at that moment of greatest joy she saw, climbing high in the midnight sky, a splinter of red light: it was the Sky Steppe, where one day her calves would roam free and without fear.

Afterwards they stood together, their hides matted, their heads touching.

126

'You know I will stay with you,' he said. 'I will guard you from the other Bulls until the end of your oestrus.'

That was the way, she knew. Mammoths are not romantic, but Lop-ear would protect his mate until the end of her oestrus period, when – she hoped – conception would occur, deep within her. Still, she could not help but mock him. '*What* other Bulls?'

'I will defend you even from the great Bull Croptail!' He raised his head, so his tusks flashed in the flat sunlight, and he danced before her as if he were about to go into battle with the Earth itself—

There was a sharp sound behind them. A cracking twig.

Mammoths' necks are short, and they cannot easily turn their heads. So Silverhair and Lop-ear lumbered about, to face behind them.

There was something here, just paces away. Like a narrow, branchless tree, casting a long midnight shadow. Silverhair could smell nothing of it.

It was a Lost.

Now it moved. With raised forelegs it lifted some kind of stick, and pointed it at them.

Lop-ear said, 'We must not show it fear. And we must not frighten it. It is only a Hotblood, like us, after all.' He hesitated. 'Perhaps it is injured. Perhaps it is hungry. That might be the meaning of the stick it carries—'

Dread filled her. 'Lop-ear, don't!'

'It's what we have come for, Silverhair.'

Lop-ear lowered his trunk, and stepped forward. From his forehead resounded the contact rumble.

The apparition took a step back, raised its stick higher. And the stick cracked.

There was a burst of light, a sound like thunder.

It was over in an instant. But that crack of light was enough to show her the strange, hairless head of the creature before her. It was the one she had met on the ice floe: the one she had called Skin-of-Ice.

Lop-ear was trumpeting in pain. She turned.

His trunk was raised, his eyes closed. And some dark liquid was gushing over the fur on his chest. It was blood, and it steamed in the cold air.

His hind legs gave way, so that he squatted like a defecating wolf, and his trunk dropped.

She raced to his side. 'What has happened to you?'

But he could not speak. Now blood spewed from his open mouth, dangling in loops from his tongue.

She ran behind him, and began to nudge at his back with her head. 'Get up! Get up!'

He tried; she could feel him padding at the ground with his hind legs, and he lifted his head.

But there was another thunder crack.

Immediately all four of Lop-ear's legs gave way and he slumped to the ground.

Silverhair staggered back, appalled, terrified. She could not understand what was happening. But she still had Lop-ear's warmth inside her, and she was drawn back to him.

There was a new sound now: a thin, high whoop, almost like a calf's immature trumpeting.

It was the creature called Skin-of-Ice, she saw. It – *he* – was holding his thunder-stick in the air above his head, and was yelping out his triumph. And he was standing on the flank of fallen Lop-ear.

Silverhair felt rage gather in her, deep and uncontrollable. She raised herself up on her hind legs, head high, and trumpeted as loudly as she could.

Skin-of-Ice raised the thunder-stick, and it cracked, again and again. Stinging, invisible insects flew around her.

Her mind crumbled into panic, and she fled.

Later, she would remember little of what followed. Only flashes, like the light from Skin-of-Ice's thunder-stick.

Sometimes she was alone, fleeing across a shadowed plain.

Sometimes the Lost pursued her, thin legs working, mysterious thunder-sticks barking.

Sometimes Lop-ear was here. She spoke to him of the future, the plans they had made. She threatened him with the punishment he would receive from Eggtusk if he didn't get up and come with her back to the Family right now.

Sometimes she saw a caterpillar, motionless on a willow branch. Then a small opening in its moist hide revealed a set of jaws: it was a larva of some still smaller insect, eating its host alive from within.

Sometimes there was only the stink of Lop-ear's cooling blood in her nostrils.

And always, always, the image of Skin-of-Ice: how the murderous Lost would look when she raised his soft, worm-like body on the tip of her tusks.

CHAPTER 4

THE RHYTHMS AND THE LOST

The sun wheeled above the horizon, never setting; the endless daylight was pitiless, for Silverhair sought only darkness.

'Silverhair. Silverhair . . .'

The words were like contact rumbles, swimming through the earth. And when she opened her eyes, unrolled her trunk so she could smell again, she could see mammoths before her: Eggtusk, Snagtooth.

With a part of her mind she knew that she had tried to find her way north, back to the Family, where they remained on the bleak plain of volcanic rock in the lee of the great Mountains at the End of the World. She recalled the walk in only fragmented glimpses: the clumps of grass she had once grazed with Lop-ear, an old hill whose eroded contours had reminded her of Lop-ear's slumped carcass.

She tried to focus on Eggtusk's words. '. . . You must listen to what I'm saying. I understand how you feel. We all do. But death is waiting for each of us. The great turning of life and death . . .'

But then the mammoths would float away from her again, like woolly clouds.

'It was the Lost,' Silverhair mumbled. 'The Lost and his thunder-stick—'

But they wouldn't listen. 'Even the Lost are part of the Cycle,' said Eggtusk. 'Though they don't know it. We are not like the Lost. Give yourself up to the Cycle, little Silverhair. Close your eyes . . .'

Silverhair felt the rocks under her feet, as if her legs were burrowing like tree-trunks to anchor her to the ground which sustained them all. And, slowly, the Cycle's calm teaching reached her.

She remembered how Wolfnose had shown her the Plain of Bones. She felt the great turning rhythms of the Earth. Her mind opened up, as if she held the topology of the whole Earth in her mind, and she saw far beyond the now, to the farthest reaches of past and future.

Her own long life, in the midst of all that epic sweep, was no more than the brief spring blossoming of a tundra flower. And Lop-ear, the same. *And yet they mattered:* just as each flower contributed to the waves of white and gold which swept across the tundra, so she and Lop-ear were inextricable parts of the great whole.

And the most important thing in the whole world was Lop-ear's warmth in her belly: the possibility, still, that she might conceive his calf.

'. . . To the Lost there is only the here and now,' Eggtusk was saying. 'They are a young species – a couple of Great-Years, no more – while we are ancient. They have no Cycle. They are just sparks of mind, isolated and frightened and soon extinguished. They never hear the greater rhythms, and never find their place in the world. That is why they disturb so much of what they touch. They are trying to forget what they are. They are dancing in the face of oblivion . . .'

Silverhair raised her head. She could feel the salt tears brim in her eyes. 'But it was my fault.'

'Lop-ear was much smarter than you are,' Eggtusk said gently. 'You couldn't have made him do anything he didn't want to do. Even *I* couldn't, and I fought him to prove the point – much as I regret that now, by Kilukpuk's cracked and festering nipples!'

'But I didn't even perform the Remembering for him.'

'No. Well, we can't very well leave him like that.' Eggtusk

laid his trunk on her head, and scratched behind her ear. 'Do you know where you are?'

She looked around, at featureless tundra. 'No,' she admitted.

'You're far from the Family. Far from anywhere. You've been wandering, Silverhair. Wandering, but not eating by the look of you. When you didn't return, Owlheart sent me to find you. It wasn't easy.'

'I – thank you, Eggtusk.'

'Never mind that. You must eat and sleep, young Silverhair. For we have a walk ahead of us. Back to the south.'

For the first time since she had lost Lop-ear, her spirits lifted. 'To Lop-ear.'

'Yes.'

'I'm surprised Owlheart let you go.'

'I had to promise we'd come back in one piece. Oh, and—'

'Yes?'

He bent so only she could hear. 'I had to take Snagtooth with me.'

The three mammoths set off at midnight. There was a layer of cloud above, but the pale-orange sun hung above the horizon in a clear strip of sky.

Heading south, the mammoths walked slowly, frequently pausing to pass dung and feed. Despite Silverhair's urgent wish to return to Lop-ear's bones, Eggtusk insisted they eat their fill. They were coming into the richest season of the year, the time when the mammoths must lay in their reserves of fat, without which they cannot survive the next winter. As Eggtusk said to Silverhair, 'I'd lick out the crusty lichen from between Kilukpuk's pus-ridden toes before I'd let you starve yourself to death. What use would that be to Lop-ear, or any of us? Eh?'

And so, under his coaxing and scolding, she cropped the grass and flowers, and the fresh buds of the dwarf willows whose branches barely grew high enough to cover her toes.

Snagtooth continued to be a problem. A growing one, in fact.

Though the stump of her smashed tusk had healed over – a great blood-red scar had formed over the gaping socket – Silverhair saw her banging her head against rock outcrops, as if trying to shake loose the pain of the tusk root. Snagtooth had a great deal of difficulty sleeping; even the back-and-forth movement of her jaw when eating seemed to hurt her.

And Snagtooth was not one to suffer in silence.

She complained, snapped, and refused to do her fair share of digging, even expecting Silverhair and Eggtusk to find her rich clumps of grass and rip them out and carry them to her ever-open mouth. Silverhair could see why Owlheart had taken the opportunity to send her away from Foxeye and the calves for a while.

'I put up with it because I can see she is suffering,' grumbled Eggtusk to Silverhair. 'Perhaps she has an abscess.'

If so, that was bad news; there was no way to treat such an agonising collection of poison in the mouth, and Snagtooth would simply have to hope it cleared up of its own accord. If it didn't, it could kill her.

Poor Eggtusk, meanwhile, was having his own trouble with warble flies. Silverhair could see maggots dropping out of red-rimmed craters in his skin, heading for the ground to pupate. Unnoticed, the flies must have laid eggs in his fur last summer. The eggs quickly hatched and the maggots burrowed into Eggtusk's tissue, migrating around the body before coming to rest near the skin of his back. Here they would have continued to grow through the winter and spring in a cavity filled with pus and blood, breathing through an air-hole gnawed in the skin. The eruption of the full-grown larvae was a cause of intense irritation to Eggtusk, who, despite his colourful cursing, was helpless to do anything about it.

And meanwhile the season bloomed around them. As the height of the brief summer approached, the tundra exploded with activity, as plants, animals, birds and insects sought to complete the crucial stages of their annual lives in this brief respite from the grip of winter. The flowers of the tundra opened: white mountain avens, yellow poppies, white heather, crimson, yellow, red, white and purple saxifrage, lousewort, pink primulas, even the orange of marigolds. All the flowers had started their cycle of growth as soon as the snow melted. And the birds were everywhere now. Snow buntings caught crane flies to feed their chicks. Skuas hunted the fledglings of turnstones and sanderlings. As she passed a cliff, Silverhair saw barnacle geese fledglings taking their first tentative steps from their parents' nests far above. This meant jumping. The chicks' stubby wings flapped uselessly, and they fell to the bottom of the cliff. Many chicks died from the fall, and others, trapped in scree, were snapped up by the eager jaws of Arctic foxes.

The silence of the winter was long gone. The air was filled with birdsong – larks and plovers, the haunting calls of loons, irritable jaeger cries – and the buzz of insects, the bark and howls of foxes and wolves. All of it was laced with the occasional agonised scream as some predator attained its goal.

It was a furious chorus of mating and death.

Through this flat, teeming landscape, Silverhair and the others walked stolidly on. When they found a rock face where they could shelter, they slept, as the summer sun scraped its way around the horizon, and the sky faded again to its deepest midnight blue.

Once Silverhair woke to find herself staring at a snowy owl, a mother perched on her nest with her brood of peeping chicks.

The mother was a white bundle of feathers, standing out clearly against grey shale. Her mate coursed over the rough vegetation, searching for lemmings to bring to his nest. The owl chicks had been born at intervals of three or four days, and the oldest chick was substantially bigger than the smallest. Silverhair knew that if some disaster occurred and the owls' food supply was threatened, the largest owlet would eat its smallest sibling – and then the next smallest, and the next.

It was brutal. But it was the owls' way of assuring that at least one youngster survived the harshest times. The little tableau, of beauty and cruelty, seemed to summarise the world, this cruel summer, to Silverhair.

The mother owl beat her broad wings slowly, and stared at Silverhair with great sulphur-yellow eyes.

As the endless day wore towards its golden noon, they drew nearer the place where Lop-ear had fallen.

They reached the low ridge near the south coast. Silverhair remembered this place. It was here she had shared Lop-ear's warmth, here they had encountered the Lost with his thunder-stick, and here she had last seen the body of Lop-ear, like a squat, fur-coated boulder.

The body was gone.

But there were Lost here.

Eggtusk led the two Cows behind an eroded outcrop of rock. The mammoths huddled together uncertainly. Eggtusk raised his trunk cautiously over the rock; the hair of his trunk streamed behind his head.

The mammoths had not been seen. The Lost didn't seem very observant; none of them was maintaining a watch for wolves – or mammoths, come to that.

The Lost were sitting in a loose circle on the ground. There were six of them. Three of them carried thunder-sticks, like the one which Skin-of-Ice had used against Lop-ear. And one of them – Silverhair could never forget that smooth, unnatural, hairless head – was Skin-of-Ice himself.

The Lost surrounded the carcass of what looked like a fox.

And they were drinking a clear fluid from flasks, which they passed from paw to paw. They sat unnaturally upright, with strange sets of loose skin over their bodies, and only a few patches of fur on their scalps and faces.

They were like wolves, she thought. Predators, working at a downed prey. But then they were *not* like wolves, for they did not work at the fox's body with their teeth and claws as wolves will. Rather, they had ice-claws – as she called them, for they were made of something that gleamed like sea ice – ice-claws that they held in their paws, and used to cut into the fox's passive body.

The Lost were grimy, listless, steeped in misery. They seemed to bicker and snap at each other, sometimes descending into clumsy fights.

All but Skin-of-Ice. He sat apart from the rest, thunder-stick on his lap, watching the others coldly.

Silverhair felt a cold, hard determination gathering inside her. All her naïve dreams of finding some opportunity to work with the Lost had evaporated with the blows inflicted on Lop-ear. These are my enemy, she thought. I will not live in a world which contains them, and I will oppose them to my dying breath.

But to do that, I must understand them.

'We're in no danger here,' said Eggtusk in a soft rumble, inaudible to the Lost. 'I'm sure they can't see us. According to the Cycle the Lost have poor hearing and smell, and we're downwind of them. And besides, three grown mammoths against six – or sixty – of those skinny creatures should be no match.'

Silverhair growled: 'They have thunder-sticks.'

'Those spindly things? What harm can they do us?'

Silverhair knew it was difficult for him to imagine, for sticks which spat fire and agony on command had no place in a mammoth's map of the world. 'Eggtusk, a thunder-stick killed Lop-ear. Skin-of-Ice didn't even have to come close to us to do it.'

'Then what should we do?'

'It's obvious,' complained Snagtooth loudly. 'We must creep away from this place of blood and Lost, and—'

Eggtusk slapped his trunk over her head. 'Quiet, you fool.'

Now, to Silverhair's bewilderment, one of the Lost – a fat brute – shucked off layers of his loose outer skin from his body. His hairless chest and forelimbs were pink and gleaming with sweat. He swung his ice-claw down through the air, hauling it with both paws. He cracked the fox's strong leg bones, tore through its skin, cut tendons, prised open ribs and ripped open the organs that had nestled inside the fox's body.

As he worked, the Lost made a noise like the caw of a gull. Almost joyous.

When he was done, this savage one opened the fox's mouth and reached inside. With a fast slash of his ice-claw he severed the fox's tongue. Then he lifted the limp, fleshy thing above his head, cawing and rubbing his big belly, as if this was the finest delicacy.

'They are like worms,' Eggtusk whispered, beside Silverhair. 'They gnaw on the meat of the dead.' Silverhair could hear the anger and disgust in his voice. 'Especially that fat one.'

'Gull-Caw,' Silverhair said.

'What?'

'We will call him Gull-Caw.'

Eggtusk was silent for a few heartbeats. Then he said, 'We must not hate them. They are Hotbloods, like us. And they have their place in the Cycle. Whatever they do. After all, it is not pleasant to watch a pack of wolves work at a seal's carcass—'

Silverhair said, 'Wolves take what they need. Even the worms do no more than that. There is none of this joy in death and the tearing apart of the body. These Lost are *not* like us, Eggtusk.'

He looked at her. 'It was you,' he reminded her, 'who wanted to seek out the Lost. Get help from them.'

'I was wrong,' she said tightly. 'I never imagined how wrong.'

Snagtooth, on Silverhair's other flank, was staring, fascinated. 'Look at the way they work together.'

'You sound as if you admire them,' Eggtusk snapped.

Snagtooth grunted. 'They are small and weak and isolated on this Island, but they are not slowly dying, as we are. They are not like us. Perhaps they are *better*.'

Silverhair, shocked more deeply by Snagtooth than she had thought possible, watched as the Lost completed their grisly butchering.

And she wondered what had become of Lop-ear. Was it possible his helpless body had received the same fate as the fox?

. . . There was a crack, like thunder.

All three mammoths raised their trunks and trumpeted.

Eggtusk had twisted his head and was staring at his shoulder. 'By Kilukpuk's oozing scabs—' Blood was seeping out of a small puncture in his hide, and spreading over his wiry hair.

But Silverhair scarcely noticed this. For, standing only a few strides downwind of them, were two of the Lost: Skin-of-Ice, and Gull-Caw. They were both holding thunder-sticks.

And they smelled of mammoth: for they had smeared themselves in mammoth dung, the rich, dark stuff clinging to their loose outer skin and their bare faces. That was how they had crept up unnoticed.

Even at this moment of peril, Silverhair felt chilled at the cunning of the Lost.

Eggtusk reared on his hind legs, raised his trunk and trumpeted. 'So you'd punch a hole in me, eh?' he roared. 'By Kilukpuk's quivering dugs, we'll see about that.' The great Bull's forefeet crashed back to the earth, and the ground shook as he lowered his head and charged.

The thunder-sticks wavered. Faced by a trumpeting, hurtling mountain of muscle, flesh and tusks, the two Lost ran, scampering across the flower-strewn plain like two Arctic hares.

Suddenly, to Silverhair, they did not seem a threat at all. But, she reminded herself, they still carried their thunder-sticks.

With Snagtooth, she ran after Eggtusk.

Skin-of-Ice fell, heavily, and cried out. When he got to his feet again he was clutching his foreleg.

Gull-Caw came back to him. The two Lost stood side by side and raised their sticks.

More thunder-cracks.

Silverhair felt something fly past her ear, a hot scorch. And another crack, and another: a series of rippling explosions like the splintering of a falling tree, sharp sounds that rolled away across the plain.

Eggtusk grunted and staggered. Silverhair saw a new splash of blood on his fleshy thigh. 'Get behind me,' Eggtusk ordered.

'But—'

'Do as he says,' snapped Snagtooth. Her eyes were wide, her smashed tusk dribbling fresh pulp.

Silverhair tucked herself, with Snagtooth, behind Eggtusk's mighty buttocks.

And now Eggtusk began to walk towards the Lost, his pace measured and deliberate. 'So you think you can kill me, do you, little maggots? We'll see about that. Do you know what I'm going to do with you? I'm going to pick you up with my trunk and drown you in the pus which oozes from Kilukpuk's suppurating mouth-ulcers. And then—'

But still the thunder-sticks barked, and the strange, invisible, deadly insects slammed into Eggtusk's giant body. One of them tore away a piece of his shoulder, and Silverhair's face was splashed by a horrific spray of hair, skin and pulped flesh.

With each impact Eggtusk staggered. But he did not fall, and he kept the Lost washed in a stream of obscene threats.

Gull-Caw was agitated. The fat one's thunder-stick no longer barked; he was scrabbling at it, frightened, frustrated.

When Skin-of-Ice saw this, he turned and ran.

Gull-Caw roared out his anger at this betrayal. Then, seeing Eggtusk remorselessly approaching, he yowled like a fox cub. He dropped his useless thunder-stick and turned to run, but he stumbled and fell on the ground.

And now Eggtusk was over him.

The great Bull reared up, raising his huge tree-trunk legs high in the air. His deformed tusk glistened, dripping with his own blood; he raised his trunk and trumpeted so loud his voice echoed off the icebergs of the distant ocean.

Silverhair reared back, terrified of him herself.

Eggtusk reached down and wrapped his trunk around the wriggling Lost. He lifted the fat body effortlessly. Eggtusk squeezed, the immense muscles of his trunk wrapped tightly around the Lost's greasy torso. Silverhair could see the Lost's eyes bulge, his short pink tongue protrude.

Then Eggtusk threw Gull-Caw into the air. The Lost briefly flew, yelling, his fat limbs writhing, his smooth, ugly skin now smeared with Eggtusk's blood.

The Lost landed heavily on his belly; Silverhair heard the crack of bone.

But still Gull-Caw tried to raise himself, to crawl away, to reach with a bloodied forelimb for his thunder-stick.

Eggtusk leaned forward and knelt on the Lost's back.

The Lost screamed as that great weight bore down. Silverhair heard the crunch of ribs and vertebrae. The Lost's scream turned to a liquid gurgle, and blood gushed from his mouth.

And then Eggtusk drove a tusk through his neck, pinning him to the ground.

The Lost twitched once, twice more. Then he was still.

CHAPTER 5
THE KETTLE HOLE

Eggtusk pulled his tusk from the body, shaking it to free it of the limp remnant flesh of the Lost. He rooted for the thunder-stick. He curled his trunk-fingers around the black, spindly thing, and lifted it high in the air. 'It feels cold.'

'It's a thing of death,' said Silverhair.

Eggtusk raised the thunder-stick and smashed it against a rock outcrop until it was bent in two, and small parts had come tumbling from it. He hurled the wreckage far into the grass. Then he wiped his tusk against the outcrop, to free it of blood and scraps of flesh.

'Now come,' said Eggtusk. 'We will honour the body of this Lost I have killed.' And he bent down, wincing slightly, and ripped yellow tundra flowers from the ground. He lumbered over to the corpse and sprinkled the flowers there. He was a fearsome sight, with his face masked in blood, one of his eyes concealed by blood-matted hair, and thunder-stick punctures over his legs and chest. Even his trunk had a bite taken out of it.

After a few heartbeats, Silverhair and Snagtooth joined in. Soon the carcass of the Lost was buried in grass and flowers. They stood over the corpse as the sun wheeled through the icy sky, Remembering the fat, ugly creature as best they could.

'Let that be an end of it,' growled Eggtusk. 'Once I des-troyed a wolf that had come stalking the Family. We never saw that pack again. The Cycle teaches that mammoths should kill only when we have to. We have frightened the

Lost so badly they'll respect us, and never come near us again . . .'

Silverhair wanted to believe that was true. But she was unsure. She had watched the way the Lost had carved slices out of that fox. There had been a *joy* in their behaviour. An evil triumph.

She couldn't help but feel that a world free of Skin-of-Ice would be a better place. And, she feared, the killing wasn't done yet.

Silverhair tried to treat Eggtusk's many wounds. They found a stream, and she bathed him with trunkfuls of cold, clear water, washing away the matted blood and dirt in his fur, and she plastered mud over the worst wounds in his flesh. But the pain of the wounds was very great. And she could see that some of them were becoming infected, despite her best ministrations with mud and leaves.

But Eggtusk was impatient to move on. 'I don't think that other worm will pose any threat to us. He can't have got far. Come on. We'll follow him.'

Silverhair was startled. 'We aren't wolves to track prey, Eggtusk.'

'And he still has the thunder-stick,' Snagtooth said, her voice without expression.

'That Lost was wounded,' Eggtusk said firmly. 'If he's died in some hole, we'll honour him. Maybe, if he's alive, we'll be able to help him.'

That seemed extremely unlikely to Silverhair. And besides, there were the other Lost to think about; what had become of them while the mammoths had chased Gull-Caw? Perhaps Eggtusk's thinking was muddled by pain . . .

But there was no more time to debate the issue; for already Eggtusk was limping off to the south, the direction Skin-of-Ice had fled.

As browsing grass-eaters, mammoths are poor trackers. As the Cycle says, *It doesn't take the skill of a wolf to sneak up on a blade of grass*. Nevertheless, it was surprisingly easy to track the progress the Lost, Skin-of-Ice, had made towards the southern coast.

Eggtusk charged ahead over the plain. 'Here is grass he crushed,' he said. 'Here is a splash of his blood, on this rock. You see? And here is a dribble of urine . . . I can still smell it . . .'

Silverhair and Snagtooth followed, more uncertainly. All Silverhair could smell right now was the stink of Eggtusk's decaying wounds.

'Of course,' said Snagtooth softly to Silverhair, 'it may be that this Lost *wants* us to find him.'

Silverhair was startled. 'But Eggtusk nearly killed him.'

'I know,' said Snagtooth. 'But who knows what goes on in the mind of a Lost?'

Silverhair kept her counsel. Perhaps Eggtusk was launching himself into this quest to take his mind off his wounds. Maybe, when his injuries had healed sufficiently for him to start thinking more clearly, she could persuade him to return to the Family, and then—

Suddenly Eggtusk trumpeted in triumph.

Silverhair slowed and stood beside him.

The Lost, Skin-of-Ice, was lying on the ground, face down, still some distance away. He wasn't moving. There was no sign of his thunder-stick. The ground between the Lost and the mammoths was hummocky, broken, tufted with grass and sprinkled with residual ice scraps.

There was no sound, no scent, and she could see the Lost only indistinctly.

The grey cap of hair on Silverhair's scalp prickled. 'I wish I knew where his thunder-stick is,' she murmured. 'We ought to be careful—'

But Eggtusk was already lumbering ahead, his trunk raised in greeting to the Lost he intended to help.

He approached a patch of ground strewn with grass and broken bushes – even a few spruce branches. Silverhair stared at the patch of ground, wondering what could have made such a mess. Wolves? Birds? But there was no scent; no scent at all.

Suddenly she was alarmed. 'Eggtusk! Take care—'

Eggtusk, his massive feet pounding at the ground, reached the debris-strewn patch.

With a cracking of twigs and branches, the ground opened up beneath his forefeet. He fell into a pit, amid an explosion of shattered branches and clumps of grass.

Silverhair charged forward. 'Eggtusk! Eggtusk!'

She could see the dome of his head and the hair of his broad back, protruding from the hole. And now his trumpeting turned to a roar of anguish.

But Snagtooth was tugging at her tail. 'Keep back! It's a kettle hole . . .'

Silverhair, despite her impatience and fear, knew that Snagtooth was right. It would help no one if she got trapped herself.

She slowed, and took measured steps towards the hole in the ground, testing each footfall. Soon she was walking over the leaves and twigs and grass which had concealed the hole.

Eggtusk was embedded in the hole, a few blades of muddy grass scattered over his back. His trunk lay on the ground, and his great tusks, stained by mud and blood, protruded uselessly before him. He was out of her reach.

As she approached he tried to lift and turn his head. He said, 'Don't come any closer.'

'Are you stuck?'

Eggtusk growled wearily. 'By Kilukpuk's snot-crusted nostril hair, what a stupid question. Of course I'm stuck. My legs are wedged in under me. I can't even move them.'

A kettle hole was a hazard of their warming times, Silverhair knew. It formed when a large block of ice was left by a retreating glacier. Sediment would settle over the ice, burying it. Then, as the ice melted, the resulting water would seep away and the sinking sediment, turning to mud, would subside to form a sticky hole in the ground.

Deadly, for any mammoth foolish enough to stray into one. But—

'Eggtusk, kettle holes are easy to spot. Only a calf would blunder into one.'

'Thank you for that,' he snorted. 'Don't you see? It's your friend Skin-of-Ice. Snagtooth was right. That wretched worm did want us to follow him. While we honoured his fallen comrade, Skin-of-Ice was preparing this trap for us. And I was fool enough to charge right in . . .'

He subsided. His breath was a rattle, and he seemed to be weakening. He tried to raise his trunk, then let it flop back feebly to the ground.

Silverhair tried to step forward, but her feet sank deeper into the mud that surrounded the hole. She felt an agitated anger; she had seen too much death this blighted summer. 'You aren't going to do this to me,' she cried. 'Not yet, you old fool!'

She scrambled back to firm ground, and forced herself to think.

She threw branches and twigs over the ground and walked forward on them. Spreading the load helped her keep out of the mud for a little further, but in the end her weight was just too great, and each time she tried to get closer to Eggtusk she was forced to back up.

Well, if she couldn't reach Eggtusk, maybe he could get himself out.

She gathered branches and threw them towards Eggtusk's head. If he could pull them into the pit he might be able to use them to get a grip with his feet.

But even when he managed to grab the branches he seemed too weak, too firmly stuck, to do anything with them.

Despairing, she looked for Snagtooth, seeking help. But

Snagtooth was gone: there was no trace of her musk on the wind, no echo of her voice.

But, Silverhair admitted, it wasn't important. Snagtooth's mind was almost as impenetrable as a Lost's, and since her injury that had only worsened. She would be no help anyhow.

. . . And Skin-of-Ice, she noticed, was gone too. Perhaps he had crawled away to die at last. Somehow she suspected it would not be so easy. But she had no time, no energy for him now.

Silverhair brought Eggtusk food, grass and twigs and herbs. But the wind scattered the grass, and Eggtusk's trunk-fingers seemed to be losing their co-ordination and were having increasing difficulty in grasping the food.

But she kept trying, over and over.

'Do not fret, little Silverhair,' he said to her, and his voice was a bubbling growl. 'You've done your best.'

'Eggtusk—'

He reached out with his trunk as if to stroke her head, but it was, of course, much too far to reach. 'Give it up. That Lost has trapped me and killed me. I am already dead.'

'No!'

'You have to go back to the Family, tell them what has happened. Owlheart will know what to do . . . Tell her I'm sorry I didn't keep my promise to bring you home. And you must tell Croptail that he is the dominant Bull now. Tell him I'm sorry I won't be there to teach him any more . . . Do it, Silverhair. Go . . .'

'I won't leave you,' she said.

'By Kilukpuk's mould-choked pores, you always were stubborn.'

'And you've always been so strong—'

'Should take more than a little hunger to kill old Eggtusk, eh? But it isn't just that. Watch now.'

With infinite difficulty, he rolled his trunk towards him,

and pushed it below his chin and into the pit, below his body. She could see the muscles of his upper trunk spasm, as if he was tugging at something.

Painfully, carefully, he pulled his trunk out of the pit. He was holding something.

It was a bone, she saw. A rib. It was crusted with dried, blackened blood – and stained with a fresher crimson.

A mammoth rib.

'The bottom of the pit is littered with them,' gasped Eggtusk. 'They stick up everywhere. Mostly into me. And I think Skin-of-Ice put some kind of poison on them.'

'They took it from the *yedoma*,' she said. Or – worse still – from Lop-ear . . . She felt bile rise in her throat. 'They are using our own bones to kill us.'

'Oh, these Lost are clever,' he said. 'Snagtooth was right about that. I couldn't have dreamed how clever.' He let the rib fall to the mud. 'Well, little Silverhair. If you're determined to hang around here, you can help me. There's something I must do while I still have the strength.'

'What?'

'Fetch a rock. As big as you can throw over to me.'

She went to an outcrop of rock and obeyed, bringing back a big sandstone boulder. She stood at the edge of the kettle hole, dug her tusks under the rock and sent it flying through the air towards Eggtusk. It landed before his face, splashing in the mud.

He raised his head, turned it sideways. And he brought his misshapen tusk crashing against the rock. The tusk cracked, but he showed no awareness of the pain.

'Eggtusk! What are you doing?'

'You needn't try to stop me,' he said, breathing hard.

'*Why?*'

'Better I do it than the Lost. Didn't you tell me how they robbed the ancient mammoth in the *yedoma*? I don't want them doing the same to me.'

And again he began to smash his magnificent deformed

148

tusk against the rock, until it had splintered and cracked at the base.

At last it tore loose, leaving only a bloody spike of ivory protruding from the socket in his face.

'Take it,' he told Silverhair, his voice thick with blood. 'You can reach it. Take it and smash it to splinters.'

She was weeping openly now. But she reached out over the mud of the kettle hole, wrapped her trunk around the tusk, and pulled it to her. It was immense: so massive she could barely lift it. Once again she appreciated the huge strength of Eggtusk – strength that was dissipating into the cold mud as she watched.

She lugged the tusk to the outcrop of sandstone, and pounded it until it had splintered and smashed to fragments.

Eggtusk rested for a time. Then he lifted his head again, and started to work on his other tusk.

When he was done, his face was half-buried in the mud, the breath whistling through his trunk; there was blood around his mouth, and pulp leaked from the stumps of his tusks.

'Eggtusk—'

'Little Silverhair. You're still here? You always were stubborn . . . Talk to me.'

'Talk to you?'

'Tell me a story. Tell me about Ganesha.'

And so she did. Gathering her strength, staying the weakening of her own voice, she told him the ancient tale of Ganesha the Wise, and how she had prepared her calf Prima to conquer the cold lands.

He grunted and sighed, seeming to respond to the rhythms of the ancient story.

. . . She woke with a start. She hadn't meant to sleep.

Eggtusk, still wedged tight in his kettle hole, was chewing on something. 'This grass is fine. Isn't it, Wolfnose? The finest I ever tasted. And this water is as clear and fresh as if it had just melted off the glacier.'

149

But she could see that only blood trickled from his mouth, and all that he chewed was a mouthful of his own hair, ripped from his back.

'Eggtusk—'

He raised his head, and the stumps of his tusks gleamed in the sun. 'Wolfnose? Remember me, Wolfnose. Remember me. I see you. I'm coming now . . .'

And his great head dropped to the earth, and did not rise again.

Silverhair felt the deepest dark of despair settle over her, an anguish of shame and frustration that she hadn't been able to help him.

Soon she must start the Remembering. She could not reach Eggtusk, or touch his body; but at least she could cover his corpse—

Suddenly there was a band of fire around her neck: a band that dug deep into her flesh. She trumpeted her shock and pain.

And the Lost were here, dancing before her, two of them, and they held sticks in their paws, sticks attached to whatever was wrapped around her neck.

Snagtooth was standing before her, apparently in no distress.

Silverhair, shocked, agonised, tried to speak. When the Lost tugged at their sticks the fire in her neck deepened, so tight she could barely breathe. 'Snagtooth . . . help me . . .'

But Snagtooth kept her trunk down. 'I brought them here.'

'You did what?'

'Don't you see? *They are smarter than we are*. Submit to them, Silverhair. It isn't so bad.'

'No—' Silverhair struggled to stay on her feet, to ignore the pain in her throat.

And beyond Snagtooth, she saw Skin-of-Ice himself. His damaged foreleg was strapped to his chest.

Light as a hare, he hopped over the mud of the kettle hole,

and came to rest on Eggtusk's broad, unmoving back. He raised his head to the sky and let loose a howl of triumph.

Then he raised an ice-claw in his paw, and drove it deep into Eggtusk's helpless back.

The thing around Silverhair's neck tightened. A red mist filled her vision.

She was forced to her knees.

CHAPTER 6
THE CAPTIVE

The Lost threw more loops and lassos at her. Many of them missed, or she shook them off easily, but gradually they caught on her tusks or trunk or around her legs. Soon her head was so heavy with ropes that she could not lift it.

Now the Lost – five or six of them, under the supervision of Skin-of-Ice – began to run around her, whooping, and beating at her flanks and legs with sticks. She tried to reach them with her tusks – she knew she could disembowel any of these weak creatures with a flick of her head – but she was pinned, and they were too clever to come close enough to give her the chance to hurt them.

She could not even lift her head to trumpet, and that shamed her more than anything else.

At last Skin-of-Ice himself came forward. His small teeth showed white in his loathsome, naked face as he bent to peer into her eyes. His mouth, a soft, round thing, was flapping and making noises.

She managed to haul herself back a pace or two. But he stood his ground, and the weight dragging at her forced her to submission once more.

Now he raised a stick, about as long as his foreleg, in the tip of which he had embedded one of his gleaming ice-claws. He held it up before her, waving it before her eyes, as if to demonstrate to her what it was.

One of the other Lost came up. He pawed at Skin-of-Ice, as if trying to restrain him. But Skin-of-Ice shook him off.

Then, with brutal suddenness, Skin-of-Ice lashed out.

He slammed the stick against her face, and the claw penetrated her cheek. The pain was liquid fire.

She kept her gaze on Skin-of-Ice, refusing even to flinch as the pain burned into her.

He threw down his goad and reached forward to her cheek. His paw came away smeared with her blood – and it cupped a brimming pool of her tears, tears she could not help but spill.

Skin-of-Ice threw the tears back in her face, so that they stung her eyes.

As the sun sank towards the horizon, the Lost gathered loose branches and twigs into a rough heap. This heap somehow erupted into flame, as if at the command of the Lost. They did not seem to fear the fire. Indeed, they fed it with more branches, which they boldly threw on to the embers, and stayed close to it, rubbing their paws as if dependent on the fire for warmth.

After a time a knot of hunger gathered in Silverhair's stomach, but the Lost would not let her feed. Even when she passed dung, which the Lost could scarcely prevent, they would kick and prod at her so that her stomach clenched, and they picked up the dung and threw it in her face.

Mammoths need a great deal of food daily, and in fact spend much of each day feeding and drinking. To be kept from doing that was a great torment to Silverhair, and she weakened rapidly.

The Lost were not organised in this. They were careless, lethargic, and seemed to spend a lot of their time asleep.

All save Skin-of-Ice. It was Skin-of-Ice who drove on the others, like a lead Bull, making them work when they would rather sleep or feed or squabble, maintaining the slow cruelty inflicted on Silverhair. All the Lost were repulsive. But it was Skin-of-Ice, she saw, who was the source of evil here.

Meanwhile, as the shadows stretched over the tundra, a group of the Lost worked in the pit which had trapped and killed Eggtusk.

Eggtusk was still upright in the pit, his legs trapped out of sight, his head supported by the stumps of his tusks. The blood that had seeped out of his wounds had soaked the ground around the pit, making it black. His body was already rigid with death, and perhaps half-frozen too.

Now the Lost slung ropes around Eggtusk and hauled. At first they could not budge the passive carcass, but they made a rhythmic noise and concerted their efforts.

At last they managed to drag Eggtusk out of the hole.

Silverhair could hear the crackle of frost-ridden fur as Eggtusk was rolled on to his back, exposing his softer under-belly, and then the more ominous crack of snapping bone. His head settled back to the cold earth, and his mouth gaped. Silverhair could see how the dried blood and dirt matted the great wounds in his chest and belly, and his stomach was swollen and hard.

It was Skin-of-Ice himself who began it.

He took an ice-claw and thrust it into Eggtusk's lower belly. Then, bracing himself and using both paws, he dragged the claw up the length of Eggtusk's body, cutting through hair and flesh, in a line from anus to throat. Silver-hair felt the incision as if it had been made in her own body.

Then, under the direction of Skin-of-Ice, the Lost reluc-tantly gathered to either side of Eggtusk. They dug their forelimbs into the new wound in his belly, grabbed his ribcage, and hauled back. The ribcage opened like a grot-esque flower, the white of bone emerging from the red-black wound.

Eggtusk was opened up, splayed.

Skin-of-Ice now climbed *inside* the body of Eggtusk. He reached down and, with his forelegs, began to dig out Egg-tusk's internal organs: heart, liver, a great rope of intestine.

Another of the Lost turned away, and vomit spilled from his mouth.

When Skin-of-Ice was done, the Lost took hold of Eggtusk's legs and hauled him away from the steaming pile of guts they had removed from the carcass. Then they turned Eggtusk over again; this time he slumped, almost shapeless, against the ground.

The Lost began to hack at the skin of Eggtusk's legs and around his neck. When it was cut through, they dug their small forelimbs inside the skin and began to haul it off the sheets of muscle and fat that coated Eggtusk's body. It came loose with a moist rip. Wherever it stuck, Skin-of-Ice or one of the others would hack at the muscle inside the skin, or else reach underneath and punch at the skin from the inside.

At last, the skin had come free from Eggtusk's back, belly and neck, a great sheet of it, bloody on the underside and dangling clumps of hair on the other. Silverhair could see it was punctured by the many wounds he had suffered.

The Lost folded up the skin and put it to one side. Eggtusk's flayed carcass was left as a mass of exposed muscle and flesh.

Now the Lost took their ice claws and began to hack in earnest at the carcass. They seemed to be trying to sever the flesh from Eggtusk's legs, belly and neck in great sections. They even cut away his tail, ears and part of his trunk.

When they were done, Eggtusk's body had been comprehensively destroyed.

But now there came a still worse horror; for the Lost began to throw lumps of dripping flesh on the fire – Eggtusk's flesh – and, when it was all but burned, they dragged it off the fire, sliced it into pieces and crammed it into their small mouths, with every expression of relish.

Silverhair forced herself to watch, to witness every cut and savour every fresh stink, and remember it all.

The Lost seemed baffled by the absence of the old Bull's

tusks, and they spent some time inspecting the bloody stumps in his face. Silverhair realised that Eggtusk had been right. For some reason the loathsome souls of these Lost cherished the theft of tusks above all, and even as he lay trapped and dying Eggtusk had defied his killers.

She clutched that to her heart, and tried to draw courage from Eggtusk's example.

But there was little time for such reflection, for the goading she endured continued, without relief. Soon her need for sleep drove all other thoughts from her mind, and the ache from the injuries to her neck and cheek refused to subside.

Snagtooth was not mistreated as Silverhair was. She was bound by a single loop of rope fixed to a stake driven into the ground. Silverhair thought that with a single yank Snagtooth could surely drag the stake out of the ground. But she seemed to have no such intention.

Skin-of-Ice came to Snagtooth, so close she could have gutted him with a single flick of her remaining tusk. But Snagtooth dipped her head and let the Lost touch her. He brought her food: pawfuls of grass which he lifted up to her, and water in a shell-like container which he carried from a stream. Passively Snagtooth dipped her trunk into the shell thing. She even lifted her trunk, and Silverhair watched her tongue slick out, pink and moist, to accept the grass from the paw of her captor.

With the watery sun once more climbing the sky, Silverhair saw, in her bleary vision, that Skin-of-Ice had come to stand before her.

He reached towards her with one paw, as if making to stroke her as he had Snagtooth. But Silverhair rumbled and pulled her head away from him.

Before she had time even to see its approach, his goad had slapped at her cheek. She could feel the scabs which had crusted over her earlier wounds break open once more, and the pain was so intense she could not help but cry out.

Now Skin-of-Ice turned to his companions and gestured with his goad.

Immediately the pressure around her throat and across her back intensified. She was forced to kneel in the dirt. Under her belly hair, she could feel the stale warmth of her own dung.

And now Skin-of-Ice stepped forward. She could feel him grab her hair, step on one prone leg, and hoist himself up on to her back so that he was sitting astride her. The Lost around her were cawing and slapping their paws together, in evident approval of Skin-of-Ice's antics.

She strained her muscles and tried to dislodge him, but she could not stand, let alone rear; she could not remove this maddening, tormenting worm from her back.

Now the pressure of the ropes lessened, and the Lost came forward and began to prod at her belly. Reluctant though she was to do anything in response to their vicious commands, she clambered slowly to her feet. As she did so, she could feel how Skin-of-Ice wrapped his paws in her long hair to keep from falling off.

The Lost moved around behind her, and she could feel a new load being added to her back: something unmoving which had to be tied in place with ropes around her belly.

She could not see what this load was. But she could smell it. It was the remnants of Eggtusk: bones, skin and dismembered meat. She tried to shake the load loose, but the ropes were too tight.

The Lost moved around her belly, loosening the ropes which bound up her legs. Skin-of-Ice pulled her ears and slapped at her with his own goad. The Lost before her were dragging at the ropes around her head and trunk.

What they intended was obvious. They wanted her to walk with them to their nest at the south of the Island, to carry the dishonoured, mutilated corpse for them.

But she stood firm. She could not escape, but, even as weak as she was, the Lost were not strong enough to haul her against her will.

Now a new rope was attached to her neck. A pair of Lost pulled it across the tundra, and attached it to the collar around Snagtooth's neck.

And Snagtooth – led by her trunk, held in the paw of one of the Lost, but otherwise under no duress or goad – began to walk, deliberately, to the south. The rope between the two mammoths stretched taut, and began to drag at Silverhair's neck. And the monster on her back lashed at her with his goad.

Silverhair's feet slipped on the dusty ground. She took one step, then another. She could resist the feeble muscles of any number of the Lost, but, weak and starved as she was, not the hauling of an adult mammoth.

She tried to call to Snagtooth: 'Why are you doing this? How can you help them?'

But her voice was weak and muffled. Snagtooth did not hear, or perhaps chose not to; she kept her face firmly turned to the south.

And, as she stumbled forward from step to step, constantly impeded by the ropes which still looped between her legs, Silverhair felt her shame was complete.

They reached the coast, not far from the place where Silverhair had first encountered Skin-of-Ice.

Silverhair was hauled along the beach.

She saw, groggily, that the season was well advanced. The sea was full of noise and motion. The remnant ice was breaking up quickly now, with bangs and cracks. Small icebergs were swept past in the current. She saw a berg strike pack ice ahead and rear up out of the water, before falling back with a ponderous splash.

She was led past a floe where a large male polar bear lay silently beside a seal's breathing hole. With startling suddenness the bear dived into the pool, and, after much thrashing, emerged with its jaws clamped around the neck of a huge ringed seal. The incautious seal was dragged through a breathing hole no wider than its head, and there was soft crunching as the bones of the seal's body were broken or dislocated against the ice. Then, with a cuff of its mighty paw, the bear slit open the seal and began to strip the rich blubber from the inside of its skin.

It seemed to Silverhair that the seal was still alive.

Silverhair was dragged away from the bear and its victim. Even the Lost, she realised, were wise enough to watch the bear with caution.

At the top of the beach, away from the reach of the tide, the Lost had made their nest.

There were more Lost here. They moved forward, hesitantly, but with curiosity. They approached Snagtooth, and she allowed them to touch her trunk and tug at the fur of her belly. Even when one of them prodded at the stump of her broken tusk, an action that must have been agonisingly painful, she did little more than flinch.

Even on first contact with the mammoths, the Lost seemed to have no fear, so secure were they in their dominance of the world around them.

Now Silverhair was dragged forward.

The beach was scarred by the blackened remains of fires. She recognised a stack of thunder-sticks, looking no more dangerous than fallen branches. There were little shelters, like caves. They were made of sheets of reddish-brown shiny stuff which appeared to have come from the monstrous hulk she had observed on the shore with Lop-ear, in a time that seemed a Great-Year remote.

There was much she did not understand. There were the straight-edged, hollowed-out boxes from which the Lost extracted their strange, odourless foods. There were the glinting, shining flasks – almost like hollowed-out icicles – from which the Lost would pour a clear liquid down their skinny throats, a liquid over which they fought, which they prized above everything else. There was the box which emitted a deafening, incessant noise, and the other box which glittered with star-like lights, into which one or other of the Lost would bark incessantly.

And all of this strange, horrific place was suffused with the smell of mammoth: dead, decaying, burned mammoth.

The Lost set up four stakes in the ground. They beat them in place with blocks of wood they held in their paws.

Silverhair was led towards the stakes.

One of the Lost walked around her on his skinny hind legs, plucked at the ropes which bound her grisly load to her belly, and stepped in front of her face to inspect her tusks—

And, stretching her ropes to the limit, she twisted her head and swiped at him. She caught him a glancing blow with the side of her tusk – he was so light and frail she could barely feel the impact – and he sprawled on the ground before her. He howled and squirmed. She raised her foreleg. In an instant she would crush the ribcage of this mewling creature.

But Skin-of-Ice was here. He grabbed the paw of the one on the ground and dragged him away from her.

Now the Lost closed rapidly around her. Commanded by Skin-of-Ice, they prodded, poked and dragged at Silverhair until the four stakes were all around her. Then they tied rope around her legs, so tightly it bit into her flesh, pinning each of her legs to a stake, and she could not move.

CHAPTER 7
THE NEST OF THE LOST

The endless day wore on.

Silverhair could not lie down, not even move. And she wasn't allowed to sleep. The Lost tormented her continually.

The stake ropes were never released. Though she chafed against them, she only rubbed raw her own flesh; she could feel how the ropes cut to the very bone of her forelegs.

The Lost would give her no water. Soon it felt as if her trunk was shrivelling like drying grass, and her chest and belly were dry as the bones which had emerged from the *yedoma*.

And they tormented her with food. One of them would hold up succulent grass before her, push it towards her mouth, perhaps even allow a blade or two to touch her tongue. But then, invariably, he would snatch the grass away.

Even when there were no Lost with her – when they were all asleep in their artificial caves, the flasks and scraps of half-chewed mammoth meat scattered around their snoring forms – they would set up one of their deafening noise-making boxes beside her, and its unending stomping ensured she could never sleep.

Snagtooth was kept tied up, in full view of Silverhair. But her tether was just a single rope, her feet were not bound so she was free to move as far as the rope would allow her, and she was fed with pawfuls of grass and containers of water.

Several times a day, Skin-of-Ice or one of the others would climb on the back of Snagtooth. The Lost would kick at the back of her ears, as if trying to drive her forward or back. Snagtooth was rewarded with mouthfuls of food if she guessed what they wanted correctly, and strikes of a goad – not as severely as they beat Silverhair – if she got it wrong. All this was greeted with hoots of laughter from the staggering, swaying Lost.

Silverhair tried to recall the Cycle, the legends of Kilukpuk and Ganesha and Longtusk; but the Cycle seemed a remote irrelevance in this place of horror. At last Silverhair's spirit seemed as if it was half-detached from her body, and even the pain of her poisoned wounds receded from her awareness.

When she was left alone, she would look beyond the camp, seeking solace. Somehow it seemed strange that the world was continuing its ancient cycles, regardless of her own suffering, and the cruel designs of the Lost. But life was carrying on.

The cliffs above this beach were crowded with thousands of eider, kittiwakes, murres and fulmars. Every ledge and crevice was packed with nesting birds, and their noise and smell was overwhelming; so many birds circled in the air they darkened the sky. At the base of the cliffs was a bright carpet of lichens and purple saxifrage, fertilised by the guano from the birds.

Silverhair saw a thick-billed murre taking its turn to sit on its single egg, freeing its partner to seek food at the ice-edge. But when the attention of the murre was distracted, a gull swooped down and easily snatched the egg, swallowing it in a single movement. The distress of the murre pair was obvious, for there might not be time in this short season to raise another egg. Silverhair, despite her own plight, felt a stab of sadness at the small tragedy.

. . . But then Skin-of-Ice would return, sometimes with a flask of liquid in his paw. He would adjust the ropes that pinned her, perhaps tightening them around some already chafed and painful spot. And then he would devise some new way to hurt her.

Some of the Lost seemed to show regret for the suffering
they caused. They would hurry past the place she was
staked, with their faces averted. Or else they would stand
before her and stare at her, their spindly forelegs dangling,
their small mouths gaping open; sometimes they would
even reach up to her hesitantly, as if to stroke her or feed
her.

But not Skin-of-Ice.

He knows I'm conscious, she thought. He knows I'm in
here.

He knows what he does hurts me. That's why he does it.
The others may kill us for food or skin or bones, but not this
one. He enjoys inflicting pain. And he enjoys humiliating.

It was a deliberate cruelty of a type she had never encountered before. And she knew it would not stop until she
bent her head to him, as had Snagtooth.

Or until one of them was dead.

'. . . Silverhair. Silverhair. Can you hear me?'

Snagtooth was a silhouette against the dying light of the
fire.

'Leave me alone,' said Silverhair.

'You don't understand.' Snagtooth was using the contact
rumble, a note so deep it was not muffled by the clatter of
the noise-maker beside Silverhair, so deep it would not
disturb the light slumbers of the Lost. But her voice sounded
oddly distorted, as if she spoke with a trunk full of water.

'What is there to understand? You have given yourself to
the Lost.'

'We can't fight them, Silverhair. Think about what the
Cycle says. Once the mammoths dominated the north of the
whole world. But then the Lost came and took it from us –
all of it, except the Island. We have to live as they want us to
live. We have no choice.'

'There is always a choice,' rumbled Silverhair.

'I think they want us to work for them. Lifting things,

moving things about, in the odd way they have of wanting to reorder everything. But it isn't so bad. When one of them climbs on your back, you don't even feel his weight after a while—'

'You do,' said Silverhair softly. 'Oh, you do.'

'They are feeding me well, Silverhair. They cleaned out my abscess. It doesn't hurt any more. Can you imagine how that *feels*?'

'Is that why you are prepared to bend before them? Because they cleaned out your tusk?'

The rumble fell silent for a long time. Then Snagtooth said, 'Silverhair, I think I understand them. I think I am like them.'

'*Like* the Lost?'

'Look around you. There are no bitches here. No cubs. These Lost are alone. Like a bachelor herd, cut off from the Families. No wonder they are so cruel and unhappy . . . Silverhair, I envy you. I can smell it from here, even above the blood and the rot of your wounds and the burning of Eggtusk's flesh—'

'Smell what?'

'The calf growing inside you.'

Silverhair, startled, listened to the slow oceanic pulsing of her own blood. *Could it be true?*

Snagtooth murmured, 'For me it's different, Silverhair. Year after year my body has absorbed the eggs of my unborn calves, even before they fully form.'

Now, in the midst of her own confusing pulse of joy, Silverhair understood. She should have known: for the Cycle teaches that sterile Cows, unable to produce calves, will sometimes grow as huge as mature Bulls, as if their bodies are seeking to make up in stature what they lack in fertility.

Snagtooth said, 'Now do you understand why I submit to the Lost? Because there is nothing else for me, Silverhair. Nothing.'

And Snagtooth turned her head, and Silverhair saw her clearly for the first time since they had arrived in this nest. 'Oh, Snagtooth . . .'

Snagtooth's trunk was *gone* – her trunk with its hundred thousand muscles, infinitely supple, immensely strong, the trunk which fed her and assuaged her thirst, the trunk which defined her identity as mammoth. Now, in the centre of her face, there was only a bloody stump, grotesquely shadowed by the fire's flickering light.

Snagtooth had allowed the Lost to sever her trunk at its root. She couldn't even feed herself or obtain water; she had made herself completely reliant on the mercy of the Lost, for whatever remained of her life.

The pain must have been blinding.

'It isn't so bad!' Snagtooth wailed thickly. 'Not so bad . . .'

The eternal Arctic day wore on.

Silverhair's stomach was so empty now, her dung so thin, she seemed to have gone beyond the pain of hunger and thirst. She couldn't even pass urine any more. The rope burns on her legs seemed to be rotting, so foul was the stench that came from them. She was giddy from lack of sleep, so much so that sometimes the pain fell away from her and she seemed to be floating, looking down on the fouled, bloody body trapped between the stakes on the ground, flying like a gull halfway to the Sky Steppe.

She tried to sense the new life budding inside her – did it have limbs yet? did it have a trunk? – but she could sense only its glowing, heavy warmth.

At last, one dark and cloudy midnight, the situation came to a head.

Skin-of-Ice approached her. She saw that he was staggering slightly. His hairless head was slick and shining with sweat. In his paw he held a glittering flask, already half empty. He raised it in his paw, almost as a mammoth would raise a trunkful of water. But he drank clumsily, as a mammoth never would, and the fluid spilled over his chin and neck.

She had no idea what the clear fluid was. It certainly wasn't water, for its smell was thin and sharp, like mould. Surely it would only serve to rot him from within. But perhaps that explained why, when the Lost forced this liquid down their throats, they would dance, shout, fight, fall into an uncomfortable sleep far from their nests near the fires or in the artificial caves. Sometimes – she could tell from the stink – they even fouled themselves.

And it was when the clear liquid was inside him that Skin-of-Ice would cause Silverhair the most pain.

He wiped away the mess on his face with his paw. He stalked before her, eyeing her, calculating. Then he turned and barked at the other Lost. Two of them emerged from one of their improvised caves, reluctant, staggering a little. They yapped at Skin-of-Ice, as if protesting. But Skin-of-Ice began to yell at them once more, pointing to the bindings on Silverhair's legs, and then pointing behind him.

Silverhair stood stolidly in her trap. It was obvious she was to face some new horror. Whatever it was, she swore to herself, though she could not mask her weakness, she would show no fear.

The Lost, reluctantly obeying Skin-of-Ice, clustered around the stakes which trapped Silverhair's legs and pulled away the ropes. Her wounds, with their encrusted blood and scab tissue, and half-healed flesh, were ripped open.

Released, her right foreleg crumpled and she dropped to one knee. The blood that flowed in her knees and hips, joints which had been held stiff and unmoving for so long, felt like fire.

But, for the first time since being brought here, Silverhair's legs were free. She stood straight with a great effort.

Now the Lost started to prod at her, and to pull at her ropes. She tried to resist, but she was so weakened now the feeble muscles of these Lost were sufficient to make her walk.

She moved one leg forward, then another. The pain in her hips and shoulders had a stabbing intensity.

But the pain began to ease.

Silverhair had always been blessed by good health, and her constitution was tough – designed, after all, to survive without shelter the rigours of an Arctic winter. Even now she could feel the first inklings of a recovery which might come quickly – if she were ever given the chance.

Her strength was returning. But she did not let her limp become less pronounced. Nor did she raise her head, or fight against the ropes. It occurred to her it might be useful if the Lost did not know how strong she was.

But still, it *hurt*.

As they passed a fire, Skin-of-Ice pulled out burning branches. He kept one himself and passed the others to his companions. Soon the patch of littered beach was illuminated by overlapping, shifting circles of blood-red light, vivid in the subdued midnight glow.

They led her past Snagtooth. Her aunt was still tied loosely by the rope dangling from her neck. The stump of her severed trunk was ugly, but it seemed to be healing over.

Snagtooth turned away.

Silverhair walked on, flanked by the Lost, led by the capering gait of Skin-of-Ice in the flickering light of the torches.

They were dragging her to another shelter: a dome shape a little bigger than the rest. The shelter stank of mammoth. She felt her dry trunk curl.

The other Lost backed away, leaving her with Skin-of-Ice. Almost trustingly, he reached up and grabbed one of the ropes that was attached to the tight noose around her neck. Feigning weakness, she allowed herself to be led forward towards the shelter.

Skin-of-Ice shielded his torch and led her through the shelter's entrance. It was so narrow her flanks brushed its sides.

She felt something soft there. *It felt like hair*: like a mammoth's winter coat.

Inside the shelter was utter darkness, relieved only slightly by a disc of indigo sky that showed through a rent in the roof. The stench of death was almost overpowering.

She wondered dully what the Lost was planning. Perhaps this was the place where Skin-of-Ice would, at last, kill her.

He bent and flicked his torch over a small pile in the middle of the floor. It looked like twigs and branches. A fire started. At first smoke billowed up, and there was a stink of fat. But then the smoke cleared, and the fire burned with a clear, steady light.

She saw that the fire was built from bone shards, smashed and broken. Mammoth bones.

The fire's light grew.

The walls of this shelter were made of some kind of skin. And the walls' supports were curved, and they gleamed, white as snow.

The supports were mammoth tusks.

The tusks had been driven into the ground, so that their tips met at the apex of the shelter. They were joined at the top by a sleeve of what looked like more bone, to make a continuous arch.

And the wall skins, too, had been taken from mammoths, she saw now: flayed from corpses, scraped and cleaned, rust-brown hair still dangling from them. As she looked down, she saw more bones – jaws and shoulder blades and leg bones as thick as tree-trunks – driven into the ground to fix the skins in place there.

Black dread settled on her as she understood. *This shelter was made entirely from mammoth hide and bone.* It was like being inside an opened-out corpse.

But the horror was not yet done. Skin-of-Ice was pointing at the ground with his paw.

Resting by the doorway was the massive skull of a mammoth. She recognised it. She was looking into the empty eye-sockets of Eggtusk.

Skin-of-Ice was confronting her, his paws spread wide, and he was cawing. She knew that he had brought her here, shown her this final horror, to complete his victory over her.

She began to speak to him. 'Skin-of-Ice, it is you who is defeated,' she said softly. 'For I will not forget what you have done here. And when I put you in the ground, the worms will crawl through your skull and inhabit your emptied chest, as you inhabit these desecrated remains.'

For a heartbeat he seemed taken aback – almost as if he understood that she was speaking to him.

Then he raised his goad.

She summoned all her strength, and reared up. The ropes around her neck and forelegs parted.

Skin-of-Ice, evidently realising his carelessness, fell backwards and sprawled before her.

At last her trunk was free. She raised it and trumpeted. She took a deliberate step towards him.

Even now he showed no fear. He raised a paw and curled it: beckoning her, daring her to approach him.

She stabbed at him with her tusk.

But he was fast. He squirmed sideways.

Her tusk drove into the earth. It hit rock buried there, and she felt its tip splinter and crack.

Skin-of-Ice wriggled away. But a splash of bright fresh red disfigured his side, soaking through the loose skins he wore.

She felt a stab of exultation. She had wounded him.

He scrambled out of the shelter.

She set about wrecking this cave of skin. She trampled on the heap of burning bones. She smashed away the supports which held up the grisly roof. When the layers of flayed skin fell over her, exposing the midnight sky, she shook them away.

All this took mere heartbeats.

Then, with her trunk, she picked up the fragments of skin, and laid them reverently over her back. She found herself breathing hard, her limited reserves of energy already depleted.

She turned to meet her fate.

Beyond the ruins of the hut there was a ring of light: a dozen burning branches held aloft by the paws of the Lost. Several of them had thunder-sticks, which they were pointing towards her. She could see their small eyes, sighting along the sticks at her head and belly.

And there was Skin-of-Ice. He was holding his side, but she could see the blood leaking through his fingers.

She tried to calculate. If she charged directly at him, even if the stinging hail from the thunder-sticks caught her, her sheer momentum could not be stopped. And Skin-of-Ice, wounded as he was, would not be able to evade her this time.

She rumbled to her calf. 'So it is over,' she said. 'But the pain will be mine, not yours. You will not see this terrible world of suffering, dominated by these monsters, these Lost. It will be brief, and then we will be together, in the aurora that burns in the sky . . .'

She lowered her head—

There was a braying, liquid roar.

The Lost scattered and ran, yelling.

A shape loomed out of the shadows: bristling with fur, one tusk held high. It was Snagtooth. Silverhair could see how she trailed the broken length of rope which had restrained her.

Without her trunk Snagtooth was unable to trumpet, but she could roar; and now she roared again. She selected one of the Lost and hurled herself straight towards him. The Lost

170

screamed and raised his thunder-stick. It spat fire, and Silverhair could see how blood splashed over Snagtooth's upper thigh. But the wound did not impede her charge.

Snagtooth's mutilated head rammed directly into the belly of the Lost.

Silverhair heard a single bloody gurgle, the crackle of crushed bone. The Lost was hurled into the air and landed far from the circle of torches.

But this victory was transient. The Lost gathered their courage and turned on Snagtooth. Soon the still air was rent by the noise of thunder-sticks.

Snagtooth reeled. She fell to her knees.

Silverhair screamed: 'Snagtooth!'

Through the storm of noise, Silverhair could hear Snagtooth's rumble. 'Remember me . . .'

And Silverhair understood. In the end, Snagtooth had thrown off her shame. She had chosen to give her life for Silverhair and her calf. Now it was up to Silverhair to get away, to accept that ultimate gift.

She turned away from the noise, the Lost, the agonised shape of Snagtooth, and slipped away into the silvery Arctic light.

The Lost closed around Snagtooth with their thunder-sticks and ice-claws.

THREE
MATRIARCH

THE STORY OF GANESHA
THE WISE

This (said Silverhair) is the story of Ganesha, who is called the Wise.

I am talking of a time many Great-Years ago – ten, twelve, perhaps more. In those days, the world was quite different, for it was warmer, and much of the land was covered in a rich Forest.

Now, in such a world you or I would be too hot, and there would be little for us to eat. But Ganesha's Family thought themselves blessed.

For Ganesha's Family, and their Clan and Kin, had lived for a hundred Great-Years in a world awash with heat, and Ganesha had no need to keep herself warm, as you do. And she ate the rich food of the Forest: grass, moss, fruit, even leaves and bark.

If Ganesha was standing before you now you would think her strange indeed.

Though she had a trunk and tusks, she had little fur; her grey skin was exposed to the cooling air, all year round. She had little fat on her lean body, and her ears were large, like huge flapping leaves. And Ganesha was tall – she would have towered over you, little Icebones!

Ganesha had two calves, both Cows, called Prima and Meridi.

Everyone agreed that Meridi was the beauty of the Family: tall, strong, lean, her skin like weathered rock, her trunk as supple as a willow branch. By comparison Prima seemed short and fat and clumsy, her ears and trunk stubby. But Ganesha, of course, loved them both equally, as mothers do.

Now, Ganesha was not called Wise for nothing. She knew the world was changing.

She walked north, to the edge of the Forest, where the trees thinned out, and she looked out over the plains: grassy, endless, stretching to the End of the World. When she was a calf, she remembered clearly, such a walk would have taken many more days.

And if Ganesha stepped out of the Forest, enduring the burning sun of that time, she could see where the Forest had once been. For the land here was littered with fallen, rotten trunks and the remnants of roots, within which insects burrowed.

And Ganesha could smell the ice on the wind, see the scudding of clouds across the sky.

The Cycle teaches us of the great Changes that sweep over the world – Changes that come, not in a year or two or ten, not even in the span of a mammoth's lifetime, but with the passing of the Great-Years.

And that is how Ganesha knew about the great Cold that was sweeping down from out of the north, and how she knew that the Forest was shrinking back to the south, just as the tide recedes from the shore.

Ganesha was concerned for her Family.

She consulted the Cycle – which, even in those days, was already ancient and rich – but she found no lesson to help her there.

However Ganesha was Wise. As she looked into the vast emptiness that was opening up in the north, Ganesha understood that a great opportunity awaited her calves.

But to take that opportunity she would have to step beyond the Cycle.

Ganesha called her calves to her.

'The Forest is dying,' she said.

Prima, squat and solid, said, 'But the Forest sustains us. What must we do?'

Meridi, tall and beautiful, scoffed at her mother. 'All you have seen is a few dead trees. You are an old fool!'

Ganesha bore this disrespect with tolerance.

'This is what we must do,' she said. 'As the Forest dies back, a new land is revealed. There are no trees, but there are grasses and bushes and other things to eat. And it stretches beyond the horizon – all the way to the End of the World.

'This land is called a Tundra. And, because it is new, the Tundra is empty. You will learn to live on the Tundra, to endure the coming Cold.

'It will not be easy,' she said to them. 'You are creatures of the Forest; to become creatures of the Tundra will be arduous and painful. But if you endure this pain your calves, and their calves, will in time cover the Tundra with great Clans, greater than any the world has seen.'

Prima lowered her trunk soberly. 'Matriarch,' she said, 'show me what to do.'

But Meridi scoffed once more. 'You are an old fool, Ganesha. None of this is in the Cycle. Soon I will be Matriarch, and there will be none of this talk of the Tundra!' And she refused to have anything to do with Ganesha's instruction.

Ganesha was saddened by this, but she said nothing.

Now (said Silverhair), to ready Prima for the Tundra took Ganesha three summers.

In the first summer, she changed Prima's skin. She bit away at Prima's great ears, reducing them to small, round flaps of skin. And she nibbled at Prima's tail, making it shorter and stubbier than her sister's, and she tugged at the skin above Prima's backside so that a flap came down over her anus.

Prima endured the pain of all this with strong silence, for she accepted her mother's wisdom. All these changes would help her skin trap the heat of her body. And so they were good.

But Meridi mocked her sister. 'You are already ugly, little Prima. Now you let Ganesha make you more so!' And Meridi tugged at Prima's distorted ears making them bleed once more.

In the second year, Ganesha made Prima fat. She gathered the richest and most luscious leaves and grass in the Forest, and crammed them into Prima's mouth.

Prima endured this. She understood that to withstand the cold a mammoth must be as round as a boulder, with as much of her body tucked on the inside as possible, and swathed in a great layer of warming fat. And so these changes were also good.

But beautiful Meridi mocked her sister's growing fatness. 'You are already ugly, little Prima, and now with your great belly and your tiny head you are as round as a pebble. Look how tall and lean I am!'

And in the third year Ganesha took Prima to a pit in the ground, left by a rotting tree stump. She bade Prima lie in the pit, then covered her with twigs and blades of grass, and caked the whole of her body with mud and stones. There Prima remained for the whole summer, with only her trunk and mouth and eyes protruding; and Ganesha brought her water and food every day.

And as the mud baked in the sun, the twigs and grasses turned into a thick layer of orange-brown fur, which Prima knew would keep her warm through the long Tundra nights. And so these changes were also good.

But again Meridi mocked her sister. 'You are fat and short, little Prima, and now you are covered with the ugliest fur I have ever seen. Look at my rock-smooth skin, and weep!'

All of this Prima endured.

At the end of the third summer Ganesha presented her two daughters to the Family.

She said: 'I will not serve as your Matriarch any longer, for I am tired and my teeth grow soft. Now, if you wish, you can choose to stay with Meridi, who will lead you deeper into the Forest. Or you can join Prima, and learn to live on the Tundra, as she has. Neither course is easy. But I have taught you that the art of travelling is to pick the least dangerous path.'

And she had Prima and Meridi stand before the assembled Family.

There was Meridi, tall and bare and lean and beautiful, promising the mammoths that if they followed her – and the teachings of the Cycle – they would enjoy rich foliage and deep-green shade, just as they had always known. And there was Prima, a squat, fat, round bundle of brown fur, who promised only hardship, and whose life would not follow the Cycle.

It will not surprise you that most of the Family chose to stay with beautiful Meridi and the Cycle.

But a few chose Prima, and the future.

So the sisters parted. They never saw each other again.

Soon the trees were dying, just as Ganesha had foreseen. Meridi and her folk were forced to venture further and further south.

At last Meridi came to a place where Cousins lived already. They were Calves of Probos like us, but they had chosen to live in the lush warm south many Great-Years ago. They called themselves *elephants*. And, though the elephants recall the Oath of Kilukpuk, they would not allow Meridi and her mammoths to share their Forest.

All of Meridi's renowned beauty made absolutely no difference.

As the Cold settled on the Earth and the Forest died away, Meridi and her Family dwindled.

Meridi died, hungry and cold and without calves.

And now not one of her beautiful kind is left on the Earth.

Meanwhile Prima took her handful of followers out on to

the Tundra. It was hard and cold, but they learned to savour the subtle flavours of the Tundra grasses, and Prima helped them become as she was – as we are now.

And her calves, and her calves' calves, roamed over the northern half of our planet.

Ganesha, you see (concluded Silverhair), was not like other Matriarchs.

Some say Ganesha was a dark figure – perhaps with something of the Lost about her – for she defied the Cycle itself. Well, if that is so, it was a fusion that brought courage and wisdom.

For Ganesha found a way for her daughter Prima to change, to become fit for the new, cold world which was emerging from inside its mask of Forest. None of this was in the Cycle before Ganesha. But she was not afraid to look beyond the Cycle if it did not help her.

And now the story of Ganesha is itself part of the Cycle, and always will be, so she can teach us with her wisdom.

Thus, through paradox, the Cycle renews itself . . .

No, Icebones (said Silverhair), the story isn't done yet. I will tell you what became of Ganesha herself!

Of course she could not follow Prima, for Ganesha had grown up in the Forest, like her mother before her, and her mother before that, in a great line spanning many hundreds of Great-Years.

And so – when the Cold came, and the Forest dwindled – Ganesha sank to her knees, and died, and her Family mourned for many days.

But as long as the Cycle is told, Ganesha will be remembered.

CHAPTER 1
THE HUDDLE

Silverhair heard the ugly cawing of the Lost.

She turned and looked back along the beach. She could see sparks of red light breaking away from the dim glow of the camp. Evidently they had done with Snagtooth, and were pursuing her once more.

She staggered along the beach. But her hind legs were still tightly bound up, and she moved with a clumsy shuffle. The stolen mammoth skin lay on her back; she could feel it, heavy as guilt.

By the low sunlight she could see the pack ice which still lingered in the Channel, ghostly blue. She could smell the sharp salt brine of the sea, and the lapping of the water on the shingle was a soothing, regular sound, so different from the days of clamour she had endured. But the cliff alongside her was steep and obviously impenetrable, even had she been fully fit.

She came to a place where the cliff face had crumbled and fallen in great cracked slabs. Perhaps a stream had once run here.

She turned and began to climb up the rough valley, away from the beach.

It was difficult, for the big stones were slippery with kelp fronds. The ropes which bound her hind legs snagged and caught at the rocks.

. . . Something exploded out of the sky.

She trumpeted in alarm. She heard a flapping like giant wings – but wings that beat faster than any bird's. And there was light, a pool of illumination that hurtled the length of the beach.

Silverhair cowered. Air gushed over her, as if from some tamed windstorm, washing over her face and back; the air stank like a tar pit.

The source of the beam was a thing of straight lines and transparent bubbles, with great wings that whirled above it. It was a huge bird, of light and noise.

The Lost had forgotten Silverhair. They went running towards the light-bird, waving their paws.

Carefully, still hobbled by the ropes on her hind legs, Silverhair limped away towards the heart of the Island.

She found a stream, trickling between an outcrop of broken, worn rocks. The first suck of water was so cold and sharp it sent lances of pain along her dry, inflamed nostrils. She raised her trunk to her mouth. She coughed, explosively; her dry throat expelled every drop of the water. When the coughing fit was done, she tried again. The water seemed to burn her throat as it coursed towards her stomach, but she swallowed hard, refusing to allow her body to reject this bounty.

She used her tusks to get the ropes off her hind legs, and then bathed her wounds. The rope burns had indeed turned brown and grey with poison. She washed them clean and caked them with the thin mud she managed to scrape from the bed of the stream.

She cast about for grass. She found it difficult to grasp the tussocks that grew sparsely here, so stiff had her abused trunk become. The grass felt dry, and her tongue, swollen and sore, could detect no flavour.

Another dry, racking cough, and the grass, half chewed, was expelled.

But she did not give up. There was a calf in her belly, sleeping calmly, trusting her to nurture it to the moment of its birth and then beyond. If she must train herself to live again, she would do it.

So she found more grass and kept trying, until she managed to keep some food in her stomach.

When she had eaten, she found a natural hollow in the ground. She reached over her shoulder for the skins and laid the pathetic remnants at the base of the hole.

She spent long heartbeats touching the skins with her trunk, trying to Remember Eggtusk, and the ancient mammoths from whom these skins had been stolen. But the strange odourless texture of the Lost lay over the skins; and the way they had been scraped and dried, punctured and stitched together, made them seem deeply unnatural.

There was little of Eggtusk left here.

When it was done she limped around the hollow, rumbling her mourning, and poked at the low mound of remains.

She longed to stay here, and she longed to sleep.

But she could feel her strength dissipating, even as she stood here. She had to return to the Family: to tell them what had become of Snagtooth and mighty Eggtusk, and to help Owlheart with whatever the matriarch decided they must do.

She turned to the north and began the long walk home.

She was a boulder of flesh and bone and fur that stomped stolidly over this blooming summer land, ignoring the shimmering belts of flowers, oblivious to the lemmings she startled from their burrows. As she walked, the warm wind from the south blew the last of her winter coat off her back, so that hair coiled into the air like spindrift from the sea.

She might have looked sullen, for she walked with her head lowered. But this is the habit of mammoths; Silverhair was inspecting the vegetation for the richest grass, which she cropped as often as she could manage.

But the food clogged in her throat as if it were a ball of hair and dirt. Her dung was hard and dry, sharp with barely digested grass. And the cold, though diminishing as the summer advanced, seemed to pierce her deeply.

Her sleep was fragmented, snatches she caught while shivering against rock outcrops, fearful of wolves and Lost.

The world map in her head was now more of a curse than a blessing. She could imagine the scope and rocky sweep of the Island, sense – from their contact rumbles and stamping – where the Family was clustered, far to the north.

She was just a pebble against this bitter panorama. And her own mind and heart – cluttered with the agonised memories of Eggtusk and Snagtooth and Lop-Ear, and with dread visions of the Lost and their light-bird, and with hopes and fears for the growing child inside her – were dwarfed, made insignificant by the pitiless immensity of the land.

As the sun wheeled in the sky she felt as if her contact with the world was loosening, as if the heavy pads of her feet were leaving the ground; she was a mammoth turning as light as the pollen of the tundra flowers which bloomed around her.

A storm descended.

A black cloud closed around her. The wind seemed to slap at her, each gust a fresh, violent blow. Her fur was plastered against her face. The ice dust hurled by the wind was sharp and dug into her flesh. She could see barely more than a few paces; she was driving herself through a bubble of light that fluctuated around her.

The storm blew out. But her strength was severely sapped.

She felt she could march no more.

She stopped, and let the sun's warmth play on her back.

After the storm, they sky was cloaked with a thin over-cast. The sun's light was diffused, so that the air shimmered brightly all around her, and nothing cast a shadow. The sun, high to the north, shone faintly through the haze, and was flanked by a ghostly pair of sun dogs, reflections from ice crystals in the air.

The shadowless light was opalescent, very strange and beautiful.

She wasn't sure where she was, which way she should go. But she could smell water here; there was a stream, and pools of icemelt, and the grass grew thickly.

It was a good place to stay. Perhaps her dung would help this place flourish.

On a ground carpeted with bright-yellow Arctic daisies, she sank to her knees. The pain in her legs ceased to clamour. She would feed soon, and drink. But first she would sleep.

She rested her tusks on the ground and closed her eyes. She could feel the spin of the rocky Earth which bore her through space, sense it carry her beneath the brightness of the sun.

But there was a deeper cold beneath, a cold that was sucking at her.

Something made her open her eyes.

She saw a strange animal, standing unnaturally on its hind legs, brandishing a stick at her. In its paws it held something that glittered like ice, small and sharp.

And now she felt a nudging around her body, under her spine and at her buttocks. Irritated, she raised her head.

A huge Bull was trying to dig his tusks under her belly. *By the oozing scabs of Kilukpuk's cracked and bleeding moles, but you're a heavy great boulder of a Cow, little Silverhair. Come on – come—*

She tried to ignore him. After all, he wasn't real. 'Go away,' she said.

But we can't, you see, child. Another mammoth – this time a massive, ancient Cow who moved stiffly, as if plagued by arthritis – stood at her other side. *It isn't your day to die. Don't you know that? Your story isn't done yet.* And she tugged at Silverhair's tusks with her trunk.

Silverhair reluctantly got to her feet. 'I'm comfortable here,' she mumbled.

You never would listen. Another voice, somewhere behind her. Turning her head sluggishly, Silverhair saw this was a strange Cow indeed, with one shattered tusk and a trunk

185

severed close to the root. The Cow was lowering her head and butting at Silverhair's buttocks, trying to nudge her forward.

The others, the Bull and the ancient Cow, had clustered to either side of her. They were huddling her, she realised.

Silverhair took a single, resentful step. 'I just want to be left alone.'

The Bull growled. *If you don't stop squealing like a calf, I'll paddle your behind. Now move.*

So, one painful step after another, her trunk dangling over the ground, Silverhair walked on. She leaned on one reassuring flank, and then the other; and the gentle nudging of the mutilated head behind her impelled her forward.

And the strange animal that walked upright stalked alongside her, just beyond reach of the mammoths, and his strange sharp objects glinted in his paw.

But it was not over. Still the land stretched ahead of her, curving over the limb of the planet.

Sometimes she thought she heard contact rumbles, and her hopes would briefly lift. But the sound was remote, uncertain, and she couldn't tell if it was real or just imagination.

She came to a place of frost heave, where ice domes as high as her belly had formed in the soil, ringed by shattered rock. This land was difficult to cross, and there was little food, for nothing could grow here.

One by one, the mammoths who had escorted her fell away: the ancient Cow, the crusty old Bull, the mutilated face that had bumped encouragingly at her rump.

Even the faint trace of contact rumbles died away. Perhaps it had only been thunder.

At last she was alone with the animal that walked upright. It glided beside her, as effortless as a shadow, waiting for her to fall.

She staggered on until the frost heave was behind her.

She stopped, and looked around dimly. She had come to a plain of black volcanic rock, barely broken even by lichen. It was a hard, uncompromising land: no place for the living.

She knelt once more, and let her chest sink to the ground, and then her tusks, which supported her head.

Here, then, she thought. Here it ends.

There was nobody here, no scent of mammoth on this barren land: no one to perform the Remembering ceremony for her and her calf. Well, then, she must do it for herself. She cast about with her trunk. But there was nothing to be had – no twigs or grass – nothing save a few loose stones, scattered over this bony landscape. She picked those up and dropped them on her back. Then she reached to her belly and tore out some hair, and scattered it over her spine.

. . . *Silverhair . . . Silverhair . . .*

There was a mammoth before her, tugging at her trunk.

She pulled back impatiently. 'Go away,' she mumbled. She had had enough of meddling ghosts.

But this mammoth was small, and it seemed to hop about before her, touching her trunk and mouth and tusks. *Silverhair, is it really you? Silverhair . . . Silverhair . . .*

'Silverhair.'

It was her nephew, Croptail. And beyond him she could see the great boulder shape of Owlheart, a cloud of flesh and fur and tusk.

She could smell them. They were real. Relief flooded her, and a great weakness fell on her, making her tremble.

She looked around, meaning to warn Owlheart about the strange upright-walking animal. But, for now, it had vanished.

Foxeye stroked her back and touched her mouth and trunk, and brought her food and water. Owlheart tended her wounds, stripping off the mud Silverhair had plastered there, washing the deepest of the cuts and covering them once more with fresh mud. She laid her trunk against

Silverhair's belly hair, listening to the small life that was growing within. Even Croptail helped, in his clumsy way.

But the little one, Sunfire, was too young even to remember her aunt; the calf stood a few paces away from this battered, bloody stranger, her eyes wide as the Moon.

Later, Silverhair would marvel at Owlheart's patience. The Matriarch must have been bursting with questions. Yet, as the sun completed many cycles in the sky, Owlheart allowed Silverhair to reserve all her energy for recovery.

Silverhair tried to understand what had happened to her on the long walk home, but even as she tried to recall fragments of it, they would slip away, like bees from a flower.

She did wonder, though, why there hadn't been a fourth ghost out there helping her: a young Bull with a damaged ear . . .

At last Owlheart came to her.

'You know you've been lucky. A couple of those wounds on your legs were down to the very bone. But now you're healing. Kilukpuk must be watching over you, child.'

Silverhair raised her trunk wearily. 'I wish she'd watch a bit more carefully then.'

'How much do you remember?'

'Everything – I think – until those Lost captured me and tied my legs to the stakes. After that it gets a little blurred. Until Snagtooth—'

'Start at the beginning.'

And so, in shards and fragments, Silverhair told the Matriarch her story.

When she was done, Owlheart was grim. 'It is just as it says in the Cycle. It was like this in the time of Longtusk, when the Lost would wait for us to die, then eat our flesh, and shelter from the rain in caves made of our skin, and burn our bones for warmth. And they will not stop there. They will take more and more, their twisted hunger never sated.'

'Then what should we do?'

Owlheart raised her trunk and sniffed the air. 'For a long time we have been sheltered, here on this Island, where few Lost ever came. But now they know we are here we can only flee.'

'Flee? But where?'

Owlheart turned her face away from the sun, and the ice-laden wind whipped at her fur.

'North,' she said. 'We must go north, as mammoths always have.'

CHAPTER 2
THE GLACIERS

The migration began the next day.

Owlheart allowed many stops, for feeding and resting and passing dung; and when the midnight sun rolled along the horizon they slept. But when the mammoths moved, Owlheart had them sweep across the tundra at a handsome pace. They ran in the thin warmth of the noon sun, and they ran in the long shadows of midnight.

Foxeye shepherded her calf Sunfire, coaxing her to feed and pass dung and sleep. Croptail strayed further afield. He would dash ahead of the rest, pawing at the grass and rock with his trunk, and run in wide circles around the group, as if to deter any wolves. Owlheart caught Silverhair's eye, and an unspoken message passed between the Cows. *He's following his instinct. What he's doing is the right thing for a young Bull. But keep an eye on him; he's no Eggtusk yet.*

It was the height of summer now. The air above the endless bogs hummed with millions of gnats, midges, mosquitoes. The mosquitoes would hover in smoke-like dancing columns, before homing in on a mammoth's body heat with remarkable accuracy, until their victim was smothered by an extremely uncomfortable cloak of insect life. Blackflies were almost as much a pest as mosquitoes, for they seemed able to penetrate the most dense layers of fur in their search for exposed skin – not just the soft parts, but even the harder skin of Silverhair's feet. They would stab their mouthparts through the skin to suck out the blood that sustained them, and the poison they injected into

Silverhair's skin to keep the blood flowing freely caused swelling and intolerable itching.

But even the mosquitoes and flies were but a minor irritant to Silverhair, as her strength gradually returned. Mammoths are not designed to be still. Silverhair found that the hours of easy movement, her muscles strengthening and her wounds healing, smoothed the pain out of her body. Even her digestion improved as the steady, normal flow of food and water through her body was restored; soon her dung passed easily and was rich and thick once more.

And as they ran, it was as if more ghosts clustered around her: this time not just two or three or four mammoths, but whole Families, young and old, Bulls and calves, running together as smoothly as the grass of the tundra ripples in the wind. It seemed to Silverhair that their rumbles were merging, sinking into the ground, so that it was as if the whole plain undulated with the mammoths' greeting calls.

But then the ghosts would fade, and Silverhair would be left alone with her diminished Family: just three Cows, one immature Bull and a suckling infant, where once millions of mammoths had roamed across the great plains.

And so, once again, the Family approached the Mountains at the End of the World.

Sheets of hard black volcanic rock thrust out of the soil. No trees grew here; nothing lived but straggling patches of grass and lichen that clung to the frost-cracked rocks. The last of the soil was frozen hard, as if winter never left this place, and the rock was slick with ice.

At last they reached the lower slopes of the Mountains themselves. Rock rose above them, dwarfing even Owlheart, the tallest of the mammoths; Silverhair could see how the rock face had been carved and shattered by frost. And the clamour of ice and shattering rock was deafening for the mammoths, making it impossible for them to sense what might lie beyond.

They walked in the lee of the Mountains, until they came to a great glacier. It lay in a valley gouged through the rock, just as a mammoth's tongue lies in her jawbone. The ice at the glacier's snout lay in greying, broken heaps across the frozen ground. But beyond, to the north, the glacier was a ribbon of dazzling white, a frozen river that disappeared into the mist of the Mountains, and it seemed to draw the staring Silverhair with it.

Foxeye said, 'We shouldn't be here. This isn't a place for mammoths. The Cycle says so . . .'

'*There is a way through the Mountains,*' said Owlheart.

'How do you know?' asked Foxeye.

Owlheart said, 'Wolfnose – my Matriarch – once told me a time when *she* was but a calf, and the Matriarch then had memories of long before . . . There was a Bull calf with more curiosity than sense. Rather like you, Silverhair. He went wandering off by himself. He followed a glacier into the Mountains, and he said it broke right through the Mountains to the northern side. Although he didn't follow it to its end—'

Suddenly Owlheart's audacious plan was clear to Silverhair. She stood before the glacier, awed. 'So this is a path broken through the Mountains by the ice. Just as mammoths will break a path through a forest.'

'And that's where we're going,' said Owlheart firmly. 'We're going beyond the Mountains at the End of the World, where no mammoth has ventured before—'

'And for good reason.' Foxeye rocked to and fro, stamping on the hard ground. 'Because it's impossible, no matter what that rogue calf said. *If* he ever existed. We don't even know what's there, land or sea or ice—'

For a heartbeat Owlheart's resolve appeared to waver. She seemed to slump, as if she were ageing through decades in an instant.

Silverhair laid her trunk on Foxeye's head. 'Enough,' she said gently. 'We must follow the Matriarch, Foxeye.'

Foxeye subsided. But her unhappiness was obvious.

Owlheart nodded to Silverhair. Her unspoken command was clear: Silverhair was to lead the way.

Heart pumping, Silverhair turned, and stepped on to the ice.

Mammoths do not spend much of the time on the bare ice, because there is no food to be had there; their habitat is the tundra. But Silverhair understood the glacier, from experience and lore.

At first she walked over cracked-off fragments of ice scattered over the rock. But soon, as she worked her way steadily forward, she found herself walking on a continuous sheet of ice. It was hard and cold under the pads of her feet, but she had little difficulty maintaining her footing.

But it was *cold*. The sun was warm on one side of her, but the immense mass of ice seemed to suck the heat from the other side of her body and her belly, and she could feel a wide and uncomfortable temperature difference from one side to the other.

She was climbing a steepening blue-white hillside, which rose above her. She enjoyed the crunchy texture of the snow underfoot. Lumps of blue ice pushed out of the snow around her, carved by the wind into fantastic shapes. Here and there shattered ice lay in fans across the white surface she was climbing. The glacier was a river of ice, seemingly motionless around her, but its downhill flow was obvious nonetheless. Lines of scoured-off rock in the ice surface marked the glacier's millennial course. The glacier's shuddering under her feet was continuous, and Silverhair could feel its agonisingly sluggish progress through its valley, and could hear the low-pitched grind and crack of the compressed ice as it forced its way through the rock, and the high-pitched scream of the rock itself being shattered and torn away.

She came to a place where the thickening ice was split by crevasses. When it flowed out of the mountains onto the tundra the glacier was able to spread out, like a stream splashing over a plain, and so it cracked open. Most of the crevasses followed the line of the glacier as it poured down its gouged-out channel in the rock. But some of them, more treacherous, cut across the line of the flow.

Most of the crevasses were narrow enough to step across. Some were bridged by tongues of ice, but Silverhair tested these carefully before leading the mammoths on to them. If a crevasse was too wide she would guide the mammoths along its length until it was narrow enough to cross in safety.

She looked into one deep crevasse. The walls were sheer blue ice, broken here and there only by a small ledge or a few frost crystals. The crevasse was cluttered by the remains of collapsed snow bridges, but past them she could see the crevasse's endless depth, the blue of the ice becoming more and more intense until it deepened to indigo and then to darkness.

In some places, where the glacier had lurched downwards, there were icefalls: miniature cliffs of ice, like frozen waterfalls. These were difficult to climb, especially where there were crevasses along the icefalls. And in some places where the glacier flowed awkwardly around a rock outcrop, the ice was shattered to blocks and shards by the shear stresses, and was very difficult to cross.

After a time, as the mammoths climbed up from the plain, there were fewer crevasses, and the going got easier. In some places the glacier was covered with hard white snow, but in others Silverhair found herself walking on clean blue unbroken ice. The blue ice wasn't flat, but was dimpled with cups and ridges. There were even frozen ripples here, their edges hard under her feet. It was exactly like walking over the frozen surface of a river.

When she looked back she could see the Family following in a ragged line: Foxeye with her two calves, and Owlheart bringing up the rear. They looked like hairy boulders, uncompromisingly brown against the blinding white of the ice.

She came to a chasm the glacier had cut deep into the mountain's rock. The mammoths were silent, even the calves, as they threaded through this cold, gloomy passage. Walls of hard blue-black rock towered above Silverhair. She could see scratches etched into the rock, and scattered over the ice there was sand, gravel, rocks, even boulders ripped out of place by the scouring ice.

At last the chasm opened out. Silverhair stepped forward cautiously, blinking as she emerged from the shadows.

She was surrounded by mountains.

She was on the lip of a natural bowl in the mountain range, a bowl which brimmed with ice; the mountain peaks, crusted with snow which would never melt, protruded above the ice like the half-buried tusks of some immense giant. The ice was trying to flow down to the plain below, but the mountains got in the way. The glaciers were the places where the ice leaked out. There were rings of frozen eddies and ripples, even waves, where the ice was pressing against the mountains' stubborn black rock faces.

The mammoths walked cautiously on to the ice bowl. There was nothing moving here but themselves, nothing before them but the plain of white ice, black rock, blue sky. But there was noise here: the distant cracks and growls and splintering crashes of ice avalanches, as great sheets broke away from the rocky faces all around them, a remote, vast, intimidating clamour. It was a clean, cold, silent place, white sprinkled with rugged black outcrops, the only smells the sharp tang of ice and the freezing musk of the mammoths themselves.

Silverhair heard her own breathing, and the squeak of the ice as it compressed under her feet. She felt small and insignificant, dwarfed by the majesty of her planet.

Owlheart stood alongside her. She was breathing hard

after the climb, and her breath steamed around her face. 'Just as the Cycle describes it. From the ice which pools here, the glaciers flow to the tundra.'

'And,' said Silverhair, 'no mammoth has ever gone further north than this.'

'No mammoth before today. *Look*.'

Silverhair followed the Matriarch's gaze. She saw that on the northern horizon the mountains were marked by a notch: another valley scoured out by glaciers. And beyond, she could see blue-grey sky.

'That's our way through,' said Owlheart.

Silverhair reached the ravine on the far side of the ice bowl, and found herself standing on the creaking mass of another glacier.

She looked down the way she must climb.

The view was startling. The glacier was a frozen torrent sweeping down its valley, turning around a bluff in the rock before spreading, flattening and shattering to shards. The rubble lines along its length made the flow obvious. They ran in parallel, turning together with each curve of the glacier. They looked like wrinkles in stretched skin.

There were even tributary glaciers running into this main body, like streams joining a river. But where the tributaries merged, the ice was cracked into crevasses, or else shattered and twisted into fields of chaotic blocks.

Despite its stillness, she could see the drama of the great ice river's gush through the broken mountains, the endless battle between the stubborn rock and irresistible ice. Where the mountains constricted the flow, the ice reared up in great shattered, frozen whirlpools; and standing ice-waves lapped at the base of black hills, truncated by millennia of frost-shatter. She heard the roar of massive avalanches, the shriek of splitting rock, the groan of the shifting ice, and the sullen voice of the wind as it moaned through the valleys of rock and ice.

It was a panorama of white ice, black rock, blue sky.

The way forward would be difficult; she knew they would be fortunate to reach the northern lands without mishap. And yet her spirit was lifted by the majesty of the landscape. Despite her troubles and her pain, she felt profoundly glad to be alive: to have her small place in the great Cycle, to have come here and witnessed *this*.

She pressed on, stepping cautiously over the shattered ice.

At first the going, over a shallow snowdrift, was easy. But then the drift disappeared, without warning, and she found herself descending a slope of steep, slick blue ice. And as she climbed down further, the horizon increasingly dropped away from her, suggesting deep ice falls or steep and fissured drops ahead.

Climbing down a glacier turned out to be much harder than climbing up one had been.

At least on the way up she had been able to see the ice falls and crevasses before she reached them; here, even the biggest obstacles were invisible, hidden by the ice's sharp falling curve, until she was on them. And with every step she took, her feet either twisted in the meltpits that marked the ancient, ribbed blue ice, or else broke through a crust of ice, jarring her already aching joints.

She came to a moraine, an unbroken wall of boulders that lay across her path. The line of debris had been deposited on the surface of the ice by centuries of glacial flow. She picked her way through the boulders, flinching when her feet landed on frost-shattered rock chips.

Now she came to a place where the ice, constricted by two towering black cliffs to either side, was shattered, split by great crevasses. In the worst areas a confusion of stresses criss-crossed the ice with crevasse after crevasse, and the land became a chaotic wilderness of giant ice pillars, linked only by fragile snow bridges.

She crept through this broken place by sticking close to the cliff to her left-hand side. The ice here, clinging to the rock, was marginally less shattered. In some places she found clear runs of blue ice, which were easier to negotiate. But even these were a mixed blessing, for the ice was ridged and hard under her feet – and it had been kept clear only by the action of a scouring wind, and when that wind rolled off the ice bowl behind her it drove billows of ice crystals into her eyes, each gust a slap.

Then she was past the crevasse field, and the rock walls opened out . . . and for the first time she could see the northern lands.

It was a plain of ice – nothing but ice, studded with trapped bergs, dotted here and there with the blue of water.

Her heart sank.

The glacier decanted on to a rocky shore littered with broken stone and scraps of ice. She walked forward. This might have been the twin of the Island's southern coast. The landfast ice was more thickly bound to the ground here than in the south, but she could see leads of clear water and dark steam clouds above them. There was no sign of vegetation, no grass or bushes or trees – nor, indeed, any exposed rock. Nothing but ice: a great sheet of it, over which nothing moved.

A huge floe was drifting close to the shore, and, cautiously, she stepped on to it. It tipped with a grand slowness, and she heard the crunch of splintering ice at its edge. The floe was pocked by steaming air-holes, through which peered the heads of seals.

As she watched, a seal reared out of the water to strike at an incautious diving sea bird, dragging it into the ocean. There was a swirl, a final, despairing squawk, and the seal's head erupted from the water with the bird's body crushed between its jaws. Then the seal thrashed its head from side to side with stunning violence, tearing the bird to pieces, literally shaking it out of its skin.

It was not a promising welcome for the mammoths, Silverhair thought.

Some distance to the west, a glacier was pushing its way into the sea ice. The pressure had made the ice fold up into great ridges around the tongue of the glacier, and in the depressions between the wind-smoothed ridges ice blocks had heaped up. At the tip of the glacier there was a sudden explosion, and a vast cloud of powdered snow shot up into the air. The roaring noise continued, and as the snow cleared a little, she saw that the snout of the glacier was splitting away, a giant ravine cracking its way down the thickness of the ice river, and a pinnacle of ice tipping away from the glacier, towards the sea. It was the long, stately birth of a new iceberg. In the low light of the sun the snow was pink, the new berg a deep sky-blue.

She could feel the ocean swelling beneath her feet, heard the groan of the shifting ice. The sky was empty save for the deep grey-blue of the far north, the colour of cold.

And she knew now that the ocean beneath her feet swept all the way to the north: all the way to the axis of the Earth.

Owlheart climbed aboard the floe beside her, making it rock. 'It's a frozen ocean,' the Matriarch said.

'Yes. We can't live here.'

'I feared as much,' said Owlheart. Her rumble was complex, troubled. 'But . . .'

Silverhair, uncertainly, wrapped her trunk around Owlheart's. She was not accustomed to comforting a Matriarch. 'I know. You had no choice but to try.'

'And now,' said Owlheart bitterly, 'at the fringe of this cursed frozen sea, we have nowhere to go.'

There was a distant clattering sound, intermittent, carried on the wind. Silverhair turned.

Something – complex, black and glittering – was flying along the beach from the west. Sweeping directly towards

199

Foxeye and her calves. Sending a clattering noise washing over the ice.

It was the light-bird of the Lost.

CHAPTER 3
THE CHASM OF ICE

The light-bird clattered over their heads like a storm. Owlheart reared up and pawed at the air. There was a stink of burning tar, a wash of downrushing wind from those whirling wings that drove the hair back from Silverhair's face. She could see Lost – two, three of them – cupped in the bird's strange crystal belly, staring down at her.

Silverhair and Owlheart hurried back to the shore, where Foxeye and her calves were waiting, cowering.

A faint scent of burning came to them on the salty breeze. The calves, huddling close to their mother, picked it up immediately; they raised their little trunks and trumpeted in alarm.

Silverhair looked along the beach, to the west, the way the bird had come. She could see movement, a strange dark rippling speckled with light. And there was a cawing, like gulls.

It was the Lost: a line of them, spread along the beach. And the light was the yellow fire of torches which they carried in their paws.

Owlheart rumbled and trumpeted; Silverhair had never seen her so angry. 'They pursue us even *here*? I'll destroy them all. I'll drag that monster from the sky and smash it to shards—'

Silverhair wrapped her trunk around the Matriarch's, and dragged her face forward. 'Matriarch. Listen to me. I've seen that light-bird before, at the camp of the Lost. It makes a lot of noise but it won't harm us. *There*—' She looked down the beach, at the approaching line of Lost. '*That* is what we must fear.'

201

'I will trample them like mangy wolves!'

'No. They will kill you before your tusks can so much as scratch them. *Think*, Matriarch.'

She could see the effort it took for Owlheart to rein in her Bull-like instincts to drive off these puny predators. 'Tell me what to do, Silverhair,' she said.

'We must run,' said Silverhair. 'We can outrun the Lost.'

'And then?' asked Owlheart bleakly.

'That is for tomorrow. First we must survive today,' said Silverhair bluntly.

'Very well. But, whatever happens today—' Owlheart tugged at Silverhair's trunk, urgently, affectionately. '*Remember me*,' she said, and she turned away.

Stunned, Silverhair watched the Matriarch's broad back recede.

The coastline here was mountainous. Black volcanic rock towered above the fleeing mammoths.

They came to another huge glacier spilling from the mountains, a cliff of ice that loomed over them. The beach was strewn with shattered ice blocks, and the glacier itself, a sculpture in green and blue, was cracked by giant ravines. The air which spilled down from within the ravines was damp and chill – cold as death, Silverhair thought.

They ran on, the three Cows panting hard, their breath steaming around their faces, the calves mewling and crying as their mother goaded them forward.

The cries of the Lost seemed to be growing louder, as if they were gaining. And still the light-bird clattered over their heads, its noise and tarry stink and distorted wind washing over them, driving them all close to panic.

Silverhair wished Lop-ear were here. He would know what to do.

Owlheart shuddered to a halt, staring along the beach. Foxeye and the calves, squealing, slowed behind her.

Silverhair came up to Owlheart. 'What is it?'

And now the wind swirled, and the stink reached Silverhair. A stink of flesh.

Strung across the beach was a series of heaps of stone and sand and ice. From each heap, oily black smoke rose up to the sky. The fire came from a thick dark substance plastered over the stones.

What burned there was mammoth.

Silverhair could smell it: bone and meat, and even some hair and skin, bound together by fat and dung. And one of the stone heaps was even crowned with a mammoth skull, devoid of flesh and skin and hair.

She recognised it immediately, and recoiled in horror and disgust. It was Eggtusk's skull.

Foxeye was standing still, shuddering. The two calves were staring wide-eyed at the fires, crying.

'We can't go through that,' growled Owlheart.

Silverhair was battling her own compulsion to flee this grisly horror. 'But we must. It's just stones and fire. We can knock those piles down, and—'

'No.' Owlheart trotted back a few paces and stared into the mouth of a great ravine in the glacier. 'We'll go this way. Maybe we'll find a way through. At least the light-bird won't be able to chase us there.' She prodded Foxeye. 'Come on. Bring the calves.'

In desperation Silverhair plucked at Owlheart's tail. 'No. Don't you see? That's what they want us to do.'

Owlheart swiped at her with her tusks, barely missing Silverhair's scarred cheek. 'This is a time to follow me, Silverhair, not to question.'

And she turned her back, deliberately, and led her Family into the canyon of ice.

Silverhair looked along the beach. One of the Lost was standing on a boulder before the others, waving his spindly forelegs in a manner of command. Silverhair could see the ice light glint from his bare scalp. It was Skin-of-Ice:

the monster of the south, come to pursue her, even here beyond the End of the World. She felt a black despair settle on her soul.

She followed her Matriarch into the ravine.

Immediately the air felt colder, piercing even the mammoths' thick coats. Immersed in ice, Silverhair felt the sting of frost in her long nostrils, and her breath crackled as it froze in the hair around her mouth.

Impatient to make haste, anxious to keep their footing, the mammoths filed through the chasm, furry boulder-shapes out of place in this realm of sculpted ice. The going was difficult; the ground was littered with slabs and blocks of cracked-off ice, dirty and eroded. With each step ice blocks clattered or cracked, and the sharp noises echoed in the huge silence.

Walls of ice loomed above Silverhair, sculpted by melt and rainfall into curtains and pinnacles. The daylight was reduced to a strip of blue-grey far above. But it wasn't dark here, for sunlight filtered through the ice, illuminating blue-green depths there.

It was almost beautiful, she thought.

Silverhair heard a clattering. She looked back to the mouth of the chasm. The light-bird hovered there, black and sinister. As Owlheart had predicted, it couldn't follow them here. Perhaps its whirling wings were too wide to fit within the narrow walls.

But on the ground she could see the skinny limbs of the Lost, the smoky light of their torches, as they clambered over ice blocks.

Owlheart had gone ahead of the others, deeper into the chasm. Now she returned, trumpeting her rage. 'There's no way out. A fall of ice has completely blocked the chasm.' She growled. 'Our luck is running out, Silverhair.'

'Luck has nothing to do with it,' said Silverhair. She felt awe: she was sure the Lost – in fact, Skin-of-Ice himself –

were behind every element of this trap: the burning fat and the skull, the driving of the mammoths into this chasm, and now the barrier at its rear. How was it possible for a mind to be so twisted as to concoct such complex schemes?

Owlheart rumbled, paced back and forth, struck the ground with her tusks. 'We aren't done yet. Listen to me. In some places, at the back of the chasm, the ice lies thin over the rock. And the rock is rotten with frost. Silverhair, go up there and dig. See if you can find a way out. If there's a way, take Foxeye and the calves. Get away from here and join up with one of the other Families.'

'Where?'

'Find them, Silverhair. It's up to you now.'

'What about you?'

Owlheart turned to face the encroaching Lost, and their fire glittered in her deep-sunken eyes. 'The Lost will have to clamber over my bloated corpse before they reach our calves.'

'Owlheart—'

'It will make a good story in the Cycle, won't it?' The Matriarch tugged at Silverhair's trunk one last time, and touched her mouth and eyes. 'Go to work, Silverhair, and hurry; you might yet save us all.'

Then she turned and faced the advancing Lost.

Silverhair turned to Foxeye, who stood over her terrified calves. 'They're trying to suckle,' Foxeye said, her voice all but inaudible. 'But I have no milk to give them. I'm too frightened, Silverhair. I can't even give them milk . . .'

'It's all right,' Silverhair said. 'We'll get out of here yet.' But the words sounded hollow to her own ears.

'They've come to destroy us, haven't they? Maybe Snagtooth was right. Maybe all we can do is throw ourselves on the mercy of the Lost.'

'The Lost *have* no mercy.'

Foxeye said bleakly, 'Then let them kill Owlheart, and spare me and my calves.'

Silverhair was shocked. 'You don't mean that. Listen to me. I'm going to save you. You and the calves. It isn't over yet, Foxeye; not while I have breath in my body.'

Foxeye hesitated. 'You promise?'

'Yes.' Silverhair shook her sister's head with her trunk. 'Yes, I promise. Wait here.'

She turned and ran, deeper into the chasm.

The ravine became so narrow that it would barely have admitted two or three mammoths abreast, and the wind, pouring down from the glacier above, was sharp with frost crystals. But Silverhair lowered her head and kept on, until she found the way jammed by the jumble of fallen ice Owl-heart had described.

The blocks here were sharp-edged and chaotically cracked, as if they had been broken off the ice walls above by the scraping of some gigantic tusk. Silverhair stared at the impassable barrier, wondering how even the Lost could have caused damage on such a scale so quickly.

She turned and worked her way back down the chasm. At last she found a patch of blue-black rock protruding through the ice walls. Perhaps the strength of the wind here had kept this outcrop free of frost and snow. But it was some distance above her head.

Before it, on the ground, there was a mound of scree – frost-shattered stone – mixed with loose snow and ice.

She stepped forward. The scree crunched and slithered under her feet. It was very tiring, like climbing up a snow bank. Small rocks began to litter the ice floor, broken off the rock face by frost, increasing with size until she found herself climbing past giant boulders.

A thunder-stick cracked.

Its sharp noise rattled from the sheer walls of the chasm. And now the screams of terrified mammoths echoed from the walls.

Every fibre in her being impelled Silverhair to lunge back

down the slope and return to her people. But she knew she must stick to her task.

She turned and resumed her climb.

When she could reach the rock face, Silverhair dug into the wall with her tusks. The rock was loosely bound and easily scraped aside. As Owlheart had predicted, the exposed rock was rotten. Water would seep into the slightest crack and then, on freezing, expand, so widening the crack. Lichen, orange and green, dug into the friable rock face, accelerating its disintegration. Gradually the rock was split open, in splinters, shards or great sheets, and over the years fragments had fallen away to form the slope of scree below her.

With growing urgency Silverhair ground her way deeper into the rotten rock. Soon she was working in a hail of frost-shattered debris, and she ignored the sharp flakes that dug into the soft skin of her trunk.

But the chasm was full of the screams of the calves, and she muttered and wept as she worked.

Then – quite suddenly – the wall fell away, and there was a deep, dark space ahead of her.

A cave.

Hope surged in her breast. With increased vigour she pounded at the rock face before her, using tusks, trunk, forehead, to widen the hole. The rock collapsed to a heap of frost-smashed rubble before her.

She reached forward with her trunk. There was no wall ahead of her. But she could feel the walls to either side, scratched and scarred. *Scarred* – by mammoth tusks? But how could that be, so deep under the ground?

There was a breath of air, blowing the hairs on her face. Air that stank of brine. Owlheart had been right; there must be a passage here, open to the air. And that was all that was important right now; mysteries of tusk-scraped walls could wait.

But would the passage prove too narrow to get through? She had to find out before she committed them all to a trap.

Scrambling over the broken rocks, she plunged into the exposed cavern. It extended deep into the rock face. There was no light here, but she could feel the cool waft of brine, hear the soft echo of her footfalls from the walls. She pushed deeper, looking for light.

And so it was that Silverhair did not see what became of Owlheart, as she confronted the troop of Lost.

The Lost advanced towards Owlheart, and their cries echoed from the walls.

The Matriarch reared up, raising her trunk and tusks, and trumpeted. Her voice, magnified by the narrow canyon walls, pealed down over the Lost, sounding like a herd of a thousand mammoths. And when she dropped back to the ground, her forefeet slammed down so hard they shook the very Earth.

But the Lost continued to advance.

After that first explosion of noise, the Lost had lowered their thunder-sticks and piled them on the ground. But now they raised up other weapons.

Here was a stick with a shard of rib or tusk embedded in its end. Here was a piece of shoulder blade, its edge sharpened cruelly, so huge it all but dwarfed the Lost who clutched it. And here were simple splinters of bone, held in paws, ready to slash and wound.

A chill settled around her heart. For they were weapons made of mammoth bone.

She put aside her primitive fear and assembled a cold determination. Whatever these Lost intended with this game of bones and sticks, the battle would surely take longer – win or lose – than if they used the thunder-sticks. If Silverhair stayed where she was and carried out her orders, they would have a chance.

Now one of the Lost came towards her. He was holding up a stick tipped with a bone shard.

She lowered her head, eyeing him. 'So,' she told him, 'you are the first to die.'

She waited for him to close with her. That thin wooden stick would be no match for her huge curved ivory tusks. She would sweep it aside, and then—

The Lost hurled his stick as hard as he could.

Utterly unexpected, it flew at her like an angry bird. The bone tip speared through her chest, unimpeded by the hair and skin and new summer fat there. She could feel it grind against a rib, and pierce her lung.

Staggering, she tried to take a breath. But it was impossible, and there was a sucking feeling at her chest.

Oddly, there was little pain: just a cold, clean sensation.

But her shock was huge. The Lost hadn't even closed with her yet – *but she knew she had taken her last breath.* As suddenly as this, with the first strike, it was over.

The Lost who had injured her knew what he had done. He was jumping up and down, waving his paws in the air in triumph.

Well, she thought, if this breath in my lungs is to be my last, I must make it count.

She plunged forward and twisted her head. The sharp tip of her right tusk cut clean through the skin and muscle of the throat of the celebrating Lost.

He looked down in disbelief as his blood spilled out over his chest and fell to the ice, steaming. Then he fell, slipping in his own blood.

Owlheart charged again, and now she was in amongst the Lost.

She reached out with her trunk, and grabbed one of them around the waist. He screamed, flailing his arms, as she lifted him high into the air. While she held him up, another bone-tipped stick was hurled at her chest. It pierced her skin but hit a rib, doing little damage. Impatiently she crashed her chest against the ice wall. There was an instant of agonising pain as the embedded sticks twisted her wounds a little further open, but then they broke away.

She tightened the grip of her mighty trunk until she felt the Lost's thin bones crack; he shuddered in her grip, then turned limp. She dropped him to the ice.

She longed to take a breath, but knew she must not try.

Two dead. She knew she would not survive this encounter, but perhaps it wasn't yet over; if she could destroy one or two more of the Lost, Silverhair and the others might still have a chance.

She looked for her next opponent. They were strung out before her, wary now, shouting, raising their sticks and shoulder blades.

She selected one of them. She raised her trunk and charged. He dropped his stick, screamed and ran. She prepared to trample him.

. . . But now another came forward. It was the hairless one, the one Silverhair called Skin-of-Ice.

He hurled a stick.

It buried itself in her mouth with such venomous power that her head was knocked sideways.

She fell. The stick caught on the ground, driving itself further into the roof of her mouth. The agony was huge.

She tried to get her legs underneath her. She knew she must rise again. But the ground was slippery, coated with some slick substance. She looked down, and saw that it was her own blood; it soaked, crimson and thick, into the broken ice beneath her.

And now the hairless Lost stood before her. He held up a shard of bone, as if to show it to her.

She gathered her strength for one last lunge with her tusk. He evaded her easily.

He stepped forward and plunged the bone into her belly, ripping at skin and muscle. Coiled viscera, black with blood, snaked on to the ice from her slashed belly. She tried to rise, but her legs were tangled in something.

Tangled in her own spilled grey guts.

She fell forward. She raised her trunk. Perhaps she could trumpet a final warning. But her breath was gone.

Within her layers of fat and thick wool, Owlheart had spent her life fighting the cold. But now, at last, her protection was breached. And the cold swept over her exposed heart.

In a cloud of rock dust, Silverhair burst out of her cavern, back into the chasm.

She was overwhelmed by the noise: the screams and trumpets of terrified mammoths, the calls and yelps of the Lost, the relentless clatter of the light-bird, all of it rattling from the sheer ice walls.

Owlheart had fallen.

Silverhair could see two of the Lost climbing over her flank. They were hauling bone-tipped sticks out of her side, and then plunging them deep into her again, as if determined to ensure she was truly dead.

But Owlheart had not given her life cheaply. Silverhair could see the unmoving forms of two of the Lost, broken and gouged.

Silverhair mourned her fallen Matriarch, and her courage. But it had not been enough. For the rest of the Lost were advancing towards Foxeye and the calves.

And Skin-of-Ice himself, bearing a giant stick tipped with sharpened bone, was leading them.

Foxeye seemed frozen by her fear. Sunfire, the infant, was all but invisible beneath the belly hairs of her mother. And Croptail, the young Bull, stepped forward; he raised his small trunk and brayed his challenge at the Lost.

Skin-of-Ice made a cawing noise, and looked to his companions. Silverhair, anger and disgust mixing with her fear, knew that the malevolent Lost, already stained with the blood of the Matriarch, was mocking the impossible bravery of this poor, trapped calf.

Silverhair raised her trunk and trumpeted. She started down the scree slope. 'Croptail! Get your mother. We can escape. Come on—'

The Lost looked up, startled. Some of them seemed afraid, she thought with satisfaction, to see another adult mammoth apparently materialise from the solid rock wall.

Perhaps that pause would give her a chance to save her Family.

The young Bull ran to his mother. He tugged at her trunk until she raised her head to face him.

But the Lost were closing, raising their sticks and claws of bone. Silverhair saw how one of them broke and ran to the thunder-sticks at the mouth of the cave. But Skin-of-Ice barked at him, and he returned. Silverhair felt cold. This was a game to Skin-of-Ice, a deadly game he meant to finish with his shards of bone and wood.

Silverhair tried to work out what chance they had. The ground was difficult for the Lost; Silverhair saw how they stumbled on the slippery, ice-coated rock, and were forced to clamber over boulders and ice chunks that the mammoths, with their greater bulk, could brush aside. And once the Family were safely in the tunnel, Silverhair would emulate Owlheart. She would make a stand and disembowel any Lost who tried to follow—

But now the shadows flickered, and an unearthly clatter rattled from the ice and exposed rock. She looked up and flinched. The light-bird was hovering over the chasm.

Two of the Lost were leaning precariously out of the bird's gleaming belly. They were holding something, like a giant sheet of skin. They dropped it into the cavern. It fell, spreading out as it did so. Silverhair saw that it was like a spider-web – but a web that was huge and strong, woven from some black rope.

And, as the Lost had surely intended, the web fell neatly over Foxeye and her calves.

Foxeye's humped head pushed upwards at the web, and

Silverhair could see the small, agitated form of Croptail. But the more the mammoths struggled, the more entangled they became. Sunfire's terrified squealing, magnified by the ice, was pitiful.

Silverhair started forward, trying to think. Perhaps she could rip the web open with her tusks—

But now there was a storm of thunder-stick shouts, a hail of the invisible stinging things they produced. Instinctively she scrambled up the scree slope to the mouth of her cave.

The fire came from the Lost leaning out of the belly of the light-bird. They were pointing thunder-sticks at her. Bits of rock exploded from the ground and walls.

Down in the chasm, the Lost were walking over the fallen webbing, holding it down with their weight where it appeared the mammoths might be breaking free. Skin-of-Ice himself clambered on top of Croptail's trapped, kneeling bulk. Almost casually, he probed through the net with his bone-tipped stick. Silverhair saw blood fount, and heard Croptail's agonised scream.

Her heart turned to ice.

. . . But the thunder-stick hail still slammed into the frost-cracked rock around her. Great shards and flakes flew into the air. She had no choice but to stumble back into her cave.

She trumpeted her defiance at the light-bird. As soon as the lethal hail diminished, she would charge.

But now there was a deeper rumbling, from above her head.

A great sheet of rock fell away from the chasm wall above the cave opening. Dust swirled over her. Then a huge chunk of the cave's roof separated and fell. She was caught in a vicious rain of rocks that pounded at her back and head, and the air became so thick with dust she could barely breathe.

Still she tried to press forward. But the falling rock drove her back, pace by pace, and the light of the chasm was hidden.

The last thing she heard was Foxeye's desperate, terrified wail. *'You promised me, Silverhair! You promised me!'*

Then, at last, Silverhair was sealed up in darkness and silence.

CHAPTER 4
THE CAVE OF SALT

Alone in the dark, Silverhair dug at the fallen boulders until she could feel the ivory of her tusks splintering against the unyielding rock, and blood seeped along her trunk from a dozen cuts and scrapes.

But the rocks, firmly wedged in place, were immovable.

She sank to her knees and rested her tusks on the invisible, uneven ground.

The calves had been captured – perhaps even now they were being butchered by the casually brutal Skin-of-Ice and his band of Lost. What was left for her now?

In the depths of her despair, she looked for guidance. And she found it in the last orders of her Matriarch.

She must seek out her Cousins: the other Families that had made up the loose-knit Clan of the Island, a Clan that had once been part of an almost infinite network of mammoth blood alliances that had spread around the world. Her way forward was clear.

. . . But what, a small voice prompted her, if there *were* no more Families to be found? What if the worst fears of Wolfnose and Lop-ear had come true?

She tried to imagine discovering such a terrible thing: how she would feel, what she would do.

She would, simply, have to cope, find a way to go on. For now she had her orders from the Matriarch, and she would follow them. And besides, she had a promise to her sister to keep.

But first she had to get out of this cave.

With new determination she got to her feet, shook off the

dust which had settled over her coat, and turned her head, seeking the breeze.

The cave was completely dark.

She moved with the utmost caution, her trunk held out before her. Her progress was slow. The floor was broken and uneven, the passage narrow and twisting, and she was afraid she might stumble over jagged rock or tumble into an unseen ravine.

And fear crowded her imagination. Mammoths, creatures of the open tundra, are not used to being enclosed; Silverhair tried not to think about the weight of rock and ice and soil that was suspended over her head.

But the echoes of her footsteps, crunching on ancient gravel, gave her a sense of a passageway stretching ahead of her. And there was the breeze: the slightest of zephyrs, laden with the sour stink of brine, somehow worming its way through cracks in the ground to this buried place.

And the breeze grew stronger, little by little, as she progressed.

But the passageway took her downwards.

As she moved deeper into the belly of the Earth, the air began to grow warmer. She heard the slow dripping of water from the walls, felt the channels those tiny drips had carved in the rock at her feet over the Great-Years. She licked the droplets from the wall. The water was cool and only a little salty, but there wasn't enough of it to quench her thirst.

At first the rising heat was comfortable – preferable, anyhow, to the dry, deathly chill of the ice chasm. Suspended here in the dark, she tried to imagine she was feeling the sun on her back, rather than the soulless, sourceless heat of deep rock.

But soon the warmth became less pleasant. She felt her heart race. She spread her ears as far as they would go, lifted her tail and opened her anus flap, opened her mouth and extended her tongue: all devices to let her body heat escape into this cloying air.

On she walked, deeper and deeper into the dark, and still the heat gathered.

At last the breeze felt a little cooler, and the quality of the echoes from the tunnel ahead changed. Underfoot the ground sloped, suddenly, much more sharply downwards.

She stopped.

The passage here, she sensed, broadened out into a wider cave. The mouth of her tunnel was set a little way above the floor of the cave. She extended her head and trunk into the empty space beyond the tunnel. The air here was much cooler, and she dropped her ears and anus flap.

With great care she worked her way down a shallow slope of scree to the floor of the cave.

She was still in complete darkness, but she could sense the great dome of this cave's ceiling far above her, like the roof of some giant mouth.

The breeze seemed to be coming from the opposite side of the cave. But she felt wary of striking out into the darkness.

So she began to feel her way along the wall.

The soft, gritty rock here was extensively scratched and scoured. She ran the sensitive tip of her trunk over furrows and grooves.

They were unmistakably the marks of mammoth tusks.

The scrapings of tusks were everywhere, even – she suspected – higher than she could reach herself. She imagined huge old Bulls reaching high up with their gigantic tusks to bring down fresh rock for their Families.

When she ventured a few paces away from the wall, she found the uneven floor littered with mammoth dung. It was obvious that the whole of this cavern had been shaped by the working of mammoths, over generations. But when she picked up some of the dung and broke it open, it crumbled, dry as dust. It was very old, and it was evident that no mammoth had been here for many years.

She used her own tusk to scrape free pebble-sized lumps of rock from the wall. She picked them up, tucked them in her mouth, ground them to sand with her huge teeth and swallowed them. The rock's flavour was deliciously sharp: perhaps born from an ancient volcano, this loose, ash-like rock was evidently rich in salt and other minerals the mammoths needed.

The reason for the mammoths' presence here was clear. Mammoths need salt and other minerals, as do other animals. But their tongues are not long enough to reach around their trunks and tusks to salt-licks, exposed out-croppings of salty minerals. So they dig them up, using their tusks to loosen the earth. This whole cavern system might once have been a simple seam of soft, salty rock into which the mammoths had dug, until at last they had shaped this giant cave and the tunnels that led to it.

Silverhair held fragments of the rock on her tongue, relishing the salty taste and the rich, ancient mammoth smell of the place, as if she were tasting the living past itself. She walked on, surrounded by the workings of her ancestors, obscurely comforted.

At last she came to a heap of scree. The fresh breeze seemed to be spilling from a hole somewhere above her head. It must be another tunnel.

She clambered on to the scree. Her feet scrabbled to get a foothold in the unstable mass; it took several efforts before she had raised herself sufficiently to get her forelegs over the lip of the tunnel. But then it was a simple matter to pull herself all the way in.

She turned her back on the salt cave and marched on, into the darkness.

She felt the tunnel floor rising. The walls closed around her uncomfortably; if she took a step to either side she brushed against warm rock. But, as she climbed, she felt a delicious, welcoming chill return to the air. The breeze she had followed continued to strengthen.

And, ahead of her now, she made out splinters of green-blue light.

Gradually, as her eyes adapted better, she saw that the pale-green glow was outlining the walls and floor and roof of her tunnel. She could even make out the larger boulders on the floor, and she was able to press forward with confidence.

At last she came to a new chamber. Like the first she had found, this chamber had evidently been hollowed out by mammoths. But this one was flooded with light. The low rocky roof had collapsed. She could see great slabs of rock scattered over the floor, gouged cruelly by the ice, and only spires and pinnacles of rock remained. But the cave was enclosed by a roof of ice.

In some places the ice was smooth and bare. Elsewhere the roof was made of snow, with thick white pillars and balls of ice crusting its under-surface, all of it glowing blue-white. Some of the roof ice had broken off and pieces of it lay scattered over the floor with the rock chunks. Perhaps this was an outlying tongue of a glacier, strong enough to bridge this hole in the ground, thin enough to let through the light.

But the light was very dim here. The sunlight was scattered by the ice and turned to a deep, extraordinary blue, translucent, richer than any colour she had seen before. Silverhair wouldn't have been surprised to see Siros, the water-loving calf of Kilukpuk, come swimming through the air towards her, her legs reduced to stubby flippers.

She worked her way around the gouged walls.

Most of the scouring was functional: simple scrapes, often ending in a ragged scar where a chunk of the salty rock had been prised away. But some of the gouging here was strange. There were marks that were small and grouped in compact patterns, and they seemed to have been made with a great deal of care. At the base of the wall she found pebbles – and even a chipped-off piece of tusk – that looked as if they had been picked up and used to mould the gouges just so.

As she stared at them, the patterns were somehow familiar.

Here was a simple series of down-scrapes – but for a heartbeat Silverhair could *see*, as if looking beyond the scrapes, a dogged mammoth standing alone in a winter storm, thick winter hair dangling around her. And here two little clusters of scrapes became a Cow with her calf, who suckled busily.

But then she lost the images, like losing her grasp on a lush strand of grass, and there were only crude gouges in the salty rock.

These markings came from a richer time: a time when there were so many mammoths on the Island they were forced to dig far underground in search of salty rock, and they were so secure they had the time and energy to record their thoughts and dreams in scrapings on the walls. It must have taken a Great-Year to make these caves, she thought; but the mammoths (before *now*, at any rate) had never been short of time.

If only she understood what she was seeing, she thought, she might find the wisdom of another Cycle here: not songs passed down from mother to calf, but messages locked for ever in the face of the rock. Lop-ear would surely have understood these images: she remembered the way he had scraped at the frost, making markings to show her the Island as a bird would see it. Lop-ear would have been happy here, she realised: happy surrounded by the frozen thoughts of his ancestors.

But all the dung was dry and odourless, very old; and the wall markings were coated by layers of hardy lichen, orange and green, fuelling their perennial growth with ice-filtered light.

It had been the scraping of mammoths that had opened up the passages she followed, even the underground caves she had found. And now it was the patient work of those long-gone mammoths that was providing her with a means of escape from the Lost. Had they known, as they dug and shaped the Earth, that their actions would have such dramatic consequences for the future?

Encouraged by the presence of her ancestors, she walked on into the dark, and the gathering breeze.

And, after only a little more time, she emerged from a rocky mouth into summer daylight.

The fresh air and the light brought her relief, but no joy.

She clung to Owlheart's instructions about seeking out help, about joining with another Family, if it could be found. So she began a wide detour towards the south-east of the Island. There was a place she had visited as a calf, many years ago, where the land was hummocky and uneven, and there were many deep, small ponds. Here – held the wisdom of the Clan – even in the hardest winter, it was often possible to smash through the thinner ice with a blow from a tusk, and reach liquid water.

And here, she hoped, she would find signs of the other Families of the Clan: if not the mammoths themselves, then at least evidence that they had been here recently, and maybe some clue about which way they had gone, and where she could find them.

If not here, she thought grimly, then nowhere.

But as she worked her way south, still she saw no signs of other mammoth Families.

She walked on, doggedly.

The tundra was still alive with flowers. There were bright-purple saxifrages, mountain avens studded with white flowers, and cushions of moss campion with their tiny white blossoms. Silverhair found a cluster of Arctic poppies, their cup-shaped yellow heads turning to the sun; they were drenched with dew where a summer fog had rolled over them, bringing them valuable moisture. Even on otherwise barren ground, the grass grew thick and green around the mouths of Arctic fox burrows, places fed by dung and food remains, perhaps for centuries.

All the plants were adapted to the extreme cold, dryness and searing winds of the Island. They grew in clumps: tussocks, carpets and rosettes, and their leaves were thick and waxy, which helped them retain their water.

But already the summer was past its peak.

The insect life was dying back. The hordes of midges, mosquitoes and blackflies were gone; the adults, having laid their eggs long ago, were all dead, leaving the larvae to winter in the soil or pond water. Spiders and mites were seeking shelter in the soil or the litter of decaying lichen and vegetation.

Birth, a brief life of light and struggle, rapid death. Silverhair sensed the mass of the baby inside her, and her heart was heavy. Would she be able to give her own child even as much as this, as the short lives of the summer creatures?

Through the briefly teeming landscape, oblivious to the riot of colour, Silverhair walked stolidly on.

Seeking to build up her strength for whatever lay ahead, she took care to feed, drink and pass dung properly. Feeding was, briefly, a pleasure at this time of year, for the berries were ripe. She munched on the bright-red cranberries, yellow cloudberries, midnight-blue bilberries and inky-black crowberries which clustered on leathery plants. But there was a tinge of sadness about this treat, for the ripening berries were another sign of the autumn that was already close.

After a few days she could hear the soft lapping of water, smell the thick scummy greenness of the life that gathered in the deep ponds of this corner of the Island.

But there was still no sign of mammoth: no stomping, no contact rumbles, no smell of fur and milk.

And at last she came to the place of the ponds, and her heart sank. For she found herself treading on the bones of a young mammoth.

When he died he – or she – must have been about the same age as Croptail. The scavengers and the frost had left little of the youngster's skin and fur, and the cartilage, tendon and ligament had been stripped from the bones, which were separated and scattered. Some of the bones bore teeth marks, and some had been broken open, she saw, by a wolf or fox eager to suck the nourishing, fatty marrow from inside.

He must have been dead for months.

She touched the scattered bones with her feet, in a brief moment of Remembering. But she knew she could not linger here. For ahead of her – between herself and the glimmering surface of the ponds – there was a field full, she saw now, of stripped and scattered bones.

She walked forward with caution and dread.

Soon there were so many bones, so badly scattered, it was impossible even to pick out individuals. But still, she could see from their size that most of those who had died here had been youngsters – even infants. And as she approached the ponds, the bones were larger – just as dead, but the bones of older calves and adults.

The tundra here was badly trampled, and all but stripped bare of grass and shrubs; even months of growth hadn't been enough for it to recover. And the bones, too, were badly scattered and trampled. She found crushed skulls, ribs smashed and scored with the marks of mammoth soles. And there were snapped-off tusks, evidence of brief and bitter battles.

There had been little Remembering here, she saw with sadness. It was as the Cycle teaches: *Where water vanishes, sanity soon follows.*

It was becoming horribly clear what had happened here.

As the pressure to find water had grown, so the discipline of this Family had broken down. Probably the youngest – pushed away from the waterholes by their older siblings, even their parents, and too small anyway to reach the water through thick ice with their little tusks – had gone first. Then the oldest and weakest of the adults.

The diminishing survivors had trampled over the bodies of their relatives – perhaps even digging through the fallen corpses to get to the precious liquid – until they, in their turn, had succumbed.

It had been a rich time for the scavengers, and the cubs of Aglu.

The destruction was not thorough; few of the bones close to the water had been gnawed by the wolves, she saw. But then there had been no need to root in rotting corpses for sustenance; the wolves had only to wait for another mammoth to fall and offer them warm, fresh meat and marrow.

At last she reached the ponds at the grisly heart of this tableau. The ponds brimmed, their surfaces thick with green summer life, swarms of insects buzzing over them. Their fecundity mocked the mammoths who must have come here in the depths of the dry winter, desperate for the water that could have kept them alive.

Silverhair realised that, but for the wisdom of Owlheart, her own Family might have succumbed like this.

Silverhair stood tall, and surveyed the tundra. The land was teeming with life, the hum of insects, the lap of water, the cries of birds and small mammals.

But nowhere was there the voice of a mammoth.

With these bones, Silverhair knew at last that the fears of Lop-ear and Wolfnose were confirmed. Ten thousand years after Longtusk had led his Family here, *there were no more mammoths on the Island*. The winter's dryness had taken the last of the Families – the last but her own.

And now those few survivors were in the hands of the remorseless Lost.

She was alone: the only mammoth in all the world who was alive, and free to act.

She shivered, for she knew that all of her people's history funnelled through her mind and heart now. If she failed, then so would the mammoths, for all time.

. . . And yet, hadn't she already failed? In her foolishness she had ignored the teaching of the Cycle, and had gone to seek out the Lost. And by doing that she had made them aware of the existence of her Family, had caused the deaths of Eggtusk and Lop-ear and Snagtooth and Owlheart, and the trapping of Foxeye and her cubs – all of it was *her fault*.

She sank to the bone-littered ground, heavy with despair.

Alone, desolate, with no Matriarch to guide her – as she'd been trained since she was a calf – she turned to the Cycle.

Mammoths have no gods, no devils. That is why they find it so hard to comprehend the danger posed by the Lost. Instead, mammoths accept their place in the great rhythms of the world, their place in past and future, as Earth's long afternoon winds through the millennia.

But mammoths have existed for a very, very long time; and, the wisdom goes, nothing that happens today is without precedent in the past. Somewhere in the Cycle lies the answer to any question. *Everybody alive is descended from somebody smart enough to survive the past:* that is the underlying message of the Cycle. *But you must not worship your ancestors. The sole purpose of your ancestors' existence was your life. And the sole purpose of your life is your calves'.*

Somehow she felt comforted. Even here, in this place of death, she was not alone; she had the wisdom of all her ancestors back to Kilukpuk, the growing heavy warmth of the creature in her womb, the promise that her calves would one day roam the Sky Steppe.

. . . And that promise, she realised, could only be kept *if Foxeye and the calves were still alive*. For, it seemed, there was no other mammoth Family left anywhere in the world, no

225

other Family which could populate that fabulous land of the future.

In that case, it was up to Silverhair – the last free mammoth – to save her Family from the Lost. She would make her way to the south of the Island, to the foul nest of the Lost. And this time she would enter it, not as a weakened, starved captive, but strong and free. She would destroy Skin-of-Ice and all his works. She would keep her promise to Foxeye and free her Family. And then—

And then, the Cycle would guide her once more into the unknown future.

Treading carefully between the scattered heaps of bones, she resumed her steady march south.

CHAPTER 5
THE UNDERSEA TUNDRA

At last, after many empty days, she reached the southern coast.

Once more she tramped along the narrow shingle beach. The sky was littered with scattered, glowing clouds, and the calm, flat seascape of floating ice pans perfectly mirrored the sky. Brown kelp streamers lay thickly on the moist stones.

She moved with great caution as she neared the site of the Lost nest, and listened hard for the clattering flap of the light-bird. Her heart pumped. She knew that her best chance would be to surprise the Lost, to charge into their camp and overwhelm them with her flashing tusks.

But there was no noise save the washing of the sea, no smell save the rich salt brine.

No sign of the Lost.

And her plans and speculations dissipated as she reached the nest site.

The camp was abandoned. Only a few blackened scars on the beach showed where the Lost had built their fires; only a few rudimentary shelters remained to show where they had hidden from the rain and wind.

Silverhair ached with frustration. She had been prepared for battle here, and there was no battle to be had. Her blood fizzed through her veins, and her tusks itched with the need to impale the soft belly of a Lost.

She found the stakes to which she had been pinned for so long, still stained black with her blood. And she found the web of black rope which had trapped Foxeye. Rust-brown calf hair was caught in the web. She held the hair to her mouth.

She could taste Sunfire. The Family had been brought here, then.

There was a clatter of whirling wings. She turned, raised her trunk and trumpeted her defiance.

The noise was indeed the light-bird. But it was far away, she saw: on the other side of the Channel, in fact, hovering over the Mainland, which was clear of fog and storm at last; its ugly noise was brought to her by the vagaries of the breezes.

She understood what had happened. The Lost had returned to the Mainland, whence they had come.

There was no sign that the Family had died here; if such a slaughter had taken place the beach would be littered with bones and hair and scraps of flesh and skin. Then – if they were not dead – the mammoths must have been taken to the Mainland too.

If she was to save them, that was where Silverhair must go.

She walked down the beach and stood at the edge of the Channel between Island and Mainland.

In stark contrast to the dry colours of the late-summer landscape, a wide stretch of sea was still white: packed solid by flat ice. Along the shoreline, however, there was a wide band of clear water interspersed with stranded icebergs, many of them grotesquely shaped by continual melting and refreezing. Ivory gulls perched on the highest bergs, and beside the smaller blocks lodged on the tide-line ran little groups of turnstone and sanderling. The wading birds pecked at crustacea among the litter of kelp. The best feeding place for the creatures of the sea was the ice-edge, where the ice met the open sea. She could see many murres working there, their high-pitched calls echoing as their thick bills bobbed into the water. The cries of the birds were overlaid with the deep, powerful breathing of beluga – white whales, their sleek bodies easily as massive as Silverhair's, and capped by a long, spiralling tusk – and narwhal, mottled grey, pods of them cruising the ice-edge or diving beneath the ice itself.

A large bearded seal broke the surface near the coast, regarded Silverhair with big sad eyes, then ducked beneath the ice-strewn water once more.

To get to the Mainland, Silverhair would have to cross this teeming water-world.

She remembered standing on this shore with Lop-ear – her reluctance even to dip her trunk in the sea – his playful calls to the Calves of Siros.

Once, Longtusk had crossed this Channel to bring his Kin to the Island. It had been a great migration, with thousands of mammoths delivered to safety. But the Cycle was silent about how Longtusk did it. Some said he flew across the water. If Silverhair could fly now, she would.

But on one point the Cycle was absolutely clear: Longtusk himself did not survive the passage.

Today, then, she must outdo Longtusk himself.

Silverhair gathered her courage. She stepped forward.

Thin landfast ice crunched around her feet. The water immediately soaked through the thick hair over her legs, and its chill reached her skin. She could feel the water seeping up the hairs dangling from her belly, and more ice broke around her chest.

She stumbled, and suddenly the water flooded over her chest and back and forced its way into her mouth. She scrambled backward, coughing, a spray of water erupting from her mouth. But she lost her footing again and slipped sideways, and suddenly her head was immersed.

She fought brief panic.

She stood straight and lifted her head out of the water, opened her mouth and took a deep draught of air. The water felt tight around her chest, like a band of ice.

Dread flooded her. She remembered the stream of runoff which had almost killed her as a calf. She had been so small then, and the stream – which she could probably ford easily now – had been a lethal torrent, no less intimidating than the Channel which faced her now. She longed to turn and flee back to the land, to abandon this quest.

But she knew this was only the beginning.

Deliberately she took another step forward. The ice, cracking, brushed against her chest. She lifted her head back as far as it could go, trying to keep her eyes and mouth out of the water. But at last the water was too deep, and it closed over her head.

The cold was shocking, like a physical blow, so intense it made her gasp.

She forced herself to open her eyes.

The water was grey-green, and its surface was a glimmering sheet above her. She could see floating ice, thin grey slabs of it over her head.

She thrust her trunk through the surface so that it protruded from the water. She blew, hard, to clear her trunk of water, and sucked in deep lungfuls of clean, salty air. She could feel her chest drag against the heavy pressure of the water, which was trying, it seemed, to crush her ribs like a trampled egg. But she could breathe.

She was floating in the water, submerged save for her trunk, her body hair waving around her. Instinctively she surged forward, dragging at the water with her forelegs, kicking with her hind legs. Soon she could see how she was pushing through the clumps of ice which littered the surface, and the air was whistling easily into her lungs.

Now all she had to do was keep this up for the unknown time it would take to cross the Channel – and overcome the savage current and whatever other dangers might lurk in the deeper water – and emerge, exhausted, on to a beach crawling with Lost . . .

Enough. She clung to the Cycle. *You can only take one*

breath at a time. Her other problems could wait until she faced them.

On she swam, into the silent dark, alone.

The sun was low to the west, and it showed as a glimmering disc suspended above the water's rippling surface. She knew that as long as she kept the sun's disc to her right side, she would continue to head south, towards the Mainland.

Away from the coast the pack ice formed a more solid mass, though there were still leads of open water, and holes broken through by melting, or perhaps by seals and bears.

She took a deep breath, pulled down her trunk, and ducked beneath the ice. She would have to swim underwater between the air holes as if she were a seal herself.

She drifted under a ceiling of ice that stretched as far as she could see. There was a carpet of green-brown algae clinging to the ceiling, turning the light a dim green; but in places where the algae grew more thinly, the light came through a clearer blue-white.

And there were creatures grazing on this inverted underwater tundra: tiny shrimp-like creatures which clung to the algae ceiling, and comb jellies which drifted by, trailing long tentacles. She could see how the tentacles were coated with fine, hair-like cilia which pulsed in the current, sparkling with fragmented colour.

The comb jellies, unperturbed by the strange, clumsy intruder, sailed off into the darker water like the shadows of clouds.

She approached an air hole. The sunlit water under the hole was bright with dust. But when she drew near she saw that the 'dust' was a crowd of tiny, translucent animals. She reached the air hole and her head bobbed out of the water's chill, oily calm into the chaotic clamour of light above—

And a polar bear's upraised paw cuffed at her head.

Silverhair trumpeted in alarm.

The bear, just as startled, slithered backwards over the ice floe, its black eyes fixed on this unexpected intruder.

Silverhair panted, her breath frosting. 'Sorry I'm not a fat seal for you,' she said. And she took another deep breath, and ducked back into the sea's oleaginous gloom.

The going got harder as she headed further out to sea.

The ice was very thick here, and huge water-carved blocks and pinnacles were suspended from the ceiling. Salty brine, trapped within the ice, was leaking down to cause this strange, beautiful effect. It was like swimming through a series of caves.

She had to swim an alarmingly long way between air holes.

Once a seal fearlessly approached Silverhair. It seemed to swim with barely a flick of its sleek body – an embarrassing comparison to Silverhair's untidy scrambling – and the ringed pattern of its skin rippled in the water. The seal studied her with jet-black eyes, then turned and swam lazily into the murky distance.

She neared the ice-edge with relief, for she would be able to breathe continually when she passed it. But there was a great deal of activity here. She glimpsed the white shapes of beluga whales sliding in a neat diamond formation through the water. Occasionally there were the brief, spectacular dives of birds hunting fish, explosions from the world of light and air above into this calm darkness.

She drove herself on, past the ice-edge, and into open water.

There was no ice above her now, and no bottom visible beneath her, and she soon left behind the busy life of the ice-edge: there was just herself, alone, suspended in an unending three-dimensional expanse of chill, resisting water.

The current here, far from the friction of the banks of the Channel, was much stronger, and she struggled to keep to her course. And, as she swam on, she could feel the heat of her body leaching out into this unforgiving sea.

As her warmth leaked away, her energy seemed to dissipate with it.

It was as if this infinity of murky, chill water was the only world she had ever known: as if the world above of air and sunlight and snow, of play and love and death, was just some gaudy dream she had enjoyed before waking to this bleak reality . . .

Suddenly her trunk filled with water. She coughed, expelling the water through her mouth. She scrabbled at the water until she was able to raise her face and mouth above the surface. She opened her mouth to take a deep, wheezing breath, and glimpsed a deep-blue sky.

She must have weakened – let herself sink – perhaps even, bizarrely, slept for a heartbeat.

But already she was sinking again.

She continued to kick, but her legs were exhausted. And when she tried to raise her trunk, she couldn't reach the air. The surface was receding from her, slow as a setting sun.

Waterlogged, she was sinking. And hope seeped out of her with the last of her warmth. She would die here, in this endless waste of water, she and her calf.

So the Cycle, after all, culminated in a lie: there would be no rescue for her Family, no glowing future for the mammoths on the Sky Steppe.

She found herself thinking of Lop-ear, that first time they had come to the southern coast: how, in the sunshine, he had teased her and tried to goad her into the water, and told her tall stories of the Calves of Siros. If she had shared Lop-ear's gift for original thinking, was there any way she could have avoided this fate?

. . . *The Calves of Siros*. Suddenly, sinking in the darkness and the cold, she had an idea.

She tried to remember the sounds Lop-ear had made when he had called for the Calves of Siros. She had to get it right;

she had only one lungful of air, and would get only one chance at this.

She began a low-pitched whistle, punctuated by higher squeals, squawks and shrieks. The sound rippled away into the black water around her. She kept up the noise until the last wisp of her air was expended.

But not even an echo replied.

She stopped kicking, and let the current carry her. She had fallen so far now the surface was reduced to a vague illumination far above. She could feel the ocean turn her slowly around, as she drifted with it.

A deeper blackness was closing around her vision. The pain in her empty lungs, the ache of her exhausted limbs, the vaguer ache of the wounds inflicted by the Lost – all of it began to recede from her, as the cold forced her to shrink deep into the core of her body.

It was almost comfortable. She knew this ordeal would not last much longer.

. . . And now a sheet of hard blackness rose from the depths beneath her. Perhaps this was death, come to meet her.

But she hadn't expected death to have sleek fur, a fluked tail, stubby flippers, and a small, seal-like head which peered up at her out of the gloom.

The rising surface pushed softly against her feet and belly. She could feel a great body swathed in fat, strong muscles working.

And suddenly she was rising again.

She burst into light and air. It was like being born. She coughed, clearing water from her trunk and mouth, and air roared into her starved lungs.

Gradually, the pain in her chest subsided. She was still floating in the water, but now her trunk lay against a great black body, and she was able to hold herself out of the ocean easily. Strong tail flukes held up her head, and the skin under her face was rough as bark.

The creature under her was huge, she realised: at least twice her own body length, and covered with the dense black hair of a seal.

A small head twisted back to look at her. She heard squeals and chirrups, alternating low whistles and high-toned bleats. It was *speech:* indistinct but nevertheless recognisable.

'. . . See you I. Paddling through water see you I. Recognise mammoth I. Mammoth better swimmer than old sea cow think I. Understand you?'

'Yes,' Silverhair said, and the effort of speech made her cough again. 'I understand. Thanks . . .'

The sea cow's long muscles rippled. To Silverhair's surprise, a gull came flapping out of the sky and landed in the middle of the sea cow's broad back. The gull started to peck at the damp hair there, plucking out parasites, and the sea cow wriggled with pleasure. 'You here are why? Not roll on tundra do sea cows.' And the sea cow raised her small muzzle and whistled at her own joke.

'I have to get to the Mainland,' said Silverhair.

'Mainland? Kelp good there. Mmm. Kelp.' The sea cow looked dreamy. 'But not there go sea cows. Why? *Lost* there.'

'You know about the Lost?'

'Lost? Find me they if, drag me from sea they, eat my kidneys they, leave handsome body for gulls they. Terrible, terrible.'

'I have met the Lost,' said Silverhair.

'Think sea cows all gone Lost. Live in seas in south some Cousins. Here think kill us Lost, long time ago gobble up our kidneys Lost. But wrong they. But not Mainland go to I, kelp or no. Stay by Island. On Island no Lost.'

'There are now,' said Silverhair grimly.

'Terrible, terrible,' said the sea cow, sounding dismayed. 'Go to Mainland you, why if Lost there?'

'I have to,' said Silverhair. 'They took my Family.'

The sea cow rolled in the water, almost throwing Silver-hair off. 'Terrible thing. Terrible Lost. Here. Hold on to me you.' And she held out a stubby, clawed flipper. Silverhair wrapped her trunk around it.

The broad flukes beat, sending up a spray which splashed over Silverhair. The sea cow's broad, streamlined bulk began to slide easily through the water, oblivious to the current which had defeated Silverhair, unimpeded even by the bulk of an adult mammoth clinging to one flipper. Soon her speed was so great that a bow wave washed around her small, determined head.

Her power was exhilarating.

The sea cow pushed easily through the loose, decaying landfast ice that fringed the shore of the Mainland.

Silverhair's feet crunched on hard shingle.

She let go of the sea cow's flipper. She stumbled forward up a steepening slope, until she had dragged herself clear of the sea. Already frost was forming on her soaked fur, and she shook herself vigorously. Soon the warmth of the after-noon summer sun was seeping into her.

The sea cow used her stubby flippers to haul herself further out of the water, so her bulk was lying on the shingle bed, her great broad back exposed. She began munching contentedly on a floating scum of brown kelp fronds. She chewed with a horny plate at the front of her mouth, for she didn't appear to have any teeth. 'Kelp. Mmm. Want some you?'

'Thanks – no.'

Now she was raised so far out of the water, Silverhair could see how strange the sea cow looked: a head and flippers much like a seal's, but trailing a great bulbous body and a powerful split fluke, as if the front half of a seal had been attached to a beluga whale. Out of the water she was ponderous and looked stranded. Silverhair could see why her kind had been such easy pickings for the Lost, before the sea cows had learned to hide and feign extinction.

Silverhair looked back at the dark, sinuous waters of the Channel. 'But for you,' she told the sea cow, 'I'd still be out there now. There for ever.'

The sea cow's fluke beat at the water. 'Oath of Kilukpuk. Hyros and Probos and Siros. Forgot that you?'

'No,' said Silverhair quietly. 'No, we haven't forgotten.' And she was filled with warmth as she realised that one of the most ancient and beautiful passages of the Cycle had been fulfilled, here on this desolate beach.

The Calves of Kilukpuk had been separated for more than fifty million years. But they hadn't forgotten their Oath.

The sea cow rolled gracefully and slid into deeper water. 'Stick to tundra next time you. Watch out for Lost you. Good luck, Cousin.' Her stubby flippers extended, and she slid beneath the ice-strewn waves.

And Silverhair, her trunk raised and every half-frozen hair prickling, walked slowly up the shingle beach, into the land of the Lost.

CHAPTER 6
THE CITY OF THE LOST

Everywhere on this ugly Mainland beach there was evidence of the Lost: chunks of rusting metal, splashes of dirty oil which stained the ice, scraps of the strange loose outer skin they wore. There were structures, long and narrow, which pushed out from the beach towards the water; at the end of these structures were more of the shell-like objects like the one she had seen on the ice floe, on her first encounter with Skin-of-Ice. But where the thing on that ice floe had been damaged, these seemed intact; they floated on the grey water, though some were embedded in the ice. Perhaps they were supposed to ferry the Lost across the water, she mused.

She walked over a line of scrubby dunes at the edge of the beach, and reached the tundra. There was grass and sedge, and even a few Arctic willows; but the ground was poor – polluted by more of the black sludgy oil which had marred the beach – and broken up by long, snaking tracks. There was a stink of tar, and a strange silence, an emptiness that was a chilling contrast to the Island's rich summer cacophony.

And everywhere there were straight lines: the hard signature of the Lost, the symbol of their dominance over the world around them.

The most gigantic line of all was a hard-edged surface set in the tundra, black and lifeless. It was a road that proceeded – straight as a shaft of sunlight – to the heart of the City of the Lost.

The City itself was the sight she had seen many times from the safety of the headland on the Island: a tangle of shining

238

tubes and tanks, randomly cross-connected, sprinkled with glowing point lights, like captive stars. From tall columns oily black smoke billowed into the air, its tarry stink overpowering even the sharp tang of brine.

The City was huge, sprawling over the tundra. It must be the Lost's prime nest, she thought. And that was where she must go.

She stepped away from the road. She found a place where the tundra wasn't quite so badly scarred, and there was grass and willow twigs to graze. She deliberately pushed the food into her mouth, ground it up and swallowed it. She found a stream. It was thin and brackish, but it tasted clean; the cold water seemed to revive her strength a little.

She noticed a carpet of lemming holes and runs, and droppings from the predator birds which hunted the little rodents. So there was life here.

And she glimpsed an Arctic fox, the last of its white winter fur clinging to its back. The fox's coat was patchy and discoloured, the nodes of its spine protruding from its back. As soon as the fox saw her, its hairs stood on end. Then it dropped its muzzle, as if in shame, and slunk away.

Silverhair thought she understood. This creature had abandoned the tundra and had learned to live in the corners of the world of the Lost. But it was a poor bargain. She wondered if, in some deep recess of its hind brain, the fox still longed for the open freedom and rich, clean silence of the tundra its ancestors had abandoned.

Her feeding done, she passed dung, the movement fast and satisfying. The world seemed vivid around her, ugly and distorted as it was here on the Mainland. If this was to be her day to die then there would be a last time for everything: to love, to eat, even to pass dung – and at last to breathe. And all of it should be cherished, for death was long.

The rich scent of her own dung filled her nostrils – and suddenly she realised that *there was no smell of mammoth here*.

The mammoths had seeped into every crevice of their Island. It wasn't possible to pull up a blade of grass which hadn't been nourished by the dung of mammoths; mammoth bones erupted from the ground everywhere as the permafrost melted; mammoths had even shaped the tundra itself, by battering down the encroaching trees of the spruce forest.

But that wasn't true here. When she raised her trunk to the air and sniffed, all she could smell was smoke and tar. And this was the place to which Foxeye and her calves had been brought: the place from which Silverhair must rescue them, or die in the attempt.

Perhaps if Lop-ear was here, she thought wistfully, he might be able to devise some plan, some way to gain an advantage over these unknowable swarms of Lost. But he wasn't here, and she had no plan. She could only rely on her strength and speed and courage and native intelligence – and the guidance of the Cycle, which had brought her this far.

She walked back to the Lost road. Its hard surface was unyielding under the pads of her feet, and its blackness soaked up the thin rays of the sun, making it feel hot. She recoiled from its strangeness.

But she raised her trunk, every sense alert, and began to walk.

The City of the Lost sprawled across the landscape, ugly, careless, uncompromising. It was a place of huge rust-stained cylinders, gigantic pipes that littered the ground, smaller tanks and boxes and heaps of strange metal shapes. As she approached the City's heart, the tallest buildings loomed over her, and she felt a helpless awe at their tall, shadowy straightness – and at the power of the worm-like creatures who had built this place.

But it was a place of waste.

She came to a pile of spruce wood, cut, evidently with

great effort, into lengths – and then abandoned on the ground to rot. And here was a heap of cracked-open cans that had been evidently simply abandoned, piled up without purpose or value. Traces of brown, rotting metal and oil had leaked into the ground, poisoning it so nothing grew here.

The Lost were *not* like the mammoths, she thought, whose very dung enriched the places they passed.

. . . And now, suddenly, she encountered her first Lost.

He came walking around one of the buildings, not looking up, his face lowered so he could peer at a sheet he carried. His outer skin was a gaudy blue, and he wore some form of orange carapace, hard and shiny, on his head.

She stood stock still, her trunk and tusks raised high above him.

His footsteps slowed, halted. Perhaps it was her smell he had noticed – or even the stink of brine which she must have carried from the sea.

He turned, slowly. He lowered his sheet, revealing cold blue eyes.

Silverhair saw herself through his eyes. Perhaps she was the first mammoth he had ever seen. She loomed before him like a fur-covered mountain, stinking of brine, her tusks alone almost as long as his body. And her face was a scarred mask, from which hard, determined eyes glowered.

The Lost yelped, comically. He threw his sheet up in the air, and stumbled backwards, landing in the mud.

He scrambled to his feet and ran away along the road, yelling. He turned a corner and disappeared into the complex, shadowy heart of the City. The sheet he had discarded blew towards her feet; she crushed it with one deliberate footstep.

Stolidly, she followed the fleeing Lost.

The buildings of the Lost loomed huge and faceless, dwarfing her. The only sounds were her own breathing, the soft slap of her footsteps – and the thumping of some distant metal heart, its low growl deeper than the deepest contact rumble. This place was *alive*, and she was willingly walking into its mouth.

And suddenly the Lost were here. Evidently Orange-Head had raised a warning. She was faced by a row of them – three, four, five, emerging from the buildings – and they all looked scared, even though they bore thunder-sticks aimed at her chest and head.

She had known this confrontation would come. She was a mammoth: not a burrowing lemming, a scurrying fox who could hide.

And she knew that from this point, the river of time, running to eternity, would split into two branches.

If the Lost chose to pump her body full of the stinging pellets of their thunder-sticks, then she would die here – though she would, she thought grimly, take as many of them with her as possible. But if not . . .

If not, if she lived and the future was still open, there was hope.

She took a deliberate step forward, towards the circle of Lost.

One thunder-stick cracked. A pellet sizzled past her ear. She couldn't help but flinch.

But it had missed her. Still she stepped forward.

Now the Lost were cawing to each other. One of them seemed to be taking command, and was waving his paws at the others. One by one, uncertainly, they lowered their thunder-sticks. Evidently they didn't want to kill her. Not yet, anyway.

Perhaps they had their own purpose for her. Well, she didn't care about that. For now, it was enough that she still breathed.

She called with the contact rumble: 'Foxeye! Croptail! Can you hear me? It's Silverhair. Foxeye, call if you hear me . . .'

She heard the thin trumpeting of a frightened calf – a trumpeting that was cut off abruptly.

Her heart hammered. At least one of them was still alive, then.

She moved forward, gliding deeper into the complex of buildings and pipes and smoking pillars. The Lost formed up behind her, their thunder-sticks never far below their shoulders, and they followed her like a gaggle of ugly calves. She called as she walked, and liquid mammoth rumbles echoed from the metal walls of this City of the Lost, and the massive, natural grace of her gait contrasted with the angular ugliness of the place.

She walked right through the City, to its far side.

Here she could see open tundra, stretching away. There were more buildings here, but their character was different. These were much rougher structures, some of them so flimsy they looked ready to fall down. Thin smoke snaked up to the grey sky, bearing the sour smell of burned meat. The ground here was churned-up, lifeless mud.

There were many Lost here, some of them emerging from the crude buildings to stare at her, some running away in fear.

And there, in a clearing at the centre of this cluster of buildings, were the mammoths. She counted quickly – Foxeye and Croptail and Sunfire – all of them alive, if miserable and bedraggled. Her heart hammered, and she longed to rush forward to her Family. But she forced herself to be still, to observe, to think.

The mammoths were held in two cages: one for Foxeye alone, the other for the two calves. When the calves saw Silverhair approach, Croptail set up an excited squealing. 'Silverhair!'

The cages, crudely constructed, were too small to allow the mammoths to move, even to turn around. They had thick ropes trailing from their roofs. Silverhair saw how distressed the calves were to be separated from their mother. Silverhair

wondered if these Lost knew how cruel that separation was –
indeed, that without her mother's milk Sunfire would soon
surely die.

Croptail was still calling. But there was a Lost beside the
calves' cage. He had a goad which he flicked cruelly through
the bars of the cage, snapping at Croptail's flank.

Silverhair rumbled threateningly.

The Lost looked at her – an unrestrained adult mammoth
– and decided not to whip the trapped calf again.

Silverhair approached Foxeye's cage. Foxeye was standing with her great head bowed, beaten and subdued, her
coat filthy. She was burdened by heavy chains which
looped around her neck and feet, fixed to stakes rammed
into the muddy ground. Silverhair reached through the bars
of the cage, and wrapped her trunk around Foxeye's.

At first Foxeye's trunk was limp. But then, slowly, it
tightened.

'I promised I'd save you,' said Silverhair. 'And here I
am.'

'We thought you were dead,' Foxeye said, almost inaud-
ibly.

'You were almost right,' said Silverhair dryly. 'But we're
still alive.'

'For now,' said Foxeye dully.

Deliberately, slowly, still trying not to alarm the Lost with
their thunder-sticks, Silverhair turned and wrapped her
trunk around the stakes which bound her sister's chains.
The stakes were fixed only loosely in the ground, and were
easy to tug free of the mud.

'Help me, Foxeye.'

'I can't . . .'

'You can. For the calves. Come on . . .'

With their sensitive trunk-fingers, the sisters explored the
cage. Silverhair found twists of thick wire; the wire was easy
to manipulate, and when it was gone, the front of the cage
fell away into the mud.

At first Foxeye cowered in the back of her open cage. But then she allowed herself to be led, by Silverhair's gentle tugs at her trunk, out of the cage.

The Lost seemed surprised by the ability of the mammoths to take the cage apart, and they were arguing, perhaps trying to decide whether to use their thunder-sticks.

Silverhair tugged Foxeye to the calves' cage. The heavy chains at Foxeye's neck and legs clanked, trailing in the mud, and as they approached, the Lost who had goaded Croptail ran off.

The calves were not chained up, and Silverhair and Foxeye simply lifted the cage up and off them. Croptail and Sunfire rushed to their mother; Sunfire immediately found a teat to suckle.

Silverhair made sure she threw the cage impressively far before letting it crash to the mud. It collapsed with a clatter of metal, sending more of the Lost fleeing.

She nudged Foxeye. 'Come on. We can't wait here.'

Croptail poked his head out from under his mother's belly hair. 'What's the plan, Silverhair?'

No plan, she thought. *I'm no Lop-ear* . . . 'We're just going to walk right out of here. Don't be afraid.'

She turned and faced the Lost. She looked around at their empty faces, their skinny bodies, their dangling jaws. She had the impression that these were not truly evil creatures – at least, not all of them. Just – Lost.

'Listen to me,' she said. 'Perhaps you can understand some of what I say. I am not going to permit you to take my Family away from their home. And if you try to stop us, I promise you your families will have to perform many Rememberings.'

But the Lost merely stared at her trumpeting, footstamping and rumbling, as if it wasn't a language at all.

She turned back to her Family. 'Go,' she said. 'You first, Croptail. That way – out to the tundra. We won't go through the City again. We'll make for the shore.'

'Then what?' demanded Croptail.

'Just do as I say.'

Bemused, frightened, Croptail obeyed. Soon, the little group of mammoths was gliding slowly towards the empty tundra.

As they walked steadily, Silverhair stared at the decrepit buildings, the rows of silent, staring Lost. 'This is a hellish place,' she said.

'Yes,' said Foxeye. 'I've been watching them. I think they want to turn the whole Earth into a gigantic city like this. Soon there will be nothing living but the Lost and the rodents that scurry for their scraps . . .'

She told Silverhair how the mammoths had been brought here.

After their capture in the ice chasm, they had been taken back to the beach and bound up tightly with ropes and chains. Then harnesses had been fixed around them, and they had been attached to the light-bird with its whirling wings – and, one by one, lifted into the sky.

'Mammoths aren't meant to fly, sister,' said Foxeye, and Silverhair could hear the dread in her voice. 'The Lost were taken away too. I think the ones who attacked us – Skin-of-Ice and the others – had been somehow stranded on the Island. The light-birds came for them when the storms cleared from the Mainland.'

'What do the Lost intend now?'

'They don't seem to want to kill us. Not right away. They have plenty to eat here, Silverhair; they don't need our flesh, nor our bones to burn . . .'

'There was rope fixed to your cage.'

'Yes. I think they were going to move us again. Fly us. Perhaps take us far from the tundra. Somewhere where there are many, many Lost, more Lost than all the mammoths who ever lived. And they would come and see us in our cages, and hit us with sticks, for they were never, ever going to let us out of there again.'

'Foxeye—'

'I'd have given up my calves,' Foxeye blurted. 'If I could have spoken to the Lost, if I thought they would have spared me, I'd have given up the calves. There: what do you think of me now?'

Silverhair rubbed her sister's filth-matted scalp. 'I think I got here just in time.'

The little group walked steadily onward, through the clutter of buildings, towards the tundra. Silverhair was dimly aware of more light-birds clattering over her head. She flinched, expecting an attack from that quarter. But none came. The birds seemed to be descending towards the City, and some of the Lost who had followed the mammoths were pointing up with their paws, muttering. Perhaps this was some new group of Lost, she thought; perhaps the Lost were divided amongst themselves.

It scarcely mattered. What was important was that still none of them tried to stop her.

Silverhair took one step after another, aware how little control she had over events, scarcely daring to hope she could take another breath. But they were still alive, and free. By Kilukpuk's hairy navel, she thought, this might actually work.

But then there was a roar like an angry god, and everything fell apart.

A Lost came running forward, face red with rage. In one paw he held a glinting flask of the clear inflaming liquid. And he carried a thunder-stick which he fired wildly.

This was a new type of stick, Silverhair realised immediately: one which spoke not with a single shout, but with a roar, and lethal insects poured out in a great cloud. Even the other Lost were forced to scatter as those deadly pellets smacked into the mud, or turned the walls of the crude dwellings into splinters.

The newcomer seemed to be berating the others. And he was turning the spitting nozzle of his thunder-stick towards the huddled Family.

This Lost wasn't going to let the mammoths go; he would obviously rather destroy them.

He was Skin-of-Ice.

Silverhair didn't even think about it. She just lowered her head and charged.

Everything slowed down, as if she were swimming through thick, ice-cold water.

She lowered her tusks, and he raised his thunder-stick, and she looked into his eyes. It was as if they were joined by that gaze, as if total communication were passing between their souls, as if there were nobody else in the universe but the two of them.

She felt a stab of regret to have come so close to freedom. But in her heart she had known it would come to this moment, that she would not survive the day.

If Skin-of-Ice had held his ground and used his thunder-stick he would surely have killed her there and then. But he didn't. In the last heartbeat, as a mountain of enraged mammoth bore down on him, he panicked.

Even as he made his thunder-stick roar, he fell backwards and rolled sideways.

Pain erupted in a line drawn across her face, chest and leg, and she felt her blood spurt, warm. One of the projectiles passed clean through her mouth, in one cheek and out through the other, splintering a tooth.

The pain was extraordinary.

She could hear the screams of Lost and mammoths alike, smell the metallic stink of her own blood. But she was still alive, still moving.

Skin-of-Ice was on the ground, scrabbling for his thunder-stick. She stood over him.

Again, in the face of her courage and strength, he made the

wrong decision. If he had abandoned the thunder-stick he might have escaped. But he did not. He had waited too long.

Silverhair lowered her tusk and speared him cleanly through the upper hind leg.

He screamed, and reached behind him to grab her tusk with his paws. She lifted her head, and Skin-of-Ice dangled on her tusk like a shred of winter hair, and she felt a fierce exultation.

But in one paw he held the thunder-stick. It sprayed its deadly fire in the air. And he kicked; his foot smashed into her forehead, and, with remarkable strength, he dragged his injured leg free of her tusk.

He fell more than twice his height to the ground.

But then he was moving again, firing his thunder-stick. The watching Lost fled, yelling.

Silverhair charged again.

Skin-of-Ice brought the thunder-stick round to point at Silverhair. But he wasn't quick enough.

As she reared over him, a hail of stings poured into her foreleg. She could feel bone shatter, muscles rip to shreds; when she tried to put her weight on that leg she stumbled.

But she had him.

She wrapped her strong trunk around his waist and, trumpeting her rage, hurled him into the air. Skin-of-Ice sailed high, twisting, writhing and firing his thunder-stick. He fell heavily, and she heard a cracking sound.

But still he pushed himself up with his forelegs. She felt a flicker of admiration for his determination. But she knew it was the stubbornness of madness.

She grabbed his hind foot with her trunk. She twisted, and heard bone crunch, ligaments snap. Skin-of-Ice screamed.

She flipped him on to his back, like a seal landing a fish on an ice floe. He still had his thunder-stick, and he raised it at her. But the stick no longer spat its venom. She could see how it was twisted and broken.

Skin-of-Ice hurled the useless stick away, his small face

distended with purple rage. Her strength and endurance had, in the end, defeated even its ugly threat.

He tried to rise, but she pushed him back with her trunk. Still he fought, clawing at her trunk as if trying to rip his way through her skin with his bare paws. She leaned forward and rested her tusk against his throat.

For a heartbeat, as Skin-of-Ice fought and spat, she held him. She thought of those who had died at his hands: Owlheart, Eggtusk, Snagtooth, Lop-ear. And she remembered her own hot dreams of destroying this monster.

A single thrust and it would be over.

She released him.

'You Lost are the dealers of death,' she said heavily. 'Not the mammoths.'

Still Skin-of-Ice tried to rise up to attack her. But other Lost came forward and dragged him back.

There were Lost all around Silverhair now, and they were raising their thunder-sticks.

She struggled to rise, to use her one good foreleg to lever herself upright. She could feel the wounds in her chest and leg tear wider, and the pain was sharp. But she would die on her feet.

She wished she could reach her Family, entwine trunks with them one last time.

She wondered why the Lost hadn't destroyed her already. She looked down at them. She saw they were hesitating; some of them had lowered their thunder-sticks.

'. . . Silverhair. Stay still. They won't harm you now. It isn't your day to die, Silverhair . . .'

It was – impossibly – the voice of an adult Bull.

She turned. A Lost was coming towards her: a new kind, all in white. He held his cupped paws up to his mouth, and he was shouting at the other Lost, making them turn their thunder-sticks away.

'. . . Don't be afraid. The Family will be safe. Nobody else will die today . . .'

And with the Lost there was a mammoth, without chains or ropes or any restraints, a mammoth who walked unhindered through the circle of thunder-sticks with this strange, posturing Lost.

It was a Bull, with one limp and damaged ear.

It was Lop-ear.

CHAPTER 7
THE CALVES OF PROBOS

Silverhair walked forward, over the soft, marshy ground of the Island.

Autumn was coming. The sun had lost its warmth, and was once more sliding beneath the horizon each night. There was no true darkness yet, but there would be long hours of spectral, indigo twilight before the sun returned. The birches, willows and other plants had started to turn to their autumn colours: crimson, ochre, yellow, vermilion, russet brown and even gold. The air was peaceful, musty with the smell of leaves and fungus. But the nights had turned cold, the frost riming the ground. And the ponds had started to freeze again, from their edges; each night's increment was marked by lines in the ice, like the growth rings of a tusk.

The land was emptying. The first migrating birds were already starting to abandon the tundra for their winter homes to the south: great flocks of swans, geese and sandpipers. Soon the silence of winter would return to the Island, and the summer's colour and noise would be as remote as a dream.

But this was like no other autumn. For Silverhair knew that the plain was barred from her by the walls the Lost had built around them: *glass*, Lop-ear had called this strange, hard, clear stuff. And in the distance she could see teams of the Lost moving about the Island's tundra, on foot or in their strange clattering vehicles.

Silverhair found a rich tuft of grass. She bent to pluck it up with her trunk, but as she tried to bend her knee her damaged leg rippled with pain. The white stuff the strange Lost had wrapped around her leg – while Lop-ear had been steadily persuading her not to gore him – was still in place, but it was threadbare and dirty, and she could see blood seeping through it.

Still, her leg was healing. There was no denying the Lost were clever. Not wise – but clever.

She heard a miniature trumpeting, a small rumble of protest. She glanced around. The calves were wrestling again; Sunfire, growing quickly, was almost as large as her brother now, and it was all Foxeye could do to separate them.

After her final battle with the Lost called Skin-of-Ice, the mammoths had been taken back to the Island across the Channel, in one of the peculiar floating metal bergs. Then – under the gentle supervision of the Lost – they had walked north, to this glassy enclosure.

The Family had never been so well fed, so safe from the attentions of predators. But Silverhair knew she would never be comfortable again, for she was living at the suffer-ance of the Lost.

Even if they had given Lop-ear back to her.

'. . . Not all the Lost are evil, Silverhair,' Lop-ear was saying. 'You must remember that. I've been observing them, trying to understand. Just as mammoths differ in personality, so do the Lost.'

'Lop-ear,' she said reasonably, 'they tried to kill you.'

'The actions of a few Lost don't reflect on the whole species. The Lost we encountered – Skin-of-Ice and his cronies – shouldn't even have been here on the Island. They are criminals. They were smuggling the clear liquid we saw them drink—'

'The stuff that makes them crazy.'

'They were blown to the Island in a storm. They were stranded here for most of the summer by the storms on the

Mainland. They were starving; they can't graze grass or hunt as the wolves can. They even tried to eat the meat of the ancient mammoths that emerge from the permafrost, but it made them ill. And so when they found us—'

'The Cycle teaches us that the belly of a wolf is a noble grave,' Silverhair growled. 'Maybe that's true of the shrivelled belly of a Lost too. It doesn't mean I have to welcome it.

'And besides, it wasn't their butchery that bothered me. Lop-ear, the Lost tried to kill you for no reason other than a lust for blood. They would have tortured me until I submitted to them like poor Snagtooth, or until I died. How can we share a world with creatures like that?'

'Because we must,' said Lop-ear bluntly. 'For the world is theirs. You have to understand there are lots of . . . *groups* among these Lost. And they pursue different goals.

'First there was Skin-of-Ice and his gang of criminals, with their angry-making water, and their need to survive. When the weather broke the criminals were rescued by another group, the workers from the City of the Lost. And the workers saw an opportunity in us. They didn't want to kill us or eat us, but they did think they could give us to others of their kind.'

'*Give* us to them? What for? Why?'

'So we could be – displayed,' he said. 'To great groups of Lost, young and old—'

Just as Foxeye had suspected. 'So,' Silverhair said bitterly, 'the Lost can mock the creatures from whom they stole the planet.'

'Something like that, I suppose. But there was *another* group of Lost, who had been here on the Island long before all the others. They built the Nest of Straight Lines. They kept others away from the Island for years, and they didn't have any curiosity about what lay in the Island's interior. They just stayed put and did their work.'

'What work?'

'How can I know that? You see, after the time of Long-tusk, the Lost thought there were no more mammoths left anywhere in the world. They thought the Island was empty, and that's why, for half a Great-Year, they didn't even come looking for us.

'And then there's *another* group – I know it's confusing, Silverhair – the ones who have saved us. And those Lost *care* about us.

'Somehow they heard that we had been discovered by the criminals. They came here, found me and saved my life – I tell you, Silverhair, after I got away from Skin-of-Ice I was ready for Remembering, I was eating my hair and speaking gibberish to the lemmings – and then they came to the Mainland to search for the rest of the Family.'

'They were nearly too late,' said Silverhair grimly.

'That's true,' he said. 'With more time the workers from the City of the Lost would have flown the others away – or else killed them. If not for you. You saved them, Silverhair. You saved the future.'

'Only to deliver us into the paws of more Lost.'

He eyed her. 'You still blame yourself, don't you?'

'If I hadn't gone seeking out the Lost in that blundering way – if I'd listened to Eggtusk and Owlheart – they might still be alive now.'

'No,' he said firmly. 'The Lost would have found us anyway. They'd already discovered the body in the *yedoma*, remember. We could no more have evaded them than we could a swarm of mosquitoes, and the mammoths would have been destroyed anyway. What you did gave us enough warning to act, to save ourselves. And besides, these new Lost—'

'These new Lost are *different*,' she said with heavy sarcasm.

'So they are,' he said, exasperated. 'Watch this.' And he trotted forward to the glass wall surrounding them, and touched it with his trunk.

The wall shimmered, and filled with light.

Silverhair gasped and stumbled backwards.

There was light all around her. A fat sun – brilliant, brighter than any Arctic sun – beat down from a washed-out brown-white sky. The ground was a baked plain, where black-leafed trees and stunted bushes struggled to grow. The horizon was muddied by a rippling shimmer of heated air. There was a smell of burning, far off on the breeze.

This was a huge, old land, she suspected.

Lop-ear was at her side. 'Don't be alarmed. It isn't real. We're still on the Island, in the glass box on the tundra. And yet—'

'What?'

'And yet it *is* real. In a way. The Lost have made this thing, this strange powerful wall, so we could see this place, even smell its dust . . .'

'What place?'

'Silverhair, this is a land far away – far to the south, where ice never comes and it never grows cold.'

A contact rumble came washing over the empty ground.

'*Mammoths,*' she hissed.

'Not exactly.'

And now she saw them: dark shapes moving easily on the horizon, like drifting boulders, huge ears flapping.

One of them turned, as if to face her. It was a Cow. She seemed to be hairless, and her bare skin was like weatherbeaten wood. She had no tusks. There was a calf at her side.

Behind her, a Family was walking. No, more than a Family – a *Clan*, perhaps, for there were hundreds of them, the young clustering around the Matriarchs, Bulls flanking the main group. Silverhair could hear liquid contact rumbles, trumpets and high-pitched squeaks; the Earth seemed to shake with the passage of those giant feet.

'They can't see us,' Lop-ear said softly.

'They are beautiful. Perhaps Meridi looked like this.'

'Yes. Perhaps.'

'Are they real?'

'Oh, yes,' said Lop-ear. 'They are real. Real – but not free, despite the way it looks. Silverhair, these are *elephants*.'

'Calves of Probos.'

'Yes. Just as we are. They are many, we are few. But, despite their greater numbers, these Cousins too are under threat from the expansion of the Lost. But the Lost have protected them, and studied them.

'Look – one Family isn't enough to continue the mammoths. Despite all we've achieved, we would die here on the Island, after another generation, two.'

'I know. We need fresh blood.'

'And it is our new Cousins who will provide it. I have seen what the Lost are trying to do, and I think I understand. These Cousins are sufficiently like us for the Lost to be able to mix our blood with theirs . . .'

'*Mix our blood?*'

'Something like that. The Lost are trying to assure our future, Silverhair.'

The big Cow turned away from them. She reached down to wrap an affectionate trunk around her suckling calf, and walked on, the calf scurrying at her feet.

Lop-ear touched the wall again and the strange scene disappeared, revealing the windswept tundra once more.

None of the elephants had tusks, Silverhair noted sadly. They had survived, but they had been forced to make their bargain with the Lost.

'Perhaps these Lost really do mean us well,' she said. 'But—'

'Yes?'

'But they will never let us go. Will they?'

'They *can't*, Silverhair. Earth is crowded with Lost. There is no room for us.'

*

At sunset, the weather broke.

Rain began to beat down, and Silverhair knew it was likely to continue for days. A grey mist hung over the green meadows, and the moisture gave the air a texture of mystery and tragedy. It was beautiful, but Silverhair knew what it meant. 'The end of another summer,' she said. 'It goes so quickly. And winter is so long . . .'

Silverhair knew her story was nearly over.

Skin-of-Ice had done her a great deal of damage – she could feel the deep unclosed wounds inside her – damage that couldn't be put right, regardless of the clever ministrations of these new Lost. There was only one more summer left in her, perhaps two. But she had no complaint; that would be enough for her to bear and suckle her calf, and teach it the stories from the Cycle.

She even knew what she would call the calf, such was its great weight in her belly. *Icebones*.

She knew she could never forgive the Lost for the things they had done to her and her Family. Perhaps it was just as well she would soon take that antiquated hatred to her grave.

For the future belonged to the calves, as it always had.

Lop-ear seemed to know what she was thinking. He stood beside her and rubbed her back with his trunk. 'We really are the last, you know. The last of the mammoths.'

'All those who had to die – Eggtusk, Owlheart, Snagtooth—'

'They did not die in vain,' he said gently. 'Every one of them died bravely, fighting to preserve the Family. We will always Remember them.

'But now we have the future ahead of us. And you're the Matriarch, Silverhair. Just as Owlheart predicted.' He rubbed her belly, over the bump of the unborn calf there. 'It's up to you to keep the Cycle alive, and help us remember the old ways. Then we'll be ready when our time comes again.'

'I don't think I have the strength any more, Lop-ear.'

'You do. You know you do. And you'll be remembered. The Cycle – our history – stretches back in time across twenty thousand great years. Its songs tell of the exploits of many heroes. But in all that immense chronicle, there is no hero to match you, Silverhair. One day our calves will run freely on the Sky Steppe, and their lives will be rich beyond our imagining. But they will envy you. For you were the most important mammoth of all. Cupped in the palm of history, caught between past and future, your actions shaped a world . . .'

She snuggled against him affectionately. 'You always did talk too much, dear Lop-ear. Hush, now.'

The rain lessened, and the scudding clouds broke up, briefly. The setting sun, swollen in the damp air, cast a pink-red glow which seemed to fill the sky, and the first stars gleamed.

'Look,' said Lop-ear softly, and he tugged her ear.

She looked up. The Sky Steppe was floating high above the moist tundra, a point of light gleaming fiery red. She stared through the glass wall at the ruddy air. It seemed to her that – just for a heartbeat – the red fire of the Sky Steppe washed down over the world, mixing with the sunset.

But then the clouds closed over the sky, and she was looking out at the dullness of the moist, rainy tundra.

Lop-ear was still talking. '. . . strange name, but the Lost—'

'What did you say?'

'I was telling you what the Lost call the Sky Steppe. For they see it better than we do, Silverhair. They know much about the land there, even about the two moons that follow it. They call it—' And he raised his head to the light in the sky, and shaped his mouth to utter the strange Lost sound.

'*Mars.*'

The sky closed over, and snow began to fall steadily. The Arctic summer was over, and Silverhair could feel the bony touch of another long, hard winter.

EPILOGUE

It is a frozen world.

Though the sun is rising, the sky above is still speckled with stars. There is a flat, sharp, close horizon, a plain of dust and rocks. The rocks are carved by the wind. Everything is stained rust brown, like dried blood, the shadows long and sharp.

And in the east there is a morning star: steady, brilliant, its delicate blue-white distinct against the violet wash of the dawn. Sharp-eyed creatures might see that this is a double star: a faint silver-grey companion circles close to its blue master.

The sun continues to strengthen. It is an elliptical patch of yellow light, suspended in a brown sky. But the sun looks small, feeble; this seems a cold, remote place. As the dawn progresses the dust suspended in the air scatters the light and suffuses everything with a pale, salmon hue. At last the gathering light masks the moons.

Two of them.

The land isn't completely flat. There are low sand dunes, and a soft shadow in the sand. It looks like a shallow ridge.

It is the wall of a crater.

It seems impossible that anything should live here. And yet there is life.

Lichen clings to the crater walls, steadily manufacturing oxygen, and there are tufts of hardy grasses. There are even dwarf willow trees, their branches hugging the ground.

. . . And there is more.

A vicious wind is rising, and lifting the dust into a storm. The horizon is lost now in a pink haze, and the world becomes a washed-out bowl of pink light.

And out of that haze something looms: a mountainous shape, seemingly too massive to move, and yet move it does. As it approaches through the obscuring mist, more of its form becomes visible: a body round as an eroded rock, head dropped down before it, the whole covered in a layer of thick red-brown hair.

The great head rears up. A trunk comes questing, and immense tusks sweep. An eye opens, warm, brown, intense, startlingly human.

The great trunk lifts, and the woolly mammoth trumpets her ancient songs of blood and wisdom.

Her name is Icebones.

BOOK 2

LONGTUSK

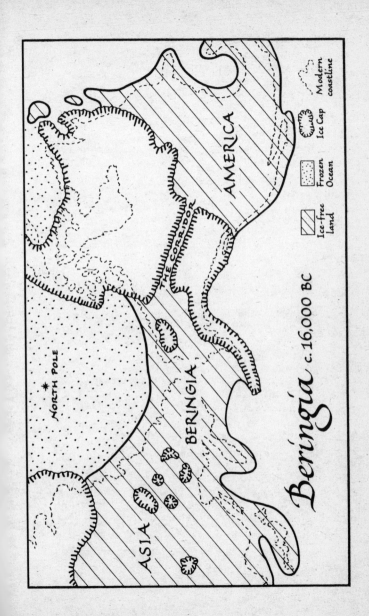

NORTH POLE

ASIA

BERINGIA

THE CORRIDOR

AMERICA

Beringia c. 16,000 BC

Ice-free land

Frozen Ocean

Ice Cap

Modern coastline

PROLOGUE

A vast sheet of ice sits on the North Pole: immense, brooding, jealously drawing the moisture from the air. Glaciers, jutting from the icecap like claws, pulverise rock layers and carve out fjords and lakes. South of the ice, immense plains sweep around the planet, darkened by herds of mighty herbivores.

The ice has drawn so much water from the oceans that the very shapes of the continents are changed. Australia is no island, but is joined to south-east Asia. And in the north, America is linked to Asia by a neck of land called Beringia, so that a single mighty continent all but circles the North Pole.

The ice is in retreat, driven back by Earth's slow thaw to its millennial fastness at the poles. But it retreats with ill grace, gouging at the land, and all around the planet there are catastrophic climatic events of a power and fury unknown to later ages. And, retreat or not, the sites of the cities of the future – Chicago, Boston, Edinburgh, Stockholm, Moscow – still lie dreaming under kilometres of ice.

The time is sixteen thousand years before the birth of Christ. And every human alive wakes to the calls of mammoths.

ONE
NOMAD

THE STORY OF LONGTUSK AND
THE SHE-CAT

Who was Longtusk?

I'll tell you who Longtusk was (Silverhair said to her daughter, Icebones). He was the greatest hero of the Cycle – and the only Bull hero in all the Cycle's long history.

My Matriarch used to say I had a little of Longtusk's spirit in me too. And I don't know why you think that's so funny, Icebones. I wasn't *always* so old and frail as this . . .

Tell you a story? Another?

Very well. I'll tell you how Longtusk defeated Teeth-of-Death, the she-cat.

This is a story of long ago, when the world was new and rich and cold, and there were no Lost, anywhere. The mammoths were the strongest and wisest of all the animals, so much so that the others grew to rely on their strength, and the way they remade the landscape, everywhere they went.

The mammoths were the Matriarchs of the world. Everybody agreed.

Well, almost everybody.

Teeth-of-Death was a she-cat. In fact she was the ruler of the sabre-tooth cats, for she was the strongest and most agile, her teeth and claws the longest and sharpest, her mind the most inventive, her cruelty the most relentless.

Every animal feared the sabre-tooth cats. Every animal feared Teeth-of-Death. Every animal save the mammoths.

The mammoths were too big, too powerful. Oh, the cats could bring down a mammoth from time to time, but only the very young or the very old or the very sick. It was not an honourable business. In fact, as they glided back and forth on their great migrations, the mammoths barely noticed the cats even existed.

This, of course, drove Teeth-of-Death insane with jealousy and hurt pride.

Now, as you know, when he was a young Bull Longtusk left his Clan and travelled far and wide: from north to south, even across the seas and the lakes and the ice. Everywhere he went he gained in wisdom and stature; everybody he met was impressed by his bearing and grace; and he had adventures which have never been forgotten.

And it was this Longtusk, Longtusk the nomad, who happened upon Teeth-of-Death.

The great cat confronted Longtusk. She said, 'This cannot go on.'

Longtusk had been feeding on a rich stand of willow. He looked down his trunk to see what was making so much noise, and there was the spitting, agitated cat. He asked reasonably, '*What* can't go on?'

'Either you rule the Earth, or I do. Not both.'

'Don't you think there are more important things to worry about than that?'

'No,' Teeth-of-Death snapped. 'Ruling is the most important thing. More important than life.'

'Nonsense,' said Longtusk. 'If it makes you happy, I hereby pronounce you the world's most fearsome animal. There. Now we don't have to argue, do we?' And he turned to walk away. For, you see, he was wise as well as brave, and he knew that an unnecessary fight should not be fought.

But that would not do for the she-cat.

With an agile bound she ran before Longtusk and confronted him. 'No,' she said. 'I cannot live while I know in my heart that you do not respect me.'

She was surely an intimidating sight: an immense cat with jaws spread wide, sharp teeth gaping, claws that with

274

a single swipe could disembowel even an adult Bull mammoth – if she ever got the chance.

'You are very foolish,' said Longtusk. But he faced her warily, for he knew he must meet her challenge.

And so it began. When news of the contest spread, all the animals of the world gathered around, pushing and staring.

Teeth-of-Death attacked Longtusk three times.

The first time she leapt at his face, reaching for his eyes and trunk. But Longtusk simply raised his tusks and pushed her away.

For her second attack Teeth-of-Death clambered up a spruce tree. She leapt down onto Longtusk's back and tried to use her great sabre teeth to gouge into his flesh. He could not reach her with his trunk to dislodge her. But she could not bite through his fur and skin. After a time he simply walked beneath a low tree and let its branches scrape the cat from his back, and that was that.

For her third attack Teeth-of-Death hid in a bank of snow. She had decided that when Longtusk came close enough she would leap at him again, trying to reach the soft flesh of his belly or trunk. It was a clever strategy and might have succeeded, even against a hero so strong as Longtusk, for cats are adept at such deception. But, obsessed with her ambition, Teeth-of-Death forced herself to lie still in her snowdrift for several days, waiting for her opportunity.

And when Longtusk at last came by, Teeth-of-Death was cold, half-starved, exhausted.

She sprang too early, made too much noise. To fend her off, Longtusk simply swept his great tusks and let their tips gouge furrows in Teeth-of-Death's beautiful golden coat.

They faced each other, Longtusk barely scratched, Teeth-of-Death bleeding and exhausted.

Longtusk said, 'Let us reach an agreement.'

Teeth-of-Death said warily, licking her wounds, 'No agreement is possible.'

For answer, he went to the snowdrift where she had been

hiding. He scraped away the snow and the hard ice that lay beneath, revealing bare earth. Then he dug deeper, and he exposed another layer of ice, hidden beneath the dirt.

'The ice comes and goes in great waves,' he said. 'This old ice was covered with dirt before it had time to melt. Now the ice has come again and covered over the land. So here we have two layers of ice in the same place, one on top of the other.'

The cat hissed, 'What relevance has this?'

'Here is my suggestion,' he said. 'We will share the world, just as these ice layers share the same patch of ground. But, just like these ice layers, we will not touch each other.

'You cats eat the meat of animals. We mammoths do not hunt; we do not covet your prey—'

'Ah,' said the cat. 'And you eat the plants and grass and trees, which we do not desire. Very well. We will share the world, as you suggest.' But her eyes narrowed.

And so it was concluded.

But when Longtusk was turning to go, the cat mocked him. 'I have tricked you,' she said. '*I* will eat the finest meat. *You*, however, must eat dirt and scrub. What kind of bargain is that? You are a fool, Longtusk.'

And Longtusk reflected.

The she-cat thought she had won: and in a way she had. She would become the steppe's ruling animal, its top predator. But Longtusk knew that though its food may be richer, a predator needs many prey to survive. Even a mighty herd of deer could support only a few cats, and the numbers of the she-cat's cubs would always be limited.

But the steppe was full of dirt and scrub, as she had called it. And Longtusk knew that thanks to his bargain it was his calves, the mammoths, who would grow in number until they filled the steppe, even to the point where they shaped it for their needs.

'Yes,' he said gently. 'I am a fool.' And he turned and walked away.

*

. . . I know what you are thinking, Icebones. Is the story true? Are *any* of the stories of Longtusk true? It seems impossible that one mammoth could cram so many acts of impossible heroism and matchless wisdom into one brief lifetime.

Well, perhaps some of the stories have become a little embellished with time. They are after all stories.

But I know this. Longtusk was real. Longtusk encountered great danger – and in the end, Longtusk sacrificed his life to save his Clan.

He was the greatest hero of them all.

CHAPTER 1

THE GATHERING

The greatest hero of them all was twelve years old, and he
was in trouble with his mother. Again.

Yellow plain, blue sky: it was a fine autumn afternoon,
here on the great steppe of Beringia. The landscape was
huge, flat, elemental, an ocean of pale grass mirrored by an
empty sky, crossed by immense herds of herbivores and the
carnivores that preyed on them. Longtusk heard the hiss of
the endless winds through the grass and sedge, the murmur
of a river some way to the west – and, under it all, the unending grind and crack of the great ice sheets that spanned
the continent to the north.

And mammoths swept over the land like clouds.

Loose wool hung around them, catching the low sunlight.
He heard the trumpeting and clash of tusks of bristling,
arguing bachelors, and the rumbles of the great Matriarchs
– complex songs with deep harmonic structure, much of
it inaudible to human ears – as they solemnly debated the
state of the world.

This was the season's last gathering of the Clan, this great
assemblage of Families, before the mammoths dispersed to
the winter pastures of the north.

And Longtusk was angry, aggrieved, ignored. He worked
the ground as he walked, tearing up grass, herbs and sedge
with his trunk and pushing them into his mouth between
the flat grinding surfaces of his teeth.

He'd gotten into a fight with his sister, Splayfoot, over a
particularly juicy dwarf willow he'd found. Just as he had
prised the branches from the ground and had begun to strip

278

them of their succulent leaves, the calf had come bustling over to him and had tried to push him away so she could get at the willow herself. *His* willow.

In response to Splayfoot's pitiful trumpeting, his mother had come across: Milkbreath, her belly already swollen with next year's calf. And of course she'd taken Splayfoot's side.

'Don't be so greedy, Longtusk! She's a growing calf. Go find your own willow. You ought to help her, not bully her . . .'

And so on. It had done Longtusk no good at all to point out, perfectly reasonably, that as *he* had found the little tree it was in fact *his* willow and the one in the wrong here was *Splayfoot*, not him. His mother had just pushed him away with a brush of her mighty flank.

The rest of the Family had been there, watching: even Skyhump the Matriarch, his own great-grandmother, head of the Family, surrounded by her daughters and grand-daughters with their calves squirming for milk and warmth and comfort. Skyhump had looked stately and magnificent, great curtains of black-brown hair sweeping down from the pronounced hump on her back that had given the Matri-arch her name. She had rumbled something to the Cows around her, and they had raised their trunks in amusement.

They had been mocking him. *Him*, Longtusk!

At twelve years old, though he still had much growing to do, Longtusk was already as tall as all but the oldest of the Cows in his Family. And his tusks were the envy of many an adult Bull – well, they would be if he ever got to meet any – great sweeping spirals of ivory that curved around before him until they almost met, a massive, tangible weight that pulled at his head.

He was Longtusk. He would live for ever, and he was destined to become a hero as great as any in the Cycle, the greatest hero of them all. He was sure of it. Look at his mighty tusks, the tusks of a warrior! He raised them now in mock challenge, even though there was no one here to see.

Couldn't those foolish Cows understand? It was just unendurable.

But now he heard his mother calling for him. Grumbling, growling, he made his way back to her.

The Cows had clustered around Skyhump, their Matriarch, and were walking northward in a loose, slow cluster. They grazed steppe grass as they walked, for mammoths must feed for most of each day, and they left behind compact trails of dung.

The Clan stretched around him as far as the eye could see, right across the landscape to east and west, a wave of muscle and fat and deep brown hair patiently washing northward. Skyhump's small Family of little more than twenty individuals – Cows with their calves and a few young males – was linked to the greater Clan by the kinship of sisters and daughters and female cousins. Where they passed, the mammoths cut swathes through the tall green-gold grass, and the ground shuddered with their footsteps.

Longtusk felt a brief surge of pride and affection. This was his Clan, and it was, after all, a magnificent thing to be part of it – to be a mammoth.

But now here was his mother, shadowed by that pest Splayfoot, and his sense of belonging dissipated.

Milkbreath slapped his rump with her trunk, as if he were still a calf himself. 'Where have you been? . . . Never mind. Can't you see we're getting separated from the Family? We have to hear what she has to say.'

'Who? Skyhump?'

Milkbreath snorted. 'No. Pinkface. The Matriarch of Matriarchs. Don't you know anything? . . . Never mind. Come *on*!'

So Longtusk hurried after his mother.

They joined a cluster of Cows, tall and old: Matriarchs all, slow and stately in their years and wisdom. He was too short to see past them.

But his mother was entranced. 'Look,' she said softly. *There she is.* They say she is a direct descendant of great Kilukpuk. They say she was burned in a great blaze made by the Fireheads, and she was the only one of her Family to survive . . .'

He could still see nothing. But when he shut out the noise – the squeal of calves, the constant background thunder of mammoths walking, eating, defecating – he could hear the Matriarchs rumbling and stamping at the ground, debating, sharing information that might sustain a few more lives through the coming winter.

Longtusk spoke quietly, with soft pipings of his trunk. 'What are they saying?'

'They're talking about the changes.' His mother's small ears stuck out of her hair as she strained to listen.

'What changes?'

'You're too young to understand,' she snapped irritably.

'Tell me.'

She growled, 'To the north the ice is shrinking back. And to the south the forests are spreading, more trees every year.'

He had heard this before. 'We can't live in the forests—'

'Not only that, there's talk that the Fireheads aren't too far to the south. And where the Fireheads go the Lost can't be far behind . . .'

Fireheads and Lost. Monsters of legend. Longtusk felt cold, as if he had drunk too much ice water.

. . . But now, without warning, the Matriarchs shifted their positions, like clouds exposing the sun. And he saw the Matriarch of Matriarchs.

She was short, her tusks long and smooth. And her face was a grotesque mask: pink and naked like a baby bird's wing, free of all but a few wisps of hair.

Longtusk burst out, 'She's too young!'

The Matriarchs stirred, like icebergs touched by wind.

Milkbreath grabbed his trunk, angry and embarrassed.

'Wisdom comes to all of us with age. But some are born wise. Wouldn't you expect that the Matriarch of Matriarchs, the wisest of all, would be special? *Wouldn't* you?'

'I don't know . . .'

'You're so much trouble to me, Longtusk! Always wandering off or getting under my feet or fighting with your sister or embarrassing me – sometimes I wish you were still in my belly, like this little one.' She stroked the heavy bulge under her belly fur.

Longtusk fumed silently.

Splayfoot came galloping up to him. His sister was a knot of fat and orange fur, with trunk like a worm and tusks like lemming bones, and her face was rounded and smoothed-out, as if unfinished. This was her first summer, and her new-born coat of coarse underfur and light brown overfur was being replaced by thicker and longer fur – though it would be her second year before her coarse guard hairs began to appear. 'You're so much trouble, Longtusk,' she squeaked up at him gleefully. She started butting his legs with her little domed forehead. 'I'll be Matriarch and you won't. Then I'll tell *you* what to do!'

He rumbled and raised his huge tusks over her head, meaning to frighten her.

The calf squealed and ran to her mother, who tucked Splayfoot under her belly. '*Will* you leave this little one alone?'

'It wasn't my fault!' Longtusk protested. 'She started it . . .'

But Milkbreath had turned away. Splayfoot burrowed at her mother's chest, seeking her dugs. But Milkbreath had little milk. So, with a deep belch, she regurgitated grass and with gentle kisses fed the warm, pulped stuff to her daughter.

As she fed, Splayfoot peered out from under a fringe of fur, mocking him silently.

It wasn't so long since Milkbreath had fed *him* that way,

murmuring about how important it was for him to eat the food that had been inside his mother's belly, for it contained marvellous substances that would help him digest. It hardly seemed any time at all.

And now look at him: pushed away, snapped at, ignored.

He stomped away, not looking back, not caring which way he went.

CHAPTER 2
THE BACHELOR HERD

He came to a track.

It was a strip of bare brown ground a little wider than his own body. Where the muddy ground was firm he could see the round print left by the tough, cracked skin of a mammoth's sole, a spidery, distinctive map.

He turned and followed the trail, curious to find where it might lead.

To human eyes the mammoth steppe would have looked featureless. It was an immense plain that swept over the north of Eurasia, across the land bridge of Beringia and into North America. But to a mammoth it was as crowded with landmarks as any human city: rubbing trees, wallows, rich feeding areas, salt licks, water holes. And these key sites were linked by trails worn by centuries of mammoth footsteps, trails embedded deep in the mind of every adult Bull and Cow, patiently taught to the calves of each new generation.

Indeed, the land itself was shaped by the mammoths, who tore out trees and trampled the ground where they passed. Other creatures lived in the shadow of the mammoths: depending on the trails they made, using the water sources they opened up with their intelligence and strength. Even the plants, in their mindless way, relied on the scattering of their seeds over great ranges in mammoth dung. Without mammoths, the steppe would not have persisted.

Longtusk stomped through his world, still angry, obsessed. But he thought over the Matriarchs' conversation: Fireheads and Lost and huge global changes . . .

He had never seen the Fireheads himself, but he'd met adults who claimed they had. The Fireheads – said to be ferocious predators, creatures of sweeping, incomprehensible danger – seemed real enough, and every young mammoth was taught at a very early age that the only response to a Firehead was to flee.

But the Lost were something else: figures of legend, a deep terror embedded at the heart of the Cycle – the nemesis of the mammoths.

It all seemed unlikely to Longtusk. The mammoths were spread in enormous herds right around the world, and even the great cats feared them. What could possibly destroy them?

And besides, his curiosity was pricked.

Why were all these changes happening *now*? How quickly would they happen? And why did the world have to become a harder place when *he* was alive? Why couldn't he have lived long ago, in a time of calm and plenty?

And, most important of all, why didn't anybody take him seriously?

Oh, he knew that there came a time when every Bull became restless with his Family; sooner or later all Bulls leave to seek out the company of other males in the bachelor herds, to learn to fight and strut and compete. But it didn't do him any good, here and now, to know that; and it drove him crazy when all this was patiently *explained* to him by some smug, pitying aunt or cousin.

After an unmeasured time he paused and looked back. Preoccupied, he hadn't been paying much attention where he walked; now he found he'd come so far he couldn't see the mammoths any more.

He heard a thin howl, perhaps of a wolf. He suffered a heartbeat of panic, which he sternly suppressed.

So he had left them behind. What of it? He was a full-grown Bull – nearly – and he could look out for himself. Perhaps this was *his* time to leave his Family – to begin the serious business of life.

Anyhow – he told himself – he was pretty sure he could find his way back if he needed to.

With a renewed sense of purpose – and with those twinges of fear firmly pushed to the back of his mind – he set off once more.

He came to a river bank.

Mammoths had been here recently. The muddy ground close to the river's edge was bare of life, pitted by footprint craters, and the trees were sparse and uniformly damaged, branches smashed, trunks splintered and pushed over.

The water was cold. This was probably a run-off stream, coming from a melting glacier to the north. He sucked up a trunkful of water and held it long enough to take off its first chill. Then he raised his trunk and let the water trickle into his mouth.

He pushed further along the cold mud of the bank. It wasn't easy going. The river had cut itself a shallow valley which offered some protection from the incessant steppe winds. As a result spruce trees grew unusually dense and tall here, and their branches clutched at him as he passed, so that he left behind clumps of ginger hair.

Then, through the trees, he glimpsed a gleam of tusks, a curling trunk, an unmistakable profile.

It was another mammoth: a massive Bull, come here to drink as he had.

Longtusk worked his way further along the bank.

The Bull, unfamiliar to Longtusk, eyed him with a vague, languid curiosity. He would have towered over any human observer, as much as three metres tall at his shoulder.

And he towered over Longtusk.

'My name,' the Bull rumbled, 'is Rockheart.'

'I'm Longtusk,' he replied nervously. 'And I—'

But the Bull had already turned away, his trunk hosing up prodigious volumes of water.

The Bull's high, domed head was large, a lever for his

powerful jaw and a support for the great trunk that snaked down before him. He had a short but distinct neck, a cylinder of muscle supporting that massive head. His shoulders were humped by a mound of fat, and his back sloped sharply down towards the pelvis at the base of his spine. His tusks curled before him, great spirals of ivory chipped and scuffed from a lifetime of digging and fighting.

And his body, muscular, stocky, round, was coated by hair: great lengths of it, dark orange and brown, that hung like a skirt from his belly, down over his legs to the horny nails on his swollen pads of feet, and even in long beard-like fringes from his chin and trunk. His tail, raised slightly, was short, but more hair made it a long, supple insect whisk. His ears were small, tucked back close to his head, all but lost in the great mass of hair there.

Suddenly the ground shuddered under Longtusk's feet, and the river water trembled.

More mammoths, a crowd of them, came spilling down the bank, pushing and jostling, clumsy giants. They were all about the same size, Longtusk saw: no Cows, no infants here.

It was a bachelor herd.

Longtusk was thrilled. He had rarely been this close to full-grown Bulls. The Bulls kept to their own herds, away from the Cow-dominated Families of mothers and sisters and calves; Longtusk had seen them only in the distance, sweeping by, powerful, independent, and he had longed to run with them.

And now, perhaps, he would.

The Bulls spread out along the river bank. Before passing on towards the water, one or two regarded Longtusk: with mild curiosity over his outsize tusks, or blank indifference, or amused contempt.

Longtusk followed, avid.

For half a day, as the sun climbed into the sky, the Bulls

moved on along the river bank, jostling, jousting, drinking and eating.

Their walk, heavy and liquid, was oddly graceful. Their feet were pads that rested easily on the ground, swelling visibly with each step. Their trunks, heavy ropes dangling from the front of their faces, pulled the mammoths' heads from side to side as they swayed. Even as they drank they fed, almost continuously. They pulled at branches of the surrounding trees with their trunks, hauling off great leaf-coated stems with hissing rustles, and crammed the foliage into their small mouths.

The soughing of their footsteps was punctuated by deep breaths, the gurgle of immense stomachs, and subterranean rumbles from the sound organs of their heads. A human observer would have made little of these deep, angry noises. But Longtusk found it easy to make out what these Bulls were saying to each other.

'. . . You are in my way. Move aside.'

'I was here in this place first. *You* move aside.'

'. . . This water is too cold. It lies heavy in my belly.'

'That is because you are old and weak. I, however, am young and strong, and I find the water pleasantly cool.'

'My tusks are not yet so old and feeble they could not crack your skull like a skua egg, calf.'

'Perhaps you should demonstrate how that could be done, old one . . .'

Longtusk, following the great Bull Rockheart, was tolerated – as long as he didn't get in anybody's way – for he was, for now, too small to be a serious competitor. His tusks were, despite his youth, larger than many of the adults' – but they only made him feel self-conscious, as if somehow he wasn't entitled to such magnificent weapons. He walked along with his head dipped, his tusks close to the ground.

Being with the Bulls was *not* like being with his Family.

Even the language was different. The Cows in the

Families used more than twenty different kinds of rumble, a basic vocabulary from which they constructed their extremely complex communications. The Bulls only had four rumbles! – and those were to do with mockery, challenge and boasting.

His Family had been protective, nurturing – a safe place to be. But the bachelor herds were looser coalitions of Bulls, more interested in contest: verbal challenges, head butts, tusk clashes. The Bulls were constantly testing each other, exploring each other's strength and weight and determination, establishing a hierarchy of dominance.

This mattered, for it was the dominant Bulls who mated the Cows in oestrus.

Right now, Longtusk was at the very bottom of this hierarchy. But one day he would, of course, climb higher – why, to the very top . . .

'You have stepped on the hair of my feet.'

Longtusk looked up at a wall of flesh, eyes like tar pits, tusks that swept over his head.

He had offended Rockheart.

The great Bull's guard hairs – dangling from his belly and trunk, long and lustrous – rippled like water, trapping the light. But loose underfur, working its way out through the layers of his guard hair in tatters around his flanks, made him look primordial, wild and unfinished.

Longtusk found himself trembling. He knew he should back down. But some of the other males nearby were watching with a lofty curiosity, and he was reminded sharply of how the Matriarch had watched his humiliation by his infant sister earlier.

If he had no place in the Family, he must find a place here. His Family had taught him how to live as a mammoth; now he must learn to be a Bull. And this was where it would begin.

So he stood his ground.

'Perhaps you have trouble understanding,' Rockheart said

with an ominous mildness. 'You see, this is where I take my water.'

'It is not your river alone,' Longtusk said at last. He raised his head, and his tusks, long and proud, waved in the face of the great Bull.

Unfortunately one curling tusk caught in a tree root. Longtusk's head was pulled sideways, making him stagger.

There was a subterranean murmur of amusement.

Rockheart simply stood his ground, unmoving, unblinking, like something which had grown out of this river bank. He said coldly, 'I admire your tusks. But you are a calf. You lack prowess in their use.'

Longtusk gathered his courage. He raised his tusks again. They were indeed long, but they were like saplings against Rockheart's stained pillars of ivory. 'Perhaps you would care to join me in combat, so that you may show me exactly where my deficiencies lie.'

And he dragged his head sideways so that his tusks clattered against Rockheart's. He felt a painful jar work its way up to his skull and neck, and the base of his tusks, where they were embedded in his face, ached violently.

Rockheart had not so much as flinched.

Longtusk raised his tusks for another strike.

With a speed that belied his bulk Rockheart stepped sideways, lowered his head and rammed it into Longtusk's midriff.

Longtusk staggered into icy mud, slipped and fell sprawling into the water.

He struggled to his feet. The hairs of his belly and trunk dangled under him in cold clinging masses.

The Bulls on the river bank were watching him, tusks raised, sniggering.

Rockheart took a last trunkful of water, sprayed it languidly over his back, and turned away. His massive feet left giant craters in the sticky mud as he walked off, utterly ignoring Longtusk and his struggles.

And now Longtusk heard a familiar, remote trumpeting . . . 'Longtusk! Longtusk! Come here right now! . . .'

'There's your mother calling you,' brayed a young Bull. 'Go back to her teat, little one. This is no place for you.'

Longtusk, head averted, humiliated, stomped out of the river and through the stand of trees. Where he walked he left a trail of mud and drips of water.

That was the end of Longtusk's first encounter with a bachelor herd.

He could not know it, but it would be a long time before he would see one of his own kind again.

Not caring which way he went, Longtusk lumbered alone over the steppe, head down, ripping at the grass and herbs and grinding their roots with angry twists of his jaw.

He couldn't go back to the herd. And he wasn't going back to his Family. Not after all that had happened today. Not after *this*.

He didn't need his Family – *or* the Bulls who had taunted him. He was Longtusk! The greatest hero in the world!

Why couldn't anybody *see* that?

He walked on, faster and further, so wrapped up in his troubles he didn't even notice the smoke until his eyes began to hurt.

CHAPTER 3
THE SHE-CAT

Startled, he looked up, blinking. Water was streaking down the hairs of his face.

Smoke billowed, acrid and dark; somewhere nearby the dry grass was burning.

Every instinct told him to flee, to get away from the blaze. But which way?

If she were with him, his mother would know what to do. Even a brutal Bull like Rockheart would guide him, for it was the way of mammoths to train and protect their young.

But they weren't here.

Now, through the smoke, he saw running creatures, silhouetted against the glow: thin, lithe, upright. They looked a little like cats. But they ran upright, as no cat did. And they seemed to carry things in their front paws. They darted back and forth, mysterious, purposeful.

Perhaps they weren't real. Perhaps they were signs of his fear.

He felt panic rise in his chest, threatening to choke him.

He turned and faced into the smoke. He thought he could see a glow there, yellow and crimson. It was the fire itself, following the bank of smoke it created, both of them driven by the wind from the south.

Then he should run to the north, away from the fire. That must be the way the other mammoths were fleeing.

But fire – sparked by lightning strikes and driven by the incessant winds – could race across the dry land. Steppe plants grew only shallowly, and were easily and quickly consumed. Mammoths were strong, stocky, round as boulders:

built for endurance, not for speed. He knew he could never outrun a steppe firestorm.

What, then?

Through his fear, he felt a pang of indignation. Was he doomed to die here, alone, in a world turned to grey and black by smoke? – he, Longtusk, the centre of the universe, the most important mammoth who ever lived?

Well, if he wanted to live, he couldn't wait around for somebody else to tell him what to do. Think, Longtusk!

The smoke seemed to clear a little. Above him, between scudding billows of smoke, the sun showed a spectral, attenuated disc.

He looked down at his feet and found he was standing in a patch of muddy ground, bare of grass and other vegetation. It was a drying river bed, the mud cut by twisted, braided channels. There was nothing to burn here; that must be why the smoke was sparse.

He looked along the line of the river. It ran almost directly south. No grass grew on this sticky, clinging mud – and where the dry river snaked off into the smoke, the glow of the fire seemed reduced, for there was nothing to burn on this mud.

If he walked *that* way, southwards into the face of the smoke, he would be walking towards the fire – but along a channel where the fire could not reach. Soon, surely, he would get through the smoke and the fire, and reach the cleaner air beyond.

He quailed from the idea. It went against every instinct he had – to walk *into* a blazing fire! But if it was the right thing to do, he must overcome his fear.

He raised his trunk at the fire and trumpeted his defiance. And, dropping his head, he began to march stolidly south.

The smoke billowed directly into his face, laced with steppe dust: hot grit that peppered his eyes and scraped in his chest. And now the fire's crackling, rushing noise rose to a roar. He felt he would go mad with fear. But he bent his head and, doggedly, one step at a time, he continued, into the teeth of the blaze.

At last the fire roared around him, and the flames leapt, dazzling white, as they consumed the thin steppe vegetation. Only a few paces away from him grass and low trees were crackling, blackening. Tufts of burning grass and bark scraps fluttered through the air. Some of them stuck to his fur, making it smoulder, and he batted them away with his trunk or his tail.

But he had been right. The fire could not reach across the mud of this river bed, and so it could not reach him.

And now there was a change. The sound of the fire seemed diminished, and he found he was breathing a little easier. Blinking, he forced open his eyes and looked down.

He was still standing in his river bed. Its surface had been dried out and cracked by the ferocious heat. To either side the ground was lifeless, marked by the smouldering stumps of ground-covering trees and the blackened remnants of grass and sedge. Near one tree he saw the scorched corpse of some small animal, perhaps a lemming, its small white bones protruding.

The stink of smoke and ash was overwhelming. The steppe, as far as he could see, had turned to a plain of scorched cinders. Smoke still curled overhead . . . but it was a thinning grey layer which no longer covered the sinking sun.

And there was no fire.

He felt a surge of elation. He had done it! Alone, he had worked out how to survive, and had stuck to his resolve in the face of overwhelming danger. Let Rockheart see him now! – for he, Longtusk, alone, had today faced down and beaten a much more savage and ruthless enemy than any Bull mammoth.

. . . *Alone*. The word came back to haunt him, like the distant cry of a ptarmigan, and his elation evaporated.

294

He turned and faced northwards. The fire was a wall across the steppe, from the eastern horizon to the west. Smoke billowed up before it in huge towering heaps, shaped by the wind. It was an awesome sight, and it cut the world in two.

He hammered at the ground with his feet, his stamps calling to the mammoths, his Family. But there was no reply, no rocky echo through the Earth. Of course not; the noise of the fire would overwhelm everything else, and before it all the mammoths must be fleeing – even the greatest of them all, the Matriarch of Matriarchs, fleeing north, ever further from Longtusk.

He would have no chance to gloat of his bravery to Rockheart, or his mother, or anyone else. For everything he knew – the Family, the Clan, the bachelor herd, *everything* – lay on the other side of that wall of fire.

He cried out, a mournful trumpet of desolation and loneliness.

He looked down at himself. He was a sorry sight, his fur laden with mud and heavily charred. And he was hungry and thirsty – in fact he had no clear memory of the last time he'd eaten.

The sun was dipping, reddening. Night would soon be here.

The last of his elation disappeared. He had thought he had won his battle by defeating the fire. But it seemed the battle was only just begun.

There was only one way for him to go: south, away from the fire. He lowered his head and began to walk.

As he marched into deepening darkness, he tried to feed, as mammoths must. But the scorched grass and sage crumbled at his touch.

His thirst was stronger than his hunger, in fact, but he found no free-standing water. He scraped hopefully at the ground with his tusks and feet. But only a little way down, the ground grew hard and cold. This was the permafrost, the deep layer of frozen soil which never thawed, even at the height of summer. He dug his trunk into the soil and sucked hopefully, but there were only drops of moisture to be had, trapped above the ice layer.

He came across a willow. It hugged the ground, low and flat, not rising higher than his knees. He prised it up with his tusks, stripped off its bark and munched the thin, dry stuff, seeking to assuage his thirst.

He knew there were places scattered around the steppe where free-standing water lay close to the surface, even in the depths of winter, and the mammoths could crack through snow and ice to reach it. The adults knew where to find such wells of life, using a deep knowledge of the land passed on from the generations before them – but Longtusk had only begun learning about the land. Now, scraping at the mud, adrift in this blackened landscape where even the trails had been scorched out of existence, he was learning how truly helpless he was.

He walked further. The trees grew more thickly, short, ancient willows and birches. Soon there were so many of them they covered the ground with a thick matting of branches. He was walking, in fact, on top of a forest. This dry, cold, wind-blasted land was not a place where trees could grow tall.

. . . He heard a hiss, deep and sibilant, somewhere behind him.

Mammoths' necks are short and inflexible, and Longtusk had to turn all the way around – slowly, clumsily, heart hammering.

The cat gazed at him, utterly still, silent.

For an instant he felt overwhelmed, his mind reeling, his courage fragmenting. He was almost irritated. The bachelor herd, the smoke, the fire – wasn't that enough? Must he face this new peril as well?

But he knew he was in deadly danger, and he forced himself to alertness.

The cat was a female, he saw. She seemed huge to Longtusk: not much less than half his own height, rippling muscle under a smooth sheen of brown fur. Her ears were small and forward-pointed, her nose small and black.

And her two sabre teeth swept down from her mouth, stained by something dark and crusted. Blood, perhaps. She must already have made a kill, of some prey animal disoriented by the fire. He could smell rotten meat on her breath.

Perhaps she had a family to feed, a brood of brawling sharp-toothed cubs. Cubs hungry for mammoth meat.

The sun, reddened by the smoky air, touched the horizon. Shadows fled across the scorched plains, and ruddy light gleamed deep in the carnivore's eye sockets.

And those eyes were fixed on Longtusk.

He raised his trunk and trumpeted. The sound rolled across the anechoic plains, purposeless.

The cat spread her claws, long and bright, and they sank into the ground. Her muscles tensed in great sheets.

Fear clamoured in his mind, threatening to drown out thought.

He tried to recall fragments of mammoth lore: that few mammoths are targeted by predators; that Bulls, not fully grown and yet driven to depart the Family – Bulls like himself – are the most vulnerable to predators like this cat; that the female cat, driven to provide for her family, is deadlier than the male.

But through all this one stark thought rattled around his awareness: *that it is at sunset that the predators hunt.*

She sprang. It was very sudden. Spitting, she soared through the air, a blur of muscle heading straight for his face, claws extended.

Blindly he raised his tusks.

She was knocked sideways, spitting and scratching.

. . . He was bleeding, he realised. There was a series of raked gashes across the front of his trunk, where a paw-swipe had caught him.

Trumpeting, he turned again.

She was crouched low, eyes on him once more, taking step after deliberate step towards him.

The mammoths evolved on open plains, where there is little cover. Under threat from a predator they adopt a ring formation, with the calves and the weak huddled at the centre.

But now Longtusk was on his own, with nobody to cover his back, utterly exposed.

He broke away and fled. He couldn't help it.

She will try to slash your trunk. Avoid this. It will cause you agonising pain and a great loss of blood. Use your tusks. Bring them down on her head to stun her, or stab her with the sharp tips. If she gets in closer, wrap your trunk around her and squeeze until her back breaks. If she gets beneath you, step on her and crush her skull. Never forget she is afraid too: you are bigger and stronger than her, and she knows it . . .

It was a comforting theory, and he recalled how he had played with other calves, mimicking attacks and defences, swiping miniature tusks back and forth. But the reality, of this spitting, stinking, single-minded cat, was very different.

And now he felt a new sharp warmth on his right hind leg. She had gouged him again. The damage was superficial, but he could feel the blood pumping out of him, weakening him. He kept running, but now he was limping.

It had been a deliberate cut. The cat was trying to shorten the chase.

He ran towards a stand of tall trees, sheltered by an outcrop of rock, their branches green-black in the fading light. Perhaps there would be cover here. He ducked into the shadow of the trees, turned—

Suddenly there was a weight on his back, a mass of spitting, squalling fur, utterly unexpected, and then stabs of sharp pain all across his back: long claws digging through his fur and into his flesh.

He trumpeted in panic. He raised his trunk and tusks, but his neck was short and he could never reach so far. *The trees*, he realised. Their black branches loomed above him. She must have climbed into the branches and dropped down onto him.

On the steppe most trees hugged the ground. Longtusk wasn't used to trees looming over him. He hadn't even considered the possibility that the cat might do such a thing.

He felt, through sharpening stabs of pain, that she was digging her claws deeper into him, and her weight shifted. He knew what she was intending; he had seen the cats at work. She was opening her gaping mouth and raising her down-pointing sabre teeth. In a moment she would use them to stab down into his helpless flesh, laying open his spine, or even his skull.

Then the pain would start.

She would not kill him quickly, he knew, for that was not the way of the cats; he would lie in blood and black agony, longing for a release to the aurora, while this cat and her foul cubs tore at his flesh—

He raised his trunk and bellowed defiance. No! He had beaten the fire. He would not be destroyed, in this dismal place, by a carrion-breathed cub of Aglu!

He charged straight at the trees. One branch, black and thick, cut across the sky, only a little above his head height.

As the branch struck her the cat yowled. The pain in his back deepened – her claws raked through his flesh as she tried to cling to him – but suddenly the pain's sharpness eased, and the weight of the cat was gone from his shoulders. Breathing hard, the wounds on his back cold, he whirled around, tusks raised, trunk tucked under his chin for protection.

The cat had vanished.

He trumpeted. His eyes, never strong, helped him little in

this fading light. And he could smell nothing – nothing but the metallic stink of his own crusting blood. Probably she had gone downwind of him.

How could she have moved so quickly, so silently? She was, he realised ruefully, much more expert at hunting than he was at being hunted.

The dark was deepening quickly. His thirst seemed to burn at his throat, a discomfort deeper even than the ache of his wounds. And he longed for shelter.

He recalled the outcrop of rock which had provided cover for these trees to grow. Clumsily, his torn leg and back aching, he lumbered around the trees. He came to a sheer wall of sandstone, perhaps twice as tall as he was, smoothly eroded, its base littered by frost-shattered scree, fallen branches and dead leaves. He moved as close to the rock face as he could, and turned to face the plains beyond.

Perhaps he could last through the night here. He might hear the cat approach if she came across the scree or the leaves. And in the morning—

There was liquid movement to his right. She had been hiding in the mound of broken wood and leaves. Now, gazing at him, she prepared to spring again.

He felt trapped in this dark, glacial moment.

He seemed to have time to study the cat's every detail: the sinuous beauty of her curved, taut muscles, the gaping, bloody maw of her mouth. Blood was crusted on her head, he noticed, a mark of his one minor victory, where he had managed to hurt her by driving her against the tree branch. But her eyes were on him, small and hard, and he could see that she knew she had won. In less than a heartbeat she would reach his soft belly with her claws, and his life would spill out on this lonely rock, far from those who had loved him.

. . . But the cat was hurled sideways and slammed into the rock face.

She fell, limp.

Time flooded over him again, and his heart hammered.

Cautiously, unable to believe he was still breathing, Longtusk crept closer. The cat lay where she had fallen, slumped in the leaves and the scree.

Blood welled from a huge wound in her temple, dark and thick, as if seeking to water the trees that grew here. The stillness of the cat was sudden, startling; this creature of motion and purpose and deadly beauty had become, in a heartbeat, a thing of the rock and the earth, her beautiful muscles slack and useless for ever.

He felt no triumph, no relief: only numbness.

Something protruded from her skull.

It was wood, a long, straight branch. It had been stripped of bark, and one end narrowed to a sharp tip. The tip looked blackened, as if it had been in a fire; but it was evidently hard, hard as a tusk – for it had pierced the cat's skull, passing through a neat puncture in her temple and out the other side. The flying stick had knocked her out of her spring; she had probably been dead, he realised, even before she collided with the rock.

There was a rustle a few paces away.

Startled, he reared up and trumpeted.

There was something out there on the darkling plain. Something small, purposeful.

But this was no cat. It walked upright, on its hind legs.

It was shorter than Longtusk, but it looked strong, with muscled legs and a broad chest. Its head was large with a wide fleshy nose, and a low brow made caves of bone from which brown eyes peered suspiciously at Longtusk. Short black hair was matted on the creature's head, and it had fur over its body – *not its own fur*, Longtusk realised with a shock, but scraps of skin from animals, deer and bison and even fox, somehow joined together.

The two of them stared at each other.

Fragments of lore drifted through Longtusk's mind. *They*

*walk upright. They wear the skin of other creatures. There is no
fighting them; only flight is possible . . .*

This creature walked upright, like a Firehead. Was it
possible? . . .

But Longtusk felt no fear now. He seemed exhausted,
done with fear.

The strange beast, cautiously, walked forward on its hind
legs towards the cat. Longtusk wondered how it kept from
toppling over. It wrapped its big front paws around the
pointed stick, stepped on the cat's inert head, and pulled
hard. With some reluctance, the stick slid out of the cat's skull.

Then, watching Longtusk, the creature jabbed with the
stick at the cat's head.

Showing him what it had done.

Slowly Longtusk understood. This creature had thrown
the stick through the air, driven it by sheer strength and
accuracy into the head of the cat – and thereby saved
Longtusk's life.

If this was a Firehead, it meant Longtusk no harm. Perhaps it was not a Firehead, but something else, something
like a Firehead, but a lesser threat.

Longtusk seemed unable to think it through, to pick
through bits of half-remembered lore.

The creature walked closer to Longtusk. Its head moved
back and forth, side to side, and its eyes were bright and
curious, even though it was obviously nervous of the
mammoth's great tusks. It worked its mouth and a strange
complex growl emerged.

Then it reached out with one of its bare front paws, and,
leaning within the radius of the tusks, stroked the long fur
on Longtusk's trunk. Longtusk flinched, but he was beyond
fear now, and he submitted to the contact. The creature
passed his fingers down through Longtusk's matted hair, the
motion oddly soothing.

But the paw came away sticky with blood, and the
creature looked at Longtusk with renewed concern.

It took its stick and began to walk away. A few paces from Longtusk, it paused and looked back.

Longtusk looked down at the shadowy form of the dead cat. Though the rock would provide him with shelter, he had no desire to stay here. This sinuous corpse, still leaking blood, would surely soon attract more predators, hyenas and foxes and maybe even other cats, before the condors descended on what was left of the carcass.

The light was all but gone, and the wind was rising.

He looked up. The upright creature was still waiting, looking back. And Longtusk had no real choice.

Slowly they walked into the night, the woolly mammoth following the Neanderthal boy.

CHAPTER 4
THE DREAMERS

They came to a shallow river valley, where running water – perhaps a tributary of the dried-out stream that had saved Longtusk from the fire – had cut its way into the hard black rock of the ground.

The upright creature scrambled down a heap of frost-shattered scree. It reached a hole of deeper darkness cut into the hillside. It was a cave, Longtusk realised.

And a glimmer of ruddy light came from within it.

Longtusk was baffled. How could there be light *inside* a cave, a place of shadows?

. . . And now Longtusk's sharp sense of smell detected the tang of smoke, carried on the light evening breeze, and he understood the source of that strange inner glow.

Fire. His upright friend had walked into fire – maybe a nest of true Fireheads!

Longtusk stood there on the river bank, torn by conflicting impulses. Should he flee, or should he rush down the bank and pull out his friend, saving the squat little creature as it had saved him from the she-cat?

But his friend had gone into the cave willingly, with no sign of fear.

The sun had not yet risen since Longtusk had been separated from his Family. And already he had endured a blizzard of new experiences. Perhaps this new vision, of fire within a cave, was simply one more strangeness he must strive to understand.

But none of that mattered. It was almost completely dark now. He was hungry, tired, thirsty – and alone once more.

Using his trunk to feel his way, he worked through the rocks to the edge of the river. He walked further, following the stream. The river bed shallowed, and he sensed a lake opening out before him: a scent of cold fresh water, a soft sweep of wind across an expansive surface. At the edge of the lake, lying along the shallow beach, he found great linear heaps of feathers left by moulting ducks and geese.

When he waded into the water its icy cold struck through the layers of fur on his legs, and he almost cried out from the pain of the wounds inflicted by the cat. But as the water lifted off the caked blood and dirt, the sharp pain turned to a wider ache, and he sensed the start of healing.

He took a trunkful of water and lifted it to his mouth; it was cool and delicious, and he drank again and again, assuaging a thirst he had nursed since the terrible moments of the fire.

He retreated to the tumbled rocks of the shore. He found a gap between two tall rock faces. He nestled there and, trying to ignore the continuing cold ache of his back and legs, waited for sleep to claim him.

In the morning, with the low sun glowing red through the last of yesterday's smoke, he made his way out of his rock cleft and down to the water.

Near the lake, the water and air and land were full of birds: many species of geese, ducks, even swans on the water, blackbirds and sparrows on the marshy land, and occasional hunters – hawks, kestrels. The short summer was ending, a time when the birds swarmed to breeding grounds like this.

A flock of geese floated on the water, a huge raft of them. They had shed all their flight feathers at once, a great catastrophic moult that had left them temporarily unable to fly, as they put all their energy into breeding and raising young and storing fat for the return journey to their winter lands in the south. All of this had to be completed in just forty or fifty days, before the snow and ice clamped down on the land again.

The rocks were covered by a fine hoar frost, so slippery that even the heavy, wrinkled pads of his feet could not find a firm footing. There was no food to be had here. Nothing grew on these rocks and pebbles and scree, all of it regularly inundated by the flooding lake, save lichen and weed. He knew, gloomily, he would have to travel far today to find the fodder he needed.

But yesterday had depleted him. The wounds on his back ached badly, and he wondered if they were festering. He felt dizzy, oddly hollow, and his eyes were gritty and sore.

Something startled the birds. Ducks and swans rose from the water, a racket of rattling, snapping wings, leaving behind the barking, flightless geese. The birds caught the light, and they seemed to glow against the dull grey of the sky, as if burning from within. There were actually many flocks, he realised, passing to and fro in a great lattice above him, as if he were standing at the bottom of an ocean through which these birds swam.

And he was still utterly, desolately, alone. He wished his Family were here.

. . . There was a splashing sound, a little way out from the lake shore. He turned slowly. He saw motion, a ripple on the water, but his eyes were too poor to make out anything more clearly.

The splashing creature stood up in the water on its two hind legs: upright, ungainly, brushing drops from the hair on its head. It was his friend of yesterday. It had discarded its furs; they lay in a neat pile on the shore. And now Longtusk could clearly see that it – *he* – was a male. His body was coated by a fine light brown hair; wet, it lay flat against the contours of his body. There was an odd patch of discoloration on his face, a jagged line across his cheek like the aurora's subtle curtain. Perhaps it was a birthmark, Longtusk speculated.

He was pushing a twig of some kind – Longtusk thought it was willow – into his mouth and expertly swivelling it around with his paw. Perhaps he was cleaning out his teeth.

Willow, he thought. That's what I will call this odd little creature. Willow.

Longtusk didn't like to admit to himself how pleased he was to see a familiar creature.

Willow let the water drain from his eyes – and he saw Longtusk clearly, standing placidly on the shore only a few paces away.

He yelped in shock, and glanced over at his pile of furs. There was a pointed stick resting there – perhaps the one he had used yesterday against the cat – but it was much too far away to reach.

But of course Longtusk meant him no harm. And when he realised this, after long heartbeats, Willow seemed to relax.

With much splashing, Willow made his way through the water to Longtusk. He reached out to scratch the mammoth's trunk hair as he had the day before. His mouth issued a stream of incomprehensible grunts; his row of teeth shone white in the morning sun.

Willow's face was round, all but bare of the light hair that coated the rest of his muscular body. His skull was long, and black hair dangled from it as from the belly of a mammoth. His nose was broad and deep, and his face seemed to protrude, almost as if it had been pulled forward by his great nostrils. His eyes gleamed like lumps of amber beneath huge bony forehead ridges.

He lifted his willow stick and offered it to Longtusk. For an instant the stubby fingers at the end of Longtusk's trunk touched Willow's palm, and Willow snatched back his paw with a frightened yelp. But then he held the stick forward again, and let Longtusk take it.

Longtusk had never seen Willow's kind before, but now,

in the light of day, his mind more clear, he knew what this creature was.

These were not Fireheads, but the cousins of Fireheads. The mammoths called them *Dreamers*.

Dreamers could be found in little pockets of habitation around the landscape, rarely travelling far from their homes. They would sometimes scavenge dead mammoths, but unlike other predators they were little threat.

And there were very few of them. Once – it was said in the Cycle – the Dreamers had covered the world. Now they were rarely encountered.

Willow ran his little paws through the long hairs on Longtusk's flank and back. When he probed at the broken flesh there, Longtusk couldn't help but flinch and growl. Willow stumbled back, his paws coated with blood and dirt.

The Dreamer cupped his paws and began to ladle water over Longtusk's back. As blood and dirt was washed away, the pain was clear and sharp, but Longtusk made himself stand stock still.

Then Willow bent over and dug. He straightened up with his paws full of black, sticky lake-bottom mud. He began to cake this liberally over Longtusk's wounds. Again this hurt – especially as the little Dreamer couldn't see what he was doing, and frequently poked a finger into a raw wound. But already Longtusk could feel how the thick mud was soothing the ache of his injuries.

There was a guttural shout from the shore. Both Longtusk and Willow turned.

It was another Dreamer, like Willow. But this one was much taller – presumably an adult, probably a male – and it, he, was dressed in thick heavy furs. There was no hair on the top of his long boulder-shaped head, which was marked with strange stripes of red and yellow.

Stripeskull, Longtusk thought.

Stripeskull had a pointed stick in his paw. This was no skinny sapling as Willow had carried, but a thick wooden shaft, its tip cruelly sharp and blackened by fire – and even Willow's little stick had been enough to bring down a cat, Longtusk recalled. Stripeskull's muscles bulged, and Longtusk had no doubt he would be able to hurl that stick hard enough to slice right through Longtusk's thick skin.

But Willow ran out of the lake, dripping glistening water, waving his forelegs in the air. Stripeskull was obviously angry and frightened – but he was hesitating, Longtusk saw.

The huge adult grabbed Willow's arm in one mighty paw and pulled him away from the lake. Again he raised his stick at Longtusk and jabbered something complex and angry. Then he turned and retreated towards the fire cave, dragging Willow with him.

Willow looked back once. Longtusk wondered if he could read regret, even longing, in the little one's manner.

It didn't matter. For Longtusk, of course, had no place here. Sadly he started to work his way out through the boulders and scree to the higher ground, seeking food.

In the days that followed, Longtusk walked far and wide.

It wasn't particularly surprising that this land was so unfamiliar to him. It was an unpromising, ugly place, all but barren – not a place for mammoths. There seemed to be a sheet of hard black rock that underlay much of the land; here and there the rock broke to the surface, and in those places nothing grew save a few hardy lichen. Even where the rock was buried it had pushed the permafrost closer to the surface, and little could grow in the thin layer of moist soil on top.

Longtusk was a big animal, and he needed to find a great deal of fodder every day. Soon he had to walk far to find a place beyond his own trample marks and decaying spoor.

Still he saw no sign of any other mammoth: no trails, no spoor save his own. He tried trumpeting, rumbling and stamping. His sensitive ears picked up only the distant howl of wolves, the slow grind of the ice sheet to the north, the moan of chill air spilling down from the North Pole.

And winter was drawing in rapidly, the days shrivelling and the nights turning into long, cold, star-frosted deserts of darkness. It was a winter Longtusk knew he would be lucky to survive, alone.

Though he roamed far, he was drawn back to the lake and the cave. After all the only being in his world who had shown him any kindness was the Dreamer cub, Willow. It was hard to leave that behind.

There was more than one cave, in fact. There was a whole string of them, right along the river bank and lake shore, gaping mouths in the rock from which the Dreamers would emerge, daily, to do their chores.

Longtusk watched them.

The males would seek out meat. With their long blackened sticks they hunted smaller animals like reindeer and red deer. They generally ignored the larger animals, like horses and aurochs. But they would often scavenge meat from an animal brought down by some more fierce predator, chasing away the hyenas and condors, slicing at the carcass with pieces of stone they held in their paws.

The males ate their meat out in the field, taking little back to the caves. Longtusk realised that like mammoth Bulls they did not provide food or protection for their cubs. That was the job of the females. Slowed by their young, often laden with infants clamped to their breasts, the females did not travel as far as the males, and so did not eat so well. They would hunt with small sticks, seeking out game like rabbits or birds. But their principal foodstuff, plucked from the lake, was aquatic plants like cattails.

The females were as strong and stocky as the males, for they worked even harder in their relentless drive to sustain and protect themselves and their cubs.

As wide as he travelled, Longtusk saw no other groups of Dreamers. This small Clan in their caves seemed utterly isolated, cut off from the rest of their kind. And yet that seemed unimportant to them. They were immersed in their small world, in themselves, in each other; they had no need for a wider web of social contacts like the mammoths' Clans.

All this Longtusk saw in glimpses, as the Moon cycled in the sky. But as a growing mammoth he was not exactly inconspicuous; and whenever the Dreamers saw him they would shout and jab sticks and hurl rocks until he went away. They were not mammoth hunters by habit, but Longtusk knew they could easily kill him if they chose, or if he seemed threatening enough. He recoiled from their weapons, and their hostility – a hostility that seemed shared by all except Willow.

Willow remained with the females and their brood. But he seemed somehow distanced, older than the rest of the infants, often the subject of an irritable cuff from one female or another. Perhaps that was why Willow's behaviour was different from the others, why he had been moved to risk his own life to save a mammoth's. Longtusk wondered if Willow, like Longtusk himself, was reaching a cusp, preparing to leave his mother and her sisters and seek out the male hunter groups.

The strange idea that he and Willow might have something in common was obscurely comforting.

As winter drew in, the nights grew long and deep, the days brief.

There was a spate of early snow storms. The air here was sucked dry by the icecap, and there was little fresh snow. But ground blizzards, with old snow picked up by heavy winds, frequently occurred. So, when it snowed, it was usually in the midst of a ferocious wind storm that might persist for days.

Longtusk endured the blizzards. He felt the snow's weight gather on his back, but he knew he was protected. His body generated its own heat by slowly burning the fat reserves he

311

had stored up during the summer. That heat was trapped with remarkable efficiency by his shell of fur and guard hairs – so well, in fact, that snow that fell on his back did not melt.

Still, in the worst of the weather, he could do nothing but stand in his shell of snow and endure. Any movement would have burned up the fat reserves whose primary use was keeping him alive. But even so, despite his hoarding of his reserves, he felt himself being depleted, bit by bit, as the winter drew in.

When the weather relented, Longtusk travelled even further than before in search of food.

In some places the wind kept patches of sun-cured summer grass free of heavy snow. When he uncovered the ground to feed, he was followed by Arctic hares or ptarmigan, seeking willow buds and insects.

But the land had emptied. The migrant animals like the deer had gone far south to warmer climes, and the Arctic foxes had retreated to sea ice, living exclusively from the remnants of polar bear kills. Some life persisted, nevertheless. There were lemmings that burrowed beneath the snow, ptarmigans that dove into drifts for insulation, even plants that managed to flourish in pockets of warm air beneath the ice.

In these days of darkness and cold and windblown snow, everything was slowed. To extend a trunk tip or open an eye, unprotected by fur, could lead to agonising pain. Any bit of moisture would turn to crystals, creating an ice fog; when he walked a cloud hung over him, shining with light.

Once he saw a snowy owl gliding silently past, and its breath trailed after it in the air.

One fiercely cold day he walked along the river valley near the Dreamers' caves, seeking water. But he found the river here had run dry.

The river had iced over. But the ice crust had broken and fallen in, and the valley floor beneath was dry. The river had first frozen over, but then the watershed further up-stream had frozen, and the water beneath the ice crust had stopped flowing. The river had drained away, leaving the unsupported crust above.

Longtusk climbed down to the river bed, the bones of fish crunching beneath his feet, grubbing for water in the cold mud.

He followed the dry bed until he reached the lake, and there, at last, he drank deeply.

But a few days later, the lake froze over.

Longtusk bent to the water's edge and tried to crack the ice with his tusks. The ice splintered and starred as he scraped. But close to the bank, where the ice clung to the muddy bottom, there was too little water beneath to satisfy his thirst. And he knew that if he ventured farther out the ice could crack under him, and he could become trapped in the mud, even drown.

He walked along the shore, seeking a place he knew where the water ran over big chunks of black rock. But even this waterfall had frozen over; great lumps and streamers of white ice clung to the rocks.

He could survive on little food – but he needed water.

He lacked a detailed knowledge of this landscape. He had no idea where he might find frozen-over ponds whose crusts might be thin enough to break with his tusks; nor did he have the skills to discover new water sources for himself.

He was cut off from the wisdom of the Clan. He knew he had much to learn about the land and how to survive – and nobody was here to teach him.

For days, lacking any better idea, he survived on nothing but dribbles of muddy, half-frozen lake bed ooze, and his strength dwindled further.

But then, when he returned hopefully to the lake, he found a wide area of it had been cleared of ice. Without hesitation Longtusk splashed out into the water, ignoring its sharp cold as it soaked into the hair of his legs. He dipped his trunk into the clear liquid and sucked it up gratefully.

The break in the ice was suspiciously neat, a half-disc like a waning Moon. Its inner rim looked chipped and scarred – as if by the paw of a Dreamer.

This cleared pool was not natural; it must be the work of his only friend, the Dreamer cub Willow, who must have seen his distress and decided to help him. Despite the chill of the brief winter day, Longtusk felt warmed.

But soon the winter's cold bit harder.

A savage wind from the north, spilling off the flanks of the ice sheet itself, howled across the battered, exposed land. Dust closed around him, shutting out the brief slivers of daylight. This storm brought little snow, but it drove great billows of dust and sand from the pulverised lands uncovered by the retreating ice.

This was an age of savage weather, dominated by the huge masses of cold air that lingered over the immense polar ice sheets, driven to instability by the accelerating warming of the climate. This hard, dry storm, Longtusk knew, might last for months.

He saw no sign of the Dreamers. They must have been sheltering in their caves.

As for himself, he could only push his body against the rocks of the river bank and try to endure.

The days of the storm wore on. He had nothing to drink but scraps of ice and snow, which anyhow chilled him as much as nourished him; and he couldn't even recall when he had last found anything to eat.

Frost gathered around his mouth and trunk tip and gummed up his eyes. A deep shivering worked its way into his bones.

It was the wind that did the damage. Still air wouldn't have been so bad, for a thin layer of warm air would have gathered around his body. But the wind, impatient and snatching, stole each scrap of heat his body produced, casting it into the south, gone, useless.

If he was with his Family they would have huddled now, gathered in a group, the youngest calves at the centre of the huddle, the adults taking their turns on the outside of the group, facing into the wind. Thanks to the Family, few mammoths would perish in such a storm.

But here, alone, Longtusk had no others to help him and protect him: only these mute, uncaring rocks.

And he knew it wasn't enough.

The shivering went away, and the cold started to penetrate deep into the core of his body. When it got there, he would quietly slide into a final sleep, not to wake again until he reached the aurora.

But perhaps that wouldn't be so bad. Perhaps there he would find his mother and his sister and even that bullying oaf Rockheart, whom he would now never get a chance to best.

As the cold gathered around his heart, he felt almost peaceful.

. . . There was something warm and soft at the tip of his trunk. It was tugging at him. He tried to open his eyes, but they were shut by ice. He shook his head, rumbling, and forced his eyelids to open with a soft crackle.

Sand and grit immediately dug into his opened eyes. The storm still raged all around him.

Something stood before him, a bundle of fur, upright. Brown eyes peered.

It was Willow. And, with one fur-wrapped paw, the Dreamer cub was tugging at Longtusk's trunk, urging him to follow.

Longtusk had almost reached the blank numbness of death, and it had been comfortable. If he returned to the land of life, he would face all its complexities: choices, hardship, pain. If only Willow let him alone . . . Just a little longer . . .

But you are Longtusk. Surely the greatest hero of them all is destined for a better death than this: alone, ignored, frozen by the mindless wind. Take your chance, Longtusk!

His trunk-fingers slipped into Willow's palm.

It was difficult to walk. His joints had become stiff, so deeply had the cold penetrated them. And when he moved out of the shelter of the rocks, the wind battered him unhindered.

But it wasn't easy for the Dreamer cub either. He felt Willow stagger, but the cub pulled himself upright against Longtusk.

They seemed to walk for a very long time.

At last they reached a place where the wind was diminished. And Longtusk felt a deep warmth radiating over his face and chest.

He was in the mouth of one of the caves. Willow was standing beside him, pulling off his furs in great frosty grit-laden bundles.

The cave was a well of red light and warmth. Flaps of animal skin had been fixed over this cave mouth. Perhaps they were supposed to drape over the entrance, keeping its warmth inside, like the flap of skin over a mammoth's anus.

The warmth came from fire, he realised suddenly: a fire that burned, smokily, in a circle of stones.

He recoiled, instinctive fear rising anew in him. But behind him, the Beringian night howled its fury.

There was no place for him out there. Despite the fire, he forced himself to stay still.

There were many Dreamers here: females, males, infants. They lay on the floor of the cave, fat and sleepy, all of them slabs of muscle. The females clustered together with their infants away from the males, who lay on their backs snoring. Some were naked; others wore light skins around their shoulders and waists. Their bare skin looked greasy, as if it had been coated by the fat of some dead animal – perhaps to keep in their bodies' warmth.

One of the dozing males stirred, perhaps disturbed by the wind that leaked in through the open skins. It was Stripe-skull, his red and yellow scalp unmistakable.

His eyes grew large as he saw a mammoth standing in the cave entrance, immense tusk shadows striped over the walls.

With surprising grace Stripeskull rolled to his feet and barked out guttural noises. Other males woke up, blinking and rubbing their eyes; when they saw Longtusk they quickly got to their hind legs, grabbing sticks of wood and sharp stones.

. . . Then the males fell back, making retching noises and waving their paws before their faces.

Longtusk realised that he had just defecated, as mammoths do many times a day, barely conscious of it. He looked back. His dung was a pile of tubular bricks, acrid, immense. He tried to push it outside the cave. But he succeeded only in smearing the hot, sticky stuff over the cave floor.

Willow was going forward to meet Stripeskull. They jabbered at each other in a fast, complex flow; they made gestures too with their heads and paws. It was obviously a language, Longtusk realised, like the mammoths' language of trumpets, growls, stomps and postures. But he had absolutely no idea what they were saying to each other. Perhaps even the frequent cuffs about the head which Stripeskull delivered to Willow were like the mammoths' subtle code of touch and rubbing. But from the way Willow was rubbing his head it was obvious the blows were also meant to hurt.

Lacking any alternative, exhausted, Longtusk stood in the cave mouth and awaited his fate.

At last Willow came to him. He reached out to Longtusk's trunk, and pushed.

Longtusk understood. He let himself be moved back out of the cave. He wasn't welcome here; it had only been a

317

childish impulse of Willow's to bring him here in the first place.

So he must suffer the wind's bony embrace once more. He felt a stab of resentment at the pain he would have to endure before he regained that numb acceptance . . .

But Willow was pulling at his trunk. He looked down. The Dreamer cub was hauling as hard as he could, his feet scraping along the ground, trying to halt the retreating mammoth.

Longtusk stopped. He was out of the cave itself, beyond the curtain of skins, but still inside its mouth. It was enough to shelter him from the wind, and the heat that leaked out of the cave seeped into his bones.

Willow held up a twig of dried wood. Longtusk had time to grab it before the cub was snatched out of sight by a glaring Stripeskull, who pulled closed the skins, shutting Longtusk out in the dark.

Longtusk munched on the twig, and – standing in the mouth of the cave, on ground imprinted by splayed Dreamer feet, bathed by stray fire warmth – he slipped easily into a deep and dreamless sleep.

CHAPTER 5
THE CAVE

The storm persisted.

Willow brought him water in a sack of skin. Longtusk drank greedily, despite a lingering stink of bison. But a mammoth is a large animal and the load of water – almost too much for Willow to carry – was downed in a couple of heartbeats.

Willow tried bringing him food. At first he produced scraps of meat, dried and salted. The stench was horrifying, and Longtusk shied back.

After that Willow brought him dried grass. There was a lot of grass in the cave; the Dreamers scattered it over the cave floor and pulled it into rough pallets to sleep on. The grass was stale and stank of the Dreamers and their fire, but it rapidly filled up his belly.

After a few days he noticed the Dreamers going out, wrapped in their furs, bringing back loads of his dung. During his brief glimpses through the parted skins, Longtusk saw that they burned the dried dung in their wide, flat hearth – along with grass, wood, bone and even bat guano, scraped from great dry heaps at the back of the cave.

The hearth – a disc of blackened earth, lined with flat stones – was the centrepiece of the cave. The adults took turns to check on the burning embers, piling on more fuel, or blowing on the glowing lumps of dung and wood and bone. The low fire kept the Dreamers alive, and maintaining it was their single most important activity.

The cave walls were pale rock, and the fire's ruddy light would glimmer from the fleshy stone, casting strange and colourful shadows.

Generally the Dreamers lived as mammoths do, Longtusk observed. The adult males kept to their own society away from the females. The males seemed to spend an inordinate amount of time belching, farting and scratching their testicles. The females grunted at each other continually and watched over their cubs with a sort of irritable affection.

Once a female came into oestrus. She walked provocatively past the indolent males, who rose from their slumbers with growls of interest. A brief contest of shouting and wrestling resolved itself in favour of Stripeskull, and he took the female by the paw and led her to the back of the cave.

The coupling of these two muscle-bound creatures was noisy and spectacular. Afterwards the pair of them returned to the hearth, sweating and exhilarated.

Most of the males carried pointed sticks, Longtusk saw. The biggest, strongest males – like Stripeskull – had the proudest sticks. Youngsters like Willow and old, bent, toothless adults had to make do with shorter sticks, some of them broken discards. But even the infants would toddle back and forth waving tiny sharpened branches and yelling.

The sticks were like the tusks of mammoth Bulls, Longtusk realised: not just useful tools, but weapons to be cherished and displayed.

One day Longtusk saw where the sticks came from.

At the back of the cave had been stacked some saplings, slim and straight. Stripeskull took one of these, stripped it of its branches and bark with stone scrapers, and then whittled down one end to a point with more chips of stone. Then he laid the sharpened end into the fire until it charred, and scraped it some more until it was fine and sharp.

He tested it by ramming it into animal carcasses hanging at the back of the cave. The exposure to fire, far from destroying the stick as Longtusk would have expected, had made it harder and more able to penetrate.

He realised now that he owed his life to this strange ingenuity – that and the courage of the cub, Willow.

But the Dreamers were capable of much stranger miracles than merely sharpening sticks.

Longtusk watched as Stripeskull took a nodule of creamy flint. He had gathered it from the river bank, where it had been washed down from chalk deposits upstream. Stripeskull sat near the hearth and laid around him other blocks of stone and bits of bone. Using one of the heavy stones, wrapped in his paw, Stripeskull began to chip at the flint block. Soon he was surrounded by a scattering of fine flakes – but he had turned his rough block of flint into a core shaped like a fat lemming, Longtusk thought, flat on the bottom and rounded on the top. Then he rubbed and ground the rim of the core, flattening it.

What came next seemed to demand great care. Stripeskull turned the core over, finally selecting a spot. Then he cupped it in one paw, raised the leg bone of a deer in the other, and gave the core a single sharp whack.

When he lifted the flint out of his paw, he left behind a round flake, very fine, its exposed surface smooth as new ice. He inspected it critically, tapped a few flakes off its edge, and tested its sharpness by rubbing it over his leg, shaving off a small patch of fur.

Then he put it to one side, returned to his core, and continued work. When he was done, he had turned a lump of unpromising flint into half a dozen fine stone blades.

He was evidently trying to teach the cub, Willow, how to work the flint. Like a mammoth calf trying to dig out his first waterhole, Willow tried to ape Stripeskull's actions. But his flint nodules just smashed and chipped, and Willow, frustrated, threw away the debris in disgust. The next day Stripeskull would sit with him, patiently, to try again.

After watching all this, Longtusk found a flint nodule just outside the cave mouth. Nearby he saw a scattering of broken flint flakes. He picked up the nodule in his trunk-fingers and turned it over and over. He tried to recall what he had seen, how these objects had been shaped by the ingenuity of Stripeskull. But already the memory of that mysterious magic was slipping from his mind.

Mammoths too could change the world: destroying trees, digging for water, clearing snow. But they would never learn to shape the things around them with the command of these strange, clumsy, upright Dreamers.

The Dreamers put the stones to use in every corner of their cave.

At the back of the cave hung the butchered carcasses of many animals – deer, reindeer, horse and bison – and their skins were stretched out to dry with stones and sticks. Sometimes one of the adults would scrape a skin with a slice of rock, over and over, working the skin to a supple smoothness. Longtusk marvelled at the way the Dreamers' powerful muscles worked, and the stone responded to their huge, dextrous fingers.

And there were even finer uses for the stones. All of the Dreamers used stone flakes to cut the hair that dangled from their heads, or to scrape their faces. Every few days Stripeskull himself would use one of his flint slices to scrape smooth the hair on his head. Then he would splash the raw skin with cold water, and draw lumps of ochre, bits of red and yellow rock, across his scalp to renew his gaudy colouring.

It was obvious from the powerful physique of all the Dreamers, males, females and cubs, that everybody here was expected to work hard throughout their lives. Many of them showed signs of old injury. But the old, the very young, the sick and the frail were cared for.

One small cub, though, was very sickly, much skinnier than others of its height. Longtusk saw how she had trouble feeding herself, despite her mother's increasingly frantic assistance.

There came a day when the cub would not stir from her pallet of grass. Her mother struggled to wake her, and she even tried to suckle the cub, though her breasts were flaccid and empty of milk.

At last the mother gave up. She came to the mouth of the cave. She tipped back her great head on its low, thick neck and raised the limp body of her cub to a stormy sky.

The other females gathered close to the distressed one, comforting her with strokes and caresses. The younger cubs pulled away to the corners of the cave, wide-eyed. The adult males, awkwardly, kept away from the females – all save two of them, who began to dig a deep hole in the ground.

When the hole was done, deep and straight-edged, Stripe-skull clambered into the pit with the body of the female cub. The little one had been washed, her hair shaved and tidied. The grieving mother dropped dried flowers over the body, and Stripeskull sprinkled powdered ochre, a red mist that floated gently down into the pit.

Then the Dreamers began to sing – adults and all but the smallest cubs – a strange, deep ululation that rolled endlessly like a river, smooth and sad.

Longtusk understood. These Dreamers, in their own way, were Remembering the cub, just as mammoths have always Remembered their own dead.

Longtusk saw that the walls of the grave pit, deep and sheer, were made up of complex layers of debris: rock, flint flakes, blackened ashy dust, bone splinters. Such detritus could only have been laid down by the Dreamers themselves. The Dreamers must have inhabited this cave – on this undistinguished river bank, making their unchanging hearths and tools – for generation upon generation upon generation: an unimaginably long time, reaching into their deepest past. Perhaps there were more bones buried here – bones a hundred thousand years deep, likewise scattered with flowers and ochre flakes – here in this trampled ground, where these strange creatures had dreamt away the unchanging millennia.

And still they sang.

Did they sing of a time when their kind had covered the world? Did they sing of their loss, their diminution to dwindling, isolated groups like this?

Did they sing of their future – and their fear?

Longtusk slipped away from the cave mouth and walked off, ignoring the driving dust, until he could hear the Dreamers' song no more.

The dust storm passed, and the cold began to ease its grip.

Heavy rain pounded the land, and glacial run-off poured along the river valley, threatening floods. The ground in front of the cave turned into a sink of oozing mud, and the adult Dreamers, slipping and sliding in the mess, complained profusely.

Longtusk knew the time was approaching when he must leave the relative security of this place. Perhaps when the weather was better he could even strike out north, and seek his Family.

So, his winter fur beginning to blow loose in a cloud around him, he took to travelling increasing distances from the cave. He was half-starved, his fat depleted, severely weakened by the harshest winter of his life.

But he still breathed. And, despite the rain and the continuing cold, life was returning to the land. The low, wind-battered trees were sprinkled with buds, full of the optimism of the new season, and the first crocuses and jonquils were showing, bright yellow and purple. Day by day, as he fed on the new growth, his strength returned.

In fact, he found he himself had grown during the bleak cold of winter. His tusks were longer still, heavier, thicker. He flashed them in the air, parrying imaginary opponents, even though there was nobody to see.

One day he found a place where a carpet of new grass,

thin green shoots, was pushing through the matted remains of last year's growth. Contentedly he began to graze.

He heard a soft mewling, like a wounded cat, coming from behind a low outcrop of hard black rock.

Pricked by curiosity, he walked over to see.

At first sight he thought it was a Dreamer cub. It was a female, wearing the ragged remains of cut and shaped skins. She was smaller in height than Willow, so presumably younger. She seemed in distress; she was huddled over on herself, clutching her spindly forelegs to her chest, and she was crying.

He ran his trunk tip over her limbs.

She was like a Dreamer, yes. But she was much thinner, her limbs weaker but more graceful. Even her head was a different shape, with a flat face, a prominent chin, a protruding forehead – no heavy eye ridges – and a compact skull. Her body seemed bare of hair: all except her head, where there was a tangled, dirty mane of fine yellow hair.

She wore something around her neck. He bent to see. Little white objects had been punctured with holes, and then strung together on what looked like a strip of sinew.

They were teeth: tiny mammoth teeth, drawn from a very new calf, perhaps even an unborn.

He rumbled in dismay.

At the noise, the cub's eyes flickered open. They were a startling blue, like steppe melt-pools. When she saw the mountain of muscle and fat and hair over her, tusk shadows looming, she yelped and tried to pull away. But she was weak, and she was trapped by the cleft of rock.

Now he could see quite how ill she was. The fingers on her paws were dead white, and her lips looked blue. But she was not shivering: the cold had penetrated deep into her body, and without help this mite would soon surely die.

He reached down with his trunk, meaning to stroke her, but she wailed feebly, unable to move.

He moved back a few paces. There was a small stand of

crocuses glowing in the lee of the rock. With his delicate trunk-fingers, he plucked out a single fat yellow bloom. He carried it to the female, and dropped it on her chest.

She seemed a little less frightened. She tried to close her paw over the flower.

Gently he wrapped his trunk under the cub and lifted her up. She was light as a feather, and her limbs dangled, unresisting. But she had managed to keep hold of her flower. He began to walk, slowly and steadily, towards the cave of the Dreamers.

After a time the cub seemed to lose her fear. She gathered pawfuls of his long trunk hairs and burrowed into them. Soon she was asleep, wrapped in the warm strength of the mammoth's trunk.

The Dreamers reacted with confusion.

This was a stranger – not one of their Clan – not even one of their kind. At first the adults seemed to have difficulty even seeing the limp cub, as if she was a thing of shadows, only half-glimpsed, too strange to comprehend. But the young were fascinated, and they clustered around, lifting aside Longtusk's trunk fur to see the sleeping cub.

Some of the males came at Longtusk with their pointed, blackened sticks, as they hadn't for some months, as if he had brought them threat in the form of this helpless cub. The females were solicitous. As soon as they realised what distress this strange cub was in, they lifted her away from Longtusk and took her towards the hearth. There they stripped away her ragged skins, rubbed grease into her skin, and huddled around her, sandwiching the cub between their own great bodies.

Willow came up to Longtusk. He rubbed Longtusk's trunk fur affectionately, and Longtusk realised that Willow, at least, thought he had done the right thing—

Somebody screamed.

It was one of the female Dreamers, an old woman, her

face twisted by an ancient burn. She was pointing at the three of them: the strange female cub, Willow and Longtusk, over and over, jabbering and growling, frightened.

She sees something, Longtusk realised, chilled. Something about the three of us.

Suddenly the cave walls, solid rock, seemed to melt away, the Dreamers dispersing like smoke, until there was only the three of them, alone, locked together. *She sees the end of my life. She thinks we will die together, we three: the yellow-haired cub, Willow, and me.*

But how can anybody know the future? And what strange fate could make such a thing happen? . . .

The old female stumbled away, scared, shouting.

And there was a howl of outrage.

Blood was pouring down Stripeskull's foreleg, where a stick protruded from his flesh. With a yell of anger and pain he dragged the stick out of his body, ripping the wound wider.

This was no simple stick of sharpened wood, Longtusk realised immediately. It had feathers attached to its base – and it was tipped, not by fire-hardened wood, but by a flake of flint, sharpened to a point much finer than any the Dreamers could manufacture.

And now shadows flitted past the cave, urgent, menacing. Stripeskull threw down the bloody stick and, with a growl of anger, marched to the mouth of the cave.

Longtusk scarcely noticed. He raised his trunk and tested the air, turning it this way and that, questing.

Longtusk was electrified. He could smell mammoth.

CHAPTER 6
THE NEWCOMERS

He stumbled out of the cave mouth to the open air.

Behind him, from the caves, he heard shouting, raised Dreamer voices. But the noises were small and far away and nothing to do with him. All that mattered was that profound and alluring smell of his own kind: musty fur and dung and even the sharp tang of musth – and, in pulses of deep sound, he thought he could hear huge, heavy strides: many of them, a Family or a bachelor herd, close by.

It was too much to hope that this was *his* Family; he knew he was far from their normal pastures. But these strangers would surely help him find his way back to his own. It was as if he had suddenly recalled who he was. How could he have spent so long, an entire winter, huddled in a mouth of eroded rock?

But the wind was swirling, and it was impossible to tell where the scents were coming from. He crashed deeper into the brush, trunk raised eagerly.

Before long, at the edge of the river, he came to a place where the stink of mammoths was very strong. He searched until he found a small, compact pile of dung.

Mammoth dung . . . perhaps.

He poked at it with his trunk, raised a fragment to his tongue to taste. It was warm and soft, obviously very recent, and its smell was strong and pungent. But its texture was strange – thicker and more fibrous than the dung of his Family – and he could taste a heavy concentration of wood and bark.

Mammoths' diets differ, according to individual taste, and

what they eat affects the quality of their dung. But Longtusk knew no mammoth whose diet was quite so skewed as to produce waste like this.

He pushed on.

He found a place where the trees were broken, the branches stripped of their bark and leaf buds, the ground trampled. Another unmistakable sign: mammoths had fed here – more than one, judging by the scale of the damage.

. . . But, like the dung, the pattern of tree damage was odd. Many of the younger saplings' trunks had been pushed aside, as if by animals who were shorter and squatter than he was. And he saw that bark and leaf buds had been taken extensively, even from above head height. Woolly mammoths will take a little bark and foliage in their diet, but they prefer the grasses and herbs of the open steppe.

Still he saw no mammoths: not so much as a silhouette glimpsed through the trees, the swish of a tail, or the curve of a tusk. He rumbled, but there was no reply.

If they were here, whoever they were, why did they not greet him?

He decided to return to the mouth of the Dreamers' cave. From there he would follow the trail that would take him back up to the steppe. Surely there, on the open plain, he would be able to find the strange mammoths.

He reached the edge of the trees, close to the Dreamers' cave – and, still in the shelter of the trees, he slowed to a halt.

Several of the Dreamers had emerged from their caves. But they were not alone.

Confronting them was a new group of creatures: standing upright like the Dreamers, but spindly, taller, much less robust.

The legs of these others were thin and taut – like those of a horse, meant for running and walking long distances. The newcomers had flat, delicate faces and high bulging skulls.

They were covered in skins, like the Dreamers, but Longtusk could see that these garments were much more finely worked than the rough creations of the Dreamers. Their paws were delicate and they held things – pointed sticks and flakes of stone – and other, incomprehensible items, like a length of wood tied up with deer sinew so that it was bent over in an arc.

And they stalked among the Dreamers with arrogance and hostility.

Longtusk spotted Stripeskull. Blood still stained his shoulder where the strange stick had punctured it. But now the big Dreamer was crouching in the dirt. He was roaring defiance, trying to stand using one of his fire-hardened sticks as a prop – but one hind leg was dragging behind him, and Longtusk saw blood pulsing from a broad gash. He was surrounded by five or six of the newcomers, and they held sticks out towards Stripeskull, threatening him.

The Dreamer females and cubs had been brought out of the cave, driven like recalcitrant calves by prods with sticks and stones. The females huddled together in a group, surrounded by the newcomers, with their cubs at the centre. They seemed bewildered as much as frightened, and their gaze slid over the newcomers that stalked amongst them – as if they were too strange even to be properly visible, as if the Clan was being overwhelmed by a party of ghosts.

Apart from Stripeskull, Longtusk could see no other Dreamer adult males. Perhaps they were off on one of their scavenging trips – or perhaps they had been driven away, by these cold, calculating others.

Longtusk watched, fascinated, repelled. He knew what he was seeing.

He had never before encountered these creatures, these distorted, hostile cousins of the Dreamers. But many of his kind had – and an understanding of the danger they posed was drummed into every young mammoth.

These were the most ferocious predators of all – more to be feared, despite their frail appearance, than even the great cats – and the only response to encountering them was flight.

For they had mastered fire itself.

And *they* were not content to let embers burn in shallow hearths, like the Dreamers; instead they used fire to drive their way across the land. Perhaps they had even been responsible for the fire which had separated him from his Family. Hadn't he glimpsed slender running forms during his dreadful flight through the smoke?

He had been wrong before, when he had first encountered Willow. About these newcomers there could be no doubt, and black dread settled on his heart.

For these were Fireheads.

One of the newcomers turned and looked directly towards him.

This one was shorter than the others, with a broad, plump belly that glistened with grease. He sniffed loudly, his small, straight nose twitching. He was, thought Longtusk, like a fat, overgrown lemming, walking comically upright on two hind legs.

He knows I'm here, Longtusk thought, hidden as I am among these trees. Or he suspects so, anyhow. He is smarter than the rest.

Now Willow spotted Longtusk too. He called out and lunged forward.

A Firehead tripped him with a stick. Willow sprawled, howling.

One of the females pushed her way out of the group and ran to Willow. Perhaps it was his mother. A Firehead confronted her. She dodged his stick and swung one mighty fist at his long, delicate face. Longtusk heard the unmistakable crack of shattering bone, and the other fell back with a gurgling cry, clutching his face.

But more of the others joined the fray. They wrestled the

female to the ground and pinned her there, a male's weight pressing down on each of her mighty limbs.

Now, from the mouth of the cave, another emerged. He was dressed in skins, like the rest, but he wore a crown of what looked like bone – *from which smoke streamed*, as if he carried burning embers cupped in scrapings in the bone. Smoke rose even from his paws, and Longtusk realised he had taken ashes from the precious hearth which the Dreamers had preserved all winter long.

Seemingly oblivious to pain, this grotesque creature raised his paws to the air and howled a cry of thin triumph. He cast the ashes to the ground, scattered them with his feet, and extinguished them in the trampled mud. The others whooped and danced, jabbing their sticks into the air.

The Dreamers looked away, bewildered and defeated.

Burning-head stalked over to the Dreamer female, who was still pinned to the ground. His teeth showing white, he leaned over her. She bellowed and tried to twist her head away. But he came closer, as if to press his lips against hers.

She hawked and spat at him. He wiped his face and threw strings of greenish phlegm back at her.

Longtusk was baffled. Was this like a fight among mammoth Bulls for access to females? But it made no sense. Even Longtusk could see that the Dreamer female was not in oestrus. Perhaps the other did not want the female, but only to demonstrate his power and dominance.

But now the ugly tableau was disturbed. Another was emerging from the Dreamer cavern: taller even than Burning-head, his head adorned by a cap of yellow-white beads – beads of mammoth ivory, Longtusk realised queasily. This one looked oddly frail, his hair a grizzled white, his skin wrinkled and weather-beaten. But he carried the limp form of the yellow-haired cub in his arms.

The rest, even Burning-head, cringed away from this new one, deferring.

Burning-head was evidently a powerful figure. But it was obvious that this new male was the true power, like the strongest Bull in a bachelor herd.

'. . . What fine tusks you have, cousin. And yet they do you little good if you stand facing into the wind.'

The voice had come from directly behind Longtusk. He whirled, trumpeting in alarm.

Now the Fireheads knew he was there; they reacted, shouting. But none of that mattered, compared to the massive looming presence suddenly here behind him.

For it was a mammoth . . . and yet it was not.

It, he, was a male. He wasn't as tall as a full-grown mammoth Bull, yet he loomed over Longtusk. He was coated with wiry black-brown hair, shorter and darker than Longtusk's, some of it stained by the grey of age. His back was flat, lacking the fleshy hump of a true mammoth, and he was heavy-set, his chest deep, his limbs and feet broad. And he had broad stubby tusks, heavily chipped and scarred.

Four of them: *four* tusks.

And, strangest of all, Longtusk made out a scar burned into his muscled flank: a strange five-pronged form, burned through the layers of hair and into his flesh, exactly like the outstretched paw of a Dreamer – or a Firehead.

The other opened his great mouth and roared. A gush of warm, foetid air billowed out over Longtusk, stinking of crushed wood and sap. The not-mammoth's teeth were cones of enamel – not flat grinding surfaces like Longtusk's, but sharp, almost like a cat's cruel fangs.

Longtusk staggered back. He crashed out of the trees and into the clearing before the caves, in full view of Fireheads and Dreamers.

There were cries of shock. Panicking, he whirled around.

All but two of the Fireheads had fallen to the ground before him. The two who remained standing – staring at him open-mouthed – were the strong leader and the grotesque Burning-head. The leader put down his cub and picked up an abandoned stick. This was fitted with a blade of something that glittered like ice. He held the stick up, pointing it at Longtusk.

In the Fireheads' distraction, the Dreamers seemed to see their chance. Even the female who had been pinned to the ground was free now. Under her lead, the females gathered their cubs and, quickly, silently, began to slip away up the trail that led to the steppe. Willow pulled Stripeskull to his feet, then let Stripeskull lean on him so that he hopped forward on his one good hind leg.

Willow cast a single regretful glance back at Longtusk, and then was gone.

But there was no time to reflect.

A powerful trumpet and a slam of broad feet into the ground told Longtusk that the strange not-mammoth was right behind him. Terrified, bewildered, overwhelmed by strangeness, Longtusk turned, trumpeting. The Fireheads cringed anew.

The other's eyes were like dark pits, embedded in wrinkled sockets of flesh.

'Do you know what that blade is, cousin? It is *quartz*. A kind of rock that's harder and sharper than almost any other. The old fellow may not look so strong, but he could throw that spear so hard that quartz tip will nestle in your heart.' The not-mammoth's accent was strange – somehow guttural, primitive – but his language, of rumbles, trumpets, growls, stamps and posture, was clear to Longtusk.

Longtusk said, 'You are not mammoth.'

'No. But I am your cousin. Don't you know your Cycle? We are all Calves of Probos. I am better than mammoth. I am *mastodont*.'

The two great proboscideans faced each other, challenging, calculating, rumbling: members of hugely ancient species,

334

separated by evolutionary paths that had diverged twenty-five million years before.

The three Fireheads were engaged in a complex three-way argument.

'We call the leader *Bedrock*,' growled the mastodont. 'For he is strong and silent as the rock on which the world is built. His cub is called *Crocus*, for the colour of her hair. And the Shaman is *Smokehat*—'

'What is a Shaman?'

Bedrock had the quartz-tipped spear raised to shoulder height, and it was still pointing at Longtusk's heart. But Crocus was pulling at Bedrock's free foreleg and was jabbering excitedly, pointing at Longtusk.

Meanwhile Smokehat, with his grotesque garb of bone and smoke, was all but dancing with impatience and rage.

'The Shaman wants you killed. Bedrock is prepared to do it. But his cub seems to think you saved her life.'

'You can understand them?'

'You pick up a little,' the mastodont said wistfully, 'if you spend long enough with them. My name is Walks With Thunder.'

Longtusk growled. 'And mine is Longtusk. Learn it for my Remembering, mastodont, for I am ready to die.'

'Oh, that isn't the idea at all.'

'What?'

The mastodont reared up, looming over Longtusk and pawing at the air.

Startled, angry, bewildered, Longtusk backed away from this terrifying opponent and plunged into the stand of trees.

He found the trail that led to the open steppe.

He turned back the way he had come and raised his trunk, sniffing the air. There was no sign of pursuit.

But there was a smell of mammoth – no, it was the sharp, wood-ash stink of the animals he must call *mastodont* – and, he realised with mounting alarm, it came from all around him.

He turned again. And there was a mastodont ahead of him.

Like Walks With Thunder, this was a squat, powerfully built male with four stubby tusks. But he sported a broad scar that ran the length of his face, a scar that all but obliterated the socket of one eye. 'Hello, little grazer,' he rumbled. 'Welcome to the herd.'

As Longtusk turned once more, trunk raised, he saw and smelled more mastodonts to his left and right, like a line of stocky, hairy boulders: a row of them, all powerful adult males.

Now, with a drumming of mighty footsteps, the mastodonts marched intently towards him, converging. Every one of them bore the strange scar sported by Walks With Thunder, a Firehead paw burned into hairless flesh. The way they moved together, as if driven by a single mind, was unnerving.

And, strangest of all, there were Fireheads with them. They carried sticks tipped with curved pieces of bone, which they used to tap the mastodonts on the head or ears or flanks. Some of the mastodonts actually had Fireheads sitting astride their backs, with their long, thin hind legs draped over their necks, feet applying sharp kicks to the mastodonts' small ears.

Soon the mastodonts were close enough for him to make out what they were saying in their heavy, strange accent.

'. . . Well, well. What have we here? Don't tell me it's a grazer.'

'I haven't seen one of those grass-chewers for a long time. I thought they had all died out.'

'It must be a Cow. Look at those pretty-pretty tusks. Any self-respecting Bull would be too embarrassed to wear skinny monstrosities like that.'

'Hey, little grazer! Can I borrow your tusks? I need a pick

to clean out my musth gland, and those spindly things are just the right size . . .'

He saw that the mastodonts had closed the circle around him.

The big scarred Bull facing him was being whipped, severely, by the Firehead with him. The Firehead was shouting, a simple, repetitive sound: '*Agit! Agit!*' It was obvious he was trying to drive the big Bull forward. This Firehead was sapling-thin with a cruel, pinched face.

The scarred Bull, seeming unaware of the multiple wounds being inflicted on him, swivelled his huge, filth-crusted rump and let out a fart of thunderous intensity. A foul brown spray knocked the skinny Firehead backwards, and the line of mastodonts reacted with stomps and growls of amusement.

The Bull walked forward nonchalantly out of his dispersing brown cloud, muscles moving under his flat brown-black coat of hair. 'Sorry about that. These Fireheads are an irritation at times.'

Longtusk stood his ground and raised his tusks. 'Come any closer and I'll rip out your other eye.'

The mastodont grunted. He reached a stand of low, twisted spruce trees. His trunk flicked out, its pink tip running over one sapling after another. Finally he settled on the biggest, strongest tree of the grove. He wrapped his trunk around its girth and, with a single flick of his huge, low-slung head, ripped the tree out of the ground, roots and all. His mouth gaped, revealing a purple tongue and teeth like miniature mountains, chipped and worn. With a crackling splinter, he bit the tree clean in half, his long jaw bones moving in a powerful up-down motion quite different from the back-and-forth grinding of a mammoth's jaw. Then he stamped on the tree, breaking it up further.

Within a few heartbeats, a healthy tree had been reduced to a few shards.

'My name is Jaw Like Rock,' said the mastodont. He

opened his huge mouth and belched; a fine spray of spittle and wood chips peppered Longtusk. 'I enjoyed that. But you grazers prefer to munch on a few blades of grass, don't you? I suppose if that's all you're strong enough to manage—'

'I'm strong enough to best you,' Longtusk said.

Jaw Like Rock looked puzzled. 'Oh, yes. It's time for me to get my eye ripped out, isn't it? We'd better get it over with.'

Unexpectedly, something barged into Longtusk's backside. Trumpeting, he tried to turn.

Here was Walks With Thunder, his broad brow dipped. 'You let me creep up on you downwind again, little grazer. You've a lot to learn.'

'I've nothing to learn from you wood-nibblers.'

Walks With Thunder's broad head once again rammed his backside, hard. Longtusk stumbled and took two or three steps forward.

Now something wrenched backward on Longtusk's left hind leg. There was a loop of hide rope knotted around his ankle, over his foot. The rope's other end was tied tightly around the roots of a tree.

He heard a yelp of triumph from his feet.

He looked down. It was the little fat Firehead, the one who had detected his presence before anybody else. He had been crawling on the ground close to Longtusk's feet, and his flabby skin was coated with something dark and pungent.

'Dung,' Longtusk said. 'Mammoth dung.'

'*Your* dung,' said Walks With Thunder easily. 'That's how Lemming crept up on you. You couldn't smell him. Oldest trick there is, little grazer. And now you're caught.'

Longtusk trumpeted his alarm. 'Why are you doing this to me? Let me go! In the name of Probos—'

Walks With Thunder exchanged a glance with Jaw Like Rock, and Longtusk thought he detected a brief sadness there.

Walks With Thunder said, 'Grazer, this has nothing to do with Probos.'

'Don't worry, lad,' Jaw said. 'We've all been through it.'

'Been through what? Let me go.' Frustrated, frightened, angry, humiliated, Longtusk tugged with all his strength at the rope. It wouldn't give. Rumbling, enraged, he fell back.

The Fireheads stood around him in a loose circle, letting the drama play itself out.

Jaw Like Rock took a heavy step forward, 'Come on then, little grazer. Let's get this over. Give me your best shot.'

Longtusk eyed Jaw Like Rock. 'There is a stink of Firehead on you,' he said. 'You have no honour.'

Jaw Like Rock stiffened.

Walks With Thunder murmured, 'I wouldn't get him angry.'

Longtusk cried, 'For Probos!' And he roared and lunged with his tusks.

The mastodont side-stepped – but not fast enough; the tip of one mammoth tusk scraped down his flank. 'Well done, little grazer,' he said, his trunk investigating the wound. 'You were too fast for me.'

Longtusk looked down, and saw a smear of bright crimson at the sharp tip of one curling spiral tusk. He felt a surge of pride. If only Rockheart could see him now! . . .

'Get it over, Jaw,' growled Walks With Thunder. 'Don't try to make him feel better about it.'

Longtusk, straining at the sinew on his leg, said, 'What does he mean?'

'Nothing,' said Jaw Like Rock, wiping blood off the tip of his trunk on the sparse grass. 'He's an old fool. Do your worst, mighty mammoth, calf of Primus!' And he trumpeted and raised his stubby tusks.

Again Longtusk lunged.

But the mastodont was standing at his side. He had moved in a blur of speed, too fast for Longtusk to see. 'Forgive me, brave grazer.' And he brought his tusks crashing down on Longtusk's head.

It was as if thunder had clapped inside his head. The light was suddenly strange, with everything suffused by a bright golden tinge. To his surprise he found he was kneeling, his trunk dangling on the grass like the discarded skin of a snake.

He tried to lift his tusks, but, oddly, they were scraping on the thin soil of the ground. With every breath he took, the golden light around him intensified.

'. . . don't understand it. It's never taken more than a single blow before. That would have felled Kilukpuk herself.'

'You aren't used to these woolly grazers, Jaw.'

'No. Perhaps all that fur—'

'More likely that wretched dome of bone on the top of his skull. Try it again, Jaw. Just make sure you don't kill him.'

A huge face loomed, a gaping jaw, the teeth surrounded by four short, squat tusks. 'Try not to move, grazer.'

Longtusk felt a wash of foetid breath, a rush of air – and again there was an explosion inside his head.

This time the world fell away, through deepening gold, into darkness.

CHAPTER 7
THE TAMING

The sun was high.

He was standing. He was conscious of hunger, an even more powerful thirst. There was a strong scent of mammoth around him . . . but not quite mammoth.

'. . . Milkbreath? Matriarch?'

'They aren't here, lad.'

The voice came from directly before him. It was a mammoth – no, a *mastodont* – short and squat, with a long narrow face and an extra pair of tusks. The mastodont seemed to swim into focus, as if ice water were draining out of his eyes.

The mastodont was a Bull, grizzled with age, and his waist and head and legs and tusks were wrapped around with lengths of rope, knotted tight and tied to the stumps of trees. Only his trunk roamed free, its pink tip questing towards Longtusk.

'Walks With Thunder,' Longtusk said slowly.

'I'm glad you know me. That oaf Jaw Like Rock is none too gentle; I feared he might have scrambled your brains for good . . . Who's Milkbreath? Your mother?'

Longtusk growled and tried to back away. But he couldn't move. He could feel ropes wrapped around his legs and torso and head.

'The ropes will tighten if you struggle. They will cut your flesh.'

Longtusk pushed hard with one leg. With a creak, the loops tightened just as Walks With Thunder had warned.

He gave up, panting, longing for water. 'Who did this?'

'Our keepers. The Fireheads.'

'I am mammoth. I have no keeper.'

'You do now, little grazer.'

'They have tied me up so I will not run away?'

'That's right.'

'. . . But why you?'

Walks With Thunder emitted a deep snort from his trunk. 'To show you it isn't so bad.'

Now a Firehead was coming towards them. It was the little fat one Walks With Thunder had called Lemming – the one who had, with stealth, slipped that first loop of rope around Longtusk's leg. He was carrying a skin bag, some dry grass.

Longtusk rumbled and lunged at the little Firehead. All over his body, the ropes creaked and tightened cruelly.

Lemming yelped and staggered backward. He dropped his skin bag, which landed with a thick gurgle.

'Let him feed you,' Walks With Thunder urged.

'I feed myself.'

'Not any more. Watch . . .'

Lemming retrieved his dropped bag, opened it up and held it out to Walks With Thunder. With a noisy slurp the mastodont sucked up a trunkful of water, draining the bag.

The smell of the water filled Longtusk's head.

Now the little Firehead started stuffing hay into Walks With Thunder's accepting mouth. The mastodont rumbled, 'It isn't so bad, Longtusk. Just accept it. You're lucky. Lemming likes you. He's one of the better ones. He goes easy with the goads. Some of the others take it too far. Like Spindle – the one Jaw farted over—'

'I won't give in.'

'You're special, are you? Different from us, smarter, stronger?'

'Yes.'

'Sniff the air, little grazer.'

342

Longtusk did so – and found he was surrounded by mastodonts: ten, eleven, twelve of them, all males, presumably the same herd who had circled him earlier. Some were pulling branches from the low trees here; but most were feeding on heaps of smashed wood left for them by the Fireheads. One mastodont was wallowing in the mud of a shallow water hole, its fringe crusted with late-winter ice. He was rolling on his side and lifting his squat feet, letting a Firehead scrape mud off his delicate soles with a piece of sharpened stone.

And now a mastodont walked past with a heavy gait. He had a passenger, a skinny Firehead who sat astride the mastodont's neck. His bare feet kicked at the animal's ears, and he struck the mastodont's broad scalp with a stick tipped with sharpened bone.

The mastodont had a broad, ugly scar across his face, eclipsing one eye.

It was Jaw Like Rock. And his rider was the keeper who had beaten him before, Spindle.

'Why does he accept that? He could throw off that creature and crush him in a moment.'

'You don't understand. Jaw has no choice. I have no choice. *You* have no choice, but to submit.'

'No.'

Walks With Thunder's trunk drooped. 'I was like you, once. Make it easy on yourself.'

'I won't listen to you.'

And Longtusk began to push against his ropes once more. They tightened around his neck and legs and belly, but still he struggled, until he was exhausted.

The Firehead keeper came to him again, with water and food; again Longtusk ignored him.

And so it went on, as the sun worked its path around the sky.

Night fell. But it was not dark, not even quiet.

The Fireheads set up huge fires in improvised hearths all around the steppe. Longtusk could feel their uncomfortable heat. The fires sent sparks up into the echoing night, and the Fireheads sat close, their faces shining in the red light, eating and drinking and laughing.

Longtusk – hungry, thirsty, exhausted, his muscles cramped from immobility – now longed for sleep. But sleep was impossible. The Fireheads would come to him and shout in his ears, or whirl pieces of bone on ropes around their heads, making a noise like a howling wind.

Walks With Thunder was still with him. 'Give in,' he urged. 'They won't stop until you do.'

'No,' mumbled Longtusk.

'Let me tell you a story,' Walks With Thunder said. 'A story from the Cycle. This is of a time deep in the past – oh, thousands of Great-Years ago, long before the ice came to the Earth. In those days there were no mammoths and mastodonts; we were a single kind, and we lived in a land of lush forests, far to the south of here.

'But the Earth cooled. The forests follow the weather, as every mastodont knows. Year by year the land became cooler and drier, and great waves of trees moved north across the Earth—'

'Why are you telling me this?'

'Just listen. Now our Matriarch, the Matriarch of all mastodonts, was called Mammut. She was a descendant of Probos, of course, but she lived long before the mother of the mammoths.'

'Ganesha.'

'Yes. Now Mammut was wise—'

'They always are in Cycle stories.'

Walks With Thunder barked his amusement at that. 'Yes. It's always easy after the fact, isn't it? . . . Mammut could see the way the forests were migrating to the north. And she said, "Just as the forests must follow the weather, so my calves must follow the forests." And so, under her leadership, her Clan followed the slow march of the forests, seeking out the marshy places beneath the great trees, for that is what mastodonts prefer. And her calves prospered and multiplied, filling the land.

'Now, much later, long after Mammut had gone to the aurora, another forest came marching across the land. A different kind of forest.'

'I don't know what you're talking about,' Longtusk mumbled.

'It was a forest of Fireheads, little grazer. And the mastodonts fled in panic.'

'That is because they were cowards.'

Walks With Thunder ignored that. 'So the mastodonts called up to the aurora, "What should we do, great Matriarch?"

'Mammut was wise. She understood.

'As the weather washes over the land, the trees must follow. As the trees wash over the land, the mastodonts must follow. And now, as the Fireheads wash over the land, the mastodonts must follow again. That is what Mammut said. And that is what we accept.'

'It isn't much of a story.'

'Well, I'm sorry. I was trying to make a point. I left out the fights and the sex scenes.'

'Anyway the Fireheads are not trees.'

Thunder growled irritably. 'The point is that the Fireheads feed us, as the trees do. They even care for us – when they choose. And we cannot be rid of them, little grazer. Any more than the land can rid itself of the trees. Accept them. Accept their food.'

Once again, Longtusk saw blearily, the Firehead, Lemming, was before him. He held up a paw, full of grasses and herbs, fragrant, freshly gathered. But Longtusk turned his head away.

It lasted three more days, three more nights.

Walks With Thunder and Jaw Like Rock were both with him.

'Your courage is astonishing, little grazer. Nobody else has ever lasted so long before.'

Longtusk, beaten down by hunger and thirst and sleeplessness, could barely see through milky, crusted eyes. 'Leave me.'

Jaw reached out and, with the pink tip of his trunk, smoothed the filth-matted fur of Longtusk's face. 'Don't let them kill you,' he said softly. 'That way they will have won.'

Longtusk closed his eyes.

After a time he felt a pressure at the side of his mouth. It was the paw of Lemming, the keeper, once more holding out sweet grasses.

'Take it, grazer. It's no defeat.'

'My name is Longtusk.'

Walks With Thunder and Jaw Like Rock thumped the ground with their trunks. 'Longtusk,' they said.

Lemming was staring at him, his eyes round, as if he understood.

Longtusk opened his mouth and took the food.

More days passed. Gradually his strength returned.

His ropes were loosened. They had burned and cut him painfully. Lemming treated the wounds with salves of fat and butter, and with water heated in the hearths. He squeezed droplets of milk from an aurochs cow into Longtusk's eyes, soothing their itching.

Five days after he had first accepted the food, more Fireheads came to see him: Bedrock the leader, the Shaman Smokehat with his grotesque headpiece of smoking bone, and the cub, Crocus.

Though Bedrock was cautious and kept hold of her paw, Crocus approached Longtusk. Her necklace of mammoth teeth gleamed in the watery spring sun. She reached past the ropes and ruffled the long hair that dangled from his trunk.

He closed his eyes, recalling how Willow, the male Dreamer cub, used to do the same thing.

He wondered where the Dreamers were now, Stripeskull and Willow and the others. Scattered, he supposed, turned out of the caves they had inhabited for uncounted generations, in the face of the advance of these Fireheads—

Pain lanced into his flank. He trumpeted and reared up, but he was contained by the ropes. There was a stink of burning flesh and hair.

The Shaman, Smokehat, held a piece of stone fixed to the end of a stick. The stone had been chipped and shaped to look like the outspread paw of a Firehead. It glowed red hot.

The mark of the Firehead, the outstretched paw, had been burned into Longtusk's flank.

Like all these others he belonged to the Fireheads, and was forever marked.

He trumpeted his anger and despair.

TWO

WARRIOR

THE STORY OF LONGTUSK AND
THE FIREHEADS

As you know, Icebones (said Silverhair), Longtusk spent most of his years as a young Bull away from other mammoths.

Everywhere he went he won friendship and respect – naturally, since he was the greatest hero of all, and even other creatures could recognise that – and in many instances he was made their leader, and led them to fruitfulness and success before passing on to continue his adventures.

And so it came to pass that Longtusk came to live with the Fireheads, and to rule them.

Now the Fireheads are the strangest creatures in all the Cycle: weak yet strong, smart yet stupid. In the summer heat they had difficulty finding the food and drink they needed, and in the winter cold they suffered because they had no winter coat.

So Longtusk decided to teach them how to live.

When they were cold, he took them to the west, where Rhino lived.

Now Rhino was a magnificent beast with a coat as thick as a mammoth's and great horns like upturned tusks (yes, she really existed, Icebones, have patience!). And Longtusk said to the Fireheads, 'You need coats like Rhino's to fend off the cold. See how warm and comfortable she is? When the wintertime is over she sheds her hair, and you may take it to make your own coats. Isn't that right, Rhino?'

And Rhino replied, 'Yes, Longtusk' – for all the creatures of the world knew Longtusk – 'my hair will be all your friends need, and they may have it.'

And the Fireheads muttered and calculated, for that is their way.

And when Longtusk's back was turned, they attacked poor Rhino, and robbed her of her fine coat, and even took her magnificent horns.

When he found out what had happened, Longtusk berated the Fireheads for their greed and impatience. 'You could have taken all you needed, if only you had waited!'

And the Fireheads said they were sorry. But in their hearts they were not.

When it rained, Longtusk took the Fireheads to the east, where Dreamer lived.

Now Dreamer was a little like the Fireheads, but she was placid and kind and accepting, and she had lived for many years in caves hollowed out of the rock of a hillside. And, of course, the caves kept the rain from her head.

And Longtusk said to the Fireheads, 'You need a cave like Dreamer's to fend off the rain. See how warm and comfortable she is? There are many caves in this hillside, and you may take them for your own shelter. Isn't that right, Dreamer?'

And Dreamer replied, 'Yes, Longtusk' – for all the creatures of the world knew Longtusk – 'the caves will be all your friends need, and they may have them.'

And the Fireheads muttered and calculated, for that is their way.

And when Longtusk's back was turned, they attacked poor Dreamer, and robbed her of her fine cave, and threw her out into the rain.

When he found out what had happened, Longtusk berated the Fireheads for their greed and impatience. 'You could have taken all you needed without stealing Dreamer's home!'

And the Fireheads said they were sorry. But in their hearts they were not.

Then the Fireheads became thirsty.

So Longtusk took them to the north, where the mammoths lived.

He brought them to a place where the mammoths, in their wisdom, knew that water seeped from deep in the ground. They were digging there with tusks and feet, bringing the water to the surface.

And Longtusk said to the Fireheads, 'You must dig for water as the mammoths do. See how much water there is? And when you have learned what the mammoths have to teach you, you can find water of your own. Isn't that right, Matriarch?'

And the Matriarch of the mammoth Family replied, 'Yes, Longtusk' – for all the mammoths knew Longtusk – 'in the ground there is all the water your friends need, and we will teach them how to find it.'

And the Fireheads muttered and calculated, for that is their way.

And when Longtusk's back was turned, they attacked the poor mammoths, and drove them away, and robbed them of their water.

When he found out what had happened, Longtusk berated the Fireheads. 'You could have found your own water without robbing the mammoths – oh, you are impossible!'

And the Fireheads said they were sorry. But in their hearts they were not.

By now Longtusk knew that all his teaching was wasted on such creatures. He had decided besides that he had spent enough time away from his Clan.

So he turned his back on the Fireheads and walked away, leaving them to fend for themselves. They called to him plaintively, begging him to return, but he would not.

And so Longtusk returned to the mammoths, and became their Patriarch, and . . .

But that's another story. Perhaps the greatest of them all.

What happened to the Fireheads without Longtusk's

wisdom, driven only by their own foolishness, cold and wet and thirsty? Nobody knows.

Some say they quickly died out.

And some say they became monsters.

CHAPTER 1

THE BONE PIT

All around Longtusk, sleeping mastodonts lay like immense boulders. In the summer they preferred to sleep on their backs, exposing their bare feet and bellies to the cool air. From time to time one of them, startled by a noise, would rise smoothly and silently to his feet, like some hairy ghost, before settling back.

But Longtusk could not sleep – even after the months he had been kept here in the Firehead settlement.

He could hear small Firehead footsteps as they pattered across the hard ground, their thin Firehead voices as they came and went on their strange, incomprehensible business. Sometimes he even heard the clear voice of the female cub, Crocus, who – in another life that was long ago and far away – he had saved from freezing.

And, worst of all, he could smell the meat they hung up on frames of wood to dry: rags of brown and purple, laced here and there by pale fat or strings of tendon, some of it even clinging to shards of white bone. Most of the meat came from deer and horse and smaller animals, but there were some larger chunks, great knobbly pieces of bone he couldn't recognise.

And he could smell the meat that burned, slowly, in the great stone-lined pits in the ground, the billowing greasy black smoke that lingered in the air.

At least he had put aside the panic he had felt continually when he had first been brought here to the Firehead settlement, as every instinct drove him to flee the smoke from the fires. But he would never grow used to that dreadful meat stink. It seemed to have seeped into his very fur, so that he was never free of it.

So Longtusk endured, waiting for morning.

The keepers came in the grey light of dawn. They talked softly and cleared their throats to alert the mastodonts of their approach. The mastodonts stirred, rumbling, and there was a rustle of leathery skin against the hobbles that bound their legs.

Most of the mastodonts were Bulls – not really a bachelor herd, for the tree-browsing mastodonts were more solitary than mammoths, Longtusk had found. But there were Families here too, Cows and calves.

The keepers approached their animals, one by one, talking softly. The mastodonts rumbled and whooshed in response, reaching out with their trunks to search the Fireheads' layers of fur for titbits of food. It was a display of affection and submission that never failed to embarrass Longtusk.

This morning the fat little keeper the mastodonts called Lemming approached Longtusk, holding out a juicy strip of bark. And, as he always did, Longtusk rumbled threateningly, curled his trunk and backed away as far as the hobbles knotted tightly around his legs would let him.

Lemming wore trousers and leggings of deer skin, moccasins and a broad hat of a tougher leather, and his clothing was stuffed with dry grass to keep him warm. Bits of grass stuck out around his wide, greasy face as he studied Longtusk, peering into the mammoth's ears and eyes and mouth.

Jaw Like Rock, his hobbles already loosened, came loping over. With a deft movement he snatched the bark from Lemming's paw and tucked it into his mouth. 'Waste of good food,' he rumbled as he munched.

'It comes from the paw of a Firehead,' Longtusk said.

'So what? Food is food.'

'I'm not like you.'

'He wasn't intending you any harm, you know. He was checking your eyes and ears for infection. And he wanted to see your tongue, too.' Jaw opened his mouth and unrolled his own tongue, a leathery sheet of muscle that dripped with saliva. 'The keepers know that a healthy mastodont has a nice pink tongue unblemished by black spots, brown eyes without a trace of white, the right number of toenails, strong and sturdy joints, a full face and broad forehead . . . You have all of that; if you were a mastodont you'd be a prize.'

Longtusk growled, impatient with the advice.

'You're the only mammoth we have here, Longtusk. The keepers don't know what to make of you. Some of them think you can't be tamed and trained, that you're too wild. And the Shaman, Smokehat, is jealous of you.'

'Jealous? Why?'

'Because the Fireheads used to believe that mammoths were gods. Some of them seem to think *you're* a god. And that takes away from the Shaman's power. Having you around gives even little Lemming a higher status. Don't you understand any of this, grazer?'

'No,' said Longtusk bluntly.

'All I'm saying is that if you give him an excuse, the Shaman will have you destroyed. Lemming is fond of you. But you're going to have to help him, to give him some sign that you'll cooperate, or else—'

But now, as if to disprove Jaw's comforting growl, his own keeper approached: Spindle, thin, ugly and brutal. He lashed at Jaw with his stick, apparently punishing the mastodont for his minor theft of the food.

Jaw didn't flinch.

'Of course,' he rumbled sourly, 'not everything's wonderful here. But there are ways to make life bearable.'

And his lifted his fat, scarred trunk and sneezed noisily. A gust of looping snot and bark chips sprayed over Spindle, who fell over backwards, yelling.

Jaw Like Rock farted contentedly and loped away.

The mastodonts were prepared for another working day. Their hobbles were removed – or merely loosened, in the case of Longtusk and a few others, mastodonts in musth and so prone to irritability. Longtusk was a special case, of course, and he wore his hobbles with a defiant pride. As they worked the keepers were careful to keep away from his tusks, so much more large and powerful than the strongest mastodont's.

Ten mastodonts, plus Longtusk, were formed up into a loose line. Walks With Thunder was at the head. Lemming sat neatly on the great mastodont's neck, his fat legs sticking out on either side of Thunder's broad head.

Lemming tapped Thunder's scalp and called out, '*Agit!*'

Walks With Thunder loped forward, trumpeting to the others to follow him.

The mastodonts obeyed. They were prompted by cries from the keepers – *Chai ghoom! Chi! Dhuth!*, Right! Left! Stop! – and they were directed by gentle taps of the keepers' goads: gentle, yes, but Longtusk had learned by hard experience that the keepers also knew exactly where to strike him to inflict a sharp burst of pain, brief and leaving no scar.

Half the mastodonts bore riders. Most of the others carried the equipment the working party would need during the day. Those without riders were led by loose harnesses of rope tied around their heads.

Longtusk, of course, had no rider, and his harness was kept tighter than the rest. Not only that, his trunk was tied to Walks With Thunder's broad tail, so that he was led along the path like an infant with his mother.

They walked slowly out of the Firehead settlement.

The Fireheads had spread far, reshaping the steppe, and they were still building. They had made themselves shelters – like the caves of the Dreamers – but of wood and rock and turf and animal skin. They built huge pits in the ground into which they hurled meat ripped from the carcasses of the creatures they hunted. And the Fireheads had built a great stockade of wood and rock, within which the mastodonts were confined. To Longtusk it was a place of distortion and strangeness, and he was habitually oppressed, crushed by a feeling of confinement and helplessness and bafflement.

But for now they were out of the stockade, and with relief Longtusk found himself on the open steppe. As the sun climbed into a cloud-dusted sky, they soon left behind the noise and stink of the settlement, and walked on steadily south.

The air was misty and full of light. Longtusk saw that it was a mist of life: vast clouds of insects, mosquitoes and blackflies and warble flies and botflies, that rose from the lakes to plague the great herbivores – including himself – and a dreamier cloud of ballooning spiders and wind-borne larvae, riding the breezes to a new land.

Through this dense air the mastodonts walked steadily, their fat low-slung rumps swaying gracefully, their tails swishing and their trunks shooting out from side to side in search of branches and leaves from the few low trees which grew here. After walking for a time they started to defecate together, a long synchronised symphony of dung-making.

Much of the land was bare, a desert of gravel and soils and a few far-flung plants. Here and there he noticed thicker tussocks of grass, speckled with wild flowers, fed by the detritus at the entrances to the dens of the Arctic foxes, and on the slight rises where owls and jaegers devoured their prey, watering the soil with blood. Steppe melt-ponds stood out boldly, bright blue against the tan and green of the plain. In the centre of the larger ponds Longtusk could see the gleam of aquamarine, cores of ice still unmelted at the height of summer.

His footsteps crunched on dead leaves, bits of flowers, fragments of twig, a thick layer of it. Some of this material might be years old. And later he came across the carcass of a wolf-killed deer. It had been lightly consumed, and now its meat had hardened, its skin turned glassy. He knew it might lie here for three or four years before being reduced to bones.

On the steppe, away from the Fireheads' frantic rhythms, time pooled, dense and slow; even decomposition worked slowly here.

He came across a golden plover, sitting on her nest on the ground. She stared back at him, defiant. The birds of the steppe had to build their nests on the ground, as there were no tall trees. Some of them – like buntings and longspurs – even lined their nests with bits of mammoth wool. This plover's nest was made of woven grass, and it contained pale, darkly speckled eggs. As the mastodonts walked by the plover got off its nest and ran back and forth, feigning a broken wing, trying to distract these possible predators from the nest itself.

Walks With Thunder, as he often did, tried to explain life to Longtusk.

'. . . The Fireheads are strange, but there is a logic to everything they do. Almost everything, anyhow. They are predators, like the wolves and foxes. So they must hunt.'

'I know that. Deer and aurochs—'

'Yes. But such animals pass by this way only infrequently, as they follow their own migrations in search of their fodder for summer or winter. And so the Fireheads must store the meat they will eat during the winter. That is the purpose of the pits – even if all those dead carcasses are repellent to us. And it explains the way they salt their meat and hang it up to dry in strips, or soak it in sour milk, and—'

'But,' Longtusk complained, 'why do they not follow the herds they prey on, as the wolves do? All their problems come from this peculiar determination to stay in one place.'

Walks With Thunder growled, 'But not every animal is

like the mastodont – or the mammoth. *We* don't mind where we roam; we go where the food is. But many animals prefer a single place to live. Like the rhinos.'

'But these Fireheads have nothing – no fat layers, hardly any hair, no way of keeping warm in the winter or digging out their food.'

'But they have their fire. They have their tools. And,' Walks With Thunder said with a trace of sadness, 'they have us.'

'Not me,' rumbled Longtusk. 'They have me trapped. But they don't have *me*.'

To that, Walks With Thunder would say nothing.

Longtusk disturbed a carpet of big yellow butterflies that burst into the air, startling him. One of the butterflies landed on the pink tip of his trunk, tickling him. He swished his trunk to and fro, but couldn't shake the butterfly free; finally, the mocking brays of the mastodonts sounding in his ears, he blew it away with a large sneeze.

They came to a river which meandered slowly between gently sloping hummocks. Vegetation grew thickly, down to the water's edge: grass, herbs and a stand of spruce forest almost tall enough to reach Longtusk's shoulders. Further downstream there were thickets of birch and even azalea, with lingering pink leaves from their spring bloom. In the longer grass wild flowers added splashes of colour: vetch, iris, primroses, mauve and blue and purple and yellow.

The mastodonts were allowed to rest. They spread out, moving through the sparse trees with a rustle of branches, tearing off foliage and shoving it into their mouths greedily. Some of them walked into the water, sucking up trunkfuls of the clear, cold liquid and spraying it over their heads and backs.

Longtusk was still hobbled. He moved a little away from the rest, seeking the grass and steppe vegetation he preferred.

He had never been here before. It seemed a congenial place – for mastodonts anyhow. But Longtusk, clad in his thick fur, was already too hot, and mosquitoes buzzed, large and voracious. He looped his trunk into his mouth, extracted a mixture of spit and water, and blew it in a fine spray over his face and head and belly.

He wondered what the Fireheads wanted from this place. Stone, perhaps. The Fireheads liked big flat slabs of stones to put inside their huts and storage pits – but he could see no rock of that kind here. Perhaps they would bring back wood; the mastodonts were strong enough to knock over and splinter as many trees as required.

The keepers came to round up the mastodonts, calling softly and tapping their scalps and flanks with their bone-tipped goads. The mastodonts cooperated with only routine rumbles of complaint.

All the mastodonts had worked here many times before, and they appeared to know what to do. The most skilful and trusted, led by Walks With Thunder, walked down towards the river. They came to a place where the grass had been worn away by deep round mastodont footprints. They began to scrape at the muddy river bank with their tusks and feet, and clouds of mosquitoes rose up around them as they toiled.

Longtusk could see that they were uncovering something: objects that gleamed white in the low sun. He wondered what they were.

. . . There was a sudden, sharp stench, a stink of death and decay, making Longtusk flinch. Some of the mastodonts trumpeted and rumbled in protest, but, under the calm, watchful eye of Walks With Thunder, they continued to work. Perhaps something had died here: a bison or rhino, its carcass washed along the river.

Soon, with the supervision of the keepers, they were dragging the large white objects from the mud. Walks With Thunder dug his tusks under one of the objects and wrapped his trunk over the top; he rammed his feet against the ground and hauled, until the clinging, cold mud gave way with a loud sucking noise, and he stumbled back.

The thing's shape was complex, full of holes. It was mostly white, but something dark brown clung to it here and there, around which mosquitoes and flies buzzed angrily.

It might have been a rock.

Jaw Like Rock stood alongside Longtusk, swishing his tail vigorously. 'I can stand the work,' the squat Bull muttered. 'It's these wretched mosquitoes that drive me to distraction.'

Longtusk asked, 'Are those rocks heavy?'

Jaw turned to look at him quizzically. 'What rocks?'

'The rocks they are pulling out of the river bank.'

Jaw hesitated. He said carefully, 'Nobody has told you what we're doing here? Thunder hasn't explained?'

'No. Aren't they rocks?'

Jaw fell silent, seeming troubled.

Longtusk found, at his feet, a patch of what looked like mammoth dung. He poked at it and it crumbled. It was dried out, stale, half frozen, obviously old. Regretfully he lifted a few crumbs to his mouth; their flavour was thin.

Since the day he had been separated from his Family by the fire storm – despite the way the Fireheads had him undertake these jaunts across the countryside – he had never seen a single one of his own kind.

But the expeditions always headed south.

He asked Jaw about this.

'Sometimes there are expeditions to the north, Longtusk,' Jaw rumbled. 'But—'

'But what?'

Jaw Like Rock hesitated, uncomfortable. 'Ask Walks With Thunder.'

Longtusk growled, 'I'm asking you.'

'It is difficult to work there. It is poor land. The ice is

retreating northwards and uncovering the land; but the new land is a rocky desert. To the south, plants and animals have lived for many generations, and the soil is rich . . .'

He's keeping something from me, Longtusk thought. Something about the northern lands, and what the Fireheads do there.

'If the south is so comfortable, why do the Fireheads live where they do? Why not stay where life is easy?'

Jaw sneezed as pollen itched at his trunk. He slid his trunk over one tusk and began to scratch, scooping out lumps of snot. 'Because to the south there are already too many Fireheads. They have burned the trees and eaten the animals, and now they fight each other for what remains. Fireheads are not like us, Longtusk. A Firehead Clan will not share its range with another.

'Bedrock tried to take the land belonging to another Clan. There was a battle. Bedrock lost. So he has come north, as far as he can, so that his Clan can carve out a new place to live.'

Longtusk tried to understand what all this meant.

He imagined a line that stretched, to east and west, right across the continent, dividing it into two utterly different zones. To the south there was little but Fireheads, mobs of them, fighting and breeding and dying. To the north the land was as it had been before, empty of Fireheads.

And that line of demarcation was sweeping north, as Firehead leaders like Bedrock sought new, empty places to live, burning across the land like the great billowing line of fire which had separated him from his Family.

It was to the north that Longtusk knew he must return one day, when the chance arose. For it was to the north – where there were no Fireheads, in the corridor of silent steppe which still encircled the planet below the ice – *that* was where the mammoth herds roamed.

The keepers approached Longtusk now. It was time to don his pack gear, he realised gloomily. He was not yet trusted with complex tasks like digging, but he was regarded as capable of carrying heavy weights.

The pack gear was substantial.

First the keepers laid over him a soft quilted pad. It extended from his withers to his rump and halfway down his sides. On top of this came a saddle of stout sacking stuffed with straw. It had a split along the back to relieve the pressure on his spine; most of the weight he had to carry would rest on his broad rib cage. And then came a platform, a flat plate of cut wood with four posts in the corners, with ropes slung between the posts to prevent his load from falling off.

The whole assembly was strapped to him by one length of thick plaited rope which went around his head and girth and up under his tail. To prevent chafing the rope was passed through lengths of hollow bone that rubbed smoothly against his chest.

And now Walks With Thunder was approaching with his mysterious, complex load, and the stench of decay grew stronger.

Longtusk became fearful.

He could see that Thunder's cargo was rounded, with two gaping sockets at the front. It seemed to have tooth marks, as if some scavenger had worked on it. The brown stuff that clung to it looked like flesh, heavily decayed and gnawed by the scavenger. There was rough skin over the scraps of flesh, and lanks of hair clung, brown and muddy.

It was bone, Longtusk realised with horror. A bone, to which decaying meat still clung.

'What's going on here, Jaw? What *is* that thing?'

'Listen to me,' said Jaw Like Rock urgently. 'It isn't what it seems . . .' He laid his trunk over Longtusk's head, trying to soothe him, but Longtusk shook it off.

The keepers began to look alarmed.

The bone thing had the stump of a tusk, broken and gnawed, sticking out of its front. A mammoth tusk.

'Nobody was killed here,' Jaw was saying. 'This wasn't the fault of the Fireheads, or anybody else. It just happened, a very long time ago . . .'

Longtusk looked again at the river bank. He saw that the white objects were *not* rocks, not one of them. They were all bones: thick leg bones and vertebrae and ribs and shoulder blades and skulls, sticking out of the mud, many of them still coated with flesh and broken and chewed by scavengers.

It was a field of corpses: the corpses of mammoths.

And here was Walks With Thunder, about to load the great vacant skull onto Longtusk's back.

Longtusk swept his tusks, knocked the skull from the grasp of an astonished Walks With Thunder, and smashed it to pieces underfoot.

He recalled little after that.

They got him under control, and brought him through the long march back to the Fireheads' settlement.

As the day wound to its close, their work done, the mastodonts were allowed to find food and water, and to mingle with the Family of Cows and calves.

Longtusk did not expect such freedom tonight.

He hadn't injured any of the Fireheads. But, despite Thunder's apologies and urging, he hadn't allowed the keepers to remount his pack gear or to place any of their grisly load on his back. The other mastodonts, some grumbling, had had to accept his share of the load. As a result he was expecting punishment.

But now the little keeper, Lemming, faced him. To Longtusk's surprise, Lemming came close, easily within range of the mammoth's great tusks. He seemed to trust Longtusk.

Lemming reached out with one small paw and touched the long hairs that grew from the centre of Longtusk's face, between his eyes. Tiny fingers pulled gently at the hairs, combing out small knots, and the Firehead spoke steadily in his thin, incomprehensible voice. He seemed regretful, as if he understood.

Now Lemming reached down and loosened the hobbles around Longtusk's ankles. Then, with the gentlest of taps from his goad, he encouraged Longtusk to wander off towards his feeding ground.

Longtusk – confused, dismayed, baffled by kindness – moved away from the trees in search of steppe grass.

The Moon was high and dazzling bright – a wintry Moon, brilliant with the reflected light of ice-laden Earth. It was Longtusk's only companion.

Even when he ate, he had to do it alone. He needed the coarse grasses and herbs of the steppe, and could tolerate little of the lush leaves and bark the mastodonts preferred. Tonight, though, he could have used a little company.

Walks With Thunder had apologised for not warning him, and tried to explain to him about the bones in the river bank. It wasn't a place of slaughter. It wasn't even the place where all those decomposing mammoths had died.

Mammoths had been drawn to the river's water over a long period of time – generations, perhaps even a significant part of a Great-Year. But a river bank could be a hazardous place. Mammoths became stuck in clinging mud and starved, or fell through thin ice and drowned. Their bodies were washed down the river, coming to rest in a meander or backwater.

Again and again this happened, the corpses washing downstream from all along the river bank, and coming to rest in the same natural trap, until a huge deposit of bodies had built up.

Sometimes the river would rise, immersing the bodies and embedding them in mud and silt, and fishes might nibble at the meat. And in dry seasons the water would drop, exposing the bodies to the air. The stench of their rot would attract flies, and larvae would burrow through the rotting flesh. Predators would come, wolverines or foxes or wolves, to gnaw on the exposed bones.

At last the bodies were buried by silt and peat, and vegetation grew over them.

But then the river's path had changed. The water began to cut away at the great natural pit of bones, exposing the corpses to the air once more . . .

'You see?' Thunder had said. 'Nobody killed those mammoths. Why, they might have died centuries ago, their bodies lying unremarked in the silt layers until now. What's left behind is just bone and rotting flesh and hair. The Fireheads imagine they have a use for all those old bones – and what harm does it do? The mammoths have gone, their spirits flown to the aurora. Strange, yes, are the ways of the Fireheads, but you'll learn to live with them. *I* have . . .'

Yes, thought Longtusk angrily, and he ripped tufts of grass roughly from the ground as he stomped along alone, all but blinded by his teeming thoughts. Yes, Thunder, you've grown used to all this. It doesn't matter what happens to my bones when I've flown to the aurora; you're right.

But you have forgotten you are a Calf of Kilukpuk. You have forgotten how we Remember those who go to the aurora before us.

I will not forget, no matter how long I live, how long I am kept here. *I* will never forget that I am mammoth.

'. . . Are you in musth?'

The contact rumble was light, shallow. Close.

Preoccupied, he looked up. A small mastodont was facing him. A calf? No, a Cow – not quite fully grown, perhaps about his own age. She was chewing on a mouthful of leaves. Her jaw was delicate and neatly symmetrical, along with the rest of her skull, and that chewing, unmammoth-like motion didn't seem as ugly and unnatural when she did it as when a big ugly Bull like Jaw Like Rock took whole branches in his maw of a mouth and—

'You're staring at me,' she said.

'What? . . . I'm sorry. What do you want?'

'I want to feed in peace,' she growled. Her four tusks were short, Moon white, and she raised them defiantly. 'And I want you to answer my question.'

'I'm not in musth.'

'The Matriarch says I must keep away from Bulls in musth. I'm not ready for oestrus yet. And even if I was—'

'I said, I'm not in musth,' he snapped, rumbling angrily.

'You act as if you are.'

'That's because—' He tried to calm down. 'It's not your fault.'

She stepped closer, cautiously. 'You're the mammoth, aren't you? The calf of Primus. I heard them talking about you. I never met a mammoth before.'

Longtusk felt confused.

What should he say to her? In his short life he had had little contact with Cows outside his immediate Family. If this was a Bull he'd know what to do; he'd just start a fight.

He snorted and lifted his head. 'What do you think of my tusks?'

She evaded his tusks, apparently unimpressed, and reached out with her slender trunk. She placed its warm, pink tip inside his mouth, startling him. Then she stepped back and lowered her trunk.

She sneezed. 'Ugh. Saxifrage.'

'I like saxifrage. Where I come from, we all eat saxifrage.'

She curled her trunk contemptuously. She turned and ambled away, her hips swaying with liquid grace, and she tore at the grass as she passed.

Good riddance, thought Longtusk.

'. . . Wait,' he called. 'What's your name?'

She raised her trunk, as if sniffing the air, and trumpeted her disdain. 'Neck Like Spruce.'

369

'My name is—'

'I know already,' she said. And she walked off into Moon-light.

CHAPTER 2
THE RIDER

All too soon the short Arctic summer was gone, and winter closed in once more.

During the day Longtusk, seeking food, would scrape aside the snow and frost to find thin grass and herbs, dead and frozen. Sometimes Fireheads would follow him and chop turf and twigs from the exposed ground, fuel to burn in their great hearths.

The mastodonts, less well adapted to the cold, needed leaves and bark from the trees. But soon all the trees close to the Firehead settlement were stripped or destroyed, and they had to travel far to find sustenance.

This became impossible as the winter closed in, and the Firehead keepers would come out of their huts to bring feed, bales of yellowed hay gathered in the summer months. Longtusk watched with contempt as the mastodonts – even strong, intelligent adults like Walks With Thunder and Jaw Like Rock – clustered around the bales, tearing into them greedily with their tusks and trunks.

The Fireheads regularly checked the mastodonts' trunks, eyes, ears and feet. Frostbite of the mastodonts' ears was common, and the Fireheads treated it with salves of fat and butter.

During the long nights, the mastodonts would huddle together for warmth, grumbling and complaining as one or another was bumped by a careless hip or prodded by a tusk. And they would regale each other with tales from their own, peculiarly distorted, version of the Cycle: legends of the heroic Mammut and her calves as they romped through the impossibly rich forests of the far south, where the sun never set and the trees grew taller than a hundred mastodonts stacked up on top of each other.

Longtusk tried to join in with tales of the heroes of mammoth legend, like Ganesha the Wise. But he'd been very young when he had heard these stories, and his memory was poor. When he jumbled up the stories the mastodonts would trumpet and rumble their amusement, nudging him and scratching his scalp with their trunks, until he stalked off in anger.

But as they talked and listened the younger mastodonts – and Longtusk – were soaking up the wisdom of their elders, embedded in such legends: how to find water in dry seasons or frozen winters, where to find salt licks, and particularly rich stands of trees.

Longtusk had left his Family at a very young age, and he found he had much to learn, even about the simple things of life.

There was a time when the toes of both his forelegs and hind legs gave him trouble, the skin cracking and becoming prone to infection.

Finally Walks With Thunder noticed and took him to one side. 'This is what you must do,' he said. The mastodont rummaged among his winter-dry fodder and selected a suitable branch. Holding it in his trunk he stripped the leaves away and peeled back the bark, munching it efficiently. Then he took the branch, broke it into four lengths and laid them out in front of him. He selected one piece and, with brisk motions, sharpened it to a point against a rock.

Then, satisfied with the shape, he began to clean methodically between his toenails, digging out the dirt, and wiping the stick clean.

'You never saw this before?' he said as he worked.

'No,' Longtusk said, embarrassed.

'Longtusk, you sweat between your toes. You must keep your toes clean or the glands will clog, causing the problems you are suffering now. It is even more important to keep your musth glands clean.' He picked up a shard of stick and, with a practised motion, dug it into one of the temporal glands on the side of his face. 'But you must be careful to use a suitable stick: one that is strong and straight and not likely to break. If it snaps and jams up your gland, it cannot discharge and it will drive you crazy.' He eyed Longtusk. 'You don't want to end up like that fool Jaw Like Rock, do you? . . .'

When the nails were clean the mastodont blew spittle on them with his trunk and polished them until they gleamed.

And so, as he grew, month on month, Longtusk's education continued, the orphan mammoth under the brusque, tender supervision of the older mastodonts.

In the worst of it, when the snow fell heavily or the wind howled, there was nothing to do but endure. Longtusk did not measure time as a human did, packaging it into regular intervals. Even in summer, time dissolved into a single glowing afternoon, speckled by moments of life and love, laughter and death. And in the long reaches of winter – when sometimes it wasn't possible even to risk moving for fear of dissipating his body's carefully hoarded heat – time slid away, featureless, meaningless, driven by the great rhythms of the world around him, and by the deep blood-red urges of his own body.

Longtusk secretly enjoyed these unmarked times, when he could stand with the others in the dark stillness and feel the shape of the turning world.

Longtusk's deep senses revealed the world beyond the horizon: in the hiss of a gale over a distant stretch of steppe, the boom of ocean breakers on a shore, the crack of ice on melting steppe ponds. And, in the deepest stillness of night, he could sense the thinness of this land bridge between the continents, with the frozen ocean to the north, the pressing seas to the south: surrounded by such immense forces, the land seemed fragile indeed.

Longtusk was learning the land on a level deeper than any human. He had to know how to use it to keep him alive, as if it was an extension of his own body, as if body and land merged into a single organism, pulsing with blood and seasons. As he matured, he would come to know Earth with a careless intimacy a human could never imagine.

Once, Longtusk woke from a heavy slumber and raised his head from a snowdrift.

Snow lay heavily, blanketing the ground. But the sky was clear, glittering with stars. The mastodonts were mounds of white. Here and there, as a mastodont stirred, snow fell away, revealing a swatch of red-black hair, a questing trunk or a peering eye.

And the aurora bloomed in the sky, an immense flat sheet of light thrown there by the wind from the sun.

It started with a gush of brightness that resolved itself into a transparent curtain, green and soft pink. Slowly its rays became more apparent, and it started to surge to east and west, like the guard hairs of some immense mammoth, developing deep folds.

It appeared at different places in the sky. When the light sheet was directly above, so that Longtusk was looking up at it, he saw rays converging on a point high above his head. And when he saw it edge-on it looked like smoke, rising from the Earth. Its huge slow movements were entrancing, endlessly fascinating, and Longtusk felt a great tenderness when he gazed at it.

Mammoths – and mastodonts – believed that their spirits flew to the aurora on death, to play in the steppes of light there. He wondered how many of his ancestors were looking down on him now – and he wondered how many of his Family, scattered and lost over the curve of the Earth, were staring up at the aurora, entranced just as he was.

The aurora moved steadily north, breaking up into isolated luminous patches, like clouds.

*

At last the days began to lengthen, and the pale ruddy sun seemed to leak a little warmth, as if grudgingly.

Life returned to the steppe.

The top layers of the frozen ground melted, and fast-growing grasses sprouted, along with sedges, small shrubs like Arctic sagebrush, and types of pea, daisy and buttercup. The grasses grew quickly and dried out, forming a kind of natural hay, swathes of it that would be sufficient to sustain, over the summer months, the herds of giant grazing herbivores that lived there.

Early in the season a herd of bison passed, not far away. Longtusk saw a cloud of soft dust thrown high into the air, and in the midst of it the great black shapes crowded together, with their humpback shoulders and enormous black horns; their stink of sweat and dung assailed Longtusk's acute sense of smell. And there were herds of steppe horses – their winter coats fraying, stripes of colour on their flanks – skittish and nervous, running together like flocks of startled birds.

In this abundance of life, death was never far away. There were wolves and the even more ferocious dholes, lynxes, tigers and leopards: carnivores to exploit the herbivores, the moving mountains of meat. Once, near an outcrop of rock, Longtusk glimpsed the greatest predator of them all – twice the size of its nearest competitor – a mighty cave cat.

And – serving as a further sign of the relentless shortness of life – condors and other carrion eaters wheeled overhead, waiting for the death of others, their huge outfolded wings black stripes against the blue sky.

Work began again. The mastodonts were set to digging and lifting and carrying for the Fireheads.

Longtusk was still restricted to crude carrying. Those who had shared his chores last season were now, by and large, tamed and trained and trusted, and had moved on to more significant work. Of last year's bearers, only Longtusk remained as a pack animal.

What was worse, during the winter he had grown. Towering over the immature, restless calves he had to work with – his mighty tusks curling before him, useless – he endured his work, and the taunts of his fellows. But a cloud of humiliation and depression gathered around him.

Longtusk realised, with shock, that he was another year older, and he had withstood yet another cycle of seasons away from his Family. But compared to the heavy brutal reality of the mastodonts around him, his Family seemed like a dream receding into the depths of his memory.

He was surrounded by restraints, he was coming to realise, and the hobbles and goads of the keepers were only the most obvious. These mastodonts had lived in captivity for generations. None of them even knew what it was to be free, to live as the Cycle taught. And his own memories – half-formed, for he had been but a calf when taken – were fading with each passing month.

Besides, he didn't want to be alone, an outsider, a rogue, a rebel. He wanted to belong. And these complacent, tamed mastodonts were the only community available to him. The keepers knew all this – the smarter ones – and used subtle ploys to reinforce the invisible barriers that restrained the mastodonts more effectively than rope or wood: pain for misbehaviour, yes, but rewards and welcoming strokes when he accepted his place.

If he could no longer imagine freedom, a life different from this, how could he ever aspire to it?

So it was that when Walks With Thunder came to him and said that the keeper, Lemming, was going to make an attempt to teach him to accept a rider, Longtusk knew the time had come to defy his instincts.

Lemming snapped, '*Baitho! Baitho!*'

Walks With Thunder murmured, 'He's saying, *Down*. Lower your trunk, you idiot. Like this.' And Thunder dipped his trunk gently, so it pooled on the ground.

Longtusk could see that all over the stockade mastodonts were turning towards him. Some of the Fireheads were pausing in their tasks to look at him, their spindly forelegs akimbo; he even spotted the blonde head of the little cub, Crocus, watching him curiously.

Longtusk growled. 'They want to see the mammoth beaten at last.'

'Ignore them,' Walks With Thunder hissed. 'They don't matter.'

The Firehead raised his stick and tapped Longtusk on the root of his trunk.

Longtusk rapped his trunk on the ground, and as the air was forced out of the trunk it emitted a deep terrifying roar.

Lemming fell back, startled.

'Try again,' Thunder urged.

I have to do this, Longtusk thought. I *can* do this.

He lowered his head and let his trunk reach the ground, as Thunder had done.

'Good lad,' said Thunder. 'It's harder to submit than to defy. Hang onto that. You're stronger than any of us, little grazer. Now you must prove it.'

The Firehead stepped onto Longtusk's trunk. Then he reached out and grabbed Longtusk's ears, his tipped stick still clutched in his paw.

Longtusk, looking forward, found he was staring straight into the Firehead's small, complex face.

This, he realised, is going to take a great deal of forbearance indeed.

'*Utha! Utha!*' cried Lemming.

'Now what?'

'He's telling you to lift him up.'

'Are you sure?'

'Just do it.'

And Longtusk pushed up with his trunk, lifting smoothly.

With a thin wail the Firehead went sailing clean over his rump.

Walks With Thunder groaned. 'Oh, Longtusk . . .'

The Firehead came bustling round in front of him. He was covered in mastodont dung, and he was jumping up and down furiously.

'At least he had a soft landing,' Longtusk murmured.

'*Baitho!*'

'He wants to try again,' Walks With Thunder said. 'Go ahead, lower your trunk. That's it. Let him climb on. Now take it easy, Longtusk. Don't throw him – *lift* him, smoothly and gently.'

Longtusk made a determined effort to keep the motions of his trunk even and steady.

But this time Lemming was thrown backwards. He completed a neat back-flip and landed on his belly in the dirt.

Other Fireheads ran forward. They lifted him up and started slapping at his furs, making great clouds of dust billow around him. They were flashing their small teeth and making the harsh noise he had come to recognise as *laughing*: not kind, perhaps, but not threatening.

But now the other keeper, Spindle, came forward. His goad, tipped with sharp bone, was long and cruel, and he walked back and forth before Longtusk, eyeing him. He was saying something, his small, cruel mouth working.

'Take it easy, Longtusk,' Walks With Thunder warned.

'What does he want?'

'If Lemming can't tame you, then Spindle will do it. *His* way—'

Suddenly Spindle's thin arm lashed out towards Longtusk. His goad fizzed through the air and cut cruelly into the soft flesh of Longtusk's cheek.

Longtusk trumpeted in anger and reared up, as high as his hobbles would allow him. He could crush Spindle with a single stamp, or run him through with a tusk. How *dare* this ugly little creature attack *him*?

But the Firehead wasn't even backing away. He was

standing before Longtusk, forelegs extended, paws tucked over as if beckoning.

'Don't, Longtusk,' Walks With Thunder rumbled urgently. 'It's what he wants. Don't you see? If you so much as scratch Spindle, they will destroy you in an instant. *It's what he wants . . .*'

Longtusk knew Thunder was right. He growled and lowered his tusks, glaring at Spindle.

The Firehead, tiny teeth gleaming, lashed out once more, and again Longtusk felt the goad cut deep into his flesh.

But suddenly it ceased.

Longtusk looked down. The girl-cub, Crocus, was standing before him. She seemed angry, distressed; tears ran down her small face. She was tugging at Spindle's foreleg, making him stop. Her father, Bedrock, and the Shaman Smokehat were standing behind her.

Spindle was hesitating, his blood-tipped goad still raised to Longtusk.

At last Bedrock gestured to Spindle. With a snort of disgust the keeper threw his goad in the dirt and stalked away.

Now Crocus stood before Longtusk, gazing up at him. She was growing taller, just as he was, and an elaborate cap of ivory beads adorned her long blonde hair, replacing the simple tooth necklace circle she had worn when younger. She seemed afraid, he saw, but she was evidently determined to master her fear.

'*Baitho*,' she said, her voice small and clear. Down, down.

And Longtusk, the warm blood still welling from his face, obeyed.

She stepped onto his trunk, reached forward, and grabbed hold of his ears.

He raised his trunk, gingerly, carefully.

Thunder was very quiet and still, as if he scarcely dared breathe. 'Right. Lower her onto your back. Gently! Recall how fragile she is . . . imagine she's a flower blossom, and you don't want to disturb a single petal.'

Rumbling, working by feel, Longtusk did his best. He felt the cub's skinny legs slide around his neck.

'How's that?'

Walks With Thunder surveyed him critically. 'Not bad. Except she's the wrong way round. She's facing your backside, Longtusk. Try again. Let her off.'

Longtusk lowered his hind legs. Crocus skidded down his back, landing with a squeal in the dirt.

'By Kilukpuk's hairy navel,' Walks With Thunder groaned, and Bedrock stepped forward, anxious.

But Crocus, though a little dusty, was unharmed. She trotted round to Longtusk's head once more. She pulled her face in the gesture he was coming to recognise as a *smile*, and she patted the blood-matted hair of his cheek. '*Baitho*,' she said quietly.

Again he lowered his trunk for her.

This time he got her the right way round. Her legs wrapped around his neck, and he felt her little paws grasping at the long hairs on top of his head. She was a small warm bundle, delicate, so light he could scarcely feel her.

Rumbling, constrained by his hobbles, Longtusk took a cautious step forward. He felt the cub's fingers digging deeper into his fur, and she squealed with alarm. He stopped, but she kicked at his flanks with her tiny feet, and called out, '*Agit!*'

'It's all right,' Walks With Thunder said. 'She's safe up there. Go forward. Just take it easy, Longtusk.'

So he stepped forward again.

Crocus laughed with pleasure. Keepers ran alongside him – as did Bedrock, still wary, but grinning. The watching mastodonts raised their trunks and trumpeted in salute.

But the Shaman, ignored by the Fireheads and their leader, was glaring, quietly furious.

*

It was all a question of practice, of course.

By the end of that first day Longtusk could lift the little Firehead onto his back, delivering her the right way round, almost without effort. And by the end of the second day he was starting to learn what Crocus wanted. A gentle kick to the left ear – maybe accompanied by a thin cry of *Chi!* – meant he should go left. *Chai Ghoom!* and a kick to the right ear meant go right. *Agit!* meant go forward; *Dhuth!* meant stop. And so on.

By the end of the third day, Longtusk was starting to learn subtler commands, transmitted to him through the cub's body movements. If Crocus stiffened her limbs and leaned back he knew he was supposed to stop. If she leaned forward and pushed his head downwards he should kneel or stoop.

Crocus never used a goad on him.

It wasn't all easy. Once he spied an exceptionally rich clump of herbs, glimpsed through the branches of a tree. He forgot what he was doing and went that way, regardless of the little creature on his back – who yelped as the branches swept her to the ground. Alternatively if Longtusk thought the path he was being told to select was uncomfortable or even dangerous – for instance, if it was littered with sharp scree that might cut his footpads – he simply wouldn't go that way, regardless of the protests of the cub.

After many days of this the keeper, Spindle, came to him, early in the morning.

Spindle raised his goad. *'Baitho! Baitho!'*

Longtusk simply glared at him, chewing his feed, refusing to comply.

The beating started then, as intense as before, and Longtusk felt old wounds opening on his cheek. But still he would not bow to Spindle.

Nobody else, he thought. Only the girl-cub Crocus.

At last Crocus came running with the other keepers. With sharp words she dismissed Spindle. Then, with Lemming's help, she applied a thick, soothing salve to the cuts Spindle had inflicted on Longtusk's cheek and thighs.

Without waiting for the command, Longtusk lowered his trunk and allowed her to climb onto his back once more.

Although Longtusk's workload didn't change, he became accustomed to meeting Crocus at the beginning or end of each day. She would ride him around the mastodont stockade, and Longtusk learned to ignore the mocking, somewhat envious jeers of the mastodonts. As she approached he would coil and uncoil his trunk with pleasure. Sometimes she brought him titbits of food, which he chewed as she talked to him steadily in her incomprehensible, complex tongue.

She seemed fascinated by his fur. Longtusk had a dense underfur of fine woolly hair that covered almost all his skin. His rump, belly, flanks, throat and trunk were covered as well by a dense layer of long, coarse guard hair that dangled to the ground, skirt-like. The guard hair melded across his shoulders with a layer of thick but less coarse hairs that came up over his shoulders from low on the neck.

Crocus spent a great deal of time examining all this, lifting his guard hairs and teasing apart its layers. As for Longtusk, he would touch Crocus's sweet face with the wet tip of his trunk, then rest against her warmth, eyes closed.

Eventually Crocus's visits became a highlight of his day – almost as welcome as, and rather less baffling than, his occasional meetings with the young mastodont Cow, Neck Like Spruce.

Once he took Crocus for a long ride across the bare steppe. They found a rock pool, and Longtusk wallowed there while Crocus played and swam. The sun was still high and warm, and he stretched out on the ground. She climbed onto his hairy belly and lay on top of him, soothed by the rumble of his stomach, plucking his hair and singing.

Even though he knew he remained a captive – even though her affection was that of an owner to the owned –

and even though the growing affection between them was only a more subtle kind of trap, harder to break than any hobbles – still, he felt as content as he had been since he had been separated from his Family.

But he was aware of the jealous glares of Spindle and Smokehat.

Longtusk grew impatient with all these obscure mental games, the strange obsessions of the Fireheads. But Thunder counselled caution.

'Be wary,' he would say, as the mastodonts gathered after a day's work. 'You have a friend now. She recalls you once saved her life. And that's good. But you're also acquiring enemies. The Shaman is jealous. It is only the power of her father, Bedrock, which is protecting you. Life is more complicated than you think, little grazer. Only death is simple . . .'

CHAPTER 3
THE SETTLEMENT

The Fireheads' numbers were growing, with many young being born, and they worked hard to feed themselves.

As spring wore into summer, Firehead hunters began making journeys into the surrounding steppe. The hunters looked for tracks and droppings. What they sought, Longtusk was told, was the spoor of wolves, for that told them that there was a migrant herd somewhere nearby, tracked by the carnivores.

And at last the first of the migrants returned: deer, some of them giants, their heads bowed under the weight of their immense spreads of antlers.

The deer trekked enormous distances between their winter range in the far south, on the fringe of the lands where trees grew thickly, and their calving grounds on the northern steppe. The calving grounds were often dismal places of fog and marshy land and bare rock. But they had the great advantage that most predators, seeking places to den themselves, would fall away long before the calving grounds were reached. And when the calves were born the deer would form into vast herds in preparation for the migration back to the south: enormous numbers of them, so many a single herd might stretch from horizon to horizon, blackening the land.

To Longtusk these great migrations, of animals and birds, seemed like breathing, a great inhalation of life.

And the Fireheads waited for the migrant animals to pass, movements as predictable as the seasons themselves, and prepared to hunt.

*

One day, late in the summer, Crocus walked with her father and the Shaman to the bone stockpile, a short distance from the mastodont stockade.

Longtusk, still not fully trusted, wasn't allowed anywhere near this grisly heap of flensed bones, gleaming in the low afternoon sun.

Crocus walked around the pile, one finger in her small mouth. She ran her paws over clutches of vertebrae, and huge shoulder blades, and bare leg bones almost as tall as she was. At last she stopped before a great skull with sweeping tusks. As the skull's long-vacant eye sockets gaped at her, the cub rubbed the flat surfaces of the mammoth's worn yellow teeth.

Longtusk wondered absently what that long-dead tusker would have made of this.

Crocus looked up at her father and the Shaman, talking rapidly and jumping up and down with excitement. This skull was evidently her choice. Bedrock and Smokehat reached down and, hauling together, dragged the skull from the heap. It was too heavy for them to lift.

Then, his absurd headdress smoking, the Shaman sang and danced around the ancient bones, sprinkling them with water and dust. Longtusk had seen this kind of behaviour before. It seemed that the Shaman was making the skull special, as if it was a living thing he could train to protect the little cub who had chosen it.

When the Shaman was done, Bedrock gestured to the mastodont trainers. Lemming and the others walked through the stockade and selected Jaw Like Rock and another strong Bull. Evidently they were to carry the skull off.

But Crocus seemed angry. She ran into the stockade herself, shouting, 'Baitho! Baitho!'

Longtusk lowered his trunk to the ground and bent his head. With the confidence of long practice she wriggled past his tusks, grabbed his ears and in a moment was sitting in her comfortable place at his neck. Then, with a sharp slap on his scalp, she urged him forward. '*Agit!*'

She was, he realised, driving him directly towards the pile of bones.

As he neared the pile an instinctive dread of those grisly remains built up in him. The other Fireheads seemed to sense his tension.

He kept walking, crossing the muddy, trampled ground, one broad step at a time.

He reached the great gaping skull where it lay on the ground. There was a lingering smell of dead mammoth about it, and it seemed to glare at him in disapproval.

Crocus tapped his head. '*A dhur! A dhur!*' She wanted him to pick it up.

I can't, he thought.

He heard a high-pitched growl around him. The hunters were approaching him with spears raised to their shoulders, all pointing at his heart.

The Shaman watched, eyes glittering like quartz pebbles.

From out of nowhere, a storm cloud of danger was gathering around Longtusk. He felt himself quiver, and in response Crocus's fingers tightened their grip on his fur.

Longtusk stared into the vacant eyes of the long-dead mammoth. What, he wondered, would *you* have me do?

It was as if a voice sounded deep in his belly. *Remember me*, it said. *That's all. Remember me.*

He understood.

He touched the vacant skull with his trunk, lifted it, let it fall back to the dirt. Then he turned.

He faced a wall of Firehead hunters. One of them actually jabbed his chest with a quartz spear tip, hard enough to break the skin. But Longtusk, descending into the slow rhythms of his kind, ignored these fluttering Fireheads, even the spark of pain at his chest.

He gathered twigs and soil and cast them on the ancient bones, and then turned backwards and touched the bones with the sensitive pads of his back feet. Longtusk was trying to Remember the spirit which had once occupied this pale bone, this Bull with no name.

The Fireheads watched with evident confusion – and the Shaman with rage, at this ceremony so much older and deeper than his own posturing. Further away, the mastodonts rumbled their approval.

The Firehead cub slid to the ground, waving back the spears of the hunters. Slowly, hesitantly, Crocus joined in. She slipped off her moccasins and touched the skull with her own small feet, and bent to scoop more dirt over the cold bones. She was copying Longtusk, trying to Remember too – or, at least, showing him she understood.

At last, Longtusk felt he was done. Now the skull was indeed just a piece of bone, discarded.

Crocus stepped up to him, rubbed the fur between his eyes, and climbed briskly onto his back. She said gently, '*A dhur.*'

Clumsily, but without hesitation, he slid his tusks under the skull and wrapped his trunk firmly over the top of it. Then he straightened his neck and lifted.

The skull wasn't as heavy as it looked; mammoth bone was porous, to make it light despite its great bulk and strength. He cradled it carefully.

Then – under the guidance of Crocus, and with Bedrock, the Shaman, and assorted keepers and spear-laden hunters following him like wolves trailing migrant deer – he carried the skull towards the Firehead settlement.

Ahead of him, smoke curled into the air from a dozen fires.

The trail to the settlement was well beaten, a rut dug into the steppe by the feet of Fireheads and mastodonts. But Longtusk had not been this way before.

He passed storage pits. Their walls were scoured by the tusks of the mastodonts who had dug out these pits, and they were lined with slabs of smooth rock. Longtusk could see the pits were half-filled with hunks of dried and salted meat, or with dried grasses to provide feed for the masto-donts; winter seemed remote, but already these clever, difficult Fireheads were planning for its rigours.

Further in towards the centre of the settlement there were many hearths: out in the open air, blackened circles on the ground everywhere, many of them smouldering with day-fires. Chunks of meat broiled on spits, filling the air with acrid smoke.

There was, in fact, a *lot* of meat in the settlement.

Some of it dangled from wooden frames, varying in con-dition from dry and curled to fresh, some even dripping blood. There were a few small animals, lemmings and rabbits and even a young fox, hung up with their necks lolling, obviously dead.

And, most of all, there were Fireheads everywhere: not the few keepers and hunters the mastodonts encountered in their stockade and during the course of their work, but many more, more than he could count. There were males and females, old ones with yellowed, gappy teeth and frost-white hair, young ones who ran, excited, even infants in their mothers' arms. They all wore thick clothing of fur and skin, stuffed with grasses and wool; all but the smallest cubs wore thick, warming moccasins.

Some of the Fireheads worked at the hearths, turning spitted meat. One female had a piece of skin staked out over the ground and she was scraping it with a sharpened stone, removing fat and clinging flesh and sinew, leaving the surface smooth and shining. He saw a male making deerskin into rope, cutting strips crosswise for strength. They seemed, in fact, to use every part of the animals they hunted: tendons were twisted into strands of sinew, and bladders, stomach and intestines were used to hold water.

They made paint, of ground-up rock mixed with animal fat, or lichen soaked in aurochs' urine. Many of them had marked their skins with stripes and circles of the red and yellow colouring, and they wore strings of beads made of pretty, pierced stones or chipped bones.

Many of the Fireheads were fascinated by Longtusk. They broke off what they were doing and followed, the adults staring, the cubs dancing and laughing.

Here was one small group of Fireheads – perhaps a family – having a meal, gathered around a sputtering fire. They had bones that had been broiled on their fire, and they cracked the bones on rocks and sucked out the soft, greasy marrow within. Longtusk wondered absently what animal the bones had come from.

As he passed – a great woolly mammoth bearing a huge skull and with the daughter of the chief clinging proudly to his back – the Fireheads stopped eating, stared, and joined the slow, gathering procession that trailed after Longtusk.

. . . Now, surrounded by Fireheads, he was aware of discomfort, a sharp prodding at his rump.

He turned. He saw the Shaman, Smokehat, bearing one of the hunters' big game spears. The quartz tip was red with blood: Longtusk's blood.

He saw calculation in the Shaman's small, pinched face. Sensing his tension, Smokehat was deliberately prodding him, trying to make him respond – perhaps by growing angry, throwing off Crocus. If that happened, if he went rogue here at the heart of the Firehead settlement, Longtusk would surely be killed.

Longtusk snorted in disgust, turned his back and continued to walk.

But the next time he felt the tell-tale prod at his rump he swished his tail, as if brushing away flies. He heard a thin mewl of complaint.

Smokehat was clutching his cheek, and blood leaked around his fingers. Longtusk's tail hairs had brushed the Firehead's face, splitting it open like a piece of old fruit. With murder in his sharp eyes, the Shaman was led away for treatment; and Longtusk, with quiet contentment, continued his steady plod.

He heard a trumpeted greeting. He slowed, startled.

There were mastodonts here: a small Family, a few adult Cows, calves holding onto their mothers' tails with their spindly little trunks. They wandered freely through the settlement, without hobbles or restraints, mingling with the Fireheads.

One of the Cows was Neck Like Spruce.

'Well, well,' she said. 'Quite a spectacle. Life getting dull out in the stockade, was it?'

When he replied, his voice was tight, his rumbles shallow. 'If you haven't anything useful to say, leave me alone.'

She sensed his tension, and glanced now at the hunters who followed him, spears still ready to fly. 'Just stay calm,' she said seriously. 'They are used to us. In fact they feel safer if we are here. Where there are mastodonts, the cats and wolves will not attack . . . Where are you going?'

He growled. 'Do I look as if I have the faintest idea?'

She trumpeted her amusement, and broke away from her Family to walk alongside him.

At last the motley procession approached the very heart of the Firehead settlement, and Longtusk slowed, uncertain.

There were larger structures here – perhaps a dozen of them, arranged in an uneven circle. They were rough domes of grey-green and white. The largest of all, and the most incomplete, was at the very centre.

Crocus slid easily to the ground. She took the tip of Longtusk's trunk in her small paw and led him into the circle of huts.

He stopped by one of the huts. It was made of turf and stretched skin and rock, piled up high. On the expanses of bare animal skin, there were strange markings, streaks and whirls of ochre and other dyes, and here and there the skin was marked with the unmistakable imprint of a Firehead paw, marked out as a silhouette in red-brown colouring.

The dome-shaped hut had a hole cut in its top, from which smoke curled up to the sky.

There were white objects arrayed around the base of the hut. White, complex shapes.

Mammoth bones.

Big skulls had been pushed into the ground by their tusk sockets, all around the hut. Curving bones, shoulder blades and pelvises, had been layered along the lower wall of the hut. There were heavier bones, femurs and bits of skulls, tied to the turf roof. And two great curving tusks had been shoved into the ground and their sharp points tied together to form an arch over a skin-flap doorway.

Some of the bones were chipped and showed signs of where they had been gnawed by predators, perhaps as they had emerged from the remote river bank where they had been mined.

Now the flap of skin parted at the front of the hut, and a woman pushed out into the colder air. She gaped at the woolly mammoth standing before her, and clutched her squealing infant tighter to her chest.

Longtusk, baffled, was filled with dread and horror. 'By Kilukpuk's last breath, what *is* this?'

'This is how the Fireheads live, Longtusk,' said Neck Like Spruce. 'The turf and rock keeps in the warmth of their fires . . .'

'But, Spruce, *the bones*. Why . . . ?'

She trumpeted her irritation at him. 'This is a cold and windy place, if you hadn't noticed, Longtusk. The Fireheads have to make their huts sturdy. They prefer wood, but there is little wood on this steppe, and what there was they have mostly burned. But there are plenty of bones.'

'Mammoth bones.'

'Yes. Longtusk, your kind have lived here for a *long* time, and the ground is full of their bones. In some ways bone is better than wood, because it is immune to frost and damp and insects. These huts are built to last a long time,

Longtusk, many seasons . . . And it does no harm,' she said softly.

'I know.' For, he realised, these mammoths had long gone to the aurora, and had no use for these discarded scraps.

There was a gentle tugging at his trunk. He glanced down. It was Crocus; she was trying to get him to come closer to the big central hut.

He rumbled and followed her.

This hut would eventually be the biggest of them all – a fitting home for Bedrock and his family, including little Crocus – but it was incomplete, without a roof.

A ring of mammoth femurs had been thrust into the ground in a circle at the base, and an elaborate pattern of shoulder blades had been piled up around the perimeter of the hut, overlapping neatly like the scales of some immense fish.

The floor had been dug away, making a shallow pit. Flat stones had been set in a circle at the centre of the hut to make a hearth. And there was a small cup of carved stone, filled with sticky animal fat, within which a length of plaited mastodont fur burned slowly, giving off a greasy smoke. With a flash of intuition he saw that it would be dark inside the hut when the roof had been completed; perhaps sputtering flames like these would give the illusion of day, even in darkness.

Under Crocus's urging, he laid down the skull he carried, just outside the circle of leg bones. Crocus jumped on it, excited, and made big swooping gestures with her skinny forelegs. Perhaps this skull would be built into the hut. Its glaring eye sockets and sweeping tusks would make an imposing entrance.

Now Crocus ran into the incomplete hut, picked up a bundle wrapped in skin, and held it up to Longtusk. When the skin wrapping fell away Longtusk saw that it was a slab of sandstone, and strange loops and whorls had been cut into its surface.

'Touch it,' called Neck Like Spruce.

Cautiously Longtusk reached forward with his trunk's fragile pink tip, and explored the surface of the rock.

'. . . It's *warm*.'

'They put the rocks in the fires to make them hot, then clutch them to their bellies in the night.'

Now Crocus was jabbering, pointing to the markings on the skin walls, streaks and whorls and lines, daubed there by Firehead fingers. The cub seemed excited.

He traced his trunk tip over the patterns, but could taste or smell nothing but ochre and animal fat. He growled, baffled.

'It's another Firehead habit,' Spruce said testily. 'Each pattern means something. Look again, Longtusk. The Fireheads aren't like us; they have poor smell and hearing, and rely on their eyes. Don't touch it or smell it. Try to look through Firehead eyes. Imagine it isn't just a sheet of skin, but a – a hole in the wall. Imagine you aren't looking at markings just in front of your face, but forms that are far away. Look with your eyes, Longtusk, just your eyes. *Now* – now what do you see?'

After a time, with Crocus chattering constantly in his ear, he managed it.

Here was a curving outline, with a smooth sheen of ochre across its interior, that became a bison, strong and proud. Here was a row of curved lines, one after the other, that was a line of deer, heads up and running. Here was a horse, dipping its head and stamping its small foot. Here was a strange creature that was half leaping stag and half Firehead, glaring out at him.

He looked around the settlement with new eyes – and he saw that there were markings *everywhere*, on every available surface: the walls of the huts, the faces of the Fireheads, the shafts of the hunters' spears, even Crocus's heated stone. And all of the markings *meant* something, showing Fireheads and animals, mountains and flowers.

The illusions were transient and flat. These 'animals' had no scent, no voices, no weight to set the Earth ringing. They were just shadows of colour and line.

Nevertheless they were here. And everywhere he looked, they danced.

The settlement was alive, transformed by the minds and paws of the Fireheads, made vibrant and rich – as if the land itself had become conscious, full of reflections of itself. It was a transformation that could not even have been imagined by any mammoth or mastodont who ever lived. He trembled at its thin, strange beauty.

How could any creatures be capable of such wonder – and, at the same time, such cruelty? These Fireheads were strange and complex beings indeed.

Now Crocus dragged his face back to the wall of her own hut. Here was a row of stocky, flat-backed shapes, with curving tusks before them.

Mastodonts. It was a line of mastodonts, their tusks, drawn with simple, confident sweeps, proud and strong.

But Crocus was pointing especially at a figure at the front of the line. It was crudely drawn, as if by a cub – by Crocus herself, he realised.

It looked like a mastodont, but its back sloped down from a hump at its neck. Its tusks were long and curved before its high head, and long hairs draped down from its trunk and belly.

He growled, confused, distressed.

'Longtusk?' Neck Like Spruce called. *'That's you*, Longtusk. Crocus made you on the wall. You see? She was trying to honour you.'

'I understand. It's just—'

'What?'

'I haven't seen a mammoth since I was separated from my Family. Neck Like Spruce, I think I'd forgotten what I look like.'

'Oh, Longtusk . . .'

Crocus came to him, perceiving his sudden distress. She wrapped her arms around his trunk, buried her face in his hair, and murmured soothing noises.

CHAPTER 4
THE HUNT

Winter succeeded summer, frost following fire.

Sometimes, Longtusk dreamt:

Yellow plain, blue sky, a landscape huge, flat, elemental, dominated by the unending grind and crack of ice. And mammoths sweeping over the land like clouds—

He would wake with a start.

All around him was order: the mastodont stockade, the spreading Firehead settlement, the smoke spiralling to the sky. *This* was the reality of his life, not that increasingly remote plain, the mammoth herds that covered the land. *That* had been no more than the start of his journey – a journey that had ended here.

Hadn't it?

After all, what else was there? Where else could he go? What else was there to do with his life, but serve the Fireheads?

Troubled, he returned to sleep.

And five years wore away.

The hunting party of Fireheads and mastodonts – and one woolly mammoth – marched proudly across the landscape. The high summer sun cast short shadows of Longtusk and his rider: Crocus, of course, now fully grown, long-legged and elegant, and as strong and brave as any of the male Firehead hunters. She was equipped for the hunt. She carried a quartz-tipped spear, and wore a broad belt slung over her shoulder, laden with stone knives and hammers, and – most prized of all – an atlatl, a dart thrower made of sculpted deer bone.

'. . . Ah,' Walks With Thunder said now, and he paused. '*Look.*'

Longtusk looked down at the ground. At first he saw nothing but an unremarkable patch of steppe grass, with a little purple saxifrage. Then he made out scattered pellets of dung.

Walks With Thunder poked at the pellets with his trunk tip. 'See the short bitten-off twigs in there? Not like mastodonts; we leave long twisted bits of fibre in our dung. And we produce neat piles too; *they* kick it around the place as it emerges . . .' He brought a piece of dung into his mouth. 'Warm. Fresh. *They* are close. Softly, now.'

Alert, evidently excited, he trotted on, and the party followed.

Over the years Longtusk had been involved in many of the Fireheads' hunts. Most of them targeted the smaller herbivores. The Fireheads would follow a herd of deer or horse and pick off a vulnerable animal – a cow slowed by pregnancy, or a juvenile, or the old or lame – and finish it quickly. Then they would butcher it with their sharpened stones and have the mastodonts carry back the dripping meat, skin and bones.

The hunts were usually brief, efficient, routine events, and only rarely would the hunters take on an animal the size of, say, a giant deer. The hunters were after all seeking food, and they tried to make their success as certain as possible, minimising the risks they took.

But today's hunt was different. Today they were going after the largest prey of all. And only the strongest and most able hunters, including Bedrock himself, had been included in the party.

Though Crocus had joined in hunts before – the only female Firehead to do so – and had become skilful with spear and stone knife, this was the first time she had been allowed by her father to take part in such an event. And so – because Longtusk still refused to allow any other rider on his back but Crocus – it was the first time for him, too.

They were heading west, and they came to a strange land.

There were pools here, but they were small and mis-shapen and filled with icy, cloudy, sour water. Trees, mostly spruce, struggled to grow, but they were stunted and leaned at drunken angles. The ground was broken and hummocky, and Longtusk had to step carefully. Here and there, in fact, the turf was no more than a thin crust over a deeper hollow. With his senses he could hear the peculiar echoes the crusty ground returned, but still an incautious footstep could lead to a stumble or worse.

Walks With Thunder, with Bedrock proudly borne on his back, loped alongside Longtusk. 'The ice is retreating to its northern fastness. But this is a place where a remnant of ice was covered over by wind-blown silt and soil before it could melt. The earth is thin; the trees can establish only shallow roots, so they grow badly. And the ice is still there, beneath us . . . Look.'

They came to a low ridge, half Longtusk's height. Under a lip of grass, he could see ice protruding above the ground, dirty, glistening with meltwater.

'The stagnant ice is slowly melting away. As it does so it leaves hollows and caverns under a crust of unsupported earth. But sometimes the rain and meltwater will work away at the ice, turning it into a honeycomb. So watch your step, little grazer, for you don't want to snap a tusk or an ankle. And you *don't* want to dump your rider on her behind.'

So Longtusk stepped carefully.

When the sun was at its highest the party paused to rest. The mastodonts were freed of their packs, hobbled loosely and allowed to wander off in search of food.

Later, some of them, Longtusk included, underwent some refresher training in preparation for the hunt, along with their riders. Jaw Like Rock, ridden by the cruel Spindle, led them.

Jaw trotted back and forth across the broken ground, and Spindle, riding Jaw's back, got cautiously to his feet. His feet were bare to improve his grip, and he kept his balance by holding out his forelegs.

Jaw kept up a commentary for the mastodonts. 'You can see he can hold his place up there. The hunters stand so they get a better leverage when they hurl their spears and darts.

'But you have to realise it isn't natural. He isn't stable. I can feel he's on the brink of falling over. He can shift his feet and hind legs to adjust his balance, and I have to try to keep my back steady as I move. See? It gets a lot harder when you're racing over this crusty ground along-side the prey . . . And if you stop working at it even for a moment—'

He stopped dead.

Spindle tried to keep his balance, waving his forelegs in the air. But without Jaw's assistance, he was helpless. With a wail, he tumbled to the ground, landing hard.

Longtusk heard his own rider, Crocus, break into peals of laughter. The mastodonts trumpeted and slapped the ground with their trunks.

Spindle was predictably furious. He got to his feet, brushing off dirt and grass blades. He picked up his goad and began to lash at Jaw's face and rump.

The other keepers turned away, as if disgusted, and the mastodonts rumbled their disapproval.

Longtusk said grimly, 'I don't know how you put up with that.'

Jaw eyed him, stolidly enduring his punishment. 'It's worth it. Anyway, nothing lasts for ever—'

A contact rumble washed over the steppe. 'Silence,' Walks With Thunder called. '*Silence*. Rhinos . . .'

*

There were three of them, Longtusk counted: two adults and a calf.

They were at the edge of a milk-white pond. One of the adults – perhaps a female – was in the water, which lapped around the fur fringing her belly. Her calf was in the pond beside her, almost afloat, sometimes putting her head under the water and paddling around her mother.

The other adult, probably a male, stood on the shore of the pond. He was grazing, trampling the grass flat and then using his big forelip to scoop it into his mouth.

They were woolly rhinos.

They were broad, fat tubes of muscle and fat. Their skin was heavy and wrinkled. On massive necks were set squat, low-slung heads with small ears and tiny black eyes. Their bodies were coated with dark brown fur, short on top but dangling in long fringes from their bellies. They had high humps over their shoulders, short tails and, strangest of all, each had two long curving horns protruding up from their noses. The bull's nasal horn in particular was long and glinting and sharp.

Small birds clustered on the bull's back, pecking, searching for mosquitoes and grubs.

Now the cow climbed out of the water, ponderous and slow, followed by her calf. Dripping, she grunted, shifted her hind legs, and emitted a spray of urine, horizontal and powerful, that splashed into the pond water and over the nearby shore. The urine came in gargantuan proportions. Longtusk saw, bemused, a series of powerful blasts, until it dwindled to a trickle down the long hairs of the cow's hind legs.

The bull, rumbling in response, immediately emptied his own bladder in a spray that covered the cow's. Then he rubbed his hind feet in the wet soil.

Thunder grunted. 'The rhinos talk through their urine and dung. When other rhinos come this way, they will be able to tell that the cow over there is in oestrus, ready to mate. But the bull has covered her marker, telling the other bulls that she is *his* . . .'

They were almost like mammoths, Longtusk thought, wondering: short, squat, deformed – nevertheless built to survive the harshness of winter.

The party of mastodonts and Fireheads began to pad softly forward.

'They haven't sensed us yet,' said Thunder. 'See the way the Bull's ears are up, his tail is low? He's at his ease. Let's hope he stays that way.'

The rhino calf was the first to notice them.

She (or he, it was impossible to tell) was prising up dead wood with her tiny bump of a horn, apparently seeking termites. Then she seemed to scent the mastodonts. She flattened her ears and lifted her tail.

She ran around her mother, prodding her with her horn. At first the mother, dozing, took no notice. But the calf put both her front feet on the mother's face and blew in her ear. The cow got to her feet, shaking her head, and rumbled a warning to the male.

The rhinos began to lumber away from the pond, in the direction of open ground. The small birds which had been working on the backs of the rhinos flew off in a brief burst of startled motion.

The mastodonts and their riders pursued, rapidly picking up speed. Those animals heavy with pack were left behind, while others lightly laden for the chase hurtled after the rhinos: they included Thunder, bearing Bedrock, Jaw with Spindle – and Longtusk, carrying Crocus, who clung to his hair, whooping her excitement as the steppe grass flew past.

'This is it,' said Thunder, tense and excited. 'We're going after the bull.'

Longtusk said, 'Why not the cow? She is slowed by the calf.'

'But she is not such a prize. See the way the bull's back is flat and straight, the cow's sagging? That shows she is old and weak. This hunt is a thing of prestige. Today these hunters are chasing honour, not the easiest meat. We go for the male.'

Soon they passed the cow and her calf. The cow flattened her ears, wrinkled her nose and half-opened her mouth, as if she was about to charge. But the mastodonts and their riders ignored her, flying onwards over the steppe in pursuit of the greater quarry.

They drew alongside the male rhino. He ran almost elegantly, Longtusk thought: like a horse, his tail high, his feet lifting over the broken ground. Even as he ran he bellowed his protest and swung his powerful horns this way and that, trying to reach the mastodonts.

With practised ease Bedrock slid to his feet on the broad back of Walks With Thunder and prepared his atlatl. He raised a dart – it was almost as long as Bedrock was tall, and its tip, pure quartz crystal, glinted cruelly – and he fitted a notch in the base of the dart to the thrower. The thrower, perhaps a third the length of the dart, was carved from the femur of a giant deer.

Longtusk could feel Crocus clambering to her feet on his back. She was unsteady, and he sensed her leaning forward, ready to grab at his hairs if she felt herself falling. Nevertheless she hefted her own dart.

And she threw first.

She hurled hard and well – but not accurately enough; the dart's tip glanced off the rhino's back, scraping through his hair, and slid onwards towards the ground.

Now her father raised his dart. He held it flat, with the thrower resting on his shoulder, his hand just behind his ear. Then, with savage force, his entire lean body whipping forward, he thrust at the dart. Longtusk saw the thin shaft bow into a curve, and then spring away from Bedrock, as if it was a live thing, hissing through the air.

The hard quartz tip shone like a falling star as it flew at

the rhino. The dart hit beneath the rhino's rib cage – exactly where it could do most damage.

The dart point had been designed and made by master craftsmen for its purpose. It was long, sharp and did not split or shatter on first impact. Instead it drove itself through the rhino's hair and layers of hide and fat, embedding itself in the soft, warm organs within.

The rhino screeched, his voice strangely high for such an immense animal. Longtusk could smell the sharp metallic tang of the blood which spurted crimson from the wound, and black fluid oozed from the rhino's lips.

But still, with awesome willpower, the rhino ran on. The pain must have been agonising as the dangling, twisting spear ripped at the wound, widening it further and deepening the internal injury.

Now another mastodont bearing a young, keen-eyed hunter called Bareface drew alongside the rhino. The hunter took careful aim and hurled his dart – not at the rhino's injured torso, but at his hind legs.

The dart sliced through fur and flesh. The rhino fell flat on the ground and rolled over, snapping off the dart that protruded from his side.

Still defiant, the rhino tried to rise. But his hind leg dangled uselessly, pumping blood, and he fell again in dirt already soaked with his own blood. Urine and dung gushed, liquid, adding to the mess in the dirt.

The mastodonts halted. The Fireheads jumped down, approaching the rhino warily.

The rhino thrashed in the dirt and bellowed his rage, slashing the air with his long horn. But he was already mortally wounded; a spray of red-black liquid shot from his mouth.

Defying the swings of that cruel horn, Bedrock leapt nimbly onto the rhino's broad back, grabbing great pawfuls of fur. With grim determination, already covered in dirt and blood, Bedrock crawled forward until he reached the base of the rhino's neck. Then he pulled from his belt a long, sharp chisel of rock. Defying the thrashings of the rhino, he stabbed the chisel into the creature's flesh, at the top of his spine. Then he produced a hammer rock from his belt.

Under Bedrock's single blow, the stone blade slid easily through the rhino's hide.

As his spine was severed the rhino's eyes widened, startled, almost curious. Then he slumped flat against the blood-stained dirt, his magnificent body reduced to a flaccid, quivering mound.

He raised his head to face Longtusk. He breathed in short sharp gasps, *whoosh, whoosh, whoosh.*

Walks With Thunder said grimly, 'He's trying to speak to you. *Who are you? Why are you doing this?*'

'How can you understand him?'

'We are all Hotbloods, grazer.'

Then, mercifully, Bedrock drove another blade into the rhino's spine.

The rhino's head slumped to the ground. His body rumbled and shuddered as its huge, complex processes closed down.

When life was gone, panting mastodonts and blood-spattered Fireheads stood away from the corpse. They seemed united by the vivid moment, stilled, as if the world pivoted on the death of this huge, defiant animal.

Then Bedrock climbed onto the rhino's back, his furs stained with blood. He raised his paws in the air and hollered his triumph, and his hunters yelled in response. They sound like wolves, Longtusk thought; it is the feral cry of the predator.

And I have run with them. For an instant an image of his mother came into his mind, her smell and warmth and touch, as clearly as if she was standing before him. Oh, Milkbreath, I have come on a long journey since I last saw you!

Bedrock jumped down and walked to the rhino's slumped

head. He gripped his hammer rock and swung it against the base of that huge horn. With a sharp crack, the horn split away from a shallow depression in the rhino's face. Bedrock raised the horn to the sky, then tucked it into his belt.

The hunters gathered around the rhino, producing their knives of stone, and began to slice through skin and fur.

Longtusk said, 'Now what? It will take a while to butcher this huge animal.'

'Oh, they aren't going to butcher it,' said Jaw Like Rock. 'It's too big a beast to haul across the steppe, too much meat to eat and store. They will dig out the liver and consume that. And, of course, Bedrock has his horn . . .'

'The horn?'

Walks With Thunder rumbled, 'Bedrock has a dozen horns already. He will take this one and have it shaped into a dagger or a drinking cup, and he will treasure it for ever, a token of his bravery. This wasn't about gathering meat. Today the Fireheads have proved, you see, what brave hunters they are . . . Look up there.'

Condors wheeled overhead, their wings stretched out, cold and black.

'*They* know,' said Thunder. 'They have seen this before, and—'

A Firehead cried out.

It was Bedrock. He stood upright, but a look of puzzlement clouded his face. And his body was quivering.

A thin, small spear protruded from his skull.

Then his eyes rolled back in his head, blood gushed from his mouth, and he collapsed as if his bones had dissolved.

Crocus rushed forward and began to keen, her voice high and thin.

Walks With Thunder said grimly, 'Circle.'

Longtusk immediately obeyed, taking his place with the others in a rough protective ring around the fallen Firehead.

It was an ancient command, millions of years old, so old it was common to both mastodonts and mammoths.

Now Longtusk could smell and hear the assailants who had so suddenly struck down Bedrock. They were Fireheads, of course – but not from the settlement. They were some way away, and they danced and stamped their delight. The skin of their small faces was coated with a fine white powder – perhaps rock flour, sieved from the shallow pools of this strange landscape – a powder that stank sharply of salt.

The young hunter, Bareface, his shaven-smooth visage twisted into an unrecognisable snarl, whipped his foreleg with suppleness and speed.

A boomerang went flying. It spun, whistling, as it soared through the thin air. It was a piece of mammoth ivory carved smooth and curved like a bird's wing, with one side preserving the convex surface of the original tusk, the other polished almost flat.

The strange Fireheads didn't even seem to see it coming – they scattered as it flew among them, like mice disturbed by an owl – but the boomerang flew unerringly to the temple of one of them, knocking him to the ground.

Jaw growled his approval. 'The one who struck down Bedrock. *He* will not live out the day . . .'

'*Whiteskins*,' Thunder muttered. 'I never thought I'd see their ugly, capering forms again.'

Longtusk said, 'You've met them before?'

'Oh, yes. Many times. But never so far north.'

Now Crocus came running to Longtusk. Her face was contorted with rage, and her blonde hair blew around her. She held the stone chisel which Bedrock had driven into the rhino's spine. '*Baitho! Baitho!*' Longtusk lowered his head and trunk, and she grabbed his ears and scrambled onto his back. '*Agit!*'

Her intention was unmistakable.

Without thought – despite rumbles of warning from the

406

mastodonts, cries of alarm from the hunters – Longtusk charged towards the Whiteskins.

Longtusk expected the Whiteskins to flee. But they held their ground. They dropped to their knees and raised weapons of some kind.

Suddenly there were more small spears of the type that had felled Bedrock flying through the air around him, fast and straight.

'They are not spears,' puffed Thunder as he ran after the mammoth, 'but *arrows*. The Whiteskins have bows – never mind, grazer! Just keep your head high when you run. *You* can take an arrow or two – but not your rider.'

And, as if in response to Thunder's warning, a small flint-tipped spear – no, an *arrow* – plunged out of nowhere into Longtusk's cheek. The pain was sharp and intense; the small blade had reached as far as his tongue.

Without breaking stride, he curled his trunk and plucked the arrow out of his cheek. Blood sprayed, but immediately the pain lessened.

Jaw Like Rock was charging past him, the keeper Spindle clinging to Jaw's hair as if for life itself, his mouth drawn back in a rictus of terror. Jaw called, 'Had a mosquito bite, grazer?'

'Something like that.'

The big tusker trumpeted his exhilaration and charged forward.

Still the strange Fireheads did not break and run.

An arrow lodged in the foreleg of Jaw Like Rock. Long-tusk could smell the sharp, coppery stink of fresh blood. Jaw screamed and pulled up, despite repeated beatings from Spindle on his back. Jaw knelt down, snapping away the arrow. Then, bellowing with rage and pain, he plunged on.

Still Spindle continued to beat him and scream in his ear.

Now they were on the Whiteskins. Mastodonts, Whiteskins

and Fireheads flew at each other in a crude, uncoordinated mêlée, and trumpets, yells and screams broke the dust-laden air.

Longtusk lunged at the Whiteskins around him with his tusks and trunk. But, nimble and light on their feet, they stayed out of his reach. They jabbed at him with their spears and rocks, aiming to slash at his trunk or belly, or trying for his legs.

Calmly, Thunder called to Longtusk: 'Watch out for those knives. These brutes have fought us before. They are trying for your hamstrings. Recall that rhino, grazer. I've no intention of carrying you back to the stockade.'

Longtusk growled his gratitude.

Jaw Like Rock, enraged by pain, feinted at a fat Whiteskin. The Firehead, evading the lunge of those tusks, got close to Jaw with his spear. But Jaw swung his tusks sideways and knocked the Whiteskin to the ground. Then, with a single ruthless motion, he placed his foot on the head of the scrambling Whiteskin.

Jaw pressed hard, and the head burst like an overripe fruit, and the Whiteskin was limp.

Through all of this Spindle clung to Jaw's back, white-eyed, obviously terrified.

But for Longtusk there was no time for reflection, or horror; for now one of the Whiteskins came directly at him, jabbing with a long spear. He was a big buck, shaven-headed and stripped to the waist, and the whole of his upper body was coated with the acrid white paste. He had a wound on his temple, a broad cut sliced deep into the greasy flesh there – as if made by a boomerang.

Crocus, on his back, yelled her anger. With a screech like a she-cat, her blonde hair flying around her, she leapt off Longtusk's back. She landed on the big Firehead, knocking him flat. She raked her nails down his bare back, leaving red gouges. The Whiteskin howled and twisted – and, despite Crocus's anger and determination, he soon began to prevail, for Crocus's strength and weight were no match for this big male.

Walks With Thunder, surrounded by his own circle of assailants, called breathlessly, 'Protect her, Longtusk. She's important now. More than you know . . .'

Longtusk had every intention of doing just that, but while the two Fireheads flailed in the dirt, he could easily harm Crocus as much as her opponent. He stood over them, trumpeting, waiting for an opportunity.

At last the Whiteskin wrestled Crocus flat on her back. He straddled her, sitting astride her belly, raising his fists to strike.

Now was Longtusk's chance.

The mammoth reached out with his trunk, meaning to grab the Whiteskin around his neck . . .

The Whiteskin jerked upright, suddenly. His paws fluttered in the air around his face, like birds, out of his control. Then he fell backwards, twitched once, and was still.

Longtusk reached down and pulled the corpse off Crocus.

He saw immediately how the Whiteskin had died. The chisel that had destroyed the rhino – still stained by the great beast's blood – had been driven upwards into the Whiteskin's face, through the soft bones in the roof of his mouth, and into his brain.

The girl got to her feet. She stared down at the creature she had killed. Then she anchored one foot on the Whiteskin's ugly, twisted face, and yanked the chisel out of his skull. The last of his blood gushed feebly.

She stepped on his chest and emitted a howl of victory – just as her father had on bringing down the rhino.

Then she fell to her knees and buried her face in her paws.

Longtusk reached out his trunk to her. She curled up, pulling the long hairs close around her, as she had as a cub, lost and alone on the steppe.

The Whiteskins were fleeing. The mastodonts trumpeted

after them, and the Firehead hunters hurled their last spears and darts.

In all, four Whiteskins had fallen. Under the watchful, contemptuous eyes of Jaw Like Rock – whose leg wound still leaked blood – the trainer, Spindle, walked from one Whiteskin corpse to the next, jabbing his spear into their defenceless cooling bodies.

Walks With Thunder came up to Longtusk. He was dusty, blood-spattered, breathing hard. 'I'm getting too old for this. Bedrock came north to find a place to live without war . . . But the world is filling up, it seems.

'Now we must attend to business. We must collect Bedrock's body. And we will walk back the way we came and retrieve the spears that were thrown. Then we will return to the settlement. Now, everything will be different . . . *Jaw!*'

Longtusk looked up in time to see it happen.

He had heard of this before. A mastodont, cruelly treated by a Firehead keeper, would not lash out in anger. Instead he would bide his time, enduring the insults and punishment, waiting for the right opportunity.

Now here was Spindle, without his goad, dancing on the bodies of already dead Whiteskins; and here was Jaw Like Rock, calmly watching him, unrestrained, not even hobbled.

In the very last instant Spindle seemed to understand the mistake he had made. He raised his paws, as if pleading.

Jaw lunged forward with a single clean, strong motion, a thrust born of experience and training, and his tusk punctured Spindle's heart.

CHAPTER 5

THE REMEMBERING

The hunting party returned to the Firehead settlement, subdued, all but silent. They moved slowly, for Jaw Like Rock was forced to walk hobbled, armed Firehead hunters shadowing his every step.

Walks With Thunder, meanwhile, moving with slow dignity, bore the bodies of Bedrock and Spindle, wrapped in fur blankets. The long nasal horn of the rhino, Bedrock's last trophy, was laid on top of his body, still caked with dried blood.

Crocus walked beside Thunder, clutching her father's cold paw.

'*War*,' growled Thunder, and he raised his trunk suddenly, as if sniffing the winds of a vanished past. 'You've been lucky to see so little of it, little grazer. Brutal and bloody it is, for Fireheads and mastodonts. They teach us special commands, and put us through mock battles to ensure we will not panic at the furious noise, the stink of blood. And they feed us drinks of fermented grass seed, a powerful potion that drives sanity from the mind, replacing it with a mist of blood . . .

'And then comes the battle.

'It can be magnificent, Longtusk! We charge into the ranks of the enemy, all but invulnerable to their arrows and axes, and scatter them. We stab with our tusks and crush with our feet. If the enemy has never seen mastodonts before they are terrified, awed out of their wits.

'But it never lasts.

'As warriors we are clumsy beasts, Longtusk. The

411

Firehead fighters learn to step aside and assail us from the sides, encircling us and separating us, striking with arrows and spears, slashing our trunks and hamstrings, killing our riders.

'And sometimes – despite the training, despite the intoxicating brews – we recall who we are. Then we panic and retreat, even trampling our own warriors.' He closed his small eyes, deep in their pits of wrinkled skin. 'I thought I had put it all behind me. Now it is coming again.'

When they reached the Firehead settlement, Bedrock's body was immediately claimed by the Shaman, Smokehat, who had it brought into his own hut of bone and turf. The Shaman berated the Firehead hunters who had been with Bedrock when he died, and even Longtusk and the mastodonts.

As for Crocus, she retreated into Bedrock's hut – hers, now – carrying the rhino horn.

As the days wore on, Crocus was forced to receive a string of visitors: older males of the Firehead tribe, there to consult, Thunder told Longtusk, about the meaning of the sudden appearance of these other Fireheads, the White-skins, on the steppe. But she did not emerge from her hut, refusing even to see Longtusk.

Longtusk felt bereft. He hadn't realised how much he had come to rely on Crocus's companionship, which seemed to fill a need not satisfied even by the mastodonts.

He threw his great muscles into the work of heavy lifting and hauling, and his companions treated him with a bluff respect. And when he wasn't working he spent much of his time in the Firehead settlement.

It was unusual for Bull mastodonts to be allowed to wander without keepers through the Firehead community, but after his long association with Crocus – during which time not a hair on her head had been harmed – Longtusk seemed to be regarded as a special case.

But he remained the only mammoth in the captive herd,

and adults gaped at him or cowered from his immense tusks, and he was constantly followed around by a small herd of goggling Firehead cubs. They collected the hair he shed, and used it to stuff their moccasins and hats and pillows. He learned to endure the perpetual tugs and strokes of the cubs, and he took great care not to step on one of those stick-thin limbs or eggshell skulls.

Work went on for Fireheads and mastodonts: hunting game for food, building and rebuilding the huts, extending and filling the storage pits for meat and hay – for the cycle of the seasons was not slowed even by death, and the inevitable approach of winter was never far from the thoughts of anybody in the community.

He watched the Fireheads butcher a deer. They took its flesh to eat and its skin to make clothing. They even used the tough skin of its forelegs for boot uppers and mittens. They made tools and weapons from its bones and antlers. They used the deer's fat and marrow for fuel for their lamps, and its blood for glue, and its sinews for bindings, lashings and thread. Gradually the deer was reduced to smaller and smaller pieces, until it was scattered around the settlement.

Longtusk saw a mother use her hair to wipe faeces from the backside of a cub.

He saw a male take the lower jawbone of a young deer, from which small sharp teeth protruded like pebbles. He sawed off the teeth at their roots, producing a series of beads almost identical in shape, size and texture, and held together by a strip of dried gum. It was a necklace.

He saw an old male pinch the tiny hearts of captive gulls, seeking to kill them without spoiling their feathers. He skinned the birds, turned the empty skins inside out, and wore the intact skins on his feet – feathers inside – within his boots.

Endless detail, endless strangeness – endless horror.

But the Fireheads went about their tasks without joy or enthusiasm. Even the cubs, when they tried to run and

413

play, were snapped at and cuffed. The settlement had become a bowl of subdued quiet, of slow footsteps.

And Longtusk felt increasingly agitated.

It was natural, he told himself. Bedrock had been the most important of the Fireheads; his death brought finality and change. Who wouldn't be disturbed?

. . . But he couldn't help feeling that his inner turmoil was something beyond that. He was aware that his mood showed in the way he walked, ripped his fodder from the ground, snarled at the Firehead cubs who got in his way or tugged too hard at his belly hairs.

At length, he came to understand what he was going through. He felt oddly ashamed, and he kept it to himself.

Still, Walks With Thunder – as so often – seemed more aware of Longtusk's moods and difficulties than anybody else. And he came to Longtusk, engaging him in a rumbling conversation as they walked, fed, defecated.

'. . . It's interesting to see how differently they treat you,' Thunder said, as he watched Firehead cubs, wide-eyed, trot after Longtusk. 'Differently from us, I mean. You have to understand that you mammoths were once worshipped as gods by these creatures.'

'Worshipped?'

'Remember when we found you at the Dreamer caves, how they threw themselves on the ground? There is little wood here. Trees struggle to grow on land freshly exposed by the ice. And so the Fireheads rely on the mammoths – especially your long-dead ancestors – for bones and skin and fur, material to build their huts and make their clothing and burn on their hearths. Without the resources of the mammoths, it's possible they couldn't survive here at all.'

Longtusk reminded Thunder of the Dreamers, who had lived so modestly in their rocky caves.

'Ah, but the Fireheads are not like the Dreamers,' said Thunder. '*They* would not be content with eking out unchanging lives like pike basking in a pool. And it is this

414

lack of contentment that drives them on . . . to greatness and to horror alike.

'They've discarded those old beliefs, I think; now, a mammoth is just another animal to them. But still you hairy beasts seem to be admired in a way they have never admired *us*, despite our long association with them. Of course that doesn't stop them from going north and—' He stopped abruptly.

The north: the old mystery, Longtusk thought, a mystery that had eluded him for years, despite his quizzing of Jaw Like Rock and other mastodonts; it was as if they had been instructed – perhaps by Thunder – to tell him nothing.

'Going north for what?' he asked now. '*What* do they seek in the north, Thunder?'

'I shouldn't have spoken . . . What's this?' Suddenly Thunder's trunk reached out to Longtusk's ear.

Longtusk couldn't help but flinch as Thunder's trunk, strong and wiry, probed in his fur until its tip emerged coated in a black, viscous liquid.

'By Kilukpuk's mighty dugs,' Thunder said. 'I thought I could smell it. The way you've been dribbling urine . . . You're in musth. Musth!'

Musth – a state of agitation associated with stress or rut; musth, in which this foul-smelling liquid would ooze from a mammoth's temporal gland; musth – when a mammoth's body was temporarily not under his full control.

'No wonder you're so agitated. And it's not the first time either, I'll wager.'

Longtusk pulled away, trumpeting his irritation. 'I'm an adult now, Thunder, a Bull. I don't need—'

'It's one thing to know what musth is and quite another to control it. And you've picked a terrible time to start oozing the black stuff. In a few days you'll play perhaps the most important role of your life.'

'What role? I don't understand.'

'With Crocus, of course. It will be tiring, difficult, stressful

415

– even frightening. Through it all you must maintain absolute control – for all our sakes. And you decide *now* is the time to go into musth . . . *Oh*. Neck Like Spruce.'

Longtusk felt his trunk curl up. 'Who?'

'You can't fool me, grazer. That's the name of the pretty little Cow you've been courting, isn't it?'

'Courting? I don't know what you're talking about.'

'Perhaps you don't. We don't always understand ourselves very well. It's true, nevertheless – and now this.' Thunder rumbled sadly. 'Longtusk, I'm just an old fool of a mastodont. I'm not even one of your kind. And I know I've filled your head with far too much advice over the years.'

Longtusk was embarrassed. 'I appreciate your help. I always have—'

'Never mind that,' said Thunder testily. 'Just listen to me, one last time. You and I – we look alike, but we're very different. Our kinds were separated, and started to grow apart, more than a thousand Great-Years ago. And that is a long, long time, ten times longer than the ice has been prowling the world.'

'Why are you telling me this?'

'While you're in musth – now and in the future – *stay away from Neck Like Spruce*. Otherwise you'll both be hurt, terribly hurt.'

'I don't understand, Thunder . . .'

But Thunder would say no more. Rumbling sadly, he walked slowly away, in search of fresh forage.

Soon the settlement, without throwing off its pall of gloom, began to bustle with activity. Longtusk learned that the Fireheads were preparing for their own form of Remembering ceremony for their fallen leader.

Everything was being rebuilt; everything was changing. It was obvious the Remembering of Bedrock would mark a great change in the affairs of the settlement – and therefore, surely, in Longtusk's own life as well, a change whose outcome was impossible to predict.

Every surface, of rock and treated skin, was scraped bare and painted with new, vibrant images. And everywhere the Fireheads made their characteristic mark, the outstretched paw. The artist would lay a bare paw, fingers open, against the rock, then suck paint into the mouth and spray it through a small tube and over the paw to make a silhouette.

The most busy Firehead, at this strange time, was an old male the mastodonts called Flamefingers. He was the manufacturer of the finest tools and ornaments of bone, ivory and stone. Flamefingers was fat and comfortable. The skills of his nimble paws had won him a long and comfortable life, insulated from the dangers of the hunt or the hard graft of the storage pits.

Flamefingers had an apprentice. This wretched male cub had to bring his master food and drink, cloths for the old Firehead to blow his cavernous nose, and even hollowed-out bison skulls, pots for the great artisan to urinate in without having to take the trouble to stand up.

Longtusk watched in fascination as the young apprentice wrestled to turn an ancient mammoth tusk – an immense spiral twice his height – into ivory strips and pieces, useful for the artisan to work.

At the tusk's narrow, sharp end, he simply chopped off pieces with a stone axe. Where the tusk was too wide for that, he chiselled a deep groove all around the tusk until only a fine neck remained, and then split it with a sharp hammer blow.

To obtain long, thin strips of ivory the apprentice had to cut channels in the tusk and then prise out the strips with chisels. Often the strips would splinter and break – an outcome which invariably won the apprentice abuse and mild beatings from his impatient master.

But the apprentice could even bend ivory, making bracelets small enough to fit around the slim wrists of Fireheads.

First he soaked a section of the tusk in a pit of foul-smelling urine. Then he wrapped the softened tusk in a fresh animal skin, soaked with water, and placed it in the hot ashes of a hearth. The skin charred and fell away in flakes. But the ivory – on extraction from the hearth with tongs made of giant deer antlers – was flexible enough to bend into loops tied off with thongs.

Flamefingers, meanwhile, made a bewildering variety of artefacts from the ivory pieces.

He made tools, whittling suitable sections into chisels, spatulas, knives, daggers and small spears. He engraved the handles of these devices with crosshatched cuts to ensure a firm grip when the tools were held in the paw, and returned the tools to the apprentice for arduous polishing with strips of leather.

But Flamefingers also made many artefacts with no obvious purpose save decoration: for example thin discs, cross-sections from the fatter end of the tusks, with elaborate carvings, pierced through the centre to take a rope of sinew or skin.

But the most remarkable artefacts of all were the figurines, of Fireheads and animals.

Flamefingers started with a raw, crudely broken lump of ivory that had been soaked for days. But despite this softening the ivory was difficult to work – easy to engrave along the grain, but not across it – and the artisan patiently scraped away at the surface with stone chisels, removing finer and finer flakes.

And, slowly, like the sun emerging from a cloud, a form emerged from the raw tusk, small and compact, coated in hairs that were elaborately etched into the grain.

Longtusk could only watch, bewildered. The artisan seemed able to *see* the object within the tusk before he had made it – as if the figure had always been there, embedded in this chunk of ancient ivory, needing only the artisan's careful fingers to release it.

The artisan held up the finished piece on his paw, blew away dust and spat on it, polishing it against his clothing.

Then he looked up at Longtusk standing over him, with the usual gaggle of Firehead cubs clutching his belly hairs.

Flamefingers smiled. He held up the figure so Longtusk could see it.

Longtusk, drawn by curiosity, reached out with the pink tip of his trunk and explored the carving. Flamefingers watched him, blue eyes gleaming, fascinated by the reaction of the woolly mammoth to the toy.

It was a mammoth, exquisitely carved.

But, though it was delicate and fine, there was a faint, lingering smell of the long-dead mammoth who had owned this tusk, overlaid by the sharp stink of the spit and sweat of Firehead.

Longtusk, intrigued but subtly repelled, rumbled softly and stepped away.

On the day of Bedrock's Remembering, Crocus at last emerged from her hut. Her bare skin was pale from her lengthy confinement. But her golden hair blazed in the light of the low sun.

All the Fireheads – even the Shaman – bowed before her. She turned and surveyed them coldly.

Today the Fireheads would do more than Remember Bedrock. Today, Longtusk had learned, the Fireheads would accept their new leader: this slim young female, Crocus, the only cub of Bedrock, and now the Matriarch of the Fireheads.

Crocus stepped forward to Longtusk. She walked confidently, as a new Matriarch should. But Longtusk could see how fragile she was from the tenseness of her lips, the softness of her eyes.

'*Baitho*,' she said softly.

Obediently he dipped his head and lowered his trunk to the ground. She climbed on his back with practised ease. He straightened up, feeling invigorated by her gentle presence at his neck once more.

He raised his trunk and trumpeted; the noise echoed from the silent steppe.

He turned and, with as much grandeur as he could muster, he began to walk towards the grave. The Fireheads and mastodonts formed up into a loose procession behind him.

And now, at a gesture from the Shaman, the music began.

They had flutes made of bird bones, hollowed out and pierced. They had bull-roarers, ovals of carved ivory which they spun around their heads on long ropes. They had instruments made of mammoth bones: drums of skulls and shoulder blades to strike and scrape, jawbones which rattled loudly, ribs which emitted a range of notes when struck with a length of femur. And they sang, raising their small mouths and ululating like wolves.

In all this noise, Longtusk and his passenger were an island of silence, towering over the rest. Her fingers twined tightly in his fur, as they had when she was a small and nervous cub just learning to ride him, and he knew that this day was extraordinarily difficult for her.

The grave was on the outskirts of the settlement, a simple straight-sided pit dug into the ground by Walks With Thunder.

Crocus slid to the ground and stood at the lip of the grave, paws folded. Longtusk stood silently beside her, the wind whipping the hair on his back.

The body of Bedrock already lay at the bottom of the pit, a small and fragile bundle wrapped in rhino hide. Bedrock's artefacts were set out around him: spears and knives and chisels and boomerangs, the tools of a home-builder and hunter, many of them made of mammoth ivory. And mammoth vertebrae and foot bones had been set out in a circle around him, as if protecting him.

But now the Shaman was here in his ridiculous smoking

hat, his skin painted with gaudy designs. He leapt into the pit and began to caper and shout. He had rattles of bone and wood that he shook over Bedrock's inert form, and he scattered flower petals and sprinkled water, raising his face and howling like a hyena.

As Crocus watched this performance she started to tremble – not from distress, Longtusk realised, but from anger. It was a rage that matched Longtusk's own musth-fuelled turmoil.

At last, it seemed, she could stand it no more. She tugged Longtusk's trunk. '*A dhur*,' she said. Pick up that thing.

Longtusk snorted in acquiescence. He knelt down, reached into the pit with his trunk, and plucked the Shaman out of the grave, burning hat and all. He set the Firehead down unharmed by the side of the pit.

Smokehat was furious. He capered and jabbered, slapping with his small paws at Longtusk's trunk.

Crocus stepped forward, eyes alight, and she screamed at the Shaman.

His defiance seemed to melt before her anger, and he withdrew, eyes glittering.

There was silence now. Crocus stepped up to the grave once more. She sat down, legs dangling over the edge of the pit.

Longtusk reached down to help her. But she pushed his trunk away; this was, it seemed, something she must do herself.

She scrambled to the pit floor. She brushed away the dirt and petals that the Shaman had scattered over her father.

She dug an object out of her clothing and laid it on top of the body. It was the rhino horn, the trophy of the last hunt – still stained with the creature's blood, as raw and unworked as when it had been smashed from the rhino's skull. Then she stroked the hide covering her father, and she picked up earth and sprinkled it over the body.

421

She was Remembering him, Longtusk realised. Her simple, tender actions, unrehearsed and personal, were – compared to the foolish ritualistic capering of the Shaman – unbearably moving.

Bedrock had been leader of the Fireheads from the moment Longtusk had first encountered these strange, complex, bewildering creatures. But here he lay, slain and silent, destroyed by a single arrow fired by a white-painted Firehead who had never known Bedrock's name, had known nothing of the complex web of power and relationships which had tangled up his life. As he gazed on the limp, passive form in the pit, Longtusk was struck by the awful simplicity of death, the conclusion to every story.

At last Crocus stood up. The Fireheads reached into the pit and lowered down bones. They were mammoth shoulder blades and pelvises. Crocus used the huge flat sheets of bone to cover the body of Bedrock. Even in death he would be protected by the strength of the mammoths, which, through their own deaths, had sustained his kind in this hostile land.

Crocus reached up to Longtusk. This time she accepted his help, and he lifted her out of the grave and set her neatly on his back. Then he began to kick at the low piles of earth which had been scooped out of the ground.

When it was done, Longtusk made his way back to the hut Crocus had shared with her father, but now inhabited alone. She slid to the ground, ruffled the fur on Longtusk's trunk with absent affection, and entered her hut, tying the skin flaps closed behind her.

When she was gone, Longtusk felt a great relief, for he thought this longest and most painful of days was at last done.

But he was wrong.

The Fireheads, having completed their mourning of their lost leader, began to celebrate the ascension of their new

Matriarch. And it was soon obvious that the celebrations were to be loud and long.

As the sun dipped towards the horizon the Fireheads opened up a pit in the ground. Here, the butchered remains of several giant deer had been smoking since the previous day. They gathered around and ripped away pieces of the meat with their bare paws, and chewed on it until their bellies were distended and the fat ran down their chins.

Then, as the cubs and females danced and sang, the males produced great pots of foul-smelling liquid, thick and fermented, which they pumped down their throats. Before long many of them were slumping over in sleep, or regurgitating the contents of their stomachs in great noxious floods. But then they would revive to begin ingesting more food and liquid, growing more raucous and uncoordinated as the evening wore on.

The mastodonts watched this, bemused.

At last, under the benevolent guidance of Walks With Thunder, the Cows gathered their calves and quietly made their way to the calm of the stockade, where all but the most trusted of the Bulls were kept.

Longtusk, his emotions still muddled and raging, followed them.

Lemming was here, bringing bales of hay from one of the storage pits. '*Lay, lay,*' he said. Eat, eat. Longtusk had noticed before that this little fat Firehead seemed happier in the company of the mastodonts than his own kind, and he felt a surge of affection.

All the mastodonts were in the stockade.

. . . All save Jaw Like Rock.

Agitated, disturbed by the throbbing noise and meat smells wafting from the Firehead settlement, Longtusk roamed the stockade. But he couldn't find the great Bull. When he asked after Jaw, he was met with blank stares.

Then – as the night approached its darkest hour, and the drumming and shouting of the Fireheads reached a climax –

he heard a single, agonised trumpeting from the depths of the settlement.

It was Jaw Like Rock.

Longtusk bellowed out a contact rumble, but there was no reply.

He sought out Walks With Thunder.

'Didn't you hear that? Jaw Like Rock called out.'

'No,' said Thunder bleakly. 'You're mistaken.'

'But I heard him—'

Thunder wrapped his trunk around Longtusk's. 'Jaw is dead. Accept it. It is the way.'

Again that trumpeting came, thin and clear and full of pain.

Longtusk, confused, distressed, blundered away from the stockade and headed into the Firehead settlement.

Tonight it had become a place of bewildering noise and stink and confusion. The Fireheads ran back and forth, full of fermented liquid and rich food – or they slept where they had fallen, curled up by the hearths in the open air. He saw one male and female coupling, energetically but clumsily, in the half-shadow of a hut wall.

Few Fireheads even seemed aware of Longtusk; he had to be careful, in fact, not to step on sleeping faces.

He persisted, pushing through the noise and mess and confusion, until he found Jaw Like Rock.

They had put him in a shallow pit, scraped roughly out of the ground and surrounded by stakes and ropes. Fire burned brightly in lamps all around the pit, making the scene as bright as day, but filling the air with stinking, greasy smoke.

It was a feeble confinement from which a great tusker like Jaw Like Rock could have escaped immediately.

But Jaw was no longer in full health.

Jaw was dragging both his hind legs. It seemed his hamstrings or tendons had been cut, so he could no longer bolt or charge. And there were darts sticking out of his flesh, over his belly and behind his ears. His skin was discoloured around the punctures, as if the darts had delivered a poison. He was wheezing, and great loops of spittle hung from his dangling tongue.

There were Fireheads all around the pit, all male, and they were stamping, clapping and hammering their drums of bone and skin. One of them was creeping into Jaw's pit, carrying a long spear. It was Bareface, Longtusk saw, the young hunter who had distinguished himself on the fatal rhino hunt. He was naked, coated in red and yellow paint.

Longtusk trumpeted. 'Jaw! Jaw Like Rock!'

Jaw's answering rumble was faint, and punctuated by gasps for breath. 'Is that you, grass chewer? Come to see the dead Bull?'

'Get out of there!'

'. . . No. It's over for me. It was over the moment I tusked that spawn of Aglu. I planned it, after all, waited for my moment . . . But it was worth it. At least Spindle will torture no more mastodonts. Or mammoths.'

'You aren't dead! You breathe, you hurt—'

'I'm dead as poor Bedrock in his hole in the ground. Don't you see? *We belong to the Fireheads.* They tend our wounds, and order our lives, and feed us. But we live and die by their whim. It is – a contract. And here, at the climax of this night of celebration, this one who creeps towards me on his belly, Bareface, will prove his courage by dispatching me to the aurora.'

'But they've already crippled you! Where is the courage in that?'

'The ways of the Fireheads are impossible to understand . . . But, yes, you're right, Longtusk. We must see some courage tonight.' Jaw raised himself on his crippled legs and trumpeted his defiance. 'Remember me, calf of Primus! Remember!'

And with a roar that shook the ground, he hurled himself forward towards Bareface.

The hunter, with lightning-fast reflexes, jammed the shaft of his spear into the ground.

Jaw's great body impaled itself. Longtusk heard flesh rip, and smelled the sour stink of Jaw's guts as they spilled, dark and steaming, to the ground.

The Fireheads roared their triumph. Longtusk trumpeted and fled.

He was in a stand of young trees in the new, growing forest that bordered the Firehead settlement. It was still deep night, dark and cloudy.

He couldn't recall where he had run, how he had got here.

But *she* was here – he could sense it through his rage, his grief and confusion, the musth that burned through his body – *she*, Neck Like Spruce, no calf now but a warm and musty presence, solid and massive as the Earth itself, here in the dark, as if she had been waiting for him.

He reached out, sensing and hearing her, and found her. Her secretions were damp on the tip of his trunk. Tasting them, he knew that she, too, was ready: in oestrus, bearing the egg that might grow into their calf.

He heard her urinate, a warm dark stream, and then she turned to face him. He found her trunk, and intertwined it with his, tugging gently, seeking its tip; the soft fingers of her trunk, so unlike his own, explored the long hairs that dangled from his belly.

For a last instant he recalled the warnings of Walks With Thunder: *Stay away from Neck Like Spruce. Stay away . . .*

Then his mouth found hers, warm tongues flickering, and the time for thinking was over.

CHAPTER 6
THE CLEANSING

Winter and summer, winter and summer . . .

As she approached the second anniversary of her father's death and her own accession to power, Crocus assembled a great war party of mastodonts and Firehead hunters. It was a time of preparation, and gathering determination – and dread.

The artisans had worked all winter, manufacturing, repairing and sharpening knives and spear points and atlatls. And every time the weather cleared sufficiently the hunters had gone out to hurl spears and boomerangs at rocks and painted animal figures – and, when they spotted them, live targets, the animals of the winter like the Arctic foxes. There were days when the settlement seemed to bristle with the Fireheads and their weapons, spears, darts and knives as dense as the spiky fur of a mastodont. But all the weapons were small and light – not designed for big game, like the giant deer or the rhino, but to pierce the flimsy hides of other Fireheads: weapons of war, not hunting.

When the preparations were complete, Crocus called for a final feast.

The Firehead hunters gorged themselves on food and drink. Longtusk watched cubs crack open big animal bones to suck out the thick marrow within, the bones returned by hunting parties that roamed north. Not for the first time Longtusk wondered what animal provided those giant snacks.

Longtusk spent his time with Neck Like Spruce, who was now heavy with calf – *his* calf.

It was unusual for a Bull, mammoth or mastodont, to remain close to his mate so long after the mating; usually a Bull would stay around just long enough to ensure conception by his seed had taken place. But Neck Like Spruce's case was different.

The calf was already overdue. Like mammoths, the oestrus cycle of these mastodonts was timed so that the calves would be born in early spring, maximising the time available for them to feed and grow strong before the calves faced the rigours of their first winter.

And throughout it had been a difficult pregnancy, despite the best attention of Lemming, the keeper, and his array of incomprehensible medicines: salves of water and hot butter for wounds, blood-red deer meat to treat inflammations, drops of milk for sore eyes . . . Spruce had become a gaunt, bony shadow, and her hair had fallen out in clumps.

It disturbed Longtusk that there was absolutely nothing he could do – and it disturbed him even more that Lemming, the undisputed Firehead expert on mastodonts and their illnesses, was at this crucial time preparing to leave, accompanying the Bulls on their northern march.

Through that last night, Longtusk stayed with Neck Like Spruce. She slept briefly. He could see the calf in her belly struggle fitfully, pushing at the skin that contained it.

The next morning, the Fireheads nursing sore heads and crammed bellies, the party assembled in a great column and began its sweep to the north. With Crocus on his back, Longtusk led the slow advance.

Since that first encounter with the Whiteskins two years before there had been several skirmishes with other bands of Fireheads. Crocus's tribe, settled for several years in their township of mammoth-bone huts, were well-fed, healthy and strong, and were able to fend off the attacks – mounted mostly by bands of desperate refugees, forced north from the overcrowded southern lands.

But this wouldn't last for ever, predicted Walks With Thunder.

'There is no limit to the number of Fireheads who might take it into their heads to come bubbling up from the south. We can defend ourselves and this settlement as long as the numbers are right. But eventually they will overrun us.'

'And then?' said Longtusk.

'And then we will have to flee – go north once again, as we have done before, and find a new and empty land. And this is what Crocus, in her wisdom, knows she must plan for; it is surely going to come in her time as Matriarch.'

So it was that Crocus was remaking herself. Still young, already skilled in hunting techniques, she had learned to use the tribe's weapons with as much skill and daring as any of the buck male warriors. And she had learned to command, to force her tribe to accept the harshest of realities.

But Longtusk thought he detected a growing hardness in her – a hardness that, when he thought of the affectionate cub who had befriended him, saddened him.

As for himself, Longtusk was now bigger and stronger than any of the mastodonts. He was no longer the butt of jokes and taunts in the stockade; no longer did the mastodonts call constant attention to his differences, his dense brown hair and strange grinding teeth. Now he was Longtusk, warrior Bull, and his immense tusks, scarred by use, were the envy of the herd.

Only Walks With Thunder still called him 'little grazer' – but Longtusk didn't mind that.

And, such was Crocus's skill in riding Longtusk – and so potent was the mammoth's own intelligence and courage – that the stunning, unexpected combination of warrior-queen and woolly mammoth leading the column could, said Walks With Thunder, prove to be the Fireheads' most important weapon of all.

During the long march, Longtusk's days were arduous. He was the first to break the new ground, and he had to be constantly on the alert for danger – not just from potential foes, but also the natural traps of the changing landscape. He paid careful attention to the deep wash of sound which echoed through the Earth in response to the mastodonts' heavy footsteps, and avoided the worst of the difficulties.

And, of course, he had to seek out food as he travelled. Firehead Matriarch on his back or not, he still needed to cram the steppe grasses and herbs into his mouth for most of every day. But the mastodonts preferred trees and shrubs, and if he found a particularly fine stand of trees he would trumpet to alert the others.

A few days out of the settlement a great storm swept down on them. The wind swirled and gusted, carrying sand from the frozen deserts at the fringe of the icecap, hundreds of days' walk away, to lash at the mastodonts' eyes and mouths, as if mocking their puny progress. Crocus walked beside Longtusk, blinded and buffeted, clinging to his long belly hairs.

At last the storm blew itself out, and they emerged into calmness under an eerie blue sky.

They found a stand of young trees that had been utterly demolished by the wind's ferocity. The mastodonts browsed the fallen branches and tumbled trunks, welcoming this unexpected bounty.

Walks With Thunder, his mouth crammed with green leaves, came to Longtusk. 'Look over there. To the east.'

Longtusk turned and squinted. It was unusual for a mastodont to tell another to 'look', so poor was their eyesight compared to other senses.

The sun, low in the south, cast long shadows across the empty land. At length Longtusk made out something: a blur of motion, white on blue, against the huge sky.

'Birds?'

'Yes. Geese, judging from their honking. But the important thing is where they come from.'

'The north-east,' Longtusk said. 'But that's impossible. There is only ice there, and nothing lives.'

'Not quite.' Walks With Thunder absently tucked leaves deeper into his mouth. 'This is a neck of land, lying between great continents to west and east. In the eastern lands, it is said, the ice has pushed much further south than in the west. But there are legends of places, called *nunataks* – refuges – islands in the ice, where living things can survive.'

'The ice would cover them over. Everything would freeze and die.'

'Possibly,' said Thunder placidly. 'But in that case, how do you explain those geese?'

'It is just a legend,' Longtusk protested.

Thunder curled his trunk over Longtusk's scalp affectionately. 'The world is a big place, and it contains many mysteries. Who knows what fragment of rumour will save our lives in the future?' He saw Crocus approaching. 'And the biggest mystery of all,' he grumbled wearily, 'is how I can persuade these old bones to plod on for another day. Lead on, Longtusk; lead on . . .'

The geese flew overhead, squawking. They were moulting, and when they had passed, white feathers fell from the sky all around Longtusk, like snowflakes.

As the days wore on they travelled further and further from the settlement.

Longtusk hadn't been this far north since he had first been captured by the Fireheads. That had been many years ago, and back then he had been little more than a confused calf.

But he was sure that the land had changed.

There were many more stands of trees than he recalled: spruce and pine and fir, growing taller than any of the dwarf

431

willows and birches that had once inhabited this windswept plain. And the steppe's complex mosaic of vegetation had been replaced by longer grass – great dull swathes of it that rippled in the wind, grass that had crowded out many of the herbs and low trees and flowers which had once illuminated the landscape. It was grass that the mastodonts consumed with relish. But for Longtusk the grass was thin, greasy stuff that clogged his bowels and made his dung slippery and smelly.

And the air was warmer – much warmer. It seemed he couldn't shed his winter coat quickly enough, and Crocus grumbled at the hair which flew into her face. But she did not complain when he sought out the snow that still lingered in shaded hollows and scooped it into his mouth to cool himself.

The world seemed a huge place, massive, imperturbable; it was hard to believe that – just as the Matriarchs had foreseen, at his Clan's Gathering so long ago – such dramatic changes could happen so quickly. And yet it must be true, for even he, young as he was, recalled a time when the land had been different.

It was an uneasy thought.

He had been separated from his Family before they had a chance to teach him about the landscape – where to find water in the winter, how to dig out the best salt licks. He had had to rely on the mastodonts for such instruction.

But such wisdom, passed from generation to generation, was acquired by long experience. And if the land was changing so quickly – so dramatically within the lifetime of a mammoth – what use was the wisdom of the years?

And in that case, what might have become of his Family?

He shuddered and rumbled, and he felt Crocus pat him, aware of his unease.

After several more days Crocus guided Longtusk down a sharp incline towards lower ground. He found himself in a valley through which a fat, strong glacial river gushed, its waters curdled white with rock flour. The column of mastodonts crept cautiously after him, avoiding the sharp gravel patches and slippery mud slopes he pointed out.

After a time the valley opened, and the river decanted into a lake, grey and glimmering.

The place seemed familiar.

Had he been here before, as a lost calf? But so much had changed! The lake water was surely much higher than it had once been, and the long grass and even the trees grew so thickly now, even down to the water's edge, that every smell and taste and sound was different.

. . . Yet there was much that nagged at his memory: the shape of a hillside here, a rock abutment there.

When he saw a row of cave mouths, black holes eroded into soft exposed rock, he knew that he had not been mistaken.

Crocus called a halt.

She and her warriors dismounted, and on all fours they crept through the thickening vegetation closer to the caves. They inspected footprints in the dirt – they were wide and splayed, Longtusk saw, more like a huge bird's than a Firehead's narrow tracks – and they rummaged through dirt and rubble.

At last, with a hiss of triumph, the hunter called Bareface picked up a shaped rock. It was obviously an axe, made and wielded by clever fingers – and it was stained with fresh blood.

And now there was a cry: a voice not quite like a Firehead's, more guttural, cruder. The mastodonts raised their trunks and sniffed the air.

A figure had come out of the nearest cave: walking upright, but limping heavily. He stood glaring in the direction of the intruders, who still cowered in the vegetation. He was short and stocky, with wide shoulders and a deep barrel chest. His clothing was heavy and coarse. His forehead sloped backwards, and an enormous bony ridge dominated his brow. His legs were short and bowed, and his feet were flat and very wide, with short stubby toes, so that he left those broad splayed footprints.

He was obviously old, his back bent, his small face a mask of wrinkles that seemed to lap around cavernous nostrils like waves around rocks. And his head was shaven bare of hair, with a broad red stripe painted down its crown.

Not a Firehead, not quite. This was the Fireheads' close cousin: a Dreamer. And Longtusk recognised him.

'He is called Stripeskull,' Longtusk rumbled to Thunder. 'I have been here before.'

'As have I. This is where we found you.'

Walks With Thunder described how, when the Fireheads had first moved north, they had sent scouting parties ahead, seeking opportunities and threats. Bedrock himself had led an expedition to this unpromising place – and Crocus had been, briefly, lost.

'The Dreamers saved her from the cold,' said Longtusk.

Thunder grunted. 'That's as maybe. We drove the Dreamers from their caves. But the land was too harsh, and we abandoned it and retreated further south.'

'And the Dreamers returned to their caves?'

'They are creatures of habit. And, back then, the Fireheads did not covet their land.'

'But now?'

'See for yourself. The land has changed. Now the Fireheads want this place . . .'

Longtusk said, 'It was so long ago.'

'For you, perhaps,' Thunder said dryly. 'For me, it seems like yesterday.'

'How did Stripeskull get so *old*?'

'Dreamers don't live long,' growled Thunder. 'And I fear this one will not grow much older.'

'What do you mean?'

But now Stripeskull seemed to have spotted the intruders.

He was shouting and gesturing. He had a short burned-wood spear at his side, and he tried to heft it, but his foreleg would not rise above the shoulder.

A spear flew at him. It neatly pierced Stripeskull's heart.

Longtusk, shocked, trumpeted and blundered forward.

Stripeskull was on the ground, and blood seeped red-black around him, viscous and slow as musth. His great head rocked forward, and ruddy spittle looped his mouth. He looked up and saw the mammoth, and his eyes widened with wonder and recognition. Then he fell back, his strength gone.

Longtusk rumbled mournfully, and touched the body with the sole of his foot. He was gone, as quickly destroyed as a pine needle on a burning tree. How could a life be destroyed so suddenly, so arbitrarily? This was Stripeskull, who had grudgingly spared his own Family's resources to save Longtusk's life; Stripeskull, with long memories of his own stretching back beyond his Family to a remote, frosty childhood – Stripeskull, gone in an instant and never to return, no matter how long the world turned.

But even while Stripeskull's body continued to spill its blood on the trampled dust, the Fireheads were moving onward, driven, busy, eager to progress.

Crocus beckoned to Longtusk. She led him to the dark mouth of the cave. '*Bowl, bowl!*' Speak . . .

With a growing feeling of unease, he raised his trunk and trumpeted. The noise echoed within the cramped rock walls of the cave, where it must have been terrifying.

A Dreamer came running out – a female, Longtusk saw, young, comparatively slim, long brown hair flying after her. She saw the mammoth, skidded to a halt and screamed.

She did not know him. The Dreamers grew quickly, as Thunder had said; perhaps this one had been an infant, or not even born, during his time here.

She tried to retreat – but the Shaman, grinning, had

moved behind her, blocking her from the cave. Her eyes widened, and for a brief moment Longtusk saw the Shaman through her eyes: ridiculously tall, with a forehead that bulged to smoothness, willow-thin legs, a nose as small and thin as a spring icicle . . .

Firehead warriors threw a net of hide rope over the female, as if she was a baby rhino, and they wrestled her to the ground. But she was strong, and was soon ripping her way through the net. So they tied more rope around her, leaving her squirming in the dirt.

The hunters fell back, panting hard; one of them was missing a chunk of his ear, bitten off by the Dreamer female. They seemed to be studying her body as she writhed and struggled.

'Perhaps they will mate with her,' Longtusk said.

'If they do it will be for pleasure only,' said Walks With Thunder. '*Their* pleasure, not hers. Something else you need to know, Longtusk. Firehead cannot seed Dreamer with cub. They are alike, you see, cousins.'

'Like mastodonts and mammoths.'

Thunder growled, oddly. 'But their blood does not mix. And so they compete, like – like two different species of gulls, seeking to nest on the same cliff face. To the Fireheads, the Dreamers are just an obstacle, something to be cleared out of the way.'

'Then what will become of the Dreamers?'

'Though they are strong, they are no match for the cunning Fireheads. If they are lucky the other Dreamers will have seen what happened here, and scattered.'

'And if not?'

Thunder snorted. 'The Fireheads are not noted for their mercy to their kin. The Dreamers will be butchered, the survivors enslaved and taken to the settlement where they will work until they die.'

Now there was a howl from the cave.

Another Dreamer emerged, this time a male. He was

young and strong, and he had a stone knife in his free paw – crude, but sharp and potent. And he had taken a captive. It was Lemming, the mastodont keeper. The Dreamer's foreleg was tight around Lemming's neck. Lemming was whimpering, and blood dripped from a wound in his upper foreleg.

The Dreamer's small eyes, glinting in their caves of bone, swivelled this way and that. He seemed to be trying to get to the female on the ground. Perhaps that was his sister, even his mate.

Crocus stepped forward. She was obviously concerned for Lemming. She held out her paws and said something in her high, liquid tongue.

The Dreamer, not understanding, jabbered back and slashed with his knife.

Longtusk acted without thinking. He slid his trunk around the Dreamer's neck and yanked so hard the Dreamer lost his grip on Lemming, and he fell back into the dirt at Longtusk's feet. The mammoth pinned him there with a tusk at the throat.

Lemming fell to the ground, limp. Crocus ran to him and called the others for help.

The Shaman stalked towards the fallen Dreamer. '*Maar thode*,' he snapped at Longtusk. '*Maar thode!*'

Break. Kill.

Longtusk leaned forward, increasing the pressure on the Dreamer's throat.

But the Dreamer was saying something too, calling in a language that was guttural and harsh, yet seemed strangely familiar.

On the Dreamer's face, under a crudely shaved veneer of stubble, there was a mark, bright red, jagged like a lightning bolt. It had faded since this Dreamer was a cub, but it was still there.

Willow, thought Longtusk. The first Dreamer I found, grown from a cub to an adult buck.

And he recognises me.

437

Crocus was close by.

Once again the three of us are united, Longtusk thought, and he felt a deep apprehension, as if the world itself was shaking beneath him. He had long forgotten the raving of the strange old Dreamer female when he had first brought Crocus here, her terror at the sight of the three of them together . . . Now that terror returned to him, a chill memory.

The Shaman hammered Longtusk's scalp with his goad, cutting into his skin. *'Maar thode!'*

Longtusk stepped back, lifting his tusk from the Dreamer's throat. Willow lay at his feet, as if stunned.

With a hasty gesture, Crocus ordered other hunters forward. They quickly bound Willow with strips of hide rope. He did not resist, though his massive muscles bulged.

The Shaman glared at Longtusk with impotent fury.

Now Crocus, accompanied by more hunters, made her way into the cave. There seemed to be no more Dreamers present, and with impunity the hunters kicked apart the crude central hearth. Under Crocus's orders, two of the hunters began to dig a pit in the ground.

'It seems we will stay here tonight,' Walks With Thunder growled. 'The cave will provide shelter. And see how the hunters are making a better hearth, one which will allow the air to blow beneath and—'

'The Dreamers have lived here for generations,' Longtusk said sharply. 'I saw it, the layers of tools and bones in the ground. Even the hearth may have been a Great-Year old. Think of that! And now, in an instant, it is gone, vanished like a snowflake on the tongue, demolished by the Fire-heads.'

'Demolished and remade,' growled Thunder. 'But that is their genius. These Dreamers lived here, as you say, for generation on generation, and it never occurred to a single one of them that there might be a different way to build a hearth.'

'But the Dreamers didn't *need* a different hearth. The one they had was sufficient.'

'But that doesn't matter, little grazer,' Thunder said. 'You and I must take the world as it is. *They* imagine how it might be different. Whether it's *better* is beside the point; to the Fireheads, change is all that matters . . .'

The two Dreamer captives, Willow and the female, huddled together on the ground, bound so tightly they couldn't even embrace. They seemed to be crying.

If Crocus recalled how the Dreamers had saved her life, Longtusk thought, she had driven it from her mind, now and for ever.

That night, when Crocus came to feed him, as she had since she was a cub, Longtusk turned away. He was distressed, angered, wanting only to be with his mate and calf in the calm of the steppe.

Crocus left him, baffled and upset.

That night – at the Shaman's insistence, because of his defiance over Willow – Longtusk was hobbled, for the first time in years.

The Fireheads stayed close to the caves for several days. Crocus sent patrols to the north, east and west, seeking Dreamers. They wished to be sure this land they coveted was cleansed of their ancient cousins before they brought any more of their own kind north.

Lemming became very ill. His wound turned swollen and shiny. The Shaman, who administered medicine to the Fireheads, applied hot cloths in an effort to draw out the poison. But the wound festered badly.

At last the bulk of the column formed up for the long journey back to the settlement. They left behind three hunters and one of the mastodonts. The captive Dreamers had to walk behind the mastodonts, their paws bound and tied to a mastodont's tail.

The hunters were heavily armed, but there had been no

sign of more Dreamers since that first encounter. Perhaps, like the mammoths, the Dreamers had learned that the Fireheads could not be fought: the only recourse was flight, leaving them to take whatever they wanted.

'Since you refused to kill the Dreamer buck,' growled Thunder as they walked, 'the Shaman has declared you untrustworthy.'

'He has always hated me,' said Longtusk indifferently.

'Yes,' said Thunder. 'He is jealous of your closeness to Crocus. And that jealousy may yet cause you great harm, Longtusk. I think you will have to prove your loyalty and trustworthiness. The Shaman is demonstrating, even now, what he does to his enemies.'

'What do you mean?'

'Lemming. The Shaman is letting him rot. His wound has festered and turned green, like the rest of his foreleg and shoulder. That is his way. The Shaman does not kill; he lets his enemies destroy themselves. Still, they die.'

'But why?'

Thunder snorted. 'Because Lemming is a favourite of Crocus's – and so he is an obstacle to the Shaman. And any such obstacle is, simply, to be removed, as the Fireheads remove the Dreamers from the land they covet. The Fireheads are vicious, calculating predators,' the old mastodont said. 'Never forget that. *The wolf's first bite is his responsibility. His second is yours* . . . Quiet.'

All the mastodonts stopped dead and fell silent. The Fireheads stared at them, puzzled.

'A contact rumble,' Walks With Thunder said at last. 'From the settlement.'

Longtusk strained to hear the fat, heavy sound waves pulsing through the very rocks of the Earth, a chthonic sound that resonated in his chest and the spaces in his skull.

'The calf,' Thunder said. 'The Cows have sung the birth

chorus. Longtusk – Neck Like Spruce has dropped her calf.'

Longtusk felt his heart hammer. 'And? Is it healthy?'

'. . . I don't think so. And Spruce—'

Longtusk, distressed, trumpeted his terror. 'I'm so far away! So far!'

Thunder tried to comfort him. 'If you were there, what could you do? This is a time for the Cows, Longtusk. Neck Like Spruce has her sisters and mother. And the keepers know what to do.'

'The best keeper is Lemming, and he is here, with us, bleeding in the dirt! Oh, Thunder, you were right. A mammoth should not mate a mastodont. We are too different – the mixed blood – like Fireheads and Dreamers.'

'Any calf of yours will be strong, Longtusk. A fighter. And Neck Like Spruce is a tough nut herself. They'll come through. You'll see.'

But Longtusk refused to be comforted.

Lemming was dead before they reached the settlement. His body, stinking with corruption, was buried under a heap of stones by a river.

And when they arrived at the settlement, Longtusk learned he was alone once more.

Neck Like Spruce had not survived the rigours of her birth. The calf, an impossible, attenuated mix of mammoth and mastodont, had not lasted long without his mother's milk.

The Remembering of mother and calf was a wash of sound and smell and touch, as if the world had dissolved around Longtusk.

When he came out of his grief, though, he felt cleansed.

He had lost a Family before, after all. If it was his destiny to be alone, then so be it. He would be strong and independent, yielding to none.

He allowed Crocus to ride him. But she sensed his change. Her affection for him dried, like a glacial river in winter.

Thus it went for the rest of that summer, and the winter thereafter.

CHAPTER 7
THE TEST

In the spring, seeking to feed the growing population of the settlement, the Fireheads organised a huge hunting drive.

It took some days' preparation.

Trackers spotted a herd of horses on the steppe. Taking pains not to disturb the animals at their placid grazing, they erected drive lines, rows of cairns made of stone and bone fragments. The mastodonts were used to carry the raw materials for these lines, spanning distances it took a day to cross. The cairns were topped by torches of brush soaked in fat.

Then came the drive.

As the horses grazed their way quietly across the steppe, still oblivious of danger, the hunters ran along the drive lines, lighting the torches. The mastodonts waited, in growing anticipation. It fell to Longtusk to keep the others in order as they scented the horses' peculiar, pungent stink, heard the light clopping of their hooves and their high whinnying.

The horses drifted into view.

Like other steppe creatures, the horses were well adapted to the cold. They were short and squat. Their bellies were coated with light hair, while their backs sprouted long, thick fur that they shed in the summer, and the two kinds of hair met in a jagged line along each beast's flank. Long manes draped over their necks and eyes, and their tails dangled to the ground.

The horses could look graceful, Longtusk supposed, and

they showed some skill at using their hooves to dig out fodder even from the deepest snow. But they were foolish creatures and would panic quickly, and so were easily hunted en masse.

At last the order came: '*Agit!*'

Longtusk raised his trunk and trumpeted loudly. The mastodonts charged, roaring and trumpeting, with tusks flashing and trunks raised.

The horses – confused, neighing – stampeded away from the awesome sight. But here came Firehead hunters, whirling noise-makers and yelling, running at the horses from either side.

All of this was designed to make the empty-headed horses run the way the hunters wanted them to go.

The horses, panicking, jostling, soon found themselves in a narrowing channel marked out by the cairns of stone. If they tried to break out of the drive lines they were met by noise-makers, spear thrusts or boomerang strikes.

The drive ended at a sharp-walled ridge, hidden from the horses by a crude blind of dry bush. The lead horses crashed through the flimsy blind and tumbled into the rocky defile. They screamed as they fell to earth, their limbs snapped and ribs crushed. Others, following, shied back, whinnying in panic. But the pressure of their fellows, pushing from behind, drove them, too, over the edge.

So, impelled by their own flight, the horses tumbled to their deaths, the herd dripping into the defile like some overflowing viscous liquid.

When the hunters decided they had culled enough, they ordered the mastodonts back, letting the depleted herd scatter and flee to safety. Then the hunters stalked among their victims, many of them still screaming and struggling to rise, and they speared hearts and slit throats.

Later would come the butchery, and the mastodonts would be employed to carry meat and hide back to the settlement. It would be hard, dull work, and the stink of the meat was repulsive to the mastodonts' finely tuned senses. But they did it anyhow – as did Longtusk, who always bore more than his share.

After the successful drive, the Fireheads celebrated, and the mastodonts were allowed a few days to rest and recover.

But Longtusk noticed the Shaman, Smokehat, spending much time at the stockade, arguing with the keepers and jabbing his small fingers towards Longtusk.

Walks With Thunder came to him. Thunder walked stiffly now, for arthritis was plaguing his joints.

Longtusk said, 'They seem to be planning another hunt.'

'No, not a hunt.'

'Then what?'

'Something simpler. More brutal . . . Something that will be difficult for you, Longtusk. The keepers are debating whether you should be allowed to lead this expedition. But the Shaman insists you go.'

'You still read them well.'

'Better than I like. Longtusk, this is it. The test. The trial the Shaman has been concocting for you for a long time – at least since that incident when you spared the life of the Dreamer.'

'I do not care for the Shaman, and I do not fear him,' said Longtusk coldly.

'Be careful, Longtusk.' Thunder quoted the Cycle. *The art of travelling is to pick the least dangerous path.*'

Longtusk growled and turned away. 'The Cycle has nothing to teach me. This is my place now. I am a creature of the Fireheads – nothing more. Isn't that what you always counselled me to become?'

Thunder was aghast. 'Longtusk, you are part of the Cycle. We all are. Forty million years—'

But Longtusk, the perennial outsider, had spent the long winter since the death of Neck Like Spruce and her calf building his solitary strength. 'Not me,' he said. 'Not any more.'

Thunder sniffed the air sadly. 'Oh, Longtusk, has your life been so hard that you care nothing for who you are?'

'Hard enough, old friend, that the Shaman with all his machinations can do nothing to hurt me. Not in my heart.'

'I hope that's true,' said Thunder. 'For it is a great test that lies ahead of you, little grazer. A great test indeed . . .'

A few days later the keepers assembled the mastodonts for the expedition. Longtusk accepted pack gear on his back, and took his customary place at the head of the column of mastodonts.

The party left the settlement, heading north. Though Crocus still sometimes participated in the drives and other expeditions, this time she was absent, and the expedition was commanded by the Shaman.

Though they followed a well-marked trail that cut across the steppe, showing this was a heavily travelled route, Longtusk had never come this way before. He did not yet know the destination or purpose of the expedition – but, he told himself, he did not need to know. His role was to work, not to understand.

The Dreamer Willow, enslaved by the Fireheads, was compelled to make the journey too. Willow's clothing was dirty and in sore need of repair, and his broad back was bent under an immense load of dried food and weapons for the hunters. The pace was easy, for the mastodonts could not sustain a high speed for long, but even so the Dreamer struggled. It was obvious his stocky frame was not designed for long journeys – unlike the taller, more supple Fireheads, whose whip-thin legs covered the steppe with grace and ease.

Over the year since his capture Willow had grown increasingly wretched. During the winter, the female Dreamer taken with him had died of an illness the Fireheads had been unable, or unwilling, to treat. Willow was not like the Fireheads. He had grown up in a society that had known no significant change for generations, a place where the most important things in all the world were the faces of his Family around him, where strangers and the unknown were mere blurs, at the edge of consciousness. Now, alone, he was immersed in strangeness, in constant change, and he always seemed on the edge of bewilderment and terror, utterly unable to comprehend the Firehead world around him.

It was said that no matter how far the Fireheads roamed they had not come across another of his kind. Longtusk supposed that just as the mammoths had been scattered and driven north by the Firehead expansion, so had the Dreamers; perhaps there were few of them left alive, anywhere in the world.

Longtusk could not release Willow from his mobile prison of toil and incomprehension. But he sensed that his own presence, a familiar, massive figure, offered Willow some comfort in his loneliness. And now, out of sight of the keepers, he let Willow rest his pack against his own broad flank and hang onto his belly hairs for support.

As the days wore away, and they drove steadily north-wards, the nature of the land began to change.

The air became chill, and the winds grew persistent and strong. Sometimes the wind flowed from west to east, and Walks With Thunder told Longtusk that such immense air currents could circle the planet, right around the fringe of the great northern icecaps.

And sometimes the wind came from the north, driving grit and ice into their faces, and that was the most difficult of all, for this was a katabatic wind: air that had lain over the ice, made cold and dry and heavy, so that it spilled like water off the ice and over the lower lands below.

They reached land recently exposed by the retreating ice. The ice had scoured away the softer soil down to bedrock, and it was a place of moraines of sand and gravel, rock smashed to fragments by the great weight of ice that had once lain here. There was little life – a few tussocks of grass, isolated trees, some lichen – struggling to survive in patches of soil, wind-blown from the warmer climes to the south.

The mastodonts became uneasy, for unlike the Fireheads they could hear the sounds of the ice pack: the crack of new crevasses, the thin rattle of glacial run-off rivers and streams, the deep grind of the glaciers as they tore slowly through the rock. To the mastodonts, the ice pack was an immense chill monster, half alive, spanning the world – and now very close.

Longtusk knew they could not stay long in this blighted land; whatever the Fireheads sought here must be a treasure indeed.

And it was as night began to fall on this wind-blasted, frozen desert that Longtusk came upon the corpse.

At first he could see only a hulked form, motionless, half covered by drifting dirt. Condors wheeled above, black stripes against the silvery twilight.

A hyena was working at the corpse's belly. It snarled at the mastodonts, but fled when a hunter hurled a boomerang.

Walks With Thunder was beside Longtusk. 'Be strong, now . . .'

It was a mammoth.

The mastodonts and hunters gathered around the huge, fallen form, awed by this immense slab of death.

It – she – was a female. She had slumped down on her belly, her legs splayed and her trunk curled on the ground before her. She was gaunt, her bones showing through her flesh at pelvis and shoulders, and her hair had come loose in great chunks, exposing dried, wrinkled skin beneath.

It was clear she was not long dead. She might have been sleeping.

But her eye sockets were bloody pits, pecked clean by the birds. Her small ears were mangled stumps. And Longtusk could see the marks of hyena teeth in the soft flesh of her trunk.

'She was pregnant,' Walks With Thunder said softly. 'See her swollen belly? The calf must have died within her. But she was starving, Longtusk. Her dugs are flaccid and thin. She would have had little milk to give her calf. In the end she simply ran out of strength. They say it is peaceful to go to the aurora that way . . .'

Longtusk stood stock still, stunned. He had seen no woolly mammoth since his separation from his Family – nothing but imperfect Firehead images of himself.

Nothing until *this*.

'We should Remember her,' he said thickly.

Thunder rumbled harshly, 'I thought you were the one who rejected the Cycle . . . Never mind. Did you know her?'

'She is old and dead. I can't recall, Thunder!'

The Fireheads were closing on the fallen mammoth with their stone axes and knives. Walks With Thunder wrapped his trunk around Longtusk's and pulled him backwards.

The Shaman's hard eyes were fixed on Longtusk, calculating, as the Fireheads butchered the mammoth.

First they wrapped ropes around her legs. Then, chanting in unison and with the help of mastodont muscles, they pulled her on her back. Longtusk heard the crackle of breaking bones as her limp mass settled.

With brisk, efficient motions, a hunter slit open her belly, reached into the cavity and hauled out guts – long tangled coils, black and faintly steaming – and dumped them on the ground. There was a stink of blood and spoiled food and rot. But there were no flies, for few insects prospered in this cold desert.

Then the hunters pulled out a flaccid sac that bulged,

449

heavy. It was the calf, Longtusk realised. Mercifully the hunters put that to one side.

The hunters cracked open her rib cage, climbed inside the body, and began to haul out more bloody organs, the heart and liver and kidneys, black lumps marbled with greasy fat.

Eviscerated, the Cow seemed to slump, hollowed.

When she was emptied, the butchers cut great slits in the Cow's skin and began to drag it off her carcass. Where the tough hide failed to rip away easily, they used knives to cut through connective tissue to separate it from the pink flesh beneath. They chopped the separated skin into manageable slices and piled it roughly.

Then, with their axes, they began to cut away the meat from the mammoth's bones. They started with the hind-quarters, making fast and powerful cuts above the knee and up the muscle masses. Then they dug bone hooks into the meat and hauled it away, exposing white, bloody bone. The bone attachments were cut through quickly, and the bones separated.

When one side of the Cow had been stripped, the ropes were attached again and the carcass turned over, to expose the other side.

The butchers were skilled and accurate, rarely cutting into the underlying bone, and the meat fell easily from the bones, leaving little behind. They assembled the meat into one immense pile, and extracted the huge bones for another heap.

When they were done the night was well advanced, and the Cow had been reduced to silhouetted piles of flesh and flensed bones, stinking of blood and decay.

The Fireheads built a fire and threw on some of the meat until the air was full of its stink. With every expression of relish they chewed slices of fat, bloody liver, heart and tongue. Even Willow, sitting alone at the fringe of the fire's circle of light, chewed noisily on the dark meat.

Then the hunters cracked open charred and heated bones and sucked hot, savoury marrow from the latticework of hollow bone within.

And at last Longtusk understood.

'I have seen them devour the contents of such bones at the settlement.'

'Yes,' said Walks With Thunder. '*They were mammoth bones*, Longtusk. Fireheads rarely hunt mammoths. You are a big, dangerous beast, grazer, and the hunters' reward, if their lives are spared, is more meat than they can carry. That's why they prefer the smaller animals for food.

'But they need mammoths. For they need fat.

'The animals they hunt regularly, the deer and the horses, are lean, with blood-red meat. But *you*, little grazer, are replete with fat, which clings to your heart and organs and swims within your bones. The Fireheads must consume it, and they need it besides for their lamps and paints and salves, and—'

'All the years I watched them trek to the north, returning with their cargoes of great bones. All those years, and I never suspected they were mammoth . . . Thunder, *why didn't you tell me?*'

'It was thought best,' said Walks With Thunder carefully, 'that you should *not* know. I made the decision; blame me. What good would it have done you to have known? But now—'

'But now, the Shaman wants me to see this. He is forcing me to confront the truth.'

'This is your test,' said Walks With Thunder. 'Will you fail, Longtusk?'

Longtusk turned away. 'No Firehead will defeat me.'

'I hope not,' Thunder said softly.

But, as it turned out, the greatest test was yet to come.

The next day the hunters walked to and fro across the

frozen desert, studying tracks and traces of dung. At last they seemed to come to a decision.

The Shaman pointed north. The mastodonts were loaded up once more.

'Why?' Longtusk rumbled. 'They have their bones and their marrow. What else can they want?'

'*More*,' called Thunder grimly. 'Fireheads always want more. And they think they know where to find it.'

It took another day's travelling.

The hunters grew increasingly excited, pointing out heaps of dry dung, trails that criss-crossed this dry land – and even, in one place, the skeleton of a mammoth, cleansed of its meat by the carrion eaters, its bones scattered over the dust.

. . . And Longtusk heard them, smelled their dung and thin urine, long before he saw them.

He rounded a low, ice-eroded hill. The land here was a muddy flat.

And around this mud seep stood mammoths.

With their high bulging heads, shoulder humps and thick, straggling hair, the mammoths looked strange in Longtusk's eyes, accustomed after so long to the sight of short, squat mastodonts; suddenly he felt acutely conscious of his own sloping back and thick hair, his *difference*.

But these mammoths were bedraggled, clearly in distress.

The mammoths gathered closely around holes in the ground. They reached with their trunks deep into the holes and sucked up the muddy, brackish water that oozed there.

They were jostling for the seeping water. But there wasn't enough for everybody.

So the mammoths fought each other, wordlessly, dully, endlessly. The plain was filled with the crack of tusk on tusk, the slap of skull on flank. Calves, thin and bony, clustered around the legs of the adults, but they were pushed away harshly. The infants wailed in protest, too weak to fight for the water they needed.

Longtusk watched all this, trembling, scarcely daring to breathe. The familiarity of them – their hair, their curling tusks – was overwhelming. And yet, what was he? *He* was not some wretched creature grubbing in the dirt for a drop of water. But if not mammoth, what had he become? He felt himself dissolve, leaving only a blackness within.

There were perhaps forty individuals – but this was not a Family or a Clan, for there were Bulls here, closer to the Cows and calves than they would be in normal times. But these were clearly not normal times. One gaunt Cow walked across the muddy flat to a place away from the others. With nervous, hasty scrapes with her feet, she began to dig out a fresh hole. Just behind her, white flensed bones rose out from the muddy ground. She stepped carelessly on a protruding skull, cracking it.

Walks With Thunder grunted softly, 'See the bones? Many have perished here already.'

Longtusk quoted the Cycle: *'Where water vanishes, sanity soon follows.'*

'Yes. But, beyond sanity, there is necessity. In times as harsh as this, mature Bulls survive, for they can travel far in search of water and food. The Cows are encumbered with their calves, perhaps unborn, and cannot flee. *But they are right to push away their calves* – so that those who do get water, those who survive, are those who can have more young in better times, in order that the Family can continue. And so the old and the young perish. Necessity . . . We did not come here by accident, Longtusk. The Fireheads knew they would find mammoths in this place of seeping water.'

'But the mammoths would not be here in this cold desert,' growled Longtusk, 'if they had not been pushed so far north by the Fireheads.'

Willow, the Dreamer, jumped into an abandoned hole. He picked up a pawful of mud and began to suck at it, slobbering greedily, smearing his face with the sticky black stuff. Unlike the mastodonts, the wretched Dreamer had no keeper to care for him, and was probably in as bad a condition as these starving mammoths.

Now the wind shifted. As the mastodonts' scent reached him one of the Bull mammoths stirred, raising his muddy trunk to sniff the air. He turned, slowly, and spotted the Fireheads and their mastodonts. He rumbled a warning.

The Bulls scattered, lumbering, trumpeting their alarm. The Cows clustered, drawing their calves in close.

But the Fireheads did not approach or threaten the mammoths. They began to unload the mastodonts and to prepare a hearth.

Gradually, thirst began to overcome the mammoths' caution. The Cows turned their attention back to the seep holes, and quickly made use of the places vacated by the Bulls. After a time, some of the Bulls came back, raising their tusks and braying a thin defiance at the mastodonts.

Longtusk stepped to the edge of an abandoned hole. There was a little seeping water, so thick with clay it was black, but the hole was all but dry.

He was aware that a Bull mammoth was approaching him. He did not turn that way; he held himself still. But he could not ignore the great creature's stink, the weight of his footsteps, his massive, encroaching presence, the deep rumble that came to him through the ground.

'. . . You smell of fat.'

Longtusk turned.

He faced a Bull: taller, older than Longtusk, but gaunt, almost skeletal. His guard hair dangled, coarse and lifeless. One of his tusks had been broken, perhaps in a fight; it terminated in a crude, dripping stump. The Bull stood listlessly; white mucus dripped from his eyes. He must barely be able to see, Longtusk realised.

Longtusk's heart was suddenly hammering. Once the Bull's accent would have been familiar to him – *for it had been the language of Longtusk's Clan*. Was it possible . . . ?

'I am not fat,' said Longtusk. 'But you are starving.'

The mammoth stepped back, growled and slapped his trunk on the ground. 'You are fat and ugly and complacent, and you stink of fire, you and these squat hairless dwarfs. You have forgotten what you are. Haven't you – Longtusk?'

'. . . *Rockheart*?'

'I'm still twice the Bull you are.' And Rockheart roared and lunged at Longtusk.

Longtusk ducked aside, and the Bull's tusks flashed uselessly through the air. Rockheart growled, stumbling, the momentum of his lunge catching him off balance. Almost effortlessly Longtusk slid his own tusks around the Bull's, and he twisted Rockheart's head. The huge Bull, roaring, slid sideways to the ground.

Longtusk placed his foot on Rockheart's temple.

He recalled how this Bull had once bested him, humiliating him in front of the bachelor herd. But Longtusk had been a mere calf then, and Rockheart a mature adult Bull. Now it was different: now it was Longtusk who was in his prime, Longtusk who had been trained to keep his courage and to fight – not just other Bulls in half-playful dominance contests, but animals as savage as charging rhinos, even hordes of scheming, clever Fireheads.

'I could crush your skull like a bird's egg,' he said softly.

'Then do it,' rumbled Rockheart. 'Do it, you Firehead monster.'

Firehead monster.

Is it true? Is that what I have become?

Longtusk lifted his foot and stepped back.

As Rockheart, gaunt and weak, scrambled to his feet and roared out his impotent rage, Longtusk walked away, saddened and horrified.

The Fireheads lingered close to the seep holes for a night and a day.

Longtusk found it increasingly difficult to bear the noise of this nightmarish place: the clash of tusks, the bleating of calves.

He said to Walks With Thunder, 'Why do the Fireheads keep us here? What do they want?'

'You know what they want,' Thunder said wearily. 'They want hearts and kidneys and livers and bones, for fat to feed to their cubs. They prefer to take their meat fresh, from the newly dead. And here, in this desolate place, they need only wait.'

'So we are waiting for a mammoth to die?'

'What did *you* think, Longtusk?'

'These Fireheads believe themselves to be mighty hunters,' Longtusk said bitterly. 'But it isn't true. They are scavengers, like the hyenas, or the condors.'

Thunder did not reply.

Somehow, in his heart, he had always imagined that his Family were still out there somewhere: just over the horizon, a little beyond the reach of a contact rumble, living on the steppe as they always had. But he had denied the changes in the land he had seen all around him, never thought through their impact on his Family. Now he faced the truth.

He recalled how so recently he had prided himself on his self-control, the fact that he was above mundane concerns, beyond pain and love and hope. He tried to cling to that control, to draw strength from it.

But the comfort was as dry and cold as the mammoths' seep holes. And he couldn't get out of his head the disgust and rage of Rockheart.

. . . The sun wheeled around the sky twice more before it happened.

There was a flurry of motion among the mammoths. The Fireheads, eating and dozing, stirred.

A mammoth Cow, barged away from a water hole, had fallen to her knees. Her breath gurgled in her chest. Other mammoths gathered around her briefly, touching her scalp and tongue with their trunks. But they were weak themselves, ground down by hunger and thirst, and had no help to offer her. Soon she was left alone, slumping deeper into the mud, as if melting.

'At last,' rumbled Walks With Thunder brutally.

With fast, efficient cries, a party of Fireheads formed up, gathering their knives and axes and spears, and set off towards the Cow.

Drawn by a hideous curiosity, Longtusk followed.

The Fireheads reached the mammoth. They started to lay their ropes on the ground, ready to pull her onto her back for gutting.

The mammoth raised her head, feebly and slowly, and her eyes opened, gummy with the milky mucus.

The Fireheads stepped back, shouting their annoyance that she was not yet dead.

While the Fireheads argued, the Cow stared at Longtusk. She spoke in a subterranean rumble so soft he could barely hear it. 'Don't you recognise me, Longtusk? Has it been so long?'

Memories swam towards him, long-buried: a calf, a ball of fluffy brown fur, not even her guard hairs grown, scampering, endlessly annoying . . .

A name.

'Splayfoot.' Splayfoot, his sister.

'You're back in time to Remember me,' she said. 'You and your Firehead friends. You were going to be the greatest hero of all, Longtusk. Wasn't that your dream? But now I can smell the stink of fire and meat on you. *What happened to you?*'

One of the hunters – Bareface – stepped forward. He had a spear in his paw, tipped by shining quartz. He hefted it, preparing for a thrust into her mouth, a single stroke that would surely kill her. Evidently the Fireheads, impatient, had decided to finish her off so they could get on with mining her body for its fat and marrow.

But this was Longtusk's own sister. His sister!

Longtusk trumpeted his rage.

With a single tusk sweep he knocked Bareface off his feet. The Firehead fell, howling, clutching his leg; bone protruded white from a bloody wound. Longtusk grabbed the spear with his trunk and drove the quartz point deep into the mud.

He went to his sister and wrapped his trunk around hers. 'Get up.'

'I can't. I'm so tired . . .'

'No! Only death is the end of possibility. By Kilukpuk's dugs, *up* . . .' And he hauled her to her feet by main force. She scrabbled at the mud, seeking a footing. Her legs were trembling, the muscles so depleted they could barely support her weight.

But now another mammoth was here – Rockheart, almost as gaunt and weakened. Nevertheless he lumbered up to Splayfoot's other side, lending his support as Longtusk tried to steady her.

And, startlingly, here was Willow, the squat little Dreamer. He jammed his shoulder under Splayfoot's heavy rump and shoved as hard as he could. He seemed to be laughing as he, too, defied the Fireheads.

The Fireheads were recovering from their shock at Longtusk's attack on Bareface. They were reaching for weapons, more of the big spears and axes that could slice through a mammoth's hide.

But now Walks With Thunder charged at them, his gait stiff and arthritic. He trumpeted, waving his huge old tusks this way and that, scattering the Fireheads. 'Go, little grazer!'

And as the water hole receded, and the motley party headed into an empty, unknown land, Longtusk could hear Thunder's call. 'Go, go, *go*!'

THREE
PATRIARCH

LONGTUSK AND THE TRUTH

There are many stories about Longtusk (said Silverhair).

There is a story that Longtusk flew over the ice, carrying his Clan to safety in a place called a nunatak.

There is a story that Longtusk dug his huge tusks into the ground, as we do when we search for water, only to find – not water – but warmth, coming out of bare rock, sufficient to drive back the ice and keep his Clan alive.

There is a story that he stamped his mighty feet and made his refuge of rock and heat fly off into the sky, carrying the mammoths with it, and the rock became the Sky Steppe, the last refuge of all. But Longtusk had to stay behind, here on Earth, to face his death . . .

Or perhaps Longtusk never died. Some say he returns, from out of the north, a hero come to save us when we face great danger. Perhaps it was he who brought our Family to the Island, before the sea rose and trapped us there. (But perhaps that was somebody else, another hero whose name we have lost, somebody inspired by Longtusk's legend . . .)

How can all the stories be true?

Can *any* of them be true?'

Oh, Icebones, I understand. You want to know. And, more than that, you *want* the stories to be true. I was just like you as a calf!

Longtusk is a wonderful hero. But we'll never know for sure. You understand that, don't you?

. . . What do I think?

Well, stories don't come out of thin air. Perhaps there's a grain of truth. Perhaps there really was a Longtusk, and something like the stories really did happen, long ago.

Perhaps. We'll never know.

If I could know one thing about Longtusk, though, it would be this.

How he died.

CHAPTER 1
THE FAMILY

Under a grey sunless sky, without shadows, every direction looked the same. Even the land was contorted, confusing, the rock bare, littered here and there by gravel and loess, lifeless save for scattered tussocks of grass.

Longtusk, trunk raised, studied the vast, empty landscape around them. *There were no Fireheads*, he realised: no storage pits, no hearths, no huts, not even a mastodont, none of it in his vision for the first time for half his lifetime.

The Fireheads had filled and defined his world for so long. Their projects – predictable or baffling, rewarding or distressing – had provided a structure to every waking moment, even when he had defied them. Now the future seemed as blank and directionless as the land that stretched around him.

He felt disoriented, like a calf who had been spun around until he was dizzy.

'I don't think they are coming after us.' He almost wished the Fireheads *would* follow him. At least that was a threat he could understand.

But it seemed he would not be given that much help. And, for the first time since his capture as a calf, he had to learn to think for himself.

'Of course not,' Rockheart was saying. 'They have no need to – save revenge, perhaps. And those dwarfish pals of yours were making trouble.'

'They aren't dwarfs,' said Longtusk. 'They are mastodonts.'

'It doesn't matter,' growled Rockheart. 'You won't be seeing them again.'

. . . Could that be true?

'You're the leader of this strange little herd of ours, Longtusk,' Rockheart said sourly. 'But I strongly suggest we head north and east.'

'Why?'

'Because we might find something to eat and drink. Although we may have to fight for it.' He eyed Longtusk. 'You aren't in your Firehead camp now, being fed hay and water by your masters . . .'

Perhaps. But Longtusk didn't want to think about a future in which he became like the mammoths he had seen at the mud seep, fighting over dribbles of brackish mud, pushing away the weak and old and young.

'North and east,' he said.

'North and east.'

So they moved on.

After a time they found a place where grass grew a little more thickly. Longtusk pulled tufts of the coarse grass into his own mouth, and helped Splayfoot to feed. Her eyes half closed, Splayfoot ground up the grass with slow, feeble movements of her jaw, but he could see her tongue was spotted with black, and she was sucking at the grass as much as eating it.

He said, 'She's very weak. She needs drink as much as food.'

Rockheart growled, 'There's no drink to be had here.'

It struck Longtusk that Rockheart himself was barely in better condition than Splayfoot. But where Splayfoot was subsiding towards death, Rockheart was still functioning, working. At the mud seep he had even been prepared to challenge Longtusk – and now here he was playing his part in this unexpected journey, which looked as if it would prove long and difficult.

His respect grew for this indomitable, arrogant Bull.

Willow, too, was hungry and thirsty. There was no water here, and the little Dreamer couldn't eat grass, like the mammoths. He prowled around the area until he found a stunted dwarf willow, clinging to the ground. He prised up its twisted branches and studied them, eventually dropping them with scorn.

Rockheart said, 'What's it doing?'

Longtusk replied, 'It – *he* – is looking for long, straight bits of wood. I expect he wants to make a spear, maybe even a fire. He might catch a lemming or a vole.'

Rockheart snorted in disgust, indifferent.

Rockheart and Splayfoot soon stopped eating, evidently having taken their fill.

Longtusk had barely scratched the surface of his hunger. He had been used to *much* more fodder than this at the Firehead settlement, and if he didn't take more he would soon be as scrawny and ragged as the others – and ill-prepared for the winter to come, when the mammoths would have to live off their stores of fat.

But to gorge himself was hardly a way to gain trust. So he took care to eat no more than Rockheart's shrunken stomach could manage.

Having fed as best they could, they moved on.

The sun was already sinking in the sky when they reached the trail.

It was just a strip of trampled land that cut across the gravel-littered rock barrens, passing roughly east to west. Longtusk, instincts dulled by captivity, might not have seen it at all. But Rockheart turned confidently onto the trail and began to head east.

Longtusk – supporting his sister, and occasionally allowing Willow to ride on his back – followed his lead.

They passed a stand of forest. The trees were firs, still young but already tall, growing fast and dense in a green swathe that stretched to the south. The forest had grown so thickly, in fact, that it had already overrun the old trail, and the mammoths had to divert north until the forest was behind them and they were cutting across open land once more.

467

Longtusk said, 'It's a long time since I was here. But I don't recall the land being like this.'

'Things have changed here, Longtusk – within the lifetime of calves a lot younger than you or me. I recall when this was all steppe, with grass, herbs, shrubs. *Now* look around: to the south you have the spreading forest, and to the north the bare rock. No place left for the steppe, eh?

'And even where there is steppe – though you might not think it – the climate is wetter than it used to be. There is more rain, more thick snow in the winter. Sometimes the land is waterlogged and boggy. In the summer nothing can grow but grass and lichens, and in the winter we struggle to keep out of snowdrifts so thick they cover our bellies. The land isn't right for us any more. Deer and moose can chew the trees, and reindeer and musk oxen browse on lichen and moss, dull cloddish brutes . . . but not *us*.

'But there are still a few places where the old steppe lingers, pockets of it here and there.'

'And that's where you're taking us.'

'That's where the mammoths live, yes – if we're lucky, friendly ones. That was the way we were heading, when we reached the mud seep. But we were weak, and . . .'

'There are fewer of us now, and I suppose in the future there will be fewer still. But we persist. We have before.'

'What do you mean?'

Rockheart eyed him. 'You've been away too long. Have you forgotten so much of your Cycle? . . .'

As winter followed summer, so the Earth had greater seasons, spanning the Great-Years. In the long winters the ice would spread, freezing the land and the air, and the mammoths could fill the expanding steppe. Now it seemed the Earth's unwelcome spring was returning, and the steppe was overrun by forests and grass – and the mammoths had to retreat, waiting out the return of the cold, as they had many times before.

It was a time of hardship. But it would pass. That was the

teaching of the Cycle. The ice had come and gone for more than two million years, and the mammoths had survived all the intervals of warmth in that immense stretch of time.

. . . But now Longtusk thought of the Fireheads: clustered around the mud seep, waiting for mammoths to die.

There were no Fireheads in the Cycle. There had been no Fireheads in the world when last the ice had retreated and advanced.

He had been away from his kind a long time, and he didn't presume to doubt Rockheart's ancient wisdom. But his experience, he was realising slowly, was wider than the old tusker's. He had seen more of the world and its ways – and he had seen the Fireheads.

And *he* did not feel so confident that the future could be the same as the past.

He kept these thoughts to himself as they pushed on.

As night closed in the clouds thickened, and the wind from the icecap was harsh. Longtusk and Rockheart huddled close around Splayfoot, trying to shelter her and give her a little of their own sparse body heat; and Longtusk allowed the Dreamer to curl up under his belly fur.

Every so often Longtusk would rouse Splayfoot and force her to walk around. He knew that there was a core of heat inside the body of each mammoth, a flicker of life and mind that must be fed like the hearths of the Fireheads. If the cold penetrated too deep, if that flame of life was extinguished, it could never be ignited again.

Splayfoot responded passively, barely conscious.

In the morning they resumed their dogged walking, following Rockheart's trail.

But soon the light changed.

Longtusk raised his trunk, sniffing the air. He could smell moisture, rain or maybe snow, and the wind was veering, coming now strongly from the east. Looking that way he saw black clouds bubbling frothily.

There was a thin honking, a soft flap of wings far above him. Birds, he saw dimly, perhaps geese, fleeing from the east, away from the coming storm. He recalled what Walks With Thunder had told him of the eastern lands, where the icecap pushed far to the south. And he recalled Thunder's obscure, half-forgotten legends of a land embedded in the ice – a place that stayed warm enough to keep off the snow, even in the depths of winter. The nunatak.

He wondered how far those birds had flown – all the way from the nunatak itself? But how could such a place exist?

The storm was rising, and he put the speculation from his mind. But he memorised the way those geese had flown, adding their track to the dynamic map of the landscape that he, like all mammoths, carried in his head.

By mid-morning the storm had hit.

The sky became a sheet of scudding grey-black clouds, utterly hiding the sun. The wind blew from the east with relentless ferocity, and carried before it a mix of snow, hail and rain, battering the mammoths' flesh hard enough to sting. Soon they were all soaked through, bedraggled, weary, their fur plastered flat, lifting their feet from one deep muddy footprint into another.

Longtusk let Rockheart lead the way, and Willow followed Rockheart, clinging to his belly fur, his small round face hidden from the wind and rain. Longtusk plodded steadily after Rockheart, being careful never to let the big tusker out of his sight, even though it meant he walked so close he was treading in Rockheart's thin, foul-smelling dung. And behind Longtusk came Splayfoot, still weak, barely able to see, clinging onto Longtusk's tail with her trunk like a calf following its mother, as sheltered as he could manage.

But when the eye of the storm approached, the wind started to swirl around. Soon Longtusk, disoriented, couldn't tell east from west, north from south – and couldn't even see the trail. But Rockheart led them confidently, probing at the muddy ground with his trunk, seeking bits of old dung and the remnants of footprints, traces that marked the trail.

And it was while the storm was still raging that they came upon the mammoths.

They looked like a clump of boulders, round and solid, plastered with soaked hair. Longtusk saw those great heads rise, tusks dripping with water, and trunks lifted into the air, sniffing out the approach of these strangers. There were a few greeting rumbles for Rockheart and Splayfoot, nothing but suspicious glares for Longtusk.

There were perhaps fifteen of them – probably just a single Family, adult Cows and older calves. The Cows were clustered around a tall, gaunt old female, presumably the Matriarch, and the calves were sheltered under their belly hair and legs.

Longtusk could see no infants. Perhaps they were at the centre of the group, out of his sight.

Rockheart lurched off the trail and led them towards the mammoths. Longtusk hadn't even been aware of the changes in the land around the trail. But now he saw grass, what looked like saxifrage, even a stand of dwarf willow clinging to the rock. It was an island of steppe in this cold desert of rock and glacial debris, just as Rockheart had described.

Willow found a shallow water hole, some distance from the mammoths, and went that way. Some of the mammoths watched him lethargically, too weak or weary to be concerned.

Rockheart and Splayfoot lumbered forward and were welcomed into the huddle with strokes of trunk and deeper, contented rumbles. Longtusk hesitated, left outside – outside, as he had been as a mammoth among mastodonts, as he had been as a mammoth at the cave of the Dreamers, and now outside even this community of mammoths.

Longtusk dredged up memories of his life with his Family, before that terrible separation. He recalled how the adults seemed so tall, their strength so huge, their command imposing, even their stink powerful. Now these wretched, bedraggled creatures seemed diminished; none of them, not even the old Matriarch at the centre, was taller than he was.

Light flared, noise roared. There was a sudden blaze to Longtusk's right, and the mammoths, startled, trumpeted and clustered, tried to run.

It was lightning, he realised, a big blue bolt. It had struck out of the low clouds and set fire to an isolated spruce tree. The tree was burning, and the stink of smoke carried to his trunk – but there was no danger; already the fire was being doused by the continuing rain.

The other mammoths had raised their trunks suspiciously at Longtusk.

He hadn't reacted. It was only lightning, an isolated blaze; in his years with the Fireheads he'd learned that fire, if contained, was nothing to fear. But he realised now that the others – even the powerful Bull Rockheart – had shown their instinctive dread.

'. . . He did not run from the fire. He didn't even flinch.'

'Look how fat he is, how tall. None of us grows fat these days.'

'See the burn on his flank. The shape of a Firehead paw . . .'

'He came with that little Dreamer.'

'He stinks of fire. And of Fireheads. That is why he wasn't afraid.'

'He isn't *natural* . . .'

But now the gaunt older Cow he had tagged as the Matriarch broke out of the group. Cautiously, ears spread and trunk raised, she approached him. Her hair was slicked down and blackened by the rain.

It had been so long, so very long. But still, there was something in the set of her head, her carriage –

Something that tugged at his heart.

Hesitantly, she reached out with her trunk and probed his face, eyes, mouth, and dug into his hair.

He knew that touch; the years fell away.

'I thought you were gone to the aurora,' she said softly.

'Do I smell of fire?'

'Whatever has become of you, the rain has washed it away. All I can smell is you, Longtusk.' She stepped forward and twined her trunk around his.

Through the rain, he could taste the sweet, milky scent of her breath.

'Come.' Milkbreath pulled him back to the group, where the huddle was reforming. The other mammoths grumbled and snorted, but Milkbreath trumpeted her anger. 'He is my son, and he is returned. Gather around him.'

Slowly, they complied. And as the day descended into night and the storm continued to rage, slow, inquisitive trunks nuzzled at his mouth and face.

He felt a surge of warm exhilaration. After all his travels and troubles he was home, home again.

But, even in this moment of warmth, he noticed that there were no small calves at his feet, here at the centre of the huddle – no infants at all, in fact.

Even as he greeted his mother, that stark fact dug deep into his mind, infecting it with worry.

CHAPTER 2
THE DECISION

The storm blew itself out.

The next day was clear and cold, the sky blue and tall. The water that had poured so enthusiastically from the sky soaked into the ground, quickly, cruelly. But the grassy turf was still waterlogged, and drinking water was easy to find. The mammoths wandered apart, feeding and defecating, shaking the moisture out of their fur.

The spruce that had been struck by lightning was blackened and broken, its ruin still smoking.

Longtusk stayed close to his sister, and, with his mother's help, encouraged her to eat and drink. Slowly her eyes grew less cloudy.

His mother's attentiveness, as if he was still a calf, filled a need in him he hadn't recognised for a long time. He answered as fully as he could all the questions he was asked about his life since he had been split from the Family, and slowly the suspicion of the others wore away. And when he told of the loss of his calf and mate, the suspicion started to turn at last to sympathy.

But there were few here who knew him.

Skyhump, the Matriarch of the Family when he had been born, was long dead now – in fact there had been another Matriarch since, his mother's elder sister, killed by a fall into a kettle hole, and his mother had succeeded her.

And there was a whole new generation, born since he had left.

There was a Bull calf, for instance, called Threetusk – for the third, spindly ivory spiral that jutted out of his right tusk socket – who seemed fascinated by Longtusk. He would follow Longtusk around, asking him endless questions about the warrior mastodonts like Jaw Like Rock, and he would raise his tusks to Longtusk's in half-hearted challenge.

Longtusk realised that Threetusk was just how *he* had been at that age: restless, unhappy with the company of his mother and the other Cows of the Family – not yet ready to join a bachelor herd, but eager to try.

But things were different now. There was no sign of a bachelor herd anywhere nearby for Threetusk to join. Perhaps there was a herd somewhere in this huge land, in another island of nourishing steppe. But how was a juvenile like Threetusk, lacking knowledge of the land, to find his way there in one piece? And if he could *not* find a herd, what would become of him?

The Family moved slowly over their patch of steppe, eating sparingly, drinking what they could find. After the first couple of days it was obvious their movements were restricted, and Longtusk took to wandering away from the rest, trying to understand the changed landscape.

He struck out south and east and west.

Each direction he travelled, the complex steppe vegetation soon dwindled out to be replaced by cold desert, or dense coniferous forests, or bland plains of grass. And to the north, of course, there was only the protesting shriek of the ice as it continued its millennial retreat.

And, hard as he listened, he heard no signs of other mammoths.

His Family was isolated in this island of steppe. Other mammoths, Families and bachelor herds, must also be restricted to steppe patches and water holes and other places where they could survive. And the nearest of those islands might be many days' walk from the others.

This isolation mattered. It made the mammoths fragile, exposed. An illness, a bad winter, even a single fall of heavy snow could take them all, with no place to run.

As they munched at their herbs and grass the others didn't seem aware of their isolation, the danger it posed for them.

And they didn't seem aware of the strangest thing of all: *there were no young calves here* – no squirming bundles of orange fur, wrestling each other or searching for their mothers' milk and tripping over their trunks.

Longtusk felt a profound sense of unease. And, when he spotted a new skein of geese flapping out of the east, it was an unease that coalesced into a new determination.

He plucked up the courage to speak to his mother.

'There was a Gathering,' he said. 'When I was a calf. Just before I got lost.'

'Yes. The whole Clan was there.'

'I saw Pinkface, the Matriarch of Matriarchs. Is she still alive?'

Milkbreath's trunk tugged at a resistant clump of grass. 'There have been several Gatherings since you were lost.'

Longtusk said slowly, 'That isn't an answer.'

Milkbreath turned to face him, and he was aware of a stiffening among the other Cows close by, his aunts and great-aunts.

He persisted. 'When was the last Gathering?'

'Many years ago. It isn't so easy to travel any more, Longtusk. Especially for the calves and—'

'At the Gathering, the last one. Were there more mammoths – or less?'

Milkbreath snorted her disapproval. 'You don't need to feed me my grass a blade at a time, Longtusk. I can see the drift of your questions.'

Rockheart was at his side. 'You shouldn't question the Matriarch. It isn't the way things are done. Not *here*.'

Milkbreath rumbled, 'It's all right, Rockheart. His education was never finished. Times are hard, Longtusk. The Matriarch of Matriarchs gave us our instructions at the last

Gathering. She could foresee the coming changes in the world, the worsening of the weather.'

'The collapse of the steppe into these little islands?'

'Yes. Even that. She knew that Gatherings would be difficult or impossible for a long time. She knew there would be fewer of us next year, and fewer still the next after that. But we have endured such changes before, many times, as the ice has come and gone. And we have always survived. It will be hard, but our bodies know the way. That's the teaching of the Cycle.'

'And what about the Fireheads? Did she speak of them?'

'Of course she spoke of the Fireheads, Longtusk. Fireheads come when we are weak and dying. They cut our corpses open for our bones and hearts . . .'

'But,' he said, 'there are no Fireheads in the Cycle. Maybe the Fireheads weren't here when the ice last retreated.'

'What does it matter?'

·'What I'm saying is that things are different now. The Fireheads are a new threat we haven't faced before . . .'

But the Matriarch continued to quote the Cycle. *'When I die, I belong to the wolves* – or the Fireheads. We must accept the Fireheads, as we accept the warming, and simply endure. In the future, all will be as it was, and there will be great Gatherings again.'

Longtusk tried another approach. 'When was the last time you heard from the Matriarch of Matriarchs?'

Rockheart growled, 'Longtusk—'

'The last Gathering?'

'. . . Yes.'

'Then she is probably dead.'

Some of the Cows rumbled and trumpeted in dismay.

'And she was wrong,' said Longtusk grimly.

Rockheart tusked the ground, rumbling his challenge. 'Do I have to fight you to shut you up?'

Longtusk ignored him. 'I have seen the Fireheads. I have seen what they do. They wait for mammoths to die. If the mammoths take too long, they finish them off with their spears . . . The Matriarch of Matriarchs was right that the mammoths have endured warming before, and recovered. *But this is not the past.* The Fireheads make everything different—'

Rockheart's blow was a mere swipe at his tusks, a loud ivory clatter that echoed over the steppe. He said grimly, 'You have forgotten your Cycle. *The Matriarch has given her orders, and we will follow.*'

Longtusk eyed Rockheart. He recalled how easily he had defeated this old tusker before – and yet here he was again, prepared to confront him, and Longtusk knew he could beat Rockheart down again, just as easily.

But that wasn't the way to succeed. Not today.

And he couldn't keep his peace, either, even though he longed to. He didn't want to be different! He only wanted to be one of the Family . . . All he had to do was stay silent.

But that wasn't the right path, either.

He summoned up the inner strength he had found during those long dark months in the Firehead camp, after the death of Neck Like Spruce and his calf.

He said, *'We cannot survive here, Matriarch.* This little patch of steppe is too small. Look around. You are thin, half-starved. A simple accident could kill us all – a flash flood, a lightning strike like the one which struck down that spruce.

'And some day the Fireheads will come here. They will – I know them! And—'

This time, Rockheart's blow was to his temple, and pain rang through his skull. He staggered sideways. He felt warm blood trickle down his flesh.

The Matriarch faced him, shifting from one foot to the other, distressed. 'End this, Longtusk.'

'Mother – Matriarch – *where are your calves?*'

Rockheart's tusks came crashing down on his. Longtusk's ivory splintered, agonisingly, as if a tooth had broken, and the tip of his right tusk cracked off and fell to the ground.

'By Kilukpuk's black heart, fight,' Rockheart rumbled.

'What makes you so wise?' Milkbreath said, upset, angry. 'What makes you different? How do you see what others don't? How do *you* know what we must do?'

Longtusk, bleeding, aching, could see Rockheart prepare for another blow, but he knew he must not respond – not even brace himself.

'. . . The calves are dead.' It was Splayfoot, his sister.

Rockheart hesitated.

Gaunt, weakened, Splayfoot came limping towards Longtusk. 'The youngest died last winter, when there was no water to be had. That's your answer, Longtusk. He *is* different, Matriarch. He has seen things none of us can imagine. And we must listen. I would have died with the others at that drying mud seep – *as would you, Rockheart* – if not for Longtusk.'

The Matriarch rumbled sadly, 'Even when we have met Bulls, even when we have mated, our bodies have not borne calves. It is the wisdom of the body. If there is too little food and water the body knows that calves should not come.'

'For how long?' Longtusk asked. 'Look around you. How long before you *all* grow too old to conceive?' He glared at them wildly, and trumpeted his challenge. 'Which of you will be the last to die here, alone?'

Rockheart, growling, prepared another lunge at Longtusk, but the Matriarch stopped him. Anguished, angry, she rumbled, 'What would you have me do?'

Longtusk said, 'There may be a way. A place to go. Beyond the reach of the ice – and even of the Fireheads.' Shuddering, trying to ignore the pain of his temple and broken tusk, he looked to the east, thinking of the geese.

Rockheart roared his disgust. 'And must we follow you, Firehead monster? Shall we call you Patriarch? There has never been such an animal. Not in all the long years of the Cycle—'

'He is right,' Splayfoot insisted. 'The spring blizzards kill our calves. The ice storms of the autumn kill Cows who are heavy with next year's calves. None of us can bear the heat of summer. And when the seeps and water holes ice over in the winter, too thickly for us to break through, we fight each other for the water, to the death . . . We can't stay here. *He is right.*'

Threetusk came pushing between them, his spindly extra tusk coated with mud. He looked up at Longtusk with trunk raised. 'Take me! Oh, take me!'

The arguments continued, for the rest of that day and into the night, and even beyond that.

The day was bright and clear and cold. The sun was surrounded by a great halo of light that arced above the horizon, bright yellow against a muddy purple sky. It was a sign of the ice cap, Longtusk knew.

It was an invitation – and a challenge.

He drew a deep breath through his trunk, and the cleanness of the air filled him with exhilaration.

'It is time,' he rumbled, loud enough for all to hear.

And the mammoths began to prepare for the separation.

The Family was to be split in two by Longtusk's project: calf separated from parent, sibling from sibling. And, though it was never stated, a deep truth was understood by all here – that the sundered Family would never be reunited, for those who walked with Longtusk into the cold mists of the east would never come back this way.

Willow pulled on all his clothing, stuffed his jacket and hat and boots with grass for insulation against the cold, and collected together his tools and strips of dried meat. Once he had understood that Longtusk was planning to move on, the Dreamer had been making his own preparations. He had made himself simple tools, spears and stone axes, and he disappeared for days at a time, returning with the fruits of his hunting: small mammals, rabbits and voles. He ate the flesh or dried it, stored the bones as raw material for tools, and used the skin, dried and scraped, to make himself new clothing.

Soon he had become as healthy and equipped as Longtusk could recall – much better than during his time as a creature of the Fireheads. It dismayed Longtusk to think that he, and the mastodonts, had received so much better treatment at the paws of the Fireheads than Willow, their close cousin.

He sought out his mother, the Matriarch.

She wrapped her trunk in his and reached out to ruffle the topknot of fur on his head, just as she had when he was a calf – even though he had grown so tall she now had to reach high up to do so. 'Such a short time,' she said. 'I've only just found you, and now we are to be parted again. And this time—'

'I know.'

'Maybe we'll both be right,' she said. 'Perhaps there really is a warm island of steppe floating in the ice cap. And maybe the Fireheads and the weather will spare those who stay here, and we will flourish again. That way there will be plenty of mammoths in the future to argue about who was right and wrong. Won't it be wonderful?'

'Mother—'

She slipped her trunk into his mouth. 'No more talking. Go.'

Go, little grazer. Was he destined always to flee, to move on from those who cared for him?

This time, he promised himself grimly, this time is the last, whatever the outcome. Wherever I finish up will be my home – and my grave.

They gathered together: Longtusk, Rockheart, Splayfoot, the bold Bull calf Threetusk, and two young Cows. Just six of them, three Bulls and three Cows, to challenge the ice cap – six mammoths, and Willow, the Dreamer.

As they stood in a dismal huddle at the fringe of the Family, the whole venture seemed impossible to Longtusk, absurd.

But here was Rockheart, the last to pledge his commitment to the trek: 'You won't get through a day without me to show you the way, you overfed milk-tusk.' Longtusk's spirit rose as he looked at the huge tusker – gaunt and bony, but a great slab of strength and determination and wisdom.

Now Rockheart raised his trunk. 'You taste that?'

'Salt water. Blown from the sea . . .'

'Yes,' said Rockheart. 'But it comes from both north and south.'

The mammoths would cross the land bridge between Asia and America much too close to its central line for Longtusk to be able to see the encroaching oceans to north and south. But sight is the least of a mammoth's senses, and, on this bright clear day, Longtusk could taste the traces of salt spray in the air, hear the rush of wind over the ocean, sense the crash of breakers on the twin shorelines.

The neck of land they had to cross seemed fragile to him, easily sundered, and he wondered again about the wisdom of what they were attempting.

But this was no time for doubt.

'From the old land to the new,' he said boldly.

'From old to new,' Rockheart rumbled.

Longtusk began to march to the east. He could feel the powerful footsteps of the others as they followed him.

It had begun.

CHAPTER 3

THE TREK

To show his own determination he chose to lead, that first day.

But at the start of the second day, without a word, he quietly deferred to Rockheart, letting the old tusker, with his superior instincts and understanding of the country, go first. That decision paid off many times – especially after the mammoth trails petered out, and the land became increasingly broken and unpredictable.

Willow preferred to walk during the day; it kept him strong and alert. But the mammoths, needing little sleep, would walk through much of the night, and then Willow would ride on Longtusk's back, muttering his strange dreams. The other mammoths watched in suspicious amazement, unable to understand how a mammoth could allow such a squat little creature onto his back.

There were animals here: musk oxen, horses, bison, even camels, passing in great herds on the horizon. They glimpsed some carnivores – wolves, lions, a sabre-tooth cat that sent a shudder of recognition through Longtusk, and a short-faced bear, fat and ugly, which came lumbering from a limestone cave. The predators watched them pass, silently speculating after the manner of their kind, seeking weakness among potential prey.

They saw no other mammoths, no Fireheads, no Dreamers.

They paused to rest and feed in an isolated island of steppe vegetation: a mosaic of grass with flowering plants and herbs like marsh marigolds, harebells and golden saxifrage, and sparse trees like ground willow, few reaching higher than a mammoth's belly hair.

At Longtusk's feet, a small face peered out of a burrow. It was a collared lemming. The little rodent, seeing that the mammoths meant him no harm, crawled out of his burrow and began to nibble at the base of an Arctic lupine.

Longtusk realised sadly that, like the mammoths, the vanishing steppe was the lemmings' only true home. But the lemming's mind, though sharp, was too small for him to discuss the issue.

Mammoth and lemming briefly regarded each other. Then the lemming ducked beneath the ground once more.

A few more days' walking brought them to a more mountainous region. To the north there was the sharp tang of ice in the air, and when he looked that way Longtusk saw a small, isolated ice cap, a gleaming dome that nestled among the mountains. It was shrinking as the world warmed; it might once have been part of a much more extensive formation.

Then they came to a place where the travelling became much more difficult. Longtusk, as the strongest, took the lead.

The land here was cut through by deep channels. These gouges ran from north to south, and so across the mammoths' eastward path. Longtusk found himself having to climb down crumbling slopes into the beds of the channels, and then up ridges on the far side, over and over. The channels seemed to have been cut right down to the rock, and there was only thin soil and scanty vegetation, broken by dunes of coarse sand and ridges of gravel. There was little water to be had, for the soil was shallow. But there was thicker growth on the top of the ridges – some of which, surrounded by the deep valleys, had smooth outlines, like the bodies of fish.

Standing on top of such a ridge, cropping the sparse grass

wearily, Longtusk looked about at the strange pattern of the land. It was like a dried-up river bed, he thought, a tracery of runnels and ridges in mud, cutting across each other so they were braided like hair, gouged out and worn smooth by running water.

But this was broader than any river valley he had ever seen. And most of the top soil and loose rock had been torn away, right down to the bedrock. If a river had ever run here it must have been wider and far more powerful than any he had encountered before.

To the north the bedrock rose, great shoulders of hard volcanic rock pushing up to either side of this channelled plain. He saw that the rocky shoulders came together in a narrow cleft. Ice gleamed white there, blocking the cleft. But it was from that cleft that these strange deep channels seemed to run.

When he raised his trunk that way he could smell water: fresh water, a vast body of it, beyond that cleft in the rock.

The mammoths discussed this briefly. The ice wedge was less than a day's walk away, and if there was water to be had the detour was surely worth the investment of their time. And besides, Longtusk admitted to himself, he was piqued by curiosity; he would like to know the story of this distorted, damaged land.

They followed one of the wider channels towards the ice plug, their muscles working steadily as the land rose.

At last Longtusk topped a ridge of rock, and he was able to look beyond the cleft and its plug of ice.

There was a lake here. It was broad and placid, and it lay in a natural hollow in the land. The water was fringed by rock and ice: the plug of ice that barred it from the damaged lands to the south, and by the shrinking ice cap which lay at its northern end.

The mammoths walked cautiously down to the lake's gravel-strewn fringe. The water was ice cold, but they sucked it into their trunks gratefully. Threetusk and the young Cows splashed out into the water, playfully blowing trunkfuls of it over each other. After a time they loped clumsily out of the water, their breath steaming, their outer fur crackling with frost.

Willow, too, made the best of the water. He threw off his furs and scampered, squat and naked, into the lake. He cried out at the cold, but immersed himself and scrubbed at the thick hair on his belly and head with bits of soft stone, getting rid of the insects that liked to make their homes there.

There seemed to be little vegetation in this placid pool. But there were signs of life by the shore, holes dug by rabbits and voles and lemmings in the long grass that fringed the water's edge. And birds wheeled overhead, ducks and gulls.

'. . . But there are no fish here,' said Rockheart. 'Strange.'

'But no fish could reach this place,' Longtusk said thoughtfully.

At the lake's northern shore, the ice gave directly onto the lake, making a cliff that gleamed white. There was a constant scrape and groan from all across the ice cliff, and Longtusk could see icebergs, small islands of blue-white ice, drifting away from the cliff. The lake water looked black beside the blinding white of the ice.

It was obvious that the ice was flowing from its mountain fastness, with hideous slowness, down towards the lake. And where the ice met the water the icebergs were calving off, great fragments of the disintegrating ice sheet.

In fact, Longtusk saw, the lake had been created by the melting of the ice sheet as it crumbled into this hollow in the rock.

'This lake is just a huge meltwater pond,' Longtusk said. 'It is fed by melting ice. There are no fish here, because there is no way for a fish to get here. And the water is kept from draining away by *that* –' The plug of ice in the rocky cleft on the lake's southern side. 'Fed by meltwater from the north, trapped by the ice plug to the south, this bowl in the land will gradually fill up—'

'Until,' Rockheart growled, 'that chunk of ice gives way.'

'Yes. And then the lake will empty itself across the land, all at once – and wash away the soil and vegetation, scouring down to the bedrock.'

'Like Kilukpuk's mighty tears.'

'Yes. No wonder the land is so damaged. But then the ice plug forms again, and the lake begins to fill once more.'

Rockheart grunted. 'If that's true, we're lucky. We're in no danger here.'

'What do you mean?'

'The water has some way to rise before it tops that ice dam.'

'You're right. We'll be long gone by then.' Good for Rockheart, Longtusk thought: practical as always, focusing on the most important issue – the mammoths' safety.

They left the lake, calling to the others.

A few more days and he could sense the broadening of the land to north and south, and he knew they had passed the narrowest point of this neck of Earth that stretched between the continents.

Thus, the mammoths walked from Asia to America.

Soon after that he could see the ice cap.

It was a line of light, straight and pure white, all along the eastern horizon, as if etched there by the ingenious paw of a Firehead. He could hear the growl and scrape as the ice flowed over the rocky land, gouging and destroying, the mighty cracks as the ice itself split and crumbled, and the steady roar of the blunt katabatic winds which spilled from its chill domed heart.

It was a frozen sheet that covered half a continent, pushing far to the south, much further south than in the land they had fled, on the far side of the land bridge. And it was this monster of ice that they must challenge before they reached safety.

He tried to maintain the pace and enthusiasm of his little group. But as they drew closer he could feel his own footsteps drag, as if the ice cap itself was drawing out his strength, just as it sucked the moisture from the air.

They reached land that had clearly been uncovered only recently by the ice.

The rock was scoured clean, laced here and there with low dunes of glacial till and sand. Only lichen grew here: patches of yellow and green, bordered by black, slowly eroding the surfaces of the rock. The lichen might be extremely ancient; it took ten years for a new colony to become visible to the eye. He wondered what slow encrusting dreams these vegetable colonists shared, what slow cold memories of the surging ice they stored.

The land became steadily more treacherous. They worked their way past moraines, heaps of rubble left by the retreating ice. The rubble was of all sizes, from gritty sand to boulders larger than a mammoth. The moraines were cut through by meltwater rivers that varied unpredictably from trickles to mighty, surging flows, and the rubble heaps were unstable, liable to slump and collapse at any time.

As they pressed further, a great wind rose, katabatic, pouring directly off the ice sheet and into their faces. It was a hard time. There was little to eat or drink and every step required a major effort, but they persisted. And Longtusk was careful to encourage his charges to gather as much strength as possible, for he knew that only harder days, if anything, lay ahead of them all.

At last they encountered the ice itself.

They reached the nose of a glacier. It was a wall of ice, cracked and dirty and forbidding. Blocks of broken ice, calved off the glacier like miniature icebergs, lay unmelting on rock that was rust-red, brown and black. Tornado-like columns of ice crystals spun across the barren rock in the wind, whipping up small lumps of sandstone that flew through the air, peppering the mammoths' hides.

This was the terminus of a huge river of ice that poured, invisibly slowly, from the vast cap that still lay to the east.

They paused to gather breath, hunted without success for food, and then began the ascent.

Longtusk picked his way onto the great ice river, stepping cautiously over a shattered, chaotic plain of deeply crevassed blue ice. The glacier was a river of raw white, its glare hurting his eyes, shining under the sky's clean blue. He could see the glacier's source, high above him, at the lip of the ice sheet itself. Where he could he chose paths free of crevasses and broken surfaces, but he could usually find easier ground near the glacier's edges, hugging the orange rock of the valley down which the glacier poured.

It was difficult going. Sometimes loose snow was whipped up by the wind and driven over the surface, obscuring everything around him up to shoulder height. But, above the snow, the sky was a deep blue.

At last the ice beneath his feet levelled out, and he realised he had reached a plateau.

It was the lip of the ice sheet.

He was standing on a sea of gleaming ice, which shone in every direction he looked, white, blue and green. The ice receded to infinity, flat white under blue sky – but perhaps his poor eyes could make out a shallow dome shape as the ice rose, sweeping away from him towards the east.

It was utterly silent and still, without life of any kind, the only sound the snort of his trunk, the only motion the fog of his breath.

He turned, ponderously, and looked back the way he had come.

This edge of the ice was marked by mountains, heavily eroded and all but buried, and he could see how the glacier spilled between the peaks towards the lower ground. Though locked into the slow passage of time, the glacier was very obviously a dynamic river of ice. Huge parallel bands flowed neatly down the valley's contours. The bands marked the merging of tributaries, smaller ice rivers that flowed into the main stream, each of them keeping the characteristic colour given them by the rock particles they had ground up and carried. Where the glacier reached the lower land it spread out, cracking, making the jumbled surface of crevasses he had struggled to cross.

Everything flowed down from here, down to the west and the lower ground, as if he had climbed to the roof of the world. He was cold, exhausted, hungry and thirsty; and he was still not confident of surviving this immense venture. But, standing here, looking down on the great frozen majesty of the ice cap and its rivers, he felt exhilarated, privileged.

He turned to face the east, ready to go on.

He stepped forward experimentally. The ice was unforgivingly cold, seeming to suck his body heat out through the thick callused pads on his feet. It was harder than any rock he had encountered – but it was not smooth. It was choppy, rippled, like the surface of a lake under the wind. But the ripples were frozen in place, and the footing was, surprisingly, quite secure, thanks to those scalloped ripples.

There is nothing to eat here, he thought dryly. There is no shelter, and if I stay too long I will surely freeze to death. But at least I won't slip up and fall.

He began to walk, and the others followed him. He could feel the ice's flow in his belly, a deep disturbing subsonic murmur as it poured with immense slowness towards the lip.

The cap was one of a string of great domes of ice that littered the northern hemisphere of the planet. At its centre the ice cap was kilometres thick, as humans would have measured it, and the bedrock beneath – ground free of life and locked in darkness – was crushed downwards through many metres.

The dome was fed by fresh falls of snow on its upper surface. The new snow crushed the softer layers beneath, forcing out the air and turning them into hard blue ice. The collapsing centre forced ice at the rim to flow down to lower altitudes, in the form of glaciers that gouged their way through river valleys. Where the ice met open water, it floated off to form immense shelves.

The ice was like a huge, subsiding mass of soft white dung, flattening and flowing, continually replenished from above.

The glaciers' flow was enormously slow – perhaps advancing by a mere mammoth footstep every year. But the ice cap was nevertheless shrinking. Less snow was falling on the ice cap than it was losing to its glaciers and ice shelves. The cap was inevitably disintegrating, though it would take an immense time to disappear.

At first, under blue skies, it was exhilarating to be here. But even from the start the ice cap was not without its dangers.

Once, Longtusk walked over a place where the ice had frozen into a thin crust that seemed to lie on deeper snow. When he took a step the surface settled abruptly. He fell – not far, just enough to startle him. And then the crust around him continued to collapse, the cracks spreading for many paces as the surface settled. The crunching, crackling noise of the ice seemed to circle him. It was eerie, like the actions of a living thing in this place where nothing could live, and he was glad to pass onto firmer ice.

. . . Even the light was strange.

Sometimes, when the sun was low, there were rings and arcs surrounding it, glimmering in the sky, and even false images of the sun to either side of it, or nestling on the horizon. It was like the blurred multiple images Longtusk would sometimes see when his eyes were wind-battered and filled with tears, so that he had to peer at the world through a lens of water.

When the nights were clear they were blue, as the Moon-light was reflected from the ice. Even when there was no Moon, and only stars shone, the nights would still be bright and blue, so powerfully did the ice capture and reflect even the stars' trickle of light.

On the third day the sky clouded over, and a white mist descended.

The light grew bright but soft, the details of the sky and even the ice under his feet blurring. Soon the horizon was invisible and the sky was joined seamlessly to the ground, as if he was walking inside some huge hollowed-out gull's egg. The light was very bright, enough to hurt his eyes, and grey-white floaters drifted like birds across his vision. There was no shadow, no relief, no texture. He could make out the line of mammoths behind him, robust stocky forms labouring across the ice, their heads wreathed in steam. They were the only objects he could see in the whole world, as if they were all floating in clouds, disengaged from the Earth.

But the mist thickened further still. In this sourceless, shadowless light, even footprints were nothing but thin tracings of blue-white against the greater white of the washed-out world, all but impossible to see with his sore and watering eyes.

They endured a day and a night in the mist: a night they spent in utter darkness, huddled together against the wind, trying to ignore their own mounting hunger and thirst and the cold of the huge thickness of ice beneath their feet, which threatened to suck every scrap of warmth from their bodies.

Doubts assailed Longtusk, suspended here in this harsh fog of ice crystals and mist. How could he have imagined that he could lead a party on such an impossible under-taking? He had only a fragment of legend to inspire him – only his memory of the flight of the birds to guide him. And in this white-out fog, even his acute mammoth senses were baffled by the clamour of wind and the creak of ice under his feet.

They were all in distress, Longtusk realised, for mammoths were not built to endure such long treks over such inhospitable terrain without food and water. It was obvious that the journey was taking a heavy toll on poor Splayfoot; she was sinking once more into that ominous half-consciousness from which he feared, one day, she might not have the strength to climb out.

And Rockheart too was suffering. He was more gaunt and bony than ever, his eyes milky and sore, his tusks protruding from the planes of his face like icicles. He had never looked older. But he wasn't feeble yet, as he proved as he propelled Splayfoot forward with a mighty shove of his forehead at her rump.

They continued. They had, after all, no choice.

At last, after another half day, the mist cleared as suddenly as it had descended. The world emerged again, reduced to elementals: a flat white surface under a blue dome, nothing but white and blue and flatness, an empty, stripped-bare land across which the mammoths toiled.

. . .. But the landscape was not quite empty.

The Dreamer Willow walked a little way away from the mammoths, blinking in the sudden glare. He peered into the east, and he pulled a strip of rabbit skin around his eyes to protect them from the sun's glare.

Then he came running to Longtusk, jabbering in his guttural, incomprehensible language, and pointed to the eastern horizon.

Longtusk squinted that way. He could see nothing but a blur where the ice merged with the sky. But that meant little; Willow's eyes, like a Firehead's, were those of a predator, much sharper than any mammoth's.

Nevertheless he felt encouraged, and they pulled forward with increased enthusiasm.

They smelled it before they saw it.

'. . . Water,' said Splayfoot, wondering. 'It smells almost warm.'

Rockheart, wheezing, walking stiffly, had raised his great scarred trunk. 'Growing things. And something else, something sour. Sulphur, perhaps.'

Willow was growing increasingly agitated. His bow legs working, he ran ahead of the mammoths and then back, urging them forward.

And then Longtusk saw it.

The mountains, protruding from the ice, seemed to float between blue sky and white ice. Grey-black scree, shattered by frost, tumbled over pure white glaciers – and, etched sharply against the black mountains, he saw pale green stripes that could only be vegetation.

It was the nunatak.

Heartened, trumpeting with excitement, he hurried forward.

Under his feet, rock began to push out of the ice and its thin covering of snow. The exposed rock was rust brown, the colour of a calf's hair. It was littered with loose snow, which was blown by the prevailing wind into white streaks.

For a time walking became a little easier. But the long, steady climb up the shallow rise added to their efforts, and soon they were all breathing hard, the young Cows trumpeting their dismay.

After a time the land began to descend once more. Longtusk found himself walking down a broad, widening valley that twisted between rounded, icebound hills. The smooth curving profiles of the hills were barely visible, the blue-white of the ice against the duller white of the sky. But here and there the land was sprinkled with fragments of black rock. The rock made it easier to see the shape of the land around him: the sweep of the valley floor, the tight rounded profiles of the hills.

He came to a piece of the black rock, lying in his path. He

nudged it cautiously with his foot. It was frothy, jet black, and sharp-edged – surely sharp enough to cut through the skin of an incautious mammoth's foot or trunk. He trumpeted a warning.

Now they left the hills behind and the valley flattened out into a wide plain. There was more rock here, he saw: dark fragments scattered across the plain, half buried by the ice. Here and there the fragments were piled up in low unstable heaps. It was as if some giant creature had burst from the land itself, scattering these lumps of rock far and wide.

Now the plain of broken rocks gave way to a broader area, smooth flat ice largely free of the rock lumps. Longtusk guessed they were approaching a frozen lake; rock lumps that fell here must have sunk to the bottom of the water and were now hidden beneath the ice layers.

Cautiously they skirted the lake, sticking to the shore.

But the land here was no longer flat. It was broken by vast bowls, like immense footprints – not of ice, Longtusk realised, but carved out of the rock itself, and coated by thin layers of ice and snow. The mammoths were forced to wend their way carefully between these craters, calling to each other when they were out of sight of one another.

Longtusk wondered what savage force had managed to punch these great wounds in the ground. This was, he thought, a strange place indeed, shaped by forces he couldn't even guess at.

At last he came to a place where the ground was bare of snow and ice. He walked forward warily.

The ground was *warm*.

He walked over a gummy brown-grey mud that clung to his footpads; here and there it was streaked orange, yellow, black. The mud was littered with shallow pools of water and rivulets which ran over sticky layers of grey scum. Where snow lay on the ground, he could see how it was melting into the hot pools and streams, folding over in huge complex swathes.

In places the water was so hot it actually boiled, the steam stained a muddy grey by particles of dirt, and there was a sour, claustrophobic stink of sulphur. The steam, curling into the air, formed towers of billows and swirls, pointlessly beautiful. In fact it rose so high it blocked out the sun, like a cloud that reached from the ground to the air, and Longtusk shivered in the reduced light.

He found a place some way from the steaming, active areas. He tasted the water. It was hot – not unpleasantly so – and it tasted sour, acidic. He spat it out.

Nearby was a place where it wasn't water that boiled but mud, grey-brown and thick. The mud had built itself a chimney, thick-walled, that rose halfway to his belly like some monstrous trunk. The steam here was laced with dark grey dust that plastered itself over the walls of the fumarole. The water had bubbled with a high rushing noise, but the slurping mud made a deeper growling sound, like the agitated rumbling of old Bull mammoths arguing over some obscure point of pride.

. . . And there was life here.

Lichen and moss clung to the bare rock, and grass, brown and flattened, struggled to survive in swathes over ground streaked yellow by sulphur. The plants were coated with layers of ice – frosted out of the steaming, moisture-laden air – as if the plants themselves were made of ice crystals.

Curiously he reached down and plucked some of the frozen scrub. The ice crumbled away, revealing thin, brittle plant material within; he crushed it with his trunk until it was soft enough to cram into his mouth. It was thin on his tongue, but nourishing.

His heart pulsed with hope and vindication. It was a harsh, unnatural place, he thought, a place of steamy claustrophobic heat and rushing noise in the middle of the stillness of this perpetual winter – *but this was the nunatak*, just as Thunder's legend had promised. He trumpeted in triumph—

But somebody was calling.

Rockheart had fallen. The Cows had clustered around him, while Threetusk and Willow stood to one side, awkward, distressed.

Longtusk hurried down the slope.

Rockheart had slumped to his knees, and his trunk drooped on the muddy ground. His breath was a rattle.

'Rockheart! What happened? Why did you fall?'

His rumbled reply was as soft as a calf's mewling. 'We made it, milk-tusk, didn't we? By Kilukpuk's dugs, you were right . . .'

And Longtusk saw it. Rockheart – understanding that Longtusk would need his experience, knowing he was too weak for the trip – had come anyway, burning up the last of his energy. He had driven the others on until they had reached this island of rocky safety.

And now he could rest at last.

Convulsed by guilt, Longtusk picked up Rockheart's trunk. 'Rockheart! You mustn't – not *now*—'

But it was too late. Rockheart's last breath bubbled out of his lungs, and he slumped to the warm rock, lifeless.

Longtusk trumpeted his grief, and his voice echoed from the rocky walls of the nunatak.

CHAPTER 4
THE NUNATAK

It was a fine bright spring morning, one of the first after the long winter. The nunatak was a bowl of black rock and green life under a blue-white sky.

Everywhere mammoths grazed.

Longtusk was working on his favourite patch of willow, which grew in the lee of a pile of sharp-edged volcanic boulders. The adults knew he favoured this spot, and left the miniature forest for him.

But the calves were another matter.

The calf called Saxifrage was playing with her mother, Horsetail, Longtusk's niece. Horsetail lay on her side, her trunk flopping, while Saxifrage tried to clamber onto her flank, pulling herself up by grasping the long fur of her mother's belly.

When she spotted Lungtusk, Saxifrage gave up her game, jumped off and approached the old tusker.

But her attention was distracted by a length of broken tusk, snapped off by some young male in an over-vigorous fight. Perhaps she had never come across such a thing before. She picked it up and began to inspect it. She grabbed it with her trunk, turned it over, and rubbed it against the underside of her trunk, making a rasping sound against the rough skin there. She put it in her mouth, chewed it carefully, and turned it over with her tongue. Then she threw it in the air and let it fall to the ground several times, listening intently to the way it rattled on the ground. At last she walked over it and touched it delicately with the tender soles of her hind feet.

Longtusk was entranced.

He couldn't help contrast the calf's deep physical exploration of the unfamiliar object with the way a Firehead cub would study something new – just *looking* at it. For a mammoth calf, the look of something was only the most superficial aspect of it: the beginning of getting to know the object, not the end.

Longtusk rumbled softly. Even after so long in the nunatak, such behaviour still charmed and fascinated him. He'd spent too much of his life away from his own kind, he thought sadly, and that had left scars on his soul that would never, surely, be healed. He wondered if there was anything more important in the world than to watch a new-born calf with her mother, lapping at a stream with her tongue, too young even to know how to use her trunk to suck up water . . .

Now Saxifrage recalled he was there. She abandoned the tusk fragment and ran to him, dashing under his belly.

He tried to turn, but his legs were stiff as tree-trunks nowadays, his great tusks so heavy they made his head droop if he wasn't careful; and in his rheumy vision the calf was just a blur of orange-brown fur, running around his feet and under his grizzled belly hair.

As the calf made another pass he looped down his trunk, grabbed her around the waist and lifted her high in the air, ignoring the protests from his neck muscles. She trumpeted her delight, a thin noise just at the edge of his hearing.

He set her down before him once more, and she stepped through the forest of his curling tusks. Her calf fur was orange, bright against his own guard hairs, blackened and grey with age.

She said, 'Longtusk, I'm going to be your mate.'

He snorted. 'I'd be impressed if I hadn't heard you say the same thing to that old buffer Threetusk yesterday.'

'I didn't! Anyway I didn't mean it. Why do they call him

Threetusk? He only has two tusks, a big one and that spindly little one.'

'Well, that's a long story,' said Longtusk. 'You see, long ago – long before you were born, even before Threetusk became the leader of the bachelor herd, in fact – he got in an argument with one of his sons, called Barktrunk—'

'Why was he called that?'

'It doesn't matter.'

'Where is Barktrunk? I never met him.'

'Well, he died. That was before you were born too. But *that's* another story. You see, the first time Barktrunk came into musth—'

'What does musth mean?'

Longtusk growled. 'Ask your mother. Now, where was I? Barktrunk. Now Barktrunk did some digging – just over there, where those rocks are piled up – and he found a new spring of water, and he said we should all drink it at once. He wanted to show us how important and clever he was, you see. Especially the Cows.'

'Why the Cows?'

'Ask your mother! Anyway – what was I saying? – yes, the water. But Threetusk, his father, came over and tasted a little of the water, just on the tip of his trunk, and he said no, this water has too much sulphur. He said so to everybody, right in front of Barktrunk.'

'I bet Barktrunk didn't like *that*.'

'He didn't. And they got into a fight. Now in those days Threetusk was big and strong, not the broken-down grass-sucking old wreck he is *now*, and you can tell him I said so. It should have been easy for Threetusk to win. But there was an accident. Barktrunk came at him like this' – he feinted stiffly – 'but Threetusk dodged, and knocked his head like *this*' – a deft sideways swipe, but slower than a glacier, he thought sourly – 'and that was when it happened. Three-tusk got one of his tusks stuck in a cleft in the rock. Just over there. When he was trying to get free the tusk broke off.

Maybe that was one of the bits of it you were playing with just now. And then—'

But Saxifrage was running around in circles, trying to catch her own tail. Longtusk rumbled softly; he had lost his audience again.

'You listen to Longtusk,' said Horsetail, Saxifrage's mother, who had come lumbering up. Named for the long graceful hairs that streamed across her rump, this daughter of Splayfoot was the Matriarch now – she had been since Splayfoot's sad death, some years ago, when Longtusk's sister's proud heart, strained by her dismal experiences, had at last failed her. Horsetail pulled her calf under her belly fur, where Saxifrage began to hunt for a nipple. 'I'm sorry, Patriarch,' she said respectfully. 'Everybody knows you need time to work on those willow leaves these days.'

'Not that much time,' he growled. 'And I do wish—'

'Try not to bite, Saxifrage!'

I do wish *you'd* listen to me, he thought.

But, thinking back, he was sure *he* had ignored almost all of what everybody had had to say to him, back when he was a calf – even Walks With Thunder, probably.

Remarkable to think that the last time he saw him, Thunder had actually been younger than Longtusk was now. How on Earth had he got so old? Where had the years gone? And . . .

And he was maundering again, and now the calf was nipping at his toes.

Saxifrage said, 'Longtusk is going to mate with me when I'm old enough.'

Horsetail rumbled her embarrassment, flapping her small ears.

Longtusk said, 'I'm flattered, Saxifrage. But you'll have to find someone closer to your own age, that's all.'

'Why? Mother says you're a great hero and will go on for ever, like the rocks of the nunatak.'

Again Horsetail harrumphed her embarrassment.

'Your mother's right about most of that,' said Longtusk wryly. 'But – not forever. Look.' He kneeled down before the calf, ignoring warning stabs of pain from his knees, and opened his mouth. 'What's in here?'

Saxifrage probed with her trunk at his teeth and huge leathery tongue. 'Grass. A bit of old twig stuck under your tongue—'

'My teeth, calf,' he growled. 'Feel my teeth.'

She reached in, and he felt the soft tip of her trunk run over the upper surfaces of his long lower teeth.

He said, 'Can you feel how worn they are? That's because of all the grass and herbs and twigs I've eaten.'

'Everybody's teeth get worn down,' said Saxifrage, wrinkling her trunk. 'You just grow more. My mother says—'

'But,' said Longtusk heavily, 'I've gotten so old I don't have more teeth to grow. This is my last set. Soon they will be too worn to eat with. And then . . .'

The calf looked confused and distressed. He reached out and stroked the topknot of her scalp with his trunk.

She said, 'Will you at least *try* to keep from dying until I'm big enough? I wouldn't have thought *that* was too much to ask.'

Longtusk eyed Saxifrage; that was one of her favourite admonitions, he knew. 'All right,' he said. 'I'll try. Just for you.'

'Now come on,' said Horsetail, tugging at her calf's trunk. 'Time for a drink. And you really mustn't bother the Patriarch so much.'

'I told you,' he said. 'She wasn't bothering me. And don't call me Patriarch. I'm just an old fool of a Bull. That Patriarch business was long ago . . .'

But Horsetail was leading her calf to a stream which bubbled from the rocks; a group of mammoths was already clustered there, their loosening winter coats rising in a cloud around them. 'Whatever you say, Patriarch.'

Longtusk growled.

Now there was a tug at his belly furs. He turned, wondering which calf was troubling his repose now.

It was the old Dreamer, Willow. Standing there in his much-patched skins, with grass crudely stuffed into his coat and hat, Willow was aged, bent almost double, his small face a mask of wrinkles. But, with a gnarled paw, he still stroked Longtusk's trunk, just as he had when they'd first met as calf and cub.

And Longtusk knew what he wanted.

Longtusk turned slowly, sniffing the air. After all these years he had learned to disregard the pervading stink of sulphur which polluted the air around this nunatak. There was little wind, and though there was a frosty sharpness to the air, there was no sign that the weather was set to change.

All in all, it was a fine day for their annual trek.

Rumbling softly, with Willow limping at his side, Longtusk set off.

Longtusk climbed a shallow rise, away from the glen where the mammoths fed. At first he walked on soil or rock, but soon his feet were pressing down on ice and loose snow.

The going got harder, the slope steepening.

At first Willow was able to keep up, limping alongside the mammoth with one paw wrapped in Longtusk's belly hair. But soon his wheezing exhaustion was obvious.

They paused for breath. Longtusk turned, looking back over the nunatak and the life sheltered there.

From afar, the mammoths were a slow drift of dark points over a field of tan grasses. Occasionally the long guard hairs of a mature Bull would catch the light, glimmering brightly. Their movements were slow, calm, dense, their attitudes full of attention. They were massive, contemplative, wise: beautiful, he thought, wonderful beautiful animals.

The nunatak was everything he could have hoped for, that fateful day when he took his leave of his own Family. But still—

But still, how brief life had been. Like a dream, or the blossoming of a spring flower on the steppe – a splash of colour, a burst of hope, and then . . .

Willow stroked his trunk absently, bringing him back.

He'd been maundering again. Morbid old fool.

With considerable effort on both their parts, Willow managed to clamber onto his back. Longtusk couldn't help but recall the liquid grace with which Crocus, the Firehead cub, had once flowed onto his back, how they had run and pranced together.

With a deep rumble he turned away and headed up the cold, forbidding slope. His breath steamed, and his ageing limbs tired quickly.

The old Dreamer was already snoring gently.

Soon Longtusk neared the crest of a ridge. The snow thinned out, and he found himself walking on rock that was bare or covered only by a scattering of snow. The land flattened out, and he stood atop the ridge, breathing hard.

He was standing on the rim of a crater.

He stepped forward cautiously. It was a great bowl, cut into the Earth, like the imprint of an immense foot. The rim curved around the huge dip in the land to close on itself, a neat circle.

The crater wall, coated with snow and ice, was sculpted to smoothness by the wind, like the sweep of a giant sand dune. The shadows were subtle and soft, white shading to blue-grey – save at the rim itself, where a layer of bare brown rock was exposed. The winds off the ice sheet kept this curving ridge swept clear of new snow falls, so that ice could not form. He let his eye be drawn to the crater's far side, where there had been an avalanche, and the smooth snow surface was marked by great ripples descending towards the crater's base.

The floor of the crater was surprisingly flat. He knew there was a lake down there. In the brief summer it would melt, turning into a placid pond of blue-grey water, cupped by the crater, visited by birds – in fact, the geese who had guided him here to the nunatak. If a mammoth were down there now, walking across that frozen surface, she would look no larger than a grain of sand, dwarfed by this immense structure of rock and ice.

Longtusk raised his trunk and trumpeted, high and thin. His voice echoed from the iced-over walls of the crater, and pealed out over the frozen lands around the nunatak.

Willow stirred on his back, grumbling, and subsided back to sleep, clinging to Longtusk's fur instinctively.

Longtusk walked a little further around the crater's rim. He came to a broad ridge in the icebound land, leading away from the crater. He walked this way now, feeling for the firm places in the piled-up snow.

Soon he saw what he was looking for. It was a splash of coal-black darkness, vivid against the snow that surrounded it. This was another crater, but little more than ten or fifteen paces wide. And further craters lay beyond, dark splashes on the snow, as if some wounded, rocky giant had limped this way.

He let himself slide over crunching rubble into the small crater. The rock was warm under his thick footpads. Where snow fell from his coat it melted quickly, and steam wisped up around him. The rock here was fragmented, crumbled. It was jet black, sharp-edged, and the fragments he picked up had tiny bubbles blown into them, like the bones of a mammoth's skull.

This crater did not have a neat rounded form, no cupped lake in its base. Its walls were just crude piles of frothy black rock. In places he could see flat plates of rock which lay over drained hollows, like the remnants of broken eggs. Everything was sharp-edged, new. This small crater was obviously much younger than its giant cousin nearby. Perhaps these small frothy rocks, frozen fragments of the Earth's chthonic blood, were the youngest rocks in the world.

And yet even in this new raw place, there was life.

He picked up a loose rock. He tasted moss and green lichen, struggling to inhabit this unpromising lump: sparse, nothing but dark green flecks that clung to the porous stuff – but it was here. And these first colonists would break up the hard cooling rock, making a sand in which plants could grow. Perhaps one day this would be a bowl of greenery within which mammoths and other animals could survive.

He came up here once a year – but always with Willow as his sole companion. Mammoths are creatures of the plains, and the members of his little Clan were suspicious of this place of hills and ice. And there wasn't a great deal to eat up here. But Longtusk embraced the stark, silent beauty of this place.

For he knew that these craters were a sign of Earth's bounty – the gift that had created this island of life and safety, here at the heart of the forbidding ice cap.

One night – many years ago – the mammoths had seen, on the fringe of their nunatak, a great gush of smoke and fire which had towered up to the clouds. The mammoths had been terrified – all but Longtusk, who had been fascinated. For at last he understood.

Over most of the world, the heat which drove life came from the sun. But here, far to the planet's north, that heat was insufficient. Even water froze here, making the ice caps that stifled the land.

Instead, here in the nunatak, the heat came from the Earth itself.

In some places it dribbled slowly from the ground, in boiling springs and mud pools. And in some places the heat gathered until it burst through the Earth's skin like a gorged parasite.

That was the meaning of the great eruption of fire and smoke they had seen. That was why the land was littered by enormous blocks of black rock, hurled there by explosions.

And the craters – even the biggest of them – were surely

the wounds left in the Earth by those giant explosions, like scars left by burst blisters. In this small crater he could actually see where smaller bubbles had formed and partially collapsed, leaving a hard skin over voids drained of rock that had been so hot it had flowed like water.

It was the Earth's heat which had shaped this strange landscape, and it was the Earth's heat which cradled and sustained the nunatak.

He left the small craters behind and began a short climb to another summit.

Soon he was breathing hard. But he'd been climbing up here every spring since they'd first arrived, and he was determined that *this* would not be the year he was finally defeated.

He reached the summit. This rocky height, windswept bare of ice like the crater rim, was one of the highest points in the nunatak, so high it seemed he could see the curve of the Earth itself.

All around the nunatak was ice.

The ice cap was a broad, vast dome of blue-white, blanketing the land. The ice was smooth and empty, as if inviting a footstep. Nothing moved there, no animals or plants lived, and he was suspended in utter silence, broken not even by the cry of a bird.

Mountains protruded from the ice sheet like buried creatures straining to emerge, their profiles softened by the overlying snow. The mountains – a chain of which this nunatak was a member – were brown and black, startling and stark against the white of the ice. Their shadows, pooled at their bases, glowed blue-white.

Over the years Longtusk had come to know the ice and its changing moods. He had learned that it was not without texture; it was rich with a chill, minimal beauty. There were low dunes and ridges, carved criss-cross by the wind, so that the ice was a complex carpet of blue-white traceries, full of irrelevant beauty. In places it had slumped into dips in the crushed land beneath, and there were ridges, long and straight, that caught the low light so that they shone a bright yellow, vivid against blue-white. Here and there he could see spindrift, clouds of ice crystals whipped up by the wind and hovering above the ground, enchantingly beautiful.

The ice was a calm flat sea of light, white and blue and yellow, that led his gaze to the horizon. The ice had a beauty and softness that belied its lethal nature, he knew; for nothing lived there, nothing outside the favoured nunatak.

But much had changed in the years – by Kilukpuk's dugs, it had been forty years or more – that he had been climbing this peak.

To the west he looked back the way they had come on their epic trek, so long ago: back across the fragile neck of land that connected the two continental landmasses. On the land bridge's northern side there was a vast, glimmering expanse of water, dark against the ice. It was where he recalled the ice-dammed lake had been.

But that lake had grown immeasurably – it was so large now it must have become an inlet of the great northern ocean itself.

Ice was melting into the oceans and the sea level was rising, as if the whole ocean were no more than a steppe pond, brimming with spring water. And the ocean was, little by little, flooding the land.

Meanwhile, on the southern horizon, there was brown and green against the ice white: a tide of warmth and life that had approached relentlessly, year by year. The exposed land formed a broad dark corridor that led off to the south – and into the new land, the huge, unknown continent that lay there – a passageway between two giant, shrinking ice sheets.

The world was remaking itself – the land reborn from the ice, the sea covering the land – all in his lifetime. It was a huge, remarkable process, stunning in scale.

And he knew that the changes he saw around him would one day have great significance for his little Clan.

He had long stepped back from his role as Patriarch. There had never before been a Patriarch in all the Cycle's long history, and he had never believed there should be one for longer than strictly necessary.

So he was no longer a leader of the Clan. Still, he had travelled further and seen more than any of the mammoths here on the nunatak.

And he knew that this nunatak would not always remain a refuge.

Sometimes he wished he had someone to discuss all this with. Somebody like Rockheart, or Walks With Thunder – even Jaw Like Rock.

But they were all gone, long gone. And Longtusk, always the outsider, now isolated by age, was forced to rely on nothing but his own experience and wisdom.

. . . Willow, on his back, was growing agitated. He was muttering something in his incomprehensible, guttural tongue. He leaned forward, over Longtusk's scalp, and pointed far to the west.

Longtusk raised his trunk, but could smell nothing on the dry air but the cold prickle of ice. He squinted, feeling the wrinkles gather around his eye sockets.

On the far horizon, he saw something new.

It was a line scratched across the ice. It ended in a complex knot, dark and massive yet dwarfed by the ice cap. And a thin thread rose up from that knot of activity, straight and true.

It was too far away to smell. But there was no doubt. *It was smoke*: smoke from a fire. And the line that cut across the ice was a trail, arrowing directly towards the nunatak.

On his back, Willow was whimpering his alarm – as well he might, Longtusk thought.

For the signs were unmistakable. After all these years, the Fireheads were coming.

As the sun sank deeper in the sky, the light on the ice grew softer, low and diffuse. Blue-grey shadows pooled in hollows, like liquid. It was stunning, beautiful. But Longtusk knew that this year he could not stay to see the sunset.

The nunatak's long dream of peace was, so quickly, coming to an end.

He turned and, with elaborate care, began his descent from the summit.

'We have no choice but to abandon the nunatak.' He looked down at the Family – the fat, complacent Cows, their playful calves, all gazing up at him, trunks raised to sniff his mood. 'We have been safe here. The nunatak has served us well. But now it is a refuge no more. And we must go.'

'You're being ridiculous,' Horsetail said severely. 'You're frightening the calves.'

'They should be frightened,' he said. 'They are in danger. Mortal danger. The Fireheads are on the western horizon. I could see their trail, and their fire. They will overrun this place, enslave you, ultimately kill you. And your calves.' He eyed them. 'Do you understand? Do you understand any of this?'

The Cows rumbled questions. 'Where should we go?' 'There is nowhere else!' 'Who is *he* to say what Cows should do? He is a Bull. And he's *old*. Why, if I—'

He had expected arguments, and he got them. It was just as it had been when he had argued with Milkbreath, his own mother, trying to convince her that the flight in search of the nunatak was necessary.

He was too old for this.

One more effort, Longtusk. Then you can rest. Think of Rockheart. *He* had kept going, despite the failure of his huge body. He pulled his shoulders square and lifted his tusks, still large and sweeping, so heavy they made his neck muscles pull.

Horsetail, the Matriarch, said sadly, 'I'm trying to understand, Longtusk. I truly am. But you must help me. *How* can they come here? We are protected by the ice.'

'But the ice is receding.'

'Where would we flee?'

'You must go south and east. At first you will cross the ice' – a rumbling of fear and discontent – 'just as your grandmothers did. Just as *I* did. But then you will reach a corridor. A passage through the ice sheets, to the warmer lands beyond, that has opened up in the years we have lived here. It won't be easy—'

'But Longtusk, *why*? Why would the Fireheads come here? On this rock, we are few. Even if these Fireheads are the savage predators you describe, why would they go to such efforts, risk their own lives, just to reach *us*?'

Now Threetusk, dominant Bull of the bachelor herd, loped towards Longtusk. He said grimly, 'Perhaps the Fireheads come because there is no room for them in the old lands. Perhaps they are seeking mammoths here because there are none left where they come from.'

There was a general bray of horror.

'Or perhaps,' Longtusk said sadly, '*it is me.*'

Horsetail rumbled, 'What do you mean?'

'I defied her,' he said, unwelcome old memories swimming to the surface of his mind.

'Who?'

'The most powerful Firehead of them all. She thought I was hers, you see. And yet I defied her . . .'

He knew it was hard for them to understand. All this was ancient history to the other mammoths, an exotic legend of times and places and creatures they had never known – maybe just another of Longtusk's tall stories, like his tales of she-cats and rhinos and Fireheads with caps of mammoth-ivory beads . . .

It was not their fault. He had wanted to bring his Clan to a safe place, and these generations of fat, complacent mammoths were what he had dreamed of seeing. It wasn't *their* fault that he had succeeded too well – that their lives of comfort and security had prepared them so badly for the ordeal ahead.

But he recalled Crocus.

He recalled how she had hunted down the Firehead who had killed her father. He knew she would not have forgotten, or forgiven.

As long as he was alive, nobody was safe here.

Horsetail and Threetusk approached him and spoke quietly so the others couldn't hear.

Horsetail said, 'You aren't the only one who has seen the corridor to the south. But it is harsh, and we don't know how long it is, or what lies at its end. Perhaps it is cold and barren all the way to the South Pole.'

'When we set off for the nunatak,' he said evenly, 'we didn't know how far that was either. We went anyway. *You* know, Threetusk – you're the only one left who does. You will have to show them how to survive.'

Horsetail said severely, 'We have old, and sickly, and calves. Many of us will not survive such a trek.'

'Nevertheless it must be made.'

'And you?' asked the Matriarch. 'Do you believe *you* could walk through the corridor?'

'Of course not.' He brayed his amusement. 'I probably wouldn't last a day. But I'm not going.'

Threetusk said, 'What?'

Briefly, briskly, he stroked their trunks. 'I know the Fireheads. And I have thought deeply on their nature. And this is what I have concluded. Listen closely, now . . .'

Saxifrage watched this, fascinated, the rumbling phrases washing over her.

Later, boldly, she stepped forward from under her mother's belly and tugged her trunk. 'What did he say? What did he say?'

But Horsetail, grave and silent, would not reply.

*

They filed past him, down the sloping rock face and onto the ice, bundles of confusion, fear and resentment – much of it directed at *him*, for even though the smoke columns from the Fireheads' hearths were now visible for all to see, they still found it impossible to believe they represented the danger he insisted.

Nonetheless, these mammoths were his Clan. He wanted to grab them all, taste each one with his trunk. For he knew he would not see them again, not a single one of them.

But he held himself back. It was best they did not think of him; the ice and the dismal corridor to the south would give them more than enough to occupy their minds.

And besides, he still had company: the little Dreamer, Willow. He had tried to push the Dreamer, gently, off the rock and after the column of mammoths. But Willow had slapped his trunk and dug his old, bent fingers in Longtusk's fur, his intentions clear.

Company, then. And a job to complete.

Longtusk waited until the long column of mammoths had shrunk to a fine scratch against the huge white expanse of the ice.

And then he turned away: towards the west, and the Fireheads.

CHAPTER 5
THE CORRIDOR

It was, Threetusk decided later, an epic to match any in the long history of the mammoths.

But it was a story he could never bear to tell: a story of suffering and loss and endless endurance, a blurred time he recalled only with pain.

It was difficult even from the beginning. Away from the warmth of the nunatak, the hard, ridged ice was cold and unyielding under their feet – crueller even than he recalled from the original trek so long ago. Where snow drifted the going was even harder.

The land itself was unsettling. The mammoths could hear the deep groaning of the ice as it flowed down from its highest points to the low land and the sea. A human would have heard only the occasional crack and grind, perhaps felt a deep shudder. To the mammoths, the agonised roar of the ice was loud and continuous, a constant reminder that this was an unstable land, a place of change and danger.

And – of course – there was nothing to eat or drink, here on the ice. They had barely travelled half a day before they had used up the reserves of water they carried in their throats, and the calves were crying for the warm rocks they had left behind.

But they kept on.

After a day and a night, they came to a high point, and they were able to see the way south.

To the left the ice was a shallow dome, its surface bright and seductively smooth. To the right, the ice lay thick over a mountain range. Black jagged peaks thrust out of the white,

defiant, and glaciers striped with dirt reached down to the
ice sheet like the trunks of immense embedded animals.

And the two great ice sheets were separated by a narrow
band of land – colourless, barren, a stripe of lifeless grey
cutting through blue-white.

It was the corridor.

They found a glacier, a tongue of ice that led them down
from the ice cap to the barren strip of land. The climb down
the glacier was more difficult than Threetusk had imagined
– especially when they got to the lower slopes, and the
glacier, spilling onto the rock, spread out and cracked,
forming immense crevasses that blocked their path.

Nevertheless they persisted, until they reached the land
itself.

Horsetail stood by Threetusk, frost on her face, her breath
billowing in a cloud around her. They gazed south at the
corridor that faced them.

They stood on bare rock, sprinkled with a little loose stone,
gravel and rock. There were deep furrows gouged into the
land, as if by huge claws. Here and there, against the ice cliffs
that bounded the corridor, there were pools of trapped meltwater, glimmering. Little grew here: only scattered clumps
of yellow grass, a single low willow, clutching the ground.

A wind blew in their faces, raising dust devils that whirled
and spat hard grey sand into their eyes. Saxifrage, the calf,
plucked at a spindly grass blade without enthusiasm, bleating her discomfort.

Threetusk said, 'It's as if the land has been scraped bare of
everything – even the soil – down to the bedrock. There
may be water, but little to eat.'

'The calves are probably too fat, as Longtusk always says,'
Horsetail said briskly. 'We'll let them rest a night. There is
some shelter, here in the lee of the glacier. Then, in the
morning—'

'We go on.'

'Yes.'

*

Longtusk had a single intention: not to allow the Fireheads to complete their journey, in pursuit of his mammoths, across the land bridge. And he believed he knew how to do it, where he must go to achieve it.

With Willow on his back snoring softly, Longtusk, with stiff arthritic limbs, picked his cautious way down off the nunatak rocks. He took a final, regretful step off the warmth of the black rock, and let his footpads settle on hard ice.

It would begin as a retracing of the great trek which had brought him here.

. . . But everything was different now.

The ice was, in places, slick with a thin layer of liquid water, making it slippery and treacherous, so that he had to choose his steps with care. And there seemed to have been a fresh frost overnight; ice crystals sparkled like tiny eyes on the blue surface of the hard older ice.

The nunatak receded behind him, becoming a hard black cone of rock, diminishing. It was as if he was leaving behind his life: his ambiguous position in the small society of the Clan, his prickly relationships with Threetusk, Horsetail and the others, the endless complexity of love and birth and death. Not for much longer would he have to carry around his heavy load of pain and loss and memory.

His life had reduced, at last, to its essence.

Soon – much sooner than he had expected – he found himself clambering down a snub of ice and onto bare rock.

He walked cautiously over rock that had been chiselled and scoured by the retreating ice. Beyond the edge of the cap itself the ice still clung in patches. But it was obvious that the ice's shrinking had proceeded apace.

He found a run-off stream. It bubbled over shallow mud, cloudy with rock flour. He walked into the brook. It barely lapped over his toes. He drank trunkfuls of the chill, sterile meltwater; it filled his belly and throat.

The water had cut miniature valleys in the flat surface of the mud. The gouges cut across each other, their muddy walls eroded away, so that the incised mud was braided with shallow clefts. Here and there a patch of ground stuck out of the stream, perhaps sheltered by a lump of rock. These tiny islands were shaped like tear-drops, their walls eroded by the continuing flow, and grasses, thin and yellow, clung to their surfaces. Longtusk found himself intrigued by the unexpected complexity of this scrap of landscape. Like so much of the world, it was intricate, beautiful – but meaningless, for there were no eyes but his to see it.

He moved on. His feet left shallow craters in the mud; downstream of where he had stood the water, bubbling, began to carve a fresh pattern of channels.

Soon he reached a new kind of landscape. It was an open forest, with evergreen trees growing in isolated clumps, and swathes of grass in between.

He let down Willow. With brisk efficiency, the Dreamer built and set simple traps of sharpened sticks and sinew. One of the traps quickly yielded a small rabbit. The Dreamer skinned it, cooked it over a small fire, ate it with every expression of enjoyment – and then, in the warmth of the afternoon, lay down and began to snore loudly.

Longtusk explored.

The trees were spruce, fir and pines, growing healthy, straight and tall. Further to the south he saw hardwoods, oak and elm and ash. There was sagebrush abundant in the grassy patches between the trees. The air was too warm for Longtusk, and he sought out snow and loose ice to chew and swallow and rub into his fur; the melting snow in his belly cooled him, and bits of ice trapped in his fur evaporated slowly, acting like sweat.

It was not long before he detected the thin scent of water: a great body of it, not much further to the west. Birds wheeled overhead, some of them gulls. And that water smell was tinged with the sharpness of salt.

It was the meltwater lake he had seen from the nunatak's summit: still dammed by its plug of ice, now joined to the ocean, grown immeasurably since he had passed by on his original trek to the nunatak. And it was his destination.

He walked back into the forest, through the shade of the young, proud trees. He saw spoor, of horses and bison and other animals. Perhaps the warmth, and the abundance of life here, had something to do with the nearness of that body of water.

But it was no place for mammoths, and the other creatures of the steppe. He felt a huge sadness, for a world was evaporating.

After a night's rest, they moved on.

The Clan walked between divergent walls of ice.

The twin ice caps were lines of white on the horizon. Sometimes they were too far away to see – but they could always be heard, groaning as if in pain at their endless collapse and crumbling.

The wind gathered strength, always coming from the south, howling in their faces, as if daring them to progress. Even if it was the ice that had made this place barren, it was the wind that kept it so; any soil which formed was whipped away in a cloud of dust, and only the hardiest plants could find root and cling to the rock.

The ground changed constantly. Where soil and dirt collected in hollows, protected from the wind, the surface was boggy and clinging. At times they had to cross islands of ice, left behind by the retreating ice caps and yet to melt. Worse, there were stretches of stagnant ice covered over by a thin crust of detritus, a crust which could conceal pits and crevasses where the underlying ice had melted and drained away.

The going became harder still.

Now they seemed to be descending a shallow slope, as if the whole land inclined to the south. The rock was cut through by valleys – some no more than narrow gullies, and some respectably large channels. Sometimes there were torrents of water, gushing down one valley or another, often carving a new course altogether. Threetusk didn't understand where these sudden floods came from; perhaps some dam of ice had burst, or a river valley's wall had been breached.

Where they could, the mammoths followed the broader valleys. But more often than not the valleys cut across their path, and they were forced to spend energy climbing over sharp-crested ridges.

Soon all the mammoths were exhausted, and several were weakening. They had plenty to drink now, but never enough to eat. Still the wind blew, harsh and fierce.

And then the first calf died.

He was a Bull, small and playful, younger than Saxifrage. He simply fell one day, his papery flesh showing the bones beneath, his eyes round and terrified.

'I have no milk!' his mother wailed. 'It's my fault. I have no milk to give him . . .'

'We have to leave him,' Threetusk said grimly to the Matriarch.

'I know,' said Horsetail. 'But after this it will be harder to keep them together. Already the Cows with small calves want to strike out alone, to find pasture they don't need to share with the others.'

'That's natural. It's what mothers do.'

'We must wait until the calf dies,' she said. 'His mother needs to Remember him. And then we go on.'

'Yes.'

After that, more deaths followed: calves, the old, and one mature Bull whose leg was crushed in a fall.

Each day the sun climbed lower in the sky. Threetusk knew the summer was ending, and if they couldn't feed and water in preparation for the cold to come, winter would kill them all as surely as any Firehead.

And still the mammoths walked on into the teeth of the unrelenting wind, leaving a trail of their dead on the unmarked land.

The land began to rise – gently at first, then more steeply. The grass-covered soil grew thin, until at last a shoulder of rock protruded, bare and forbidding. Still Longtusk climbed, the air growing colder. He stepped with caution up the steepening slopes, avoiding heaps of sharp, frost-shattered scree.

He recalled this place from the trek. He had reached the range of low, glacier-eroded hills which marked the southern border of the ice-melt lake. And as he climbed, the land opened up around him, and he saw the great ice dam before him, lodged in its cleft in the hillside – still containing its mass of meltwater, after all these years.

To his right, to the north, he saw the lake itself – much bigger than he recalled, a shining sheet of grey-blue water stretching to a perfectly sharp horizon. There was ice scattered on it, floes and slushy melt and even a few eroded-smooth icebergs. But the ice cap which had first created this lake was much receded now.

The water lapped at a shallow shore of gravel and bare rock, and he saw birds, coons and ducks, swimming among reeds. There were gulls nesting in the steeper cliffs below him. And he could smell the tang of salt, much more strongly now. The northern ocean, which ran all the way to the pole itself, must have broken in on this lake, turning it into an immense pool of brine, an inlet of the ocean itself.

To his left – to the south of the hills – the land swept away. It was a rough plain, marked here and there by the sky-blue glimmer of pools and the glaring bone-white of old ice. Far away he could see a flowing dark patch, clouded by dust, that might be horses or bison. If he listened closely he could hear the thunder of hooves, feel the heavy stamp of that moving ocean of meat.

But this blanket of life – grown much thicker since the last time he passed here – did not conceal the deeper rocky truth of this landscape. He could see how the land was folded, wrinkled, cut deeply by channels and gorges. Most of these channels were dry, though thin ribbons of water gleamed in some of them. They flowed south, away from the lake-ocean behind him, and in places they cut across each other, braided like tangled hair.

It was a land shaped by running water – just like the muddy rivulet where he had drunk. But no rivulet had made this land, not even a great river; only the mightiest of floods could have shaped this immense panorama.

He turned back and forth, trunk raised, sniffing the air, understanding the land.

He knew what he must do here. And he knew, at last, how he would die.

He set off for the ice dam itself.

'. . . Threetusk.'

He paused, lifting bleary, wind-scarred eyes. The wind had eased, for the first time in – how long?

He raised his trunk and looked back at the column of mammoths, wearily trudging in his footsteps. They had been walking over a rocky plateau that had been even more barren and unforgiving than the rest of the corridor. Had they lost anyone else since he last counted? But he couldn't even recall the names of those who had fallen . . .

Horsetail was pulling at his trunk. He saw how thin she had become, the bones of her skull pushing through tangled fur.

But she was saying, 'Threetusk – *smell*.'

Wearily he raised his trunk and sniffed the air.

There was water, and grass, and the dung of many animals.

They blundered forward.

They came to a ridge. He stepped forward cautiously.

The land fell away before him, a steep wall of tumbled rocks. To his left, a waterfall thundered. It was glacier melt: the ghost of snows that might have fallen a Great-Year ago, now surging into the land below.

And that land, he saw, was green.

Pools glimmered in the light of the low sun. He saw clouds of birds over some of the pools, so far away they might have been insects. The land around the pools, laced by gleaming streams, was steppe: coarse grass, herbs, lichen, moss, stunted trees.

And there were animals here, he saw dimly: horses, what looked like camels – and, stalking a stray camel, a pack of what appeared to be giant wolves.

'We made it,' he said, wondering. 'The end of the corridor. We had to battle through the breath of Kilukpuk herself. But we made it. We have to tell Longtusk – tell him he was right.'

Horsetail looked at him sadly. 'Where Longtusk has gone, I don't think even a contact rumble would reach him.' She sniffed at the ground, probing with her trunk. 'We need to find a way down from here . . .'

Threetusk looked back, troubled. The journey had been so hard that it had been some time since he had thought of the defiant old tusker they had left behind.

What *had* become of Longtusk?

CHAPTER 6
THE TEARS OF KILUKPUK

Cautiously, Longtusk walked forward onto the ice dam. In places the ice, melting, had formed shallow pools; some of these were crusted over, and more than once a careless step plunged his foot into cold, gritty water.

He reached the centre of this wall of ice, where it was thinnest – and weakest.

The ice dam was old.

On its dry southern side its upper surface was gritty and dirty, in places worn to a greyish sheen by years of rain. Its northern side had been hollowed out by lapping water, so that a great lip of ice hung over a long, concave wall. The ice under the lip gleamed white and blue, and more ice, half-melted and refrozen, gushed over the lip to dangle in the air, caught in mid-flow, elaborate icicles glistening.

He could feel the groan of this thinning dam under the weight of the water – a weight that must be rising, inexorably, as the sea level rose, spilling into the lake. The ice dam settled, seeking comfort, like a working mastodont labouring under some bone-cracking load. But there was little comfort to be had.

Instability – yes, he thought; that was the key.

A memory drifted into his mind: how Jaw Like Rock had taken that foolish keeper – what was his name? Spindle? – riding on his back standing up. Jaw had stopped dead, and stood square on the broken ground. Spindle had tried to keep his balance, but without Jaw's assistance he was helpless, and he had fallen.

It had been funny, comical, cruel – and relevant. For the

water of the lake was poised high above the lower land, contained only by this fragile dam, just as the keeper's weight had been suspended over Jaw.

Strange, he hadn't thought of old Jaw for years . . .

'. . . *Baitho! Baitho!*'

Fireheads were approaching Longtusk, stepping onto the narrow rim of this worn ice dam. And one was calling to him in a thin, high voice.

On his back Willow hissed, full of hatred and fear.

Longtusk could see them now. There was a knot of Firehead hunters with their thick, well-worked clothing thrown open, exposing naked skin to the warmth of the air. Most of them had held back on the rocky ridge. But two Fireheads were coming forward to meet him, treading carefully over the ice dam, holding each others' paws.

And beyond the Fireheads, snaking back to the west, there was a column of mastodonts. Longtusk could hear the low rumbles of their squat, boulder-like bodies, feel the soft pound of their big broad feet on bare rock.

Ignoring the Fireheads, he sent out a deep contact rumble. 'Mastodonts. I am Longtusk.'

Replies came as slow pulses of deep sound, washing through the air.

'Longtusk. None here knows you.'

'That is true. We are young and strong, and you must be old and weak.'

'But we know of you.'

The voices were coloured by the rich, peculiar accent of the mastodonts, brought with them all the way from the thick forests of their own deep past.

'Walks With Thunder,' Longtusk called. 'Is he with you?'

'Walks With Thunder has gone to the aurora.'

'It was a magnificent Remembering.'

'He died well . . .'

He growled, and a little more sadness crowded into his

weary heart. But perhaps that was all he could have hoped for, after so long.

'Longtusk. There are legends of your courage and strength, of your mighty tusks. My name is Shoulder Of Bedrock. Perhaps you have heard of my prowess as a warrior. I would welcome sharpening my tusks on yours . . .'

He rumbled, 'I regret I have not heard of you, Shoulder of Bedrock, though I have no doubt your fame has spread far. I would welcome a contest with you. But I fear it must wait until we meet in the aurora.'

The mastodonts rumbled their disappointment.

'Until the aurora,' they called.

'Until the aurora . . .'

The two Fireheads approached him. One wore a coat of thick mammoth hide, to which much black-brown fur still clung, and it – no, *he* – wore a hat of bone from which smoke curled into the air. And the other, smaller, slighter, wore a coat that gleamed with the blue-white of mammoth ivory.

The male was Smokehat, of course. The Shaman's face was a weather-beaten, wizened mask, etched deep by re-sentment and hatred. The Shaman's tunic was made of an oddly shaped, almost hairless piece of hide. It had two broad holes, a flap of skin sewn over what looked like the root of a trunk and its hair had been burned away in patches, exposing skin that was pink and scarred . . .

It was a face, Longtusk realised – the face of a mammoth, pulled off the skull, the trunk cut away and stretched out so that empty eye holes gaped. And not just any face: that swathe of purple-pink hairless scarring was unmistakable. This was a remnant of Pinkface, the Matriarch of Matri-archs.

This one brutal trophy, brandished by Smokehat, told him all he needed to know about the fate of the mammoths in the old land to the west.

And with the Shaman was Crocus, Matriarch of the

Fireheads, the only Firehead in all history to ride a woolly mammoth. Her hair blew free in the slight wind – once fiery yellow, now a mass of stringy grey, dry and broken. Long-tusk felt a touch of sadness.

There was a sharp pain at his cheek, a gush of warm blood. He looked down in disbelief.

Smokehat's goad, long and bone-tipped, was splashed with Longtusk's blood. The Shaman had slapped him as if he were an unruly calf.

'*Baitho!*' On your knees . . .

Longtusk reached down with his trunk, plucked the goad from the Shaman's paw, and hurled it far into the dammed lake.

The Shaman was furious. He waved a bony fist in Long-tusk's face with impotent anger.

But now a stream of golden fluid arced from over Long-tusk's head and neatly landed on the Shaman's bone hat. Smokehat, startled, stood stock still. The burning embers in his hat started to hiss, and thick yellow fluid trickled down his face.

There was a bellow of guttural triumph from Longtusk's back. It was Willow, of course. With surprising skill, he was urinating into the Shaman's hat.

The Shaman, howling with rage, dragged the hat from his head and threw it to the ground. He jumped up and down on it, smashing the bones and scattering the embers. But then he yelped in pain – perhaps he had trodden on a burning coal or a shard of bone – and he fled, limping and yelling, acrid urine trickling over his bare scalp.

Crocus covered her face with her paws, her shoulders shaking. Longtusk recalled this strange behaviour. She was laughing.

Now she looked up at him, blue eyes made only a little rheumy by age, startlingly familiar. She reached out and buried her fingers in the long fur dangling from his trunk. She made cooing noises, like a mother bird, and he rumbled his contentment. The years evaporated, and he was a grow-ing calf, she a cub freezing to death in the snow, a vibrant young female riding his back with unprecedented skill.

But her face was a mask of wrinkles, and he saw bitter-ness etched there: bitterness and disappointment and anger. Her life – the demands of leadership, the hard choices she had had to make – all of it had soured her.

And her coat was grotesque.

He recalled the simple tooth necklace she had worn when he first found her. But now, as if it had grown out of that necklace like some monstrous fungus, her coat, draped down to the ground, was sewn with many thousands of beads. There were strings of them across her forehead and in a great sheet that followed her hair down her back; there were rows and whorls sewn into the panels at front and back; there were more strings that dangled from her fore-legs and belly to the ground, like the long hairs of a mammoth.

And every one of the beads was of mammoth ivory.

Within her suit she shone, blue-white like the ice. But Longtusk felt sure that not all the mammoths who had sacrificed their tusks for this monstrosity had gone to the aurora Great-Years before, abandoning their bones to the silt of a river bank. If the Fireheads had ever respected the mammoths, it was long ago. This coat was a thing of excess, not beauty: a symbol of power, not respect.

The Crocus he had known would never have worn such a monstrosity. Perhaps that girl had died at the moment her father fell to the Whiteskins' arrow, all those years ago. Perhaps what had lived on was another creature: the body alive, the spirit flown to the aurora.

Now she dug beneath her coat and pulled out a double loop of thick plaited rope. She held it towards him, cooing.

It was a hobble.

It was a hated thing, a symbol of his long submission, and he realised he had been right: she had pursued the mammoths such immense distances so that she could regain her dominance over him.

He lifted his tusks and roared, and his voice echoed from the curving dam of ice.

Crocus looked up at him, her eyes hardening. Perhaps she intended to call her hunters to put him down, to end once and for all the life of this unruly mammoth.

But it didn't matter. For she didn't know, couldn't know, that his life was already over.

He stamped his foot. The ice cracked.

The surface of the ice immediately crumbled, cracking in great sheets around them. He felt himself fall, his legs sinking into deeper loose material beneath.

Willow tumbled off his back and landed in the soft ice. Crocus fell to her knees, her heavy bead suit weighing her down, old and bewildered.

Longtusk shook himself free of the loose ice and continued to stamp, here at the dam's narrowest and weakest point.

Compared to the forces here – the weight of water, the power of this huge ice dam – even the strength of a powerful Bull mammoth was as nothing, of course. But what was important was how he applied that strength – for, like Spindle riding the back of Jaw Like Rock, the ice dam was unstable, overloaded by the brimming lake.

And he heard the dam groan.

Worn thin by years of erosion, already under immense pressure from the weight of the water it contained, stress cracks began to spread through its weakening structure, and Longtusk, in the deep senses of his bones, felt the rhythm of those cracks, and changed his stamping to speed their propagation.

There were ripples on the lake. Birds were taking to the air, alarmed.

And on the other side, water began to gush out of the

dam's dirty, eroded face – just a fine spray at first, noisy rather than voluminous; but soon the cracks from which it emerged were widening, the water flow increasing.

Willow got to his feet, and he reached out with a hairy paw to help Crocus. Crocus hesitated, then took his paw in her own. Then the two of them grabbed onto Longtusk's belly fur.

And so the three of them were locked together, Longtusk realised – Longtusk, Willow and Crocus; mammoth, Dreamer and Firehead – locked together at the end of their lives, just as had once been foreseen by a Dreamer female, long, long ago.

He wondered if they understood what he had done.

The centre of the dam collapsed.

Huge slabs and boulders of ice arced into the air, followed by a powerful torrent of water. Suddenly the air was filled with noise: the roar of the water, the shriek of tortured ice. The dam was high, and the first blocks took a long time to fall to the green land below, fanning out amid a spray of rumbling, frothing, grey-blue water. Longtusk thought he saw a deer there, immense antlers protruding proudly from his head, looking up in utter bewilderment at the strange rain descending on him.

The first ice blocks hit the ground, exploding into fragments and gouging out deep earth-brown craters. But the craters lasted only a heartbeat, for when the waters splashed over the earth the land turned to shapeless mud and washed away.

The deer had vanished. He had been the first to die today. He would not be the last, Longtusk knew.

The dam, once broken, was crumbling quickly. Grey-brown water cut down through the unresisting ice like a stone knife slicing through the flesh of a mammoth. And as the breach widened, so the gush of water extended, deepening and broadening. But its violence did not diminish, for the great mass of water pressed against the dam with an eagerness born of centuries of containment. It shot through the breach horizontally, darkening the land before falling in a shattering rain.

Willow was tugging at Longtusk's fur and pointing back the way they had come, towards the rocky hillside.

The Dreamer was right. It would be safer if they returned there, away from the collapsing ice dam itself.

Longtusk turned and began to make his cautious way back along the shuddering dam. The whole ice surface was cracking and unstable now. Low and squat, Willow seemed to find it easier to stand on the dam's shaking surface than the taller, more elegant Firehead. Crocus was whimpering with fear, and the Dreamer put his strong arm around her, in this last extreme helping this distant cousin to safety.

Above the rush of water, the scream of the cracking ice, Longtusk heard a remote, thin trumpet. It was a mastodont. He looked back, and saw that the mastodonts and their Firehead keepers had fled to the safety of the land, and were fanning out over the hillside there. He couldn't see if the Shaman was among them. He didn't suppose it mattered; with Crocus gone, so was his grisly power.

He hoped the mastodonts would survive, and find freedom.

At last the three of them scrambled onto the rocky hillside. It felt scarcely less unsteady than the ice, so powerfully did the gushing water shake it.

He looked over the flooding land to the south. New rivers surged along the dry old valleys, like blood surging through a mammoth's veins. Already the ridges of soil and gravel, slowly and painfully colonised by the plants, were being overwhelmed and swept away.

But now the ice dam collapsed further. Immense blocks, blocks the size of icebergs, calved off the eroded walls and fell grandly to the battered land – and the flooding reached a new intensity.

A wall of grey water surged from the huge breach, a river

trying to empty a sea. This new mighty flow simply over-whelmed the puny canyons and valleys hit by the first flooding, drowning them as if they had never been. A great bank of mist and fog rolled outwards from the breached dam, looming up to the sky as swirling clouds.

Beyond the advancing wave front, bizarrely, the sun still shone, and the land was a placid blanket of folded earth peppered with trees. Longtusk saw a herd of bison, a black lake of muscle and fur. They looked up from their feeding at the wall of water that advanced on them, towering higher than the tallest trees.

The herd was gone in an instant, thousands of lives snuffed out as their world turned from placid green to crushing black.

And still the water came, that front of grey advancing without pity over the green, spreading out over the land in a great fan from the breached dam, as if trying to emulate the sea from which it had emerged.

. . . Now, though, the flow began to diminish, and the water surging over the land began to drain away. Longtusk saw that the breached dam had, if briefly, reformed; slabs of ice and boulders, presumably torn from the basin of the trapped lake, had jammed themselves into the breach, stemming the flow, which bubbled and roared its frustration at this blockage.

As the flood waters subsided, draining into shallow pools and river valleys, the drowned land emerged, glistening.

It was unrecognisable.

Where before there had been green, now there was only the red-brown and black of the bedrock. Under the dam, where the water had fallen to the ground, a great pit had been dug out, gouged as if by some immense mammoth tusk, already flooded with water and littered with ice blocks. It was not that the surface of the land had been washed away, a few trees uprooted – *all* of it, all the animals and trees and grass and the soil that had sustained them had been scoured clean off, down to the bony bedrock, and then the bedrock itself broken and blasted away. Even the hills had been reshaped, he saw, their flanks eroded and cut away. It was as if a face had been flensed, scraped clean of hair and skin and flesh down to the skull.

Mighty rivers flowed through the new channels, and in folds of the land lakes glimmered – huge expanses, lakes that would have taken days to walk around. It was a new landscape, a new world that hadn't existed heartbeats before. But he knew there was no life in those rivers and lakes, no plants or fish, not even insects hovering over their surfaces. This was a world of water and rock.

And now there was a new explosion of shattered rock and crushed ice. The temporary dam had failed. The water leapt through and engulfed the land anew, immediately overcoming the lakes and rivers that had formed and gleamed so briefly, a world made and unmade as he watched.

Surely this mighty flood would not rest until it had gouged its way across this narrow neck of land to reach the brother ocean to the south, sundering the continents, cutting off the new lands from the old.

And with the Fireheads trapped in the old world, the mammoths would be safe in the new.

But such small calculations scarcely seemed important. Longtusk felt the shuddering of the planet in his bones, a deep, wild disturbance. The Earth was reshaping itself around him, the sea asserting its mighty fluid dominance over the land. Before such mighty forces his life was a flicker, no more significant than a droplet of spume thrown up as the water surged through the broken dam.

. . . And yet he lived, he realised, wondering. They still stood here – the three of them, Willow, Crocus and himself, the Firehead and the Dreamer still clutching his soaked fur.

For a heartbeat he wondered if they might, after all, live through this.

But now Crocus cried out, pointing.

The hillside they stood on was crumbling. Its surface was cracking, falling away into the grey-brown torrent that gushed below. And the exposed grey-black rock was crumbling too, exploding outwards, great shards of it being hurled horizontally by the power of the water. Its lower slopes must have been undercut by the flood.

The land itself was disappearing out from under him, faster than any of them could run.

So it is time, he thought.

Willow plucked at his ears. He bent his head, and the Dreamer slid proudly onto his back. Another story was ending here, thought Longtusk: this squat, aged Dreamer was probably the last of his kind, the last in all the world, and with his death his ancestors' long patient Dreams would end for ever.

Crocus was weeping. She was frightened, like the cub he had once found in the snow, lost and freezing and bewildered. She looked up at Longtusk, seeking comfort.

He wrapped his trunk around her. She curled up in the shelter of his powerful muscles, pulling his long thick fur around her. She closed her eyes, as if sleeping.

. . . The land disappeared with a soft implosion, startlingly quickly, and there was nothing under his feet.

He was falling, the Dreamer's legs locked around his neck, Crocus cradled in his trunk. The air gushed around him, laden with noise and moisture.

He could hear the rush of water beneath him, smell its triumphant brine stink as the sea burst across this narrow neck of land, sundering continent from continent.

Is this how it feels to die? Is this how it feels to be born?

Defiantly he lifted his mighty tusks. *Milkbreath! Thunder! Spruce!*

And then—

CHAPTER 7
THE COUSINS

It was later – much later – before Threetusk truly understood what had happened. And, as he grew older yet, the
strange events of those days plagued his mind more and
more.

He found her cropping grass with the painful, slow care of
the old.

'You look terrible,' said Saxifrage, as she always did.

'And, Matriarch or not, you're just as uppity as when you
were a calf and I could lift you in the air with my trunk.'

She snorted with contempt. 'Like to see you try it now.'
But she reached up and nuzzled her trunk tip into his
mouth.

Her flavour was thin, stale, old – yet deliciously familiar to
Threetusk. They had sired four calves together. Threetusk
had known other mates, of course – and so, he knew, had
Saxifrage – but none of his couplings had given him such
warm joy as those with her. And (he knew, though she
would never say so) she felt the same way about him.

But Saxifrage was a Matriarch now, and her Family stood
close by her: daughters and granddaughters and nieces,
calves playing at the feet of their mothers, happy, well-fed
and innocent.

Even in this huge and empty new land birth and life and
death had followed their usual round for the mammoths,
and Threetusk found the world increasingly crowded by
unfamiliar faces. Sometimes he was startled to discover just
how old he was: when he tried to kneel in the water of a
spring, for instance, and his knees lanced with arthritic pain;

or when he grumbled about the smoothness of his teeth – and then recalled they were the last he would ever grow.

He settled in beside her, and pulled at the grass. 'I've been thinking,' he said. 'We're the only ones who recall it all. The crossing. The only ones who were *there*. To these youngsters, all of it – Longtusk, the refuge, the corridor – is as remote as a story in the Cycle.'

'It already *is* in the Cycle.'

'Yes,' he said. 'And if I knew Longtusk he'd bury his head in a mud seep rather than hear some of the legends that are growing up around him.'

'But he *was* a hero . . . You know, you never told me the last thing Longtusk said to you. That day when he announced we had to leave the nunatak, and he took aside you and my mother, Horsetail.'

'I've been thinking,' he said again.

She rumbled, irritated at his evasion. 'Bad habit at your age.'

'About ice and land bridges and corridors . . . You see, it isn't so easy to reach this new land of ours. First you have to cross the land bridge, *and* you have to get through the ice corridor. You have to time it just right; most of the time one or other of them will be closed, by sea or ice—'

'So what?'

'So it's difficult, but not impossible, for others to make the crossing. Although for now we're protected by the ocean, there might come a time in the future when the land bridge opens again, and *they* come pouring across . . .'

Saxifrage shivered, evidently as disturbed as he was by the notion that the Fireheads might come scouring down this innocent country, burning and hunting and building and *changing*.

'It won't happen in our time,' Saxifrage said. 'And—'

But they were interrupted by a thin trumpeting on the fringe of the gathering. It sounded like a calf – a badly frightened calf.

'*Circle!*'

Saxifrage's Family immediately formed a defensive ring around their Matriarch.

Impatiently Saxifrage pushed her way out of the ring, determined to see what was going on. Threetusk followed in her wake.

A calf stood in the protection of her mother's legs, agitated, still squealing with fright. It was immediately obvious why she was distressed.

The Family was standing at the edge of an open, grassy flood plain. A forest bounded the southern side of the plain. And something had emerged from the fringe of trees on the far side of the clearing.

It might have been a mammoth – it was about the size of a healthy adult Bull, Threetusk supposed – but it was almost hairless. Its skin was dark brown and heavily wrinkled, and it sprouted patches of wiry black hair. Its head was strangely small, and its trunk was short and inflexible.

And it had four short, straight tusks, one pair in the upper jaw, one in the lower.

It was staring at the herd of mammoths, clearly as surprised and alarmed as they were.

'It's a calf of Probos,' said Saxifrage, wondering. 'A cousin of the mammoths – like Longtusk's mastodonts. There have been rumours of creatures like us here: distant sightings, contact rumbles dimly heard. But . . .'

A young Bull mammoth had gone to challenge the strange animal.

Threetusk struggled to hear their encounter. 'His language is strange. I can barely understand him. *Gomphothere*. His kind are called gomphotheres. We are cousins. But we have been apart a long, long time—'

Saxifrage grabbed his trunk. 'Threetusk, don't you see? *This is proof.* Your ideas about the bridge and the corridor opening and closing *must be right*. The way must have opened in the past and let through that gomphothere thing – or his ancestors anyhow. And if the way opened in the past, it will surely open again in the future. Oh, Threetusk, you were right. It won't happen in our lifetimes. But the Fireheads are coming.' She shuddered. 'And then what will become of us?'

'. . . We shouldn't call them Fireheads,' he said slowly.

'What?'

'That's what Longtusk said to Horsetail and me. On that last day.' He closed his eyes and thought of Longtusk. It was as if the years peeled away like winter fur.

We know their true name. They are already in the Cycle. Driven by emptiness inside, they will never stop until they have covered the Earth, and no animal is left alive but them – heap upon heap of them, with their painted faces and their tools and their weapons. They are the demon we use to scare our calves; they are the nemesis of the mammoths. They are the Lost . . .

Saxifrage said, 'Some day in the future the ice will return, and the steppe will spread across the planet once more. It will be a world made for mammoths. But will there be any mammoths left alive to see it?'

The young mammoth's tusks clashed with the gompho-there's, a sharp, precise ivory sound. The gomphothere trumpeted and disappeared into the forest.

EPILOGUE

On this world, a single large ocean spans much of the northern hemisphere. There are many smaller lakes and seas confined within circular craters, connected by rivers and canals. Much of the land is covered by dark green forest and by broad, sweeping grasslands and steppe.

But ice is gathering at the poles. The oceans and lakes are crawling back into great underground aquifers. Soon the air will start to snow out.

The grip of the ice persisted for billions of years before being loosened, it seemed for ever. And yet it comes again.

This is the Sky Steppe.

This is Mars.

The time is three thousand years after the birth of Christ. And in all this world there is no human to hear the calls of the mammoths.

BOOK 3

ICEBONES

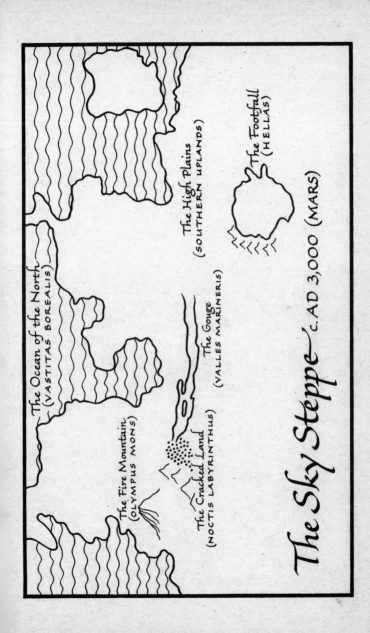

The Ocean of the North
(VASTITAS BOREALIS)

The High Plains
(SOUTHERN UPLANDS)

The Footfall
(HELLAS)

The Gouge
(VALLES MARINERIS)

The Fire Mountain
(OLYMPUS MONS)

The Cracked Land
(NOCTIS LABYRINTHUS)

The Sky Steppe — c. AD 3,000 (MARS)

PROLOGUE

There is a flat, sharp, close horizon, a plain of dust and rocks. The rocks are carved by the wind. Everything is stained rust brown, like dried blood, the shadows long and sharp.

This is not Earth.

Though the sun is rising, the sky above is still speckled with stars. And in the east there is a morning star: steady, brilliant, its delicate blue-white distinct against the violet wash of the dawn. Sharp-eyed creatures might see that this is a double star; a faint silver-grey companion circles close to its blue master.

The sun continues to strengthen. Now it is an elliptical patch of yellow light, suspended in a brown sky. But the sun looks small, feeble; this seems a cold, remote place. As the dawn progresses the dust suspended in the air scatters the light and suffuses everything with a pale, salmon hue.

At last the gathering light masks the moons. Two of them.

On this world, a single large ocean spans much of the northern hemisphere. There are smaller lakes and seas: many of them circular, confined within craters, linked by rivers and canals. Much of the land is covered by dark green forest and by broad, sweeping grasslands and steppe.

But ice is gathering at the poles. The oceans and lakes are crawling back into ancient underground aquifers.

The grip of the ice persisted for billions of years. Now it comes again.

Soon the air itself will start to snow out.

This is the Sky Steppe.

This is Mars.

The time is three thousand years after the birth of Christ.

The rocky land rings to the calls of the mammoths. But there is no human to hear them.

ONE
MOUNTAIN

THE STORY OF THE LANGUAGE OF KILUKPUK

This is a story Kilukpuk told Silverhair, at the end of her life.

All this happened a long time ago, long before mammoths came to this place, which we call the Sky Steppe. It is a story of Kilukpuk herself, the Matriarch of Matriarchs, who was born in a burrow in the time of the Reptiles. But at the time of this story the Reptiles were long gone, and the world was young and warm and empty.

Kilukpuk had been alive for a very long time. She had become so huge that her body had sunk into the ground, turning it into a Swamp within which she dwelled.

But she had a womb as fertile as the sea. And every year she bore Calves.

Kilukpuk was concerned that her Calves were foolish.

Now, in those days, no Calves could talk. Oh, they made noises: chirps and barks and rumbles and snores and trumpets, just as Calves will make today. But what the Calves chattered to each other didn't *mean* anything. They made the noises in play, or without thinking, or from pain or joy.

Kilukpuk decided to change this.

One year Kilukpuk bore three Calves.

As they suckled at her mighty dugs, she took each of them aside. She said, 'If you want to suckle, you must make this sound.' And she made the suckling cry. And then, when the Calves were no longer hungry, she pushed them away.

The next day all the Calves were hungry again, and Kilukpuk waited in her Swamp.

The first Calf was silent, for she had forgotten the cry Kilukpuk taught her. And so she received no milk.

And she died.

The second Calf made the suckling cry, but made many other noises besides, for she thought that the cry was as meaningless as any other chatter. And so she received no milk.

And she died.

The third Calf, observing the fate of her sisters, made the suckling cry correctly. And Kilukpuk gathered her to her teat, and suckled her, and that Calf lived to grow strong.

When she grew up, that Calf had three Calves of her own. And all of them were born knowing the suckling cry.

Now Kilukpuk gathered the three Calves of her Calf. She said, 'If you ever lose your mother, you must make this sound.' And she made the lost cry. And then she pushed the Calves away.

A few days later, the playful Calves lost their mother – as Calves will – and Kilukpuk waited in her Swamp.

The first Calf was silent, for she had forgotten the cry Kilukpuk taught her. And so she stayed lost, and the wolves got her.

And she died.

The second Calf made the lost cry, but made many other noises besides, for she thought that the cry was as meaningless as any other chatter. And so she stayed lost, and the wolves got her.

And she died.

The third Calf, observing the fate of her sisters, made the lost cry correctly. And Kilukpuk gathered her up in her trunk and delivered her to her mother, who suckled her, and that Calf lived to grow strong.

And when she grew up, that Calf had three Calves of her own. And all of them were born knowing the suckling cry, and the lost cry.

And the next generation of Calves were born knowing the suckling cry, and the lost cry, and the 'Let's go' rumble.

And the next generation after that were born knowing the suckling cry, and the lost cry, and the 'Let's go' rumble, and the contact rumble.

And so it went, as Kilukpuk instructed each new generation. Calves who learned the new calls were bound tightly together, and Kilukpuk's Family grew stronger.

Calves who did not learn the new calls died. And still Kilukpuk's Family grew stronger.

That is how the language of mammoths and their Cousins came about. And that is why every new Calf is born with the language of Kilukpuk in her head.

Yes, it was cruel, and Kilukpuk mourned every one of those Calves who died. But it is the truth.

The Cycle is the wisdom of uncounted generations of mammoths. Nothing in there is false. For if it had been false, it would have been removed.

Just as the foolish Calves who would not learn were removed, by death.

CHAPTER 1
THE AWAKENING

Icebones was cold.

She was trapped in chill darkness. She couldn't feel her legs, her tail, even her trunk. She could hear nothing, see nothing.

She tried to call out to her mother, Silverhair, by rumbling, trumpeting, stamping. She couldn't even do that. It was like being immersed in thick cold mud.

And the cold was deep, deeper than she had ever known, soaking into the core of her body, reaching the warm centre under her layers of hair and fat and flesh and bone, the core heat every mammoth had to protect, all her life.

Perhaps this was the aurora, where mammoths believed their souls rose when they died.

. . . But, she thought resentfully, she was only fifteen years old. She had never mated, never borne a calf. How could *she* have died?

Besides, much was wrong. The aurora was full of light, but there was no light here. The aurora was full of the scent of growing grass, but there was no scent here.

And things were changing.

She had been – *asleep* – and now she was awake. *That* had changed.

She recalled a time before this darkness, when she had been with Silverhair. They had walked across the cold steppe of the Island, surrounded by the Lost and their incomprehensible gadgetry, perturbed and yet not harmed by them. She recalled what her mother had been saying: 'You will be a Matriarch some day, little Icebones. You will be the greatest of them all. But responsibility will lie heavily on you . . .' Icebones hadn't understood.

With her mother, then, on the Island. Now here. *Change*. A time asleep. Now, awake in the dark. Change, change, change.

Everyone knew that in the aurora nothing changed. In the aurora mammoths gathered in the calm warm presence of Kilukpuk, immersed in Family, and there was no day or night, no hunger or thirst, no *I*: merely a continual, endless moment of belonging.

This was *not* the aurora. I am not dead, she realised. My long walk continues.

But with life came hope and fear, and dread settled on her.

She made the lost cry, like a calf. But she couldn't even hear that.

Thunder cracked. Light flashed in sharp lines above and below her. She felt a shuddering, deep in her belly, as if the ground itself was stirring.

She tried to retreat, to rumble her alarm, but still she could not move.

The close darkness receded. Great hard sheets of blackness, like dark ice, fell away. She was suddenly immersed in pink-red light.

And now the feeling returned to her legs and trunk, belly and back, all in a rush. It was like being drenched suddenly in ice water. She staggered, her legs stiff and remote. She tried to trumpet, but her trunk was heavy, and a thick, briny liquid gushed out of it, like sea water.

When her nostrils were clear she took a deep, shuddering breath. The air was cold and sharp – and *thin*. It made her gasp, hurting her raw lungs. Her weak eyes prickled, suddenly streaming with salty water. But she rejoiced, for she was whole again, immersed in her body, and the world.

But it was not the world she had known.

The sky was pink, like a dawn, or a sunset.

She was standing on a shallow slope. She ran her soft trunk tip over the ground. It was hard smooth rock, blue-red. Its surface was rippled and lobed, as if it had melted and refrozen.

This broad plain of rock descended as far as she could see, all the way to the horizon. She must be standing on the flank of a giant mountain, she thought. She turned to look up towards the summit, and she saw a great pillar of black smoke thrusting up to the sky, billows caught in their motion as if frozen.

Her patch of rock, soiled by her watery vomit, was surrounded by sheets of dense blackness that lay on the ground. When she touched this black stuff, she found it was hard and cold and lacking in scent and taste, quite unlike the rock in its chilling smoothness. And the sheets had sharp, straight edges. It was the crust of darkness that had contained her when she had woken from her strange Sleep, and it filled her with renewed dread.

She stepped reluctantly over the smooth black sheets, until she had reached the comparative comfort of the solid rock. But the rock's lobes and ridges were hard under her feet, and every time she took a step she had a strange, dream-like sensation of floating.

Nothing grew here: no herbs, no trees. There was nothing to eat, not so much as a blade of grass.

The air stank of smoke and sulphur. The sun was small and dim and shrunken. The ground shuddered, as if some immense beast buried there were snoring softly in its sleep.

I am in a strange place indeed, she thought. Her brief euphoria evaporated, and disorientation and fear returned.

A contact rumble reached her, resonating deep in her belly. *She was not alone*: relief flooded her.

She turned sharply. Pain prickled in her knees and back and neck, and in the pads of her feet.

A mammoth was approaching – a Bull, taller than she was.

As he walked his powerful shoulders rose and fell, and his head nodded and swayed, his trunk a tangible weight that pulled at his neck. His underfur was light brown, but yellow-white around his rump and belly. His tough overlying guard hairs were much darker, nearly black on his rump and flanks, but shading to a deep brown flecked with crimson on his forequarters. The hairs that dangled from his trunk and chin and feet were paler, in places almost white. His tusks curled before him, heavy and proud. He walked slowly, languidly, as if dazed or ill.

She could see him only dimly, through air laden with mist and smoke. But she could smell the deep warmth of his layered hair, feel the steady press of his footsteps against the hard ground.

He was *mammuthus primigenius*: a woolly mammoth, as she was.

She didn't know him.

The two of them began to growl and stomp, facing each other and turning away, touching tusks and trunks, even emitting high, bird-like chirrups from their trunks. The moist pink tip of his trunk reached out and explored her mouth, scalp and eyes. She ran her own trunk fingers through his long guard hairs, finding the woolly underfur beneath.

In this way, touching and singing and listening and smelling, the two mammoths shared a complex, rich exchange of information.

'. . . Who are you? Where are you from?'

'My name is Icebones—'

'Do you know where the food is? We're all hungry here.'

She stumbled back, confused. He was hard to understand, his sounds and postures and gestures a distortion of the language she was used to, as if he had come from a different Clan, not related to her own. And his manner was strange –

eager, clumsy, more befitting a callow calf than a grown
Bull.

She realised immediately, *He is frightened*.

Discreetly she probed the area of his temple between his
eyes and his small ears where he would secrete musth fluid,
if it was his time. But she found nothing.

'I don't know anything about food.'

He growled. 'But you came out of *that*.' He probed at the
black sheets around her.

She didn't know what to say to him.

Baffled, disturbed, she stepped forward, ignoring the continuing stiffness in her legs, and walked down the featureless slope. The Bull followed her, demanding food noisily,
like a calf pursuing his mother.

She reached a shallow ridge. She paused there, raised her
trunk and sniffed, studying the world.

She saw how this Mountain's vast shadow spilled across
the rocky plains below. Looking beyond the shadow to
where the land was still sunlit, she saw splashes of grey-
green – steppe, perhaps, or forest. And beyond that she saw
the broad shoulders of two more vast, shallow mountains,
pushing above the horizon, mighty twins of the Mountain
under her feet, made grey and colourless by distance and
mist. Close to the horizon thin clouds glowed, bright blue,
stark against the pink sky.

There was a moon in the sky. But it was not *the* Moon,
which had floated above the night lands of the Island. This
moon was a small white disc, and it was climbing into
the smoky sky as she watched – *visibly moving*, moment by
moment, with a strange, disturbing speed. As it climbed, approaching the sun, it turned into a crescent, a cup of darkness, that finally disappeared.

And then the moon's shadow passed over the sun itself, a
dark spot like a passing cloud.

Icebones cringed.

With her deep mammoth's senses she could hear the

songs of the planet: the growl of earthquakes and volcanoes, the howl of wind and thunder, the angry surge of ocean storms, all the noises of earth, air, fire and water. And she could tell that this world was small, round, hard – and strange.

She raised her trunk higher, trying to smell mammoths, her Family, Silverhair. She could smell nothing but the stink of sulphur and ash.

Wherever she was, however she had got here, she was far from her Family. Without her Family she was incomplete – for a mammoth Cow could no more live apart from her Family than a trunk or leg or tusk could survive if cut off the body.

The Bull continued to pursue her.

She turned on him. 'Why are you following me? I am not in oestrus. Can't you tell that? And you are not in musth.'

His eyes gleamed, amber pebbles in pits of wrinkled skin. 'What is *oestrus*? What is *musth*?'

She growled. 'My name is Icebones. What is your name? Where is your bachelor herd?'

'Do you know where the food is? Please, I am *very* hungry.'

She came closer to him, curiosity warring with her anger and confusion. She explored his face with her trunk. How could he know so little? How could he not have a *name*?

And – where *was* she? This strange place of pink mountains was like nowhere she had ever heard of, nowhere spoken of even in the Cycle, the mammoths' great and ancient body of lore . . .

Nowhere, except one place.

'*The Sky Steppe*. That's where we are, isn't it?' The Sky Steppe, the Island in the sky where – according to the Cycle – mammoths would one day find a world of their own, far from the predations and cruelty of the Lost, a world of calm and plenty.

But this place of barren rock and smoky air didn't seem so plentiful to her, and nor was it calm.

The Bull ignored her questions. 'I'm hungry,' he repeated.

She turned her back on him deliberately.

She heard him grunt and snort, the soft uncertain pads of his footsteps recede. She felt relief – then renewed anxiety.

I'm hungry too, she realised. And I'm thirsty. And, after all, the strange, infuriating Bull was the only mammoth she had seen here.

She turned. His broad back, long guard hairs shining, was still visible over a blue-black ridge that poked like a bone out of the hard ground.

She hurried after him.

Walking was difficult. The hard ground crumpled into folds, as if it had once flowed like congealing ice, and great gullies had been raked out of the side of the Mountain.

Her strength seemed sapped. She struggled to climb the ridges, and slithered on her splayed feet down slopes where she could not get a purchase. The air was smoky and thin, and her chest heaved at it.

She found a gully that was roofed over by a layer of rock. She probed with brief curiosity into a kind of cave, much taller than she was, that receded into the darkness like a vast nostril. Perhaps all the gullies here had once been long tubular caves like this, but their rocky roofs had collapsed.

In one place the ground had cracked open, like burned skin, and steam billowed. Mud, grey and liquid, boiled inside the crack, and it built up tall, skinny vents, like trunks sticking out of the ground. The air around the mud pool was hot and dense with smoke and ash, making it even harder to draw a breath.

Grit settled on her eyes, making them weep. She longed for the soft earth of the Island in summer, for grass and herbs and bushes.

But the Bull was striding on, his gait still languidly slow to her eyes. He was confident, used to the vagaries of the ground where she was uncertain, healthy and strong where she still felt stiff and disoriented. She hurried after him.

And now, as she came over a last ridge, she saw that he had joined a group of mammoths.

They were all Cows, she saw instantly. She felt a surge of relief to see a Family here – even if it was not *her* Family. She hurried forward, trumpeting a greeting.

They turned, sniffing the air. The mammoths stood close together, and the wind made their long guard hairs swirl around them in a single wave, like a curtain of falling water.

There were three young-looking Cows, so similar they must have been sisters. One appeared to be carrying a calf: her belly was heavy and low, and her dugs were swollen. An older Cow might have been their mother – her posture was tense and uncertain – and a still older Cow, moving stiffly as if her bones ached, might be *her* mother, grandmother to the sisters – and so, surely, the Matriarch of the Family. Icebones thought they all seemed agitated, uncertain.

Icebones watched as the Cow she had tagged as the mother lumbered over to the Bull and cuffed his scalp affectionately with her trunk . . . *And the mother towered over the Bull.*

That didn't make sense, Icebones thought, bewildered. Adult Bulls were taller than Cows. This Bull had been much taller than Icebones, and Icebones, at fifteen years old, was nearly her full adult height. So how could this older Cow tower over *him* as if he was a calf?

There was one more Cow here, Icebones saw now, standing a little way away from the clustered Family. This Cow was different. Her hair was very fine – so fine that in places Icebones could see her skin, which was pale grey, mottled pink. Her tusks were short and straight, lacking the usual curling sweep of mammoth tusks, and her ears were large and floppy.

This Cow was staring straight at Icebones as she approached, her trunk held high as she sniffed the air. Her posture was hard and still, as if she were a musth Bull challenging a younger rival.

'I am Icebones,' she said.

The others did not reply. She walked forward.

The mammoths seemed to grow taller and taller, their legs extending like shadows cast by a setting sun, until they loomed over her, as if she too was reduced to the dimensions of a calf.

Icebones felt reluctant, increasingly nervous. Must everything be strange here?

She approached the grandmother. Though she too was much taller than Icebones, this old one's hair was discoloured black and grey and her head was lean, the skin and hair sunken around her eyes and temples, so that the shape of the skull was clearly visible. Icebones reached out and slipped her trunk into the grandmother's mouth, and tasted staleness and blood. She is very old, Icebones realised with dismay.

She said, 'You are the Matriarch. My Matriarch is Silverhair. But my Family is far from here . . .'

'Matriarch,' said the grandmother. 'Family.' She gazed at Icebones. 'Silverhair. These are old words, words buried deep in our heads, our bellies. I am no Matriarch, child.'

Icebones was confused. 'Every Family has a Matriarch.'

The grandmother growled. 'This is my daughter. These are her children, these three Cows. And *this* one carries a calf of her own – another generation, if I live to see it . . . But we are not a Family.' She sneezed, her limp trunk flexing, and blood-stained mucus splashed over the rock at her feet.

Icebones shrank back. 'I never heard of mammoths without names, a Family that wasn't a Family, Cows without a Matriarch.'

One of the three tall sisters approached Icebones curiously. Her tusks were handsome symmetrical spirals before her face. Her legs were skinny and extended. Even her head was large, Icebones saw, the delicate skull expansive above the fringe of hair that draped down from her chin.

She reached out with her trunk and probed at Icebones's hair and mouth and ears, just as if Icebones was a calf. 'I know who you are.'

Icebones recoiled.

But now the others were all around her – the other sisters, the mother, the Bull.

'We were told you would come.'

'I am thirsty. I want water.'

'My baby is stirring. I am hungry.'

The strange, tall mammoths clamoured at her, like calves seeking dugs to suckle, plucking at the hair on her back and legs, even the clumps on her stubby tail.

She trumpeted, backing off. 'Get away from me!'

The other – the Ragged One, stub-tusked, pink-spotted – came lumbering over the rocky slope to stand close to Icebones. 'You mustn't mind them. They think *you* might be the Matriarch, you see. That's what they've been promised.'

Now the Bull-calf came loping towards her, oddly slow, ungainly. He said to Icebones, 'Show us how to find food. That's what Matriarchs are supposed to do.'

I'm no Matriarch, she thought. I've never even had a calf. I've never mated. I'm little older than you are, for all your size . . . 'You must find food for yourself,' she said.

'But he can't,' the Ragged One said slyly. 'Let me show you.'

And she turned and began to follow a trail, lightly worn into the hard rock, that led over a further ridge.

Confused, apprehensive, Icebones followed.

The Ragged One brought her to a shallow pit that had been sliced into the flank of the Mountain. At the back of the pit was a vertical wall, like a cliff face, into which sockets had been cut, showing dark and empty spaces beyond.

And, strangest of all, on a raised outcrop at the centre of the levelled floor stood a mammoth – but it was not a mammoth. It, he or she, was merely a heap of bones, painstakingly reassembled to mimic life, with not a scrap of flesh or fat or hair. The naked skeleton raised great yellow tusks challengingly to the pink sky.

Icebones recognised the nature of this place immediately: the harsh straight lines and level planes of its construction, the casual horror of the bony monument at the centre. 'This is a place of the Lost,' she said. 'We should get away from here.'

The Ragged One gazed at her with eyes that were too orange, too bright. 'You really don't understand, do you? The Lost aren't the problem. The problem is, *the Lost have gone.*' She circled her trunk around Icebones's, and began to tug her, gently but relentlessly, towards the shallow, open pit.

Icebones walked forward, one heavy step after another, straining to detect the presence of the Lost. But her sense of smell was scrambled by the stink of the smoky air.

'Where were you born?'

'On the Island,' Icebones said. 'A steppe. A land of grass and bushes and water.'

The Ragged One growled. 'Your Island, if it ever existed, is long ago and far away. *Here* – this is where I was born. And my mother before me – and her mother – and hers. Here, in this place of the Lost. What do you think of that?'

Icebones looked up at the cavernous rooms cut into the wall. 'And was a Lost your Matriarch? Did the Lost give you your names?'

'We had no Matriarch,' the Ragged One said simply. 'We had no need of Families. We had no need of names. For we only had to do what the Lost showed us, and we would be kept well and happy. Look.' The Ragged One stalked over to a low trough set in the sheer wall. A flap of shining stone dangled before it, like the curtain of guard hairs beneath the belly of a mammoth. The Ragged One pushed the tip of her trunk under the flap, which lifted up. When she withdrew her trunk, she held it up before Icebones. Save for a little dust, her pink trunk tip was empty.

Icebones was baffled by this mysterious behaviour. And she saw that the trunk had just a single nostril.

The Ragged One said, 'Every day since I was born I came to this place and pushed my trunk in the hole, and was rewarded with food. Grass, herbs, bark, twigs. *Every day*. And from other holes in this wall I have drawn water to drink – as much as I like. But not today, and not for several days.'

'How can food grow in a hole?'

The old grandmother came limping towards them, her gaunt head heavy. 'It doesn't grow there, child. The Lost put it there with their paws.'

'And now,' the Ragged One said, 'the Lost are gone. All of them. And so there is no more food in the hole, no more water. *Now* can you see why we are frightened?'

The old one, with a weary effort, lifted her trunk and laid it on Icebones's scalp. 'I don't know who you are, or where you came from. But we have a legend. One day the Lost would leave this place, and the great empty spaces of this world would be ours. And on that day, one would come who would lead us, and show us how to live: how to eat, how to drink, how to survive the heat of the summer and the cold of the winter.'

'A Matriarch,' Icebones said softly.

The grandmother murmured, 'It has been a very long time – more generations than there are stars in the sky. So they say . . .'

'But now,' the Ragged One said, 'the Lost are gone, and we are hungry. Are you to be our Matriarch, Icebones?'

Icebones lifted her trunk from one to the other. The grandmother seemed to be gazing at her expectantly, as if with hope, but there was only envy and ambition in the stance of the Ragged One.

'I am no Matriarch,' Icebones said.

The Ragged One snorted contempt. 'Then must we die here—?'

Her words were drowned by a roar louder than any mammoth's. The ground shuddered sharply under Icebones's feet, and she stumbled.

Dark smoke thrust out of the higher slopes of the Mountain. The huge black column was shot through with fire, and lumps of burning rock flew high. The air became thick and dark, full of the stink of sulphur, and darkness fell over them.

'Ah,' said the Ragged One, as if satisfied. 'This old monster is waking up at last.'

Flakes of ash were falling through the muddy air, like snowflakes, settling on the mammoths' outer hair. It was a strange, distracting sight. Icebones caught one flake on her trunk tip. It was hot enough to burn, and she flicked it away.

A mammoth trumpeted, piercingly.

Icebones hurried back, trying to ignore the sting of ash flakes on her exposed skin, and the stink of her own singed hair.

She met a mammoth, running in panic. It was one of the three sisters, and the long hairs that dangled from her belly were smouldering. 'Help me! Oh, help me!' Even as she ran, Icebones was struck by the liquid slowness of her gait, the languid way her hair flopped over her face.

The injured one, confused, agitated, ran back to the others. Icebones hurried after her and beat at the Cow's scorched and smouldering fur with her trunk.

The others stood around helplessly. The mammoths, coated in dirty ash, were turning grey, as if transmuting into rock themselves.

At last the smouldering was stopped. The injured Cow was weeping thick tears of pain, and Icebones saw that she would have a scarred patch on her belly.

Icebones asked, 'How did this happen to you . . . ?'

There was a predatory howl, and light glared from the sky. The mammoths cringed and trumpeted.

A giant rock fell from the smoke-filled sky. It slammed into the floor, sending smaller flaming fragments flying far, and the ground shuddered again. Beneath a thin crust of black stone, the fallen rock was glowing red-hot.

With a clatter, the patiently reconstructed skeleton of the long-dead mammoth fell to pieces.

'*That* is how I was burned,' the injured sister said resentfully.

More of the lethal glowing rocks began to fall from the sky, each of them howling like a descending raptor, and where they fell the stony ground splashed like soft ice.

The mother lumbered up. 'We have to get out of this rain of rocks,' she said grimly.

'The feeding place,' gasped the injured sister.

'No,' growled the mother. '*Look*.'

Icebones peered through curling smoke and the steady drizzle of ash flakes. A falling rock had smashed into the place of feeding, breaking open the thin wall as a mammoth's foot might crush a skull.

The Ragged One was watching Icebones, as if this was a trial of strength. She said slyly, 'The Lost have abandoned us. Must we all die here? Tell us what to do, Matriarch.'

Icebones, dizzy, disoriented, tried to think. Did these spindly mammoths really believe she was a Matriarch? And whatever they believed, what was she to do, in this strange upside-down world where it rained ash and fiery rock? Surely Silverhair would have known . . .

The grandmother, through a trunk clogged with ash and dirt, was struggling to speak.

Her daughter stepped closer. 'What did you say?'

'The tube,' the old one said. 'The lava tube.'

The others seemed baffled, but Icebones understood. 'The great nostril of rock . . . It is not far.' I should have thought of it. Silverhair would have thought of it. But I am not Silverhair. I am only Icebones.

She waited for the grandmother to give her command to proceed. But, of course, this old one was no Matriarch. The mammoths milled about, uncertain.

'We must not leave here,' said the burned sister. 'What if the Lost return? They will help us.'

At last her mother stepped forward and slapped her sharply on the scalp with her trunk. 'We must go to the lava tube. Come now.' She turned and began to lead the way. The others followed, the Bull pacing ahead with foolish boldness, the three sisters clustered together. The Ragged One tracked them at a distance, more like an adolescent Bull than a Cow.

As they toiled away into the thickening grey murk, Icebones realised that the grandmother was not following.

She turned back. To find her way she had to probe with her trunk through the murk. The smoke and ash was so thick now it was hard to breathe.

The grandmother had slumped to her knees, and her belly was flat on the ground, guard hairs trailing around her. Her eyes were closed, her trunk coiled limply before her, and her breath was a shallow laboured scratch.

'You must get up. Come on.' Icebones nudged the old one's rump with her forehead, trying to force her to stand. She trumpeted to the others. 'Help her!'

The grandmother's rumble was weak, deep, almost inaudible over the shuddering of the rocky ground. 'Let them go.' She slumped again, her breath bubbling, her body turning into a shapeless grey mound under the ash.

Icebones feverishly probed at the old one's face and mouth with her trunk. 'I will see you in the aurora.'

One eye opened, like a stone embedded in broken flesh and scorched hair. 'There is no aurora in this place, child.'

Icebones was shocked. 'Then where do we go when we die?'

The old one closed her eyes. 'I suppose I'll soon find out.' Her chest was heaving as she strained at the hot, filthy air. She raised her trunk, limply, and pushed at Icebones's face. 'Go. Your mother would be proud of you.'

Icebones backed away. She was immersed in strangeness and peril, far from her Family – and now she was confronted by death. 'I will Remember you.'

But the grandmother, subsiding as if into sleep, did not seem to hear, and Icebones turned away.

It was the greatest volcano in the solar system. It had been dormant for tens of millions of years. Now it was active once more, and its voice could be heard all around this small world.

And, across the volcano's mighty flanks, the small band of mammoths toiled through fire and ash, seeking shelter.

CHAPTER 2

THE SONGS OF THE WORLD

The blazing rocks continued to fall from the sky, splashing against the stolid ground.

The rocky tube shuddered and groaned. Sometimes dust or larger fragments of the inner roof came loose, and the mammoths, huddled together, squealed in terror. But the tube held, protecting them.

The darkness of night closed in. Still the ash snow fell thickly. The cave grew black. The mammoths tried to ignore the hunger and thirst that gnawed at them all.

Sometimes, in the darkness, Icebones heard the others snore or mumble. Icebones felt weariness weigh on her too. But she was reluctant to fall back into the dark, having emerged from that timeless, dreamless Sleep so recently.

She felt compassion for these wretched nameless ones – but at the same time her own fear deepened, for it was apparent that there was nobody here who could help *her*, no Family or Matriarch or even an experienced, battle-scarred old Bull.

She wished with all her heart that Silverhair was here.

The morning came at last, bringing a thin pinkish light that only slowly dispelled the purple-black of night. But the ash continued to fall, and there was a renewed round of rock falls.

The mammoths were forced to stay cooped up together in the lava tube, bickering and trying to avoid each other's dung, which was thin and stinking of malnourishment.

By mid-afternoon, thirst drove them out. They had to

push their way through ash which had piled up against the mouth of their long cave.

The world had turned grey.

A cloud of thick noxious gas continued to pump out of the summit of this immense Fire Mountain, and a grey-black lid of it hung beneath the pink sky, darkening the day. Ash drifted down, turning the rocky ground into a field of grey smoothness over which the mammoths toiled like fat brown ghosts, every footfall leaving a crater in fine grey layers.

Everything moved slowly here, Icebones observed. As she walked her steps felt light, as if in a dream, or as if she was wading through some deep pond. When she kicked up ash flakes they fell back with an eerie calmness. Even the guard hairs of the mammoths rippled languidly.

Trying to ignore the strangeness, Icebones walked with exaggerated caution. If she must be called a Matriarch, she should fulfil the role. 'The ash hides the rock's folds and crevices,' she said. 'You must be careful not to injure your-selves.' She showed the others how to probe at the ground ahead with their trunks, feeling out hidden traps.

But the Ragged One stalked alongside her, her posture stiff and mocking. 'So you know all about ash. You know better than I do, after I have spent my whole life here on this Fire Mountain.'

'No,' said Icebones evenly. 'But I have seen how snow covers the ground. And the dangers are surely alike.'

The Ragged One growled. '*There*,' she said. 'There are dangers in this place you have never imagined.'

Icebones saw that a new river was making its way down the broad flank of the Mountain. It was a river of fire.

Glowing red, it flowed stickily and slowly, like blood. It was crusted over by a dark brown scum that continually crumbled, broke and congealed again. Flames licked all along the length of the flow, and wispy yellow smoke coiled. In one place the flow cut through a frozen pond, and a vast cloud of yellow-white steam rose with a harsh hissing.

Icebones could smell the burning stench of the molten rock river, feel its huge rumble as it churned its way down the slope, cutting through layers of ancient rock as if they were no more substantial than ice. 'We were fortunate,' she said softly. 'If that rock river had chosen to flow a little more to the east—'

'It would have overwhelmed our lava tube,' said the Ragged One. 'Yes. We would have been scorched, or buried alive, or crushed . . .'

'It is a shame the rock flow is destroying the pool. We could have drunk there.'

The Ragged One snorted. 'In your wisdom you will find us more water.'

Icebones, irritated, walked up the rocky slope. 'Very well. Let's find water.'

Reluctantly the Ragged One followed.

Icebones came to an area where the ash was a little less thick. She walked back and forth across the rock, stamping, scraping exposed outcrops with her tusks and slapping them with her trunk, listening hard.

The young Bull approached, ungainly on his oddly elongated legs. 'What are you doing?'

Feeling like a foolish infant – she had to remind herself that this towering Bull was only a calf himself – she said, 'I'm looking for water.'

'There is no water here.'

'Yes, there is. But it's deep underground. Can't you hear it?'

Comically, he cocked his small ears. 'No,' he said.

'Listen with your belly and feet and chest.' She stamped again. 'The ground here is hard and it rings well. And the water that flows deep makes the rock shudder . . .' To Icebones, the rumble of the deep water was a distinct noise under the frothy din of the surface world, like the far-off call of a thunderstorm, or the giant crack of a distant glacier calving an iceberg.

The Bull raised his trunk, as if to smell the deep-buried water. He rammed his tusks against the hard, rippled rock, but they rebounded, and he yelped with pain.

'We must find a place where the water comes closer to the surface.' She walked down the hillside, pausing to stamp and listen, tracking the path of the underground river.

The others followed, the Bull with eagerness, the rest with incomprehension or resentment, but all driven by their thirst.

She came to a place where a vast pipe thrust out of the ground. It stalked away over the rocky slope on spindly legs, like some immense centipede. The pipe was as wide as three or four mammoths standing side by side, and its surface was slick and white, like a tusk.

The pipe was obviously a creation of the Lost. But its purpose did not interest her – for she could hear water running through it.

She began to probe at the ground just above the pipe. The rock was shattered here; underneath a surface layer of dust there was fine rubble. And, when she dug into this with her trunk, she could smell water.

The Bull could smell it too. 'Let me drink! Give me the water!'

Icebones growled. 'I am not your Lost keeper, here to nurse you. The water is here, but you must work for it.' She trumpeted to the others. 'Come, now. Watch what I do.'

She bent her head and cleared away surface debris with brisk swipes of her tusks. Then she stood square and began to dig her way into the rubble with her trunk.

The Ragged One snorted sceptically, but the others crowded closer.

Icebones soon grew tired, but she ignored her discomfort and kept digging.

Perhaps half a trunk's length deep the rubble began to

turn into sticky, half-dried mud, and she gratefully sucked out the first droplets of water.

After that the others quickly settled to work around her. They grumbled and complained as they scraped their tusks or caught their sensitive trunk fingers on sharp rock fragments. But the scent of water lured them on, and soon their complaints turned to a murmur of mutual encouragement.

Icebones could sense warmth rising from the ground here. Perhaps that had something to do with the rivers of rock which had gushed from this Mountain; perhaps that deep warmth had kept the underground water from freezing here.

At last Icebones dug deep enough to find soil soaked to mud. She had to kneel on her front legs to reach. With her trunk tip she hollowed out a chamber deep beneath the ground. She let the hole fill with seeping water, which she sucked out in a great trunk load and emptied into her mouth. The water was hot, a little salty, and it fizzed oddly in her throat – but it was delicious.

The others, working less expertly, were slower, but her success drove them on. At length they were all pumping out muddy, brownish water and filling their mouths.

Working together at the rock face was the nearest this strange, fractured bunch had come to behaving like a Family, Icebones thought. She allowed herself to relish this moment of immersion: the shuffling of feet and the scrape of tusk on rock, the soft rustle of the mammoths' thick hair, and the myriad small sounds, farts and hums and squeals and rumbles, that emanated from the mammoths' immense torsos as they drank.

When she had drunk her fill, Icebones walked away from the others.

The rock beneath her feet came in layers, she found, exploring it with her trunk: layers of red overlying grey, grey overlying blue, blue overlying black. Here and there this stratified rock was pocked by craters, huge circular scars.

Perhaps all of this vast Mountain was made up of layer after layer of hardened rock, vomited from the summit over many years.

When she urinated, the rock and dust fizzed and hissed where her water splashed it. She sniffed at this new peculiarity, baffled and disturbed. The very dust was strange here.

She found a steep-sided ridge and climbed it stiffly, the mild exertion making her gasp for air. The ash had drifted away from the top of the broad ridge, leaving hard exposed rock.

Standing on the ridge, she was suspended between purple sky and a land that glowed red.

The flank of the Fire Mountain swept away beneath her. The sun was setting behind her, already hidden by the Mountain – she was looking east, then – and the sky was a stark dome of bruised purple, showing a few stars at the zenith. The Mountain thrust out of the belly of this world, as if some monstrous planetary calf were struggling to be born. And, on the eastern horizon, she saw those other rocky cones, mountains almost as vast, their sunlit faces glowing red.

There was a layer of clouds *beneath* her. The clouds were tall thunderheads, flat and smooth and black beneath, topped by huge pink-white mounds, and they sailed like icebergs on some invisible sea of thicker, moister air. I really am very high, she thought.

Below the clouds, on the deeper land beneath, she saw swathes of pale green and grey: the mark of life, grasslands or steppe. Raising her trunk she thought she could smell water, far away, far below.

We must go there, she thought, down to that plain. For we surely cannot stay here, on this barren slope.

She could see the giant water-bearing pipe, at the roof of

which the mammoths still dug for water. When she climbed a little higher she saw that more pipes thrust out of the bulk of the Mountain and spread around it across the rocky land. They were thin lines that shone pink in the last of the sunlight.

In a way this great structure was magnificent, she thought, the huge shining trunks stretching straight and far, farther than many mammoth trails. But she wondered if that was why this old Fire Mountain had come to life. The Lost were always thirsty for water. Perhaps, like a greedy mammoth who drains the ground beneath her feet, the Lost had sucked away too much of the water which had gathered here, disturbing the Mountain.

Now the light was fading fast, and the immense shadow of the Fire Mountain stretched across the land. Soon she could hear calls, rising from the hidden depths of the landscape, drifting on the thin, cold air. They were clearly the voices of predators – wolves, perhaps, or cats – marking out their killing territories. Though the predators' calls made her tense and alert, there was something reassuring in the thought that she and her motley band of mammoths were not the only living things in this strange, cold world.

As the light faded further, she heard more subtle sounds: the hiss of wind over mountains and forests and steppe, the deep, subtle murmur of an ocean, the groan of glaciers and the crackling of ice sheets, the murmur of liquid rock within the Fire Mountain, the deeper churning of this world's hot core. When she stamped her feet, she could hear washes of sound echoing back and forth through the deep foundations of the land.

The sunset and the dawn were the times sound carried best. And so she listened, with every aspect of her being, her ears and belly and chest, to the deeper sounds, the songs of the world. And gradually she built up an image, in sounds and echoes, of the spinning rocky ball to which she clung.

This was a small, cold world. It was made of rock, rock

that was hard deep into its being – unlike that other world, the world of her birth, whose rocky skin was laid thin over a churning liquid body, like thin ice on a pond.

But the cold here would suit mammoths, she thought. And the hardness of the rocks made the world's songs easy to hear.

The world was round, like a ball of dung. But it was a misshapen ball. To the north it was flattened, as if a massive foot had stamped down there, cracking and compressing the rock across half the world. The giant pit made by that stamping was, she sensed, filled with water, a world-girdling ocean. The southern lands were higher, but they, too, had been struck a series of immense, damaging blows. One of those slamming impacts had been so powerful it had punched a great pit into the hide of the world – and the impact had caused a rebounding upthrust of rock *here*, in the lands beneath her feet. The huge Fire Mountain itself stood over that rock mound.

This world was a small, swollen, battered place, she saw, born in unimaginable violence, bruised by ancient blows from which it had never healed.

And the world was dying.

She could hear water freezing over, or flowing into deep basins, or seeping into the ground. She could hear the crack of ice spreading over that vast northern ocean. Even the air was settling out. She could hear its moan as it pooled, cooling, like water running downhill, reaching at last the lowest places of all – like that immense punched-in depression on the far side of the world.

The world was growing cold, and its air and water were shrivelling away – and, she supposed, all life with them . . .

And it was not the world where she had been born. The songs of this small world and the songs of that other place – massive, liquid, alive – were unmistakably different.

But how could that be? How could there be a place *here* that was not *there*? It was beyond her imagination.

And – *why* had she been brought here?

She recalled the Island, her Family. It was as if she had been with them yesterday, listening to Silverhair's patient account of how, when she was no older than Icebones now, the Lost had found the Island and nearly killed them off, the last of all the mammoths. All her life, Silverhair had told Icebones she would one day be a Matriarch. And she had steadily coached her daughter in the wisdom of the mammoths, teaching her the songs of the Cycle, imparting a deep sense of blood and land . . .

Yes, one day I will be a Matriarch, Icebones thought. I have always accepted my destiny. But not here. Not now. I am not ready!

But, ready or not, what was she to do next?

She sucked the thin, dry air through her trunk, felt its cold prickle in her lungs, smelled the lingering tang of ash. Alone, longing for the warmth of her Family, she began to sing: 'I am Icebones. My Matriarch was Silverhair, my mother. And her Matriarch was Owlheart. And her Matriarch was Wolfnose . . .'

She called with deep rumbles. She sensed a fluttering of skin over her forehead, the membranes stretched tight over the hollows in her skull that made her voice's deepest sounds. And she stamped, too, a rhythmic thumping that sent acoustic pulses out through the hard rocky ground.

Icebones. Icebones . . .

She gasped and turned around, trunk held high. But she was alone.

Her name had come not through the air, but as deep sound through the hard rock of the ground.

She stamped out, 'I am Icebones, daughter of Silverhair. Who are you?'

Long heartbeats later came a reply. *I am strong and my tusks are powerful. More powerful than my brother's. Are you in oestrus? Are you with calf? Are you suckling?*

Icebones snorted. It was a Bull, then: intent only on

rivalry with his fellows and on mating with any receptive Cow – just like all Bulls, who, some Cows would say, are calves all their lives.

'I am not in oestrus. Where are you?'

It is a cold place. By the shore of a round sea. There is little to eat. Snow falls. There are few of us. Predators stalk us.

She raised her trunk and sniffed the air. She could smell only the rock, the thin, dry air and her own dung. There was no scent of Bull – and an adult Bull in musth, dribbling from his temple glands and trickling urine, emitted a powerful scent indeed. 'You must be far away, very far.'

But my tusks are long and powerful, almost as long as my . . .

His last word was indistinct.

'And you have no need of a name?'

Names? None of us have names.

She snorted. 'I will call you Boaster.'

The steppe is sparse. We walk far to graze. Once we were many, like daisies on the steppe. Now we are few.

'We must find each other,' she said immediately, rapping her message into the deep rock.

A Family of Cows, with no adult Bulls, could not prosper: without Bulls to impregnate the Cows, it would be extinct within a generation. And likewise an isolated bachelor herd without Cows would soon die, unable to reproduce itself. It was a deeper layer of peril, she realised, lurking beyond the dangers of the fires that belched into the air.

Yes. I am ready for you, Icebones. I have no need to wait for musth. But now his words were becoming indistinct. Perhaps he was walking over softer ground, or a storm on that northern ocean was making the rocks too noisy. . . . *Follow the water*, she caught. . . . *Water and the thick warm air . . . the lowest place . . .*

And then he was gone, and she was alone again.

The light was ebbing out of the sky now. The sun had long vanished behind the Mountain, and an ocean of shadow was pooling at its base, obscuring those stretches of steppe and forest, turning them grey and lifeless. The stars were emerging through a great disc of blackness that spread down from the zenith towards the horizon, revealing a huge, clear sky.

There was a presence beside her, a trunk pulling at hers. Eager for company, she clung to it gratefully. But she felt sparse, stiff hair on that trunk, and tasted bitterness.

It was the Ragged One. 'You must come back. The others want you.'

'Why?'

'They want to Remember the old one. As you told them they should.'

Icebones told the Ragged One of the Bull she had spoken to.

The Ragged One seemed to understand little. 'The Bulls were brought here, to the Mountain, to us. And if one of them was in musth, and one of us in oestrus, there would be a mating. That was all we needed to know about Bulls.'

'And you would sing the Song of Oestrus?'

But the Ragged One knew nothing of that. 'Once there were many of us. Many like you, many like *me*. The Lost did not mean to keep us for ever. They were making the world, you see. They were covering it with oceans and steppe and forests. One day there would be room for us to roam, in Clans. But then the Sickness came . . .'

She described an horrific illness among the mammoths. It would begin with blood in urine. Then would come waves of heat and cold, and growths that would sprout from mouth and feet and anus. Finally, after a suffusion of great pain, there would be death.

'And if one caught it, all would fall.' She turned to Icebones, growling. 'I know you think we have been kept by the Lost, that we are like calves. But we heard the mammoths calling to each other, all over this quiet world, Icebones. We heard the cries of the carnivores too, as they broke through fences no longer maintained by the Lost. We heard their joy at the ease of the kills they made, and later their disappointment at how little meat remained.

'And one by one those distant mammoth voices fell silent.

'Can you imagine how that was? Perhaps you should indeed teach us to Remember. Perhaps that is why you have been sent among us – to Remember all who died.'

Icebones was horrified. But she said, '*We* aren't dead yet. On this Mountain there is no food, and precious little water. We must go down to the plains.'

The Ragged One snorted. 'You are a fool. The world is growing cold, yes. *Because the Lost have gone.*'

Icebones was baffled. 'Where did they go?'

'They went up, into the sky,' the Ragged One said. 'And that is where *we* must go. Not down. *Up*.' She said this decisively, and stalked away stiff-legged.

The Remembering was simple.

Icebones had the mammoths help her dig out the body of their grandmother. It had been scorched and dried by its immersion in the ash. Much of the hair was blackened and curling, and the skin was drawn tight. The eyelids, gruesomely, had fallen open, and the eyes had become globes of cloudy, fibrous material, sightless.

Icebones said, 'Watch now, and learn.' She scraped at the bare ground with her tusks. Then she picked up a fingerful of grit and ash and dropped it on the grandmother's unresponding flank.

The mother reached down, picked up a loose rock, and stepped forward to do the same.

Soon they were all using their trunks and feet to cover the inert body with ash, dust and stones – all save the Ragged One, who stayed on the edge of the group, unwilling to participate, and yet unable to turn away.

As they worked, Icebones felt a deeper calm settle on her

soul. The Cycle said this was how the mammoths had always honoured their dead.

Silverhair had told her of a place on the Island called the Plain of Bones, where the ground was thick with the bones of mammoths – of Icebones's ancestors, who had walked across the land for uncounted generations before her. She wondered how many mammoth bones lay beneath the hard rocky ground of this small new world.

CHAPTER 3
THE SKY TRAIL

At dawn the world glowed its brightest red. It was as if the dust and the rocks caught the red light of the rising sun and hurled it back with vigour. Even the mammoths' hair trapped the all-pervasive red light, their guard hairs glowing as if they were on fire. On the plains far below, pools or rivers looked jet black, and the green of life was scattered, irrelevant in this mighty redness.

Icebones longed for a scrap of blue sky.

It was apparent that the mammoths, lacking any better idea, were prepared to go along with the Ragged One's scheme. Though Icebones felt nothing but dread at the very notion of pursuing Lost, she had no better suggestion either.

When the light was adequate, the Ragged One simply set off up the flank of the Mountain. The others followed only haphazardly, paying no attention to each other, with none of the calm discipline of a true Family.

Icebones took a place at the back of their rough line.

The Mountain's slope was shallow, and the mammoths climbed steadily. With their strong hind legs mammoths were well suited to climbing – though descending a slope was always harder, as that meant all a mammoth's weight was supported by her front legs.

Here and there mosses, lichens and even clumps of grass protruded from cracks in the hard red-black ground. Icebones pulled up grass tufts, wrapping her trunk lips around the thin-tasting goodies. But the grass was sparse and yellowed, struggling for life.

And there was no water to be found, none at all. She

could tell from the rock's deep echoes that the groundwater was buried deep here, far beneath a lid of rock much too thick and hard for any mammoth tusk to penetrate.

The dung of the other mammoths was thin and watery. These mammoths had built up a reserve of fat from the ambiguous generosity of their Lost keepers. But it had clearly been a long time since they had fed properly.

As for herself, Icebones had no real idea how long it had been since she had last tasted the Island's lush autumn grass. What a strange thought that was . . . We must find proper grazing soon, she thought.

At length the mammoths reached something new. A line of shining silver stood above the rust-red rock, running parallel to the line of the slope. It stood above the ground on legs like spindly tree trunks.

The line swept down from the humped slope of the Mountain, down towards the hummocked plain below, down as far as Icebones could see until it dwindled to a silvery thread invisible against the red-blue clutter of the layered rock.

Icebones felt cold, deep inside. A thing of clean surfaces and hard sharp edges, this was clearly the work of the Lost.

But the others showed no fear – indeed they seemed curious, and they walked around the skinny supports, probing with pink trunk tips.

The Ragged One came to Icebones. 'This is the south side of the Fire Mountain. The sunlight lingers here. You see the green further below, smell the tang of the leaves? The Lost grew vines there. But now the vines are dying.'

Icebones asked, 'What would you have us do?'

'This is the path the Lost took to the sky,' the Ragged One said simply. 'We must follow it. That way we will find the Lost again.'

Paths worn by mammoths in the steppe were simple trails of bare and compacted earth. This shining aerial band looked like no path Icebones had ever seen. She said starkly,

'Perhaps the Lost don't want you to find them. Have you thought of that? If they wanted you, they would have taken you with them.'

The Ragged One growled and clashed her stubby tusks against Icebones's. 'You should crawl back into the cave of darkness you came from. I will lead these others. When we find the Lost we will be safe.' And she turned her back on Icebones and stalked away, trunk folded beneath her face.

Icebones, fighting her instincts, trailed behind.

As day followed day, the mammoths climbed the endless shallow slope, following the Sky Trail. They grew still more weary, hungry, thirsty, and their joints ached, the soft pads of their feet protesting at the hard cold rock beneath them. Icebones learned to concentrate on each footfall, one after another, letting her strength carry her upward even when it seemed that there was too little air in her aching lungs to sustain her.

The sky above was never brighter than a deep purple-red, even at midday. In the morning there would be a thick blanket of frost that turned the ground pink-white, covering the living things. But as the sun rose the frost quickly burned off, faster than they could scrape it up with their trunks. Even here, life clung to the rock. Grass was sparse, but moss and lichen coated the crimson rock. But as they climbed higher the last traces of ground cover evaporated.

Soon there was only the rock, red and hard and unforgiving. It was as if the land's skull was emerging from beneath a fragile skin of life.

And the higher they climbed, the more the world opened out.

This Fire Mountain was a vast, flattened dome of rock. A sharp cliff surrounded its circular base, with walls that cast long shadows in the light of the dipping sun. Icebones could follow the line of the strange shining Sky Trail down the slope. It passed through a cleft in that forbidding base cliff and strode on into the remote plain, until it dwindled to invisibility amid the thickening green of vegetation.

The land beyond the Fire Mountain was rough and broken, ribbed with sharp ridges. Though littered with patches of green and glinting with water, it would surely be difficult country to cross.

Further away still, she glimpsed an immense valley running almost directly east. The valley was heavily shadowed by this swollen land of giant Fire Mountains, but it ran to the horizon, vanishing in the mist there.

And to the north she saw a gleaming line of ice, flat and pure. The ice spanned the world from horizon to horizon, and she knew she was seeing an ocean, thick with pack ice: it was the ocean whose presence she had sensed, the ocean that had pooled in the great depression that had shaped the northern hemisphere of this world.

It was a vast landscape of shaped rock, red and shadowed grey, pitted with shallow craters – and only thinly marked by the green of life.

There was nothing for Icebones here.

This is not my world, she thought. And it never could be. Why had she been taken from her home, stranded on this alien ball of rock with all its strangeness, where insane moons careened across the sky? Who had done it – the Lost? What twisted cruelty had caused them to plunge her into this strange madness . . . ?

There was a flurry of movement above her. She stood still, raising her tusks suspiciously.

She found herself facing a goat. An ibex, perhaps. It carried proud antlers, and was coated with thick white wool. Its chest was immense, swelling in the thin, dry air. The ibex appeared to have been digging into a patch of black ice with one spindly hoof.

The goat seemed to be limping. The skin over one of its feet was blackened.

'Frostbite,' Icebones said. It was a dread fear of all

mammoths. 'That goat has been incautious. It may lose that foot, and then the stump will turn infected, if it lives that long.'

'No,' growled the Ragged One. 'The frostbitten skin will harden and fall away, leaving new pink skin that will quickly toughen.'

'No creature can recover from frostbite.'

'You cannot,' said the Ragged One. '*I* cannot. But this goat can. It is not like the creatures you have met before, Icebones. Just as this is not the world you knew.'

Icebones watched the goat hobble away, and she wondered if the clever paws of the Lost had made these disturbing changes, even in goats.

The mammoths approached the goat's abandoned ice patch. This had been a pond, Icebones found. In places the ice was clear, so that she could see through it to the black mud at the bottom. On the shallow bank around the pond she found dead vegetation, fronds of grass and pond plants, deep brown and frozen to the mud. When she touched the plants she could taste nothing but icy dirt.

Once it was warm here, she thought, even at this great height. But this world has grown colder, and the pond froze, right down to its base.

The pregnant Cow mewled, 'Nothing can live here. This is no place for us.'

The Ragged One rumbled deeply. 'We should get on.'

But all the mammoths were weary and agitated. Icebones could smell blood and milk in the pregnant Cow's musky scent. Her sisters clustered close around their mother, reluctant to move further. The Bull stomped back and forth, agitated.

'This is foolish,' said the mother, with a sharp slap of her trunk on the ground. 'Enough. We are cold and tired, and it is hard to breathe. We should not climb further.'

The Ragged One regarded them with contempt. She said simply, 'Then I will go on alone.' And she turned her back and, with trunk held high, stood beneath the shining Sky Trail.

'Wait,' Icebones called.

The Ragged One snorted. 'Will you make me stop? You are no Matriarch.'

Icebones said, 'I will come with you. It is not safe for you to go alone. But,' she said carefully, 'if we do not find the Lost, you will come down with me.'

The Ragged One rumbled, hesitating.

Icebones took a step forward, trying to conceal her reluctance to continue this futile climb. The others were watching her sombrely.

The Ragged One proceeded up the slope. Icebones followed.

After a few paces Icebones looked back at the others. Already they were diminished to rust-brown specks on the vast, darkling hillside.

They had long risen far above the sounds of life: the rumbling of the mammoths, the call of birds, the rustle of the thin breeze in the sparse grass. Here there was to be heard only the voice of the Mountain itself. Occasionally Icebones would hear a deep, startling crack, a rattle of distant echoes, as rock broke and fell and an avalanche tumbled down some slab of crimson hillside.

The Sky Trail, ignoring the toiling mammoths beneath it, strode on confidently towards the still-hidden summit of the Mountain.

The ground was complex now, covered by many ancient lava flows: this Mountain had spewed out liquid rock over and over. In places the rock flows had bunched into broad terraces, perhaps shaped by some underlying feature in the mighty slope. The walking was a little easier on the terraces, though the steps between them made for a difficult climb, and Icebones did not relish the prospect of the return.

There were many craters, on this shoulder of rock. Some

of them were vast pits filled with sharp-edged rubble, while others were dents little larger than the footfalls Icebones might make in a field of mud. Some of the larger craters were filled with hard, level pools of fresh rock, and rivers of frozen rock snaked from one pit to another.

Ice had gathered in scattered pocks in the twisted rock face, black and hard, resistant to the probe of her tusks.

These scattered pockets grew larger until they merged, filling shallow depressions between low ridges. Soon Icebones was forced to walk on ice: hard, ridged, wind-sculpted ice, it creaked under her feet as it compressed.

If anything this was worse than the rock. On this pitted surface there was no food, no liquid water to drink – nothing but the ice, its deep cold ever willing to suck a mammoth's heat from her. And the air was thinner and colder than ever, and Icebones's lungs ached unbearably with every step she took.

She heard grunting. The Ragged One was working at a patch of ice with sharp scrapes of her tusks. Her hair, frosted white, stuck out at random angles from her body.

Icebones lumbered up the slope to join her. To her surprise she saw that a tree had grown there. It had a thick trunk that protruded from the ice, and its branches, almost flat against the ice, were laden with a kind of fruit – a black, leathery berry, broad but flaccid, about the size of a mammoth's foot pad.

She asked, 'Is it a willow?' But she knew that no willow could grow on ice.

'Not a willow,' the Ragged One said, panting hard. 'It is a breathing tree. Help me.'

Icebones saw that the Ragged One had been trying to prise some of the broad black fruit out of the ice. Icebones bent to help, lowering her tusks.

One of the fruit popped out of its ice pit, and the Ragged One pulled it to her greedily. Icebones watched curiously as she used her trunk fingers to pull a plug of a hard, shell-like

587

material from the husk of the fruit, and pushed her trunk into a dark, pulp-filled cavity revealed beneath. The fruit quickly collapsed, shrivelling as if thrown on a fire, but the Ragged One closed her eyes, her pleasure evident. Then she cast aside the fruit and began to prise loose another.

'Is it good to eat?'

'Just try it,' said the Ragged One, not sparing attention from her task.

On her first attempt Icebones punctured the fruit's skin, and it deflated quickly with a thin wail. But with her second try she got her fruit safely out of the ice. When she plunged her trunk tip into the soft pulpy cavity, she was startled by a gush of thick, warm, moist air. It was unexpected, remarkable, delicious. She closed her mouth and tried to suck all the air into her lungs, but she got a nostrilful of odourless fruit pulp, and sneezed, wasting most of the air.

She found another fruit and tried again.

For a time the two mammoths worked at the tree, side by side.

The Ragged One poked at an empty skin. 'The tree breathes in during the day, drawing its warmth from the sun and the rock, and it makes the air thick and wet. And at night the fruit breathes out again. In, out, like a sleeping mammoth – but each fruit takes only one breath a day.

'The breathing tree was the first tree that grew here. That is the legend of my kind. The breathing tree makes the air a little warmer and sweeter, so that grass and bushes and birds and ibexes and *we* can live here.'

This meant nothing to Icebones. A *breathing tree*? A fruit that could make a dead world live . . . ?

'Your kind? Where are your kind now?'

The Ragged One's trunk lifted towards Icebones, its mottled skin ugly beneath sparse hair. 'Gone. Dead. I am alone. And so are you. I am not like the others. *They* are all calves of the calves of Silverhair, the last of the mammoths of the Old Steppe.'

Icebones stopped dead. '*Silverhair*?'

'Have you heard of her?'

'She was my mother.'

The Ragged One snorted. 'You are her calf? She *suckled* you?'

'Yes!'

'Then where is she?'

'I don't know,' said Icebones miserably. 'Far from here.'

The Ragged One said slowly, 'Listen to me. Silverhair was the mother of all the mammoths of this Sky Steppe. She was the mother of their mothers, and the mother of their mothers before them . . . and on, back and back. Silverhair has been bones, dust, for a very long time. So how can she have borne *you*, who are standing here before me? You must have slept in your box of darkness for an age, squat one.'

Icebones, bewildered, tried to comprehend all this. *Was it possible?* Could it really be that she had somehow slept away the generations, as calf grew to mother and Matriarch and fell away into death, over and over – as her mother's calves grew to a mighty horde that covered this world – while she, daughter of their first ancestor, had stayed young and childless?

'If what you say is true,' she said, 'you must be a daughter of Silverhair too.'

'Not me,' said the Ragged One, discarding the emptied husk of the last fruit. And she strode on without explanation.

Icebones felt a deep, unaccountable revulsion towards the Ragged One. But she hurried after her, following the pale shadow of the Sky Trail.

Within a few steps, all the warmth and air she had garnered from the breathing tree had dissipated, and she was exhausted again.

*

Icebones marched grimly on through her hunger and thirst, through the gathering pain in her lungs and the aching cold that sucked at the pads of her feet.

At first she was not even aware that the Ragged One had stopped again. It was only when she made out the other's grim, mournful lowing that she realised something was wrong.

The Sky Trail had fallen.

Icebones walked carefully over hard ridges of wind-sculpted ice.

Although those mighty legs still cast their gaunt, clean shadows over the Mountain's slope, the silvery thread of the path itself had crumbled and fallen. It lay over the icy rocks like a length of shining spider-web. When she looked back down the Mountain's flank she saw how the path dangled from the last leg to which it was attached, lank and limp as a mammoth's belly hairs.

The fallen Sky Trail lay in short, sharp-edged segments, shattered and separated. When she probed at the wreckage with her trunk it was cold, hard and without taste or odour, like most of what the Lost produced.

The Ragged One was standing beside a great pod, long, narrow, like a huge broken-open nut. It seemed to be made of the same odourless, gleaming stuff as the Sky Trail itself.

And it contained bodies.

Icebones recognised them immediately. The stubby limbs, the round heads and hairless faces, all enclosed in complex, worked skins. *They were Lost.* And they were dead, that much was clear: there was frost on their faces and in their clouded eyes and opened mouths.

The Ragged One stood over the silent, motionless tableau, probing uselessly at faces and claw-like paws with her trunk. The wind howled thinly through the structure of the leg towers around her.

Icebones said, 'They have been dead a long time. See how the skin of this one is dried out, shrunken on the bone. If not for the height here, the wolves and other scavengers would surely—'

'They were trying to leave,' the Ragged One blurted. 'Perhaps they were the last. And they died when they spilled out of the warmth of their pod on to this cold Mountain.'

'Where were they going?'

'I don't know. How can I know?'

'We should Remember them,' Icebones said.

But the Ragged One snapped harshly, 'No. It is not their way.'

The shrunken sun was approaching the western horizon, and its light was spreading into a broad pale band across the sky. The light glimmered from the ice line of the distant ocean, and the tangled thread of the wrecked Sky Trail, and the tusks of the mammoths. Soon it would be dark.

Icebones said, 'Listen to me. The Lost are gone or dead, and we cannot follow them. And we cannot stay on this Fire Mountain.'

The Ragged One growled and stamped her feet, making the hard rock ring.

Icebones felt immensely tired. 'I don't want to fight you. I have no wish to lead. *You* lead. But you must lead us to a place we can live. You must lead us down from this Mountain of death. Down to where the air pools, like morning mist in a hollow.'

The Ragged One stood silently. Then she said reluctantly, 'You don't understand. I am afraid. I have lived my whole life on this Mountain. I have lived my whole life with the Lost. I don't know how else life can be.'

Impulsively Icebones grabbed her trunk. 'You are not alone. We are all Cousins, and we are bound by the ancient Oath of Kilukpuk, one to the other . . .'

But the Ragged One had never heard of Kilukpuk, or the vows that bound her descendants, whether they climbed the trees or swam the ocean or walked the land with heavy tusks dangling. She pulled away from Icebones's touch.

Still suffused by that deep physical revulsion, Icebones nevertheless felt oddly bound to this pale, malformed creature. For all her strangeness, the Ragged One seemed to have more in common with Icebones than any of the other mammoths here. Only the Ragged One seemed to understand that Icebones was truly *different* – had come from a different place, perhaps even a different time. Only the Ragged One seemed to understand that the world had not always been the same as this – that there were other ways for mammoths to live.

And yet the Ragged One seemed intent on becoming Icebones's enemy.

The Ragged One dropped her head dolefully, emitting a slow, sad murmur. She was clearly unwilling to leave these sad remains, all that was left of the Lost.

Alone, Icebones trudged further up the shallow slope.

The ice thinned. Higher up the slope it began to break up and dissipate altogether, as if she had come so high that even the ice could not survive, and there was only the bare rock. The texture of the rock itself was austere and beautiful, if deadly: it was a bony ground of red and crimson and orange, with not a scrap of white or green, no water or life, not an ice crystal or the smallest patch of lichen.

From here she could see that the eastern flank of the Mountain was a swathe of smooth crimson rock, marked here and there by the black cracks of gullies, or by narrow white threads that were frozen streams. But to the west she saw the white stripes of huge glaciers spilling down towards the lower plains from great bowls of ice.

The ground flattened out to afford her broadening views of the landscape: that gleaming white of ocean ice, the grey-green land below, the Fire Mountain's twin sisters. The land had been distorted and broken by the vast uplift that had created the volcanoes here. In places the rock was wrinkled, covered with sharp ridges that ran around the base of the Mountain, and even cracked open like dried-out skin. The greatest crack of all, running directly to the east away from the Mountain, was that immense valley that stretched far to the horizon, extending around the curve of the world.

And soon she could see the caldera at the very summit of this Mountain-continent, the crater from which burning rock had so recently gushed. It was no simple pit, but a vast walled landscape of pits and craters. On its complex floor molten rock pooled, glowing bright red. The far side of the caldera was a long flat-topped cliff marked by layers, some black, some brown, some pinkish red. Immense caverns had worn into the softer rock, between harder, protective layers.

It was a pit big enough itself to swallow a mountain.

She stood there, listening to the quiet subterranean murmur of the Mountain. The sky faded to a deep purple and then a blue-black above. In that huge blueness, even though the sun still lingered above the horizon, stars swam. The ground under her feet was red-black, cracked and smashed, as if it had been battered by mighty feet, over and over.

She felt humbled by the immensity of this rock beast. The Lost had stolen the water that had lain frozen in its interior, and by doing so had woken its ancient rage. But the Lost's puny devices were no more than scrapes on the Mountain's mighty ancient bulk, the bite of an insect on a mammoth's broad flank.

She returned, carefully, down the slope to where the Ragged One still stood beside the wreckage of the Lost seed pod.

CHAPTER 4
THE DESCENT

The sky was crossed – not by one abnormal moon – but *two*.

The twin moons climbed rapidly in the daylit sky. But without warning they would wink into darkness, as if entering some huge mouth. Or, just as unexpectedly, they flickered into brightness in the middle of the night sky. One of them, which moved more rapidly, had a lumpish shape, like a rock or a bit of dung, not like a real Moon at all. But the other moon was, if anything, stranger still: just a pin-point of light, like a meandering star.

The moons were eerie, unpredictable, and utterly strange. Icebones felt disturbed every time she glimpsed them.

It took days for the two of them to climb back down to the other mammoths.

One cold dawn, longing for company, Icebones stepped away from the Ragged One, who browsed fitfully, still half-asleep.

Icebones stamped hard. 'Boaster! Boaster . . . !'

I hear you, Icebones. It is bright day here.

High on this Fire Mountain it was not yet morning. The pinkish light of the dawn had turned the Mountain's bulk into a deep black silhouette above her, and she could see the spreading plain at the foot of the Mountain as a jumble of shadows, lifeless, intimidating.

This Boaster and his companions must be far away, far around the curve of the world. She felt a twinge of regret. It seemed impossible that she would ever meet her immodest friend.

She said, 'It is cold and dry.'

Here the land is flat but it is frozen. I am tall and strong, but even my great weight leaves no foot marks, and my heavy tusks will not scratch the ice. Nothing lives. Nothing but the carnivores, who stalk us. Their bellies brush the ground, for the pickings are easy for them in this harsh land . . . We seek deeper places.

Yes, she thought, with new determination. Yes, that is what we must do.

Boaster said now, *Yesterday there was a duel. Neither Bull would back down. One was gored, the other's head was crushed.*

'Were they in musth?'

Yes, both in musth, in deep musth.

With no Cows, the rivalry battles in that isolated bachelor herd were futile, so must be all the more savage. Frustrated, the Bulls were fighting themselves to death.

But now Boaster was saying, *Be wary, little Icebones. Even as an infant I was mighty. My calf will weigh you down, like a boulder in the belly. Are you in oestrus yet?*

No, she thought. Not yet. And when she probed that deep oceanic part of herself, she detected no sign that oestrus was near. She felt well enough. Perhaps it was simply not her time.

When I am in musth, my dribble smells sweet. It will make you wonder, before I mount you.

'If I permit you . . .'

They talked on, as the planet turned.

Icebones and the Ragged One returned, weary, to the group.

It seemed to Icebones that in just a few days the air had grown distinctly colder. And it was clear to all the mammoths that they couldn't stay here.

But to Icebones's dismay the mammoths bickered about what to do.

The mother wanted them to descend from this high Mountain shoulder. Perhaps they should make for the sea, the mother suggested, for there at least they would find water.

Icebones kept her counsel. To descend was in accord with her own instincts. She knew that the seas around the Island had been salty – no use for drinking – but perhaps here the seas were different, like so much else.

The pregnant sister kept apart. Obsessed and worried about the dependent creature growing within her, she had turned inward. The Cow needed the support and guidance of her Family as at no other time in her life. But such support was not forthcoming, for her relatives did not know how to give it.

Sometimes the infant kicked and murmured, and Icebones knew it was enduring bad dreams of its life to come.

Like the Ragged One, the other sisters seemed intent on seeking out the vanished Lost. The older of them – a tall, vain creature with tightly spiralling tusks – demanded they roam around the Mountain. Her younger sister, dominated by the vain one, rumbled eager agreement. It was the younger who had been scorched by the Mountain's falling rock, and she still bore a pink, hairless patch of healing skin.

As for the Bull, he seemed intent only on adventure. He charged back and forth across the bleak rock slope, trumpeting and brandishing his tusks, in pursuit of imaginary enemies and rivals.

Icebones growled her frustration. In a true Family at a time of decision making, all would be entitled to their say, but all would know their place. A good Matriarch would listen calmly, and then make her decision – or rather, speak the Family's decision for them.

In a Family everybody knew what to do, from instinct and a lifetime's training. Here, it seemed, nobody knew their roles, or how to behave. And as Icebones listened to the bickering she heard a deeper truth: without the cocoon of

Lost which had protected them all their lives, these mammoths were bewildered, all but helpless, and very, very afraid.

She drew the mother aside. 'You must lead them.'

The mother raised her trunk sorrowfully and probed at Icebones's scalp hairs. Her scent was rich and smoky, like the last leaves of autumn. 'You want me to be a Matriarch.'

'You must make them into a Family. A Family is always there – from the day you are born, to the day you die . . .' Icebones recalled wistfully how her own mother, Silverhair, had been with her as she grew up, with her for every heartbeat of her young life. 'And without a Family—' Without my Family, she thought, I am not complete. She quoted the Cycle. '*In the Family, I becomes We.*'

The mother said wistfully, 'We don't have Families here. The Lost saw to that.'

Icebones said harshly, 'The Lost are gone now. I saw them up on that mountainside – the last of them, their dried-out corpses. They cannot help you. You are the mother of these squabbling calves. Tell them what you have decided, and then lead them.'

The mother seemed dubious. But she stood before the younger mammoths and slapped the ground with her trunk.

The sisters and the Bull turned, rumbling in soft alarm.

The mother said, 'We must go down to the lower places. There will be warmth, and grass to eat. We will go to the shore of the great northern sea, and drink its water.'

For a frozen moment the mammoths fell silent. The sisters regarded their mother. The Bull pawed the ground and growled softly.

The Ragged One stood aloof, head turned away, the thin wind raising the loose hairs of her back. She said: '*Which way?*'

Icebones saw the mother was hesitating. It wasn't a trivial

question: Icebones had seen from the summit that this
dome-shaped Mountain was surrounded by a scarp of tall,
impassable cliffs. But she knew there was a way through.

She stepped up to the mother. As if she was addressing a
true Matriarch, she said respectfully, 'If we follow the Sky
Trail down the Mountain, we will find a way through the
cliffs.'

The mother, with relief, replied, 'Yes. We will follow the
Sky Trail. It will be many days' walk. The sooner we begin,
the sooner we will reach the sea.' And she stepped forward
with confidence.

Grumbling, resentful – but perhaps inwardly relieved that
somebody was taking the lead – her daughters fell in behind
her. Icebones took the rear of the little line, while the Bull
ran alongside, keeping his separation from the group of
Cows, as a growing Bull should.

At least we are trying, Icebones thought. And, wherever I
die, at least it will not be here, on this dismal rocky slope.

As the little group made its way down the Mountain,
following the strange straight-line shadow of the shining
Sky Trail, the Ragged One followed them, distant, silent.

The rock beneath their feet was unyielding. Sometimes,
when the land was gouged and scarred by ancient flows of
molten rock, they had to detour far from the Sky Trail.

The only water was to be found in hollows where rain or
snow had gathered. Most of these puddles were frozen to
their bases, but as they descended they found a few larger
ponds where some liquid water persisted beneath a thick
shell of ice. Gratefully the mammoths cracked the ice lids
with their tusks or feet and sucked up the dirty, brackish
water.

But the taller, spiral-tusked sister complained about the
foul stink of the pond water compared to the cool, clean
stuff the Lost used to provide for them.

At night, when the shrunken sun had fallen away and the

cold clear stars emerged from the purple sky, they mostly kept walking, their trunks seeking out water and scraps of vegetation. They would pause only briefly to sleep, and Icebones encouraged them to gather close together, the pregnant one at the centre, so that they shared and trapped the warmth of their bodies.

It was very disturbing to Icebones to walk over new land: land where there were no mammoth trails, no memories in her head, nobody to lead. It was the mammoths' way to learn the land, to build it into their memories and wisdom, and to teach it to their young. That way the land's perils could be avoided and its riches sought. That learning had never happened here. And it troubled her that every step she took was into strangeness – and unknown danger.

After a few days they reached the terminus of the Sky Trail. The shining line sank into a kind of cave, a place of hard straight lines and smooth walls. Icebones shrank from it. But the others clumped forward eagerly and explored every cold surface and every sharp straight edge, as if saying goodbye.

They walked on.

Below the Sky Trail terminus, the rock was just as barren and sparse of life as it had been at higher altitude. But Icebones felt her spirits lift subtly, as if the looming Sky Trail, the mark of the Lost, had been weighing on her spirit.

The Bull came to walk with her. His coat was glossy and thick, and he held his growing tusks high. 'Why must we call you Icebones?'

'Because it is my name.'

He thought about that. 'Very well. But why not Boulder, or Snowflake, or Pond?'

'My mother said I was heavy and cold in her womb. As if she'd swallowed a lump of ice, she told me. And so she called me Icebones. A name is part of a mammoth—'

'I have no name,' he said.

'I know.'

'Will you give me a name?'

Intrigued, she asked, 'What kind of name?'

'I am strong and fierce,' he said, illustrating this with a comically deep growl. 'I will be a brave hero, and I will mate all the Cows in the world. Silverhair was brave and strong. Perhaps my name should be Silverhair.'

She snorted her amusement. 'That was the name of my mother. She was indeed brave and strong. But you are a Bull, and you need the name of a Bull.'

'I don't know the names of any Bulls.'

'The Cycle tells of the bravest and strongest Bull who ever lived. His name was Longtusk. He lived long ago, in a time when the steppe was full of mammoths. He lived alone among the animals, and he even lived among the Lost – for it is the fate of Bulls, you know, to leave their Families and travel far. But then at last he found his Clan and led them on a great journey, to a place where they could live without fear. In the end he gave his life to save them.'

The Bull trumpeted his appreciation. 'I would like to be called Longtusk,' he growled. 'But I am no hero. Not yet, anyway.'

She pondered. 'Your voice is deep and carries far, like the thunder. Longtusk had a faithful companion called Walks With Thunder. *Thunder*. There. That shall be your name.'

'Thunder, Thunder!' The towering Bull, with his spindly legs and thin, immature tusks, ran after the Cows to tell them his exciting news.

The next morning, the Cow with the spiral-shaped tusks came up to Icebones, trailed, as always, by her smaller sister. The older one said diffidently, 'That fool of a Bull says you have given him a name.'

'He has found his name,' Icebones said.

The Cow snorted. '*I* have no need of a name – not from a mammoth. The Lost liked me, you see. They used to admire my tusks and my long hair. Their cubs would brush my belly hairs with their paws, and I would let the older ones climb on my back while I walked.'

Icebones tried not to show her revulsion.

'They would talk to me all the time,' said the Cow. 'Not the way a mammoth talks, of course. They had a funny jabber they made with their mouths, and they didn't use their bellies or feet or foreheads at all. But you could tell they were talking even so.' She walked oddly as she said this, as if showing off her hair and fine muscles for an invisible audience of Lost. 'So I am quite sure the Lost had their own name for *me*.'

Icebones stayed silent, watching her.

At length the Cow said, 'But if you *were* to give me a name – a mammoth name, I mean – what would it be?'

Most mammoth names reflected a deep characteristic of their holder: an attribute of her body, her smell or taste or noise – even her weight, like Icebones's. Few were to do with the way a mammoth *looked*: Silverhair, yes, for that lank of grey on her forehead had been such a startling characteristic. But Icebones knew that sight was the most important sense of all for the Lost. And so for this one, the way she had looked in the eyes of the Lost was the key to her character.

'Your name will be Spiral,' Icebones said. 'For your tusks twist around in spirals, the one like the other.'

'*Spiral*.' The Cow wandered away, admiring her own tusks.

Her sister made to follow Spiral as usual, but she hesitated. 'Icebones, what about my mother?'

It is not my place to name these mammoths, Icebones thought. I am not their Matriarch, or their mother. But if not me, who? She thought of the smell of the older Cow, her tangy, smoky musk. 'Autumn,' Icebones said impulsively. 'For she smells of the last, delicious grass of summer.'

The Cow seemed pleased. 'And my other sister, the one with calf?'

'I would call her Breeze—'

'For her hair is loose and whips in the wind, like the grass on a windblown steppe!'

'Yes.' This little one isn't so bad, Icebones thought, when she gets away from her foolish sister. 'Will you tell them for me?'

'Yes, I will.'

'And what about you?'

'Me?' The Cow was transfixed, as if she hadn't imagined such an honour could be applied to her. 'You choose, Icebones.'

Icebones probed at the young Cow's mouth, and tasted sweetness. 'Shoot,' she said at last. 'For you taste of young, fresh grass.'

The Cow seemed delighted. 'Thank you, Icebones . . . But what about *her*?'

She meant the Ragged One, who grazed alone as usual, irritably dragging at grass tufts and willow tips, her rough hair a cloud of captured sunlight around her.

'She is the Ragged One,' said Icebones. 'No other name would suit.'

But the little Cow had already scampered away, after her sister.

They approached the lip of the Mountain-base cliff. The wall was heavily eroded, and very steep – what they could see of it; none of them cared to approach the edge.

At last Icebones found a steep gully that cut deep into the ground. Its floor was strewn with boulders and frost-shattered rubble, as if a river had once flowed there. It would not be an easy route, but this cleft, cutting deep into the rock behind the cliffs, offered a way down to the plains below.

Cautiously, reluctantly, the mammoths filed into the gully.

The rock that made up the walls was grey-red and very hard, its surface covered with sharp-edged protruding lumps, speckled with glimmering minerals of green and black. Moss grew in cracks in the walls and over some of the loose rocks. The wind tumbling off the Fire Mountain's broad flanks poured through this gap, and mercilessly sucked out the mammoths' heat. Icebones could hear the rumbles of complaint echoing back from the tall, sheer walls.

A pair of birds flew up and down the gully, graceful, large-winged. Perhaps they were swallows.

The mammoths found a place where the rocky floor was broken by small crevices, which provided shelter for succulent grass clumps and even herbs. The mammoths fell on this feast and ate greedily.

Leaving the feeding mammoths, Icebones came to a broad ledge that led out to the face of the cliff itself. She walked along the ledge, curious, probing at the smooth rock with her trunk . . . and the cliff face opened out around her.

She realised that looking down from the Mountain's summit she had had no real idea of the vast size of this cliff. Seen from here, there was *only* the cliff: a wall of blue-red rock that rose above her and out of sight, and fell away beneath her to a blur of red tinged with grey-green that might have been the ground. There was cloud both above her *and* below: a layer of pink-grey cirrus far above, and a smooth rippling sea below.

The world was simple: cloud above and below, and this hard vertical cliff face, like an upturned landscape.

She spotted a waterfall, where an underground river burst out of the rock face into the air. But the water fell with an eerie slowness, as if the air was too thick to allow it to pass, and it broke up into myriad red-glimmering droplets that dispersed in the air. This was a waterfall that would never reach the ground, she realised.

. . . And then it struck her how *high* she was here, higher than clouds, higher than birds – and how unprotected. Mammoths were plain animals, unused to heights. Vertigo overwhelmed her, and she inched back along the ledge towards the others, and safety.

As they neared the base of the gully, it began to broaden and flatten, its eroded walls diminishing. But its floor was littered with rocks. The mammoths had to work their way past boulders which towered over them, and under their feet was a litter of loose rock, scree and talus that sometimes gave way under an incautious step. But the big rocks were pitted and carved by the wind, and many of the looser small rocks underfoot were worn smooth by wind or water also.

Icebones was the first to break out of the gully, and walk beyond the cliff. She stepped forward carefully, relishing the openness around her. Sandpipers fled from her, screeching in protest.

She found herself walking over dwarf willows, a flattened, ground-hugging forest that crunched under her feet. A red-black river meandered sluggishly across a ruddy plain. Two cranes stood by the river, still and watchful, as many creatures of the steppe habitually were. As she approached a longspur, it sat as still as a stone on its nest of woven grass, watching her with black eyes. She could see the bird's eggs, which glowed with a smooth pink light.

Away from the river small lakes stood out, purple-black. In the larger ponds Icebones could see a gleam of green: cores of ice that survived from the last winter, and would probably persist to the next.

In the shimmering, complex light, this land at the foot of the cliff was a bowl of life. She saw more willows and sedges, their green vivid against the underlying crimson of the rock. And even the bare outcropping rock was stained yellow or orange by lichen.

It was a typical steppe. It was a place of stillness and

watchfulness, for the land was ungenerous. But, unlike the bare wall of the Mountain, this land was *alive*, and Icebones felt her soul expand into its familiar silence.

She turned and looked back towards the cliff. Its base was fringed by conifer forest. Compared to the mammoths grazing at their bases, these trees grew very tall, Icebones saw immediately: they were slender, but they soared fifty, even a hundred times the height of a mammoth, so that their upper branches were a blur of greenery.

But the trees, huge as they were, were utterly dwarfed by the wall of rock that banded the base of the Fire Mountain.

Bright red, extensively fluted and carved by the wind, the tremendous cliff soared high above the broken ground. The columns and vertical chasms of its face glowed a deep burnt orange in the light of the setting sun. The gully the mammoths had climbed down was a black crack, barely visible.

So immense was its length that the cliff looked like a flat, unbending wall, marching from horizon to horizon. The cliff was a wall that cut the sky in half, and it was oppressive, crushing: like a wall of time, she thought, separating her from her Family, like death, which would one day part her from everything she knew and loved.

The mammoths stayed at the base of the cliff for a night, grazing and resting.

The sun, easing west, passed over the cliff's rim not long after midday, and shadows spilled over the ground. The cliff turned purple-red, and the air immediately started to feel colder. Although the day was only half gone – a glance at the bright pale pink sky told Icebones that – here at the foot of this mighty barrier it was already twilight. She noticed now how spindly the conifer trees were, as if they were straining for the light they could never hope to reach.

And in the dawn, with the sky barely paled by the rising sun, the light caught the top of the cliff, so that a great band of orange rock shone high in the sky directly above her. It was like a smeared-out rocky sun, and it actually cast a little light – though no warmth – over the night-darkened plains at the cliff's base.

It was a relief to walk away from the cliff's brooding mass, and out of its pool of shadow.

CHAPTER 5
THE OCEAN OF THE NORTH

The mammoths worked their way steadily northwards, seeking the ocean.

The going was slow, for the land, folded and broken, was covered by lobes and ridges and collapsed rocky tunnels, and the mammoths were frequently forced to turn away from their northern heading. Icebones was acutely aware that every diversion lengthened the journey they must complete.

But she was not aware of any change of the season. The last she recalled of the Island it had been autumn – but that fading memory seemed to have no relevance here. The mammoths were not shedding any winter coat, so she supposed it must be late summer or autumn. But she sensed no drawing-in of the nights, no gathering cold. Perhaps even time ran slowly here, slow as falling water, slow as coagulating blood.

The days wore away.

At length the mammoths reached a new land.

It was an ocean of dust: a flat red plain, a line of ice close to the northern horizon, a dome of pinkish sky in which the small sun sailed. Where bare rock was exposed, it was dark and tinged with blue or purple, sheets of it eroded almost flat.

The higher land they were leaving, to the south, curved in a great arc, a coast for this sea of dust. The 'shore' was littered with gravel bars and drifts of red dust.

There were structures on this higher ground – blocky,

straight-edged shelters that were obviously the work of the Lost.

The mammoths looked around these buildings desultorily. They were boxes pierced by straight-edged holes. Dust had drifted up against the walls of the buildings, and had filtered inside, covering their inner floors with a fine red carpet. The mammoths' broad feet left shallow cone-shaped tracks in the dust, which flowed quickly back where they had disturbed it. Near the buildings a stand of trees poked out of the bright red ground. They might have been oaks. But they were clearly long dead, their bare branches skeletal and gaunt and their trunks hollowed out, and any last leaves that had fallen had long been buried or driven away by the wind.

The Ragged One had walked a little way further to the north, on to the dust plain. She was probing at something black and ropy on the ground. It was clearly dead, and it crumbled and broke.

'See this?' she said to Icebones. 'Seaweed. Once the sea covered all this dust and sand. But now the sea is far away. Look – you can see where the shore used to be.'

Icebones made out rippled ridges in the sand, the footprint of the vanished sea.

'And look at this.' The Ragged One walked a little deeper into the plain. She came to a set of smooth, rounded shapes that protruded from the dust. She blew on the shapes with her trunk and exposed wood, scuffed and pitted by wind-blown sand.

'More work of the Lost,' said Icebones.

'Yes.' The Ragged One dug her tusks under one of the objects and, with a heave, flipped it on its back, sending dust flying. It was like a bird's nest, sculpted in smooth wood. 'The Lost would sit in such things as these, and float upon the water. As was their right. For they made these floating things – *and they made the ocean itself*, brought the water here to cover the land, brought the fish and worms and even the seaweed to live here. But now the world is drying like a corpse – the water has gone—'

'And so have the Lost.'

'Yes. And so have the Lost.' The Ragged One ran her trunk tip longingly over the eroded lines of the stranded boat. The red dust had stained the pale ivory of her tusks a subtle, rusty pink.

Icebones felt a sudden surge of sympathy for her. She reached out and wrapped her trunk around the head of the other, ignoring the now-familiar stale stink. 'Come,' she said. 'We must cross this dried-out seabed. If we start, the others will follow.'

Briefly the Ragged One closed her eyes, rumbling a kind of contentment at Icebones's touch. Then, sharply, she pulled away. 'Yes. We must go to the water.'

Side by side, Icebones and the Ragged One began to plod across the bone-dry plain.

The land remained utterly flat, a beach left stranded by a last fatal tide. When Icebones walked, windblown dust would billow around her, as if dancing in memory of the waters that had once washed over this place.

When she walked over more compact dust or exposed rock, she felt her footsteps ring through the rocky foundation of this ancient sea. And she could tell that this plain, overlaid by the shrunken sea to the north, encompassed the whole top half of this world, a wasteland that stretched all the way to the north pole and down almost to the equator. It was remarkable, enormous, intimidating, and by comparison she was like a beetle crawling across the textured footprint of a mammoth.

If the water was gone, then this had become a sea of light.

Broad, shallow, wave-like dunes crossed from horizon to horizon. As the sun descended, the low light shone brightly from the west-facing slopes of the dunes, and shadows lengthened behind them, so that Icebones was surrounded by bands of shining ochre light. And when she looked at the soft ground at her feet she saw how each dust grain shone grey or red, as if defying the dying of the light.

Here and there rocks littered the surface. Some of the rocks were half buried by dust, and their buried edges were generally sharper than those exposed to the erosion of wind and rain. She learned caution where she stepped, not wishing to cut her foot pads. Sometimes the remnants of living things clung to an exposed rock: fronds of dried-up, blackened seaweed, or small white shells.

The dust was thick and clinging, but it had its uses. All the mammoths were plagued by ticks and lice – Icebones suspected the Lost had groomed them, keeping them clear of such parasites – and she had to show them how to rub dust and dirt into their skin to scrub away the irritants.

It seemed very strange to have to teach a calf's skills to a tall old Cow like Autumn.

But there was nothing to drink here, nothing to eat. The dust clogged her trunk and throat, sucking out the moisture, making her even more thirsty. The dust stank, of blood and iron.

As they continued to walk steadily north the character of the ground changed. In places the land shone, coated with fine flat sheets of some white, glittering substance. When she tasted this, she found it was salt, another relic of the vanished sea.

Soon her footfalls were breaking through an upper layer of dust, exposing frosty, damp mud, rust-coloured. There was water here, not far beneath the surface.

And now there was vegetation, grass sprouting out of the dirty red mud. It was nothing but tough dune grass. But the mammoths, who had eaten nothing for half a day, fell on the wiry yellow stuff as if it was the finest browse.

Gulls hopped among the spindly grass tufts or circled overhead, their caws thin and clear in the cold, still air. Icebones thought the gulls seemed huge – their bobbing heads rose higher than her own belly hairs – much larger than any birds she recalled from the Island.

At last the land sloped down sharply, forming a beach strewn with rust-red gravel and littered with scraps of dusty frost.

The mammoths stepped forward cautiously.

Beyond the beach, just a few paces away, water lapped, black and oily. It was a half-frozen ocean. Here and there ice sheets clung to the beach. Further out floes of ice drifted on the water, colliding with slow, grinding crashes. Some of the ice was stained brown, perhaps where floes had been flipped over by bears or seals, exposing the weeds that crusted their lower surface. Stretches of exposed water made a complex pattern of cracks and scrapings like the wrinkled skin of a very old mammoth, shaped by wind and current. The exposed water was as black as night. Here and there traces of fog and even windblown snow curled tiredly.

Birds wheeled exuberantly. She spied huge-winged kittiwakes, fulmars and jet-black guillemots. Every so often one of them would plunge into the dark water, seeking plankton or cod.

There was more life here, crowded close to this shore, than anywhere else Icebones had seen on this small world.

She heard an angry screeching. There was a bloody carcass on the ice – perhaps it was a seal, or even a bear cub. Petrels soared over it trailing arched wings, their tails fanned out to ward off rivals. Landing on the ice, they tucked their heads right inside the corpse, emerging with their heads and necks gleaming bright red, only their pale, angry eyes showing white.

The light of the pinkish sky turned the ice rust red, the exposed water a deep purple-black. The sea rolled with huge, languid waves, much taller and slower than anything on the oceans around the Island. The ice seemed to moan and wail like a living thing, as, riding the ocean's tremendous waves, it warped and cracked.

In this setting even the mammoths looked strange, transformed: they were stolid blocks of fur and fat, their tusks shining red-pink, their bodies surrounded by crimson-glowing haloes where the sunlight caught their guard hairs.

This was not like the coast of the Island. To Icebones this rust-red shore was a strange and alien scene indeed.

She spotted a bear, swimming through a lead of open water. His head was white as bone, and he cut steadily through the black water, trailing a fine wake behind him. He reached an ice floe and, in a single powerful lunge, pulled himself out of the water, his back feet catching the lip of the ice without hesitation. He shook himself, and water flew off his fur in a cloud of spray.

The bear turned and glared at the mammoths with small black eyes.

His fur caught the light, so that subtle reds and pink-whites gleamed from his guard hairs. Icebones saw that his hips were wider than his shoulder, his long neck sinuous, so that he was a wedge of muscle and power that faced her with a deadly concentration. And he was huge, she saw: much larger than any bear she ever saw off the coast of the Island.

He crossed to the other side of his floe, his great clawed paws swinging, and slid back into the water, silently.

She was in a hunting ground. Her underfur prickled, and she raised her trunk suspiciously.

She stepped down to the water's edge. A few paces from the sea, petrels had dug their burrows into the unfrozen earth. When Icebones trod on a burrow inadvertently, collapsing it, a soft-plumed adult bird blinked up at her in silent protest.

Icebones let the sea water soak into the long hairs that dangled over her feet. The water itself was cold and sharp.

She sucked up a cautious trunkful and dipped her trunk tip into her mouth. It seemed to fizz, oddly, making bubbles in her nostrils, as if air dissolved in it were struggling to escape.

It was a bitter brine.

And in the air that blew off the face of the ocean, soft but very cold, she could smell salt.

Of course this tremendous world sea would be full of salt, just like the ocean that had surrounded the Island. This Ocean of the North was nothing but sour undrinkable brine, all the way to the pole of the world.

She sensed in their hunched postures that the other mammoths knew this as well as she did. It was as she had expected, but she felt disappointed nonetheless.

As if to put on a brave swagger, the Bull, Thunder, trumpeted and charged forward into open water. Spray danced up around his legs, quickly soaking his fur, and ice crackled against his chest. 'Come on,' he yelled. 'At least we can get rid of this foul dust for a while!' And he plunged his trunk into the water and sprayed it high in the air.

Shoot ran after the Bull into the deeper water, lumbering and squealing. The little Cow stumbled, immersing her head, but she came up squirting water from her trunk brightly. 'It's cold! And it gets deep, just here. Watch out—'

'Thunder. Call me Thunder!' And the Bull rapped his trunk into the water, sending spray over the Cow. Vigorously, Shoot splashed back.

Haughty Spiral stayed close to her mother and sister Breeze, watching the antics of the others with disdain.

Droplets of brine, caught on the wind, spattered into Icebones's face and stung her eyes.

A flash of motion further from the shore caught her eye. It had looked, oddly, like a tusk – but it had been straight and sharp, not like a mammoth's ivory spiral. There it was again, a fine twisted cone that rolled languidly through the air. And now she saw a vast grey body sliding through a dark lead of open water, turning slowly. She heard a moan, and then a harsh screech, accompanied by a spray of water. Perhaps this was some strange whale.

The Ragged One came to stand beside Icebones. 'The water is foul,' she rumbled. 'I suppose you will tell us now you always knew it would be like this.'

'This is not my world,' Icebones said levelly. 'I know nothing of its oceans.'

The Ragged One growled.

'This is not the time to argue,' Icebones said. 'We cannot stay here. That much is obvious.' She turned, trunk raised, seeking Autumn.

But there was a sharp trumpet from the water.

All the mammoths turned.

Shoot was floundering, hair soaked, struggling to keep her head above the water. Icebones could see the black triangle of her small mouth beneath her raised trunk.

But the trumpet had come not from Shoot, but from Thunder. The Bull was splashing his way out of the water as fast as he could, trunk held high, eyes ringed white with panic.

Now there was a surge behind Shoot, like a huge wave gathering.

Abruptly a mass burst out of the water, scattering smashed ice that tumbled back with a clatter. Icebones glimpsed a blunt head with a smooth, rounded forehead, and that strange twisted tusk thrust out through the upper lip of the opened mouth, on the left side. The tusk alone would have dwarfed Icebones. But even the head was small in comparison with a vast body: grey and marbled, marked with spots and streaks, grey as dead flesh, with small front flippers, and a crumpled ridge along its back. When the whole of that body had lifted out of the water, the flukes of its powerful tail beat the water with great slaps.

By Kilukpuk's mercy, Icebones thought, bewildered.

The whale fell back into the water, writhing, with a vast

languid splash. Shoot was engulfed, and Icebones wondered if she had already been taken in that vast mouth.

But when the water subsided, Icebones saw that Shoot was still alive, gamely trying to swim in the churning water. 'Help me!' she called, with high, thin chirps of her trunk.

Without thinking further, Icebones rushed into the water. She ran past Thunder, who stood shivering on the shore. But the Ragged One ran with her.

Icebones slowed when the water reached her chest and soaked into her heavy hairs, and the sea-bottom ooze clumped around her feet. The Ragged One, taller and with longer legs, was able to make faster progress, and she reached Shoot first.

The whale made another run. Water surged. A school of silver fish came flying from the water before splashing back, dead or stunned. Fulmars and kittiwakes fell on this unexpected bounty, screeching.

The Ragged One had wrapped her trunk around Shoot's, and was hauling her towards the shore. Icebones hurried to the Cow's rear, half-swimming in the rapidly deepening water, and rammed at Shoot's rump with her forehead.

The whale lunged out of the water, and that huge twisted tusk was held high above the mammoths, ugly and sharp.

For a heartbeat Icebones found herself peering into the whale's ugly purple mouth. Its lips barely covered its rows of cone-shaped teeth. Its eyes were set at the corners of the mouth – and, though a dark intelligence glimmered there, Icebones saw that the eyes could not move in their sockets.

In its way it was beautiful, Icebones couldn't help thinking: a solitary killer, stripped of the social complexity of a mammoth's life, its whole being intent only on killing – beautiful, and terrible.

The whale fell back.

As they struggled on towards the shore, with her head immersed in the murky, icy brine, Icebones rammed at Shoot's backside with increased urgency.

But the snap of jaws around her did not come. At last the mammoths found themselves in shallower water, beyond the reach of those immense teeth.

Shoot's sisters hurried to her and ran their trunks over her head and into her mouth, cherishing her survival. Shoot, shaking herself free of water, showed no signs of injury from her ordeal, though the whale's teeth must have missed her by no more than a hair's-breadth.

The Ragged One stood with Icebones by the edge of the suddenly treacherous sea. The whale's tusk broke the surface and cruised to and fro, as if seeking to lure an unwary mammoth back into the water, and where it passed, sheets of ice were cracked and lifted and brushed aside.

'If the Lost created this ocean,' Icebones said, 'why would they put in it such a monster as that?'

'Perhaps they didn't,' the Ragged One said. 'Perhaps it has cruised the waters of this world ocean, eating all the smaller creatures, devouring its rivals, growing larger and larger as it feeds – devouring until nothing was left to challenge it . . . A monster to suit a giant ocean. If the Lost were here they would surely destroy it.'

'But they are not here.'

'No.'

'You did well,' Icebones said.

The Ragged One slapped the water with her trunk, irritably. Evidently she did not welcome Icebones's praise. 'This is not your world,' the Ragged One growled. 'Just as you said.'

Thunder was strutting to and fro, raising and lowering his tusks, his posture an odd mixture of aggression and submission.

Icebones approached him cautiously. 'Thunder?'

'Don't call me that!' He scuffed the dusty beach angrily. 'Shoot was threatened, and I ran from danger. I am not Thunder. I am not even a Bull. I am nothing.'

'I know that the heart of a great Bull beats inside you. And you are part of this Family, just as much as the others.'

'I have no Family. I was taken from my mother when I was a calf.'

'Taken? Why?'

'That is what the Lost do. What does it matter?'

'It matters a great deal. A calf should be with his mother.'

'I have no Family,' he repeated. 'You despise me.'

'You followed your instinct,' she said harshly. '*The mammoth dies, but mammoths live on*. That's what the Cycle says. There are times when it is right to sacrifice another's life to save your own.'

The Bull growled bitterly, 'Even if that's true, *you saved Shoot*, where I failed.'

She reached out to him, but he flinched, muttering and rumbling, and stalked away.

She sought out Autumn. The tall, clear-eyed Cow was standing alone.

'The Bull-calf blames himself,' Autumn said. 'But *I* led us here, to this vile and useless sea.'

'How could you have known? You have lived all your life on your Mountain. It was a worthwhile gamble—'

'Because I led us here my daughter was nearly killed, and we will all starve or die of thirst. If some new monster does not burst out of the ground to devour us first.'

Icebones grabbed her trunk. 'You must lead us.'

Autumn probed at Icebones's face. 'Don't you understand? I was the Matriarch, for a few brief days, and I have killed us all.' And she stumbled away.

The Ragged One, standing alone by the shore, was remote, withdrawn as ever, still mourning her failure to find the Lost on the mountain summit. Thunder and Autumn were both immersed in their private worlds of self-loathing and anger. Breeze was standing at the water's edge, lost in herself, her swollen belly brushing the languid

617

waves. Shoot was pursuing her sister, regaling her with lurid tales of her encounter with the monster from the sea, while Spiral trotted haughtily away.

None of them will lead, Icebones realised, dismayed. They will stay here on this desolate beach, sulking or fretting or boasting, as the sun rises and falls, and we grow still more thirsty and hungry.

No, Icebones thought. I am not prepared to die. Not yet.

She drew herself up to her full height, and emitted a commanding rumble, as loudly as she could.

The other mammoths turned towards her.

Silverhair, be with me now, she prayed.

'You will pay attention to me,' she said.

A flock of ivory gulls, startled by her call, lifted into the air on vast translucent wings.

She kept her voice as deep and loud as she could – although, before these towering mammoths, she felt small and inferior, a squat, noisy calf.

'You were right in your first guesses, when I emerged from my cave of Sleep. I am indeed a Matriarch. On the Old Steppe, where I lived, I was Matriarch of a Family of many mammoths, despite my youth. I led them well, and I was loved and respected.'

The Ragged One said slyly, 'If this is so, why didn't you say so before?'

'I wanted to see if you were fit to join my new Family.' She raised her trunk, as if sniffing them all. 'And I have decided that you are strong mammoths with good hearts. I am your Matriarch. I will listen to you, but you will do as I say.'

Autumn had turned away, and Thunder looked merely confused.

Breeze asked, 'What should we do?'

'We cannot stay here. There is no food, and the water is foul. The world is growing cold, day by day. But the air, like the water, flows to the deep places. There is a place, far from here, which is deeper than anywhere in the world.'

The Ragged One rumbled suspiciously, 'Where is this place?'

And Icebones described the great pit on the other side of the world – a hole gouged by a giant impact, a blow so powerful it had made the rocks rise up here, on the planet's opposite side. 'It is called the Footfall of Kilukpuk,' she said, thinking fast. 'And that is where we will go. There will be pasture for you and your calves. There will even be Bulls for you to run with, Thunder, and for you others to mate with.'

The Ragged One brayed. 'And this wonderful place is on *the other side of the world*? So you have never seen or smelled it?'

It was as if she was articulating Icebones's own doubts.

But Icebones said firmly, 'I will lead you there.' She raised her trunk, sniffing the air. 'We must walk away from the setting sun. We will keep walking east, and in the end we will reach the Footfall. Let's go,' she said, as she had heard her mother say many times to her own Family. 'Let's go, let's go.'

But the mammoths simply watched her, baffled.

So she raised her trunk and trumpeted, and began to walk east, following the line of the old coast, towards a sky that was already turning a deepening purple.

After a few paces she paused and turned. The three sisters, huddled together, were walking after her slowly, tracking her moist footsteps in the dusty sand. A little behind them came Autumn and Thunder, each still distracted, but submissively following the lead Icebones had given.

But now the Ragged One lumbered up to her. 'You cannot make this rabble into a Family just by saying it. And you cannot make yourself a Matriarch.'

'If you wish to stay here,' Icebones said, her voice a deep, coarse rumble, 'I will not oppose you.'

The Ragged One growled, 'If you fail – when you fail – I will be there to remind you of this day.'

I know you will, Icebones thought.

The wind was rising now. She saw that it was swirling over the pack ice, lifting spray and bits of loose ice and snow into a great grey spiral, angry and intimidating. The scavenging petrels left their bloody meals and rose into the sky, cawing angrily, their feathers stained red.

CHAPTER 6
THE ICE BEETLE

Heading towards the light of the rising sun, they skirted the shore of the giant ocean. There was better forage to be had a little way to the south, away from the barren coast itself, where soil and water had gathered in hollows.

But the landscape, distorted by the volcanic uplift that lay beneath the Fire Mountain, was flawed and difficult. Deep, sharp-walled valleys cut across their path. Conversely, sometimes the mammoths found themselves labouring over networks of ridges that rose one after the other, like wrinkles in aged flesh.

As leader, Icebones was able to impose a rhythm appropriate for a Family on the move. She had the mammoths walk slowly but steadily, all day and most of each night, probing at the ground with their trunks, foraging for grass and herbs and water. At first the others complained, for this was an alien way of life for creatures used to being fed as they needed it. But Icebones knew that this steady progress was better suited to a mammoth's internal constitution. And when after a few days the others got used to the steady, satisfying rhythm, and food passed pleasingly through their systems, the level of complaints dwindled.

But they were not yet a Family.

A Family was supposed to walk in coordination, led by its Matriarch and the senior Cows, all of them watching out for each other, in case of predators or natural traps like mud holes. *This* untidy rabble rambled over the broken ground as if they were rogue Bulls, as if the others did not exist, or matter.

Icebones knew it would take a long time to teach them habits that should have been ingrained since birth, and it seemed presumptuous even to imagine that she, young and inexperienced, was the one to do it. But, she reminded herself, there was nobody else.

So she persisted.

Sometimes Spiral would walk alongside Icebones, with Shoot prancing in her wake. The tall, elegant Cow would regale Icebones with unwelcome tales of her time with the Lost, when they had tied shining ribbons to her hair, or rode on her back, or had encouraged her to do tricks, picking up fruit and walking backwards and bowing at their behest.

This irritated Icebones immensely. 'You are mammoth,' she said sternly. 'You are not a creature of the Lost. You should not boast of your foolish dancing. And you should not ignore your sister. You should watch out for her, as she watches out for you. That is what it is to be Family.'

'Ah, the Family,' Spiral said. 'But what is there for me in your Family, Icebones? I am beautiful and clever and I smell fine, while *you* are small and squat. Will a Family stop you being ugly?'

Icebones reached up and tugged at Spiral's pretty tusks. 'It does not matter what I look like – or what *you* look or smell like. You will not always be healthy and pretty, Spiral. And someday you will have a calf of your own – perhaps many calves – just as your sister is carrying now. And then you too will have to rely on others.'

For a brief moment Spiral seemed to be listening hard, and her trunk tip shyly probed at Icebones's mouth. But then she pulled away, trumpeting brightly, and lumbered off, Shoot as ever trailing her eagerly.

They came to a place where enormous valleys cut across their path. The mammoths climbed down shallow banks and worked their way across rubble-strewn floors.

These tremendous channels were littered with huge

eroded boulders, pitted and scoured by water and wind, around which the mammoths had to pick their way. Perhaps water had once flowed from the high southern lands into the basin of the north, cutting these channels and depositing this debris. But those vanished rivers must have been mighty indeed. And these huge channels were clearly very ancient, for many of them were pitted by craters, or even cut through by younger channels.

The great age of the land was obvious, the complexity of its formation recalled in the folded rock around them.

They found a flooded crater, a shallow circular lake in a pit smashed into a channel bottom. The mammoths welcomed this easily accessible pool, though they had to break through layers of ice to reach the dark, cold water beneath.

At the water's circular edge, Icebones found clumps of grass. She would twist her trunk around a clump of stems and kick at its base to dislodge it. After beating the grass against her knees to knock off the dirt, she pushed it into her mouth, and her trunk explored for new clumps as she chewed.

She inspected the ice on the crater pond. Much of it was hard and blue. Mammoths learned about ice. Icebones knew that fresh ice first appeared as a film of oily crystals, almost as dark as the water itself. When it thickened it would turn grey and opaque, and thicken slowly. If it lasted to a second winter it would harden and turn a cold white-blue.

So the ice covering this pool was persisting through the long summer of this strange world. It was another sign that the world was cooling, and the tide of warmth and water and life was withdrawing, step by step.

Spiral lumbered up to her, complaining. 'Icebones, that's not fair. You are taking the best grass!'

Icebones slapped Spiral's cheek with her trunk tip – not hard, but enough to sting, and to make the others turn to listen. 'I am the Matriarch,' she growled. 'I take the first, and the best. Your mother is next. And then the rest of you. It is the way,' The pecking-order she was striving to teach Spiral was part of every Family's internal structure – although no mature Family would stick to it rigidly, with food being apportioned according to need.

Spiral grumbled, 'If this is what it means to be in a Family I would rather the Lost returned.' But she backed away, deferring to Icebones's tentative authority.

Beyond the flooded crater, the ground began to drop in altitude. Though it was still broken and often difficult to negotiate, the soil was richer here, and steppe plants flourished. There were even stretches of forest, conifer trees so tall they seemed to stretch up to the pale pink sky. And there was plenty to eat now: grass, coltsfoot, mountain sorrel, lousewort, sedge, dwarf birch.

Covering ground that was rich in loam and easy under their feet, their stomachs filling up, the mammoths' spirits seemed to lift, and they walked on more vigorously.

Icebones noticed that as they got used to the fodder of the steppe the mammoths' tastes were starting to diverge: Thunder sought out a type of willow with small diamond leaves, while Spiral preferred the sedge. They were starting to forget the rich food the Lost had provided for them, she realised with some relief.

But now Icebones became aware of a dark smudge, like low cloud, on the horizon directly ahead of her, to the east. And she smelled smoke.

Fire ahead. The mammoths drew closer, trunks raised.

Fire was a natural thing, of course – it could be caused by flowing lava, or lightning strikes – but in mammoths' minds fire was primarily a thing of the Lost. *Where there is smoke, there are the Lost* – so went the wisdom of the Cycle.

They walked on, into the thickening smoke.

They came to a shallow crater rim. The smoke was pouring sluggishly into the air from the crater's belly.

It was an easy climb up the crater wall to its narrow crest.

But now the smoke was thick, making their eyes stream and filling their nostrils with its stink. The mammoths were agitated, for the scent of fire sparked deep instincts of fear and flight in them all.

The crater was a big one, surrounded by a ring of eroded hillocks that stretched to the horizon. A bank of smoke hung thick and dense over the crater basin.

And the basin was full of trees: fallen, burning trees, with flames licking ponderously. There were so many that they lapped up against the crater walls, and trunks lay thick on the ground like shed pine needles. But each of these 'needles' was the trunk of a great conifer, stripped of its branches.

Autumn growled, 'We can't walk through that. We would suffocate in the smoke, or get trapped beneath the burning trunks, or—'

'You're right.' Icebones raised her trunk, trying to sense the lie of the land despite the distraction of the smoke, and the steady rumble of collapsing, burned-out logs. 'The wind comes this way.' She took a step towards the southern crater rim. 'We will walk around these circular walls. The smoke will blow away from us, not over us.'

'It is out of our way,' the Ragged One pointed out sourly.

Icebones snapped, 'We have no choice. Be careful where you step. Help each other. Let's go, let's go.' And without further discussion she set off, following the narrow ridge that ran around the crater rim.

She didn't look back, but she could tell from their footfalls and rumbles that the mammoths were following her.

The going wasn't difficult, though in places the rim wall broke up into separate eroded hillocks, and they had to climb through narrow gulches or over crumbled rock. But there was no water to be had on this bare rock wall. Soon the air, hot and dry and laden with the stink of wood smoke, burned in her nostrils and throat.

The wind veered and a gust of smoke washed over her, blinding her eyes and flooding her sensitive nostrils, so that she had to work her way over the lumpy ground by touch alone.

When the smoke cleared she saw something moving, dimly visible through the thinning grey veils of smoke.

She stopped dead, trunk raised. She sensed the other mammoths gathering around her, curious, nervous. She could see something shining, like ice, a vast bulk moving. And she could feel how its weight made the ground shudder.

Now it emerged from the smoke.

A vast boxy shape was crawling laboriously up the side of the crater. It was more like a great slab of rock than any living thing. On its back was a kind of shell, like an insect's carapace, but the shell was flat and a pale silvery-grey, and it was liberally covered with caked-on dust and dried mud. It would have been big enough for all seven of the mammoths to stand side by side on its back. The beast moved forward, not on legs, but on its underbelly, leaving tracks cut deep in the rock of the crater rim. But those tracks were well worn, Icebones saw. Wherever this strange creature was heading, it had made this journey many times.

'It is like a beetle,' Breeze said. 'With a shell of ice. An ice beetle.'

The ice beetle trailed huge long limbs – far longer but less mobile than a mammoth's trunk. And in a set of shining fingers it grasped a tree-trunk. The tree had been dragged over the dusty plain from a stand of conifer forest. In that forest stood a number of stumps, where trunks had been neatly cut away from their roots.

Icebones could smell, under the dominant stink of the fire, the sap of the tree trunk and the iron tang of the red dust. But she could smell nothing of the beetle, nothing at all.

As the mammoths watched, the ice beetle, in dour silence,

hauled the tree-trunk up the side of the steep crater wall. Dust rose up in clouds. Then the beetle spun slowly around and let the tree-trunk fall into the crater, where the flames would soon reach it.

The beetle, its trunk-arms empty, seemed to rest, as if exhausted. Then it roused itself. It swivelled and began to edge its way back down the crater rim wall.

Autumn growled, 'Once mammoths did this. Hauling trees from forests to pits in the ground, where they would be burned and buried. Now, it seems, the Lost have stronger servants even than us.'

'Perhaps it is like mammoth dung,' Icebones mused. 'Where mammoths pass, new life sprouts, for our dung enriches the ground. Maybe the Lost – or at least their servants – are working to build the world, to build life. But why does it continue, now the Lost have vanished?'

'Because it doesn't know what else to do,' the Ragged One said. 'Because nobody told it to stop. Because it is mad, or stupid.'

'Everything about the Lost is a mystery to us,' said Autumn grimly. Spiral made to protest, but Autumn insisted, 'We lived with them, and accepted their gifts of food and water. But we never understood them. It is the truth, daughter.'

As the beetle passed, Shoot reached out tentatively with her trunk tip and brushed the sharp edge of its carapace. 'It is cold. But it is not wet like ice. And it smells of nothing.' She sneezed sharply, sending dust flying. 'It is covered in dust.' She began to blow at the carapace, ridding a corner of dust, and exposing a clean, shining surface.

Spiral stepped forward and joined her. So did Icebones, without being sure why. They blew away the dust, or, where mud was caked, they picked at it with their trunk fingers and brushed it off.

Icebones noticed that Breeze hung back, distracted, evidently uncomfortable from the weight of her calf.

The ice beetle continued to work its way down the hillside, its great body tipping up clumsily. It did not react to the mammoths' attention.

When it reached the level ground outside the crater the beetle began to trundle away, back towards the forest. But now its exposed carapace gleamed silver, free of dust and mud save for a few streaks.

'Do you think it's moving a little faster?' Autumn asked. 'Maybe it needs the sunlight, like a flower.'

'I never saw a flower like *that*,' Icebones said sceptically.

'True, true.'

There was nothing for the mammoths here, nothing but this insane abandoned creature and its endless, meaningless task. Icebones said, 'Let's go.' She took a step forward, meaning to climb down from the crater rim.

But, behind her, Breeze gasped. She had fallen to her knees, her stubby trunk lying pooled and limp on the ground. 'Help me.'

Autumn growled, 'It is the calf. *It is time.*'

Spiral turned to Icebones. 'What must we do? Oh, what must we do?'

Icebones felt her stomach turn as cold as a lump of ice. 'I suppose the Lost helped you even with this.'

Spiral fell back, growling dismally, and Icebones felt a stab of shame.

Autumn said, 'The Lost were with us always . . . But there are no Lost here.'

Close at Icebones's side like a guilty conscience, the Ragged One said softly, 'If not you, who else?'

Icebones gathered her courage and stepped forward. Breeze, still slumped to her knees, was straining, her belly distended. 'You must stand,' Icebones said.

'I can't.'

'Help her,' Icebones ordered.

Briskly Spiral and Shoot stepped forward. They dug their

trunks and foreheads under their sister's belly, while Icebones pushed at her rump.

In a few heartbeats Breeze had staggered to her feet, but her legs were shuddering. The two sisters stood close to Breeze, keeping her upright with nudges of their bodies. Even Thunder gently pushed Breeze's rump, rumbling encouragement.

Breeze, panting hard, leaned forward so her back legs were stretched out behind her. Icebones thought she could see the calf moving within its cave of flesh.

Breeze raised her trunk and trumpeted, straining. There was a sudden eruption of blood and water, a stink of urine and milk.

'I can see it!' Shoot called suddenly. 'Look! The calf is coming!'

And Icebones saw it too: in a gush of water and blood, two legs had pushed from Breeze's vagina. Now a small head and the bulk of a little body was squeezed out, wrapped in a clear, shimmering sheet. For a moment it dangled by its hind legs. Then Breeze gave a final heave.

The calf shot out and plopped to the ground.

Shoot and Spiral, suddenly aunts, hurried forward to the baby, which lay wrapped in its blood-streaked sac on the ground.

Icebones stayed with Breeze, who staggered forward. 'You must stay on your feet.'

'It hurts, Icebones,' Breeze said.

'It's all right. Just a little longer. Push hard, Breeze. Push—'

Now the afterbirth emerged, a sodden bloody lump that fell limp to the ground.

Breeze sighed, eyes closing, and she fell to her knees. Thunder curled his trunk over her protectively.

'The calf's not moving,' Shoot wailed. 'Is it dead?'

Icebones pushed past Shoot and Spiral. The calf still lay where it had fallen. 'We have to get it out of the birth sac.'

She leaned and tried to catch the membrane with her tusk tips, ripping and pulling it. 'Help me – but do not hurt the calf.'

It seemed to take long heartbeats, but at last they had the amniotic sac free. Shoot hurled the bloody sheet away with an impulsive shake of her head.

Icebones leaned forward to the calf, inspecting it – him! – with her trunk tip. He was a bundle of pale orange fur that was soaked and flattened by amniotic fluid. His legs were spindly stalks, his trunk was a mere thread, and his head was smooth and round, as if not yet formed. He was breathing shallowly, his little chest rising and falling rapidly, and his breath steamed around his face.

Icebones wrapped her trunk underneath the calf, and encouraged Shoot and Spiral to help her. Soon they had him set upright on his skinny, trembling legs. His little eyes opened with a moist pop, and Icebones saw they were bright red. But now he threw back his tiny trunk so it lay on his forehead, and opened his mouth.

'Hungry,' he said, his voice a thin, choked mewl. 'Cold. Hungry. Oh, let me back . . . !'

CHAPTER 7
THE CRACKED LAND

The calf made the suckling cry, over and over, as if he had been taught it by Kilukpuk herself.

'He needs milk,' Icebones said. She hurried to Breeze, who still lay on the ground.

Breeze's eyes were closed, and she was breathing hard, obviously exhausted. 'Woodsmoke,' she murmured.

'What?'

'That is what he will be called. For when he was born my head was full of smoke . . .'

'You must come,' Icebones said gently.

'Let me sleep, Icebones . . .'

The calf opened his mouth and wailed, his voice thin and high. 'Cold, cold!'

And now, at last, Icebones was at a loss. 'Without milk he will die,' she said. 'I don't know what to do.'

Autumn came forward, her gait stiff. 'Let me.' And she gathered the little creature in her trunk and guided him forward, pulling him beneath her legs. Blindly, he snuggled at her belly fur until he found the dugs that dangled between her forelegs. Driven by instinct he clamped his mouth to a nipple and began to suckle greedily.

Icebones, astonished, saw thin, pale milk dribble down his cheek. 'Autumn – you have milk. But you are not with calf.'

'It began when I saw how weak Breeze was becoming. I don't know why.' She eyed Icebones. 'You may be Matriarch,' she rumbled softly. 'But you don't know everything, it seems.'

'I know that you are a good mother,' said Icebones. 'For

you were there when your daughter, and her calf, needed you most.'

The calf – Woodsmoke – squeaked his contentment, and Autumn rumbled softly.

It was strange, Icebones thought: just heartbeats old, and yet the calf had already achieved something immensely important, by redeeming Autumn, his grandmother . . . Perhaps it was an omen of his life to come.

Spiral and Shoot gathered around their mother protectively, rumbling reassurance. Further away, Thunder stayed with Breeze, stroking her hair with gentle motions of his trunk.

It was a moment of tenderness, of contentment, of togetherness.

But Icebones could not help but look east, trunk raised, towards the difficult country that lay ahead – a country through which she would now have to bring a calf, and a weakened mother.

A wind rose, droning through the clefts in the crater wall, drowning out the reassuring rumbles of the Cows.

Further east, the ground rose steadily. The steppe vegetation grew thinner, and any water was frozen over.

Icebones's chest began to ache as she took each breath, as it had not since she was high on the Fire Mountain.

They came to a land covered by vast pits.

The pits were shallow and rounded, and dust pooled deep in them. They were like footprints around a dried mud hole – but these 'footprints' were huge, taking many paces to cross. In some places the pits were overwhelmed by frozen rock flows, as if the pitted landscape had been formed long ago, and then this younger rock poured over it to harden in place.

It was difficult country. But Icebones feared that the terrain further east of here might be more difficult still.

Looking that way from the higher ridges, she could see deep shadows and broken walls, hear complex, booming echoes.

And at night she thought she heard the low rumble of some vast animal, echoing from tortuous cliffs.

Difficult, yes. And now they had the calf to consider.

Woodsmoke trotted beside his mother or his grand-mother, stumbling frequently. He was still coated with the short underfur from his birth, topped now by a thin layer of pink-red overfur. His back was round, lacking the slope and distinctive shoulder hump he would develop later in life. Though he had been born with the ancient language of all Kilukpuk's children, there were many things he had to learn. He couldn't yet use his trunk to gather food, or even to drink. For now he was completely dependent on milk, which he drew from his mother's nipple with his mouth – the only time in his life when he would use his mouth directly to feed.

The calf slowed them down: there was no doubt about that. They had had to wait several days at the birthing place while mother and calf recovered, and even now the group could walk no faster than the calf could manage.

But Icebones would not have done without him. Wood-smoke was quickly becoming the focus of the group, this nascent Family. He would run from one to the other, ignorant and uncaring of their obscure adult disputes. Only the Ragged One refused to respond to his unformed charms.

His favourite was his aunt, Spiral.

She would lower her trunk and let him clamber on it or pull it. Or she would lie on the ground and let him climb up over her belly, digging his tiny feet into her guard hairs, determined and dogged, as if she was some great warm rock. In her turn, Spiral would forgive Woodsmoke anything – even when he dribbled urine into her fine coat, of which she was so proud.

Icebones was surprised by this; it showed a side of Spiral

she hadn't suspected. Finally, she thought she understood. She sought an opportunity to speak to the Cow.

'Spiral – *you've had a calf of your own*. That's why you're so close to Woodsmoke, isn't it?'

At first Spiral would not reply. She walked along with something of her old haughtiness, head held high, her handsome tusks bright in the cold sunlight. But at length she said, 'Yes. If you must know. I have given birth to two calves. Both Bulls. I watched the calves learn to walk, and I suckled them. But soon, when they were no older than Woodsmoke is now, they were taken away.' She said this flatly, without emotion.

'They were taken by the Lost? What cruelty.'

'They were not – cruel. They were taking the calves to a place that would be better for them.' She shook her head, and her delicate trunk rippled. 'And when my calves were gone, each time, I was stroked and praised by the Lost, and given treats, and—'

'Where are the calves now?'

'Surely they are dead,' she said harshly. 'The Sickness killed so many.'

'You can't know that.'

'It does not hurt.' And she trumpeted brightly, as if joyful. But it was a thin, cold sound.

The little calf came blundering over to Spiral in his tangled, uncoordinated way, seeking to play. But she pushed him away with a gentle shove of her trunk. 'I have no need of *him*,' she snapped.

Icebones brought him back. 'I know,' she said carefully. 'But he needs you.'

And, tentatively, Spiral wrapped her trunk around the little calf's small, smooth head.

The pits in the ground became deeper and more fragmented, and began to merge. Soon Icebones was walking through a deepening gully. The walls grew steadily steeper around her, and the floor, littered with broken rocks, tilted downwards sharply. Soon Icebones's front legs were aching, and her foot pads and trunk tip were scratched raw by the hard-edged rocks.

The gully gave way to a more complex landscape still, a place of branching chasms and tall cliffs. It was the cracked land she had sensed from afar, and dreaded.

Icebones found herself walking through a flat-bottomed valley so deep and sheer-walled that she was immersed in cold shadow, even though she could see a stripe of pinkish daylight sky far above her. The walls, steep above her, were heavily eroded. They were made of layers of hard red-grey sandstone and blue-black lava, and here and there they had slumped tiredly into landslides.

In some places the walls had collapsed altogether, leaving spires and isolated mesas, so that she wandered through a forest of rock, carved into eerie, spindly shapes by the endless wind.

In the weak light the mammoths were rounded, indistinct forms, shuffling gloomily. The ground was littered with sand dunes and rock from the crumbled walls, so the going was difficult and slow. They were all unhappy: mammoths were creatures of the open steppe, and it was against their instincts to be enclosed by high walls.

But the chasm was short. Soon it opened out – but only into a branching array of more deep gorges, separated by tall, sharp-edged walls. Icebones stamped her feet and rumbled. But the walls of this increasingly complex maze sent back only muddled and confusing echoes.

The nights were the worst. The stars and disconcerting moons crossed the sky, but the mammoths were stranded in a deep shadowed darkness.

Icebones tried to keep them moving. But because of the calf's weariness that proved to be impossible, and they were forced to endure the dark huddled closely around Breeze, while her calf napped peacefully in the forest of her legs.

In the darkest night, Icebones heard deep, brooding rumbles. All the mammoths heard it, she thought, but none would speak of it, as if fearful of making it real.

In the daytime Icebones, weary and befuddled, strove to keep moving east.

This maze of chasms was a pattern of grooves cut deep into the land, as if by the claws of some great predator, so that the plain high above their heads was cut into sunlit islands, each separate from the others.

Spiral said, 'I have become a creature of the ground like a lemming, able only to peer up at the sunlight above.' And her grumble was joined by the others.

It was as if it was somehow Icebones's fault that they were having such difficulties. It was utterly unfair, of course. But then, she thought gloomily, nobody had promised her that being a Matriarch was anything to do with fairness.

'I will tell you stories from the Cycle.'

That met with a general groan.

But Icebones said, 'The Cycle is our story – *your* story. This Cracked Land is difficult. But the Cycle is full of stories of mammoths who faced difficulties, for it is the times of hardship that shape us.' And she began to tell them the story of Longtusk. 'It is said that when Longtusk was a calf the mammoths roamed free, great Clans of them, all across the northern steppes. But Longtusk's Family was forced to flee, northwards, ever north, for the Lost were encroaching from the south, breeding and squabbling and building . . .'

The mammoths still grumbled, but the noise was subdued, and suffused by the soft pads of their feet, the growls of their bellies, gentle burps and farts. Even the little calf trotting at Icebones's side listened intently. Woodsmoke was still too young to understand much of what she said. But he was responding to the rhythm of her language, as she hoped they all would.

The Ragged One continued to keep apart.

'At last,' Icebones went on, 'the mammoths had nowhere

else to go. The land gave way to a great frozen ocean where nothing could live but seals and other ugly creatures. It seemed that soon the mammoths would be overwhelmed by the Lost.

'But Longtusk found a way. There was a bridge of land that spanned the ocean, from one great steppe to another. And, on the far side of the bridge, there were no Lost – only open steppe, where the mammoths could grow and breed and live. So Longtusk gathered the mammoths of his Clan, and said to them—'

Something dropped before her, huge and heavy and dark. It opened a cavernous mouth and screamed. She glimpsed rows of sharp teeth.

Without thinking she lunged forward – she felt the rasp of fur on her tusks, the squelch of soft flesh breaking – and the creature screamed louder yet.

And then, in an instant, it was gone, leaving her with the stink of blood in her nostrils, and the echo of that deadly scream rattling from the walls around her.

She stood there, shaking like a frightened calf.

The mammoths had scattered. The calf had been left alone, and he was turning back and forth, little trunk raised, mewling pitifully. 'Scared . . . scared . . .'

Icebones said, 'We must stay together. That – thing – was probably after the calf.'

Spiral was stiff with rage and fear. 'Enough of your talk,' she said. 'The Ragged One is right. This is not your world, Icebones. You did not know we would meet such a creature here, did you?'

'If we squabble it will pick us off one by one.' Icebones raised her tusks, which still dripped red blood. 'Is that what you want?'

At last Autumn rumbled, 'She is right. The calf is probably its main target, for he is weakest, and slowest. Breeze, come to him.'

Breeze stepped forward and tucked her calf beneath her legs. Woodsmoke tried to suckle, but Breeze pushed him back. The rest of the mammoths clustered around mother and calf.

'We will go on,' insisted Icebones. 'This warren of chasms will not last for ever. If everyone keeps their trunk high, we will survive.'

They were reluctant, fretful, afraid. But nobody had a better suggestion. And so they began to move forward once more. The calf's mewling was muffled by the legs and belly fur of its mother, and the adult mammoths rumbled uneasily, their deep sounds echoing heavily from the sheer ravine walls.

Thunder walked beside Icebones. 'What do you think it was?'

'Perhaps it was some kind of cat. There are stories of great cats in the Cycle – Longtusk himself fought such a beast. Perhaps it has grown fat by destroying everything else living here, like the whale in the Ocean of the North. But I have never seen a cat, for none lived on the Island. Many of the animals mentioned in the old Cycle stories are long gone . . .'

Icebones saw that the stripe of sky visible far above her head was already fading to a deep orange-pink.

'Soon it will be dark,' the Ragged One said softly. 'And then we will make a story of our own. Won't we, Matriarch?'

They came to another branch in the chasm system. This time Icebones faced three intersecting ravines, each sheer-walled and littered with loose rock, each leading only to further complexity – and each empty, as far as she could see.

We must continue east, she told herself. If we don't achieve that much, everything else is lost. She stepped forward and led them into the central chasm.

There was a bellow. The mammoths stumbled back, trunks raised in alarm.

This time the creature had dropped from above, on to Autumn's back. The mammoth was pawing the ground and trumpeting. She lifted her head in a vain effort to reach her tormentor with her tusks or trunk.

The creature was only dimly visible in the shadows, but Icebones glimpsed hard, front-facing yellow eyes, that black bloody mouth, and claws that gleamed white and dug deep into Autumn's flesh, causing blood to well and drip down her heavy hair.

Autumn blundered against the chasm wall. The cat creature yowled its protest. But it was ripped away from her back, its claws leaving a final set of gouges.

Icebones lunged forward, trumpeting, tusks held high.

The cat raised itself to its full height, yellow eyes fixed on Icebones. It was spindly, but its body was a sleek slab of muscle. It opened its huge mouth and hissed. And it leapt with astonishing agility up the chasm wall.

Again the mammoths were left in sudden silence.

'It lives on the walls,' Shoot said, wondering.

Spiral had her head dipped, her trunk wrapped over her forehead. 'I can't stand it,' she whimpered. 'I am so afraid.'

Icebones herself was shaken to her core. Mammoths were used to facing predators, but as a creature of the open steppe, Icebones had no experience of threats dropping down on her from out of the sky.

She walked up to Autumn. 'Your back is hurt.' She probed with her trunk fingers at the slash wounds. The covering hair was matted with blood. 'We will find mud to bathe your wounds.'

'No,' Autumn growled, pulling back. 'We must get out of this place before dark.'

Thunder said softly, *'Which way?'*

For a terrible moment Icebones realised that she did not know – the chasm looked identical before her and behind her – she had been turned around several times, and the stripe of pink sky above her gave no clues as to the direction of the sun.

The Ragged One was watching her, waiting for her to fail.

At last Icebones spotted a small heap of mammoth dung, still steaming gently, a few paces away. 'That is the way we have come. So we will go the other way – to the east.'

Thunder growled, 'But that is the way the cat went.'

A high-pitched yowl echoed from the chasm walls. The mammoths peered that way fearfully, raising their trunks to sniff the air. 'Where is it?' 'Is it close?' 'I think it came from that way.' 'No, *that* way . . .' But the echoes thrown by the complex walls of the chasm system masked the source of the call – as perhaps the cat intended, Icebones thought.

The Ragged One stood before Icebones. 'It can track us by our dung, and our footprints, and our scent. How can we throw it off? You don't know what to do, do you? You are no Matriarch. You have not told us the truth – not since the moment you woke up inside your cave of darkness. And now you have led us into deadly peril.'

Icebones, desperate, her head full of alarm, thought, Not *now* . . . But she was tired of strangeness, of unpredictable dangers, of dragging this recalcitrant group across a barren rocky world, of the Ragged One's unrelenting hostility.

'All right,' she said sharply. 'You want the truth – then here it is. *I am no Matriarch.* I think my mother intended me to come here to this place and lead you someday . . . but not yet. Not until I was grown, and had calves of my own, and had become a true Matriarch. I don't know what happened – I don't know why I found myself here, now. *I don't want to be here.* But here I am.'

The mammoths rumbled, tense, unhappy.

Thunder reached to her hesitantly. 'You *lied*? But you named us, Icebones.'

She glared at them all. 'Yes, I lied. I had no choice. If I hadn't, you would have died on the shore of that salt-filled ocean.'

Autumn's rumble was tinged with pain. 'Enough of this. It won't make any difference if Icebones is a liar or not if we are all dead by sundown. *Which way?*'

Two chasms led from this point. One was straight, its walls sheer and clean, but the other was a jumble of rocks.

Icebones snapped, 'We go down there.' She meant the jumbled, difficult route.

Autumn growled, 'Are you sure? The other looks much easier.'

The Ragged One said, 'What does it matter? Icebones is a fool. The cat can follow us wherever we go.'

Icebones said, 'You must listen to me. Listen to me because I am Icebones – for who you know me to be, not for who you wish me to be. Go now, that way, as I told you.'

Slowly, sullenly, the mammoths began to move towards the more crowded chasm.

But Icebones called Autumn back. 'Wait, Autumn. Forgive me.' And she dug into the wounds on Autumn's back, breaking open the clots and covering her trunk fingers with blood.

Autumn bore this stoically. Perhaps she understood what Icebones intended.

As the mammoths filed into the crowded chasm, Icebones set off, alone, into the other, cleaner defile. Where she trod she made sure she left clear footprints in the dust and scattered rock, and even squeezed out a little dung and urine. And she took care to smear Autumn's blood on the rocky walls.

Then she backed out of the chasm, trying to step in the tracks she had already made.

Just as she reached the junction of the chasm, she heard a cold yowl – glimpsed a black form shimmering over the rock above her head – saw yellow predator's eyes. The cat hurtled, black and lithe, into the chasm she had seeded, away from the mammoths.

Quickly she ducked after the others. 'Try not to drop dung for a while – I know that is hard – and try to be quiet . . .'

Thunder asked, subdued, 'How did you know what the cat would do?'

'I hoped that blood would be a stronger lure than the smell of our waste and hair. The other chasm is long, and it will take a while for the cat to explore it. But soon enough it will know that we have tricked it, and come looking for us once more.'

So they proceeded through the shadowed complexity of the chasm, picking their way between huge fallen boulders and over smaller sharp-edged rocks.

Icebones glanced at the Ragged One. But the Ragged One's posture spoke only of resentment and fury. Icebones knew that in the days to come the dynamics of her little band would be even more difficult, and that a final confrontation was yet to come.

After several more days – dismal days, frightening, bereft of food and water – the mammoths emerged at last from the Cracked Land.

With relief they fanned out under a pale, open sky, over a shallow slope of scree and broken rock. There was even food to be had, tufts of grass and scrubby trees growing in the sudden flood of light.

From here they should go south and east, for that was the direction to the Footfall. But when she looked that way, Icebones saw that the ground ended in a sharp line, much closer than the horizon, as if there was a dip beyond.

Leaving the mammoths to feed, she walked that way. Soon she had reached the break in the ground – and she recoiled, shocked.

It was a sheer drop.

She was on the lip of a chasm. But this immense feature

would have dwarfed the mazy ravines through which she had guided the mammoths.

As if scoured out by a vast tusk, it was a mighty gouge in the land. And it was in her way.

TWO

GOUGE

THE STORY OF THE FAMILY OF KILUKPUK

This is a story Kilukpuk told Silverhair.

Now, as you know, Kilukpuk was born at a time when the world belonged to the Reptiles. The Reptiles were the greatest beasts ever seen – so huge they made the land itself shake with their footfalls – and they were cunning and savage hunters.

In those days our ancestors called themselves Hotbloods.

The Hotbloods were small timid creatures who lived underground, in burrows, the way lemmings do. They had huge, frightened eyes, for they would only emerge from their burrows at night, a time when the Reptiles were less active and less able to hunt them. They all looked alike, and rarely even argued, for their world was dominated by the constant threat of the Reptiles.

The ancestors of every warm-blooded creature you see today lived in those cramped dens: bear with seal, wolf with mammoth.

It was into this world that Kilukpuk, the first of all Matriarchs, was born. If you could have seen her, small and cautious like the rest, you would never have imagined the mighty races which would one day spring from her loins. But, despite her smallness, Kilukpuk was destined to become the mother of us all.

Kilukpuk had many brothers and sisters.

One was called Aglu. Secretive and sly, his blood runs in the veins of all the creatures that eat the flesh of others, like the wolves.

One was called Ursu. Fierce and aloof, she became the mother of all the bears.

One was called Equu. Foolish and vain, she became the mother of all the horses.

One was called Purga. Strange and clever with paws that could grasp and manipulate, he . . .

Yes, yes, there is a story here, and I will get to it!

Now after the Reptiles had gone, the Hotbloods emerged from their burrows. For a long time they were timid, as if they feared the Reptiles might return. But at last they grew confident, and their calves and cubs and foals grew fat and strong and tall.

And by the time Longtusk was born, much later, a time when the ice crowded down from the north of the Old Steppe, there were many bears and horses and wolves, and many mammoths.

But only mammoths, the Calves of Kilukpuk, had Families.

Now at one time in his life Longtusk lived alone, and he wandered the land. Everywhere he went he won friendship and respect – naturally, since he was the greatest hero of all, and even other, stupid creatures could recognise that.

One spring day Longtusk, wandering the land, happened to come by a snow bank. He saw a bear alone, mourning loudly.

Now a cub of Ursu likes to live alone, in caves she digs out of snow banks with her paws. She will spend her winter in the snow, nursing her cubs, until they come out in the spring to play and hunt.

Longtusk called, 'What is wrong?'

And the bear said, 'My cub has grown sickly and died. My milk was sour, and I could not feed him.'

And Longtusk was saddened. But he knew that if a mammoth's milk soured, she would ask the others of her Family, her mother and sisters and aunts, to suckle the calf for her, and the calf would not die. But the bear lived alone, and had no Family to help care for her cubs.

Longtusk stayed with the bear a day and a night, comforting her, and then he walked on.

In the summer Longtusk, wandering the land, happened to come upon a horse as she cropped a stand of grass. She was mourning loudly.

Now the foals of Equu like to run together in herds, but they have no Matriarch, and no true Family.

Longtusk called, 'What is wrong?'

And the horse said, 'I was running with my brothers and sisters and our foals when we ran into a bank of smoke. It was a fire, lit by the Lost. Well, we turned and ran, as fast as we could. But we ran to a cliff's edge and fell – all but me – and the Lost have taken the flesh and the skin of my brothers and sisters and foals, and I am alone.'

And Longtusk was saddened. But he knew that if Lost hunters tried to panic a mammoth Family, the wisdom of the Matriarch and her sisters would keep them from falling into such a simple trap.

Longtusk stayed with the horse a day and a night, comforting her, and then he walked on.

In the autumn Longtusk, wandering the land, happened to come upon a wolf as she chewed on a scrap of meat. She was mourning loudly.

Now the wolves run together in packs. But they have no true Family.

Though Longtusk was rightly wary of any cub of Aglu, he approached the wolf. He called, 'What is wrong?'

And the wolf said, 'We were hunting. My brother was injured and he died. My parents and my sister and my cubs fell on him, and I joined them, and we fought over the entrails we dragged from his stomach. But the meat tasted sour in my mouth, and I am still hungry, and my brother is gone, and I am alone.'

And Longtusk was saddened. But he knew that when a

mammoth died, her Family would Remember her properly, and those who had to live on were soothed. But when a wolf died he became nothing but another piece of meat between the teeth of his pack.

Longtusk stayed with the wolf a day and a night, comforting her, and then he walked on.

If you are a Cow you are born into a Family, and you live in that Family, and you die in that Family. All your life. A Family must share in the care and protection of the calves. A Family must respect the wisdom of its elders, and especially the Matriarch. A Family must Remember its dead. In a Family, *I* becomes *We*.

All these things Longtusk knew. All these things Kilukpuk taught us, and more.

. . . I know, I know. I have not said what became of Purga, brother of Kilukpuk.

Well, Purga sired clever creatures who climbed and ran and hunted and built and fought and killed. And *they* became the Lost.

But that is another story.

CHAPTER 1
THE BRIDGE

The mammoths spent a night on the lip of the great cliff, huddled under a sky littered with hard, bright stars. Icebones was surrounded by the warm gurgles of the mammoths' bellies, their soft belches and farts. Sometimes she heard a rustle as Woodsmoke scrambled through belly hair and sought a teat to suckle.

But every time sleep approached Icebones imagined she was back in the maze of rock, and that a lithe black creature, all teeth and claws, was preparing to spring out of the air.

It was with relief that she saw the dawn approaching. Finding a stream, she took a trunkful of ice-cold water and tipped it into her mouth. The mammoths were already drifting away in search of the first of the day's forage. The place they had stood for much of the night was littered with dung.

Autumn's wounds still seeped blood that leaked into her ragged guard hairs. Shoot cleaned the wounds of blood and dirt with water, and plastered mud into the deepest cuts.

Breeze encouraged her calf to pop fragments of the adults' dung into his mouth, for it would help his digestion. But his control of his trunk was still clumsy, and he smeared the warm, salty dung liberally over his mouth. He was growing rapidly. His legs, to which tufts of orange hair clung, were spindly and long, and he was already half Icebones's height.

Finished with the dung, Woodsmoke trotted from one adult to another, chirping his simple phrases: 'I am hungry! I am not cold!' – and, most of all: 'Look at me! Look at what

I am doing!' Autumn grumbled wearily that it might be better for the nerves of the adults if calves did not speak from the moment they were born. But Icebones knew she didn't mean it.

Icebones walked to the edge of the Gouge.

The canyon was vast, magnificent, austere. It stretched from east to west, passing beyond the horizon in either direction. Its walls, glowing red and crimson and ochre, were nothing but rock, cracked and seamed by heat and frost and wind. Peering down, she saw grey clouds drifting through the canyon, feathery rafts floating on the languid river of air that flowed between those mighty walls.

The wall beneath her was huge, tall enough to dwarf many mountains. Its face was cut into columns and gullies, carved and fluted by water and wind, the detail dwindling to a dim darkness at its base.

But the Gouge's far southern wall was a mere line of darkness on the horizon. She imagined a mammoth like herself standing on that southern wall, peering north across this immense feature. To such an observer, Icebones would be quite invisible.

The Gouge's floor was visible beneath the flowing grey cloud. She made out the ripple of dunes, the snaking glint of a river, and the crowded grey-green of forests or steppe – all very different from the high, frozen plain on which she stood. The Gouge was so deep that the very weather was different on its sunken floor.

Thunder, the young Bull, stood beside her. 'The valley is big,' he said simply.

'Yes. Do you see? It is light *there*, to the east, but it is still dark *there*, to the west.' It was true. The morning sun, a shrunken yellow disc immersed in pale pink light, seemed to be rising from out of the Gouge's eastern extremity. Long, sharp shadows stretched across the Gouge floor, and mist pooled white in valleys and depressions. And, as she looked further to the west, she saw that the floor there still lay in deep darkness, still in the shadow of the world. 'The Gouge is so big that it can contain both day and night.'

Thunder growled. 'It is too big to understand.'

Gently, she prodded his trunk. 'No. Feel the ground. Smell it, listen to it. Hear the wind gushing along this great trench, fleeing the sun's heat. Listen to the rumble of the rivers, flowing along the plain, far below. And listen to the rocks . . .'

'The rocks?'

She stamped, hard. 'You are not a Lost, who is nothing but a pair of eyes. You can hear much more than you can see, if you try. The shape of the world is in the rocks' song.' She walked back and forth, listening to the ringing of the ground. She could feel the spin of the world, and the huge slow echoes that came back from the massive volcanic rise to the east.

And she could feel how this valley stretched on and on, far beyond the horizon. It was like a great wound, she thought, a wound that stretched around a quarter of the planet's belly.

Now Thunder was trotting back and forth, trunk high, eyes half-closed, slamming his clumsy feet into the ground. 'I *can* feel it.' He trumpeted his pleasure. 'The Lost showed me nothing like *this*.'

'The Lost do not understand. This is mammoth.'

Growling, stamping, he stalked away.

Autumn walked up to Icebones. She moved stiffly. 'You are kind to him.'

Icebones rumbled, 'He has a good heart.'

Autumn walked carefully to the lip of the valley. 'It must have been a giant river which carved this valley.'

'Perhaps not a river,' Icebones said. She recalled how she had stood atop the Fire Mountain with the Ragged One, and had seen how the land was uplifted. 'Perhaps the ground was simply broken open.'

'However it was formed, this tusk-gouge lies across our path. Can we walk around it?'

'The Gouge stretches far to the east of here. The land at its edge is high and cold and barren. It would be a difficult trek.'

Autumn raised her trunk and sniffed the warming air that rose from the Gouge. 'I smell water, and grass, and trees,' she said. 'There is life down there.'

'Yes,' Icebones mused. 'If we can reach the floor, perhaps we will find nourishment. We can follow its length, cutting south across the higher land when we near the Footfall itself.'

Autumn walked gingerly along the lip of the Gouge. 'There,' she said.

Icebones made out an immense slope of tumbled rock, piled up against the Gouge wall, reaching from the deep floor almost to its upper surface. As the sun rose further, casting its wan, pink light, the rock slope cast huge shadows. Perhaps there had been a landslide, she thought, the rocks of the wall shaken free by a tremor of the ground.

She murmured doubtfully, 'The rock looks loose and treacherous.'

'Yes. But there might be a way. And—'

A piercing trumpet startled them both. The Ragged One came lumbering up to them.

'I heard what you are saying,' the Ragged One gasped. 'But your trunk does not sniff far, Icebones. There is no need to clamber down into that Gouge and toil along its muddy length.'

Autumn asked mildly, 'Shall we *fly* over?'

The Ragged One snorted. 'We will walk.' And she turned to the west.

When Icebones looked that way she saw a band of pinkish white, picked out by the clear light of the rising sun. It rose from the northern side of the Gouge, on which she stood, and arced smoothly through the air – and it came to rest on the Gouge's far side.

It was a bridge.

Like everything about this immense canyon, the bridge was huge, and it was far away. It took them half a day just to walk to its foot.

The bridge turned out to be a broad shining sheet that emerged from the pink dust as if it had grown there. It sloped sharply upwards, steeply at first, before levelling off. It was wide enough to accommodate four or five mammoths walking abreast.

Icebones probed at its surface with her trunk tip. It was smooth and cold and hard and smelled of nothing. 'The Lost made this,' she said.

'Of course they did,' snapped the Ragged One. 'Impatient with the Gouge's depth and length, they hurled this mighty bridge right across it. What ambition! What vision!'

'They didn't put anything to eat or drink on it,' Autumn said reasonably.

Thunder stepped forward on to the bridge itself, and stamped heavily at its surface. Where he trod, his dirty foot pads left huge round prints on the gleaming floor. 'It is fragile, like thin ice. What if it is cracked by frost? This bridge was meant for the Lost. They were small creatures, much smaller than us. If we walk on it, perhaps it will fall.'

Icebones rumbled her approval, for the Bull was using the listening skills she had shown him.

But the Ragged One said, 'We will rest the night and feed. We will reach the far side in a day's walk, no more.'

Autumn growled doubtfully.

'No,' Icebones said decisively. 'We should keep away from the things of the Lost. We will climb down the landslide, and—'

'You are a coward and a fool.' The Ragged One's language and posture were clear and determined.

Icebones felt her heart sink. Was this festering sore in their community to be broken open again?

STEPHEN BAXTER

Thunder stepped forward angrily. 'Listen to her. The bridge is not safe.'

'Safe? What is *safe*? Did your precious hero Longtusk ask himself if that famous bridge of land was *safe*?'

'This is not the bridge of Longtusk,' Icebones said steadily. 'And you are not Longtusk.'

The Ragged One stepped back. 'I have endured your posturing, Icebones, when it did us no harm. But by your own admission you are no Matriarch. And now your foolish arrogance threatens to lead us into disaster. You others should follow me, not her,' she said bluntly.

Autumn, rumbling threateningly, stood by the shoulder of Icebones. 'This one is strange to us,' she said. 'Perhaps she is not yet a Matriarch. But she has displayed wisdom and leadership. And now she is right. There is no need to take the risk of crossing your bridge.'

'Icebones gave me my name,' Thunder said. 'I follow her. *You* are the arrogant one if you cannot tell this bridge is unsafe.' He stood alongside Icebones, and she touched his trunk.

Breeze lumbered towards her mother, her calf tucked safely between her legs. 'You are wrong to divide us. This fighting wastes our energy and time.'

Icebones rumbled, relieved, gratified by their unexpected support. 'Breeze is right. Let us put this behind us—'

'No.' The older sister, Spiral, had spoken. 'We must finish this terrible journey before we all die of hunger, and before another monster leaps out of the sea or sky or ground to consume us. And the quickest way is to take the bridge.'

'*It is not safe*,' Icebones growled.

'So *you* say,' Spiral said angrily. 'But it was made by the Lost. What do you know of the Lost, Icebones? They looked after our every need for a long time – for generations – long before you ever came here.' And, for a moment, behind the gaunt face and the dirty, matted hair, Icebones saw once

656

again the vain, spoiled creature she had first met. 'Shoot? Will you come with me?'

Shoot looked from her mother to her sister and back, dismayed. Then, hesitantly, she stepped up to Spiral.

The Ragged One raised her stubby tusks in triumph. 'We will cross the bridge, we three.'

'No,' Icebones said, gravely anxious. She had not anticipated this turn of events. 'We must not break up the Family.'

'This is no Family here,' said the Ragged One, contemptuous.

'If we stay together we can watch over each other. By splitting us, you endanger us all.'

'If that is so, you must drop your foolish pride and let me lead you, like these two.'

Icebones rumbled, 'I can't. Because you are leading them to their deaths.'

'Then there is nothing more to be said.' The Ragged One turned to face the arcing bridge and stalked away. Spiral followed.

Shoot glanced back at her mother, obviously distressed. But she followed her sister's lead – as, perhaps, she had all her life.

It was another long and difficult night, and it granted Icebones little sleep.

As pink light began to wash over the eastern lands, she walked alone to the edge of the canyon. It was a river of darkness. She listened to the soft chthonic breathing of the rocks beneath her feet, and the gentle ticking of frost, and she strained to hear the rhythm of distant mammoth footsteps.

She called out with deep vibrations of her head and belly and feet: 'Boaster. Can you hear me? It is me, Icebones. Boaster, Boaster . . .'

Icebones. I hear you.

She felt a profound relief, as if she was no longer alone.

We are walking. Every day we walk. The sun is hidden. It rains. We have come to a huge walled plain covered by something that glitters in the light, even the light of this grey sky. There is nothing to eat on it.

'It is ice.'

No. It is not cold and there is no moisture under my trunk tip.

She shuddered. 'It is a thing of the Lost.'

Yes. There is a great beast, like a beetle, which tends it. The beast wipes away the dust on the floor. My brother challenged the beetle. It turned away.

'Your brother defeated it?'

My brother is brave and strong. But not so brave as me. And he is smaller than me in many ways. Much smaller. For example, his—

'I can guess,' Icebones said dryly. She told him she had decided to head for the basin she had called the Footfall of Kilukpuk. 'But we face many obstacles.' And she told him about the Gouge, and tried to tell him of the mammoths' confusion and dissent.

You think you have problems, he called back. *Imagine how it is for me. All the time I slip up in my own musth dribble, and I trip over my long, erect—*

'You cannot still be in musth.'

Wait until we meet at the Footfall. You will see my musth flow, and you will be awed at its mighty gush. Are you in oestrus yet?

'No,' Icebones said, with a shiver of sadness.

Good, came Boaster's voice, deep-whispering through the rock. *It would be a waste. Wait until we meet at the Footfall. I must go. We have found a dwarf willow and the others are stripping it like wolf cubs, leaving none for me. Be brave, little Icebones. We will meet at the Footfall. Goodbye, goodbye . . .*

Icebones stood alone in the chill, bloody light of dawn, listening to the last of his words wash through the rock.

*

The Ragged One stepped on to the smooth slope of the bridge. She stamped hard on the cold surface, as if testing it under her weight.

The bridge rang hollowly.

More tentatively Shoot followed, and then, at last, Spiral.

Autumn growled, her voice filled with sadness as she watched her daughters walk out into emptiness.

'This is wrong,' Icebones said. 'Wrong, wrong. Mammoths are creatures of the steppe, and the open sky. They are not meant to hover like birds high above the ground.'

But none of the three rebels was listening.

Soon the mammoths had gone so far that they looked like beetles, crawling over the mighty band of the bridge. The sun was still low in the sky, and the three toiling mammoths cast long shadows across the bridge's smooth, pink-lit surface.

Icebones could hear the deep thrumming vibrations of the bridge as it bent and bowed in response to the mammoths' weight.

The Ragged One turned. She trumpeted, her voice dwarfed by the Gouge beneath her. 'You are wrong, all of you. The bridge will protect us. See?' And she raised her foot –

Icebones trumpeted, 'No!'

– and the Ragged One began to stamp, hard, at the shining surface of the bridge.

Icebones heard the cracking long before she could see it. It sounded like pack ice over a swelling sea, or a fragment of bone beneath a clumsy mammoth foot pad.

A spider-web of cracks spread over the pale pink surface. The whole bridge was quivering, and already slivers of it were crumbling off its edges and falling, to be lost far below.

Autumn trumpeted, an ancient, wordless cry, and she ran forward to the edge of the bridge.

Shoot turned back and faced her sister. 'Go back! We must go back!'

But Spiral, last in line, would not move. She stood on the

trembling bridge, feet splayed and trunk dipped, as if frozen in place.

'She is terrified,' Breeze said. 'And if she does not move, the others cannot.'

Thunder tossed his head skittishly. 'I will go out there. I will save them.' But there was terror in the white rims of his eyes.

'Your place is here,' Icebones said firmly. 'You must protect these others, and the calf. That is your duty now.'

He tried to hide his relief. 'Yes,' he said. 'That is my duty.'

And my duty, Icebones thought, is to bring the others back – or die trying.

Without thinking about it she stepped on to the cold surface of the bridge. She could feel the deep, dismal resonance of the bridge as it shuddered and shook. The frequent cracks were sharp detonations, carrying clearly to her ears and belly.

She stepped forward gingerly.

Autumn growled, but did not try to stop her.

Soon Icebones had passed beyond the edge of the land, and she could look down into the depths of the Gouge. The rising sun cast deep pink shadows from the layers of cloud, obscuring the brown-grey ground far beneath. She was standing *above* the clouds, she thought, and all that kept her from that immense drop was the fragile thinness of the bridge; her stomach clenched, tight as the jaws of a cat.

At last she reached Spiral. Icebones tugged at her tail until she yelped.

'You must turn around. We have to go back.'

'I can't,' Spiral said, whimpering. The Cow stood rooted as solid as a tree to the thin bridge floor.

Shoot picked her way back along the shuddering bridge. She slapped Spiral's head with her trunk, and even clattered her tusks against her sister's.

At last, under this double assault, Spiral, moaning softly, began to turn. Each footfall was as tentative and nervous as a newborn calf's. Step by step, Icebones led Spiral back towards the cliff top.

They had almost reached the hard, secure rock when there was a harsh trumpet.

Autumn called, '*Shoot!*'

A section of the shuddering bridge had crumbled and fallen away. Icebones could see bits of it falling through the air, sparkling as they spun, diminishing to snowflakes.

And there was nothing beneath Shoot's hind feet.

Shoot fell back, oddly slowly. For a heartbeat she clung to the broken edge of the bridge with her forelegs, and she scrabbled with her trunk. Then she slid back, as smoothly as a drop of water sliding off the tip of a tusk. She wailed, once.

Icebones glimpsed her sprawled in the air, almost absurdly, limbs and trunks and tusks flapping like the wings of a clumsy, misshapen bird. Her fall was agonisingly slow, slow enough for Icebones to hear every whimper and cry, even to smell the urine that gushed into the air around Shoot's legs.

Then she was lost in cloud, and Icebones was grateful.

She heard the trumpeting cry of Spiral, and Autumn's answering wail.

Icebones inspected the crack. It was wide, and getting wider as more chunks of bridge structure fell away like sharp-edged snowflakes.

The Ragged One stood on the far side of the crack, backing away slowly. The damaged bridge was like a great tongue lolling from the remote far side of the Gouge. But as the bridge swung up and down beneath her the Ragged One kept her footing easily.

'You cannot return,' Icebones called.

'I do not choose to return.'

'You will be alone.'

The Ragged One snorted, and stepped back again as more of the bridge fell away. 'I have always been alone. Don't you know that yet?'

'We will meet at the Footfall.'

'Perhaps.' And the Ragged One turned away.

Icebones watched her recede. For all the tragedy and renewed danger her shrunken band would face from now on, a secret part of her was glad that the Ragged One was gone – at least for now.

The bridge trembled and cracked further.

Autumn was still trumpeting, her voice thin and sharp. 'The morning is barely begun. But already my daughter is dead. How can this be?'

The sun rose higher, shining brighter as the blue morning clouds dispersed.

CHAPTER 2
THE WALK DOWN FROM THE SKY

By midday the mammoths had reached the top of the landslide. Subdued, weary, they scattered in search of forage.

Icebones and Thunder stood at the very edge of the cliff. The Gouge was a river of pink light below them, laced with cloud. The line of the cliff itself was cut back in great scallops, as if some huge animal had taken bites out of it. In one place a broad, deep channel came to an end at the cliff, as if the greater Gouge had simply been cut into the land, leaving the older valley hanging.

The landslide was a great pile of broken rock that fell away into the depths of the Gouge until it disappeared beneath a layer of thin cloud. The slope was pitted by craters, its scree and talus smashed and compressed to a glassy smoothness. Even this landslide was ancient, Icebones realised, old enough to have accumulated the scars of such powerful blows. This was an old world indeed, old upon old.

'We should go *that* way,' Thunder said, looking down at a point where the landslide slope looked particularly flat and easy. 'And then we can follow that trail.' He meant a rough ridge that had formed in the heaped rubble, zigzagging towards the Gouge floor.

Icebones said, 'But I doubt that any mammoths have walked here before.' Trails made by mammoths had been proven reliable and safe, perhaps over generations. Mammoth trails were part of their deep memory of the world. But there was no memory here. This 'trail' of Thunder's was nothing but a random heaping of rocks. She said at last, 'We cannot move from this place today. The others are not ready for such a challenge.'

'But to lose another day—'

'Your mind is sharp, Thunder. Theirs are crowded by grief. For now, you must continue to study our path. We will rely on you.'

'You are wise,' he said, and resumed his inspection of the path.

That day seemed terribly long – and when it was done, the night seemed even longer.

Autumn had withdrawn into herself once more. Breeze took refuge in the calf, who blundered about oblivious of the greater tragedy around him.

Spiral seemed the worst affected.

At first the tall Cow wailed out her grief loudly. Icebones meant to go to her to comfort her, but Autumn held her back. 'This is how she was with the Lost,' she said harshly. 'When she was hurting, or hungry, or just wanted attention. They would come running to her. We should not go running now. She must bear the burden of what has happened.'

Icebones bowed to the wisdom of the older Cow.

When none of the mammoths responded, Spiral's wails ceased abruptly. She withdrew from the others, seeking out forage in a distracted, half-hearted manner. Then, after a time, she began to make deep, mournful groans, so deep they carried better through the ground than the air, and Icebones saw salty tears well in Spiral's small eyes. At last she was truly grieving, as a mammoth should.

And now Autumn came to her, and wrapped her trunk around her daughter's bowed head.

Icebones, feeling very young, was bemused and distressed by the complexity of the emotions spilling here.

Icebones walked to the edge of the cliff, gathered her courage, and stepped off.

Rubble crunched and compressed under her front feet.

Cautiously she stepped further, bringing her back legs on to the rocky slope. The footing seemed good, and the rock fragments slipped over each other less than she had feared. The surface rocks were worn smooth by dust or water or frost, but some of them were loosely bound together by mats of moss and lichen.

She soon tired, her front legs aching, for it was never comfortable for mammoths to walk downhill. But she persisted, doggedly following the rubble trail Thunder had picked out, listening to the rumbles and grunts of the mammoths who followed her.

The wall of the Gouge loomed behind her. It was striped with bands of varying colour, shades of red and brown, like the rings of a fallen tree. The topmost layer was the thickest, an orange blanket of what appeared to be loose dust. And the wall was carved vertically, marked with huge upright grooves and pillars of rock, perhaps made by rock falls or running water. The grooves cut through the flat strata to make a complex criss-cross pattern. Great flat lids of harder rock stuck out of the wall, sheltering hollowed-out caverns that she climbed past. She made out rustles of movement: birds, perhaps, nesting in these high caves.

This tremendous wall was a complex formation in its own right, she saw, shaped by the vast, slow, inexorable movements of rock and air and water. With its endless detail of strata and carvings and nesting birds, it went on as far as she could see, a vertical world, all the way to the horizon, where it merged in the mist with its remote, parallel twin.

Now she found herself walking into clouds. They were thin, wispy streaks, and they rested on an invisible layer in the air.

She soon passed through the strange cloud lid, into air that was tinged blue, full of mist. The air was noticeably thicker, warmer and moist, and she breathed in deep satisfying lungfuls of it.

The mammoths came to a flat, dusty ledge, still high above the Gouge floor. They fanned out, seeking forage.

Icebones, probing at the ground, found there was vegetation here: yellow and red lichen, mosses, even a little grass. But it was sparse, and the only water was trapped under layers of ice difficult to crack. She knew they must go much deeper before they could be comfortable.

She prepared to move on.

But the calf had other ideas. Woodsmoke reached up to his mother's front leg, lifted his trunk over his fuzzy head, and clamped his mouth to her heavy breast. Icebones could smell the milk that trickled from his mouth. When he was done, he knelt down in his mother's shade and slumped sideways, his eyes closing. His belly rose as he breathed, and his mouth popped open, a circle of darkness.

Time for a nap, it seems, Icebones thought wryly.

The other mammoths gathered around Breeze and her calf. Autumn lifted her heavy trunk and rested it on her tusks. The others let their trunks dangle before them. Only Icebones, in this tall company, was short enough that her trunk reached the ground without her having to dip her head to reach.

The mammoths' bodies swayed gently, in unison. Filled with dust, their thick outer hair caught the pink sunlight, so that each of them was surrounded by a halo of pink-white light.

Immersed in the deep soft breathing of the others, Icebones closed her eyes.

She was woken by a soft, subtle movement.

Spiral had gone to the limit of the ledge, her foot pads compressing soundlessly. Trying not to disturb the others, Icebones followed her.

The afternoon air had grown more clear, and now the deepest world of the Gouge revealed itself. The floor was carved into a series of terraces, and broken up by smaller chasms or chains of hills. And in the deepest section of all she saw the pale glint of water. But it was a straight-line slash that ran right down the length of the Gouge, even cutting through what looked like natural lakes and river tributaries. It was no river but a canal: an artefact of the paws of the Lost.

With trunk raised, Spiral was staring fixedly towards the west. Icebones squinted, trying to make her poor eyes work better.

Over the green-grey floor of the Gouge lay a fine white line. It crossed the valley from one side to the other, like a scratch through a layer of lichen.

'It is the fallen bridge.'

'Yes,' said Spiral. 'And that is where Shoot lies, crushed like an egg. Should we go back and look for her corpse? That is your way, isn't it? The wolves and birds will have taken the meat and guts and eyes by now. But if the bones are not too scattered—'

'Stop this,' Icebones snapped, with all the Matriarchal command she could muster. 'You must not think of your sister in death. Think of *her*.'

Spiral reached forward with her trunk, as if seeking the ghost of her vanished sister. Hesitantly she said, 'She was – funny. She was loyal. She always stuck by me. Sometimes that would annoy me. Some of the Lost thought she was cuter than me and would give her attention . . .'

'I can see how that would irritate you,' Icebones said gently.

Spiral had the grace to snort, mocking herself. 'She followed me. *Me*. And I betrayed her trust by leading her to her death.'

Icebones groped for something to say. 'Sometimes we have no choice about how we act. Sometimes, *we cannot save even those we love*. That is what the Cycle tells us, over and over.' And that hard fact would be the most unpalatable truth of all for these untutored mammoths, if they ever had to face it.

But Spiral was still distant, wounded, and the Cycle seemed a dusty abstraction.

Icebones thought, Thunder, Autumn, Spiral: all of them suffused by guilt, agonised by the mistakes they felt they had made. It was because they had always been under the care of the Lost. It was because they had never had to act for themselves.

Wisdom must be earned, through pain and loss. That was what these mammoths were struggling to learn.

The mammoths were beginning to stir, blowing dust from their trunks. The calf, revived and excited, bumped against their legs.

They reached a new, steep slope of loose talus. It was more difficult to climb down, but it delivered them to the warmer, moister air more quickly, and they pushed forward with enthusiasm.

Abruptly they emerged on to a broad terrace. Stepping forward stiffly, relieved to be on flat ground again, Icebones immediately felt a soft crackle beneath one foot pad. It was the sprawled-out branch of a dwarf birch. Looking ahead, she could see that the ground was littered with patches of open water.

The mammoths fanned out, emitting grunts of pleasure as they found tufts of grass and clumps of herbs.

Icebones walked to the crumbled lip of the terrace, and found herself in a strange world.

The Gouge's mighty walls ran roughly straight, but they were complex even from this perspective, full of great scraped-out bays separated by knife-sharp ridges. Everywhere she saw landslides: rock skirts, sloping sharply, leaning against the walls. In one place, she saw, a giant landslide had swept right across the wide Gouge floor and come washing up against the far wall.

The walls were so tall they rose up above the clouds. And

they were still visible even at the horizon, as if a notch had been taken out of the very planet.

Thin, high cries fell on her like snowflakes. Peering up, she saw geese flying away from the sun in a vast, crowded formation, skimming through the strip of sky enclosed by the walls. The wall itself was pocked with ledges and pits where birds nested: guillemots, murres, kittiwakes and gulls. The birds flew back and forth against the cliff face, their wings flashing bright against the huge wall's brooding crimson.

Below the level of this terrace, the steppe-like terrain gave way to a forest of spruce, pine, aspen: cold-resistant trees so tall they seemed to be straining to reach the sky. And beyond them she saw the glimmer of water. It was the canal, the straight-line cut through the Gouge's deepest part. Alongside the canal more trees grew, but these were fat, water-rich broadleaf trees, oak and elm and maple, basking in the comparative warmth of those depths. She glimpsed a sea of shining black washing along the valley – a herd of migrant animals: bison, reindeer, maybe even horses.

The air over these deeper parts of the Gouge floor shone pink-gold, full of moisture and dust, and the green and blue of water and life overlaid the strong red colour of the underlying rock, making a startling contrast. But the thin scraping of life was utterly overwhelmed by the mighty geology that bounded it. And every sound she heard, every rumble that came to her through the ground, was shaped by those tremendous cliffs.

This was a walled world.

Woodsmoke came running floppily before her, his fuzzy-haired head bobbing up and down, his trunk exploring the ground as he ran. 'Which way? Which way, Icebones? Which way?'

Icebones peered east, away from the setting sun. Her

shadow fled along the ground before her, straight along the Gouge floor, a thing of spindly legs and stretched-out body – just like a native-born mammoth, she thought.

She scratched the calf's scalp with her trunk fingers. 'Follow your shadow, Woodsmoke.'

The calf lolloped away, trumpeting his excitement, and his thin cries echoed from the Gouge's mighty walls.

CHAPTER 3
THE WALLED WORLD

The Gouge's floor was carved by lesser valleys and twisting ridges. Lakes pooled, linked by the cruel gash of that central canal. The lakes were crowded with reeds and littered with ducks and geese. Around their shores forests grew, mighty oaks that stretched up so high their upper branches were lost in mist.

The mammoths would come down to the lakes' gravelly beaches to sip water that was mostly free of salt, even if it fizzed uncomfortably in Icebones's trunk. But the lower ground was softer and frequently boggy, and nothing grew there but bland uninterrupted grasses, or tall coniferous trees, neither of which provided food that sustained mammoths well. They generally kept to higher ground, where grew a rich mosaic vegetation of grass, herbs, shrubs and trees, providing a healthy diet.

They often glimpsed other animals: Icebones recognised reindeer, horses, bison and musk oxen, lemmings and rabbits, and she saw the spoor of creatures who fed off the grazing herds, like wolves and foxes. The smaller animals seemed about the size she recalled from the Island. But the reindeer and horses were very tall, with spindly legs that scarcely seemed capable of supporting their weight.

The long-legged rabbits could bound spectacularly high into the air. But they fell back with eerie slowness, making them tempting targets for diving raptor birds.

For a while an arctic fox followed the mammoths, sniffing their dung. The fox was in his winter coat, a gleaming white so intense it was almost blue. The fox moved with anxious, purposeful movements over a network of trails, undetectable to Icebones. He was no threat to the mammoths, but the fox was an efficient scavenger of food, a hunter of lemmings and eggs and helpless chicks who might fall from a cliff-side nest. Somehow she found it reassuring to see this familiar rogue prospering in this peculiar landscape.

But still, though the Gouge was crowded with life compared to the upper plains from which they had descended, on the higher ground they passed lakes that had dried up, leaving only bowls of cracked mud. Even here, in this strange walled world, the tide of life was inexorably receding.

Icebones inspected one such mud bowl gloomily. It was churned by many hoof marks, and littered with bits of bone, cracked and scored by the teeth and beaks of scavengers. When the water had vanished, animals, dying of thirst, had congregated here to die – and had then provided easy meat for the predators. She tried to imagine the scenes here as adult jostled with adult, fighting for water, maddened by thirst, and the young and old and weak were pushed aside. And she wondered if any of these bits of well-chewed bone had once belonged to mammoths.

She kept these reflections to herself – but she sensed from Autumn's reflective silence that the older Cow at least understood this.

But meanwhile the walking was steady, the weather on the Gouge floor calm, the grazing good. The mammoths gradually became more confident, their bellies filling, and the steady rhythms of life banished their lingering grief over the loss of Shoot.

The calf helped, of course.

His scrawny little body filled out, becoming almost burly. His newborn's hair was growing out, his underfur thicker, his coarser overfur longer. But his hair was still a bright pink-brown, much lighter than that of adult mammoths. He would gallop on stiff legs, leaving an uneven set of clumsy tracks – only to come to a sudden halt, trunk raised to sniff the air, his low forehead wrinkled with concentration. Or he would scoop up loose grass, suck, sniff, blow out dust, and run about as if trying to explore every detail of the ground they crossed. He picked dust and earth and insects from his thickening coat, and with wide-eyed curiosity he would pop each item into his mouth, more often than not spitting it out again.

He was still dependent on his mother's milk, but Icebones made sure he was happy to be cared for by the others. Spiral, in particular, relished looking after him – so much so, in fact, that Icebones sometimes wondered if she was growing jealous that he wasn't her own.

Though Icebones never spoke it out loud, all of this was a preparation against the dire possibility that Woodsmoke might lose his mother. No mammoth was more vulnerable than a calf without a mother.

But for now, Woodsmoke was secure and happy, and busy with his exploration of the intriguing world in which he found himself.

One day the calf began to play with a lemming that had, unwisely, not retreated to its burrow as the mammoths' heavy footfalls approached.

'That lemming is not happy,' commented Thunder.

Icebones recalled the Cycle. '*No animal likes to be disturbed.*'

Thunder rumbled deeply. 'You often quote your Cycle. But how do you *know* the Cycle is true?'

She noticed he was walking stiffly. He held his head high, and his legs were stiff, as if sore. Everything about him seemed larger than usual. And, she thought, there was an odd smell about him: something sweet, pervasive, sharp.

He went on, '*You* didn't live in the times of long ago when herds of mammoths darkened the steppe. *You* never met Longtusk or Ganesha or Kilukpuk or any of the rest. Perhaps it is all the murmurings of calves, or foolish old Bulls.'

She bridled at that. No mammoth should speak so

disrespectfully of the Cycle, the heart of mammoth culture. But then, she reminded herself, Thunder had been brought up in ignorance. It wasn't his fault, and it was her role to put that right.

'Thunder, you must understand that every mammoth alive today is descended from survivors: mammoths who mastered the world well enough to reach adulthood and raise healthy calves, who grew up in their turn. The Cycle is the wisdom of that great chain of survivors, accumulated over more generations than there are stars in the sky.'

'But *this is a different place*. You say that yourself. Perhaps no mammoths lived here before the Lost brought us. What use is the Cycle to us?'

'While we live, we must not be afraid to *add* to the Cycle. Ganesha taught us that, and Longtusk. The Cycle will never be complete. Not while mammoths live and learn. There is completeness only in extinction . . .'

But she felt that such comfort, embedded in the Cycle itself, was thin.

And perhaps Thunder was right.

This Sky Steppe was itself a part of the Cycle. But whereas the rest of the Cycle was a memory of the past, the Sky Steppe had always been a vision of the *future*: a glittering, succulent promise of days to come.

Sometimes, when this small red world seemed so strange, she wondered if perhaps nothing around her was real. Maybe she was living in a moment embedded in the vision, of a mammoth long dead – Kilukpuk herself, perhaps. *And in that case she was part of that dream too*. She was living thoughts, just a concoction of memories and dreams, with no more life than the reconstructed bones of the mammoth on the Fire Mountain.

But now Woodsmoke brayed and yelled, 'I am a great Bull. I will mate you all, you Cows!' His thin cries and milky scent, and the iron stink of the dust he kicked up, were sharp intrusions of reality into her maundering.

The calf started dancing in a tight circle around the lemming. The little rodent sat as if frozen, clearly wishing this huge monster would go away. Then Woodsmoke made a mock charge, head lowered. The lemming, snapping out of its trance, turned tail and shot across the ground, a muddy brown blur, until it reached a hole and disappeared.

Woodsmoke's mother cuffed him affectionately and tucked him under her belly, where the great Bull was soon seeking out his mother's milk.

Thunder growled. 'That little scrap is mocking me.'

'He is playing at what he will become.'

'But he was threatening a *lemming*.'

'He has to start somewhere. If there were other calves here, he would wrestle with them and stage little tusk-clashes. It is all part of his preparation for the battles he must wage as an adult.'

Thunder growled again. 'Perhaps. But when that wretched calf approaches me, reaching up with his grass-blade trunk to wrestle, I want to throw him out of the Gouge . . .'

Suspicious now, she sniffed at the ground over which Thunder had walked, smelling his urine, which was hissing slightly as it settled into the red dust. And she probed at the thick hair before his ears with her trunk fingers. She found a dark, sticky liquid trickling from his temporal gland.

'Thunder – you are in musth!'

He rumbled deeply. It was the musth call, she realised. Without understanding it he was calling to oestrus Cows, if any had been here to listen. 'I thought I was ill.'

'Not ill.' She stroked the temporal glands on both sides of his head. They were swollen. 'You are sore here.' Gently she lifted his trunk and had him coil it so it rested on its tusks. 'That will relieve the pressure on one side of your face at least.'

'Icebones, what is happening to me? I roam around this Gouge listening, but I don't know what for. The Cows keep their distance from me – even you.'

It was true, she realised. She had responded to his calls without thinking. She said carefully, 'Musth means that you are ready to mate. Your smell, and the rumbles you make, announce your readiness to any receptive Cows. The aggression you feel is meant to be turned on other Bulls, for Bulls must always fight to prove they are fit to sire calves. But here there are no Bulls for you to fight – none save Woodsmoke, and you have shown the correct restraint.'

He growled, 'But there are Cows.'

'None of us is in oestrus, Thunder,' she said gently. 'You will learn to tell that from the smell of our urine. None of us is ready.'

She felt his trunk probe at her belly. 'Not even you?'

'Not even me, Thunder. I am sorry.' Again she was struck by the fact that she had still not come into oestrus, had felt not so much as a single twinge of that great inner warmth in all the time she had been here. 'Don't worry. In a few days this will pass and you will feel normal again.'

He grunted. 'I hope so.'

In fact she suspected that even if one of the Cows were in oestrus, right here and right now, still Thunder would fail to find himself a mate. He was clearly young and immature, and no Cow would willingly accept a mating with such a Bull. If there were other Bulls here he wouldn't even get a chance, of course. For his first few musth seasons Thunder would simply be overpowered by the older, mature Bulls.

He pulled away, grumbling his disappointment. He raised his tusks into the shining sunlit air, and a swarm of insects, rising from a muddy pond, buzzed around his head, glowing with light. 'I feel as if my belly will burst like an overripe fruit. Why, if she were here before me now, I would mate with old Kilukpuk herself—'

'Who speaks of Kilukpuk?'

Thunder brayed, startled, and stopped dead. The voice – like a mammoth's, but shallow and indistinct – had seemed to come from the reaches of the pond ahead of them.

*

'What is it?' Thunder asked softly. 'Can there be mammoths here?'

Icebones grunted. 'What kind of mammoth lives in the middle of a pond?'

'Kilukpuk, Kilukpuk . . . How is it I know that name?'

And a trunk poked up out of the water, and two wide nostrils twitched. It was short, hairless, stubby, but nevertheless indubitably a trunk.

Icebones stepped forward. The mud squeezed between her toes, unpleasantly thick, cold and moist. 'I am Icebones, daughter of Silverhair. If you are mammoth, show yourself.'

A head broke above the surface of the water. Icebones saw a smooth brow with two small eyes set on top, peering at her. 'Mammoth? I never heard of such things. *Bones-Of-Ice?* What kind of name is that?' The creature sniffed loudly. 'Don't drop your dung in my pond.'

Thunder growled, 'If you don't show yourself I will come in there and drag you out. *Before* I fill up your pond with my dung.'

Thunder's musth-fuelled aggression was out of place, Icebones thought. But it seemed to do the trick.

There was a loud, indignant gurgle. With a powerful heave, a squat body broke through the languidly rippling water.

It stood out of the water on four stubby legs. It had powerful shoulders and rump, and a long skull topped by those small, glittering eyes. It wasn't quite hairless, for fine downy hairs lay plastered over its skin, smoothed back like the scales of a fish. But the whole body was so heavily coated in crimson-brown mud that it was hard to see anything at all.

It was like no mammoth Icebones had ever seen. And yet it had a trunk, and even two small tusks that protruded from its mouth, curling slightly and pointing downwards.

And it gazed at Icebones with frank curiosity, its stubby trunk raised.

More of the hog-like creatures came drifting through the water. They looked like floating logs, Icebones thought, though thick bubbles showed where they belched or farted.

Meanwhile the other mammoths gathered around Icebones and Thunder – all save the calf. Woodsmoke, quickly bored, had splashed into the mud at the fringe of the pond and was digging out lumps of it with his tusks.

Spiral asked, 'What *is* it?'

The creature in the pond said, '*It* is Chaser-Of-Frogs. I am the Mother of the Family that lives here.'

Evidently, Icebones thought dryly, her dignity was easily hurt. '*Mother?* You are a Matriarch?'

Chaser-Of-Frogs eyed Icebones suspiciously. 'I do not know you, Bones-Of-Ice. Do you come from the Pond of Evening?'

She must mean one of the lakes to the west of here, Icebones thought. She said, 'I come from a place far from here, which—'

Chaser-Of-Frogs grunted and buried her snout-like trunk in pond-bottom mud. 'Always making trouble, that lot from Evening. Even though my own daughter mated with one of them. When you go back you can tell them that Chaser-Of-Frogs said—'

Thunder growled and stepped forward. 'Listen to her, you floating fool. We come from no pond. *We are not like you*.'

'And yet we are,' Icebones said, drawn to the pond's edge, trunk raised. She could smell foetid mud, laced with thin dung. 'You have tusks and a trunk. You are my Cousin.'

'Cousin?' The glittering eyes of the not-mammoth stared back at her, curious in their own way. 'Tell me of Kilukpuk. I know that name . . . and yet I do not.'

'It is an old name,' Icebones said. 'Mammoths and their Cousins are born with it on their tongues.' And Icebones spoke of Kilukpuk, and of Kilukpuk's rivalry with her brother, Aglu, and of Kilukpuk's calves, Hyros and Siros, who had squabbled and fought in their jealousy, of Kilukpuk's favourite, Probos, and how Probos had become Matriarch of all the mammoths and their Cousins . . .

Her own nascent Family clustered around her. The log-like bodies in the pond drifted close to the shallow muddy beach, tiny ears pricked, the silence broken only by occasional gulping farts that broke the surface of the water.

'I have never heard such tales,' mused Chaser-Of-Frogs. 'But it is apt. I sink in the mud, as did Kilukpuk in her swamp. I browse on the plants that grow in the pond-bottom ooze, as she must have done. I am as she was.' She seemed proud – but she was so caked in mud it was hard to tell.

How strange, Icebones thought. Could it be that these Swamp-Mammoths really were ancient forms, remade for this new world? Perhaps they had been moulded from mammoths, the way Woodsmoke was moulding lumps of mud.

Only the Lost would do such a thing, of course. And only the Lost knew *why*.

'You mammoths,' said Chaser-Of-Frogs now. 'Tell me where you are going.'

'To the east,' Thunder said promptly. 'We are walking around the belly of the world. We are seeking a place we call the Footfall of Kilukpuk—'

'You will not get far,' Chaser-Of-Frogs said firmly. 'Not unless you know your way through the Nest of the Lost.'

Thunder growled, 'What Nest?'

Chaser-Of-Frogs snorted, and bits of snot and mud flew into the air. 'You've never even heard of it? Then you will soon be running like a calf for her mother's teat.' She sank into her mud, submerging save for the crest of her back and the tip of her trunk.

Then she rose again lazily, as if having second thoughts. 'I will show you. Tomorrow. It is in gratitude for the stories, which I enjoyed. Today I will rest and eat, making myself ready.'

Thunder said, 'You fat log, you look as if you have spent your whole life resting and eating.'

Autumn slapped his forehead. 'She will hear you.'

Chaser-Of-Frogs surfaced again. 'Don't forget. No dung in the pond. Those disease-ridden scoundrels from Evening are always playing that trick. I won't have it, you hear?'

'We won't,' said Icebones.

Chaser-Of-Frogs slid beneath the dirty brown water and, with a final valedictory fart, swam away.

CHAPTER 4
THE NEST OF THE LOST

The ground stank of night things: of roots, of dew, of worms, of the tiny reptiles and mammals that burrowed through it.

All the mammoths found it difficult to settle. They were deeper into the Gouge than they were accustomed to. The air felt moist and sticky, and was full of the stink of murky pond water. The vegetation was too thick and wet for a mammoth's gut, and soon all of their stomachs were growling in protest.

Icebones could sense the deep wash of fat log-like bodies as the Swamp-Mammoths swam and rolled in their sticky water. Not a heartbeat went by without a fart or belch or muddy splash, or a grumble about a neighbour's crowding or stealing food.

And, as the light faded from the western sky, a new light rose in the east to take its place: a false dawn, Icebones thought, a glowing dome of dusty air, eerily yellow. It was the Nest of the Lost, of course, just as Chaser-Of-Frogs had warned.

Autumn, Breeze and Thunder faced the yellow light, sniffing the air with suspicious raised trunks. It pleased Icebones to see that they were starting to find their true instincts, buried under generations of the Lost's unwelcome attention.

Not Spiral, though. She started trotting to and fro, lifting her head and raising her fine tusks so they shone in the unnatural light.

*

As the true dawn approached, Icebones heard the pad of clumsy footsteps. It was Chaser-Of-Frogs.

In the pink-grey half-light the Swamp-Mammoth stood before them, her stubby trunk raised. Her barrel of a body was coated in mud that crackled with frost, her breath steamed around her face, and her broad feet left round damp marks where she passed. 'Are you ready? *Urgh*. Your dung stinks.'

'The food here is bad for us,' Autumn growled.

'Just as well you're leaving, then,' Chaser-Of-Frogs said. 'Go drop a little of that foul stuff in the Pond of Evening, will you? Hey! What's this?'

Woodsmoke had run around to Chaser-Of-Frogs's side and was scrambling on her back. He was taller than she was. He already had his legs hooked over her spine, and he was pulling with his trunk at the sparse hair that grew there. 'I am a Bull, strong and fierce. What are you? If you are a Cow I will mate with you.'

'Get him off! Get him off!' Chaser-Of-Frogs turned her head this way and that, trying to reach him, but her neck was too rigid, her trunk much too small.

Autumn stalked forward and, with an imperious gesture, wrapped her trunk around the calf and lifted him up in the air.

Woodsmoke's little face peered out through a forest of trunk hair. 'I want to mate with it!'

Chaser-Of-Frogs growled and backed away. 'Try it and I'll kick you so hard you'll finish up beyond the next pond, you little guano lump.'

'He's only a calf,' Breeze rumbled.

'I know. I've had four of my own. Just keep him from being a calf around me.'

Icebones said gravely, 'We saw the lights. The Nest of the Lost. We need your guidance, Chaser-Of-Frogs. Please.'

Chaser-Of-Frogs growled again, but evidently her dignity wasn't too badly bruised. She sniffed the breeze. 'Let's go.

We must keep up a good pace, for there's nothing to eat in there. But keep this in mind. Whatever you see – *there's nothing to fear.*'

And, without hesitation, she set off across the swampy ground to the east.

Icebones, suppressing her own uneasiness, strode purposefully after her. She could hear the massive shuffle of the mammoths as they gathered in a loose line behind her.

The mammoths followed the bank of the canal. The waterway arrowed straight east, so that the rising sun hung directly over the lapping water, as if to guide their way.

The Gouge here lacked the tidy clarity of its western sections. The walls were broken and eroded, as if they had been drowned beneath an immense, catastrophic flood. The floor terrain was difficult, broken land, littered with huge, eroded rock fragments or covered in steep dust dunes.

But the land close to the canal was levelled: as smooth as the surface of Chaser-Of-Frogs's mud pond.

'I've heard of this place,' said Autumn. 'Once mammoths were bound up with rope, and made to pull great floating things along the length of this shining water.'

Icebones rumbled uncomfortably. She sensed that even Autumn missed something of the certainty of those days, when the Lost ran the world and everything in it.

There was movement on the canal's oily waters. Thunder backed away from the water's edge, perhaps recalling the whale that had come so close to taking Shoot in the Ocean of the North.

But this was no whale. It swam over the surface of the water, a massive straight-edged slab. It had no eyes or ears or trunk or feet. Huge slow waves trailed after it, feathering gracefully.

Autumn growled to Icebones, 'It is obviously a thing of the Lost. And, look – it has a shining shell, like the ice beetle in the crater.'

The huge water beetle drifted to a halt against the canal bank. A straight-edged hole in its side opened up, like a mouth, and a tongue of shining material stuck out and nuzzled against the land. Then the beetle waited, bobbing gently as the waves it had made rippled under it, and its carapace glistened in the dusty sunlight.

Nothing climbed aboard the beetle, and nothing came out of its mouth.

After a time the beetle rolled in its tongue, shut its strange mouth, and pushed its way gently further down the canal. After a time it stopped again, and Icebones saw that once more it opened its mouth, waiting, waiting.

Chaser-Of-Frogs growled, 'Every morning it is the same. This water-thing toils up and down the canal, sticking out its tongue. This is the way of things here. Everything you see will be strange and useless. Nothing will do you harm. Come now.' She stumped on.

They followed, walking beside the shore of the canal, while the waves of the beetle slowly rippled and subsided.

Soon they approached vast spires, slender and impossibly tall, taller than the greatest tree even on this tall planet. The gathering sunlight seeped into the spires, so they were filled with glowing pink light.

As they approached these glittering visions all the mammoths grew perturbed.

When Icebones looked into a spire she was startled to see another mammoth gazing back at her: a somewhat ragged, sunken-eyed, ill-fed Cow staring back at her from the depths of a glimmering pink pool. The mammoth had no smell and made no noise – for it was herself, of course, a reflection just as if she was staring into a pool of still water. But this 'pool' had been set on edge by the strange arts of the Lost, and its strangeness disturbed her, right to the warm core of her being.

Woodsmoke came running from between his mother's legs, trumpeting a shrill greeting. He ran straight into the shining wall and went sprawling, a mess of legs and trunk. Mewling a protest, he got up and trotted back to the wall. He raised his trunk at the mammoth calf he could see there, and the other calf raised its trunk back. With a comical growl, Woodsmoke tried to butt the other mammoth, only to find himself clattering against the wall again.

He might have kept that up all day, Icebones thought, if his mother hadn't come to tuck him between her legs again.

'I am bigger than him. Did you see? My tusks were bigger than his. He was frightened of me. He ran away.'

'Yes. Yes, he ran away.'

There were buildings all around them now, of all sizes and shapes and colours, all characterised by hard, cold straight lines. And there were tall angular shapes, like trees denuded of their branches. These 'trees' had a single fat fruit suspended from their top. Many of the fruit had fallen and smashed, but from others an eerie yellow light glowed, perhaps the source of the light Icebones had observed during the night.

The trails between the buildings were littered with red dust, and as the mammoths passed, their feet left clear round imprints. Many of the buildings showed signs of damage, their walls broken by huge rough-edged holes. In corners of the great avenues there were heaps of debris, branches and dust and bones, smashed up and dumped here as if by some great storm. It was evident that this place had been abandoned for some time.

Icebones was aware of Spiral's growing, silent dismay; she would not find the Lost here.

Suddenly, from all over the Nest, boxy beetles came scurrying.

The mammoths stopped dead, and Breeze trumpeted alarm.

The beetles began to rush from one silent building to another. A mouth would open in the hide of a beetle, and another would open to greet it in the gleaming side of the building, and the beetle would wait – just as the water-beetle had waited by the side of the canal. But nothing came to climb into or out of the beetle, no matter how long it waited. At last the beetle would close itself up again and scuttle off to its next fruitless rendezvous.

As suddenly as it had begun, the swarm of beetles thinned out. The last beetles shut their mouths and hurtled off out of sight.

But now another crowd of toiling beetles hurried between the buildings. These creatures sprouted arms and scrapers and trunk-like hoses, and they swept at the dust, making it rise in billowing red clouds into the air. But the dust would merely settle again once they had passed.

One toiling beetle scurried after the mammoths. It scraped up their dung and placed it into a wide mouth in its own side, and then polished at the floor until no trace of the dung was left. Thunder went up to the beetle and kicked it so hard that he opened up a new mouth in its side. After that, mewling to itself, the beetle moved only in tight circles, endlessly polishing the same piece of ground.

As the sun climbed higher in the sky, they moved away from the spires and scurrying beetles and reached an open area. This abutted the bank of the canal, and it was surrounded by a half-circle of low structures, like a row of wolf's teeth. The floor surface here was hard under their feet, and the light glimmered from it, pink and bright.

Suddenly, all at the same instant, the structures snapped open, revealing black, cavernous interiors. And all the mammoths recoiled, for they smelled the greasy stink of scorched flesh.

From nowhere gulls appeared, cawing. They soared down on huge filmy wings and pecked at the small buildings and the floor around them. Icebones even spotted a fox that came padding silently across the shining floor. The gulls cawed in protest at this intruder.

Spiral cast to and fro, nervous, skittish. 'It is the smell of food.'

'Broiled flesh?' Icebones said. 'What kind of food is that?'

'It is the food of the Lost,' Autumn said grimly.

Breeze said, 'Maybe this is a place where the Lost would come to feed.'

'But if that's so,' Spiral said anxiously, 'where are they?'

'Long gone,' Autumn said. She reached for her daughter.

But Spiral pulled away. Trumpeting, as if calling the small-eared Lost, she ran clumsily from structure to structure.

No Lost came to eat. After a time the structures snapped closed once more, scattering the gulls.

Chaser-Of-Frogs sneezed, and dusty snot gushed out of her trunk. She said brightly, 'All this talk of food is making me thirsty. Come. Let us find water.' Briskly, she turned and began to plod steadily down the canal bank, squat, solid, determined.

Following the canal, they came to a new set of structures, situated at the base of a broad valley. From all over the valley, fat pipes, heavily swathed by some silvery skin, erupted from the ground and converged on this place.

One structure was an inverted wedge of dull grey. It had grilles along its sides, and it was tipped by four giant tubes from which white steam plumed with a continual rushing noise. Icebones saw that water, condensing from the billowing steam, dribbled down the walls. Chaser-Of-Frogs lapped at this with her trunk.

Icebones did likewise, with less enthusiasm. The water was fine, she supposed, but it was too warm, and it tasted of sulphur and iron, and of something else indefinable – *something of the Lost*, she thought.

But she was thirsty, and forced herself to drink her fill.

Soon the others joined her and drank with more apparent enjoyment, for they were more used to accepting water from the Lost than she was.

Chaser-Of-Frogs called, 'Bones-Of-Ice. Come stand here.'

Icebones complied, and, following Chaser-Of-Frogs's urging, leaned gently against a pipe that was almost as tall as she was. The pipe was warm.

Chaser-Of-Frogs barked amusement. 'The pipe contains warm water. The water comes from lodes of warmth buried deep under the skin of the world. And that is what keeps the Nest alive,' she said. 'You see?'

'Not really,' admitted Icebones.

'I do,' said Thunder unexpectedly. 'Didn't Longtusk stamp his feet and draw heat from the ground, to keep his Family alive . . . ?'

Now Chaser-Of-Frogs wandered away from the water plant. Grunting, she began pawing at the ground with her forefeet. With clumsy swipes, the Swamp-Mammoth had soon wiped clear a wide area of the floor.

Icebones saw there were shapes embedded in the shining floor. She leaned down to see better, and blew away more dust with delicate sweeps of her trunk.

She saw leaves, stuck inside the shining floor surface. The leaves were grey and colourless, and they lay in thick sheets, one over the other. She stroked the floor with her trunk, but she touched only the hard, odourless floor surface.

'What do you think of *that*?' Chaser-Of-Frogs demanded proudly.

'They are like no tree I have ever seen.'

'Now look over here.' The Swamp-Mammoth led Icebones to another place, where she swept aside the dust once more.

Here, inside the floor, Icebones saw the shells of animals from the sea – and bones. They were pretty, regular shapes, she thought, sharing a six-fold pattern: six leaves, six stubby limbs, six petals.

Chaser-Of-Frogs said gently, 'These are the bones of creatures who lived here long, long ago – before the Lost ever came here. When you die, Bones-Of-Ice, you will be covered by mud and dust that will squeeze you flat. Until—'

'Until I become like *this*,' Icebones said, awed. 'Where I was born, the bones of mammoths lay thick in the ground. I thought there were no bones here – just as there are no mammoth trails. But I was wrong.'

'These are not the bones of our kind, Cousin. I was not always the Mother of the Big Pond. The Mother before me said that *her* Mother saw the Lost and their toiling beetles dig this strange bone-filled rock out of the Gouge wall – deep down, at its lowest layers. These squashed animals died long ago, you see. And nothing lived after them, so nothing was laid down over them but bare, dead rock, a great thickness of it. And the Lost took the bony rock and put it here.'

'Why?'

Chaser-Of-Frogs grunted. 'Who knows why the Lost do as they do?'

Icebones pondered the meaning of the rock. She pressed, frustrated, at the impenetrable surface, longing to touch and smell the ancient plants, to hear the voices of the animals.

Long ago there was life here. There had been trees, and living oceans, and beasts that roamed the crimson lands. But their world died. The oceans froze over and dried up, and the air cooled, and the last rain fell, and the last snow . . . Now all that was left of them was here, in this rock, compressed flat by time.

Clumsily, self-consciously, Chaser-Of-Frogs turned her back and pawed at the ground, trying to touch the bones with her hind feet.

'You are Remembering,' Icebones said.

Chaser-Of-Frogs stopped, panting – used to her lethargic life in the mud, she got out of breath easily – and she looked up at Icebones with her small hard eyes. 'Do you think we are foolish?'

'No. I think you are wise.'

Chaser-Of-Frogs eyed her. 'Bones-Of-Ice, I am done here. I am a poor fighter of wolves. I must go back before dark. You will go on. Just follow the canal.'

Suddenly the thought of being without the squat, humorous, courageous Swamp-Mammoth seemed unbearable. Impulsively Icebones twined her trunk around the other's. 'Come with us.'

Chaser-Of-Frogs snorted. 'What for, Cousin?'

'The world is dying – just as it died before, ending the lives of those buried creatures . . .' Icebones explained how she was leading the mammoths to the basin she had called the Footfall of Kilukpuk, the deepest place in the world, where she hoped enough air and water would pool to keep the mammoths alive. 'Come with us.'

'Me?' Chaser-Of-Frogs grunted, self-deprecating. 'Look at me. I can scarcely trudge over an ice-flat plain for half a day before I am exhausted. How could I walk around the world?'

'I'm serious—'

'So am I,' Chaser-Of-Frogs snapped. 'Bones-Of-Ice, I am no fool. I can smell it myself. Every year the line of trees creeps further down the Gouge wall. Every year our ponds shrink, just that bit more. Every year I see more animals migrate one way up the Gouge than come back the other. But look at me, Bones-Of-Ice. I could not contemplate such a trek as yours . . . Not yet, anyhow. I smell wisdom on you, young Bones-Of-Ice, but you have much to learn. You see, my calves are not yet *desperate* enough.'

'I don't see what desperation has to do with it.'

Chaser-Of-Frogs said bluntly, 'A trek to your Footfall pit would kill most of us. That is the truth. And *that* is why we must be desperate before we accept such suffering.'

Icebones was taken aback. 'We will help you.'

'Why should you? You never knew us before. We aren't your kind. We aren't even like you.'

'We are Cousins, and we are bound by the Oath of Kilukpuk.'

Chaser-Of-Frogs grunted. 'My dear Bones-Of-Ice, you have enough to do.' The Swamp-Mammoth waddled away, towards the light of the setting sun. 'I'll tell you what. I will seek out your scent at the Footfall. And if those piss-drinkers from the Pond of Evening get there before me, make sure you save the best pond for me . . .'

The next morning the Lost-made canal, which had guided them eastward for so long, finished its course.

Icebones stood at its head, before a square-edged termination whose regularity made her shudder. From here the canal arced back towards the west, a line of water straight as a sunbeam all the way to the horizon. She glimpsed the Nest of the Lost. In the uncertain light of morning, the fruits of the light-trees were glowing in broken rows. Beetles clanked to and fro once more, opening their mouths for anybody who wanted to ride in them, and the food places opened, sending out thick smells of meat and drink for anybody who cared to call. But nobody came, nobody but the gulls.

There was a flash of light, a distant crack like thunder.

Flinching, Icebones raised her trunk.

The sun was buried in a dense layer of mist and blue ice clouds at the eastern horizon, a band of light framed by the Gouge's silhouetted walls. The sky was clear, the world as peaceful as it ever got. What storm comes out of a clear sky . . . ?

Now there was another flash. She peered to the east, where she thought the flash had come from.

The sun was swimming in the sky, sliding from side to side and pulsating in size. A line of light darted down from the sun's disc, connecting it to the ground, like a huge glowing trunk reaching down through the dusty air. She heard a remote sound, deep and complex – like a landslide, or the cracking of a rock under frost or heat.

She blinked her eyes, seeking to clear them of water. When she stared again into the sun she could see its disc quite clearly, whole and round and unperturbed.

She lowered her head, searching for grass and water, trying to forget the strangeness, to put aside her deep unease.

CHAPTER 5

THE SKUA

They were in difficult country.

The Gouge floor was crumpled into ridges and eroded hillocks, pitted by depressions where water pooled, and littered with vast pocked boulders. Progress was slow, and all the mammoths were weary and fractious.

The Gouge walls were now further apart and badly defined. The nearest wall was a band of deep shadow, striped by orange dawn light at its crest. And it was pocked by huge round holes, as regular as the pits left by raindrops in sand. Inside the holes the wall surface looked glassy, as if coated in ice.

The holes were surely too regular to be natural. Icebones thought they must be the work of the Lost – though what there was to be gained by digging such immense pits in a rock wall, and how they had done it, was beyond her. Sometimes during the day she made out movement in those huge pits, heard the peep of chicks. Birds had made their nests there, high above the attention of the scavengers and predators of the Gouge floor.

One early dawn, Icebones was woken, disturbed. She raised her trunk.

The sun was still below the eastern horizon, where the sky was streaked with pink-grey. The other mammoths had fanned out over a patch of steppe. The only sounds they made were the soft rustle of their hair as they walked, or the rip of grass, and the occasional chirping snore from Woodsmoke, who was napping beneath his mother's legs.

She heard the gaunt honking of geese. Sometimes their

isolated barks rose until they became a single outcry, pealing from the sky. Now she saw the birds in the first daylight, their huge wings seeming to glow against the lightening sky.

But it wasn't the geese that had disturbed her.

She turned, sniffing the air. It seemed to her that the light was strange this morning, the air filled with a peculiar orange-grey glow. And there was an odd scent in the breeze that raised her guard hairs: a thin iron tang, like the taste of ocean air.

She looked west, where night still lay thick on the Gouge as it curled around the belly of the world. A band of deeper darkness was smeared across the Gouge floor, and a wind blew stronger in her face, soft but steady.

She felt the hairs on her scalp rise.

Spiral was digging with her trunk under Breeze's belly. 'Let me have him. Let me!' She was trying to get hold of Woodsmoke, who, wide awake now, was cowering under his mother's belly.

'Get away,' Breeze said. 'Leave us alone, Spiral . . .' Breeze pushed her sister away, but she was smaller, weaker. And the calf was becoming increasingly agitated by the pushing and barging of the huge creatures that loomed over him.

Autumn walked to her squabbling daughters, stately and massive. 'What is this trouble you are making?'

The calf, mewling and unhappy, wanted to run to his grandmother, but Breeze kept a firm hold on him with her skinny trunk. 'Make her go away.'

'She is selfish,' Spiral protested. 'He loves me as well as her.'

'Enough,' Autumn said. 'You are both making the calf unhappy. How does that show love . . . ? Breeze, you must let the calf go to Spiral.'

'*No!*'

'It is her right.'

Yes. Because Spiral is senior, Icebones thought, watching.

'But,' Autumn said, 'you must let his mother feed him, Spiral.'

'I can feed him,' Spiral protested.

Autumn said gently, 'No, you can't. He still needs milk. Come now.' Deliberately she stepped between the two Cows, and wrapped her trunk around Woodsmoke's head, soothing him. And, with judicious nudges, she arranged the three of them so that the calf was in the centre.

The two competing Cows stood face to face. They laid their trunks over Woodsmoke's back, soothing and warming him.

After a few heartbeats, now that the tussle was resolved, Woodsmoke snorted contentedly and lay down to nap, half-buried under the Cows' heavy trunks.

The wind picked up further, ruffling Icebones's hair. Far above, a bird hovered, wings widespread. Perhaps it was a skua.

She looked to the west again. The light continued to seep slowly into the sky, but she could see that the band of darkness had grown heavier and denser, filling the canyon from side to side, as if some immense wave was approaching. But she could hear nothing: no rustling of trees or moaning of wind through rock.

Autumn joined Icebones. 'Taste this.' She held up her trunk tip to Icebones's mouth.

Icebones tasted milk.

'I found it on Spiral's breast. She stole it from Breeze, to lure the calf.' Autumn rumbled unhappily. 'Of all of us, I think it is Spiral who suffers the most.'

Icebones wrapped her trunk around Autumn's. 'Then we must help her, as much as we can.'

Icebones knew that Autumn's instinct had been good. In a Family, it was not uncommon for a senior Cow to adopt the calf of another – whether the true mother liked it or not. The whole Family was responsible for the care of each calf, and calves and adults knew it on some deep-buried level. But under the stifling care of the Lost these Cows had never learned to understand their instincts, and were now driven by emotions they probably could not name, let alone understand.

But now Thunder came trumpeting. He was breathing hard, his eyes rimmed by white. 'Icebones! Icebones!' He turned to face west, his trunk raised high.

That wall of crimson darkness had grown, astonishingly quickly. It filled the Gouge from side to side, and towered high up the walls. And now Icebones could hear the first moans of wind, the crack of rock and wood, and she could feel the shuddering of the ground.

Something hovered briefly before the storm front, hurled high in the air, green and brown, before being dashed to the ground and smashing to splinters. It was a mighty conifer tree, uprooted and destroyed as casually as a mammoth's trunk would toss a willow twig.

'By Kilukpuk's eyes,' Autumn said softly.

Icebones trumpeted, 'Circle!'

The adults gathered around Breeze and her calf. Icebones prodded them until they all had their backs to the wind, with Autumn, Thunder and Icebones herself at the rear of the group.

There was a moment of eerie silence. The ground's shaking stopped, and even the wind died.

But still the storm front bore down on them. Its upper reaches were wispy smoke, and its dense front churned and bubbled, like a vast river approaching.

Icebones, pressed between Thunder and Autumn, felt the rapid breathing of the mammoths, smelled their dung and urine and milk and fear. 'Hold your places,' she said. 'Hold your places—'

Suddenly the storm was on them.

Perhaps it had something to do with night and day.

The Gouge was so long that while its eastern end was in day, its western extremity was still in night. Icebones imagined the battle between the cold of night and warmth of day, as the line of dawn worked its slow way along the great channel. Was it so surprising that such a tremendous daily conflict should throw off a few storms?

But the *why* scarcely mattered.

The wind was red-black and solid and icy cold. It battered at Icebones's back and legs. Dust and bits of stone scoured at her skin, working through her layers of hair and grinding at any exposed flesh, her ears and trunk tip and even her feet.

Now a thick sleety snow began to pelt her back. Soon her fur was soaked through with icy melt, and the cold deepened, as if the wind was determined to suck away every last bit of her body heat. The ground itself was shuddering, making it impossible for her rumbles or stamping to reach the others.

She risked opening one eye.

It was like looking into a tunnel lined by soggy snow, rain, crimson dust and rock fragments that drove almost horizontally ahead of her. She could even see a kind of shadow, a gap in the driving storm, cast by the mammoths' huge bulk.

She had seen this vast storm approaching since it was just a line on the bleak horizon. How was it she hadn't heard its howl, or even felt the rumble of its destruction? Perhaps the storm was so violent, so rapid, that it outran even its own mighty roar.

But by standing together the mammoths were defeating the storm, she thought with a stab of exultation. However soaked and battered and cold, they would emerge from this latest crisis stronger and more united as a Family—

There was a noise like thunder, a blow like a strike from Kilukpuk's mighty tusk.

The world spun around, and she was flying, *flying*,

through the driven snow and the dust. She could feel her legs and trunk dangling, helpless, not a single one of her feet in contact with the ground, lost in the air like poor Shoot. She could smell blood – no, she could taste it.

But there was no pain, not even fear. How strange, she thought.

A wall, dark red and hard, loomed before her.

She slammed into rock. Pain stabbed in her right shoulder.

She slid down the wall to the ground. Hard-edged rock ripped at her belly and legs and face.

And then she fell into darkness.

She could feel cold rock beneath her belly.

She opened her eyes.

She glimpsed a dim sun through smoky dust, and the round shapes of mammoths, their hair licking around them. A gust battered her face, and she squeezed her eyes shut.

But the storm had diminished.

She was resting on her front, her legs folded beneath her, as a mammoth would lie when preparing to die. She tried to pull her forefeet under her, so she could rise. Pain exploded in her right shoulder, and she stumbled flat again, sprawling like a clumsy calf.

But then there was a trunk under her, strong and supple. 'Lean on me.' Autumn stood over her, a massive silhouette against a crimson sky. 'The storm has gone to find somebody else to torment. But you are hurt.'

High above Autumn, a bird wheeled through dusty red light.

Icebones tried again to stand. The pain in her shoulder betrayed her once more. But this time Autumn's strong trunk helped her, and she managed to stay upright, shakily, her three good legs taking her weight.

The mammoths shook themselves and tugged at their hair, trying to get out the worst of the grit and dust and water. The calf, none the worse for his experience, was trotting from one adult to another, his little trunk held up as he tried to help them groom. Icebones saw that crimson dust had piled up where the mammoths had been standing, making a low dune.

The land showed the passing of the storm. Dust and gravel lay everywhere, and new red-black streaks along the rocky ground showing where the winds had passed. Bushes and bits of trees lay scattered. There was even the broken corpse of a small, young deer, Icebones saw, bent so badly it was almost unrecognisable.

She wondered what damage this storm would have done in the Nest of the Lost. Surely no trace of the mammoths' footsteps in the littered dust would remain.

A shadow arced over the mammoths. Icebones saw that bird still wheeling overhead, wings outstretched. She looked like a skua, hunting a lemming. Perhaps she nested in those great spherical caves in the cliff face. Icebones raised her trunk, but could smell nothing but iron dust and her own blood.

She took a step forward. Pain jarred in her shoulder, making her cry softly.

'Everybody's safe,' Autumn said sternly. 'Everybody but you. Your shoulder is damaged. We will rest here, until your healing begins.'

'We must reach the Footfall—'

'We cannot reach this Footfall of yours at all without you, Icebones. So we will wait, whether you like it or not.'

'I am sorry,' Icebones said softly.

'If you are sorry you are a fool. Maybe we should go back to the ponds. I bet Chaser-Of-Frogs was comfortable in her mud, with only the tip of her trunk sticking out into the storm. What do you think . . . ?'

The bird was descending, Icebones saw, curious despite her pain. Her body was stone grey, her beak bluish, and her wings had white flashes across them. She had webbed feet, spread beneath her, pointing at the ground – webbed, with claws.

She was descending, and descending, and descending. Coming out of the storm, unperturbed by the remnant winds.

Coming straight towards the mammoths.

Growing huge.

The calf was alone, grubbing at a fallen tree.

Icebones roared, 'Watch out!' She tried to run. Her shoulder seared and she fell sprawling, as if her leg had been cut away. Still the mammoths did not look up. And still Icebones tried to stand, pushing herself forward, for the shadow was becoming larger. 'The bird!' she called again. 'The bird . . . !'

A roof of feathers and bone slid over her, rustling, and there was a smell like scorched flesh. She glimpsed a blue-grey beak, and black eyes, flecked with yellow, peered into hers. Those great wings beat once, lazily and powerfully, and air gushed.

Icebones cringed. All the dust-stained mammoths were in the bird's shadow now, standing like blocks of sandstone.

The webbed feet spread, talons reaching out of the sky. The calf ran for his mother, trunk raised, mewling.

The talons closed. Woodsmoke trumpeted as the claws pricked his sides, and blood spurted, gushing over his spiky hair.

The bird screeched, a sound like rock cracking, as she struggled to lift her prey. With every beat of the wings, dust and bits of rock were sent flying, and the ground shuddered. It was a nightmare of noise and dust, shadow and blood, the stink of feathers.

If the skua succeeded in getting off the ground, she would surely carry the calf away to some high, remote nest, where he would be devoured alive, piece by bloody piece, by a clutch of monstrous chicks. Icebones roared her anguish. But, pinned by her injury to the ground, she could do nothing.

Breeze came rushing in, tusks raised, trumpeting, utterly fearless. She got close enough to swipe at the bird with her tusks, and she grabbed a wing with her trunk. The bird screamed and beat her wings, pulling free, leaving long, greasy black feathers fluttering in the air. A beak the size of a mammoth's thigh bone slashed down.

Breeze staggered back, trumpeting. Icebones saw that her back had been laid open. The Cow slumped to the ground, legs splayed.

The bird was flapping harder now, and gushes of rock and dust billowed out from beneath her immense, rustling wings. At last she raised the struggling calf off the ground, and was straining for the sky.

Thunder ran forward. He was waving an uprooted bush over his head, his trunk wrapped around its roots. A cloud of red dust flew around his head.

The skua shrieked and stabbed with her beak, for the bush made Thunder look much larger than he was. He hurled the bush at her head and ran trumpeting into the shadow of her wings, slashing his tusks back and forth.

The bird screeched again – and Icebones knew the Bull had reached flesh.

The skua tried one last time to lift herself. But the calf continued to squirm, and Icebones could see Thunder whirling like a dust devil, striking over and over with blood-stained tusks at the soft feathers of the bird's chest.

At last, with a final angry scream, the bird released Woodsmoke. The calf fell to the ground with a soft impact. The great wings beat, and Icebones saw that Thunder was knocked aside.

But now the bird was rising, diminishing in the sky, becoming a small black speck that wheeled away towards the cliffs.

The calf mewled. His mother rushed to him, uncaring of her own wounds.

*

They sought shelter under an overhang of rock, a place where no more nightmares could come wheeling down from the sky.

Thunder was sore from heavy bruises inflicted on his flanks by the beating wings of the bird. Breeze's back had been laid open so badly that the white of bone showed in a valley of ripped red flesh, and Autumn laboriously plastered it with mud. The calf had suffered puncture-marks in his side left by the bird's talons, ripped wider by his struggles to get free. Spiral worked with his grandmother to clean them up for him, and to soothe his wailing misery.

All the mammoths were subdued, bombarded as they had been by the storm and the attack of the bird so soon after. Icebones suspected it had been no coincidence. The bird must prefer to hunt after such a storm, when animals, dead or injured or simply bewildered, were most vulnerable to her mighty talons.

Skuas on the Island had fed on rodents, like lemmings, and the chicks of other birds. There had been nothing like this monster. She recalled the birds she had seen nesting in the cliff hollows – but she realised now that she had totally misjudged their size, fooled by the vastness of the cliff. Perhaps such a cliff bred birds of this immense size to suit its mighty scale.

Icebones felt a dread gather in her heart. Perhaps this is how Kilukpuk felt at the beginning of her life, she thought, when she lived in a burrow under the ground, and the Reptiles stalked overhead. But the mammoths had grown huge since those days. Nothing threatened them, for the mammoths were the greatest creatures in the world . . .

But not *this* world, she thought.

As the sun slid down the sky, Icebones limped up to the young Bull. 'Walk with me, Thunder. Let me lean on you.'

Growling uncertainly, he settled in at her right side, and she leaned her shoulder on his comfortably massive bulk. When they emerged from the shelter of the rock overhang,

Thunder raised his trunk higher. 'It is not safe,' he rumbled. 'The bird has blood on her talons now.'

'Yes,' she said. 'And I cannot run fast. But I have you to protect me. Don't I, Thunder?'

'I did nothing,' he growled.

Standing awkwardly, she wrapped her trunk around his. 'You defied your instincts. Mammoths are not used to being preyed upon – and certainly not by a bird, an ugly thing which flaps out of the sky. But you fought her off. You are brave beyond your years, and your strength.'

'I abandoned Shoot when the sea beast threatened. I would not walk on to the bridge after Spiral. You saw my fear—'

'But you saved Woodsmoke. You are what you do, Thunder. And so you are a hero.' He tried to pull away, so she slapped him gently. 'I want you to call somebody now. I cannot, for I cannot stamp . . . There is a Bull I know. He is far from here, but I hope we will meet him someday. He is called Boaster.'

'Boaster?'

'Call him now. Call him as deep and as loud as you can.'

So Thunder called, his massive chest shuddering and his broad feet slamming against the ground.

After a time, Icebones heard the answering call washing through the rock. *Icebones? Is that you?*

'Tell him you are Thunder.'

Hesitantly, Thunder complied.

A Bull? Are you in musth? Keep away from Icebones, for she is mine. For myself, though Icebones calls me Boaster, my relatives and rivals, for obvious reasons, call me Long—

'Never mind that,' said Icebones hastily. 'Tell him what you did today.'

Still hesitant, awkward, Thunder stamped out, 'I killed a bird.'

After a long delay, the reply came: *A bird? What did you do, sneeze on it?*

Thunder trumpeted his anger. 'The bird was vast. So vast its wings spanned this Gouge through which we walk. It descended like a storm and grabbed a calf in its mighty talons . . .'

While Boaster was listening respectfully, Icebones limped away, leaving Thunder standing proud, telling of his deeds to other Bulls – which was just what Bulls were supposed to do.

But as she withdrew she watched the darkling sky.

CHAPTER 6
THE SHINING TUSK

The character of the landscape slowly changed. The walls became more shallow and broken. It was evident that they were, at last, rising out of the mighty Gouge.

One morning the mammoths found themselves facing a valley that cut across the main body of the Gouge. The valley appeared to flow from the high, dry uplands of the southern hemisphere into the immense ocean basin that was the north, as if from higher ground to lower.

The mammoths clambered down a shallow slope. The light of the rising sun cast long shadows from the rubble strewn on the surface, making the ground seem complex and treacherous.

If walking along the flat ground had been difficult for Icebones, working down a slope like this – where she had to rest her weight on her forelegs and damaged shoulder – was particularly agonising. And even on the floor of the outflow valley, she found she had to tread carefully: a flat surface layer of dust and loose gravel covered much larger rocks beneath, their edges sharp enough to gash a mammoth's foot.

It didn't help that the day seemed peculiarly hot and bright. The rising sun was swollen and oddly misshapen, and the air was full of light.

Icebones knew she should give a lead to the others. But it took all her strength just to keep moving. She plodded on in silence, locked in her own world of determination and pain: *Just this step. Now just one more . . .*

She found a small, deep pond, frozen over. Impatiently

she pressed on the ice until it cracked into thick, angular chunks, and she sucked up trunkfuls of cold, black water, ignoring the thin slimy texture of vegetation. Soon she had washed the dust out of her throat and trunk, and was trickling soothing water over her aching shoulder.

The others still bore injuries. Breeze nursed the brutal slashes in her back. The calf was fascinated by his wounds, and his grandmother often caught him picking at the scabs that had formed there.

But the one who slowed them down the most was Icebones herself, to her regret and shame.

Thunder stood very still, listening carefully to the deep song of the rocks, as she had taught him. 'This is a damaged country,' he said.

'Yes.' She forced herself to raise her head.

To the north, the valley branched into a series of smaller channels, like a delta. The waters must once have flowed that way. The valley floor was smoothly carved, textured with sandbars that followed the path of the vanished flood. She saw what must have been an island in the flow, flat-topped, shaped like the body of a fish to push aside the water. To the south, where the water must have come from, the landscape was quite different: littered with blocks and domes and low hills, all of them frost-cracked, water-eroded and streaked with lichen, their outlines softened by layers of windblown dust. But many of these blocks were immense, much larger than any mammoth. It was just like the bottom of a huge dried-up river.

All this was drenched in a pink-white glow, and she could feel the sun's heat on her back. She squinted up, wondering if she would find the sun misshapen again, as she had seen it days before, close to the canal's terminus. But the light was too bright, and it dazzled her. She turned away, eyes watering.

Thunder said, 'There is water under the ground. A great lake of it, trapped under a cap of ice. I can *feel* it. Can you?'

'Yes—'

'But it is very deep.' He seemed excited as his awakened instincts pieced together the story of this land. 'Perhaps the water broke out in a huge gush, as the waters broke out of Breeze's belly when Woodsmoke was ready to be born. Then it flooded over the land, seeking the sea to the north. The water carved out this valley. See how it washed across the ground here, shaping it, and surged around that island . . . Perhaps the land to the south simply collapsed. If you suck the water out of a hole in the ice on a frozen pond, sometimes the ice will crack and fall, under its own weight . . .'

Maybe he was right. But whatever water had marked this land was vanished a long time ago. She saw craters punched into the ancient valley floor, themselves eroded by wind and time.

Thunder was still talking. But his words blurred, becoming an indistinguishable growl. The air was now drenched by a dazzling light that picked out every stray dust mote around her.

'I'm sorry, Thunder. What did you say? I am hot, and the day is bright.'

But Thunder's pink tongue was lolling. 'It is the sky,' he said. 'Look, Icebones. There is nothing wrong with you. It is the sky!'

The sun had grown huge – and was getting larger. With every extension of that pale, ragged disc, the heat and the brilliance around her increased. It was silent, eerie, and profoundly disturbing.

There was a nudge at her side, an alarmed trumpet. Icebones made out Spiral, a shimmering ghost in the pink-stained brilliance. 'Come away! You are in great danger here. Hurry . . . !' Spiral began to barge vigorously at Icebones's flank.

Icebones needed little further urging.

The ground was littered with scree and, unable to see, she

stumbled frequently. Her shoulder hurt profoundly, and she felt as if she would melt from the heat. Though she was half-blinded, she could hear as clearly as ever: Spiral's blaring, the scrape of her foot pads over the loose rock, even the scratchy, shallow breathing of the other mammoths further away.

That flaring sun expanded still further. Eventually it became a great disc draped over the sky, its blurred rim reaching halfway to the horizon.

It was horrifying, bewildering, unreal, a new impossible unreality in this unreal world. *The sun does not behave like that*. If I am the frozen dream of some long-dead seer, she thought, then perhaps the dream is breaking down; perhaps this is the light of the truth, breaking through the crumbling dream . . .

But now the heat began to fade, suddenly. There was a soft breeze, carrying the tang of ice. The light, too, seemed dimmer.

Her thoughts cleared, like a fever dream receding. Here was Autumn, a blocky, ill-defined silhouette before her.

'If that was summer,' Icebones said, 'it was the shortest I've ever known.'

'This is no joke.' Autumn pushed her trunk into Icebones's mouth. 'You're too hot. Come now, quickly.' So Icebones was forced to walk again, in the footsteps of hurrying Autumn.

They reached a tall, eroded rock, crusted with yellow lichen. In its shade there was a patch of snow, laced pink by dust. Autumn reached down, scooped up snow with her trunk and began to push it into Icebones's mouth.

Icebones lumbered forward and let the cool pink-white stuff lap up to her belly. Mammoths did not sweat, and using frost or snow like this was an essential means of keeping cool. Icebones only wished that the snow were deep enough to cover her completely.

When she felt a little better, she staggered wearily out of

the ice. Slush dripped from guard hairs that were still hot to the touch of her trunk tip.

The place where she had been standing with Thunder, bathed in light, glowed a bright pink-white. Threads of steam and smoke rose from the red dust. The stink of burning vegetation and scorched-hot rock reached her nostrils.

Above the glowing ground a column of shining, swirling dust motes rose into the air. It was a perfect, soft-edged cylinder that slanted towards the sun – but Icebones had never seen a sunbeam of such intensity, nor one cast by such a powerful and misshapen sun.

Away from the sun itself, the sky seemed somehow diminished. Close to the zenith, she could even make out stars. It was as if all the light in the world had been concentrated into that single intense pulse.

An overheated rock cracked open with an explosive percussion, making all the mammoths flinch and grumble.

'If we were still standing there,' Thunder said grimly, 'we too would be burning.'

Spiral nudged him affectionately. 'And your fat would flow like water, you big tusker, and we would all swim away.'

But now the shining pillar of light dispersed, abruptly, leaving dust motes churning, and the intense glow dissipated as if it had never been. When she peered up, Icebones saw the sun was restored to its normal intensity, small and shrunken.

'It is a thing of the Lost,' she said. 'This great tusk of light that stirs and breaks the rock.'

'Yes,' said Autumn. 'Somehow they can gather the light of the sun itself and hurl it down where they choose. From the Fire Mountain I saw it stab at the land, over and over, carving out pits and valleys.'

'Like the canal in the Gouge,' Icebones said.

'But now it is scratching the land as foolishly as Woodsmoke trying out his milk tusks. The Lost are gone, and it doesn't know what to do.'

The cloudy deformation of the sun was gathering again, and the light beam was slicing down once more, this time on the higher land to the south, above the escarpment at the head of the valley. Where it rested the rock cracked and melted.

The ground shuddered – a single sharp pulse – and the mammoths rumbled their unease.

Autumn said, 'I think—'

'Hush!' The brief, peremptory trumpet came from Thunder. 'Listen. Can't you hear that? Can't you, Icebones?'

Breeze said impatiently, 'I hear the burning grass, the hiss of the melting rock—'

'No. Deeper than that. *Listen.*'

Icebones stood square on the ground, pressing her weight on to all her four legs, despite the stabs of pain in her shoulder. And then she heard it: a subterranean growl, deep and menacing.

'We have to get to the higher ground,' she said immediately. They were halfway across the valley, she saw, and the eastern slope looked marginally easier to climb. 'Let's go, let's go. *Now.*' She began to limp that way, her damaged shoulder stinging with pain.

The mammoths milled uncertainly.

'Why?' Breeze asked. 'What are we fleeing?'

'Water,' said Icebones. 'A vast quantity of water, an underground sea locked into the ground. Like the great flood that once burst across this land, scraping out the valley you stand in. And now—'

'And now,' said Thunder urgently, 'thanks to the shining tusk, that underground sea is awakening, stretching its muscles. Come *on.*'

At last they understood. They began to lumber across the plain towards the eastern wall, trunks and tails swaying.

The ground above the escarpment cracked with a report

that echoed down the walls of the valley, and steam gushed into the air. The vast body of water beneath, vigorous on its release after a billion years locked beneath a cap of perma-frost ice, was rising at the commanding touch of the great orbiting lens – rising with relentless determination, seeking the air.

CHAPTER 7
THE FLOOD

Though the ground was broken and their way was impeded by half-buried lumps of debris, they all made faster time than Icebones – even the calf, who clung to his mother's tail.

A giant explosion shook the ground.

Her foreleg folded beneath her. She crashed forward on to her knees, pain stabbing through her shoulder.

From the great scribbled scar inflicted by the tusk of light, a vast fountain of steam gushed into the pale sky. Vapour and debris drifted across the sun, turning it into a pale pink smear.

I'm not going to make it, she thought.

And now dust rained down like a dense, gritty snow. Icebones snorted to clear her trunk, and she tasted the blood flavour of the hot, iron-rich dust.

Suddenly she was alone in a shell of murky dust. And the mammoths were no more than crimson blurs in the distance, fast receding.

She supposed it was for the best that the others had not looked back. She had never wanted to become a burden.

She found herself staring at a rock – staring with fascination, for it might be the last thing she would ever see. It was heavily weathered, eroded, pitted and cracked. Its colour was burnt orange, but there were streaks of blue-red on its north-facing surfaces, which had been exposed to sunlight longer. It was made of a lumpy conglomerate, pebbles trapped in a mix of hardened sand.

Pebbles and sand, she thought. Pebbles and sand that must

have formed in fast-flowing rivers, and then compressed into this mottled rock on some ocean bed. All of it ancient, all of it long gone.

She ran her trunk fingers over the rock's pocked surface. She found a series of small, shallow pits, a row of them, each just large enough to take her trunk-tip.

. . . *They were footprints*, locked into the surface of the hardened rock. She probed more carefully at the nearest print. It had six toes. No living animal had six toes. Now its kind was lost, leaving no trace save these accidentally preserved prints.

She felt a surge of wonder. Despite the noise, her pain, despite the imminent danger, despite the rock's shuddering, she longed to know where that ancient animal had been going – what it had wanted, how it had died.

But she would never know, and might live no more than a few more heartbeats, not even long enough to savour such wonder.

The dusty debris falling over her was becoming more liquid, she thought, and warmer too. The flood was nearing. The ground shook. She huddled closer to her rock.

But a long, powerful trunk wrapped under her belly.

It was Spiral. The young Cow loomed over Icebones as a mother would loom over her calf. She was coated in red dust, and her guard hairs were already damp.

Icebones said, 'You shouldn't have come back. You'll die, like me. The flood is coming.'

Spiral rumbled, loudly enough to make herself heard over the noise of the water. 'Yes, the flood comes . . . like the tears of Kilukpuk.'

Icebones felt weary amusement. '*You* talk now of Kilukpuk?'

'I'm hoping you'll tell me more of those old tales, Icebones.'

'It's too late. We can't get to the bank.'

'No. But there is an island, further to the north, that

might stay above the waters.' She grabbed Icebones's tusks and began to drag her along the bed of the ancient channel.

Icebones tried to resist, digging her feet into the ground, but the pain in her shoulder was too great even for that.

'You must not do this,' she said.

'Icebones, help me or we'll both drown.'

Icebones forced herself to her feet.

To the north, the way the ancient waters had once flowed, the land was covered by scour marks, braided channels, heavily eroded islands, sand bars, the scars left by flowing water. The island Spiral had selected was shaped like a vast teardrop, its steep, layered sides polished to smoothness by ancient floods.

Climbing the island's crumbling walls was one of the most difficult things Icebones had ever done. The strata cracked and gave way, coming loose under her in a shower of rock and pebbles and dust, and each fall brought lancing pain in her shoulder that made her trumpet in protest. But Spiral stayed with her every step, ramming Icebones's rump with her head, as if driving her up the slope with sheer strength and willpower.

At last they reached the lip of the wall. With a final, agonising effort Icebones dragged her carcass on to the island's flat top. She crumpled, falling on to her knees. The surface was smooth hard mudstone, a fragment of the floor of some ancient sea, she thought.

Spiral stood before her, breathing hard, caked with orange dust, her hair ragged: tall and wild, she was a figure from a nightmare. 'You are a heavy burden to haul.'

Icebones gasped, 'You should have left me.'

'Too late for that.'

And now, through the murky, sodden gloom, more mammoths approached: Autumn, Thunder, Breeze, the calf.

Icebones growled, 'What are you doing here?'

'We are waiting for you,' said Thunder. 'Did you think we

would go on without you? And when we saw Spiral bringing you here—'

Lightning flashed. The mammoths flinched.

Where the sky tusk had broken the ground, dust and steam still gushed, crimson red, and over the towering clouds of dust and steam, lightning cracked. Now water was beginning to pulse out of the ground, stained pink by the ubiquitous dust.

Instinctively the mammoths gathered closer, nuzzling and bumping.

Icebones was surrounded by the rich smell of their hair, and they loomed over her as if she was a calf. She snorted. 'Some Matriarch. I did not understand the tusk of the sun. I did not hear the movement of the water under the ground until we were in danger. I am the slowest of us all, and have put you at risk.'

Autumn said, 'But *I* understood the meaning of the tusk. And Thunder with his sharp hearing heard the water, and understood, and warned us in time. And Spiral used her strength to save you – just as you have used your strength to aid others of us in the past.'

'But the Cycle teaches—'

'Is the Cycle more important than the instincts of the mammoths around you?'

'. . . No,' Icebones conceded.

'So you have not failed,' Autumn whispered. 'We are Family. We are what you made us. *My strength is your strength.*'

'It doesn't always work like that,' Icebones said grimly. '*Sometimes it is right to abandon the weak . . .*'

Autumn pushed her trunk into Icebones's mouth. 'No more lessons.'

All the mammoths began to murmur, a deep rumble of reassurance as if to soothe a frightened calf. Their rumbles merged subtly, becoming like the single voice of a vaster creature.

Icebones let her self sink into that comforting pit of sound. She felt her doubts and fears and anxieties dissolve – and her sense of self washed away with them. *She was Family*: she heard the world through Thunder's sharp ears, and felt Spiral's tall strength suffuse her own limbs, and Autumn's deep knowledge and unknowing wisdom filled her head, and she shared Breeze's deep love for her calf, who became as precious to her as her own core warmth.

She had never forgotten how bleakly bereft she had felt on that rocky hillside, when she first woke from her un-natural sleep, bombarded by strangeness – alone, as she had never been in her life. But now a new Family had built around her – *I* had become *We* – and she was whole again.

With a final shuddering tremble, the ground around the great fracture gave way. Layers of rock lifted like a lid. Angry water spilled into the valley, pounding on the eroded boulders, shattering ancient stones that might not have been disturbed since the world was young.

A wall of dirty, rust-brown water fell on them, hard and heavy.

As the setting sun began finally to glint through the rem-nant haze, the mammoths separated stiffly. They were cold, hungry, bruised, utterly bedraggled.

Water, turbulent and red-brown with mud, still surged around their island. Immense waves, echoes of the mighty fracture, surged up and down the ancient valley.

But already the flood water had begun to recede. Much of it was draining away through the ancient channels to the Ocean of the North. The rest was simply soaking away into the dust, vanishing back into the thirsty red ground as rapidly as it had emerged. The revealed ground, slick with crimson mud and remnant puddles, sparkled in the low sunlight, as red and wet as skinned flesh.

The very shape of this island had changed, its battered walls crumbled away under the onslaught.

The Lost remake worlds, Icebones thought. But they do not stay remade. Soon the things the Lost have built here, all the bridges and pipelines and Nests and the toiling beetles, will collapse and erode away. And when the dust has silted up even their marvellous straight-edged canal, the ancient face of the Sky Steppe will emerge once more, timeless and indomitable.

The Lost are powerful. But the making of a world will forever be beyond them, a foolish dream.

By the light of a fat, dust-laden pink sunset, the mammoths scrambled down the island's newly carved sides, and across the valley floor. By the time they got to the higher ground they were so coated in sticky red-black mud Icebones could barely raise her legs.

'What now, Matriarch?' 'What should we do?' 'Where should we go?'

These questions emerged from a continuing communal rumble, for the voices of a true Family were always raised together, in an unending wash of communication – as if, emerging from consensus, every phrase began with the pronoun 'we'.

'Thunder, you are our ears and nostrils. Which way?'

He stood straight and still, sniffing the wind, feeling the shape of the world. At length he said, 'South. South and east. That way lies the Footfall of Kilukpuk.'

'Very well. Spiral, you are our strength. Shall we begin the walk?'

'We are ready, Matriarch.'

Icebones made the summons rumble, a long, drawn-out growl: 'Let's go, let's go.'

Gradually their rumbles merged once more, as they tasted readiness on each other's breath. 'We are ready.' 'We are together.' 'Let's go.' 'Let's go, let's go.'

Icebones strode forward, ignoring the pain in her shoulder – which, since it now affected only a small part of her greater, shared body, was as nothing. The other mammoths began to move with her, their trunks exploring the rocky red ground beneath their feet, just as a true Family should. Icebones felt affirmed, exulting.

But as they climbed away from the valley, and as Icebones made out the high bleak land that still lay before them, she sensed that they would yet need to call on all their shared strength and courage if they were to survive.

. . . And then, clinging to an outcrop of rock at the fringe of this harsh southern upland, she found a fragment of hair: pale brown, ragged, snagged from some creature who had come this way. She pulled the hair loose with her trunk and tasted it curiously. Though it was soaked through, the hair had a stale, burning smell that she recognised immediately.

The hair had belonged to the Ragged One.

THREE
FOOTFALL

THE STORY OF THE GREAT CROSSING

The Cycle is made up of the oldest stories in the world. It tells all that has befallen the mammoths, and its wisdom is as perfect as time can make it.

But now I want to tell you one of the youngest stories in the Cycle. It is the story of how the mammoths came to the Sky Steppe.

It is the story of Silverhair, who was the last Matriarch of the Old Steppe.

It is the story of the first Matriarch of the Sky Steppe.

It is a story of mammoths, and Lost.

For generations the last mammoths had lived on an Island. Silverhair was their Matriarch.

The Lost were everywhere. But the Lost had never found the Island, and the mammoths lived undisturbed.

No mammoth lived anywhere else. Not one.

But now, at last, the Lost had come to the Island.

Though most of these Lost showed no wish to hunt the mammoths or kill them or drive them away, they kept them in boxes and watched them with their predators' eyes, all day and all night.

Silverhair knew that mammoths cannot share land with Lost.

But Silverhair was old and tired. She had spent all her strength keeping her Family alive. She was in despair, and ashamed of her weakness.

One night Kilukpuk came down from the aurora. And

Kilukpuk said Silverhair must not be ashamed, for she had fought hard all her life. And she must not despair.

Silverhair snorted. 'This world is full of Lost. We have nowhere to live. What is there left for me but despair?'

'But there is another world,' Kilukpuk told her. 'It is a place where there will be room for many mammoths. And mammoths will live there until the sun itself grows cold.'

Silverhair asked tiredly, 'Where is this marvellous place?'

And Kilukpuk said, 'Why, have you forgotten your Cycle? It is the Sky Steppe.'

Silverhair knew about the Sky Steppe, of course. She had seen it float in the sky, bright and red – just as her world, which we call the Old Steppe, once floated in our sky, bright and blue. And, indeed, the Cycle promised that one day mammoths would walk free on the Sky Steppe.

But Silverhair was weary and old, for she could not believe even mighty Kilukpuk. She said, 'And how are the mammoths to get there? Will they sprout wings and fly like geese?'

'No,' said Kilukpuk gently. 'There is a way. But it is hard.'

It would be the work of the Lost, said Kilukpuk. What else could it be? For the Lost owned the world, all of it.

Calves would be taken from their mothers' bodies, un-born. They would be put in ice, and sent into the sky in shining seeds, and taken to the Sky Steppe. That way many calves could be carried, to be spilled out on the red soil of the Sky Steppe, as if being born.

The bereft mothers would never know their calves, and the calves never know their mothers.

This was very strange – typical of the Lost's eerie clever-ness – and Silverhair could not understand. 'How will the calves learn how to use their trunks, how to find water and food? If they have no Matriarch, who will lead and protect them?'

'That is the second thing I have to tell you,' said Kilukpuk. 'And this too is very hard.'

And Kilukpuk said that Silverhair's calf – her only calf – would also be taken. For that calf, already half-grown, was to be Matriarch to all the new calves who would tumble from the shining seeds to the red soil. That calf, daughter of the last Matriarch of the Old Steppe, would be the first Matriarch of the Sky Steppe.

'You must teach her, Silverhair,' said Kilukpuk. 'As I taught my Calves to speak, and to find water and food, and to live as a Family. You must teach her to be a Matriarch, so she can teach those who follow her.'

Silverhair spun around and scuffed the ground. 'My calf is all I have. I will not give her up. How can I live?'

But she knew that Kilukpuk was right.

Silverhair listened to Kilukpuk's wisdom. And she passed on that wisdom to her calf. And, when the time came, she gave her calf to Kilukpuk, and the Lost.

For that one sacrifice alone, we know Silverhair as great a hero as any in the Cycle's long course. For if she had not, and if she had not taught her calf well, none of us alive today would ever have been born.

Even though, as is the way of the Lost's clever-clever schemes, many things went wrong, and the calf-Matriarch was kept in a box of cold and dark for much longer than she should have been – so long that before she emerged, generations of mammoths had lived and died on the Sky Steppe . . .

Well, that was how the Great Crossing was made. But the story is not done.

For Kilukpuk taught Silverhair another truth of the Cycle: that sometimes we cannot spare even those we love.

The Crossing was hard and dangerous indeed. And Silverhair's calf would herself have a dread price to pay for making that Crossing.

That calf's name, as you know, was Icebones.

CHAPTER 1
THE HIGH PLAINS

The land was a tortured wilderness: nothing but blood-red rock, rugged, cracked and pitted, under a sky that shone yellow-pink.

And it was dominated by craters.

The largest of them were walled plains, their rims so heavily eroded they were reduced to low, sullen mounds lined up in rough arcs. The smaller craters were sharper, and when the mammoths ploughed their way over rim ridges, their neat circular shapes were clearly visible. In places the craters crowded so close together that their walls overlapped and merged, so that the mammoths were forced to climb over one smooth fold in the land after another, like waves on some vast rust-red ocean.

Icebones listened to the rumbling echoes that the mammoths' footfalls returned from the distorted ground. She sensed giant rubble lying crammed there. She tried to imagine the mighty blows which must have rained down on this land long ago – mighty enough to shatter rock into immense pieces far beneath her feet, mighty enough to make the rock itself rise up in great circular ripples as if it were as fluid as water.

But the land had been shaped by more than the crater-forming blows. In some places the rock had melted and flowed. Craters had been overwhelmed, their walls buried and their interiors flooded with ponds of hard, cold, red-black basalt.

And water had run here, creating channels and valleys. Some of these cut right through the crater walls and even spilled into their floors. The channels themselves were overlaid by the round stamps of craters, and sometimes cut across by more recent channels and valleys.

Dust lay scattered everywhere, piled up against crater walls or inside their rims and against the larger boulders, streaked light and dark. The dust was constantly reshaped by the wind: each dawn Icebones would peer around as the rocky wilderness emerged from the darkness, startled by how different it looked.

It was as if she was walking through layers of time: everything that had ever happened to this land was recorded here in a rocky scar or wrinkle or protrusion or dust heap.

. . . Sometimes, toiling across this unforgiving land of rock, thirsty, hungry, weary, sore, Icebones imagined she was *old*: with eroded molars and aching bones, in a place of moist green, surrounded by calves. Sometimes these waking dreams were so vivid that she wondered if *this* time of redness and desolation was merely a recollection. Perhaps this was not the vision of a long-dead prophet of the past, but a memory from the unknown future. Perhaps she *was* that very old Cow, on her last molars, returning to her youth in memory. Perhaps the Icebones she imagined herself to be was only a thing of memory, walking through a remembered land.

But if that was so, she thought dimly, then it must mean she would survive these harsh days, survive to grow old and bear calves . . . . mustn't it?

Troubled, she walked on, as best she could, waiting for the dream to end, the memory to disperse – for herself to wake up, old and safe and content.

But the dream, or memory, did not end.

So the days wore away on the High Plains, where land and sky glowed red in a great monotonous dialogue.

One day they found a narrow valley where a pool of water

had gathered. Trapped under a thin crust of ice, the water was brackish and briny. But it was the first liquid water the mammoths had encountered for days, and they smashed the ice and sucked it up gratefully.

Woodsmoke worked his way along the pond's rocky edge, exploring the water's deeper reaches. Suddenly a ledge of eroded rock crumbled beneath him. Rock fragments tumbled into the water, quickly followed by Woodsmoke's hind legs. He scrabbled at the rocky ground with his trunk and feet, but the crumbling rock offered little purchase. The calf slid into the freezing water until he was submerged save for his head and forelegs.

He trumpeted, his hair floating in the water around him.

The mammoths came running, water dribbling out of their mouths.

Breeze and Autumn fell to their knees beside the calf. They reached under his belly to lift him out with their trunks. Icebones and Spiral hurried to help – but the calf was too heavy to lift out, and it was impossible to get a purchase on his soaked, slippery hair. As they struggled, the calf's high-pitched bellows echoed from the rocky land around them.

At last Autumn ordered the others back. Carefully she looped her trunk around Woodsmoke's neck, and drew him towards the pond's shallower end. When the water was shallow enough for his hind feet to touch the pond bed, he quickly clambered out.

The calf shook himself to rid his fur of stinking pond scum, and his mother hurried close to nuzzle him. But he was frightened and angry. 'Why are we in this horrible place? Why don't we go back to the valley? There was water and stuff to eat . . .' The mammoths rumbled in unison, seeking to reassure him and persuade him to continue.

Autumn growled to Icebones, 'He thinks we were safe in the Gouge. He can't see that the world is changing, because it has not changed while he is alive. He thinks it will be the same for ever.'

Icebones, disturbed by the incident, wondered if that was true. What if *she* hadn't emerged so suddenly from her mysterious Sleep? What if *she* didn't have her memories of the Island and the Old Steppe, of such a very different time and place? Would she even perceive the changes from which she was fleeing – and which had already cost these mammoths so much?

And as the featureless days wore away, and the mammoths grew steadily more weary and cold and hungry and thirsty, darker doubts gathered.

It seemed audacious, absurd, for her to lead her mammoths across this high, silent, dead place. Perhaps it was simpler to suppose that the fault lay in her own head and heart, and not in the world around her. Perhaps she was leading these mammoths – not to salvation – but to their doom.

But then she would think of the dried mud and bones around the ponds of the Gouge, and the wide salt flats that bordered the Ocean of the North. This world was indeed changing for the worse – *she was right* – and she must continue to confront that truth, and she must gather her strength of body and mind, and work to bring these mammoths to safety, as best she knew how.

One evening, as the dark drew in, Icebones hauled her weary legs up the shallow rim of yet another crater. She was limping, favouring her damaged shoulder where pain still stabbed.

She reached the summit of a low, eroded rim mountain – and found herself facing a surface so smooth and flat she wondered briefly if it might be liquid water. But her nostrils were full of the tang of red dust. And as she looked more closely she saw rippling dunes, like frozen waves, and sharp-edged boulders littered here and there. There was no motion, no ripple, no scudding wave: this was a lake of dust, not water, and a faint disappointment tugged at her.

Thunder stood beside her. 'How strange. The other wall of this crater is buried.'

Icebones saw that it was true. The smooth, flat lake of crimson dust washed away to the south, submerging the crater's far wall. Perhaps this crater had formed on a slope, and had been partly buried when the dust gathered. Further away she saw fragmentary ridges and arcs poking out of the dust field: bits of more drowned craters. But the dust sea did not extend far. Beyond the submerged craters was more of the broken, jumbled, very ancient landscape they had become used to.

She raised her trunk and sniffed the air. It was dry, cold, and it smelled of nothing but iron dust: no moisture, no life. 'This raised ridge is not a good place to find water.'

'We need rest,' Thunder sighed. 'Rest and peace, even more than we need food. Let us stay here until morning, Icebones.'

Icebones understood: at least here on the ridge no walls of rock loomed around them. Under an open, empty sky, creatures of the steppe could rest easy, if hungrily. 'You are right,' she said. 'We should call the others.'

Night fell quickly here. Shadows fled across the broken land, and pools of blackness grew and merged, as if a tide of dark was rising all around them. The stars burned hard in the blackness, not disturbed by a wisp of mist or a scrap of cloud, and the silence stretched out into the dark, huge and complete, as if concealing greater secrets.

A mammoth broke from the group and padded to the edge of the crater-rim ridge. Though he was just black on black, a shadow in the night, Icebones could smell Thunder.

Trying not to disturb the others, who were clustered around the snoring calf, Icebones followed him.

Thunder held his trunk high in the air, peering over the

dust-flooded crater. She stood beside him, trunk raised and ears spread, listening.

. . . And now she thought she heard a thin, high scraping, like the scrabbling paw of some tiny animal, coming from the surface of the dust sea. It was very soft, so quiet she would never have noticed it if not for the high, lifeless stillness of this place. But in the silent dark it was as loud to her as the bark of a wolf.

The scratching vanished.

Then it returned, a little further away.

She rumbled, 'Perhaps it is a lemming.'

Thunder said bluntly, 'No lemming hops from place to place over great bounds as this invisible scratcher does.'

The two mammoths waited on the ridge, side by side, as the night wore away, and the invisible scratcher drifted, seemingly at random, around the dust bowl.

And when the first bruised-purple light began to seep into the eastern sky, they saw it.

An immense sac hovered in the air, just above the dust. It was like the skin of some huge fruit. At first it was pitch black, silhouetted against the dawn sky. It trailed a tendril, more pliant than the branch of a willow, that coiled on the ground like the trunk of a resting mammoth. But as the sac drifted, the trailing tendril scraped along the ground, making the scratching noise she had heard.

Thunder said, 'Is it a bird?'

'It's no bird I ever saw. Look, it has no wings, although it flies . . . I think it is floating like the feathers of a moulting goose, or as seeds are blown on the breeze.'

'What mighty tree will grow when that vast seed falls?'

Now pale dawn light diffused over the dust pool and shone into the heart of the sac, making it glow from within, pink and grey. The floating thing was made of some smooth shining translucent substance, Icebones saw, but it was slack and loose, like the skin around the eyes of a very old mammoth. And its trailing tendril dragged something knotty and silver across the dust, exploring like a trunk, leaving a shallow trench.

Now that the light was striking the sac it was starting to swell and rise, its surface unfolding with a slow, rustling languor. The silver knot scraped over the dust as the tendril slowly uncoiled.

'Perhaps it rises in the day and flies on the wind,' Icebones mused. 'And then it sinks at night and scrapes its silver fruit on the ground.'

'But it has no bones or head,' said Thunder. 'It cannot choose where it travels, as a mammoth can. It is blown on the wind. What does it travel *for*? What is it hoping to find?'

Icebones blew dust out of her trunk. 'That we will never know—'

The sea's placid surface erupted before them. Dunes flowed and disintegrated. A great black cylinder rose, and dust fell away with a soft rustle all around.

Icebones stumbled back, and she made to trumpet a warning. But so profound was her shock at this sudden apparition that her throat and trunk seemed to freeze. And besides, what warning could she give?

The cylinder of black-red flesh, twisting out of the dust, was crusted with hard segmented plates. At its apex was a nostril, or mouth: a pit, black as night, lined with six inward-pointing teeth. Dust was falling into that gaping maw, but whatever immense creature lay beneath the surface seemed indifferent. The great mouth folded around the lower portion of the floating sac. Huge, sharp teeth meshed together with a noise like rock on rock, and the sac's fabric was ground apart effortlessly.

Then the vast pillar twisted and fell back into the dust. It sank quickly out of sight, dragging half the sac and the trailing cable with it.

There were no ripples or waves. The dust ocean was immediately still, with only a new pattern of dunes left to show where the beast had been. The severed upper half of the sac drifted away, tumbling, on breezes that were gathering strength in the morning air.

For heartbeats the two mammoths stood side by side, saying nothing, stunned.

'It was a beast,' said Thunder fervently.

'Like a worm. Or a snake.'

'Do you think the Lost brought it here from the Old Steppe?'

'I don't think it has anything to do with the Lost, Thunder. Did it smell of the Lost – or any animal you know? Did you see its teeth?'

'They were very sharp and long.'

'*But it had six*: six teeth, set in a ring.' Just as the footprints she saw in the ancient outflow-channel had had six toes. Just as the creatures buried in the rock floor of the Nest of the Lost had six leaves and limbs and petals . . .

She stepped forward, sniffing the chill, thin mist pooling over the flooded crater. 'I think our sand worm was here long before the coming of the Lost.' Surviving in the dust, where creatures of water and air froze and died as the world cooled – perhaps sleeping away countless years, as the tide of life withdrew from the red rock of the world, waiting patiently until chance brought it a morsel of water or food . . . 'Perhaps the Lost never even knew it was here,' she said.

'If they had known they would probably have tried to kill it,' said Thunder mournfully. 'We should not seek to cross this dust pool.'

'No,' said Icebones. 'No, we shouldn't do that.'

Now the other mammoths were starting to wake. The dawn was filled with the soft sounds of yawns and belches, and the rumbling of half-empty guts.

Icebones and Thunder rejoined their Family.

731

CHAPTER 2
THE BLOOD WEED

The land, folded and cracked and cratered, continued to rise inexorably. There was no water save for occasional patches of dirty, hard-frozen ice, and the rocks were bare even of lichen and mosses. The sky was a deep purple-pink, even at noon, and there was never a cloud to be seen.

Icebone's shoulder ached with ice-hard clarity, all day and all night. She limped, favouring the shoulder. But over time that only caused secondary aches in the muscles of her legs and back and neck. And if she ever over-exerted herself she paid the price in racking, wheezing breaths, aching lungs, and an ominous blackness that closed around her vision.

One day, she thought grimly, that fringe would close completely, and once more she would be immersed in cold darkness – just as she had been before setting foot on this crimson plain – but this time, she feared, it was a darkness that would never clear.

It was a relief for them all when they crested a ridge and found themselves looking down on a deeply incised channel. For the valley contained a flat plain that showed, here and there, the unmistakable white glitter of ice.

Woodsmoke trumpeted loudly. Ignoring his mother's warning rumbles, the calf ran pell-mell down the rocky slope, scattering dust and bits of loose rock beneath his feet. He reached the ice and began to scrape with his stubby tusks.

The others followed more circumspectly, testing the ground with probing trunk tips before each step. But

Thunder was soon enthusiastically spearing the ice with his tusks. More hesitantly, Spiral and Breeze copied him.

Icebones recalled how she had had to show the mammoths how water could be dug out from beneath the mud. To Woodsmoke, born during this great migration, it was a natural thing, something he had grown up with. And perhaps *his* calves, learning from him, would approach the skill and expertise once enjoyed by the mammoths of her Island.

Icebones longed to join in, but knew she must conserve her strength. To her shame the weakness of the Matriarch had become a constant unspoken truth among the mammoths.

Alone, she walked cautiously on to the ice.

The frozen lake stretched to the end of the valley. To either side red-brown valley walls rose up to jagged ridges. The ice itself, tortured by wind and sunlight, was contorted into towers, pinnacles, gullies and pits, like the surface of a sea frozen in an instant. Heavily laced with dust and bits of rock, the ice was stained pale pink, and the colour was deepened by the cold salmon colour of the sky: even here on the ice, as everywhere else on these High Plains, she was immersed in redness.

Soon Thunder trumpeted in triumph, 'I am through!'

He had dug a roughly circular pit in the ice. The pit, its walls showing the scrape of mammoth tusks, was filled with dirty green-brown water.

All of them hesitated, for by now they had absorbed many Cycle lessons about the dangers of drinking foul water.

At least I can do this much for them, Icebones thought. 'I will be first,' she said.

With determination she stepped forward and lowered her trunk into the pit. The water was ice cold and smelled stale. Nevertheless she sucked up a trunkful and, with resolution, swallowed it. She said, 'It is full of green living things. But I think it is good for us to drink.' And she took another long, slow trunkful, as was her right as Matriarch.

Defying Family protocol, as calves often would, Woodsmoke hurried forward, knelt down on the gritty ice, and was next to dip his trunk into the ragged hole. But he could not reach, and he squeaked his frustration.

Autumn brushed him aside and dipped her own mighty trunk into the hole. She took a luxurious mouthful, chewing it slightly and spitting out a residue of slimy green stuff. Then she took another trunk's load and carefully dribbled the water into Woodsmoke's eager mouth.

After that, the others crowded around to take their turn.

When they had all drunk their fill, Thunder returned to his pit. He knelt down and reached deep into the water. Icebones could see the big muscles at the top of his trunk working as he explored. The modest pride in his bearing was becoming, Icebones thought. He was growing into a fine Bull, strong in body and mind.

With an effort, he hauled out a mass of slimy green vegetation. He dumped it on the ice. It steamed, rapidly frosting over. He shook his trunk to rid it of tendrils of green murk. 'This is what grows beneath the ice,' he said. 'I could feel sheets of it, waving in the water like the skirt of some drowned mammoth. I think the sheets are held together by that revolting mucus.'

Spiral probed at the mat with her trunk, the tense posture of her body expressing exquisite disgust. 'We cannot eat this,' she said.

Autumn growled, 'You will if you have to.'

'No, Spiral is right,' Icebones said. 'If we are driven to eat this green scum, it will be because we are starving – and we are not that yet.' She sniffed the air. It was not yet midday. 'We will stay here today and tonight, for at least we can drink our fill.'

The mammoths fanned out over the valley, probing at the

ice, seeking scraps of food in the wind-carved rock of the walls.

Icebones came to an odd pit in the ice, round and smooth-sided.

She probed into the pit – it was a little wider than her trunk – and she found, nestling at the bottom, a bit of hard black rock. When she dug out the rock and set it on the surface, it felt a little warmer than the surrounding ice. Perhaps it was made warmer than the sun, and that way melted its tunnel into the ice surface, at last falling through to the water beneath, and settling to the lake's dark bed.

She found more of the pits, each of them plunging straight down into the ice. The smaller the stone, the deeper the pit it dug. Driven by absent curiosity she pulled out the rocks wherever she could. Perhaps the rocks would start to dig new pits from where she had set them down, each in its own slow way. And perhaps some other curious mammoth of the future would wonder why some pits had stones in them, and some were empty.

Close to one valley wall she found a stand of squat trees. They had broad roots, well-founded in frozen mud, and their branches were bent over, like a willow's, so that they clung to the rock wall. But the fruit they bore was fat and black and leathery.

They were breathing trees.

She began to pull the leathery fruit off the low, clinging branches. She recalled how the Ragged One had shown her how to extract a mouthful of air from those thick-coated fruit. Each charge of air was invigorating but disappointingly brief, and afterwards her lungs were left aching almost as hard as before.

Thunder called her with a deep rumble. He was standing on the shore's frozen mud, close to a line of low mounds. She left the trees and walked slowly over to him.

The mud was dried and hardened and cracked. She could

see how low ridges paralleled the lake's ragged shore: water marks, where the receding lake had churned up the mud at its rim.

She pointed this out to Thunder. 'It is a sign that the lake has been drying for a long time.'

'Yes,' he growled. 'And so is this.' He swept his tusks through one of the mounds. It was just a heap of rocks, she saw, with larger fragments making a loose shell over smaller bits of rubble. But its shape had been smoothly rounded, and inside there were bits of yellow skin that crumbled when Thunder probed at them. 'I think this mound was made in the lake.'

She tried to pick up a fragment of one skin-like flake. It crumbled, and it was dry, flavourless. 'Perhaps this was once alive. Like the mats you found under the ice.'

'The lake is dying, Icebones. Soon it will be frozen to its base, and then the ice will wear away, and there will be nothing left – nothing but rock, and dried-up flakes like this.'

They walked a little further, following the muddy shore.

In one place the lake bank was shallow, and easily climbed. Icebones clambered up that way. The land beyond was unbroken, harsh. But it was scarred by something hard and shining that marched from one horizon to the other: glimmering, glowing, an immense straight edge imposed on the world.

Icebones and Thunder approached cautiously. 'It is a fence,' he said.

'A thing of the Lost.'

'Yes. A thing to keep animals out – or to keep them in.'

That made no sense to Icebones. The land beyond the fence seemed just as empty and desolate as the land on this side of it. There was nothing to be separated, as far as she could see.

Thunder probed the fence with his tusk. Icebones saw that it was a thing of shining thread, full of little holes. The holes were too small to pass a trunk tip, but she could see through the fence to what lay beyond.

And what she saw there was bones: a great linear heap of them, strewn at the base of the fence.

The mammoths walked further, peering up and down the fence, trying to touch the bones through the mesh.

'I don't think any of them are mammoth,' Icebones said.

Thunder said tightly, 'The animals could smell the water. They couldn't get through the fence. But they couldn't leave; the world was drying, and they couldn't get away from that maddening smell.'

'So they stayed here until they died.'

'Yes.' And he barged the fence with his forehead, ramming it until a section of it gave way. Then he tramped it flat into the dust.

But there were no animals to come charging through in search of water; nothing but the dust of bones rose up in acknowledgement of his strength.

She tugged his trunk, making him come away.

From the lake came a soft crushing sound, a muffled trumpet.

The mammoths whirled.

Icebones looked first for the calf: there he was, safely close by his mother's side, though both Breeze and Woodsmoke were standing stock still, wary.

But of Autumn there was no sign.

Ignoring the pain in her straining lungs, Icebones hurried stiffly on to the ice. 'Where is she? What happened?'

'I don't know,' Breeze called. 'She was at the far side of the lake, seeking clearer water. And then—'

'Keep the calf safe.'

Thunder immediately began to charge ahead.

Icebones grabbed his tail and, with an effort, held him back. 'We may all be in danger. Slowly, Thunder.'

He growled, but he said, 'Lead, Matriarch.'

Trying to restrain her own impatience, Icebones led Thunder and Spiral across the frozen lake, step by step, exploring the complex red-streaked surface with her trunk tip.

She heard a low rumble.

She stopped, listening. The others had heard it too. With more purpose now, but with the same careful step-by-step checking, the three mammoths made their way towards the source of the call.

At last they came to a wide pit, dug or melted into the ice. And here they found Autumn.

She lay on her side, as if asleep. But her body was covered with broad streaks of blood red, as if she had been gouged open by the claws of some huge beast. Her face, too, was hidden in redness, from her mouth to the top of her trunk.

'She is bleeding!' cried Spiral. 'She is dead! She is dead!' Her wails echoed from the high rock walls of the valley.

But Icebones could see that Autumn's small amber eyes were open, and they were fixed on Icebones: intelligent, angry, alert.

Icebones reached down and touched one of the bloody streaks with her trunk. This was not broken flesh. Instead she found a cold, leathery surface that gave when she pushed it, like the skin of a ripe fruit.

'This is a plant,' she said. 'It has grabbed on to Autumn, the way a willow tree grabs on to a rock.' She knelt and leaned into the pit. She stabbed at the plant with her tusk, piercing it easily.

Crimson liquid gushed out stickily, splashing her face. The tendril she had pierced pulled back, the spilled fluid already freezing over.

The plant closed tighter around Autumn, and the Cow groaned.

Spiral touched Icebones's dirtied face curiously and lifted her trunk tip to her mouth. '*It is blood.*'

Thunder growled, 'What manner of plant has blood

instead of sap? What manner of plant attacks a full-grown mammoth?'

'She cannot breathe,' Icebones said. 'She will soon die . . .' She reached down and began to stab, carefully and delicately, at the tendrils wrapped over Autumn's mouth. More of the bloody sap spurted. But the plant's grip tightened on Autumn's body, as the trunk of a mammoth closes on a tuft of grass, and Icebones heard the ominous crack of bone.

At last she got Autumn's mouth free. The older Cow took deep, gasping breaths. 'My air,' she said now. 'It sucks out my air! Get it off. Oh, get it off . . .'

Icebones and Thunder began to stab and prise at the bloody tendrils. The eerie blood-sap pumped out and spilled into the pit, and soon their tusks and the hair on their faces were soaked with the thick crimson fluid. But wherever they cut away a tendril more would come sliding out of the mass beneath Autumn – and with every fresh stab or slice the tendrils tightened further.

'Enough,' Icebones said. She straightened up and, with a blood-stained trunk, pulled Thunder back.

Woodsmoke stood with Breeze a little way away from the pit. He trumpeted in dismay. 'You aren't going to let her die.'

It struck Icebones then that Woodsmoke had never seen anybody die. She wiped her bloody trunk on the ice, then touched the calf's scalp. 'We can't fight it, little one. If we hurt the blood weed it hurts Autumn more.'

'Then find some way to get it off her without hurting it.'

Thunder rumbled, from the majesty of his adolescence, 'When you grow up you'll learn that sometimes there are only hard choices, calf—'

But Icebones shouldered him aside, her mind working furiously. 'What do you mean, Woodsmoke? *How* can we get the weed to leave Autumn alone?'

Woodsmoke pondered, his little trunk wrinkling. 'Why does it want Autumn?'

'We think it is stealing her breath.'

'Then give it something it wants more than Autumn's breath. I like grass,' he said. 'But I like saxifrage better. If I see saxifrage I will leave the grass and take the saxifrage . . .'

Icebones turned to Thunder. 'What else could we offer it?'

Thunder said, 'Another mammoth's breath. *My* breath. Icebones, if you wish it—'

'No,' she said reluctantly. 'I don't want to lose anybody else. But what else . . . ?'

Even as she framed the notion herself, Thunder trumpeted excitedly. '*The breathing trees*,' they shouted together.

'Get the fruit,' said Icebones. 'You and Spiral. You are faster than I am. *Go*.'

Without hesitation the two young mammoths lumbered over the folded ice towards the breathing trees, where they clung to the lake's rocky shore.

Autumn moaned again. 'Oh, it hurts . . . I am sorry . . .'

'Don't be sorry,' said Woodsmoke mournfully.

'It is my fault,' Autumn gasped. 'The plant lay over the pit. It was a neat trap . . . I did not check . . . I walked across it without even thinking, and when I fell, it wrapped itself around me . . . Oh! It is very tight on my ribs . . .'

'Don't talk,' said Icebones. Her voice lapsed into a wordless, reassuring rumble. Breeze joined in, and even Woodsmoke added his shallow growl.

Perhaps the pit had been melted into the ice by a stone, Icebones thought. Perhaps the blood weed, driven by some dark red instinct, had learned to use such pits as a trap. And it waited, and waited . . .

Autumn lay still, her eyes closed, her breath coming in thin, hasty gasps. But Icebones could see that the blood weed was covering her mouth once more.

This blood weed, like the breathing tree, was a plant of the cold and airlessness of the desiccated heights of this world. It was as alien to her as the birds of the air or the worms that crawled in lake-bottom mud – and yet it killed.

'. . . We got it! We got it, Icebones!' Thunder and Spiral came charging across the ice. Thunder bore in his trunk the top half of a breathing tree, spindly black branches laden with the strange dark fruit. He threw the tree down on the ice, close to the pit. 'Now what?'

Icebones grabbed a fruit with her trunk, lowered it into the pit, and, with a determined squeeze, popped it over the prone body of Autumn.

A little gust of fog burst from the fruit.

The tendrils of the blood weed slithered over the mammoth's hair. Autumn gasped, as if the pressure on her ribs was relieved a little. But the weed had not let go, and already the fruit's air had dissipated.

'More,' said Icebones. 'Thunder, hold the tree over the pit.'

So Thunder held out the broken branches while Spiral, Icebones and Breeze all worked to pluck and pop the fat fruits.

With every brief gust of air the agitation of the weed increased. But they were soon running out of fruit, and Autumn's eyes were rolling upwards. Icebones growled, despairing.

And then, quite suddenly, the weed slid away from Autumn. With an eerie sucking noise its tendrils reached up, like blood-gorged worms, to the dark breathing-tree branches above it.

'Let it have the branches, Thunder! But keep hold of the root—'

The weed knotted itself around the branches, moving with a slow, slithering, eerie stealth.

When the last of its tendrils had slid off Autumn's prone form, Spiral and Thunder hurled the tree as hard and as far as they could. The tangle of branches went spinning through the thin air, taking the crimson mass of the weed with it. Its blood-sap leaked in a cold rain that froze as soon as it touched the ice.

CHAPTER 3
THE ICE MAMMOTHS

They were suspended in dense, eerie silence – not a bird cry, not the scuffle of a lemming or the call of a fox – nothing but bright red rock and purple sky and six toiling mammoths.

There was nothing to eat, nothing to drink.

All of them were gaunt now, their hair thinning. Their ribs and shoulder blades and knees stuck out of their flesh, and their bony heads looked huge, as if they were gaining wisdom, even as their bodies shrivelled.

And day after day wore away.

They came to another lake, much smaller. They walked down to it, slow and weary.

This time the water was frozen down to its base. The ice was worn away – not melted, but sublimated: over the years the ice had evaporated without first turning to water. The mammoths ground at this stone-hard, deeply cold stuff, seeking crushed fragments they could pop into their mouths.

Around the lake they found scraps of vegetation. But the trees were dead, without leaves, and their trunks were hollowed out, and the grass blades broke easily in trunk fingers, dried out like straw.

Thunder, frustrated, picked up a rock and slammed it against another. Both rocks broke open with sharp cracks.

Icebones explored the exposed surfaces, sniffing. There was green in the rock, she saw: a thin layer of it, shading to yellow-brown, buried a little way inside the rock itself, following the eroded contours of its surface. Perhaps it was lichen, or moss. The green growing things must shelter here, trapping sunlight and whatever scraps of water settled on the rock. But when Icebones scraped out some of the green-stained rock with a tusk tip, she found nothing but salty grains that ground against her molars, with not a trace of water or nourishment.

She flung away the rock. She felt angry, resentful at being reduced to scraping at a bit of stone. And then she felt a twinge of shame at having destroyed the refuge of this tiny, patient scrap of life.

The lake was fringed by dried and cracked mud. Walking there, Icebones found herself picking over the scattered and gnawed bones of deer, bison, lemmings, horses, and they spoke to her of the grisly story that had unfolded here.

But there was hope, she saw. Some footprints in the mud led *away* from the deadly betrayal of the pond and off to the south, before vanishing into the red dust. Perhaps some instinct among these frightened, foolish animals had guided them the way Icebones knew the mammoths must travel, to the deep sanctuary of the Footfall.

Exploring the mud with her trunk tip, Icebones found one very strange set of prints. They were round, like mammoth footprints, but much smaller and smoother. These creatures had come here after the rest had died off, for bits of bone were to be found crushed into the strange prints. And, here and there, these anonymous visitors had dug deep holes – like water holes, but deeper than she could reach with her trunk.

She noticed Spiral. The tall Cow was standing alone on the ice at the edge of the lake, her trunk tucked defensively under her head. She was gazing at a brown, shapeless lump that lay huddled on the rocky shore.

Thunder stood by her, wrapping his trunk over Spiral's head to comfort her.

Spiral said, 'I was working the ice. I didn't even notice *that* at first. It doesn't even *smell* . . .'

That was a dead animal. It was a goat, Icebones thought –

or rather it had once been a goat, for it was clearly long dead. It lay on its back, its head held up stiffly into the air as if it was staring at the sky. Its skin seemed to be mostly intact, even retaining much of its hair, but it was drawn tight over bones and lumpy flesh. The goat's mouth was open. The skin of its face had drawn back, exposing the teeth and a white sheet of jaw bone.

The goat had even kept its eyes. Exposed by the shrinking-back of its skin, the eyeballs were just globes of yellow-white, with a texture like soft fungus.

'It must have lost its way,' said Thunder gently.

'It died here,' said Icebones. 'But there are no wolves or foxes or carrion birds to eat its flesh. Not even the flies which feast on the dead. And its body dried out.'

Spiral prodded the corpse with her spiralling tusks. It shifted and rocked, rigid, like a piece of wood. 'Will we finish up dried out and dead like this? And then who will Remember us?'

'We are not lost,' Thunder growled. 'We are not goats. We are mammoth. We will find the way.'

They stayed a day and a night at the pond, gnawing at bitter ice.

Then they moved on.

They frequently came across blood weed.

It was difficult to spot. The weed gave off little odour, and its blood-red colour almost exactly matched the harsh crimson of the underlying rock and dust – which was probably no accident.

The mammoths found bits of bone, cleansed of flesh, in the weeds' traps, but all such traces were old. Even the weeds had not fed or drunk for a long time. Icebones wondered if these plants could last for ever, waiting for the occasional fall of unwary migrant animals into their patient maws.

Icebones came across a new kind of plant, nestled in a

hollow. It was like a flower blossom, cupped like an up-turned skull, and its tight-folded petals were waxy and stiff. The whole thing was as wide as a mammoth's footprint, and about as deep. A sheet of some shining, translucent sub-stance coated the top of the blossom, sealing it off. Under the translucent sheet Icebones thought she saw a glint of green.

Cautiously she popped the covering sheet with the tip of her tusk. The sheet shrivelled back, breaking up into threads that dried and snapped. A small puff of moisture escaped, a trace of water that instantly frosted on the petals. A spider scuttled at the base of the blossom.

Icebones scraped off the frost eagerly and plunged her moist trunk tip into her mouth. It was barely a trace, but it tasted delicious, reviving her spirit a great deal more than it nourished her body. She picked the flower apart and chewed it carefully. Despite that trace of green there was little flavour or nourishment to be had, and she spat it out.

She called the others, and they soon found more of the plants.

Each plant sheltered spiders, which made the moisture-trapping lids that allowed the green hearts of the plants to grow. So each flower was like a tiny Family, she thought, spiders and plant working together to keep each other alive.

It was Thunder who came up with the best way to use the flowers. He opened his mouth wide and pushed the whole plant in, lid first. Then he bit to pop the lid, and so was able to suck down every bit of the trapped moisture. But he had to scrape off bits of spider-web that clung to his mouth and trunk, and Icebones saw spiders scrambling away into his fur.

Spiral made a hoot of disgust. 'Eating spider-web. How disgusting.'

Icebones found another plant and, deliberately, plucked it and thrust it into her mouth. 'Spiders won't kill you. Thirst will. You will all do as Thunder does—'

Suddenly Thunder stood tall, trunk raised, his small ears spread.

The others froze in their tracks – every one of them, flighty Spiral, Autumn with her aching ribs, Breeze with her scored back, even restless, growing, ever-hungry Woodsmoke, as still as if they had been shaped from the ancient rock itself. Icebones found a moment to be proud of them, for a disciplined silence, vital to any prey animal, was a characteristic of a well-run Family.

And then she heard what had disturbed Thunder. It was a scraping, as if something was digging deep into the ground.

'But,' Autumn murmured, 'what kind of animal makes burrowing noises like that?'

Thunder said, 'There is a crater rim ahead. It hides us from the source of the noise. I will go ahead alone, and—'

'No, brave Thunder. We are safer together.' Icebones stepped towards the crater ridge. 'Let's go, let's go.'

The other mammoths quickly formed up behind her. They climbed the shallow, much-eroded crater rim.

Icebones paused when she got to the rim's flattened top, her trunk raised.

In the crater basin, heavy heads lifted slowly.

Thunder pealed out a bright trumpet. He hurried forward, scattering dust and bits of rock. Icebones, more warily, clambered down the slope, keeping her trunk raised.

Mammoths – at least that was her first impression. They were heavy, dark, hairy creatures, spread over the basin. She saw several adults – Cows? – clustered together around a stand of breathing trees, digging at the roots. A black-faced calf poked its head out through the dense hairs beneath its mother's belly, curious like all calves. Further away there were looser groupings of what she supposed were Bulls.

As Thunder approached, the Cows lifted their trunks out of the holes they had dug. Their trunks were broad but very long, longer than any adult mammoth Icebones had met before. Their tusks were short and stubby. They huddled closer together, the adults forming a solid phalanx before the stand of trees.

They looked like mammoths. They behaved as mammoths might. But they did not *smell* like mammoths. And as Icebones worked her way down the slope, her sense of unease deepened.

Woodsmoke had wandered away from his mother. Two calves peered at him from a forest of thick black hair. The adults watched him suspiciously, but no mammoth would be hostile to a calf, however strange. Soon Woodsmoke had locked his trunk around a calf's trunk, and was tugging vigorously.

Icebones announced clearly, 'I am Icebones, daughter of Silverhair. Who is Matriarch here?'

The strange mammoths rumbled, heads nodding and bodies swaying, as if in confusion.

At length a mammoth stepped forward. 'My name is Cold-As-Sky. I do not know you. You are not of our Clan.'

Cold-As-Sky was about Icebones's size, as round and solid as a boulder. Her hair was black and thick. There was a thick ridged brow on her forehead, sheltering small orange eyes. She had a broad hump on her back, and when she took a breath, deep and slow, that hump swelled up, as if she carried a second set of lungs there. Her long trunk lay thickly coiled on the rock at her feet. Her voice was as deep as the ground's own songs.

Icebones stepped forward tentatively. 'We have come far.'

'You are not like us.'

'No,' Icebones said sadly. 'We are not like you.' As unlike, in a different way, as the Swamp-Mammoths had been unlike Icebones and her Family. 'And yet we are Cousins. You speak the language of Kilukpuk.'

Just as Chaser-Of-Frogs had reacted to the ancient name, so Cold-As-Sky looked briefly startled. But her curiosity was soon replaced by her apparently customary hostility. 'We speak as we have always spoken.'

Her language, in fact, was indistinct. This Ice Mammoth spoke only with the deep thrumming of her chest and belly, omitting the higher sounds, the chirrups and snorts and mewls a mammoth would make with her trunk and throat. But her voice, deep and vibrant, would carry easily through the rocks, Icebones realised. This was a mammoth made for this high cold place, where the air was thin, and only rocks could be heard.

Cold-As-Sky said now, 'You call yourself my Cousin. What are you doing here? Do you intend to steal my air trees?'

Air trees – breathing trees? 'No,' said Icebones wearily. 'But we are hungry and thirsty.'

'Go back to where you came from.'

'We cannot go back,' Thunder said.

Icebones stepped forward and reached out with her trunk. '*We are Cousins.*'

Cold-As-Sky growled, but did not back away.

Icebones probed at the other's face. That black hair was dense and slippery, and as cold as the rock beneath her feet. She finally found flesh, deep within the layers of hair. The flesh was cold and hard, and covered in fine, criss-cross ridges. She pinched it with her trunk fingers. The other did not react – as if the flesh was without sensation, like scar tissue. The trunk itself was very wide and bulbous near the face, with vast black nostrils.

To her shock, Icebones saw that Cold-As-Sky's trunk tip was lined with small white teeth. The teeth were set in a bony jaw, like a tiny mouth at the end of her trunk.

Cold-As-Sky's mouth was a gaping blue-black cavern. Even her tongue was blue. Icebones touched that tongue now – and tasted water.

Cold-As-Sky growled again, pulling back. 'Your trunk is hot and wet. You are a creature of the warmth and the thick air and the running water.' Her immense trunk folded up, becoming a fat, stubby tube. 'This is not your place.'

Icebones's anger battled with pride – and desperation. '*I tasted water on your lips.* Please, Cousin—'

'And you have water,' Thunder said, stepping forward menacingly.

Cold-As-Sky snorted contempt, a hollow sound which echoed from the recesses of vast sinuses. 'If you want water, take it. Come.' And she turned and began to push her way through the solid wall her Family had made.

Wary, Icebones followed, with Thunder at her side.

They came to the stand of breathing trees. Icebones saw that the Ice Mammoths had burrowed into the hard rocky ground at their roots. One Cow was kneeling, her body a black ball of shining hair, and her trunk was stretched out, pushed deep into the ground.

Icebones probed into one of the holes with her own trunk. It was much deeper than she could reach. But, around its rim, she saw traces of frost.

Icebones imagined those strange trunk-tip teeth digging into the rock and permafrost, chipping bit by bit towards the water that lay far, far below. With such a long trunk, Icebones saw, mammoths could survive even in this frozen wasteland, where the water lay very deep indeed.

'If you want water,' Cold-As-Sky said, 'dig for it as we do.'

Now Autumn walked up, grand, dignified, rumbling. 'You can see that is impossible for us.'

'Then you will go thirsty.'

'*You* have calves,' Autumn said harshly. '*You* are mammoth.'

Cold-As-Sky flinched, and Icebones saw that the Oath of Kilukpuk, which demanded loyalty between Cousins, was not forgotten here.

But nevertheless Cold-As-Sky said, 'Your calves are not my calves. Your kind has come this way before – a strange ragged-haired one, mumbling—'

Autumn said sharply, '*She* has been this way?'

Icebones said, 'If you will not give us water, will you guide us? We are going south. We seek a great pit in the ground, where the warmth may linger.'

'I have heard its song in the rocks.' Cold-As-Sky stamped the ground and nodded her head. 'You will fall into the pit and its rocks will cover your bones . . . if you ever reach it, for the way is hard.'

'*Which way?*'

Cold-As-Sky turned to the south-east. Icebones looked, and felt the slow wash of echoes from the hard folded landscapes there.

'I can feel it,' Thunder said, dismayed. 'Broken land . . . Great chains of mountains . . . One crater rim after another . . . It will be the hardest land we have encountered yet.'

Autumn said grimly, 'The Footfall of Kilukpuk made a mighty splash.'

'No matter how difficult, that is our trail,' said Icebones.

Woodsmoke had been playing with a calf of the Ice Mammoths, pulling at her trunk as if trying to drag the other out from the forest of her parents' legs. Now Breeze pulled him away. Woodsmoke looked back regretfully to a small round face, a pair of wistful orange eyes.

Autumn said to Cold-As-Sky, 'Why are you so hostile? We have done you no harm.'

'This world was ours,' growled Cold-As-Sky, her voice deep as thunder. 'Once it was all like this. The blood weed and the air tree flourished everywhere, and there were vast Clans, covering the land . . . Then the warmth came, and *you* came. And we were forced to retreat to this hard, rocky land, where our calves fall into the pits of the blood weed. But now the warmth is dying, and you are dying with it. And soon I will walk on your bones, and the bones of your calves.'

That strange perversion of the rite of Remembering made

Icebones shudder. But she said, 'We did not bring the warmth. We did not banish the cold. If you are hurt, we did not hurt you. We are your Cousins.'

It seemed to Icebones that Cold-As-Sky was about to respond. But then she turned away, and the Ice Mammoths returned to their deep holes in the ground.

Icebones said, 'Let's go, let's go.' And, with one determined footstep after another, she began the steady plod towards the south-east, where distant mountains cast long jagged shadows.

CHAPTER 4
THE DUST

I know it is hard, little Icebones. But you have walked your mammoths around the world. And there is only a little further to go.

'But that last "little further" may be the hardest of all, Boaster.'

Don't call me Boaster! Tell me about the land . . .

And she hesitated, for this land was like nothing she had experienced, either in her old life before the Sleep, or even here in this strange, cold world. For this land had been warped by the great impact which had created the Footfall of Kilukpuk itself.

She stood at the head of an ancient water-carved channel. The ground was broken into heaped-up fragments, as if the water, draining away, had left behind a vast underground cavern into which the land had collapsed. But the fallen rocks were very old, heavily pitted and eroded and covered with dust. And when the mammoths dug deeper into the ground they found it riddled with broad tunnels – but they were dry, hollowed out like ancient bones, as if the water that made them had long disappeared.

All around her there were hills, great clumps of them, grouped into chains like the wrinkles of an ancient mammoth. But the mountains were eroded to a weary smoothness, and they were extensively punctured and smashed by younger, smaller craters.

Thunder, his listening skills developing all the time, said he thought that around the central basin there were – not the single chain of rim mountains that surrounded most craters –

five concentric rings of mountains, vast ripples in the rock thrown up by the giant primordial splash. Lacing through these rim-mountain chains were vast, shallow channels, apparently cut by water in the deep past. The channels themselves were covered in crater punctures, or pierced by sharper, litter-filled channels.

Around Icebones, the Family were rooting desultorily at the unpromising, hummocky ground. Icebones felt an unreasonable stab of impatience with this little group of gaunt, helpless mammoths.

She thought of the Clan gatherings Silverhair had told her of, when Families and bachelor herds would congregate on great green-waving steppes, so many mammoths they turned the air golden with their shining hair, and for days on end they would talk and fight and mate . . .

But such gatherings had been even before Silverhair's time. This starving group were perhaps the only true mammoths in half a world, and Icebones knew she had no choice but to accept her lot.

Boaster rumbled softly, still waiting for her reply.

'It is a very old land, Boaster,' she said at last. 'And, like an old mammoth, it is ill-tempered when disturbed.'

It is an old world, I think, much disturbed by the Lost.

But now Thunder was calling, his voice a deep uncomfortable growl.

'I must go. Graze well, Boaster.'

And you, little Icebones . . .

Thunder was standing on a slight rise, staring to the south, trunk raised. She saw that a wind, blowing from that direction, was ruffling the hair around his face. 'Can you taste it?'

Peering south, she made out a hard black line that spread right along the horizon, separating the crimson land from the purple sky. The wind touched her face. It was harsh and gritty. She raised her trunk, exposing its sensitive tip. When she put the tip in her mouth she could taste iron.

'Dust,' she said. 'Like the storm in the Gouge.'

'Yes. It is a storm, and it carries a vast cloud of dust. And it is coming towards us.'

Icebones felt her strength dissipate, like water running into the dust. No more, she thought: we have endured enough.

'You are alert, Thunder. We rely on your senses.'

But this time her praise made little impact, for his worry was profound.

The light grew muddled, as if the day itself was confused. Gradually the wind picked up, blustering in their faces and whipping dust devils before it.

The storm front grew into a towering wall, a curtain that was deep crimson-black at its base and a wispy pink-grey at the top, hanging from the sky like the guard hairs of some vast mammoth. Icebones could hear the crack and grumble of thunder, and the ragged wisps at the top of the sheet of air whipped and churned angrily. It was an awesome display of raw power.

Icebones had decided that the mammoths should not try to move. They were already badly weakened by hunger and thirst and cold. She tried to ensure they rested, gathering their energy, just as the storm did.

The mammoths had nothing to say to each other. They merely stood, bruised, dismayed, waiting for the storm to break on them.

There was a moment of stillness. Even the wind died briefly. Icebones could see her own shadow at her feet.

When she looked up she could see the sun. It shone fitfully through veils of black cloud and dust that raced across the sky, churning and thrashing.

And then the sun vanished, and the air exploded.

Gusts as hard as rock battered at Icebones's face and legs and neck, and the dust they carried scoured mercilessly at her hair and exposed flesh. It was as if she was in a bubble inside the dust, a bubble that was flying sideways through the air. The sun showed only in glimpses between tall, scudding clouds, and lightning crackled far above her, casting deep purple glows through layers of cloud and dust.

She was immersed in vast layers of noise: the crack of thunder, the howl of the air over the rock, the relentless scraping of the dust. Her sound impressions broke up into chaotic shards. She lost her deep mammoth's sense of the land, and she felt lost, bewildered.

And – unlike the storm they had endured in the Gouge – this wind was *dry*, as dry as the dust it carried, and it seemed to suck the moisture from her blood.

The mammoths were around her, and she felt the tension of their muscles as they fought the storm. But she knew she was burning her last reserves of strength just to stay standing against the pressure of the wind.

Autumn was beside her, trumpeting: 'It will take half a day for this storm to wash over us, for it stretches deep into the southern lands.'

'I did not imagine it could be so bad. If we stay here our bones will be worn to dust . . .'

'We must find shelter.' That was Thunder, his Bull's growl almost lost in the howl of the air. 'There is a crater rim, some way to the south.'

'We must try,' Icebones said. 'But how will we find it?'

'The storm comes from the south. If we head into it, we will find our ridge.'

Autumn rumbled, 'It is hard enough just to stand. To walk into that horror—'

'Nevertheless we must,' Icebones said. 'Thunder, you go first. The next in line grab his tail. If anyone loses hold we stop immediately. Thunder, you will not have to lead for long. We will take turns.'

Thunder said, 'I will endure—'

'We will do it the way I say. And be wary of the blood

756

weed.' Trying to project confidence, she trumpeted, 'Let us begin. Let's go, let's go . . .'

To break their huddled formation, to expose themselves to the wind, was hard. No matter how she tucked her trunk under her face, no matter how tightly she squeezed shut her eyes, still the dust lashed at her as if it was a living thing, malevolent, determined to injure. The calf was deeply unhappy, trumpeting his discomfort into the wind, continually trying to push his way back under his mother's guard hairs.

As if from a vast distance she heard Thunder's thin, readying trumpet cry.

A few heartbeats later, Spiral began to move, her steady footsteps determined, her buttocks swaying. At the end of the line, Icebones, keeping a careful hold on Spiral's tail, followed behind.

They walked into howling darkness. Icebones could tell nothing of the land around her, smell nothing but the harsh iron tang of the dust that clogged her nostrils and mouth. It was a shameful, selfish relief to shelter behind Spiral's huge bulk.

Spiral stopped abruptly. Icebones's head rammed into her thighs.

Icebones felt her way along the line to sniff out the problem.

It was the calf. Wailing, terrified, Woodsmoke had slumped to the ground.

With much cajoling and lifting by the strong trunks of Autumn and Icebones, Woodsmoke finally got to his feet. But Icebones could feel how uncertain his legs were, as weak as if he was a newborn again.

They managed only a few more steps before the calf collapsed once more.

Icebones had the mammoths form up into a wedge shape facing the storm, with one of the adults at the apex, and the calf and his mother sheltered at the rear.

'His strength is gone, Icebones,' Breeze cried through the storm's noise. 'He is hungry and thirsty and I have no milk to give him. We must stay here with him until the storm is over.'

'But,' Thunder growled, 'we *cannot* stay here. This foul dust sucks the last moisture out of my body.'

'We can't stay and we can't go on,' Spiral said. 'What must we do, Matriarch?'

Battered by the storm's violence, blinded, deafened, her own strength wearing down, Icebones knew how she must answer. And she knew that she must test her new Family's resolve as it had not been tested before.

. . . But I am just Icebones, she thought desperately. I am little more than a calf myself. Who am I to inflict such pain on these patient, loyal, suffering mammoths? *How do I know this is right?* Oh, Silverhair, if only you were here!

But her mother was not here. And her course was clear. She was Matriarch. And, like generations of Matriarchs before her, she reached into the Cycle, the ancient wisdom of mammoths who had learned to survive.

'Autumn, Thunder – do you think we could reach the crater rim, if not for the calf?'

Thunder seemed baffled. 'But we have the calf—'

'Just tell me.'

'Yes. We are strong enough for that, Matriarch.'

Icebones said gravely, '*The mammoth dies, but mammoths live on.*'

Spiral understood first. She wailed, 'Do you see what this monster is saying? She wants us to abandon the calf. We must go to the crater rim, and save ourselves, while he dies alone in the storm. *Alone.*'

'No!' Breeze wrapped her trunk around her fallen calf.

Autumn spoke, and there was a huge, impressive sadness in her voice. 'Daughter, you can bear other calves. Others who will grow strong, and continue the Family . . . *You* are more important than Woodsmoke, because of those other calves.'

'Kilukpuk will care for him,' said Icebones. *'If a mammoth dies young, it is easy for him to throw off his coat of earth, and to play in the light of the aurora . . .'*

'There is no aurora here,' Spiral said bleakly.

'Would you sacrifice him, Icebones?' Breeze trumpeted. 'Would *you*, mother, if this was your calf?'

The moment stretched, the tension between the mammoths palpable.

This was the crux, Icebones knew. And Autumn was the key. If Autumn maintained her resolve, then they would abandon the calf, and go on. And if she did not, they would all die, here in this screaming storm.

Autumn sighed, a deep rumble that carried through the storm. 'No,' she said at last. 'No, I could not abandon my calf.'

And Icebones, with a deep, failing regret, knew they were lost.

Breeze clutched her calf, and her sister came close, both of them stroking and reassuring the calf as best they could.

'I am sorry,' Autumn said, huddling close to Icebones. 'I did not have the strength. It is hard to be mammoth.'

'Yes. Yes, it is hard.'

'We have been toys of the Lost too long . . .'

'Let us huddle. Perhaps we will defeat this storm yet.'

But she knew that wasn't possible. And, from the tense, subdued postures of Autumn and Thunder beside her, she sensed they knew it too.

The continent-sized dust storm continued, relentless, cruel, oblivious to the mammoths' despair.

The dust clogged her trunk and mouth, until she was as dry as a corpse. And still the storm went on, so dense she no longer knew if it was day or night. Perhaps she even slept a while, exhausted, her body battling the storm without her conscious control.

I tried, Silverhair. But they just weren't ready to be a Family – a true Family, able to face the hard truths as well as the easy ones . . .

No. *I* was not ready. *I* have failed.

But it hardly mattered now. After a few days, when they were reduced to scoured-clean bones, nobody would ever know what happened here.

She felt a new, hard form beside her. She turned sluggishly, trying to lift her trunk.

She sensed a stocky body, hair that was dense and slick, crimson against the storm's dark light.

'You are Cold-As-Sky,' she said, her voice thick with dust.

The other did not reply.

'There is no water here.'

'No,' said the Ice Mammoth, her voice somehow clear through the storm. 'This land is very old. Even the deep-buried ice has sublimated away.'

'But you live.'

'But I live. I carry water in my throat, and in a hump on my back, enough to let me survive the longest dust storm.'

'My trunk is clogged,' Icebones said softly. 'All I can taste is dust. Cousin, give me water.'

Cold-As-Sky ignored her. '*This* is the truth of this world. This is how it was before the Lost came here. The planet itself is trying to kill you now. You are meant to die. Just as *we* were meant to die. Did you know that?'

Icebones did not reply, wishing only that Cold-As-Sky would leave her alone with her blackness and despair.

But Cold-As-Sky went on, 'It is true. The first of us who awoke found that all the world was like this high, broken plain. There were no soft green things, no pockets of thick wet air to clog the lungs . . . Only the clean rock and the red sky. And the only water was buried deep in the dust, where it should lie, where it is safe.

'And we were the only living things. We Ice Mammoths, and the blood weed, and the air trees, and the spider-flowers.

'Many calves died, gasping for air as they were born. But we endured. Slowly the trees made the air thicker, and slowly the spider-flowers captured the water. And we Ice Mammoths dug ancient water out of the ground, and broke up the rock with our tusks, and made the red dust rich with our dung.

'You call yourself a Matriarch. I was born knowing that word. And I was born knowing that *we* had no Matriarch to teach us, to show us how to dig the roots of the breathing trees, or to drink the blood of the weed. We had to learn it all, learn for ourselves. And every scrap of wisdom was earned at the cost of a life. What do you think of that? Where is your Kilukpuk now?'

Icebones, enduring, said nothing; the Ice Mammoth's voice, low and harsh, was like the voice of the engulfing storm itself.

'The Lost were already here, huddling in caves. They had shining beetles that dug and crawled and crushed rock, and a great tusk in the sky that burned channels into the ground. But we were more important than any of that. We knew it. *That* is why the Lost made us, and put us here. We broke the land for them. And we had many calves, and we spread—'

'And you changed the world,' said Icebones.

'Yes,' Cold-As-Sky said bitterly. 'Our tusks and our dung made the land ready for creatures like *you*, with your green plants we could not eat, and your thick wet air we could not even breathe . . . And with every scrap of land that was changed there was a little less room left for *us*. Many died – the old and the very young first – and each year there are fewer calves than the last . . .'

'I am sorry.'

'You do not understand,' Cold-As-Sky said bleakly. 'It was

761

our destiny to die. To make the land, and then die away, leaving it for *you*.

'But then the Lost flew off into the sky in their shining seeds.

'The green things started to blacken and die. The ponds of murky water sank back into the ground and froze over. The ancient cold returned. The dust was freed, and the world-spanning storms began again. And we touched each other's mouths, and tasted hope for the first time in memory.'

'And that is why we are dying,' Icebones said.

'*This is not your land*. If you live, I die.'

'We are Cousins, Calves of Kilukpuk,' Icebones growled. 'You know the Oath. Every mammoth is born with the Oath, just as she is born knowing the name of Kilukpuk, and the tongue she taught us. And so you know that if the Oath is broken, the dream of Kilukpuk will die at last . . . But enough. I am weary. I have come far, Cousin, and I am ready to die, if I must. Leave me.'

And, as the dust swirled around her, it seemed she drifted into blankness once more, as if letting go of her hold on the world's tail.

But then something probed at her mouth: a trunk, strong, leathery, cold. And water trickled into her throat.

She sucked at the trunk, like a calf at her mother's breast. The water, ice cold, washed away the dust that had caked over her tongue.

But then, though her thirst still raged, she pushed the trunk away. 'The calf,' she gasped.

She sensed the vast bulk of the Ice Mammoth move off into the howling storm, seeking Woodsmoke.

CHAPTER 5
THE FOOTFALL

Icebones breasted a ridge, exhausted, her shoulder a clear icicle of pain. She paused at the crest.

She saw that they had reached a place where the land descended sharply. A new vista opened up before her: a landscape sunk deep beneath the level of this high, broken plain. Within huge concentric systems of rock, she saw a puddle of green and water-blue.

It was a tremendous crater. It was the Footfall of Kilukpuk.

And, even from this high vantage, still suspended in the thin air, Icebones could hear the call of mammoths.

Eagerly, her breath a rattle in her throat, she walked on, step by painful step.

The Family climbed down through crumpled, eroded rim mountains.

On the horizon Icebones made out complex purple shadows that must be the rim walls on the far side of this great crater. They seemed impossibly far away. And the wall systems were extensively damaged. In one place a fire mountain towered from beyond the horizon, a vast, flat cone. The rim mountains before it were broken, as if rivers of rock had long ago washed them away and flooded stretches of the central plain. Further to the east, the rim mountains were pierced by giant notches. They were valleys, perhaps, cut by immense floods. Everything here was ancient, Icebones realised: ancient and remade, over and over.

Plodding steadily, the mammoths left the terrain of the

rim mountains. They reached a belt of land around the central basin itself, a hard red-black rock, folded and wrinkled into ridges and gullies and stubby isolated mesas.

Icebones could hear the broken song of the ground beneath her, feel the deep shattering it had endured, deep beyond the limits of her perception. But since it had formed, this ancient scar tissue had been crumpled and folded and eroded. Every rocky protrusion was carved and shaped by wind and rain, and dust was everywhere, heaped up against the larger rocks and ridges.

But even here they found stands of grass and struggling herbs and trees, and shallow ponds which were not frozen all the way to their base. Already the bony rockscape over which they had struggled for so long, with its killer weed and breathing trees and distorted, resentful Ice Mammoths, seemed a foul dream, and the habitual ache in Icebones's chest began to fade.

After many days' walking over this ridged plain, the mammoths at last reached the basin itself.

Quite suddenly, Icebones found herself stepping on to thick loam that gave gently under her weight. When she lifted her foot she could see how she had left a neat round print; the soil here was thick and dense with life.

All around her the green of living things lapped between crimson ridges and mesas, like a rising tide.

The mammoths fanned out over the soft ground, ripping eagerly at mouthfuls of grass, grunting their pleasure and relief.

This lowest basin was a cupped land, a secret land of hills and valleys and glimmering ponds. Icebones made out the rippling sheen of grass, herbivore herds which moved like brown clouds over the ground, and flocks of birds glimmering in the air. And, right at the centre of the basin, there was an immense, dense forest, a squat pillar of dark brown that thrust out of the ground, huge indeed to be visible at this distance.

Here, all the ancient drama of impacts and rocks and water had become a setting for the smaller triumphs and tragedies of life.

Woodsmoke ran stiff-legged to the shore of a small lake where geese padded back and forth on ice floes. The mammoth calf went hurtling into the water, trumpeting, hair flying, splashing everywhere. The geese squawked their annoyance and rose in a cloud of rippling wings.

Icebones watched him, envying his vigour.

Woodsmoke, shaking water out of a cloud of new-sprouting guard hairs, ran to Breeze. The calf wrapped his trunk around his mother's leg, a signal that he wished to feed. Welcoming, she lifted her leg, and he raised his trunk and clambered beneath her belly fur, seeking to clamp his mouth on her warm dug.

Icebones might have left him to die on the High Plains.

Warily she explored her own feelings. Woodsmoke's death would have left a hole in her that would never have healed, she thought. But she knew, too, that it would have been right – that she would make the same decision again.

Autumn, more sedately, came to Icebones. 'It is a good place. You were right, Icebones.'

Together they walked back towards the foothills of the high rocky plain. At the fringe of the broad pool of steppe there was a stretch of mud, frozen hard and bearing the imprint of many vanished hooves and feet.

Icebones sniffed the air. 'Yes. It is a good place. But look at this. Even here the tide of life is receding – even here, in the Footfall itself.'

Autumn wrapped her trunk over Icebones's. 'We are exhausted, Icebones, and so are you. Tomorrow's problems can wait until we are stronger. For today, enjoy the water and the grass and the sweet willow twigs.'

'Yes,' Icebones said. 'You are wise, Autumn, as always—'

They heard a mammoth's greeting rumble.

Immediately both Cows turned that way, trunks raised.

It was a Bull. He was walking out of the central steppe plain towards them. He was no youth like Thunder, but a mature Bull in the prime of his life, a pillar of muscle and rust-brown hair, with two magnificent tusks that curled before his face. He towered over Icebones – taller than any of the mammoths of her Family, taller than any mammoth she had ever encountered before her Sleep.

He gazed down at her, curious, excited. '. . . Icebones?' His voice was complex, like the voice of every mammoth, a mixture of trunk chirps and snorts, rumblings from his head and chest, and the stamping of his feet. But she recognised the deep undertones that had carried to her around half a world.

'Boaster – *Boaster*!'

Boaster pressed his forehead against hers. Icebones grasped his trunk and pulled at him this way and that. Then she let go, and they roared and bellowed and ran around each other until they could bump their rumps. Then they stood side by side, swaying, urinating and making dung urgently.

He touched her lips, and lifted his trunk tip to his mouth, tasting her. 'It is indeed you, little Icebones.'

'Littler than you imagined,' she said dryly.

'Yes. But *I* am not.' And he swung around, showing her what hung from his underbelly. 'There. Isn't *that* magnificent?'

She realised, awestruck, that he hadn't been boasting after all . . . But she said, 'You will always be Boaster to me.'

He growled. 'You are not in oestrus, little Icebones. Have I missed your flowering? Must I wait? Who took you – not that *calf*?'

Thunder rumbled. 'I am no calf. Would you like me to prove it?' And he raised his tusks, challenging the huge Bull.

But Boaster ignored the challenge. He ran his trunk over

the younger Bull's head to test his temporal gland and his ears. 'You need to do some filling out. But you are a fine, strong Bull. Some day our tusks will clash over a Cow. But not today.' And, symbolically, he clicked his tusks against Thunder's.

Thunder backed away, not displeased.

Now more Bulls followed Boaster, fanning out around the Family. Some of them trunk-checked Thunder. 'Ah, Thunder. We have heard of you. The great bird killer!' 'You are just skin and bones!' 'What was it you bested – just a chick, or a full-grown duck?'

Thunder growled and threw his tusks threateningly. 'It was a mighty bird whose wings darkened the sky, and whose beak could have cut out *your* flimsy heart in a moment, weakling . . .' And he launched into the story of his battle with the skua, only a little elaborated. Gradually the other Bulls drifted closer, at first rumbling and snorting their scepticism, but growing quieter and more respectful as he developed his tale.

Autumn walked up to Icebones. 'He will have to defend the reputation he makes for himself. He is not among calves now.'

'He is a strong and proud Bull, and he will prosper.'

'And there is somebody else who is looking rather proud of herself,' Autumn said.

She meant Spiral.

Two of the older Bulls had broken away from the herd, watching each other warily. One of them boldly approached Spiral, trunk outstretched.

Spiral backed away, shaking her head. But she allowed him to place his trunk in her mouth.

The Bull lifted his trunk tip into his own mouth, touching it to a special patch of sensitive tissue there, and inhaled. Immediately he rumbled, 'Soon you will be in oestrus. And then I will mate you—'

'*I* will be the one,' said the other Bull. 'My brother is weak and foolish.' And he nudged his brother with his forehead, pushing him aside.

But now another Bull emerged from the herd, a giant who even outsized Boaster, with yellowed tusks chipped from fighting. 'What's this about oestrus? Is it this pretty one? Ignore these calves, pretty Cow. See my tusks. See my strength . . .'

Spiral turned and trotted away, trunk held high. The huge tusker followed her, still offering his gruff blandishments, and the younger Bulls followed, keeping a wary distance from the tusker and from each other.

'She has barely met an adult Bull in her life,' Autumn said. 'Yet she plays with them as a calf plays with lumps of mud. She always did relish being the centre of attention.'

'But the attention of Bulls is better than to be a toy of the Lost.'

Now Boaster was tugging at Icebones's tusks. She saw sadly that Boaster, too, was distracted by the scent of imminent oestrus that came from Spiral – that part of him longed to abandon Icebones and her dry belly, to run after the other Bulls and join in the eternal mating contests. But, loyally, he stayed with her, and his manner was urgent, eager.

'Icebones, come. There is something I must show you. Bring your Family. Come, please . . .'

She rumbled to the Family a gentle 'Let's go', and began to walk at Boaster's side.

After a time, the various members of her Family disengaged themselves from their various concerns, and formed up into a loose line and trotted after her: Autumn alongside Breeze, who shepherded Woodsmoke, and then came Spiral, still followed by her retinue of hopeful Bull attendants.

The only one who did not follow was Thunder, who was already becoming immersed in the society of the Bulls. Icebones felt a stab of sadness and turned away.

Boaster walked easily and gracefully, his belly and trunk swaying, and his guard hairs shone in the sunlight, full of health. But he walked slowly alongside Icebones, in sympathy with the battered, exhausted mammoth who had come so far.

It took days to walk into the centre of the basin.

The land opened out around Icebones. This tremendous crater was more than large enough for its walls to be invisible, hidden by the horizon. Soon Icebones would never have guessed that she was crossing a deep hollow punched into the hide of the world.

It was full of life. Icebones saw the tracks of herds of horses and bison, and the burrowing of lemmings, and the nests of birds. But folds of ancient, tortured rock showed through the rich lapping soil. And in the stillness of the night, beneath the calls of the wolves and the rumblings of contented mammoths, Icebones could sense the deep fractures that lay beneath the surface of this hugely wounded land.

After a few days the central forest came pushing over the horizon. Soon it was looming high over their heads, a dense mass of wood, topped by foliage that glowed silver-green in the light.

'I don't understand,' Icebones said to Boaster. 'Mammoths are creatures of the steppe. We like the dwarf trees that grow over the permafrost – willows and birches . . . What interest have we in a tall forest like this?'

'But it is not a forest,' he said gently.

Now Breeze came crowding forward. '*It is not a forest*,' she said. 'Icebones, can't you see? Can't you feel its roots? *It is a tree* – a single, mighty tree!'

Icebones walked forward and peered at the 'forest', and she saw that Breeze was right. There were no gaps to be seen in that dense mass of wood. Its single tremendous trunk was supported by huge buttress-like roots. And when she looked up, she saw that the trunk ran tall and clean far beyond the reach of any mammoth, and the tree's foliage was lost, high above her – lost in a wisp of low cloud, she realised, shocked.

'It is a tree higher than the sky,' she said. 'All the trees here grow tall. But this is the mightiest of all.'

Boaster growled. 'If it could talk, it might be called Boaster too – what do you think, Icebones? But this is a special tree. Its fruit draws in air.'

'It is a breathing tree.' She described the trees they had encountered on the High Plain.

'Yes,' Boaster said. 'But this is their giant cousin. This Breathing Tree is a mammoth among trees.' He touched her trunk. 'I know how hard your journey was. But this Tree shows that the mightiest of living things can prosper here . . . If the Tree survives, so will we.'

She moved closer to him and wrapped his trunk in hers. 'The journey was hard. But you gave me strength when I had none left.'

He pulled away, puzzled. '*I* inspired *you*? Come with me.' He tugged at her trunk. 'Come, come and see.'

They walked a little away around the Tree's vast cylindrical trunk. It was like walking around a huge rock formation.

And suddenly, before her, there were mammoths.

There were huge old Bulls with chipped tusks, bits of grass clinging to the hairs of their faces, giant scars crossing their flanks and backs. And fat, slow Cows, round-faced calves running at their feet. And young Bulls, their adult tusks just beginning to show like gleams of ice in rock folds. And leaner, loose-haired mammoths whose journey here looked as if it had been as hard as Icebones's.

Around her was the sound of mammoths: the click of tusks, the dry rustle of intertwined trunks, the hiss of their hair and tails – many, many mammoths.

'Can you smell them?' Boaster asked gently. 'Can you *hear* them?'

Icebones was stunned. 'Where do they come from?'

'They came from all over this little world. They were abandoned by the Lost, and they were helpless, just as your Family was. If they had stayed in their Lost cages, they would have starved or submitted to the cold – but they didn't know what else to do.

'But your Family was different. *They had you.* And when you made your decision to bring them here to the Footfall, I knew I had to follow you, with my bachelor herd. Not that I didn't have to crack a few tusks to make them see sense . . .

'And then, with our calls and stamping, we spread the word to all the mammoths who can hear. Some were reluctant to come, some didn't understand, and some were simply frightened. But none of them faced so hard a journey as you.

'And one by one, Family by Family, they began the great walk, from north, south, west, east . . .'

'All of these mammoths are here because of *me*?'

Autumn was at her side. 'Because of you, Icebones, Matriarch. Your achievement was mighty. You walked your mammoths around the world. You walked them from the highest place of all, the peak of the Fire Mountain, to the deepest place, this Footfall. It is an achievement that will live for ever in the songs of the Cycle.'

Weak, overtired, hungry, thirsty, Icebones tried to take in all this – and failed. She wished Silverhair could see her now. She would, at last, be proud.

But there was room in her heart for a stab of doubt. She recalled the fringe of the crater basin, the dried mud there where the tide of life had receded. Could it be that she had drawn these mammoths here on a promise of life and security that, in the end, would not be fulfilled? Perhaps what she had achieved was not an inspiration – but a betrayal.

But now Breeze came trotting up to her, her manner

urgent and tense. 'Thunder is calling from the edge of the steppe. Can you hear him? Icebones, he says *she* is coming.'

Icebones immediately knew who she meant. And she realised that, whatever her triumph in bringing the mammoths here to the navel of the world, she must gather up her strength for one more challenge.

For, out of the harsh High Plains, the Ragged One was approaching.

CHAPTER 6

THE BREATHING TREE

Icebones – still limping, still favouring the shoulder she now suspected would never properly heal – liked to walk beside the Tree. Around it the air was dense with the life of the long summer. A great misty fog of aerial plankton, ballooning spiders and delicate larvae drifted over the land in search of places to live.

She stroked the Tree's deep brown bark and listened to the currents of sap that ran within it, considering its mysteries. She sensed how this Tree was dragging heat and water up from the world's depths.

And, slowly, as she began to understand its purpose, she came to believe that this vast Tree was the core of everything . . .

It took many days for the Ragged One to cross the Footfall.

And she was not alone. She had entered the crater with a mysterious herd of her own. And as she crossed the plain more mammoths were joining her. A determined force was trekking steadily towards the Tree, and Icebones.

Autumn and Boaster stayed with her, her closest companions.

Boaster said, 'You do not have to face this *Ragged One*, little Icebones. Let me drive her off with a thrust of my tusks.' And he dipped his head and lunged at an imaginary opponent.

She stroked his face fondly. She knew that though she was slowly regaining some of her health, she would never be as strong as she had been before. She had left her strength and youth, it seemed, up on the High Plains.

But she knew it was her duty to face the Ragged One.

Autumn and Boaster knew it too, of course.

Autumn growled, 'It would help if we knew what that wretched creature wanted. I'm sure it has nothing to do with being mammoth.'

Boaster rumbled, 'It is disturbing how many here think back nostalgically to the days when the Lost ran our lives for us. That is why those addled fools follow her.'

Icebones said, 'But the way of the Cycle is often harsh. Even we, on the High Plains, turned back from confronting the final truth . . . I cannot blame these others.'

She spotted Breeze, who had come into oestrus. She was walking fast, holding her head tall. Her eyes were wide amber drops. She was being pursued by a large, grizzled Bull, his tusks scarred and chipped. Dark fluid leaked from his musth glands and down his face, and he dribbled urine as he walked.

A little further away, two younger Bulls were challenging each other, raising their tusks and shaking their heads. But they both must know that whoever won their battle would not gain access to Breeze while the battered old tusker claimed her.

Breeze and the victorious tusker began a kind of dance. She would walk away, glancing over her shoulder, and he would follow, rumbling. But then he would hold back, as if testing her willingness and desire, and in response she slowed.

Beyond this central pair and the two young competing Bulls was a ring of more males, eight or ten of them – some of them massive, many sporting savage scars and shattered tusks. Further away still more Bulls watched the central couple jealously, standing still as rocks.

The whole circle of Bulls, young and old, was held in place around Breeze, trapped by invisible forces of lust and jealousy and fear.

'It is the consort,' Autumn observed. 'So the ancient dance continues.'

'As it should,' Icebones said.

Boaster growled and pawed the ground, his huge trunk swaying. A sad unspoken thought passed between Boaster and Icebones: she had still not come into oestrus, and they both feared now that the dryness at her core would never be broken.

Autumn, oblivious to this, said, 'I only wish that Spiral could find some happiness too.'

Icebones understood her regret. Spiral had come into oestrus soon after Icebones's mammoths had arrived here in the Footfall. She was tall and handsome, and the Bulls could tell from her complex scents that she had borne healthy calves before. But though Spiral had attracted an even larger consort retinue than Breeze, in the end she had brayed at her winning suitor and fled, refusing his advances.

'She will come to no harm,' said Boaster. 'She is proud and difficult, but she is beautiful.'

'Ah,' Autumn said, rather grandly. 'But she wrestles with problems you may not imagine, child . . .'

'Just as,' came a muddy voice, 'you big hairy animals can barely imagine the troubles *I* have.'

Icebones turned. A squat creature was waddling towards her, its peculiarly naked skin covered in drying mud. It raised a small stubby trunk.

Icebones limped forward, inordinately pleased. 'Chaser-Of-Frogs!'

The Mother of the Swamp-Mammoths looked up at Boaster with small black eyes and burped proudly. Boaster trumpeted, startled, and he backed away from the stubby form.

Chaser-Of-Frogs said, 'Without me, you know, these clumsy oafs would be blundering around that Gouge still.' She reached up with her trunk and probed at Icebones's belly. 'But your journey was hard too. You are a bag of skin. And,' she said more gently, probing at Icebones's dry dugs, 'you have other problems, I fear.'

Icebones gave a brief rumble of regret. But she insisted, 'What of you, Chaser-Of-Frogs? I thought you would never leave that muddy pond.'

'My Family have found a new pond now.' She raised her trunk towards a shallow lake nearby.

Icebones heard and smelled more Swamp-Mammoths burrowing gratefully into the muddy pond floor. Their wet backs gleamed in the sun like logs, and their protruding eyes blinked slowly. Mammoths stood around these new arrivals, trunks raised in curiosity, and a clutch of ducks swam away indignantly.

There were perhaps a dozen Swamp-Mammoths in the lake.

Icebones said softly, 'This is all?'

Chaser-Of-Frogs said grimly, 'We both knew how it would be, Bones-Of-Ice. Most would not follow. Of those who set out, those who died first were the old and the young, our calves . . . It was hard, Bones-Of-Ice. So hard.'

Autumn rumbled, 'We faced the same choice – and failed – and our bones would now be scoured by the dust storms of the high plain, our line extinct, if not for good fortune . . .'

'*The mammoth dies, but mammoths live on,*' Icebones said softly.

But now Boaster stiffened. He was looking to the north, his tusks raised, and he trumpeted.

There was a sound of feet, purposefully walking. And on the northern horizon a black cloud hugged the ground, like the approach of a storm.

Icebones, with deep reluctance, turned that way. When she raised her trunk she could smell a tang of blood and staleness.

It was no storm. It was mammoth: a great herd of them, and they walked through the billowing crimson dust raised by their own powerful footfalls.

Calves ran squealing in search of their mothers. Bulls

broke off from their jousting and backed away, grumbling. Even Breeze's consort circle was broken up.

'It is as if a cloud has come across the sun,' Autumn said.

But Icebones stood straight. For, in the lead of the marching mammoths, grey hair flying wispy in the wind, was the Ragged One.

It was time. Relief flooded Icebones.

One more trial, Icebones. Just one more. Then you can rest.

She gathered her strength.

The Ragged One trumpeted, her loose hair wafting around her strange grey-pink face. She was gaunt, her ribs protruding beneath her sparse hair. Her face was scarred, her tusks badly chipped.

'So, Icebones,' the Ragged One said, 'you survived. And you did not kill any more mammoths on your journey.'

Before Icebones could reply, Autumn raised her trunk. 'Spiral,' she said softly. 'Daughter – is that *you*?'

From behind the Ragged One, Spiral stepped forward, head held high, her beautiful tusks gleaming.

Autumn rumbled her dismay.

Icebones growled to the Ragged One, 'Say what it is you want here. And say what you have promised these mammoths who follow you.'

'That is simple,' the Ragged One said. '*I have told them I will bring back the Lost.*'

Icebones immediately sensed the hopeful, longing mood of the mass of mammoths who had followed Icebones – and, to her shock, she even sensed a stirring of doubt in Boaster, who stood at her side.

For a heartbeat she felt giddy, weak, as if she might fall. This was a dangerous moment indeed: a moment that could decide the future of the species, here on this rocky steppe – and all that she could bring to bear was her own failing strength.

Spiral called thinly, 'The Lost gave us life, Icebones. What have you to offer us but a jumble of myths, suffering and death – as my own sister died, as *we* nearly died?'

There was a great rumbling from the mass of mammoths behind her.

'I have nothing to offer you,' Icebones said. 'Nothing but the truth, and dignity.'

The Ragged One snorted contempt. 'I cannot eat truth. I cannot drink dignity.'

Autumn demanded, '*How* do you imagine you will call back the Lost from the sky?'

The Ragged One walked up to the giant Breathing Tree. Its mottled bark loomed above her like a wall. Grunting, she slashed at the bark with her tusks.

The gouged wood leaked a blood-red sap.

'I am one mammoth, with a single pair of tusks. But I can cut and slash. And when I am exhausted, another will come and cut after me, and then another, and another . . . It might take a season, a whole year. But we are mammoths, and we are strong. And we will destroy this Tree, as we can destroy any other.'

'You are a fool,' said Autumn. 'How will that help you bring back the Lost?'

'You are old and your mind is addled,' said the Ragged One. 'You are the fool. Look at this Tree. Smell it. Hear its roots worming into the earth. Is there another such Tree in the whole of the world? No, there is not. *Because this Tree is a creation of the Lost* – their mightiest work, destined to outlive the Nests, and the beetle things that toil and burn. And if we destroy the Tree, the Lost will wish to restore it – *and they will return.*'

A wave of excited trumpeting rippled through the crowd of her followers, and the noise was briefly deafening.

Before the Ragged One's intense anger and determination, Icebones felt weak, like a figure in a dissolving dream. But she knew she must act. 'I will stop you.'

'And if you try,' hissed the Ragged One, 'I will kill you.'

'Then that is what you will have to do, for I will oppose you to my last breath.'

'Why?' Autumn asked. 'Icebones, it is only a tree.'

'No,' Icebones said. 'I have thought deeply on this, and I believe I understand the Tree's true importance – *as do you, Cold-As-Sky*. Show yourself now.'

Out from the crowd beyond Spiral, a squat, rounded form shouldered her way: mammoth, yes, but with a hump and covered in black, sticky hair, and with small feet and tiny pointed ears, and a pair of eyes that glowed orange.

The mammoths around her recoiled, rumbling uncertainly.

'I am here, Icebones,' said the Matriarch of the Ice Mammoths. 'I followed your Ragged One. I come here despite the thickness of the air, and the stench of water and your fat green growing things . . .'

Icebones said, 'Cousin. You saved my Family on the High Plains. And yet now you seek to destroy a world.'

Cold-As-Sky said harshly, 'I come not to destroy, but to make the world as it once was.'

'I don't understand any of this,' Autumn said.

Icebones spoke loudly enough for every mammoth in the Footfall to hear.

'This one is right, that the Tree is a gift of the Lost – their last gift to this world. But the Lost have gone, and the Tree remains. And now its meaning has nothing to do with the Lost, but with the Cycle – *with us*.

'When Longtusk led his Family away from the advancing Lost and over the great bridge, he reached a land of ice, where nothing could live. But Longtusk had heard of a place called a *nunatak*. It was a refuge, a place where heat bubbled from the ground, keeping back the ice, and green things lived, even in the depths of winter. There the mammoths survived.'

'These are fables for calves,' said the Ragged One sourly.

Icebones walked up to the Breathing Tree and stroked its cut-through bark. 'Like Longtusk's Family, we are stranded in a world of ice. But this Footfall is our *nunatak*.' She stamped her feet, challenging the mammoths. 'Listen to the song of the rocks. Feel how the ground is shattered and compressed. This is the deepest pit in the world, where the rock has been pushed far down – so far that the inner heat of the world, which lies beneath the plants and soil and rocks, is close. Can you feel it? Can you hear the mud that bubbles, the liquid water that gurgles?'

There were rumbles of doubt and surprise among the gathered mammoths. Icebones could hear them pawing at the ground, listening for the secret songs that welled there.

'The heat is deeper than any of us could reach,' said Icebones. *'But the roots of this Tree will reach deeper than any mammoth's trunk.* Even yours, Cold-As-Sky. One day this Tree will draw up the heat of the world. It will breathe rich air, and weep water – and the world will live.'

'One day?' Boaster asked wistfully.

'Not yet,' Icebones said gently. 'This Tree, mighty as it towers over us poor mammoths, is but a sapling. Can't you tell, Boaster?'

The Ragged One trumpeted desperately, 'If we destroy the Tree, the Lost will return.'

'No,' Icebones said. 'You showed me yourself how the Lost abandoned this world. Wherever they have gone, it has nothing to do with us. But if you destroy the Tree, you destroy yourselves – and your calves, and their calves after them.' She raised her tusks. 'This is the truth. If I am the only one opposed, then you must kill me first.'

There was an expectant silence, a forest of raised trunks.

Icebones stood alone. She had done all she could. And so she waited in the thin, high sunlight, with the tang of red dust strong in her nostrils.

The small world spun around her, and heat gathered in her head.

Autumn came to stand behind Icebones.

Breeze joined her.

And even the calf faced the crowd of mammoths, his tiny tusks upraised as if he was ready to take them all on.

'We are your Family, Icebones,' Autumn said. 'On that long journey, *I* became *We*. And now we stand with you.'

'And me,' growled Boaster, adding his massive presence. Icebones touched his trunk with affection and gratitude.

Chaser-Of-Frogs came waddling up, scattering drying mud. 'None of you is as handsome as me. But Bones-Of-Ice taught me we are all Cousins, and she spoke the truth – and that truth saved me. I am proud to be your Family, Bones-Of-Ice. *I* become *We*.'

Autumn trumpeted, 'Spiral. Join us.'

But Spiral, standing close to the Ice Mammoths, postured and pranced, as if for an invisible audience of Lost.

But now Thunder emerged from the crowd. He approached Spiral. Another young Bull followed him, unknown to Icebones.

Thunder called, 'I recall how it was for you on that distant Mountain, Spiral. The Lost pampered you and praised you – *but they took away your calves*.'

'It is true,' Autumn said. 'Daughter, you recall the Lost with affection. But in truth they hurt you as no mother should be hurt.'

Spiral trumpeted, 'Leave me alone – oh, leave me alone!'

The other Bull stepped forward. His tusks, though still immature, were long and smooth – and they made neat curls that were, Icebones saw, an exact match of Spiral's own. He walked awkwardly up to Spiral. He reached out with his trunk, and probed her mouth and trunk tip and breasts. 'But *I* cannot leave you alone,' he said thickly. 'Have you forgotten me, mother?'

Spiral stood stiff and silent, eyes wide. Then she cried out, pain mixed with joy, and wrapped her trunk around her son's face.

STEPHEN BAXTER

Icebones pealed, 'This is how it is to be mammoth: mother with calf, Families together, herds of Bulls strong and proud. We have no need of the Lost. All we need is each other. Join me now. Join my Clan.'

And, like an ice floe slowly melting, the group beyond the Ragged One lost its cohesion. One by one mammoths broke away from the disciplined mass, to join Icebones and her Family.

Spiral came lumbering stiffly to her mother, her trunk still wrapped tightly around the head of the calf that had been taken from her long ago. Autumn embraced her daughter gruffly.

A massive tusker came up, dribbling stinking musth. He tried to get close to Breeze, whose oestrus smell was still powerful. Curtly Autumn shielded her daughter from his attention.

A part of Icebones was amused that even now the deeper story of life went on.

Thunder joined Icebones. She nuzzled his mouth affectionately. 'Well done,' she said. 'You have made the difference, I think . . .'

'I thought it would work,' Thunder said softly.

'What do you mean?'

'I thought Spiral might have run off to join that ranting fool. I found the calf two days ago. I thought he might come in useful. So I kept him distracted until now.'

Icebones was astonished. 'How can you think in such a devious way?'

'Just be glad I am on your side,' Thunder said modestly.

Cold-As-Sky snorted. 'But what of us, Icebones?' The Ice Mammoths were breathing fast, their blue tongues lolling. To them, Icebones recalled, the thin, clean air of the Footfall was dense and clammy and much, much too hot. Cold-As-Sky said, 'If I join you, I die. If the Tree makes your world, it destroys ours.'

Autumn turned on the Ragged One. 'You see why they

782

followed you? Even these strange creatures cared nothing for the Lost, for your dreams. *All they wanted was to smash the Tree*, for they understood its importance, as Icebones did. You are a fool – you let them use you—'

Icebones touched Autumn's trunk to still her.

Thunder said unexpectedly, 'But you need not die, Cold-As-Sky.'

The Ice Mammoths inspected him suspiciously.

In brief phrases – illustrated with much stamping and growling – he told them of the Fire Mountain, where he had been born. 'It is high,' he said. 'Higher than your High Plains, the highest place in all the world. No matter how hard this Tree breathes, that Mountain's summit will still be a place of cold and thinness and ice.'

Cold-As-Sky said to Icebones, 'Is this true?'

Icebones glanced at the Ragged One. '*She* knows it to be true. We walked to the summit, and saw breathing trees . . . Yes, you could live there, Cold-As-Sky.'

'But it is half a world away.'

Now Breeze's calf stepped forward. 'I will lead you,' said Woodsmoke brightly. '*I* have walked half the world. I will show you how.'

Breeze cuffed him affectionately but proudly, for he stood tall and determined.

Cold-As-Sky rumbled, and her Ice Mammoths clustered around her.

Then, hesitantly, Cold-As-Sky stepped forward and stood behind Icebones. Her Family followed.

The Ice Mammoths smelled of ice and iron.

At last the Ragged One was left isolated.

It is done, Icebones thought. Her sense of relief was overwhelming, leaving her weak.

'You have defeated me,' said the Ragged One bleakly.

'No. We are not Bulls battling over a Cow. There is no defeat, no victory. Be with our Family.'

'You don't understand,' said the Ragged One. 'You have never understood. *I* cannot become part of your *We*.'

'That isn't true—'

'But it is, in a way,' said Chaser-Of-Frogs.

'This muddy thing is right, Icebones,' said Cold-As-Sky, ignoring Chaser-Of-Frogs's bristling. 'She is mammoth, yet she is not – *just as we are.*

'I told you we have our own legend, our own memories. We know we were set down on a world where nothing could live – nothing but ourselves, and the blood weed and other plants which feed us. And we recall the first of us all – *for those first had no mothers.*'

Chaser-Of-Frogs said grimly, 'I hate to ally myself with one so ugly as this, but our memory is the same. In the beginning there were no mothers. There was no Cow, no oestrus, no consort dance, no mating . . .'

'Then how did you come to be?'

'The Lost made us,' Cold-As-Sky said simply. 'They took the bones of mammoths who died long ago, and ground them in the blood of others – remote Cousins called *elephants* who lived in the warm places. And, out of the mixing, came—'

'Us,' said Chaser-Of-Frogs sourly.

'It was not enough for the Lost that they brought mammoths to this place,' said Cold-As-Sky bitterly. 'They had to make us into things of their own.'

Icebones asked, 'But *why*? Why would they do this?'

Autumn growled, 'Perhaps they were in musth, and sought to impress their females.'

'No,' said the Ragged One. 'They loved us. They loved the *idea* of us. That is what I believe. They wanted to remake us, to bring us back from the extinction to which they almost drove us, to give us this new world where there would be room for us to browse.'

Autumn walked up to the Ragged One and ruffled her sparse, untidy hair. 'If it was love, they loved us too much,' she said gruffly.

'And that is why you sought to wreck the world,' Icebones said, understanding at last. 'That is why you wanted the Lost back so badly. *Because they made you.*'

'Enough,' said Autumn. 'Give this up. Join us now.'

The Ragged One hesitated, agitated, distressed. She reached out to Autumn, raising her trunk – and, briefly, Icebones believed it might be possible.

But then the Ragged One trumpeted wildly. She pushed past the Ice Mammoths and lumbered away.

Icebones made to go after her, but Autumn held her back with her long, strong trunk. In a moment the Ragged One was lost among the mammoths – and Icebones sensed that she would never see her again.

The mammoths began to disperse.

'It is done, Icebones,' Autumn said. 'The shadow of the Lost is gone at last. This is our world now.'

'Yes. It is done . . .'

And the last of Icebones's strength drained into the red dust. The colours leached out of the world, and her head filled with a sharp ringing. She would have fallen, if not for the support of her Family.

A watching human would only have seen the mammoths gather, heard nothing but an intense and mysterious rumbling and growling and stamping and clicking of tusks.

She would never have known that the destiny of a world had been tested, and determined.

CHAPTER 7
THE DREAM OF KILUKPUK

The Song of Oestrus disturbed Icebones, startling her awake.

She sniffed the air querulously.

It was cold and damp. The sun was dim, or so it seemed to her. Perhaps another winter was coming, though it seemed no more than heartbeats since spring was done.

But then the seasons were shorter on this hard little world. Or were they longer? She could not recall.

Time flowed strangely here; like water, like blood. Sometimes it seemed that her life had fled as rapidly as the fleeting summers, for here she was, suddenly a last-molar, barely able to chew the softest grass any more, her senses and her memories as eroded as her teeth.

Ah, but sometimes she thought she was young again, young and *imagining* how it would be to be a broken-down old mammoth, here in this green hollow, the navel of the world.

Young dreaming of old age, or dotard dreaming of youth? Perhaps, in the end, it made no difference. Perhaps there was no past or present, young or old; perhaps life was just a single moment, a unity, like a pebble taken into the mouth to ward off thirst, inspected by the tongue from every angle . . .

Anyhow, whether the world was growing cold or not, *she* certainly was.

She lumbered towards the Breathing Tree.

Soon she was wheezing with the effort of the walk, and her shoulder ached, never properly healed from its ancient injury. Close to the Tree's roots, where hot air gushed and warm water flowed, the Swamp-Mammoths had made their wallows. She would find some company there, and perhaps would try a little grass, or even a willow bud. And she would ruminate a while with Autumn. Ah, but poor, stolid Autumn was long dead, and she had forgotten again.

She saw a herd of caribou. They preferred to live out their lives at the fringe of the great forests of warmer climes, but came to the steppe to breed. They crossed a stream, splashing and pawing at the water, so that sunlit droplets rose up all around them. Their movements were hasty, nervous, skittish, like horses.

She found the source of the oestrus call. On a small rise a Bull had mounted a young Cow, laying his trunk over her back and the top of her head, and gripping her hips with his forelegs.

When he lumbered away from her, the Cow's song was loud, a series of deep swooping notes repeated over and over, rising out of silence then fracturing into nothing. Soon more Cows joined her to celebrate, trumpeting and making urine together, and they reached out crisscrossing trunks to explore the ground, seeking the strong smell of the mating.

But Icebones's battered old trunk could smell nothing, and the oestrus songs were fuzzy in her hearing – and even her heart felt only the smallest pang of jealousy. She, of course, had never come into oestrus, not once in her long life since she had woken from her strange, half-forgotten Sleep on that remote mountainside. It didn't seem to matter any more. Perhaps her heart had grown calluses, like the broken pads on her feet.

She walked on, labouring to breathe, heading for the Tree.

There were mammoths everywhere. They walked steadily through long grass that swirled in their wake. One of them stopped to graze, and the swaying grass fell still at the same time as the rippling of his hair.

There was a sense of stillness about the mammoths, Icebones thought: of meditation, patience, their calmness as solid and pervasive as the crimson rock beneath her feet. All creatures of the steppe knew stillness.

Where the mammoths walked, ground-nesters like plovers and jaegers flew up angrily if they threatened to step in their nests. But snow buntings and longspurs were making their nests of discarded mammoth wool. And in the winters the snow-clearing of the mammoths exposed grass for hares and willow buds for ptarmigans, and the wells they dug were used by wolves and foxes and others, and even now the insects stirred up by the mammoths' passage served as food for the birds.

It was as it had always been, as the Cycle proudly proclaimed: *Where mammoths walk, they bring life*. It was right, and it was good.

The mammoths reached out to her with absent affection. But they were strangers to her.

Of course they were. By comparison with their spindly liquid grace she felt like a lump of earth, grey and dull. These were mammoths shaped by this new world. The grass grew from the blood-red dust, and the mammoths ate the grass, so that the red dust of the Sky Steppe coursed in their veins. Changing, shimmering, these new mammoths moved past her like tall shadows, shifting, growing stranger with every new generation.

And none of them were her children, or grandchildren: not one.

Taken from her mother on the Island, she had devoted her life to a quest for Family. Well, she had succeeded. She had built the mammoths into a Family, into Clans. But now the Sky Steppe was taking them away.

. . . *Icebones*.

She stopped, struggling to raise her heavy old trunk. The calling voice had been unfamiliar, and it had seemed to come neither from left or right, nor before or behind.

The colours leached out of the world. She felt herself sway.

Icebones. Icebones. '. . . Icebones.'

She looked up. A Bull stood before her – little more than a calf, no taller than she was, his tusks still stubby and untested.

'Woodsmoke?'

'No,' he said patiently. 'Woodsmoke was the mate of my grandmother, Matriarch. I am Tang-Of-Dust. You recall – as an infant I loved to roll in dust dunes and—'

'Ah, Tang-Of-Dust.' But his smell was indistinct, his form in her eyes only a wavering outline. 'Always eat the tall grass,' she said.

'Matriarch?'

'You are what you eat. That much is obvious to everyone. And the tallest grass dreams of touching the sky, of reaching the aurora. So that is what you must eat . . .'

Here was a pretty stand of tussock grass. Forgetting Tang-Of-Dust, she bent to inspect it. The tall thin leaves grew as high as her shoulder, rising out of a pedestal of old leaves and roots. Between the tussock clumps burnet grass grew. This sported round red flower heads that swayed gracefully in the breeze. There were other plants scattered more thinly, like ferns and buttercups and dandelions, and many clumps of fungus, some of them bright red or white, their colours a startling contrast to the deep green of the grass.

Just a stand of grass. She couldn't even smell or taste it. All she could do was see it, as if with age she was turning into one of the Lost. But it was beautiful, intricate, like so much of the world.

She was still herself. She was Icebones, daughter of Silverhair. Nothing would erode *that* away: the last thing she would retain, even when the world had worn away like her molars.

She said, 'He went away, you know.'

'Matriarch?'

'Woodsmoke. He was born on the great Migration – did you know that? I suppose wandering was in his blood . . . At first it wasn't possible, of course. The world away from the Footfall just got too cold for anything to live. Anything like us, anyhow. But gradually that changed, and off he went. But they say that where his dung fell, grass and trees grew, and the animals and birds that live on them followed. Isn't that wonderful, Woodsmoke? As if life is spreading out from this deep warm place. He never came back, of course . . .'

'Yes, Matriarch,' the calf said respectfully. But he was growing impatient. 'Matriarch, *it has changed*. In the sky.'

She grumbled, '*What* has changed?'

'The blue star that flies near the sun.'

She squinted, compressing failing eyes.

The calf was right, she saw. The familiar blue spark had been replaced by a sliver of silver light.

. . . And now, quite suddenly, the silver grain winked out – vanished completely, as if it had never been. Its small brown companion, abandoned, sailed alone in the sky.

She raised her trunk but could smell nothing, hear nothing. How strange, she thought.

Tang-Of-Dust asked, 'What does it mean?'

'I don't know, child.'

'They say that the Lost went there. To the blue light.'

'It might be true,' she said. And she wondered where they had gone now.

'Some say the Lost were insane. Or evil.'

She lowered her heavy head. 'No, not evil, not insane . . . But not like us. In many ways they were arrogant and foolish. But the Lost brought life here. Think of that. We existed a long time before the Lost came, and we will exist for a long time now that they are gone. Theirs was just a brief moment of pain and change and death – but in that moment they gave us a new world. Even if this world is nothing but a dream of Kilukpuk . . .' She slumped forward, to her knees, and her trunk pooled in the dust. 'And, I suppose, by redeeming us, the Lost redeemed themselves. Isn't that wonderful?'

The calf reached out uncertainly. 'Matriarch. Are you ill?'

Her belly settled on to the dust, and she closed her eyes. 'Just tired, Woodsmoke. In a moment we will talk—'

But now there was an explosion of pain in her chest. She gasped and fell forward.

She saw legs all around her, a forest of them, as if she was a newborn calf surrounded by her mother and aunts. That was absurd, for she could hardly be more different from a calf.

She closed her eyes again.

A memory of old age, or a dream of youth? But she tasted blood – or perhaps it was the dry dust of this red world – not a dream, then . . .

Or perhaps the dream was over.

'Icebones . . . Icebones . . .'

Icebones.

She tried to lift her head, to open her eyes, but could not. And yet she thought she saw a mammoth before her: a vast mammoth with dugs the size of mountains, and feet that could stamp great pits in the rock, and tusks like glaciers, and a voice like the song of a world. A mammoth who shone, even though Icebones's eyes were closed.

Do you know who you are?

'I am Icebones, daughter of Silverhair.' That much remained. 'I am very tired.'

You know who I am?

'Yes. Yes, I know who you are, Kilukpuk.'

It's time to go, little one.

'But my Family needs me.'

Now I need you. And Icebones felt a trunk wrap around her head and probe into her dry mouth.

She was lifted up, shedding her body as every spring she had shed her winter coat.

'I am not fit, Matriarch . . .'

No one is more fit than you. And no one paid a greater price than you. The Lost brought you here, in your Sleep, across a vast gulf. And in that gulf a hard light shines. And you were – damaged.

And Icebones knew Kilukpuk meant her dry womb. 'That is why I have no calves.'

But every mammoth who lives is your calf. You saved your kind in every way it is possible to be saved: you gave them life, and you gave them back their selves.

'Will there be soft browse? My molars aren't what they were.'

I will show you the softest, sweetest browse that ever was.

'There is no aurora here. Where are we going?'

To where Silverhair is waiting for you. No more questions, now.

The great shining mammoth drew away.

Effortlessly, Icebones followed. And the small red world receded beneath her, folding over on itself until it became a crimson ball splashed with green and blue, before it disappeared into the dark.

EPILOGUE

Ice still swathes much of the northern ocean, and the southern pole. But the ice is receding. In the ancient highlands of the south the flooded craters and rivers and canals glow blue-green once more. Much of the land is covered by dark forest and broad, sweeping grasslands and steppe – but the primordial crimson of the dust still shines through the green.

This will always be a cold, dry place. This world is too small, too far from the sun. But life is spreading here, year by year: life first brought here by vanished, clever creatures with silver ships and toiling machines, but life now finding its own way on the hard, ancient plains, led by the stately beasts whose calls echo around the planet.

But those calls will never be heard on the summit of the Fire Mountain. That obstinate shoulder of rock still pushes out of the thickening air, just as it always has. From its barren summit the stars can be seen, even at midday.

Here, in the thin air, not even the hardy Ice Mammoths venture. Here, nothing grows.

Nothing, that is, save a solitary dwarf willow, a single splash of green-brown against the ancient crimson rock. Against all odds, the willow's windblown seed has found a trace of water here, high on the Fire Mountain: enough to germinate, and survive.

Just a trace of water, trapped in the buried skull of a mammoth.